THE
OXFORD BOOK OF
DETECTIVE STORIES

Patricia Craig is a freelance critic and reviewer and has edited several anthologies including Oxford Books of *English Detective Stories*, *Modern Women's Stories*, *Travel Stories*, and *Ireland*. She lives in Northern Ireland and is currently working on a biography of Brian Moore.

THE
OXFORD BOOK OF
DETECTIVE
STORIES

Edited by

PATRICIA CRAIG

OXFORD
UNIVERSITY PRESS

*This book has been printed digitally and produced in a standard specification
in order to ensure its continuing availability*

OXFORD
UNIVERSITY PRESS

Great Clarendon Street, Oxford OX2 6DP

Oxford University Press is a department of the University of Oxford.
It furthers the University's objective of excellence in research, scholarship,
and education by publishing worldwide in

Oxford New York

Auckland Cape Town Dar es Salaam Hong Kong Karachi
Kuala Lumpur Madrid Melbourne Mexico City Nairobi
New Delhi Shanghai Taipei Toronto
With offices in
Argentina Austria Brazil Chile Czech Republic France Greece
Guatemala Hungary Italy Japan South Korea Poland Portugal
Singapore Switzerland Thailand Turkey Ukraine Vietnam

Oxford is a registered trade mark of Oxford University Press
in the UK and in certain other countries

Published in the United States
by Oxford University Press Inc., New York

Introduction, biographical notes, and selection © Patricia Craig 2000

The moral rights of the author have been asserted

Database right Oxford University Press (maker)

Reprinted 2008

ISBN 978-0-19-280371-9

CONTENTS

INTRODUCTION

THINGS have changed somewhat since the last general Oxford collection of crime and detective stories was published in 1926.[1] The editor of that volume, E. M. Wrong, did not have an abundance of material at his disposal. Between Poe and Pain—his opening and closing contributors—he mustered only seven detective writers proper, and a couple of pranksters (Barry Pain is one). Conan Doyle, R. Austin Freeman . . . these will, undoubtedly, seem sedate and old-fashioned to a present-day detective addict; however, they come saturated with the charm of a bygone era, as well as pointing up the strengths of the detective story, as it evolved into a distinctive form. This new *Oxford Book of Detective Stories* aims to show the scope of the genre, historically and geographically; and therefore it includes two of Wrong's authors—founding fathers—before branching out in various directions to indicate how the story involving some dramatic misdemeanour was being treated at different times over the last hundred years or so, and in different countries. Inevitably, at least half of the stories selected for this volume have been written during the last thirty or forty years, and come right up to the present to give some sense of the astonishing developments which have taken place as the genre has become full-fledged—in spite of predictions that it would never attain maturity because of in-built defects such as a formulaic framework and otiose assumptions. In fact, it has proved immeasurably resilient. However many times it has been pronounced antiquated, at its last gasp, the detective story has gone on to confound its critics by simply refusing to fade away, and indeed turning round every now and then to perform some feat of adaptability or reanimation. In all its guises, thriller, puzzler, shocker, entertainer, or whatever, it goes on thriving.

It is not just a matter of the abandonment of traditional restraints, the fact that no one any longer balks at detached body parts, say, or sexual enormities, details of autopsies, obscenities, tortures, horrendous serial killings, or what-have-you, all in the name of entertainment (and often adding up to superb entertainment, a circumstance the Christie generation might have found impossible to envisage).

[1] In the World's Classics series

What gets between such exorbitant ingredients and their potentially harrowing effect is, indeed, as ever, the narrative tone, which must be carefully judged to have the most constructive impact on readers. This particular genre, it's true, has, at its best, consistently distilled the atmosphere, priorities, and preoccupations of each successive era—and detective fiction in recent years (stories as well as novels) has intertwined itself with urgent contemporary anxieties and facts of life. As the world becomes more and more global, glossy, technological, urban, drug-ridden, and prone to vandalism of all kinds, it is fitting that the most compelling exercises in detection should take account of these departures, and others, and turn them to felicitous account.

Detective fiction has either a long or a relatively short ancestry, depending on how you look at it. There used to be a fashion among commentators to enlist unlikely practitioners to its ranks, retrospectively, and partly as a counterblast to imputations of triviality, trashiness, and so forth, which frequently bedevilled it. Hence, it was vouchsafed a lineage going back to the Old Testament, and taking in Aristotle, Herodotus, Voltaire, Defoe, Alexander Dumas, and many others along the way—all interesting and thought-provoking, if a trifle tongue-in-cheek. Everyone knows that the category, as we understand it, was invented by Poe in 1841, and subsequently refined by Conan Doyle in the 1890s—after which the way was open for a deluge of detective stories, with each age imposing its own stamp and topical variations over the basic formula. As far as historical antecedents are concerned—it's true that a collection of quasi-detective stories by Keui Wan Yung was assembled in China as long ago as 1211, under the title *Trials Held Beneath a Pear Tree*—and from China, too, came the eighteenth-century account of three cases solved by Judge Dee, a bigwig of the Tang dynasty (618–907); in the present century, this was translated into Dutch by the diplomat and sinologist Robert Van Gulik, who then appropriated the character for a series of novels and stories of his own (complete with English translations). The Judge Dee stories—of which I've included 'The Murder on the Lotus Pond' here—give a good, though inevitably westernized, impression of an almost unimaginably remote period in China's history, as well as being adroit detective tales in their own right.

It is unusual, indeed, to find a 'historical' detective story that isn't scuppered by an excessively high dosage of period colouring; the two genres don't blend easily, but seem instead, when fused together, to let themselves be swamped by a kind of facile romanticism or wooden-ness. Superficial effects are gained too easily, while genuine effectiveness is sabotaged. Detective writers should approach with caution any period but their own. There are, however, some shining exceptions to this general historical benightedness, as readers of the *Oxford Book of Detective Stories* will discover. Not only Judge Dee, but the figures of authority in Gwendoline Butler's story, 'Bloody Windsor'—Major Mears and Sergeant Denny—come imbued with a proper understanding of the era in question. Castle Hill, the Marlborough Arms, a child spinning a hoop, young girls in jeopardy . . . add a severed head to these constituents of Georgian Windsor, and you get a full measure of this author's articulation of the sprightly and sinister—and a Dickens connection to boot.

Possibly the least problematic way to tackle 'historical' detective writing is to cast it in the form of parody, whether parody of some contemporary vogue, or of a particular author. Ruth Dudley Edwards's 'Father Brown in Muncie, Indiana', for example, is a charming and hilarious *jeu d'esprit*, while Sara Paretsky's *faux*-Chandler exercise, 'Dealer's Choice', stays close to the spirit of the prototype while adding a pace and exhilaration of its own. Nothing has the edge on this except perhaps the genuine article—and the story I've selected for this anthology, 'No Crime in the Mountains', is vintage Raymond Chandler: ironic and laconic and abundant in a kind of West Coast throwaway glamour. 'About a mile or so beyond the meadows a dirt road wound out toward a long point covered with junipers. Close inshore there was a lighted dance pavilion . . .'

The strongest distillation of a particular time and place, or, in a word, atmosphere: this is one of the two main qualities I've borne in mind while putting this collection together (that the other is ingenuity of plot hardly needs to be specified, since this is a *sine qua non* of the genre). When W. H. Auden, in his famous essay 'The Guilty Vicarage', claims to have difficulty in reading 'any detective story that is not set in rural England', he was expressing a preference for one kind of pungent 'fantasy' detection, that perfected by Agatha Christie, with its horrors-among-the-hollyhocks and sanitized sense of evil, its emphasis on 'the puzzle pure and complex' (in Julian Symons's phrase). Rural England, with all its quaintness and cupidity, is represented here by R. Austin Freeman, while Christie herself merrily shifts the scene to Egypt to give us the trappings of an archaeological dig, complete with Mummy's Curse. (Even rural England, that figment of detective writers, occasionally allows in an arresting social detail. Freeman's 'A Puzzle of the Sand-Hills', for example, is set at a time when the poor of Broadstairs might be seen scavenging for coal along the Thanet shore.)

One story in this collection, John Charles Dent's 'The Gerrard Street Mystery', fails to comply with 'pure' detective requirements by allowing in an element of the supernatural; however, it is a striking account of a strange occurrence, as well as providing an enticing evocation of nineteenth-century Toronto, and so I have relaxed my own rules to include it here. (I've also bent the rules a bit with the Simenon contribution which comes from *Maigret's Memoirs*: this proved irresistible with its enumeration of policemen's discomforts, mundane detective work, and disquisition on the Gare du Nord. Besides, it does contain a crime and its resolution.) The Sherlock Holmes story, 'The Adventure of the Blue Carbuncle'—which *is*, quintessentially, a piece of pure detection—is likewise rich in atmosphere: Baker Street *c*.1890, two days after Christmas—'It was a bitter night, so we drew on our ulsters and wrapped cravats about our throats . . . We passed across Holborn, down Endell-street, and so through a zigzag of slums to Covent Garden Market.' *Someone's* goose is about to be cooked, you can be sure of that.

Before Sherlock Holmes came on the scene, the detective story looked as though it might reach its fullest flowering in France, where Émile Gaboriau was setting his detective characters to investigating criminal goings-on among the Paris *bourgeoisie*: the story 'Missing!', for example, efficiently elucidates the disappearance of a tall bald jeweller from his premises in the Marais district of the city. But France, despite the advent of authors like Leblanc and Leroux, lost out first to England, and then to America, though the *roman policier*—culminating in the present century in the doings of Inspector Maigret,[2] whose name is on a level with that of Sherlock Holmes—was sufficiently robust to hold its own.

Most histories of the genre, such as Howard Haycraft's *Murder for Pleasure* of 1942, are in agreement that the form only really took root in these three countries, England, France, and America—which raises interesting questions about why, in Haycraft's words, it should always have been 'essentially a democratic institution; produced on [a] large

---

[2] Though Maigret's creator, Georges Simenon, is not French but Belgian, the stories are strongly associated with Paris and its environs.

scale only in democracies'. I suppose the simple answer is that it upholds freedoms dear to the heart of liberal thinking—the freedom to have yourself cleared of a wrong suspicion, as it may be, or to nurture a belief that some kind of cosmic justice is operating. No one gets away with murder in fictions of the old school.

England, France, America: there were, it's true, in the early years, some authors of other nationalities, like the Danish Palle Rosenkrantz, who made the form their own—Rosenkrantz's 'A Sensible Course of Action', a beautifully judged story dated precisely to 1905, concerns some histrionic Russians and an officer of the Copenhagen police. But on the whole, foreign countries with a taste for detective fiction had to rely on translations from the English until comparatively recent times: Japan, for instance, only developed a native tradition after 1923 (when the first indigenous story, 'The Two Sen Copper Coin' by 'Edogawa Rampo', appeared). Matsumoto and his much younger compatriot Shizuko Natsuki are distinguished exemplars of that tradition. The Japanese Superintendent Otani, though, is the creation of an Englishman, James Melville, who spent some years in Japan as a cultural diplomat. Melville's Christmas offering, 'Santa-San Solves It', is a mills-of-God story with a resonant punch-line. To return to Europe: from Czechoslovakia comes Josef Škorecký's 'The Classic Semerák Case', which is humorous, succinct, and cleverly constructed. And the Dutchman Janwillem van de Wetering (represented here by 'The Deadly Egg') takes a cheerful and dexterous approach to murder in Amsterdam.

The Georgia author Jacques Futrelle, who lost his life in the *Titanic* shipwreck of 1912, might be said to exemplify one strand in American detective writing—urbane and intricate—a strand which was continued by (for example) the Canadian Harvey J. O'Higgins, and later embraced and expanded by authors such as Amanda Cross or the more demotic Sue Grafton (for a comparable *English* urbanity, we might look to Sarah Caudwell with her lawyer's *finesse*). The other special North American style was of course the Hammett hard-boiled—or, in the hands of William MacHarg and others, the simultaneously pared-down and souped-up. Not all American writers fall into one or other of these categories, of course—there is Erle Stanley Gardner from Massachusetts, for example, whose 'The Case of the Irate Witness' (the first Perry Mason short story) is a splendid example of court-room showmanship, not to mention the unclassifiable Ellery Queen: to whom, incidentally, every compiler of a detective anthology must be tremendously indebted. No one else has provided so consistent an outlet for the detective-story writer in the present century. *Ellery Queen's Mystery Magazine*, endless volumes, *Queen's Quorum*, specialist issues devoted to one particular grouping after another . . . it adds up to a storehouse for the enthusiast, especially the enthusiast of short fiction. The Queen story included here, 'My Queer Dean!', is undeniably a bagatelle, but, I would contend, an appealing bagatelle. And Stuart M. Kaminsky's missing-person investigation, set in Sarasota, Florida, overturns all the reader's expectations, to invigorating effect.

There is no area of the world, it seems, that hasn't in the end had a go at producing its own version of the murder-and-detection tale, whether or not a whole new tradition, with native variations, subsequently came into being. The Italian story included here, for example, Paolo Levi's 'The Ravine', owes a good deal to the classic English model of the 1920s and 1930s, with its knowing investigator, small circle of suspects, and twist in the tail; while the Finnish contribution, from Pentti Kirstilä, 'Brown Eyes and Green Hair', employs a method which most English-speaking readers will find intriguingly unfamiliar. In compiling this collection, I have tried to cast my net as widely as possible, though I don't pretend to have scrutinized a body of detective stories from *every* country; there is first of all the language problem, and then the fact that some sources of material simply suggest themselves more readily than others. But I would hope that, within certain inescapable limitations, a good range of detective stories has been brought together here; and certainly, just to mention, at random, rural England, ancient China, post-war Czechoslovakia, present-day Dublin, Edwardian Boston, and provincial Ontario (the setting for Ted Wood's engaging 'Pit Bull', which concerns illegal dog-fighting, a stolen pet, and the doughty owner who takes matters into his own hands)—just to cite these locations gives some idea of the scope and variety of *The Oxford Book of Detective Stories*.

With the involvement in the genre of the Argentinian author Jorge Luis Borges, the detective story is pushed to its limits in one direction, to end with a flourish by disappearing up its own conventions. Hebrew scholarship, cabalistic mysteries, a compass and a pair of dividers as aids to detection—these are among the features of the extraordinary story, 'Death and the Compass', in which Inspector Lonnröt not only perceives the pattern underlying a series of slayings, but is himself crucial to this deadly pattern. Borges treats the form as a kind of labyrinth for the intellect; the other self-reflexive story in this collection (well, aside from Thurber's very funny 'The Macbeth Murder Mystery', which is included in a spirit of high jinks)—'My Brother Jack' by the Australian Garry Disher, is constructed on a more down-to-earth plane but is none the less striking in its expertise and playful elaboration of the rules.

It is important to stress that rules still apply, however much relaxation has been effected in the areas of decorum, verisimilitude, and so forth, or however much we're impressed by one instance after another of breath-taking present-day manipulation of the rules. A detective story still requires a crime, some puzzlement, and some kind of solution. It is remarkable, though, what different authors can make of these essential features. Peter Robinson, in 'Summer Rain', has a person coming to Inspector Banks to demand an investigation of his own past murder—in another incarnation. (This story has no truck whatever with hocus-pocus.) And the Scottish author Ian Rankin's compelling 'The Dean Curse' has an up-to-date device—a car bomb—at its centre.

Running my eye down the contents list of what seems to me a very vigorous collection, I am somewhat embarrassed—as the editor of *The Oxford Book of Modern Women's Stories* among other things—I am embarrassed to note the disproportion between male and female detective authors. Men predominate. I must confess it—I failed to hold in mind any supplementary objective while compiling this anthology. I was simply on the look-out for top-notch work, whatever its provenance. Some years ago, I fell with absolute eagerness on a book of detective stories by women—only to conclude, reluctantly, that the editor's admirable purpose had swamped her judgement. Anna Katharine Green, Carolyn Wells, L. T. Meade, Baroness Orczy, Mignon Eberhart, and others: some of these are better when writing at novel length, and some are simply better forgotten. Their stories embody all kinds of topical flaws, weakness of construction, absurdity, melodrama, sentimentality, or what-have-you. Not until the appearance of the great Christie did women writers start to come into their own. Things are vastly different at present, of course, and for every story in this collection by a male author published after 1980 (say), one of equal virtuosity by a woman could have been found. However, as with any anthology, it boils down to a matter of personal choice, and the stories here are those which have made the strongest impact on me. With all their diversity—of location, mood, approach, type of case assigned to the detective for solving, and so on—they enable us, as readers, to applaud their authors' endlessly paradoxical ability to construct the most diverting and engrossing narratives out of episodes of violence, derangement, and brutality.

I should like to thank the following for their considerable assistance at all stages of this project: John Kennedy Melling, Rolando Pieraccini, Judith Luna, Naomi May, David Torrens, Gerry Keenan, Nora T. Craig; and I am, as ever, indebted to Jeffrey Morgan for the most resourceful advice and unfailing encouragement.

THE

OXFORD BOOK OF

DETECTIVE

STORIES

ÉMILE GABORIAU (1833–1873)

Missing!

―――――――

I

ONE Sunday afternoon, not long ago, the whole district of the Marais—that busy quarter of Paris which nowadays is but one vast workshop from the Temple to the Rue Saint Antoine, from the Bastille to the Rue Turbigo—was in a state of most unwonted excitement. Bustling as it may be on week-days, when all the bronze factories re-echo to the sound of toil, when the heavy vans roll over the pavement from druggists to toy-dealers, taking at each halt some fresh consignment for despatch by rail, when work-people and customers crowd the thousand and one establishments where every description of '*article de Paris*' is produced for a value of many millions of francs per annum—on Sundays, at least, the Marais usually relapses into silence. Were it not for the multitudinous inscriptions which cover all the houses from garret to basement chronicling the names of manufacturers, dealers, and commission agents, one might fancy oneself in the old times, when the Marais was inhabited solely by the *rentier* class, by worthy old couples retired from business on fairly decent incomes, or by relics of the ancient nobility, scarcely wealthy enough to reside in the Faubourg St Germain. Such, indeed, was the Marais fifty years ago—a quiet and secluded district—and thus have Honoré de Balzac and Paul de Kock described it in their novels. But, nowadays, it is a vast hive of industry, whence peace and quiet are utterly banished during the six days set apart for toil. It is only on the Sabbath, when workshops and store-rooms are closed, when the week-day toilers are making merry in their native Belleville, or chinking glasses in the *bosquets* of Montreuil, that it regains a semblance of its old tranquillity.

And yet, on the particular Sunday we have mentioned, the usual 'Sabbath-hush' was wanting. True enough, no heavily laden vans were rolling through the narrow streets; no din of hammers and anvils came from the closed *ateliers*. The footways were not bestrewn with packing-cases, and no crowd of commissionaires and receivers, clerks, and commercial travellers, hurried hither and thither peripatetically proving the truth of the axiom that 'Time is money.' But then, there were unusually animated groups of customers in all the wine-shops, unwonted knots of people at the street corners, gatherings of housewives in front of the fruiterers' stores, and conclaves of doorkeepers and kindred scandalmongers in every convenient alley.

Something very extraordinary must have happened, as passers-by correctly opined. The fact is, that one of the most honourable manufacturers of the Rue du Roi de Sicile had disappeared, and all efforts to find him had so far proved unsuccessful. The grocer at the corner of the Rue Saint Louis possessed full information on the subject—information obtained first hand from the cook of the missing gentleman—and his shop was most extensively patronised that afternoon, even by people who pretended that he mixed dust with his pepper, and sweetened his jam with glucose. For once in a way, they put up with his adulterations to enjoy the benefit of his conversation. 'It was yesterday evening,' repeated the worthy grocer over and over again, as he assisted in weighing pounds of sugar and penn'orths of salt, 'yesterday evening just after dinner, our neighbour M. Jandidier went down to his cellar to get up a bottle of old wine, and since then no one has seen him. The cellar door was found wide open, but M. Jandidier had disappeared, vanished, evaporated!'

From time to time it happens that mysterious disappearances are spoken of. Alarm is spread in various directions, and prudent people invest money in sword-sticks and revolvers. But as a rule the police shrug their shoulders when these occurrences are mentioned. They are acquainted with the 'seamy side' of the cunningly embroidered canvas. They start an investigation and discover the truth, so different to popular exaggeration: in lieu of a romance, they come upon some sad story.

However, to a certain extent the grocer of the Rue Saint Louis spoke the truth. It was a fact that M. Jandidier, who did a most extensive business as a manufacturer of imitation jewellery, had altogether disappeared since the previous night.

M. Théodore Jandidier was some fifty-eight years old. He was very tall and very bald, gifted with fairly good manners and deportment, and according to popular report, possessed of a very considerable fortune. This was not to be wondered at, for in Paris the trade in imitation jewellery is simply enormous, and some manufacturers like the Bourguignons and others, whose creations are exported all over the world, are simply millionaires. One could not say as much concerning M. Jandidier, but he was, nevertheless, a man of means. A pretty little collection of scrip and bonds were said to yield him an income of twenty thousand francs a year, and his business brought him an average annual profit of another fifty thousand. He was esteemed and liked in the neighbourhood, for his probity was above all question, and his morals perfectly exemplary. When five-and-thirty, he had married a portionless cousin, who had proved a happy and faithful wife.

This worthy couple possessed an only daughter named Thérèse, who was literally idolised by her father. At one time it had been said that she was to marry M. Gustave Schmidt, the eldest son of the senior partner in the great banking house of Schmidt, Gubenheim, and Worb, but somehow or other—no one knew why—the marriage had been broken off; and this had caused all the more surprise, as the young folks were apparently very much in love with each other.

Some friends of the Jandidier family pretended that old Schmidt, the father, the most avaricious of all our Parisian financiers, and an inveterate 'fleecer,' had requested that Mademoiselle Thérèse should bring her husband a preposterously large dowry, such as her father could not possibly furnish despite his comparative wealth. However, this was only a rumour which nothing had so far authenticated.

On this Sunday afternoon, when the news of M. Jandidier's disappearance spread through the Marais, all the incidents of his past life which the gossips were acquainted with were duly recorded and submitted to public appreciation. A hundred stories of his honesty and good nature were told. He had been an honour to the district, an excellent worthy man in every respect. Given his rigid morals, it was altogether impossible to imagine that he had 'gone off on the loose.' His family ties were too strong for him to have abandoned his wife and daughter. No, he must have fallen a victim to some base scoundrel—he must have received a foul blow; and the honour of the Marais required that his remains should be recovered and fittingly interred, and that his murderer should be brought to justice.

So thus, during that Sunday afternoon, the rumours flew through the district, spreading in every ear and growing on every tongue, till, at last, having learned the reports from his agents, the district commissary of police considered it his duty to repair to the missing gentleman's residence with the view to obtaining precise information.

He was ushered into the grand drawing-room which was in a state of semi-obscurity, the shutters being half closed and the curtains drawn. Both Madame Jandidier and her daughter were distracted with grief, and he had considerable difficulty in calming them and inducing them to answer his questions. However, he was at length placed in possession of these particulars.

On the previous evening (Saturday) M. Jandidier had dined as usual with his family. He had made, however, but a poor meal, for he was troubled with a bad headache. After dinner he had gone downstairs—not to the wine cellar as the grocer of the Rue Saint Louis pretended—but to his warehouse, where a couple of *employés* were still at work. Having given them some orders, he retired for a short time into his private room, occupied himself, no doubt, with various business matters, and then came upstairs again and told his wife that he was going out for a stroll. From that stroll he had never returned.

The commissary of police carefully noted down these particulars, and then asked Madame Jandidier if he could speak with her alone for a few minutes. She looked at him with some surprise but finally signified her assent, and Mademoiselle Thérèse discreetly left the room.

'You must excuse the question I am about to ask you, madame,' exclaimed the commissary, as the young lady closed the door behind her. 'But this is a serious affair, and if we, the officials of justice, are to clear up the mystery, we must know the whole truth. Excuse my indiscretion, I beg you, but can you tell me whether M. Jandidier, your husband, ever had—to your knowledge—what shall I say? Well, any passing fancy, any feminine acquaintance away from home?'

Madame Jandidier sprang to her feet as if impelled by a spring. Anger had dried her tears, and it was in a snappish voice that she answered, 'I have been married three-and-twenty years, monsieur. Never on any one occasion has my husband given cause for such a supposition. If I was not with him of an evening, he never returned home later than ten o'clock.'

'Well, madame, was your husband in the habit of frequenting any club?' asked the commissary. 'Had he any special café where he met his friends?'

'I should not have allowed such habits,' curtly replied the lady.

'Do you know if he was accustomed to carry large sums about his person, madame?'

'On that point I can give you no information. I have always attended to my household, and not to my husband's business affairs.'

The commissary found it impossible to obtain any further information, for the worthy dame's grief was now blended with a strong admixture of anger and resentment. The supposition that her husband might have a mistress revolted her feelings as a wife, and the barely veiled insinuation that he might frequent a club, and no doubt gamble there, incensed her as an attack on his recognised probity and integrity. However, despite Madame Jandidier's stiff air, the commissary thought it only right to try and assuage her affliction by repeating a few hackneyed 'compliments of condolence,' and then, with a profound bow, he retired.

Before leaving the house, however, he considered it his duty to question the servants, and their statements, which generally corroborated Madame Jandidier's, made him feel somewhat anxious. He began to think that a crime had really been committed.

A few hours later he sent his report to the Prefecture of Police, and the same evening the case was submitted to the consideration of the Public Prosecutor. The latter, in his turn, delegated an investigating magistrate to examine the affair, and on the Monday morning the famous detective Retiveau, better known in the Rue de Jérusalem by his nickname of 'Maître Magloire,' received orders to scour Paris, and if needs be, the provinces, in search of M. Jandidier—or his corpse. A capital photograph of the manufacturer, taken only a short time previously, was handed to the detective, who at once commenced his difficult task.

II

Maître Magloire was a man of no little energy, and a fervent believer in the value of time. His alacrity was proverbial, so that the investigating magistrate entrusted with the Jandidier affair was by no means surprised when, on the Monday afternoon, his usher announced that the detective wished to speak with him, having already obtained some important information.

The magistrate at once gave orders for the police agent to be admitted. 'Here already, M. Magloire,' said he. 'So you have fresh news, eh?'

'I am on the scent, monsieur.'

'Well, tell me what you have ascertained.'

'To begin, monsieur, I have learned that M. Jandidier did not leave home at half-past six on Saturday evening, but at seven o'clock precisely.'

'Precisely?'

'Well, yes. My information comes from a clock-maker, in the immediate neighbourhood of M. Jandidier's house. This clock-maker knew him well, and noticed that he paused in front of his shop. In fact, M. Jandidier pulled out his watch and compared time with the clock above the door. The circumstance induced the clock-maker to look at the time himself, and he recollects perfectly well that it was then exactly two minutes past seven. Those two minutes would have amply sufficed for M. Jandidier to walk from his house as far as this shop. It is fortunate that he should have paused to compare time, for this apparently trivial circumstance has guided me to all my subsequent discoveries. For instance, the clock-maker noticed that M. Jandidier was munching an unlighted cigar. It occurred to me that he must ultimately have lighted it, and I asked myself where and how? Had he a box of lucifers in his pocket? No; for I learned at his house that a little silver-plated box he usually carried about with him had been found on the mantelshelf in his room since his disappearance. In this case, I reasoned, he must probably have gone into some tobacconist's shop to get a light.'

'Yes, no doubt,' opined the magistrate.

'I had considerable difficulty in finding the shop in question,' resumed the detective; 'but as the course taken by M. Jandidier from his residence to the clock-maker's shop seemed to indicate that he was going towards the boulevards, I went in that direction. To my delight, just as I reached the Boulevard du Temple, sure enough I came upon a tobacconist's shop. I went in and made inquiries. The woman behind the counter was well acquainted with M. Jandidier, and she recollected perfectly that he came in on Saturday evening to get a light. She was all the more certain on the point for, at the same time, he purchased a packet of *londrès extra*, which greatly surprised her, as he usually smoked very cheap cigars.'

'How did he seem?'

'The woman told me that he looked preoccupied. I obtained from her an important piece of information, which shows that Madame Jandidier was altogether wrong when she told the commissary of police that her husband did not go to any particular café. However, husbands don't always tell everything to their wives; and according to the tobacconist, M. Jandidier frequently went to the Café Turc, which is hard-by. I went there and questioned the waiters. Two of them remembered having seen him on Saturday evening. He drank two small glasses of brandy neat, and talked with some friends who were there. He seemed sad. The waiter who served at his table told me that he and his friends talked all the while about life insurances. It was half-past eight when he went away, accompanied by one of his friends, M. Blandureau, a merchant of the neighbourhood. I immediately went to M. Blandureau's warehouse and questioned him. He told me that on Saturday evening he walked down the boulevards with M. Jandidier, as far as the corner of the Rue de Richelieu, where M. Jandidier left him, saying that he had business to attend to. He was not at all in his usual frame of mind, M. Blandureau tells me; he seemed out of sorts and worried with melancholy presentiments.'

'Very good, so far,' muttered the magistrate.

'On leaving M. Blandureau,' continued Maître Magloire, 'I returned to the Rue du Roi de Sicile to inquire of the people of the house if M. Jandidier had, to their knowledge, any customers or friends, might be even a mistress, in the Rue de Richelieu. I more particularly questioned the man-servant, who generally did his master's errands, but all he could tell me was that M. Jandidier's tailor lived in that street. I thought it, after all, advisable to go and see this tailor. "Yes," said he, "M. Jandidier came to see me on Saturday. He came to order a pair of trousers, it was past nine o'clock." It seems that whilst he was being measured a button fell from his waistcoat, and he asked the tailor to sew it on again. For this to be done, he took off his coat, and at the same time removed a packet of papers and a note-book from the breast-pocket. Holding these papers in his hand he half sorted them, and the tailor noticed that they comprised several bank-notes!'

'Ah! That's a clue. So he had a large sum on his person?'

'Large? Well not so, perhaps, for a man of his position; but still a fair amount. The tailor thinks there must have been twelve or fourteen hundred francs in notes.'

'Continue,' said the investigating magistrate.

'While the button of his waistcoat was being sewn on again, M. Jandidier suddenly left off sorting his papers and complained of indisposition. The tailor had already noticed that he looked far from well; and at his customer's request he despatched an apprentice to fetch a cab. M. Jandidier said that he had to go as far as the Halle aux Vins to see one of his work-people who lived hard-by. Unfortunately the apprentice could not tell me the number of the cab he fetched, but on the other hand he recollected that it had yellow wheels, and was drawn by a big black horse. The yellow wheels proved that the vehicle did not come from the stables of the Cab Company, but that it belonged to some petty job-master. I sent a circular note to all the authorised cab-keepers, and a few hours ago I had the satisfaction of learning that the vehicle in question was No. 6,007. The driver remembered that on Saturday evening he was hailed by a lad in the Rue de Richelieu, and that for ten minutes or so he waited outside the shop of a tailor named Gouin. I asked him if he would be able to recognise the gentleman he drove to the Halle aux Vins, and he told me that he thought he would. Thereupon, I showed him five photographs, and he at once picked out M. Jandidier's portrait. There was a bright moonlight on Saturday evening, he said, and whilst the gentleman was counting out the money to pay his fare he had a good look at him.'

Maître Magloire paused and noted with satisfaction the approbative expression on the magistrate's face.

'Well,' said he, 'this cabby drove M. Jandidier to the immediate vicinity of the Halle aux Vins, to No. 48, in the Rue d'Arras-Saint-Victor; and in this house there lives a workman, whom M. Jandidier employed, a workman of the name of Jules Tarot.'

The significant manner in which Maître Magloire articulated these words, 'Jules Tarot,' was well calculated to impress the investigating magistrate.

'Have you any suspicions?' asked the latter, giving the detective a keen look.

'Not precisely; but still, here are the facts. On reaching the Rue d'Arras, M. Jandidier discharged his cab. He asked the doorkeeper if Tarot was at home, and on receiving an affirmative reply he went upstairs. It was then about ten o'clock. Half an hour afterwards the doorkeeper went to bed, and he was just falling asleep when he heard Tarot come downstairs. Tarot called to him to pull the rope which opens the door, and, thanks to the night light, the doorkeeper perceived that the workman was accompanied by the gentleman who had called. They went out together; and shortly after midnight Tarot returned home alone.'

'And M. Jandidier?' asked the magistrate.

'Ah! I have been unable to trace him any further,' replied Maître Magloire.

'That seems significant; suspicious even.'

'Yes, monsieur. I fancy it's a bad job. Of course, I could not question Tarot; it would have put him on his guard.'

'Have you found out what kind of man this fellow Tarot is?'

'Oh! On that point I questioned the doorkeeper. Tarot, he told me, is a mother-of-pearl worker. He polishes the shells, and is most skilful in imparting the proper nacreous iridescence. Altogether, he seems to be a clever fellow, and he and his wife together—for he has taught her the work—earn at times as much as a hundred francs a week.'

'So they are well off, for people of their class.'

'Well, no, monsieur. They are both of them young, both of them Parisians born and bred, they have no children, and so they amuse themselves. Not content with Sunday relaxation and pleasure, they habitually make Monday a fête day, after the fashion of so many work-people, and the result is, that long before pay-day arrives they are desperately hard up.'

'H'm,' said the magistrate, stroking his chin with a pensive air. 'All this seems very suspicious—very suspicious indeed. So the Tarots lead rather a loose life? Their purse is often empty; and very likely they are in debt. Those twelve hundred francs that M. Jandidier had about him, no doubt, excited their covetousness. He probably called on Tarot to entrust him with some work, and no doubt pulled out his pocket-book to make a memorandum. Tarot must have seen the bank-notes. And no trace, you say, can be found of M. Jandidier after he left the house with his workman at eleven o'clock at night?'

'No, monsieur, no trace at all,' answered the detective. 'I have made diligent inquiries in all directions but without result.'

'Very strange, very suspicious,' muttered the magistrate; and then in a louder key he added: 'I must say, M. Magloire, that you have conducted this inquiry admirably. Guided by M. Jandidier's unlighted cigar, you have traced him to—well, to the man who is probably his murderer. Yes, his murderer, I have very strong suspicions on the point.'

A brief pause ensued, and then the magistrate asked: 'Was Tarot at home when you made these inquiries this afternoon?'

'Oh, no, monsieur. He and his wife had gone off. It's Monday, remember.'

'Are you certain that they had merely gone off holiday-making?'

'Why, yes, monsieur; the doorkeeper said they had left early in the morning with a couple of friends, two of Tarot's comrades, I believe. They were going to picnic near Chaville.'

'Ah! That was a splendid opportunity to make a perquisition in their absence, Maître Magloire.'

'Certainly, monsieur, but I had no search warrant, and besides, it was only an hour or so ago that I went to the Rue d'Arras.'

'I suppose that doorkeeper is to be depended upon?'

'Oh, yes, monsieur. He's affiliated at the Prefecture, No. 920.'[1]

'Then he's safe. Did you leave him any instructions as to what he ought to do, if the Tarots returned home before you saw him again?'

'I did better than that, monsieur, I left a comrade at the house to wait and watch.'

'Very good. Well, M. Magloire, we must have a perquisition; and here are a couple of warrants which you can use if occasion requires. Be here at eight o'clock to-morrow morning.'

So saying, the magistrate returned to some documents he had been perusing when the detective arrived. The latter pocketed the warrants, made a deep bow, and hastened out of the room.

III

It was already six o'clock, and before repairing to the Rue d'Arras-Saint-Victor it was necessary that Maître Magloire should call at the office of the district commissary of police, show him his instructions, and request him to preside at the perquisition. As the commissary was away at his dinner, some little time was lost. 'We must have a locksmith,' the detective reflected, 'for the Tarots will hardly have returned, and it will be necessary to force open the door.' A locksmith was accordingly procured, a couple of *gardiens de la Paix* were summoned to serve as an escort, and on the commissary's return the party set off.

At the corner of the street the detective asked his companions to wait a moment, and then went ahead. It was necessary that he should reconnoitre the ground, and ascertain from the comrade whom he had left with the doorkeeper if anything noteworthy had occurred during his absence.

---

[1] It should be remembered that a very large number of Parisian doorkeepers, or *concierges*, are secret-agents of the Prefecture de Police.—*Trans.*

As he entered the house he heard heavy steps climbing the stairs, and a man and a woman singing a gay refrain. 'Have they returned?' thought Maître Magloire, and he hurried into the doorkeeper's room.

His comrade was there, and on perceiving him raised his forefinger to his lips: 'Hush, they've just come home. They are only half-way upstairs.'

'They are singing loud enough,' rejoined Maître Magloire in an undertone. 'I must say that they are unusually gay for—for murderers.'

'Oh!' replied his comrade. 'The wine has got into their heads. As for their gaiety we'll see about that by and by.'

Despite this rejoinder Magloire remained for a moment pensive. 'Am I mistaken?' he asked himself. 'But, then——' However, his hesitation was of short duration. 'At all events we must clear up the mystery,' he added, and leaving the house he went in search of the commissary.

Joyful the Tarots had certainly seemed as they climbed the stairs, singing a popular ditty. They were laden with field flowers, which the wife tastefully arranged in two large blue vases as soon as they had entered their lodging.

'Now, Clementina,' called the husband, 'you must make haste with the supper, or else the concert will be over by the time we get there.'

Both Tarot and his wife were very partial to the entertainments given at a little *café concert* in the neighbourhood, and it was with the view of going there that evening that they had returned so early from their excursion.

'Oh! I've only the stew to warm,' answered the wife; 'but, Eugène, while I light the fire would you mind running down to fetch a quart of wine?'

The husband took an empty bottle from a corner in the kitchen and went toward the outer door of the apartment, but when only half-way he paused with surprise.

Rat-tat-tat, rat-tat-tat. Some very noisy visitor indeed demanded admittance.

'Who's there?' cried Tarot.

'Open, in the name of the law,' answered a stern voice.

Husband and wife turned pale with terror.

'Open, in the name of the law,' repeated the same voice.

Still Tarot did not budge. Fear seemed to root him to the spot.

There was no further parleying, for at that moment Maître Magloire perceived that the key had been left in the door outside. So he just turned it and walked in, followed by his comrade and the commissary of police.

On perceiving the latter functionary, whose stomach was spanned with his broad tricolour sash of office, Tarot and his wife were seized with a nervous trembling, of which Maître Magloire took careful note.

'Why didn't you open the door?' sternly asked the commissary of police.

'I was so surprised—monsieur—I didn't know—I——' stammered Tarot.

'Ah, you look as if you had something on your conscience,' retorted the functionary. 'I suppose you know what has brought us here?'

Tarot gave the commissary an anxious look, and stammered an incomprehensible answer.

'We have come to make a perquisition,' said Maître Magloire. 'Do you know that your employer, M. Jandidier of the Rue du Roi de Sicile, has disappeared? He was last seen in your company late on Saturday night.'

Both Tarot and his wife were too overwhelmed to speak.

'Come, give us the keys of all your drawers and cupboards,' said the commissary; and as the wife timidly drew them from her pocket he added, turning to the detective: 'There you are, Maître Magloire, you may set about your task.'

The search was a protracted and a difficult one, for dusk had now set in, and a careful scrutiny could scarcely be made by lamplight. However, all the drawers were turned out, and all the cupboards carefully explored. Magloire ferreted in every nook and corner, ripped up the mattresses and pillows on the bed, tried the stuffing of the chairs, but all to no avail. Nothing suspicious could be found.

'It's singular,' muttered the detective; and he once more asked himself, 'Have I been mistaken after all?'

At this moment it occurred to him to look at the Tarots who stood by, watching the proceedings in silence. Perhaps their demeanour might give him a clue; otherwise he and his companions would have no other resource but to apologise and withdraw. At first he observed nothing particular, save an expression of affright in their looks, but as he carefully followed the direction of the wife's glance, he noticed that it was fixed on a birdcage hanging near the window. 'Eureka!' he cried. 'I have it!'

Springing toward the cage he unhooked it, and, careless of the canary roosting on the perch, he examined it in every sense. As in most cages there was a movable floor which drew out to admit of proper cleansing, and, sure enough, between the thin boards, Maître Magloire found a sum of twelve hundred francs in bank-notes.

The Tarots exchanged looks of terror. The husband seemed overwhelmed, but the wife broke out into piteous lamentations, repeating again and again that she and her husband were innocent.

However, the commissary and Magloire paid little or no attention to her wailings. 'You had much better make a clear breast of it,' exclaimed the detective, 'instead of kicking up that row.' Whereupon both husband and wife answered in piteous tones: 'Oh! we are innocent, sir, we are innocent!'

This time the detective shrugged his shoulders. 'In the name of the law, I arrest you,' said he. 'I charge you with the murder of M. Jandidier.' And he called to the two *gardiens de la Paix*, waiting below, to come upstairs.

The Tarots showed no signs of resistance, but as they were charged with a capital offence, the commissary thought it prudent to have them handcuffed. They passively allowed themselves to be removed to a cab which was sent for, and half an hour later they crossed the threshold of the Dépôt, and were duly locked into separate cells.

Magloire was fairly elated, and, forgetful of discipline, hurried off to the private residence of the investigating magistrate, to acquaint him with the capture and the recovery of M. Jandidier's money. The magistrate was pleased to express his approval, and renewed the appointment for the following morning at his office at the Palais de Justice.

The Tarots were interrogated separately. They both looked pale and careworn when they entered the magistrate's office, but, after passing the night under lock and key in a prison cell, this was only natural. However, they had both found their tongues again, and apparently they had preconcerted a system of defence, for their answers were identical.

They admitted that M. Jandidier had called on them on the Saturday evening. He seemed very poorly, and they asked him if he would not like to take a drop of something, but he refused the offer.

'What was the object of his visit?' asked the magistrate.

'He wished us to execute an important order, and proposed that we should take work-people on our own account.'

'That's singular. Had he not numerous workmen of his own?'

'Yes, but he said that his health was failing him, that he could no longer give his usual attention to business, and should prefer to transfer the order to us.'

'And what was your answer?'

'We told him that we lacked the capital to execute it.'

'Ah!—ah! And what then?'

'Why, he replied, "Oh, that's of no consequence. I'll advance you enough money"; and he pulled out his pocket-book, and laid twelve hundred francs in bank-notes on the table.'

'Had he so much confidence as that in you?'

'Well, he knew we worked fairly well.'

'Yes, but you have dissipated habits. You spend your money faster than you earn it. Your story is altogether improbable. M. Jandidier must have known how prodigal you both were. Well, did you at least give him a receipt?'

'Yes, monsieur.'

'Who signed it?'

'We both did.'

'H'm, and what then?'

'After that,' answered Tarot, 'M. Jandidier asked me to see him further on. He said he was going in the direction of the Faubourg St Antoine.'

'And where did you leave him?'

'At the Place de la Bastille. We crossed the Constantine foot bridge and followed the canal.'

'Ah! you followed the canal?' exclaimed the magistrate, eyeing Tarot attentively. 'And you reached the Place de la Bastille safely?'

'Certainly we did, monsieur,' answered the workman, with a flushed face.

Naturally enough, the magistrate asked both the husband and the wife to explain why they had hidden the money in the birdcage, and they each gave the same answer. On the Sunday night, as they were going home, Tarot met a comrade who, while he was playing cards in a wine-shop in the Marais during the afternoon, had heard of M. Jandidier's disappearance. The news greatly frightened them, and Tarot said to his wife, 'If it were known that he came here on Saturday night, it would be a bad job for us. Didn't we cross the bridge together, and walk along the banks of the canal? The police would certainly suspect me, and if those twelve hundred francs were found in our possession, we should be altogether lost.'

'We didn't sleep all Sunday night,' said Tarot's wife; 'we lay awake thinking about M. Jandidier. And we certainly shouldn't have gone out on the Monday, if one of my husband's cousins hadn't come to fetch us according to arrangement. However, in the country we almost forgot about the matter, and as the detective says, we were no doubt gay when we came home. Before going out, I wanted to burn the bank-notes, but Tarot wouldn't let me. He meant to refund the money to M. Jandidier's family, he said; and besides, as he explained, we might have put ourselves in a bad position by destroying the notes, for, even if M. Jandidier were dead, his body might be found with our receipt in his pocket, and then we should have to refund the money; and how could we do so if the notes were destroyed?'

The magistrate listened attentively to this explanation, which was plausible if not probable, and the prisoners' line of defence struck him as a very artful one. 'How did you know,' he asked at length, 'how did you know that M. Jandidier's body had not been found when the police searched your place? It might have been recovered, and the detectives might have had your receipt with them. It was your duty to produce that money at once. Why didn't you do so?'

'We didn't know what to do or what to think, monsieur; we were too frightened.'

'Innocent persons have no reason to feel frightened,' sententiously retorted the magistrate. 'Justice knows how to distinguish between the innocent and the guilty.'

He said this, and yet, at that very moment, he was asking himself in sore perplexity, 'Are these people culpable or not?' After all, there was nothing to corroborate the explanation of the Tarots, and it was utterly impossible for him to content himself with their mere word. A further search must be made for M. Jandidier. Perhaps his body might be found, and then it would be possible to form a positive opinion. In the meanwhile, the workman and his wife must be retained in custody.

IV

A week elapsed, and the magistrate was still in the same perplexity. The Tarots had each been re-examined three times, but nothing fresh had been elicited from them, and their later statements failed to contradict their earlier version. Were they innocent, then? Or had they merely cleverly preconcerted a plausible system of defence?

M. Jandidier's remains had been searched for far and wide. The Seine and the canal had been dragged. The missing manufacturer's photograph had been sent all over France, but utterly without result. In this situation, the magistrate asked himself what course he ought to pursue. If he sent the prisoners to the assizes they would very likely be acquitted for want of sufficient proofs, especially if they were defended by a skilful advocate. No doubt there was the circumstance of those twelve hundred francs found in their possession; but would that suffice to ensure a conviction? The prisoners explained their possession of this money in a most artful fashion, and, besides, the true *corpus delicti* was wanting. What should the magistrate do then?

He was asking himself this question for the hundredth time, when a strange, almost incredible report reached his ears. The well-known firm of Jandidier *ainé* had suspended payment, and was going into bankruptcy! 'Who would have expected that!' grumbled the magistrate. 'Well, perhaps, we are coming to the truth.'

On the morrow a detective who had been duly instructed, brought him a full report of circumstances which none of M. Jandidier's family had ever dreamed of. The revelation was an astounding one, and had caused immense surprise throughout the district of the Marais where M. Jandidier had been so respected and esteemed. In fact, the man whom the denizens of the Rue du Roi de Sicile so delighted to honour, the idol of the trade in imitation jewellery, had fallen from his pedestal with a crash. People had imagined he was wealthy, and yet in reality he was ruined—utterly ruined: and during the last three years he had only kept up his credit by means of expedients. Less than a thousand francs had been found in his safe, and on the Saturday after his disappearance, bills for sixty-seven thousand five hundred francs were presented for payment by the Bank of France. Yes, Jandidier, the man of severe morality, gambled at the Bourse; the virtuous husband kept a mistress!

The magistrate could scarcely believe his ears, and was giving vent to his astonishment when Maître Magloire appeared, quite out of breath.

'You know the news, monsieur?' asked the detective as he crossed the threshold.

'Yes, I have just been told everything.'

'The Tarots are innocent!'

'I think so—and yet that visit Jandidier paid them—how do you explain that visit?'

The detective sighed. 'Ah, monsieur,' said he, 'I was a fool, as my colleague Monsieur Lecoq, has just shown me. You will recollect that at the Café Turc, Jandidier and his friends talked all the time about life assurances?'

'Yes, I remember; but what connection——'

'Ah, monsieur, that was the point I ought to have kept in mind! Jandidier's life was assured for 200,000 francs.'

'Indeed!'

'Yes, and as you are aware, monsieur, in France assurance companies don't pay when the holder of the policy commits suicide. Now, Jandidier was no doubt anxious to provide for his family; and so he made it appear as if he had been murdered, in hopes that the companies would pay his wife.'

'Do you think he has destroyed himself?'

'I cannot say, monsieur. At all events we cannot find his remains. Maybe he has simply taken himself off. And yet I don't know; he can only have had very little money with him, and at his age a man scarcely has the courage to begin life over again. At all events, he certainly laid a trap for poor Tarot, and would have sent him to the guillotine for the sake of his policies being paid.'

'What a scamp!' growled the magistrate; and he took up his pen to sign an order for the release of the workman and his wife.

Thanks to M. Gustave Schmidt—of the great house of Schmidt, Gubenheim, and Worb—the firm of Jandidier did not go into bankruptcy. Old Schmidt had just died, most opportunely, and M. Gustave was able to dispose of the paternal inheritance as he pleased, and more than that, he means to dispose of himself as well, for the papers announce that he and Mademoiselle Thérèse Jandidier are to be married next month.

Tarot and his wife have set up in business, thanks to the twelve hundred francs returned to them at M. Gustave's request; and, mindful of the investigating magistrate's reproaches anent their 'prodigality' and 'dissipated habits,' they have quite given up 'merry-making' on Mondays.

But what has become of M. Jandidier? Is he dead, or has he gone to America? If any of our readers are acquainted with his whereabouts, they may communicate with the authorities, who offer a thousand francs reward!

JOHN CHARLES DENT (1841–1888)

The Gerrard Street Mystery

————

I

My name is William Francis Furlong. My occupation is that of a commission merchant, and my place of business is on St Paul Street, in the City of Montreal. I have resided in Montreal ever since shortly after my marriage, in 1862, to my cousin, Alice Playter, of Toronto. My name may not be familiar to the present generation of Torontonians, though I was born in Toronto, and passed the early years of my life there. Since the days of my youth my visits to the Upper Province have been few, and—with one exception—very brief; so that I have doubtless passed out of the remembrance of many persons with whom I was once on terms of intimacy. Still there are several residents of Toronto whom I am happy to number among my warmest personal friends at the present day. There are also a good many persons of middle age, not in Toronto only, but scattered here and there throughout various parts of Ontario, who will have no difficulty in recalling my name as that of one of their fellow-students at Upper Canada College. The name of my late uncle, Richard Yardington, is of course well known to all residents of Toronto, where he spent the last thirty-two years of his life. He settled there in the year 1829, when the place was still known as Little York. He opened a small store on Yonge Street, and his commercial career was a reasonably prosperous one. By steady degrees the small store developed into what, in those times, was regarded as a considerable establishment. In the course of years the owner acquired a competency, and in 1854 retired from business altogether. From that time up to the day of his death he lived in his own house on Gerrard Street.

After mature deliberation, I have resolved to give to the Canadian public an account of some rather singular circumstances connected with my residence in Toronto. Though repeatedly urged to do so, I have hitherto refrained from giving any extended publicity to those circumstances, in consequence of my inability to see any good to be served thereby. The only person, however, whose reputation can be injuriously affected by the details has been dead for some years. He has left behind him no one whose feelings can be shocked by the disclosure, and the story is in itself sufficiently remarkable to be worth the telling. Told, accordingly, it shall be; and the only fictitious element introduced into the narrative shall be the name of one of the persons most immediately concerned in it.

At the time of taking up his abode in Toronto—or rather in Little York—my uncle Richard was a widower, and childless; his wife having died several months previously. His only relatives on this side of the Atlantic were two maiden sisters, a few years younger than himself. He never contracted a second matrimonial alliance, and for some time after his arrival here his sisters lived in his house, and were dependent upon him for support. After the lapse of a few years both of them married and settled down in homes of their own. The elder of them subsequently became my mother. She was left a widow when I was a mere boy, and survived my father only a few months. I was an only child, and as my parents had been in humble circumstances, the charge of my maintenance devolved upon my uncle, to whose kindness I am indebted for such educational training as I have received. After sending me to school and college for several years, he took me into his store, and gave me my first insight into commercial life. I lived with him, and both then and always received at his hands the kindness of a father, in which light I eventually almost came to regard him. His younger sister, who was married to a watchmaker called Elias Playter, lived at Quebec from the time of her marriage until her death, which took place in 1846. Her husband had been unsuccessful in business, and was moreover of dissipated habits. He was left with one child—a daughter—on his hands; and as my uncle was averse to the idea of his sister's child remaining under the control of one so unfit to provide for her welfare, he proposed to adopt the little girl as his own. To this proposition Mr Elias Playter readily assented, and little Alice was soon domiciled with her uncle and myself in Toronto.

Brought up, as we were, under the same roof, and seeing each other every day of our lives, a childish attachment sprang up between my cousin Alice and myself. As the years rolled by, this attachment ripened into a tender affection, which eventually resulted in an engagement between us. Our engagement was made with the full and cordial approval of my uncle, who did not share the prejudice entertained by many persons against marriages between cousins. He stipulated, however, that our marriage should be deferred until I had seen somewhat more of the world, and until we had both reached an age when we might reasonably be presumed to know our own minds. He was also, not unnaturally, desirous that before taking upon myself the responsibility of marriage I should give some evidence of my ability to provide for a wife, and for other contingencies usually consequent upon matrimony. He made no secret of his intention to divide his property between Alice and myself at his death; and the fact that no actual division would be necessary in the event of our marriage with each other was doubtless one reason for his ready acquiescence in our engagement. He was, however, of a vigorous constitution, strictly regular and methodical in all his habits, and likely to live to an advanced age. He could hardly be called parsimonious, but, like most men who have successfully fought their own way through life, he was rather fond of authority, and little disposed to divest himself of his wealth until he should have no further occasion for it. He expressed his willingness to establish me in business, either in Toronto or elsewhere, and to give me the benefit of his experience in all mercantile transactions.

When matters had reached this pass I had just completed my twenty-first year, my cousin being three years younger. Since my uncle's retirement I had engaged in one or two little speculations on my own account, which had turned out fairly successful, but I had not devoted myself to any regular or fixed pursuit. Before any definite arrangements had been concluded as to the course of my future life, a circumstance occurred which seemed to open a way for me to turn to good account such mercantile talent as I possessed. An old friend of my uncle's opportunely arrived in Toronto from Melbourne, Australia, where, in the course of a few years, he had risen from the position of a junior clerk to that of senior partner in a prominent commercial house. He painted the land of his adoption in glowing colours, and assured my uncle and myself that it presented an inviting field for a young man of energy and business capacity, more especially if he had a small capital at his command. The matter was carefully debated in our domestic circle. I was naturally averse to a separation from Alice, but my imagination took fire at Mr Redpath's glowing account of his own splendid success. I pictured myself returning to Canada after an absence of four or five years with a mountain of gold at my command, as the result of my own energy and acuteness. In imagination, I saw myself settled down with Alice in a palatial mansion on Jarvis Street, and living in affluence all the rest of my days. My uncle bade me consult my own judgment in the matter, but rather encouraged the idea than otherwise. He offered to advance me £500, and I had about half that sum as the result of my own speculations. Mr Redpath, who was just about returning to Melbourne, promised to aid me to the extent of his power with his local knowledge and advice. In less than a fortnight from that time he and I were on our way to the other side of the globe.

We reached our destination early in the month of September, 1857. My life in Australia has no direct bearing upon the course of events to be related, and may be passed over in a very few words. I engaged in various enterprises, and achieved a certain measure of success. If none of my ventures proved eminently prosperous, I at least met with no serious disasters. At the end of four years—that is to say, in September, 1861—I made up my account with the world, and found I was worth ten thousand dollars. I had, however, become terribly homesick, and longed for the termination of my voluntary exile. I had, of course, kept up a regular correspondence with Alice and Uncle Richard, and of late they had both pressed me to return home. 'You have enough,' wrote my uncle, 'to give you a start in Toronto, and I see no reason why Alice and you should keep apart any longer. You will have no housekeeping expenses, for I intend you to live with me. I am getting old, and shall be glad of your companionship in my declining years. You will have a comfortable home while I live and when I die you will get all I have between you. Write as soon as you receive this, and let us know how soon you can be here—the sooner the better.'

The letter containing this pressing invitation found me in a mood very much disposed to accept it. The only enterprise I had on hand which would be likely to delay me was a transaction in wool, which, as I believed, would be closed by the end of January or the beginning of February. By the first of March I should certainly be in a condition to start on my homeward voyage, and I determined that my departure should take place about that time. I wrote both to Alice and my uncle, apprising them of my intention, and announcing my expectation to reach Toronto not later than the middle of May.

The letters so written were posted on the 19th of September, in time for the mail which left on the following day. On the 27th, to my huge surprise and gratification, the wool transaction referred to was unexpectedly concluded, and I was at liberty, if so disposed, to start for home by the next fast mail steamer, the *Southern Cross*, leaving Melbourne on the 11th of October. I *was* so disposed, and made my preparations accordingly. It was useless, I reflected, to write to my uncle or to Alice, acquainting them with the change in my plans, for I should take the shortest route home, and should probably be in Toronto as soon as a letter could get there. I resolved to telegraph from New York, upon my arrival there, so as not to take them altogether by surprise.

The morning of the 11th of October found me on board the *Southern Cross*, where I shook hands with Mr Redpath and several other friends who accompanied me on board for a last farewell. The particulars of the voyage to England are not pertinent to the story, and may be given very briefly. I took the Red Sea route, and arrived at Marseilles about two o'clock in the afternoon of the 29th of November. From Marseilles I travelled by rail to Calais, and so impatient was I to reach my journey's end without loss of time, that I did not even stay over to behold the glories of Paris. I had a commission to execute in London, which, however, delayed me there only a few hours, and I hurried down to Liverpool, in the hope of catching the Cunard Steamer for New York. I missed it by about two hours, but the *Persia* was detailed to start on a special trip to Boston on the following day. I secured a berth, and at eight o'clock the next morning steamed out of the Mersey on my way homeward.

The voyage from Liverpool to Boston consumed fourteen days. All I need say about it is, that before arriving at the latter port I formed an intimate acquaintance with one of the passengers—Mr Junius H. Gridley, a Boston merchant, who was returning from a hurried business trip to Europe. He was—and is—a most agreeable companion. We were thrown together a good deal during the voyage, and we then laid the foundation of a friendship which has ever since subsisted between us. Before the dome of the State House loomed in sight he had extracted a promise from me to spend a night with him before pursuing my journey. We landed at the wharf in East Boston on the evening of the 17th of December, and I accompanied him to his house on West Newton Street, where I remained until the following morning. Upon consulting the time-table, we found that the Albany express would leave at 11.30 a.m. This left several hours at my disposal, and we sallied forth immediately after breakfast to visit some of the lions of the American Athens.

In the course of our peregrinations through the streets, we dropped into the post office, which had recently been established in the Merchant's Exchange Building, on State Street. Seeing the countless piles of mail-matter, I jestingly remarked to my friend that there seemed to be letters enough there to go around the whole human family. He replied in the same mood, whereupon I banteringly suggested the probability that among so many letters, surely there ought to be one for me.

'Nothing more reasonable,' he replied. 'We Bostonians are always bountiful to strangers. Here is the General Delivery, and here is the department where letters addressed to the Furlong family are kept in stock. Pray inquire for yourself.'

The joke I confess was not a very brilliant one; but with a grave countenance I stepped up to the wicket and asked the young lady in attendance:

'Anything for W. F. Furlong?'

She took from a pigeon-hole a handful of correspondence, and proceeded to run her eye over the addresses. When about half the pile had been exhausted she stopped, and propounded the usual inquiry in the case of strangers:

'Where do you expect letters from?'

'From Toronto,' I replied.

To my no small astonishment she immediately handed me a letter, bearing the Toronto post-mark. The address was in the peculiar and well-known handwriting of my uncle Richard.

Scarcely crediting the evidence of my senses I tore open the envelope, and read as follows:—

'TORONTO, 9th December, 1861.

'MY DEAR WILLIAM—I am so glad to know that you are coming home so much sooner than you expected when you wrote last, and that you will eat your Christmas dinner with us. For reasons which you will learn when you arrive, it will not be a very merry Christmas at our house, but your presence will make it much more bearable than it would be without you. I have not told Alice that you are coming. Let it be a joyful surprise for her, as some compensation for the sorrows she has had to endure lately. You needn't telegraph. I will meet you at the G.W.R. station.

'Your affectionate uncle,
RICHARD YARDINGTON.'

'Why, what's the matter?' asked my friend, seeing the blank look of surprise on my face. 'Of course the letter is not for you; why on earth did you open it?'

'It *is* for me,' I answered. 'See here, Gridley, old man; have you been playing me a trick? If you haven't, this is the strangest thing I ever knew in my life.'

Of course he hadn't been playing me a trick. A moment's reflection showed me that such a thing was impossible. Here was the envelope, with the Toronto post-mark of the 9th of December, at which time he had been with me on board the *Persia*, on the Banks of Newfoundland. Besides, he was a gentleman, and would not have played so poor and stupid a joke upon a guest. And, to put the matter beyond all possibility of doubt, I remembered that I had never mentioned my cousin's name in his hearing.

I handed him the letter. He read it carefully through twice over, and was as much mystified at its contents as myself; for during our passage across the Atlantic I had explained to him the circumstance under which I was returning home.

By what conceivable means had my uncle been made aware of my departure from Melbourne? Had Mr Redpath written to him as soon as I acquainted that gentleman with my intentions? But even if such were the case, the letter could not have left before I did, and could not possibly have reached Toronto by the 9th of December. Had I been seen in England by some one who knew me, and had not one written from there? Most unlikely; and even if such a thing had happened, it was impossible that the letter could have reached Toronto by the 9th. I need hardly inform the reader that there was no telegraphic communication at that time. And how could my uncle know that I would take the Boston route? And if he *had* known, how could he foresee that I would do anything so absurd as to call at the Boston post office and inquire for letters? '*I will meet you at the G.W.R. station.*' How was he to know by what train I would reach Toronto, unless I notified him by telegraph? And that he expressly stated to be unnecessary.

We did no more sight-seeing. I obeyed the hint contained in the letter, and sent no telegram. My friend accompanied me down to the Boston and Albany station, where I waited in feverish impatience for the departure of the train. We talked over the matter until 11.30, in the vain hope of finding some clue to the mystery. Then I started on my journey. Mr Gridley's curiosity was aroused and I promised to send him an explanation immediately upon my arrival at home.

No sooner had the train glided out of the station than I settled myself in my seat, drew the tantalizing letter from my pocket, and proceeded to read and re-read it again and again. A very few perusals sufficed to fix its contents in my memory, so that I could repeat every word with my eyes shut. Still I continued to scrutinize the paper, the penmanship, and even the tint of the ink. For what purpose, do you ask? For no purpose, except that I hoped, in some mysterious manner, to obtain more light on the subject. No light came, however. The more I scrutinized and pondered, the greater was my mystification. The paper was a simple sheet of white letter-paper, of the kind ordinarily used by my uncle in his correspondence. So far as I could see, there was nothing peculiar about the ink. Anyone familiar with my uncle's writing could have sworn that no hand but his had penned the lines. His well-known signature, a masterpiece of involved hieroglyphics, was there in all its indistinctness, written as no one but himself could ever have written it. And yet, for some unaccountable reason, I was half disposed to suspect forgery. Forgery! What nonsense. Anyone clever enough to imitate Richard Yardington's handwriting would have employed his talents more profitably than indulging in a mischievous and purposeless jest. Not a bank in Toronto but would have discounted a note with that signature affixed to it.

Desisting from all attempts to solve these problems, I then tried to fathom the meaning of other points in the letter. What misfortune had happened to mar the Christmas festivities at my uncle's house? And what could the reference to my cousin Alice's sorrows mean? She was not ill. *That*, I thought, might be taken for granted. My uncle would hardly have referred to her illness as 'one of the sorrows she had to endure lately.' Certainly, illness may be regarded in the light of a sorrow; but 'sorrow' was not precisely the word which a straightforward man like Uncle Richard would have applied to it. I could conceive of no other cause of affliction in her case. My uncle was well, as was evinced by his having written the letter, and by his avowed intention to meet me at the station. Her father had died long before I started for Australia. She had no other near relation except myself, and she had no cause for anxiety, much less for 'sorrow,' on my account. I thought it singular, too, that my uncle, having in some strange manner become acquainted with my movements, had withheld the knowledge from Alice. It did not

square with my pre-conceived ideas of him that he would derive any
satisfaction from taking his niece by surprise.

All was a muddle together, and as my temples throbbed with the
intensity of my thoughts, I was half disposed to believe myself in a
troubled dream from which I should presently awake. Meanwhile, on
glided the train.

A heavy snow-storm delayed us for several hours, and we reached
Hamilton too late for the mid-day express for Toronto. We got there,
however, in time for the accommodation leaving at 3.15 p.m., and we
would reach Toronto at 5.05. I walked from one end of the train to the
other in hopes of finding someone I knew, from whom I could make
enquiries about home. Not a soul. I saw several persons whom I knew
to be residents of Toronto, but none with whom I had ever been
personally acquainted, and none of them would be likely to know
anything about my uncle's domestic arrangements. All that remained
to be done under these circumstances was to restrain my curiosity as
well as I could until reaching Toronto. By the by, would my uncle
really meet me at the station, according to his promise? Surely not. By
what means could he possibly know that I would arrive by this train?
Still, he seemed to have such accurate information respecting my
proceedings that there was no saying where his knowledge began or
ended. I tried not to think about the matter, but as the train
approached Toronto my impatience became positively feverish in its
intensity. We were not more than three minutes behind time, as we
glided in front of the Union Station. I passed out on to the platform
of the car, and peered intently through the darkness. Suddenly my
heart gave a great bound. There, sure enough, standing in front of the
door of the waiting-room, was my uncle, plainly discernible by the
fitful glare of the overhanging lamps. Before the train came to a
stand-still, I sprang from the car and advanced towards him. He was
looking out for me, but his eyes not being as young as mine, he did
not recognize me until I grasped him by the hand. He greeted me
warmly, seizing me by the waist, and almost raising me from the
ground. I at once noticed several changes in his appearance; changes
for which I was wholly unprepared. He had aged very much since I
had last seen him, and the lines about his mouth had deepened
considerably. The iron-grey hair which I remembered so well had disappeared, its place being supplied with a new and rather dandified-
looking wig. The oldfashioned great-coat which he had worn ever
since I could remember, had been supplanted by a modern frock of

spruce cut, with seal-skin collar and cuffs. All this I noticed in the first hurried greetings that passed between us.

'Never mind your luggage, my boy,' he remarked. 'Leave it till tomorrow, when we will send down for it. If you are not tired we'll walk home instead of taking a cab. I have a good deal to say to you before we get there.'

I had not slept since leaving Boston, but was too much excited to be conscious of fatigue, and as will readily be believed, I was anxious enough to hear what he had to say. We passed from the station, and proceeded up York Street, arm in arm.

'And now, Uncle Richard,' I said, as soon as we were well clear of the crowd, 'keep me no longer in suspense. First and foremost, is Alice well?'

'Quite well, but for reasons you will soon understand, she is in deep grief. You must know that—'

'But,' I interrupted, 'tell me, in the name of all that's wonderful, how you knew I was coming by this train; and how did you come to write to me at Boston?'

Just then we came to the corner of Front Street, where was a lamp-post. As we reached the spot where the light of the lamp was most brilliant, he turned half round, looked me full in the face, and smiled a sort of wintry smile. The expression of his countenance was almost ghastly.

'Uncle,' I quickly said, 'what's the matter? Are you not well?'

'I am not as strong as I used to be, and I have had a good deal to try me of late. Have patience and I will tell you all. Let us walk more slowly, or I shall not finish before we get home. In order that you may clearly understand how matters are, I had better begin at the beginning, and I hope you will not interrupt me with any questions till I have done. How I knew you would call at the Boston post-office, and that you would arrive in Toronto by this train, will come last in order. By the by, have you my letter with you?'

'The one you wrote me at Boston? Yes, here it is,' I replied, taking it from my pocket-book.

'Let me have it.'

I handed it to him, and he put it into the breast pocket of his inside coat. I wondered at this proceeding on his part, but made no remark upon it.

We moderated our pace, and he began his narration. Of course I don't pretend to remember his exact words, but they were to this effect.

During the winter following my departure to Melbourne, he had formed the acquaintance of a gentleman who had then recently settled in Toronto. The name of this gentleman was Marcus Weatherley, who had commenced business as a wholesale provision merchant immediately upon his arrival, and had been engaged in it ever since. For more than three years the acquaintance between him and my uncle had been very slight, but during the last summer they had had some real estate transactions together, and had become intimate. Weatherley, who was comparatively a young man and unmarried, had been invited to the house on Gerrard Street, where he had more recently become a pretty frequent visitor. More recently still, his visits had become so frequent that my uncle suspected him of a desire to be attentive to my cousin, and had thought proper to enlighten him as to her engagement with me. From that day his visits had been voluntarily discontinued. My uncle had not given much consideration to the subject until a fortnight afterwards, when he had accidentally become aware of the fact that Weatherley was in embarrassed circumstances.

Here my uncle paused in his narrative to take breath. He then added, in a low tone, and putting his mouth almost close to my ear:

'And, Willie, my boy, I have at last found out something else. He has forty-two thousand dollars falling due here and in Montreal within the next ten days, and *he has forged my signature to acceptances for thirty-nine thousand seven hundred and sixteen dollars and twenty-four cents.*'

Those, to the best of my belief, were his exact words. We had walked up York Street to Queen, and then had gone down Queen to Yonge, when we turned up the east side on our way homeward. At the moment when the last words were uttered we had got a few yards north of Crookshank Street, immediately in front of a chemist's shop which was, I think, the third house from the corner. The window of this shop was well lighted, and its brightness was reflected on the sidewalk in front. Just then, two gentlemen walking rapidly in the opposite direction to that we were taking brushed by us; but I was too deeply absorbed in my uncle's communication to pay much attention to passers-by. Scarcely had they passed, however, ere one of them stopped and exclaimed:

'Surely that is Willie Furlong!'

I turned, and recognized Johnny Grey, one of my oldest friends. I relinquished my uncle's arm for a moment and shook hands with Grey, who said:

'I am surprised to see you. I heard only a few days ago, that you were not to be here till next spring.'

'I am here,' I remarked, 'somewhat in advance of my own expectation.' I then hurriedly enquired after several of our common friends, to which enquiries he briefly replied.

'All well,' he said; 'but you are in a hurry, and so am I. Don't let me detain you. Be sure and look in on me tomorrow. You will find me at the old place, in the Romain Buildings.'

We again shook hands, and he passed on down the street with the gentleman who accompanied him. I then turned to re-possess myself of my uncle's arm. The old gentleman had evidently walked on, for he was not in sight. I hurried along, making sure of overtaking him before reaching Gould Street, for my interview with Grey had occupied barely a minute. In another minute I was at the corner of Gould Street. No signs of Uncle Richard. I quickened my pace to a run, which soon brought me to Gerrard Street. Still no signs of my uncle. I had certainly not passed him on my way, and he could not have got farther on his homeward route than here. He must have called in at one of the stores; a strange thing for him to do under the circumstances. I retraced my steps all the way to the front of the chemist's shop, peering into every window and doorway as I passed along. No one in the least resembling him was to be seen.

I stood still for a moment, and reflected. Even if he had run at full speed—a thing most unseemly for him to do—he could not have reached the corner of Gerrard Street before I had done so. And what should he run for? He certainly did not wish to avoid me, for he had more to tell me before reaching home. Perhaps he had turned down Gould Street. At any rate, there was no use waiting for him. I might as well go home at once. And I did.

Upon reaching the old familiar spot, I opened the gate, passed on up the steps to the front door, and rang the bell. The door was opened by a domestic who had not formed part of the establishment in my time, and who did not know me; but Alice happened to be passing through the hall and heard my voice as I inquired for Uncle Richard. Another moment and she was in my arms. With a strange foreboding at my heart I noticed that she was in deep mourning. We passed into the dining-room, where the table was laid for dinner.

'Has Uncle Richard come in?' I asked, as soon as we were alone. 'Why did he run away from me?'

'Who?' exclaimed Alice, with a start; 'what do you mean, Willie? Is it possible you have not heard?'

'Heard what?'

'I see you have *not* heard,' she replied. 'Sit down, Willie, and prepare yourself for painful news. But first tell me what you meant by saying what you did just now,—who was it that ran away from you?'

'Well, perhaps I should hardly call it running away, but he certainly disappeared most mysteriously, down here near the corner of Yonge and Crookshank Streets.'

'Of whom are you speaking?'

'Of Uncle Richard, of course.'

'Uncle Richard! The corner of Yonge and Crookshank Streets! When did you see him there?'

'When? A quarter of an hour ago. He met me at the station and we walked up together till I met Johnny Grey. I turned to speak to Johnny for a moment, when—'

'Willie, what on earth are you talking about? You are labouring under some strange delusion. *Uncle Richard died of apoplexy more than six weeks ago, and lies buried in St James's Cemetery.*'

II

I don't know how long I sat there, trying to think, with my face buried in my hands. My mind had been kept on a strain during the last thirty hours, and the succession of surprises to which I had been subjected had temporarily paralyzed my faculties. For a few moments after Alice's announcement I must have been in a sort of stupor. My imagination, I remember, ran riot about everything in general, and nothing in particular. My cousin's momentary impression was that I had met with an accident of some kind, which had unhinged my brain. The first distinct remembrance I have after this is, that I suddenly awoke from my stupor to find Alice kneeling at my feet, and holding me by the hand. Then my mental powers came back to me, and I recalled all the incidents of the evening.

'When did uncle's death take place?' I asked.

'On the 3rd of November, about four o'clock in the afternoon. It was quite unexpected, though he had not enjoyed his usual health for some weeks before. He fell down in the hall, just as he was returning from a walk, and died within two hours. He never spoke or recognized any one after his seizure.'

'What has become of his old overcoat?' I asked.

'His old overcoat, Willie—what a question,' replied Alice, evidently thinking that I was again drifting back into insensibility.

'Did he continue to wear it up to the day of his death?' I asked.

'No. Cold weather set in very early this last fall, and he was compelled to don his winter clothing earlier than usual. He had a new overcoat made within a fortnight before he died. He had it on at the time of his seizure. But why do you ask?'

'Was the new coat cut by a fashionable tailor, and had it a fur collar and cuffs?'

'It was cut at Stovel's, I think. It had a fur collar and cuffs.'

'When did he begin to wear a wig?'

'About the same time that he began to wear his new overcoat. I wrote you a letter at the time, making merry over his youthful appearance and hinting—of course only in jest—that he was looking out for a young wife. But you surely did not receive my letter. You must have been on your way home before it was written.'

'I left Melbourne on the 11th of October. The wig, I suppose, was buried with him?'

'Yes.'

'And where is the overcoat?'

'In the wardrobe upstairs, in uncle's room.'

'Come and show it to me.'

I led the way upstairs, my cousin following. In the hall on the first floor we encountered my old friend Mrs Daly, the housekeeper. She threw up her hands in surprise at seeing me. Our greeting was brief; I was too intent on solving the problem which had exercised my mind ever since receiving the letter at Boston, to pay much attention to anything else. Two words, however, explained to her where we were going, and at our request she accompanied us. We passed into my uncle's room. My cousin drew the key of the wardrobe from a drawer where it was kept, and unlocked the door. There hung the overcoat. A single glance was sufficient. It was the same.

The dazed sensation in my head began to make itself felt again. The atmosphere of the room seemed to oppress me, and closing the door of the wardrobe, I led the way down stairs again to the dining-room, followed by my cousin. Mrs Daly had sense enough to perceive that we were discussing family matters, and retired to her own room.

I took my cousin's hand in mine, and asked:

'Will you tell me what you know of Mr Marcus Weatherley?'

This was evidently another surprise for her. How could I have heard of Marcus Weatherley? She answered, however, without hesitation:

'I know very little of him. Uncle Richard and he had some dealings a few months since, and in that way he became a visitor here. After a while he began to call pretty often, but his visits suddenly ceased a short time before uncle's death. I need not affect any reserve with you. Uncle Richard thought he came after me, and gave him a hint that you had a prior claim. He never called afterwards. I am rather glad that he didn't, for there is something about him that I don't quite like. I am at a loss to say what the something is; but his manner always impressed me with the idea that he was not exactly what he seemed to be on the surface. Perhaps I misjudged him. Indeed, I think I must have done so, for he stands well with everybody, and is highly respected.'

I looked at the clock on the mantel piece. It was ten minutes to seven. I rose from my seat.

'I will ask you to excuse me for an hour or two, Alice. I must find Johnny Grey.'

'But you will not leave me, Willie, until you have give me some clue to your unexpected arrival, and to the strange questions you have been asking? Dinner is ready, and can be served at once. Pray don't go out again till you have dined.'

She clung to my arm. It was evident that she considered me mad, and thought it probable that I might make away with myself. This I could not bear. As for eating any dinner, that was simply impossible in my then frame of mind, although I had not tasted food since leaving Rochester. I resolved to tell her all. I resumed my seat. She placed herself on a stool at my feet, and listened while I told her all that I have set down as happening to me subsequently to my last letter to her from Melbourne.

'And now, Alice, you know why I wish to see Johnny Grey.'

She would have accompanied me, but I thought it better to prosecute my inquiries alone. I promised to return some time during the night, and tell her the result of my interview with Grey. That gentleman had married and become a householder on his own account during my absence in Australia. Alice knew his address, and gave me the number of his house, which was on Church Street. A few minutes' rapid walking brought me to his door. I had no great expectation of finding him at home, as I deemed it probable he had not returned from wherever he had been going when I met him; but I should be able to find out when he was expected, and would either wait or go in search of him. Fortune favored me for once, however; he had returned more than an hour before. I was ushered into the drawing-room, where I found him playing cribbage with his wife.

'Why, Willie,' he exclaimed, advancing to welcome me, 'this is kinder than I expected. I hardly looked for you before tomorrow. All the better; we have just been speaking of you. Ellen, this is my old friend, Willie Furlong, the returned convict, whose banishment you have so often heard me deplore.'

After exchanging brief courtesies with Mrs Grey, I returned to her husband.

'Johnny, did you notice anything remarkable about the old gentleman who was with me when we met on Yonge Street this evening?'

'Old gentleman? Who? There was no one with you when I met you.'

'Think again. He and I were walking arm in arm, and you had passed us before you recognized me, and mentioned my name.'

He looked hard in my face for a moment, and then said positively:

'You are wrong, Willie. You were certainly alone when we met. You were walking slowly, and I must have noticed if any one had been with you.'

'It is you who are wrong,' I retorted, almost sternly. 'I was accompanied by an elderly gentleman, who wore a great coat with fur collar and cuffs, and we were conversing earnestly together when you passed us.'

He hesitated an instant, and seemed to consider, but there was no shade of doubt on his face.

'Have it your own way, old boy,' he said. 'All I can say is, that I saw no one but yourself, and neither did Charley Leitch, who was with me. After parting from you we commented upon your evident abstraction, and the sombre expression of your countenance, which we attributed to your having only recently heard of the sudden death of your Uncle Richard. If any old gentleman had been with you we could not possibly have failed to notice him.'

Without a single word by way of explanation or apology, I jumped from my seat, passed out into the hall, seized my hat, and left the house.

III

Out into the street I rushed like a madman, banging the door after me. I knew that Johnny would follow me for an explanation so I ran like lightning round the next corner, and thence down to Yonge

Street. Then I dropped into a walk, regained my breath, and asked myself what I should do next.

Suddenly I bethought me of Dr Marsden, an old friend of my uncle's. I hailed a passing cab, and drove to his house. The doctor was in his consultation-room, and alone.

Of course he was surprised to see me, and gave expression to some appropriate words of sympathy at my bereavement. 'But how is it that I see you so soon?' he asked—'I understood that you were not expected for some months to come.'

Then I began my story, which I related with great circumstantiality of detail, bringing it down to the moment of my arrival at his house. He listened with the closest attention, never interrupting me by a single exclamation until I had finished. Then he began to ask questions, some of which I thought strangely irrelevant.

'Have you enjoyed your usual good health during your residence abroad?'

'Never better in my life. I have not had a moment's illness since you last saw me.'

'And how have you prospered in your business enterprises?'

'Reasonably well; but pray doctor, let us confine ourselves to the matter in hand. I have come for friendly, not professional, advice.'

'All in good time, my boy,' he calmly remarked. This was tantalizing. My strange narrative did not seem to have disturbed his serenity in the least degree.

'Did you have a pleasant passage?' he asked, after a brief pause. 'The ocean, I believe, is generally rough at this time of year.'

'I felt a little squeamish for a day or two after leaving Melbourne,' I replied, 'but I soon got over it, and it was not very bad even while it lasted. I am a tolerably good sailor.'

'And you have had no special ground of anxiety of late? At least not until you received this wonderful letter'—he added, with a perceptible contraction of his lips, as though trying to repress a smile.

Then I saw what he was driving at.

'Doctor,' I exclaimed, with some exasperation in my tone—'pray dismiss from your mind the idea that what I have told you is the result of diseased imagination. I am as sane as you are. The letter itself affords sufficient evidence that I am not quite such a fool as you take me for.'

'My dear boy, I don't take you for a fool at all, although you are a little excited just at present. But I thought you said you returned the letter to—ahem—your uncle.'

For a moment I had forgotten that important fact. But I was not altogether without evidence that I had not been the victim of a disordered brain. My friend Gridley could corroborate the receipt of the letter and its contents. My cousin could bear witness that I had displayed an acquaintance with facts which I would not have been likely to learn from any one but my uncle. I had referred to his wig and overcoat, and had mentioned to her the name of Mr Marcus Weatherley—a name which I had never heard before in my life. I called Dr Marsden's attention to these matters, and asked him to explain them if he could.

'I admit,' said the doctor, 'that I don't quite see my way to a satisfactory explanation just at present. But let us look the matter squarely in the face. During an acquaintance of nearly thirty years, I always found your uncle a truthful man, who was cautious enough to make no statements about his neighbours that he was not able to prove. Your informant, on the other hand, does not seem to have confined himself to facts. He made a charge of forgery against a gentleman whose moral and commercial integrity are unquestioned by all who know him. I know Marcus Weatherley pretty well, and am not disposed to pronounce him a forger and a scoundrel upon the unsupported evidence of a shadowy old gentleman who appears and disappears in the most mysterious manner, and who cannot be laid hold of and held responsible for his slanders in a court of law. And it is not true, as far as I know and believe, that Marcus Weatherley is embarrassed in his circumstances. Such confidence have I in his solvency and integrity that I would not be afraid to take up all his outstanding paper without asking a question. If you will make inquiry, you will find that my opinion is shared by all the bankers in the city. And I have no hesitation in saying that you will find no acceptances with your uncle's name to them, either in this market or elsewhere.'

'That I will try to ascertain tomorrow,' I replied. 'Meanwhile, Dr Marsden, will you oblige your old friend's nephew by writing to Mr Junius Gridley, and asking him to acquaint you with the contents of the letter, and the circumstances under which I received it?'

'It seems an absurd thing to do,' he said, 'but I will if you like. What shall I say?' and he sat down at his desk to write the letter.

It was written in less than five minutes. It simply asked for the desired information, and requested an immediate reply. Below the doctor's signature I added a short postscript in these words:—

'My story about the letter and its contents is discredited. Pray answer fully, and at once.—W.F.F.'

At my request the doctor accompanied me to the post office, on Toronto Street, and dropped the letter into the box with his own hands. I bade him good night, and repaired to the Rossin House. I did not feel like encountering Alice again until I could place myself in a more satisfactory light before her. I dispatched a messenger to her with a short note stating that I had not discovered anything important, and requesting her not to wait up for me. Then I engaged a room and went to bed.

But not to sleep. All night long I tossed about from one side of the bed to the other; and at daylight, feverish and unrefreshed, I strolled out. I returned in time for breakfast, but ate little or nothing. I longed for the arrival of ten o'clock when the banks would open.

After breakfast I sat down in the reading-room of the hotel, and vainly tried to fix my attention upon the local columns of the morning's paper. I remember reading over several items time after time, without any comprehension of their meaning. After that I remember—nothing.

Nothing? All was blank for more than five weeks. When consciousness came back to me I found myself in bed in my own old room, in the house on Gerrard Street, and Alice and Dr Marsden were standing by my bedside.

No need to tell how my hair had been removed, nor about the bags of ice that had been applied to my head. No need to linger over any details of the 'pitiless fever that burned in my brain.' No need, either, to linger over my progress back to convalescence, and thence to complete recovery. In a week from the time I have mentioned, I was permitted to sit up in bed, propped up by a mountain of pillows. My impatience would brook no further delay, and I was allowed to ask questions about what had happened in the interval which had elapsed since my over-wrought nerves gave way under the prolonged strain upon them. First, Junius Gridley's letter in reply to Dr Marsden was placed in my hands. I have it still in my possession, and I transcribe the following copy from the original now lying before me:—

Boston, Dec. 22nd, 1861.
Dr Marsden:

'In reply to your letter, which has just been received, I have to say that Mr Furlong and myself became acquainted for the first time during our recent passage from Liverpool to Boston, in the *Persia*, which arrived here Monday last. Mr Furlong accompanied me home, and remained until Tuesday morning, when I took him to see the Public Library, the State House, the Athenaeum, Faneuil Hall, and other points of interest. We casually dropped into the post-office, and he remarked upon the great number of letters there. At my instigation—made, of course, in jest—he applied at the General Delivery for letters for himself. He received one bearing the Toronto postmark. He was naturally very much surprised at receiving it, and was not less so at its contents. After reading it he handed it to me, and I also read it carefully. I cannot recollect it word for word, but it professed to come from his affectionate uncle, Richard Yardington. It expressed pleasure at his coming home sooner than had been anticipated, and hinted in rather vague terms at some calamity. He referred to a lady called Alice, and stated that she had not been informed of Mr Furlong's intended arrival. There was something too, about his presence at home being a recompense to her for recent grief which she had sustained. It also expressed the writer's intention to meet his nephew at the Toronto railway station upon his arrival, and stated that no telegram need be sent. This, as nearly as I can remember, was about all there was in the letter. Mr Furlong professed to recognize the handwriting as his uncle's. It was a cramped hand, not easy to read, and the signature was so peculiarly formed that I was hardly able to decipher it. The peculiarity consisted of the extreme irregularity in the formation of the letters, no two of which were of equal size; and capitals were interspersed promiscuously, more especially throughout the surname.

'Mr Furlong was much agitated by the contents of the letter, and was anxious for the arrival of the time of his departure. He left by the B. & A. train at 11.30. This is really all I know about the matter, and I have been anxiously expecting to hear from him ever since he left. I confess that I feel curious, and should be glad to hear from him—that is, of course, unless something is involved which it would be impertinent for a comparative stranger to pry into.

Yours, &c.,
'Junius H. Gridley.'

So that my friend had completely corroborated my account, so far as the letter was concerned. My account, however, stood in no need of corroboration, as will presently appear.

When I was stricken down, Alice and Dr Marsden were the only persons to whom I had communicated what my uncle had said to me during our walk from the station. They both maintained silence in the matter, except to each other. Between themselves, in the early days of my illness, they discussed it with a good deal of feeling on each side. Alice implicitly believed my story from first to last. She was wise enough to see that I had been made acquainted with matters that I could not possibly have learned through any ordinary channels of communication. In short, she was not so enamoured of professional jargon as to have lost her common sense. The doctor, however, with the mole-blindness of many of his tribe, refused to believe. Nothing of this kind had previously come within the range of his own experience, and it was therefore impossible. He accounted for it all upon the hypothesis of my impending fever. He is not the only physician who mistakes cause for effect, and *vice versa*.

During the second week of my prostration, Mr Marcus Weatherley absconded. This event so totally unlooked for by those who had had dealings with him, at once brought his financial condition to light. It was found that he had been really insolvent for several months past. The day after his departure a number of his acceptances became due. These acceptances proved to be four in number, amounting to exactly forty-two thousand dollars. So that that part of my uncle's story was confirmed. One of the acceptances was payable in Montreal, and was for $2,283.76. The other three were payable at different banks in Toronto. These last had been drawn at sixty days, and each of them bore a signature presumed to be that of Richard Yardington. One of them was for $8,972.11; another was for $10,114.63; and the third and last was for $20,629.50. A short sum in simple addition will show us the aggregate of these three amounts—

$$\begin{array}{r} \$8{,}972 \quad 11 \\ 10{,}114 \quad 63 \\ 20{,}629 \quad 50 \\ \hline \$39{,}716 \quad 24 \end{array}$$

which was the amount for which my uncle claimed that his name had been forged.

Within a week after these things came to light a letter addressed to the manager of one of the leading banking institutions of Toronto arrived from Mr Marcus Weatherley. He wrote from New York, but stated that he should leave there within an hour from the time of posting his letter. He voluntarily admitted having forged the name of my uncle to three of the acceptances above referred to and entered into other details about his affairs, which, though interesting enough to his creditors at that time, would have no special interest to the public at the present day. The banks where the acceptances had been discounted were wise after the fact, and detected numerous little details wherein the forged signatures differed from the genuine signatures of my Uncle Richard. In each case they pocketed the loss and held their tongues, and I dare say they will not thank me for calling attention to the matter, even at this distance of time.

There is not much more to tell. Marcus Weatherley, the forger, met his fate within a few days after writing his letter from New York. He took passage at New Bedford, Massachusetts, in a sailing vessel called the *Petrel* bound for Havana. The *Petrel* sailed from port on the 12th of January, 1862, and went down in mid-ocean with all hands on the 23rd of the same month. She sank in full sight of the captain and crew of the *City of Baltimore* (Inman Line), but the hurricane prevailing was such that the latter were unable to render any assistance, or to save one of the ill-fated crew from the fury of the waves.

At an early stage in the story I mentioned that the only fictitious element should be the name of one of the characters introduced. The name is that of Marcus Weatherley himself. The person whom I have so designated really bore a different name—one that is still remembered by scores of people in Toronto. He has paid the penalty of his misdeeds, and I see nothing to be gained by perpetuating them in connection with his own proper name. In all other particulars the foregoing narrative is as true as a tolerably retentive memory has enabled me to record it.

I don't propose to attempt any psychological explanation of the events here recorded, for the very sufficient reason that only one explanation is possible. The weird letter and its contents, as has been seen, do not rest upon my testimony alone. With respect to my walk from the station with Uncle Richard, and the communication made by him to me, all the details are as real to my mind as any other incidents of my life. The only obvious deduction is, that I was made the recipient of a communication of the kind which the world is accustomed to regard as supernatural.

Mr Owen's publishers have my full permission to appropriate this story in the next edition of his 'Debatable Land between this World and the Next.' Should they do so, their readers will doubtless be favoured with an elaborate analysis of the facts, and with a pseudo-philosophic theory about spiritual communication with human beings. My wife, who is an enthusiastic student of electro-biology, is disposed to believe that Weatherley's mind, overweighted by the knowledge of his forgery, was in some occult manner, and unconsciously to himself, constrained to act upon my own senses. I prefer, however, simply to narrate the facts. I may or may not have my own theory about those facts. The reader is at perfect liberty to form one of his own if he so pleases. I may mention that Dr Marsden professes to believe to the present day that my mind was disordered by the approach of the fever which eventually struck me down, and that all I have described was merely the result of what he, with delightful periphrasis, calls 'an abnormal condition of the system, induced by causes too remote for specific diagnosis.'

It will be observed that, whether I was under an hallucination or not, the information supposed to be derived from my uncle was strictly accurate in all its details. The fact that the disclosure subsequently became unnecessary through the confession of Weatherley does not seem to me to afford any argument for the hallucination theory. My uncle's communication was important at the time when it was given to me; and we have no reason for believing that 'those who are gone before' are universally gifted with a knowledge of the future.

It was open to me to make the facts public as soon as they became known to me, and had I done so, Marcus Weatherley might have been arrested and punished for his crime. Had not my illness supervened, I think I should have made discoveries in the course of the day following my arrival in Toronto which would have led to his arrest.

Such speculations are profitless enough, but they have often formed the topic of discussion between my wife and myself. Gridley, too, whenever he pays us a visit, invariably revives the subject, which he long ago christened, 'The Gerrard Street Mystery,' or, 'The Mystery of the Union Station.' He has urged me a hundred times over to publish the story; and now, after all these years, I follow his counsel, and adopt his nomenclature in the title.

ARTHUR CONAN DOYLE (1859–1930)

The Adventure of the Blue Carbuncle

———

I HAD called upon my friend Sherlock Holmes upon the second morning after Christmas, with the intention of wishing him the compliments of the season. He was lounging upon the sofa in a purple dressing-gown, a pipe-rack within his reach upon the right, and a pile of crumpled morning papers, evidently newly studied, near at hand. Beside the couch was a wooden chair, and on the angle of the back hung a very seedy and disreputable hard felt hat, much the worse for wear, and cracked in several places. A lens and a forceps lying upon the seat of the chair suggested that the hat had been suspended in this manner for the purpose of examination.

'You are engaged,' said I; 'perhaps I interrupt you.'

'Not at all. I am glad to have a friend with whom I can discuss my results. The matter is a perfectly trivial one' (he jerked his thumb in the direction of the old hat), 'but there are points in connection with it which are not entirely devoid of interest, and even of instruction.'

I seated myself in his armchair, and warmed my hands before his crackling fire, for a sharp frost had set in, and the windows were thick with the ice crystals. 'I suppose,' I remarked, 'that, homely as it looks, this thing has some deadly story linked on to it—that it is the clue which will guide you in the solution of some mystery, and the punishment of some crime.'

'No, no. No crime,' said Sherlock Holmes, laughing. 'Only one of those whimsical little incidents which will happen when you have four million human beings all jostling each other within the space of a few square miles. Amid the action and reaction of so dense a swarm of humanity, every possible combination of events may be expected to take place, and many a little problem will be presented which may be striking and bizarre without being criminal. We have already had experience of such.'

'So much so,' I remarked, 'that, of the last six cases which I have added to my notes, three have been entirely free of any legal crime.'

'Precisely. You allude to my attempt to recover the Irene Adler papers, to the singular case of Miss Mary Sutherland, and to the adventure of the man with the twisted lip. Well, I have no doubt that this small matter will fall into the same innocent category. You know Peterson, the commissionaire?'

'Yes.'

'It is to him that this trophy belongs.'

'It is his hat.'

'No, no; he found it. Its owner is unknown. I beg that you will look upon it, not as a battered billycock, but as an intellectual problem. And, first, as to how it came here. It arrived upon Christmas morning, in company with a good fat goose, which is, I have no doubt, roasting at this moment in front of Peterson's fire. The facts are these. About four o'clock on Christmas morning, Peterson, who, as you know, is a very honest fellow, was returning from some small jollification, and was making his way homewards down Tottenham Court-road. In front of him he saw, in the gaslight, a tallish man, walking with a slight stagger, and carrying a white goose slung over his shoulder. As he reached the corner of Goodge-street, a row broke out between this stranger and a little knot of roughs. One of the latter knocked off the man's hat, on which he raised his stick to defend himself, and, swinging it over his head, smashed the shop window behind him. Peterson had rushed forward to protect the stranger from his assailants, but the man, shocked at having broken the window, and seeing an official-looking person in uniform rushing towards him, dropped his goose, took to his heels, and vanished amid the labyrinth of small streets which lie at the back of Tottenham Court-road. The roughs had also fled at the appearance of Peterson, so that he was left in possession of the field of battle, and also of the spoils of victory in the shape of this battered hat and a most unimpeachable Christmas goose.'

'Which surely he restored to their owner?'

'My dear fellow, there lies the problem. It is true that "For Mrs Henry Baker" was printed upon a small card which was tied to the bird's left leg, and it is also true that the initials "H.B." are legible upon the lining of this hat; but, as there are some thousands of Bakers, and some hundreds of Henry Bakers in this city of ours, it is not easy to restore lost property to any one of them.'

'What, then, did Peterson do?'

'He brought round both hat and goose to me on Christmas morning, knowing that even the smallest problems are of interest to me. The goose we retained until this morning, when there were signs that, in spite of the slight frost, it would be well that it should be eaten without unnecessary delay. Its finder has carried it off, therefore, to fulfil the ultimate destiny of a goose, while I continue to retain the hat of the unknown gentleman who lost his Christmas dinner.'

'Did he not advertise?'

'No.'

'Then, what clue could you have as to his identity?'

'Only as much as we can deduce.'

'From his hat?'

'Precisely.'

'But you are joking. What can you gather from this old battered felt?'

'Here is my lens. You know my methods. What can you gather yourself as to the individuality of the man who has worn this article?'

I took the tattered object in my hands, and turned it over rather ruefully. It was a very ordinary black hat of the usual round shape, hard, and much the worse for wear. The lining had been of red silk, but was a good deal discoloured. There was no maker's name; but, as Holmes had remarked, the initials 'H.B.' were scrawled upon one side. It was pierced in the brim for a hat-securer, but the elastic was missing. For the rest, it was cracked, exceedingly dusty, and spotted in several places, although there seemed to have been some attempt to hide the discoloured patches by smearing them with ink.

'I can see nothing,' said I, handing it back to my friend.

'On the contrary, Watson, you can see everything. You fail, however, to reason from what you see. You are too timid in drawing your inferences.'

'Then, pray tell me what it is that you can infer from this hat?'

He picked it up, and gazed at it in the peculiar introspective fashion which was characteristic of him. 'It is perhaps less suggestive than it might have been,' he remarked, 'and yet there are a few inferences which are very distinct, and a few others which represent at least a strong balance of probability. That the man was highly intellectual is of course obvious upon the face of it, and also that he was fairly well-to-do within the last three years, although he has now fallen upon evil days. He had foresight, but has less now than formerly, pointing to a moral retrogression, which, when taken with the decline of his fortunes, seems to indicate some evil influence, probably drink, at work upon him. This may account also for the obvious fact that his wife has ceased to love him.'

'My dear Holmes!'

'He has, however, retained some degree of self-respect,' he continued, disregarding my remonstrance. 'He is a man who leads a sedentary life, goes out little, is out of training entirely, is middle-aged, has grizzled hair which he has had cut within the last few days, and which he anoints with lime-cream. These are the more patent facts which are to be deduced from his hat. Also, by the way, that it is extremely improbable that he has gas laid on in his house.'

'You are certainly joking, Holmes.'

'Not in the least. Is it possible that even now when I give you these results you are unable to see how they are attained?'

'I have no doubt that I am very stupid; but I must confess that I am unable to follow you. For example, how did you deduce that this man was intellectual?'

For answer Holmes clapped the hat upon his head. It came right over the forehead and settled upon the bridge of his nose. 'It is a question of cubic capacity,' said he: 'a man with so large a brain must have something in it.'

'The decline in his fortunes, then?'

'This hat is three years old. These flat brims curled at the edge came in then. It is a hat of the very best quality. Look at the band of ribbed silk, and the excellent lining. If this man could afford to buy so expensive a hat three years ago, and has had no hat since, then he has assuredly gone down in the world.'

'Well, that is clear enough, certainly. But how about the foresight, and the moral retrogression?'

Sherlock Holmes laughed. 'Here is the foresight,' said he, putting his finger upon the little disc and loop of the hat-securer. 'They are never sold upon hats. If this man ordered one, it is a sign of a certain amount of foresight, since he went out of his way to take this precaution against the wind. But since we see that he has broken the elastic, and has not troubled to replace it, it is obvious that he has less foresight now than formerly, which is a distinct proof of a weakening nature. On the other hand, he has endeavoured to conceal some of these stains upon the felt by daubing them with ink, which is a sign that he has not entirely lost his self-respect.'

'Your reasoning is certainly plausible.'

'The further points, that he is middle-aged, that his hair is grizzled, that it has been recently cut, and that he uses lime-cream, are all to be gathered from a close examination of the lower part of the lining. The lens discloses a large number of hair ends, clean cut by the scissors of the barber. They all appear to be adhesive, and there is a distinct odour of lime-cream. This dust, you will observe, is not the gritty, grey dust of the street, but the fluffy brown dust of the house, show-ing that it has been hung up indoors most of the time; while the marks of moisture upon the inside are proof positive that the wearer perspired very freely, and could, therefore, hardly be in the best of training.'

'But his wife—you said that she had ceased to love him.'

'This hat has not been brushed for weeks. When I see you, my dear Watson, with a week's accumulation of dust upon your hat, and when your wife allows you to go out in such a state, I shall fear that you also have been unfortunate enough to lose your wife's affection.'

'But he might be a bachelor.'

'Nay, he was bringing home the goose as a peace-offering to his wife. Remember the card upon the bird's leg.'

'You have an answer to everything. But how on earth do you deduce that the gas is not laid on in the house?'

'One tallow stain, or even two, might come by chance; but, when I see no less than five, I think that there can be little doubt that the individual must be brought into frequent contact with burning tallow—walks upstairs at night probably with his hat in one hand and a guttering candle in the other. Anyhow, he never got tallow stains from a gas jet. Are you satisfied?'

'Well, it is very ingenious,' said I, laughing; 'but since, as you said just now, there has been no crime committed, and no harm done save the loss of a goose, all this seems to be rather a waste of energy.'

Sherlock Holmes had opened his mouth to reply, when the door flew open, and Peterson the commissionaire rushed into the apart-ment with flushed cheeks and the face of a man who is dazed with astonishment.

'The goose, Mr Holmes! The goose, sir!' he gasped.

'Eh! What of it, then? Has it returned to life, and flapped off through the kitchen window?' Holmes twisted himself round upon the sofa to get a fairer view of the man's excited face.

'See here, sir! See what my wife found in its crop!' He held out his hand, and displayed upon the centre of the palm a brilliantly scintillating blue stone, rather smaller than a bean in size, but of such purity and radiance that it twinkled like an electric point in the dark hollow of his hand.

Sherlock Holmes sat up with a whistle. 'By Jove, Peterson,' said he, 'this is treasure trove indeed. I suppose you know what you have got?'

'A diamond, sir! A precious stone! It cuts into glass as though it were putty.'

'It's more than a precious stone. It's *the* precious stone.'

'Not the Countess of Morcar's blue carbuncle!' I ejaculated.

'Precisely so. I ought to know its size and shape, seeing that I have read the advertisement about it in *The Times* every day lately. It is absolutely unique, and its value can only be conjectured, but the reward offered of a thousand pounds is certainly not within a twentieth part of the market price.'

'A thousand pounds! Great Lord of mercy!' The commissionaire plumped down into a chair, and stared from one to the other of us.

'That is the reward, and I have reason to know that there are sentimental considerations in the background which would induce the Countess to part with half of her fortune if she could but recover the gem.'

'It was lost, if I remember aright, at the Hotel Cosmopolitan,' I remarked.

'Precisely so, on the twenty-second of December, just five days ago. John Horner, a plumber, was accused of having abstracted it from the lady's jewel case. The evidence against him was so strong that the case has been referred to the Assizes. I have some account of the matter here, I believe.' He rummaged amid his newspapers, glancing over the dates, until at last he smoothed one out, doubled it over, and read the following paragraph:—

'Hotel Cosmopolitan Jewel Robbery. John Horner, 26, plumber, was brought up upon the charge of having upon the 22nd inst. abstracted from the jewel case of the Countess of Morcar the valuable gem known as the blue carbuncle. James Ryder, upper-attendant at the hotel, gave his evidence to the effect that he had shown Horner up to the dressing-room of the Countess of Morcar upon the day of the robbery, in order that he might solder the second bar of the grate, which was loose. He had remained with Horner some little time but had finally been called away. On returning he found that Horner had disappeared, that the bureau had been forced open, and that the small morocco casket in which, as it afterwards transpired, the Countess was accustomed to keep her jewel was lying empty upon the dressing-table. Ryder instantly gave the alarm, and Horner was arrested the same evening; but the stone could not be found either upon his person or in his rooms. Catherine Cusack, maid to the Countess, deposed to having heard Ryder's cry of dismay on discovering the robbery, and to having rushed into the room, where she found matters as described by the last witness. Inspector Bradstreet, B division, gave evidence as to the arrest of Horner, who struggled frantically, and protested his innocence in the strongest terms. Evidence of a previous conviction for robbery having been given against the prisoner, the magistrate refused to deal summarily with the offence, but referred it to the Assizes. Horner, who had shown signs of intense emotion during the proceedings, fainted away at the conclusion, and was carried out of court.'

'Hum! So much for the police-court,' said Holmes, thoughtfully, tossing aside the paper. 'The question for us now to solve is the sequence of events leading from a rifled jewel case at one end to the crop of a goose in Tottenham Court-road at the other. You see, Watson, our little deductions have suddenly assumed a much more important and less innocent aspect. Here is the stone; the stone came from the goose, and the goose came from Mr Henry Baker, the gentleman with the bad hat and all the other characteristics with which I have bored you. So now we must set ourselves very seriously to finding this gentleman, and ascertaining what part he has played in this little mystery. To do this, we must try the simplest means first, and these lie undoubtedly in an advertisement in all the evening papers. If this fail, I shall have recourse to other methods.'

'What will you say?'

'Give me a pencil, and that slip of paper. Now, then: "Found at the corner of Goodge-street, a goose and a black felt hat. Mr Henry Baker can have the same by applying at 6.30 this evening at 221B, Baker-street." That is clear and concise.'

'Very. But will he see it?'

'Well, he is sure to keep an eye on the papers, since, to a poor man, the loss was a heavy one. He was clearly so scared by his mischance in breaking the window, and by the approach of Peterson, that he thought of nothing but flight; but since then he must have bitterly regretted the impulse which caused him to drop his bird. Then, again, the introduction of his name will cause him to see it, for every one who knows him will direct his attention to it. Here you are, Peterson, run down to the advertising agency, and have this put in the evening papers.'

'In which, sir?'

'Oh, in the *Globe, Star, Pall Mall, St James's Gazette, Evening News, Standard, Echo,* and any others that occur to you.'

'Very well, sir. And this stone?'

'Ah, yes, I shall keep the stone. Thank you. And, I say, Peterson, just buy a goose on your way back, and leave it here with me, for we must have one to give to this gentleman in place of the one which your family is now devouring.'

When the commissionaire had gone, Holmes took up the stone and held it against the light. 'It's a bonny thing,' said he. 'Just see how it glints and sparkles. Of course it is a nucleus and focus of crime. Every good stone is. They are the devil's pet baits. In the larger and older jewels every facet may stand for a bloody deed. This stone is not yet twenty years old. It was found in the banks of the Amoy river in Southern China, and is remarkable in having every characteristic of the carbuncle, save that it is blue in shade, instead of ruby red. In spite of its youth, it has already a sinister history. There have been two murders, a vitriol-throwing, a suicide, and several robberies brought about for the sake of this forty-grain weight of crystallised charcoal. Who would think that so pretty a toy would be a purveyor to the gallows and the prison? I'll lock it up in my strong-box now, and drop a line to the Countess to say that we have it.'

'Do you think this man Horner is innocent?'

'I cannot tell.'

'Well, then, do you imagine that this other one, Henry Baker, had anything to do with the matter?'

'It is, I think, much more likely that Henry Baker is an absolutely innocent man, who had no idea that the bird which he was carrying was of considerably more value than if it were made of solid gold. That, however, I shall determine by a very simple test, if we have an answer to our advertisement.'

'And you can do nothing until then?'

'Nothing.'

'In that case I shall continue my professional round. But I shall come back in the evening at the hour you have mentioned, for I should like to see the solution of so tangled a business.'

'Very glad to see you. I dine at seven. There is a woodcook,

I believe. By the way, in view of recent occurrences, perhaps I ought to ask Mrs Hudson to examine its crop.'

I had been delayed at a case, and it was a little after half-past six when I found myself in Baker-street once more. As I approached the house I saw a tall man in a Scotch bonnet, with a coat which was buttoned up to his chin, waiting outside in the bright semicircle which was thrown from the fanlight. Just as I arrived, the door was opened, and we were shown up together to Holmes' room.

'Mr Henry Baker, I believe,' said he, rising from his armchair, and greeting his visitor with the easy air of geniality which he could so readily assume. 'Pray take this chair by the fire, Mr Baker. It is a cold night, and I observe that your circulation is more adapted for summer than for winter. Ah, Watson, you have just come at the right time. Is that your hat, Mr Baker?'

'Yes, sir, that is undoubtedly my hat.'

He was a large man, with rounded shoulders, a massive head, and a broad, intelligent face, sloping down to a pointed beard of grizzled brown. A touch of red in nose and cheeks, with a slight tremor of his extended hand, recalled Holmes' surmise as to his habits. His rusty black frock-coat was buttoned right up in front, with the collar turned up, and his lank wrists protruded from his sleeves without a sign of cuff or shirt. He spoke in a low staccato fashion, choosing his words with care, and gave the impression generally of a man of learning and letters who had had ill-usage at the hands of fortune.

'We have retained these things for some days,' said Holmes, 'because we expected to see an advertisement from you giving your address. I am at a loss to know now why you did not advertise.'

Our visitor gave a rather shame-faced laugh. 'Shillings have not been so plentiful with me as they once were,' he remarked. 'I had no doubt that the gang of roughs who assaulted me had carried off both my hat and the bird. I did not care to spend more money in a hopeless attempt at recovering them.'

'Very naturally. By the way, about the bird, we were compelled to eat it.'

'To eat it!' Our visitor half rose from his chair in his excitement.

'Yes, it would have been no use to anyone had we not done so. But I presume that this other goose upon the sideboard, which is about the same weight and perfectly fresh, will answer your purpose equally well?'

'Oh, certainly, certainly!' answered Mr Baker, with a sigh of relief.

'Of course, we still have the feathers, legs, crop, and so on of your own bird, so if you wish——'

The man burst into a hearty laugh. 'They might be useful to me as relics of my adventure,' said he, 'but beyond that I can hardly see what use the *disjecta membra* of my late acquaintance are going to be to me. No, sir, I think that, with your permission, I will confine my attentions to the excellent bird which I perceive upon the sideboard.'

Sherlock Holmes glanced sharply across at me with a slight shrug of his shoulders.

'There is your hat, then, and there your bird,' said he. 'By the way, would it bore you to tell me where you got the other one from? I am somewhat of a fowl fancier, and I have seldom seen a better-grown goose.'

'Certainly, sir,' said Baker, who had risen and tucked his newly-gained property under his arm. 'There are a few of us who frequent the "Alpha" Inn, near the Museum—we are to be found in the Museum itself during the day, you understand. This year our good host, Windigate by name, instituted a goose-club, by which, on consideration of some few pence every week, we were each to receive a bird at Christmas. My pence were duly paid, and the rest is familiar to you. I am much indebted to you, sir, for a Scotch bonnet is fitted neither to my years nor my gravity.' With a comical pomposity of manner he bowed solemnly to both of us, and strode off upon his way.

'So much for Mr Henry Baker,' said Holmes, when he had closed the door behind him. 'It is quite certain that he knows nothing whatever about the matter. Are you hungry, Watson?'

'Not particularly.'

'Then I suggest that we turn our dinner into a supper, and follow up this clue while it is still hot.'

'By all means.'

It was a bitter night, so we drew on our ulsters and wrapped cravats about our throats. Outside, the stars were shining coldly in a cloudless sky, and the breath of the passers-by blew out into smoke like so many pistol shots. Our footfalls rang out crisply and loudly as we swung through the Doctors' quarter, Wimpole-street, Harley-street, and so through Wigmore-street into Oxford-street. In a quarter of an hour we were in Bloomsbury at the 'Alpha' Inn, which is a small public-house at the corner of one of the streets which runs down into Holborn. Holmes pushed open the door of the private bar, and ordered two glasses of beer from the ruddy-faced, white-aproned landlord.

'Your beer should be excellent if it is as good as your geese,' said he.

'My geese!' The man seemed surprised.

'Yes. I was speaking only half an hour ago to Mr Henry Baker, who was a member of your goose-club.'

'Ah! yes, I see. But you see, sir, them's not *our* geese.'

'Indeed! Whose, then?'

'Well, I got the two dozen from a salesman in Covent Garden.'

'Indeed! I know some of them. Which was it?'

'Breckinridge is his name.'

'Ah! I don't know him. Well, here's your good health, landlord, and prosperity to your house. Good-night.'

'Now for Mr Breckinridge,' he continued, buttoning up his coat, as we came out into the frosty air. 'Remember, Watson, that though we have so homely a thing as a goose at one end of this chain, we have at the other a man who will certainly get seven years' penal servitude, unless we can establish his innocence. It is possible that our inquiry may but confirm his guilt; but, in any case, we have a line of investigation which has been missed by the police, and which a singular chance has placed in our hands. Let us follow it out to the bitter end. Faces to the south, then, and quick march!'

We passed across Holborn, down Endell-street, and so through a zigzag of slums to Covent Garden Market. One of the largest stalls bore the name of Breckinridge upon it, and the proprietor, a horsey-looking man, with a sharp face and trim side-whiskers, was helping a boy to put up the shutters.

'Good evening. It's a cold night,' said Holmes.

The salesman nodded, and shot a questioning glance at my companion.

'Sold out of geese, I see,' continued Holmes, pointing at the bare slabs of marble.

'Let you have five hundred to-morrow morning.'

'That's no good.'

'Well, there are some on the stall with the gas flare.'

'Ah, but I was recommended to you.'

'Who by?'

'The landlord of the "Alpha." '

'Oh, yes; I sent him a couple of dozen.'

'Fine birds they were, too. Now where did you get them from?'

To my surprise the question provoked a burst of anger from the salesman.

'Now, then, mister,' said he, with his head cocked and his arms akimbo, 'what are you driving at? Let's have it straight, now.'

'It is straight enough. I should like to know who sold you the geese which you supplied to the "Alpha." '

'Well, then, I shan't tell you. So now!'

'Oh, it is a matter of no importance; but I don't know why you should be so warm over such a trifle.'

'Warm! You'd be as warm, maybe, if you were as pestered as I am. When I pay good money for a good article there should be an end of the business; but it's "Where are the geese?" and "Who did you sell the geese to?" and "What will you take for the geese?" One would think they were the only geese in the world, to hear the fuss that is made over them.'

'Well, I have no connection with any other people who have been making inquiries,' said Holmes carelessly. 'If you won't tell us the bet is off, that is all. But I'm always ready to back my opinion on a matter of fowls, and I have a fiver on it that the bird I ate is country bred.'

'Well, then, you've lost your fiver, for it's town bred,' snapped the salesman.

'It's nothing of the kind.'

'I say it is.'

'I don't believe it.'

'D'you think you know more about fowls than I, who have handled them ever since I was a nipper? I tell you, all those birds that went to the "Alpha" were town bred.'

'You'll never persuade me to believe that.'

'Will you bet, then?'

'It's merely taking your money, for I know that I am right. But I'll have a sovereign on with you, just to teach you not to be obstinate.'

The salesman chuckled grimly. 'Bring me the books, Bill,' said he.

The small boy brought round a small thin volume and a great greasy-backed one, laying them out together beneath the hanging lamp.

'Now then, Mr Cocksure,' said the salesman, 'I thought that I was out of geese, but before I finish you'll find that there is still one left in my shop. You see this little book?'

'Well?'

'That's the list of the folk from whom I buy. D'you see? Well, then, here on this page are the country folk, and the numbers after their names are where their accounts are in the big ledger. Now, then! You see this other page in red ink? Well, that is a list of my town suppliers. Now, look at that third name. Just read it out to me.'

'Mrs Oakshott, 117, Brixton-road—249,' read Holmes.

'Quite so. Now turn that up in the ledger.'

Holmes turned to the page indicated. 'Here you are, "Mrs Oakshott, 117, Brixton-road, egg and poultry supplier." '

'Now, then, what's the last entry?'

' "December 22. Twenty-four geese at 7s. 6d." '

'Quite so. There you are. And underneath?'

' "Sold to Mr Windigate of the 'Alpha' at 12s." '

'What have you to say now?'

Sherlock Holmes looked deeply chagrined. He drew a sovereign from his pocket and threw it down upon the slab, turning away with the air of a man whose disgust is too deep for words. A few yards off he stopped under a lamp-post, and laughed in the hearty, noiseless fashion which was peculiar to him.

'When you see a man with whiskers of that cut and the "pink 'un" protruding out of his pocket, you can always draw him by a bet,' said he. 'I daresay that if I had put a hundred pounds down in front of him that man would not have given me such complete information as was drawn from him by the idea that he was doing me on a wager. Well, Watson, we are, I fancy, nearing the end of our quest, and the only point which remains to be determined is whether we should go on to this Mrs Oakshott to-night, or whether we should reserve it for to-morrow. It is clear from what that surly fellow said that there are others besides ourselves who are anxious about the matter, and I should——'

His remarks were suddenly cut short by a loud hubbub which broke out from the stall which we had just left. Turning round we saw a little rat-faced fellow standing in the centre of the circle of yellow light which was thrown by the swinging lamp, while Breckinridge the salesman, framed in the door of his stall, was shaking his fists fiercely at the cringing figure.

'I've had enough of you and your geese,' he shouted. 'I wish you were all at the devil together. If you come pestering me any more with your silly talk I'll set the dog on you. You bring Mrs Oakshott here and I'll answer her, but what have you to do with it? Did I buy the geese off you?'

'No; but one of them was mine all the same,' whined the little man.

'Well, then, ask Mrs Oakshott for it.'

'She told me to ask you.'

'Well, you can ask the King of Proosia for all I care. I've had enough of it. Get out of this!' He rushed fiercely forward, and the inquirer flitted away into the darkness.

'Ha, this may save us a visit to Brixton-road,' whispered Holmes. 'Come with me, and we will see what is to be made of this fellow.' Striding through the scattered knots of people who lounged round the flaring stalls, my companion speedily overtook the little man and touched him upon the shoulder. He sprang round, and I could see in the gaslight that every vestige of colour had been driven from his face.

'Who are you, then? What do you want?' he asked in a quavering voice.

'You will excuse me,' said Holmes, blandly, 'but I could not help overhearing the questions which you put to the salesman just now. I think that I could be of assistance to you.'

'You? Who are you? How could you know anything of the matter?'

'My name is Sherlock Holmes. It is my business to know what other people don't know.'

'But you can know nothing of this?'

'Excuse me, I know everything of it. You are endeavouring to trace some geese which were sold by Mrs Oakshott, of Brixton-road, to a salesman named Breckinridge, by him in turn to Mr Windigate, of the "Alpha," and by him to his club, of which Mr Henry Baker is a member.'

'Oh, sir, you are the very man whom I have longed to meet,' cried the little fellow, with outstretched hands and quivering fingers. 'I can hardly explain to you how interested I am in this matter.'

Sherlock Holmes hailed a four-wheeler which was passing. 'In that case we had better discuss it in a cosy room rather than in this windswept market-place,' said he. 'But pray tell me, before we go further, who it is that I have pleasure of assisting.'

The man hesitated for an instant. 'My name is John Robinson,' he answered, with a sidelong glance.

'No, no; the real name,' said Holmes, sweetly. 'It is always awkward doing business with an *alias*.'

A flush sprang to the white cheeks of the stranger. 'Well then,' said he, 'my real name is James Ryder.'

'Precisely so. Head attendant at the Hotel Cosmopolitan. Pray step into the cab, and I shall soon be able to tell you everything which you would wish to know.'

The little man stood glancing from one to the other of us with half-frightened, half-hopeful eyes, as one who is not sure whether he is on the verge of a windfall or of a catastrophe. Then he stepped into the cab, and in half an hour we were back in the sitting-room at Baker-street. Nothing had been said during our drive, but the high, thin breathing of our new companion, and the claspings and unclaspings of his hands, spoke of the nervous tension within him.

'Here we are!' said Holmes, cheerily, as we filed into the room. 'The fire looks very seasonable in this weather. You look cold, Mr Ryder. Pray take the basket chair. I will just put on my slippers before we settle this little matter of yours. Now, then! You want to know what became of those geese?'

'Yes, sir.'

'Or rather, I fancy, of that goose. It was one bird, I imagine, in which you were interested—white, with a black bar across the tail.'

Ryder quivered with emotion. 'Oh, sir,' he cried, 'can you tell me where it went to?'

'It came here.'

'Here?'

'Yes, and a most remarkable bird it proved. I don't wonder that you should take an interest in it. It laid an egg after it was dead—the bonniest, brightest little blue egg that ever was seen. I have it here in my museum.'

Our visitor staggered to his feet, and clutched the mantelpiece with his right hand. Holmes unlocked his strong box, and held up the blue carbuncle, which shone out like a star, with a cold, brilliant, many-pointed radiance. Ryder stood glaring with a drawn face, uncertain whether to claim or to disown it.

'The game's up, Ryder,' said Holmes, quietly. 'Hold up, man, or you'll be into the fire. Give him an arm back into his chair, Watson. He's not got blood enough to go in for felony with impunity. Give him a dash of brandy. So! Now he looks a little more human. What a shrimp it is, to be sure!'

For a moment he had staggered and nearly fallen, but the brandy brought a tinge of colour into his cheeks, and he sat staring with frightened eyes at his accuser.

'I have almost every link in my hands, and all the proofs which I could possibly need, so there is little which you need tell me. Still that little may as well be cleared up to make the case complete. You had heard, Ryder, of this blue stone of the Countess of Morcar's?'

'It was Catherine Cusack who told me of it,' said he, in a crackling voice.

'I see. Her ladyship's waiting-maid. Well, the temptation of sudden wealth so easily acquired was too much for you, as it has been for better men before you; but you were not very scrupulous in the means you used. It seems to me, Ryder, that there is the making of a very pretty villain in you. You knew that this man Horner, the plumber, had been concerned in some such matter before, and that suspicion would rest the more readily upon him. What did you do, then? You made some small job in my lady's room—you and your confederate Cusack—and you managed that he should be the man sent for. Then, when he had left, you rifled the jewel case, raised the alarm, and had this unfortunate man arrested. You then——'

Ryder threw himself down suddenly upon the rug, and clutched at my companion's knees. 'For God's sake, have mercy!' he shrieked. 'Think of my father! Of my mother! It would break their hearts. I never went wrong before! I never will again. I swear it. I'll swear it on a Bible. Oh, don't bring it into court! For Christ's sake, don't!'

'Get back into your chair!' said Holmes, sternly. 'It is very well to cringe and crawl now, but you thought little enough of this poor Horner in the dock for a crime of which he knew nothing.'

'I will fly, Mr Holmes. I will leave the country, sir. Then the charge against him will break down.'

'Hum! We will talk about that. And now let us hear a true account of the next act. How came the stone into the goose, and how came the goose into the open market? Tell us the truth, for therein lies your only hope of safety.'

Ryder passed his tongue over his parched lips. 'I will tell you it just as it happened, sir,' said he. 'When Horner had been arrested, it seemed to me that it would be best for me to get away with the stone at once, for I did not know at what moment the police might not take it into their heads to search me and my room. There was no place about the hotel where it would be safe. I went out, as if on some commission, and I made for my sister's house. She had married a man named Oakshott, and lived in Brixton-road, where she fattened fowls for the market. All the way there every man I met seemed to me to be a policeman or a detective, and for all that it was a cold night, the sweat was pouring down my face before I came to the Brixton-road. My sister asked me what was the matter, and why I was so pale; but I told her that I had been upset by the jewel robbery at the hotel. Then I went into the back yard, and smoked a pipe, and wondered what it would be best to do.

'I had a friend once called Maudsley, who went to the bad, and has just been serving his time in Pentonville. One day he had met me, and fell into talk about the ways of thieves and how they could get rid of what they stole. I knew that he would be true to me, for I knew one or two things about him, so I made up my mind to go right on to Kilburn, where he lived, and take him into my confidence. He would show me how to turn the stone into money. But how to get to him in safety. I thought of the agonies I had gone through in coming from the hotel. I might at any moment be seized and searched, and there would be the stone in my waistcoat pocket. I was leaning against the wall at the time, and looking at the geese which were waddling about round my feet, and suddenly an idea came into my head which showed me how I could beat the best detective that ever lived.

'My sister had told me some weeks before that I might have the pick of her geese for a Christmas present, and I knew that she was always as good as her word. I would take my goose now, and in it I would carry my stone to Kilburn. There was a little shed in the yard, and behind this I drove one of the birds, a fine big one, white, with a barred tail. I caught it, and, prising its bill open, I thrust the stone down its throat as far as my finger could reach. The bird gave a gulp, and I felt the stone pass along its gullet and down into its crop. But the creature flapped and struggled, and out came my sister to know what was the matter. As I turned to speak to her the brute broke loose, and fluttered off among the others.

' "Whatever were you doing with that bird, Jem?" says she.

' "Well," said I, "you said you'd give me one for Christmas, and I was feeling which was the fattest."

' "Oh," says she, "we've set yours aside for you. Jem's bird, we call it. It's the big, white one over yonder. There's twenty-six of them, which makes one for you, and one for us, and two dozen for the market."

' "Thank you, Maggie," says I; "but if it is all the same to you I'd rather have that one I was handling just now."

' "The other is a good three pound heavier," she said, "and we fattened it expressly for you."

' "Never mind. I'll have the other, and I'll take it now," said I.

' "Oh, just as you like," said she, a little huffed. "Which is it you want, then?"

' "That white one, with the barred tail, right in the middle of the flock."

' "Oh, very well. Kill it and take it with you."

'Well, I did what she said, Mr Holmes, and I carried the bird all the way to Kilburn. I told my pal what I had done, for he was a man that it was easy to tell a thing like that to. He laughed until he choked, and we got a knife and opened the goose. My heart turned to water, for there was no sign of the stone, and I knew that some terrible mistake had occurred. I left the bird, rushed back to my sister's, and hurried into the back yard. There was not a bird to be seen there.

' "Where are they all, Maggie?" I cried.

' "Gone to the dealer's."

' "Which dealer's?"

' "Breckinridge, of Covent Garden."

' "But was there another with a barred tail?" I asked, "the same as the one I chose?"

' "Yes, Jem, there were two barred-tailed ones, and I could never tell them apart."

'Well, then, of course, I saw it all, and I ran off as hard as my feet would carry me to this man Breckinridge; but he had sold the lot at once, and not one word would he tell me as to where they had gone. You heard him yourselves to-night. Well, he has always answered me like that. My sister thinks that I am going mad. Sometimes I think that I am myself. And now—and now I am myself a branded thief, without ever having touched the wealth for which I sold my character. God help me! God help me!' He burst into convulsive sobbing, with his face buried in his hands.

There was a long silence, broken only by his heavy breathing, and by the measured tapping of Sherlock Holmes' finger-tips upon the edge of the table. Then my friend rose, and threw open the door.

'Get out!' said he.

'What, sir! Oh, heaven bless you!'

'No more words. Get out!'

And no more words were needed. There was a rush, a clatter upon the stairs, the bang of a door, and the crisp rattle of running footfalls from the street.

'After all, Watson,' said Holmes, reaching up his hand for his clay pipe, 'I am not retained by the police to supply their deficiencies. If Horner were in danger it would be another thing, but this fellow will not appear against him, and the case must collapse. I suppose that I am committing a felony, but it is just possible that I am saving a soul. This fellow will not go wrong again. He is too terribly frightened. Send him to gaol now, and you make him a gaol-bird for life. Besides, it is the season of forgiveness. Chance has put in our way a most singular and whimsical problem, and its solution is its own reward. If you will have the goodness to touch the bell, Doctor, we will begin another investigation, in which also a bird will be the chief feature.'

R. AUSTIN FREEMAN (1862–1943)

A Mystery of the Sand-Hills

I HAVE occasionally wondered how often Mystery and Romance present themselves to us ordinary men of affairs only to be passed by without recognition. More often, I suspect, than most of us imagine. The uncanny tendency of my talented friend John Thorndyke to become involved in strange, mysterious and abnormal circumstances has almost become a joke against him. But yet, on reflection, I am disposed to think that his experiences have not differed essentially from those of other men, but that his extraordinary powers of observation and rapid inference have enabled him to detect abnormal elements in what, to ordinary men, appeared to be quite commonplace occurrences. Certainly this was so in the singular Roscoff case, in which, if I had been alone, I should assuredly have seen nothing to merit more than a passing attention.

It happened that on a certain summer morning—it was the fourteenth of August, to be exact—we were discussing this very subject as we walked across the golf-links from Sandwich towards the sea. I was spending a holiday in the old town with my wife, in order that she might paint the ancient streets, and we had induced Thorndyke to come down and stay with us for a few days. This was his last morning, and we had come forth betimes to stroll across the sand-hills to Shellness.

It was a solitary place in those days. When we came off the sand-hills on to the smooth, sandy beach, there was not a soul in sight, and our own footprints were the first to mark the firm strip of sand between high-water mark and the edge of the quiet surf.

We had walked a hundred yards or so when Thorndyke stopped and looked down at the dry sand above tide-marks and then along the wet beach.

'Would that be a shrimper?' he cogitated, referring to some

impressions of bare feet in the sand. 'If so, he couldn't have come from Pegwell, for the River Stour bars the way. But he came out of the sea and seems to have made straight for the sand-hills.'

'Then he probably was a shrimper,' said I, not deeply interested.

'Yet,' said Thorndyke, 'it was an odd time for a shrimper to be at work.'

'What was an odd time?' I demanded. 'When was he at work?'

'He came out of the sea at this place,' Thorndyke replied, glancing at his watch, 'at about half-past eleven last night, or from that to twelve.'

'Good Lord, Thorndyke!' I exclaimed, 'how on earth do you know that?'

'But it is obvious, Anstey,' he replied. 'It is now half-past nine, and it will be high-water at eleven, as we ascertained before we came out. Now, if you look at those footprints on the sand, you see that they stop short—or rather begin—about two-thirds of the distance from high-water mark to the edge of the surf. Since they are visible and distinct, they must have been made after last high-water. But since they do not extend to the water's edge, they must have been made when the tide was going out; and the place where they begin is the place where the edge of the surf was when the footprints were made. But the place is, as we see, about an hour below the high-water mark. Therefore, when the man came out of the sea, the tide had been going down for an hour, roughly. As it is high-water at eleven this morning, it was high-water at about ten-forty last night; and as the man came out of the sea about an hour after high-water, he must have come out at, or about, eleven-forty. Isn't that obvious?'

'Perfectly,' I replied, laughing. 'It is as simple as sucking eggs when you think it out. But how the deuce do you manage always to spot these obvious things at a glance? Most men would have just glanced at those footprints and passed them without a second thought.'

'That,' he replied, 'is a mere matter of habit; the habit of trying to extract the significance of simple appearances. It has become almost automatic with me.'

During our discussion we had been walking forward slowly, straying on to the edge of the sand-hills. Suddenly, in a hollow between the hills, my eye lighted upon a heap of clothes, apparently, to judge by their orderly disposal, those of a bather. Thorndyke also had observed them and we approached together and looked down on them curiously.

'Here is another problem for you,' said I. 'Find the bather. I don't see him anywhere.'

'You won't find him here,' said Thorndyke. 'These clothes have been out all night. Do you see the little spider's web on the boots with a few dewdrops still clinging to it? There has been no dew forming for a good many hours. Let us have a look at the beach.'

We strode out through the loose sand and stiff, reedy grass to the smooth beach, and here we could plainly see a line of prints of naked feet leading straight down to the sea, but ending abruptly about two-thirds of the way to the water's edge.

'This looks like our nocturnal shrimper,' said I. 'He seems to have gone into the sea here and come out at the other place. But if they are the same footprints, he must have forgotten to dress before he went home. It is a quaint affair.'

'It is a most remarkable affair,' Thorndyke agreed; 'and if the footprints are not the same it will be still more inexplicable.'

He produced from his pocket a small spring tape-measure with which he carefully took the lengths of two of the most distinct footprints and the length of the stride. Then we walked back along the beach to the other set of tracks, two of which he measured in the same manner.

'Apparently they are the same,' he said, putting away his tape; 'indeed, they could hardly be otherwise. But the mystery is, what has become of the man? He couldn't have gone away without his clothes, unless he is a lunatic, which his proceedings rather suggest. There is just the possibility that he went into the sea again and was drowned. Shall we walk along towards Shellness and see if we can find any further traces?'

We walked nearly half a mile along the beach, but the smooth surface of the sand was everywhere unbroken. At length we turned to retrace our steps; and at this moment I observed two men advancing across the sand-hills. By the time we had reached the mysterious heap of garments they were quite near, and, attracted no doubt by the intentness with which we were regarding the clothes, they altered their course to see what we were looking at. As they approached, I recognized one of them as a barrister named Hallett, a neighbour of mine in the Temple, whom I had already met in the town, and we exchanged greetings.

'What is the excitement?' he asked, looking at the heap of clothes and then glancing along the deserted beach; 'and where is the owner of the togs? I don't see him anywhere.'

'That is the problem,' said I. 'He seems to have disappeared.'

'Gad!' exclaimed Hallett, 'if he has gone home without his clothes, he'll create a sensation in the town! What?'

Here the other man, who carried a set of golf clubs, stooped over the clothes with a look of keen interest.

'I believe I recognize these things, Hallett; in fact, I am sure I do. That waistcoat, for instance. You must have noticed that waistcoat. I saw you playing with the chap a couple of days ago. Tall, clean-shaven, dark fellow. Temporary member, you know. What was his name? Popoff, or something like that?'

'Roscoff,' said Hallett. 'Yes, by Jove, I believe you are right. And now I come to think of it, he mentioned to me that he sometimes came up here for a swim. He said he particularly liked a paddle by moonlight, and I told him he was a fool to run the risk of bathing in a lonely place like this, especially at night.'

'Well, that is what he seems to have done,' said Thorndyke, 'for these clothes have certainly been here all night, as you can see by the spider's web.'

'Then he has come to grief, poor beggar!' said Hallett; 'probably got carried away by the current. There is a devil of a tide here on the flood.'

He started to walk towards the beach, and the other man, dropping his clubs, followed.

'Yes,' said Hallett, 'that is what has happened. You can see his foot-prints plainly enough going down to the sea; but there are no tracks coming back.'

'There are some tracks of bare feet coming out of the sea farther up the beach,' said I, 'which seem to be his.'

Hallett shook his head. 'They can't be his,' he said, 'for it is obvious that he never did come back. Probably they are the tracks of some shrimper. The question is, what are we to do? Better take his things to the dormy-house and then let the police know what has happened.'

We went back and began to gather up the clothes, each of us taking one or two articles.

'You were right, Morris,' said Hallett, as he picked up the shirt. 'Here's his name, "P. Roscoff", and I see it is on the vest and the shorts, too. And I recognize the stick now—not that that matters, as the clothes are marked.'

On our way across the links to the dormy-house mutual introductions took place. Morris was a London solicitor, and both he and Hallett knew Thorndyke by name.

'The coroner will have an expert witness,' Hallett remarked as we entered the house. 'Rather a waste in a simple case like this. We had better put the things in here.'

He opened the door of a small room furnished with a good-sized table and a set of lockers, into one of which he inserted a key.

'Before we lock them up,' said Thorndyke, 'I suggest that we make and sign a list of them and of the contents of the pockets to put with them.'

'Very well,' agreed Hallett. 'You know the ropes in these cases. I'll write down the descriptions, if you will call them out.'

Thorndyke looked over the collection and first enumerated the articles: a tweed jacket and trousers, light, knitted wool waistcoat, black and yellow stripes, blue cotton shirt, net vest and shorts, marked in ink 'P. Roscoff', brown merino socks, brown shoes, tweed cap, and a walking-stick—a mottled Malacca cane with a horn crooked handle. When Hallett had written down the list, Thorndyke laid the clothes on the table and began to empty the pockets, one at a time, dictating the descriptions of the articles to Hallett while Morris took them from him and laid them on a sheet of newspaper. In the jacket pockets were a handkerchief, marked 'P.R.'; a letter-case containing a few stamps, one or two hotel bills and local tradesmen's receipts, and some visiting cards inscribed 'Mr Peter Roscoff, Bell Hotel, Sandwich'; a leather cigarette-case, a 3B pencil fitted with a point-protector, and a fragment of what Thorndyke decided to be vine charcoal.

'That lot is not very illuminating,' remarked Morris, peering into the pockets of the letter-case. 'No letter or anything indicating his permanent address. However, that isn't our concern.' He laid aside the letter-case, and picking up a pocket-knife that Thorndyke had just taken from the trousers pocket, examined it curiously. 'Queer knife, that,' he remarked. 'Steel blade—mighty sharp, too—nail file and an ivory blade. Silly arrangement, it seems. A paper-knife is more convenient carried loose, and you don't want a handle to it.'

'Perhaps it was meant for a fruit-knife,' suggested Hallett, adding it to the list and glancing at a little heap of silver coins that Thorndyke had just laid down. 'I wonder,' he added, 'what has made that money turn so black. Looks as if he had been taking some medicine containing sulphur. What do you think, doctor?'

'It is quite a probable explanation,' replied Thorndyke, 'though we haven't the means of testing it. But you notice that this vesta-box from the other pocket is quite bright, which is rather against your theory.'

He held out a little silver box bearing the engraved monogram 'P.R.', the burnished surface of which contrasted strongly with the dull brownish-black of the coins. Hallett looked at it with an affirmative grunt, and having entered it in his list and added a bunch of keys and a watch from the waistcoat pocket, laid down his pen.

'That's the lot, is it?' said he, rising and beginning to gather up the clothes. 'My word! Look at the sand on the table! Isn't it astonishing how saturated with sand one's clothes become after a day on the links here? When I undress at night, the bathroom floor is like the bottom of a bird-cage. Shall I put the things in the locker now?'

'I think,' said Thorndyke, 'that, as I may have to give evidence, I should like to look them over before you put them away.'

Hallett grinned. 'There's going to be some expert evidence after all,' he said. 'Well, fire away, and let me know when you have finished. I am going to smoke a cigarette outside.'

With this, he and Morris sauntered out, and I thought it best to go with them, though I was a little curious as to my colleague's object in examining these derelicts. However, my curiosity was not entirely baulked, for my friends went no farther than the little garden that surrounded the house, and from the place where we stood I was able to look in through the window and observe Thorndyke's proceedings.

Very methodical they were. First he laid on the table a sheet of newspaper and on this deposited the jacket, which he examined carefully all over, picking some small object off the inside near the front, and giving special attention to a thick smear of paint which I had noticed on the left cuff. Then, with his spring tape he measured the sleeves and other principal dimensions. Finally, holding the jacket upside down, he beat it gently with his stick, causing a shower of sand to fall on the paper. He then laid the jacket aside, and, taking from his pocket one or two seed envelopes (which I believe he always carried), very carefully shot the sand from the paper into one of them and wrote a few words on it—presumably the source of the sand—and similarly disposing of the small object that he had picked off the surface.

This rather odd procedure was repeated with the other garments— a fresh sheet of newspaper being used for each and with the socks, shoes, and cap. The latter he examined minutely, especially as to the inside, from which he picked out two or three small objects, which I could not see, but assumed to be hairs. Even the walking-stick was inspected and measured, and the articles from the pockets scrutinized afresh, particularly the curious pocket-knife, the ivory blade of which he examined on both sides through his lens.

Hallett and Morris glanced in at him from time to time with indulgent smiles, and the former remarked:

'I like the hopeful enthusiasm of the real pukka expert, and the way he refuses to admit the existence of the ordinary and commonplace. I wonder what he has found out from those things. But here he is. Well, doctor, what's the verdict? Was it temporary insanity or misadventure?'

Thorndyke shook his head. 'The inquiry is adjourned pending the production of fresh evidence,' he replied, adding: 'I have folded the clothes up and put all the effects together in a paper parcel, excepting the stick.'

When Hallett had deposited the derelicts in the locker, he came out and looked across the links with an air of indecision.

'I suppose,' said he, 'we ought to notify the police. I'll do that. When do you think the body is likely to wash up, and where?'

'It is impossible to say,' replied Thorndyke. 'The set of the current is towards the Thames, but the body might wash up anywhere along the coast. A case is recorded of a bather drowned off Brighton whose body came up six weeks later at Walton-on-the-Naze. But that was quite exceptional. I shall send the coroner and the Chief Constable a note with my address, and I should think you had better do the same. And that is all that we can do, until we get the summons for the inquest, if there ever is one.'

To this we all agreed; and as the morning was now spent we walked back together across the links to the town, where we encountered my wife returning homeward with her sketching kit. This Thorndyke and I took possession of, and having parted from Hallett and Morris opposite the Barbican, we made our way to our lodgings in quest of lunch. Naturally, the events of the morning were related to my wife and discussed by us all, but I noted that Thorndyke made no reference to his inspection of the clothes, and accordingly I said nothing about the matter before my wife; and no opportunity of opening the subject occurred until the evening, when I accompanied him to the station. Then, as we paced the platform while waiting for his train, I put my question:

'By the way, did you extract any information from those garments? I saw you going through them very thoroughly.'

'I got a suggestion from them,' he replied, 'but it is such an odd one that I hardly like to mention it. Taking the appearances at their face value, the suggestion was that the clothes were not all those of the same man. There seemed to be traces of two men, one of whom appeared to belong to this district, while the other would seem to have been associated with the eastern coast of Thanet between Ramsgate and Margate, and by preference, on the scale of probabilities, to Dumpton or Broadstairs.'

'How on earth did you arrive at the localities?' I asked.

'Principally,' he replied, 'by the peculiarities of the sand which fell from the garments and which was not the same in all of them. You see, Anstey,' he continued, 'sand is analogous to dust. Both consist of minute fragments detached from larger masses; and just as, by examining microscopically the dust of a room, you can ascertain the colour and material of the carpets, curtains, furniture coverings, and other textiles, detached particles of which form the dust of that room, so, by examining sand, you can judge of the character of the cliffs, rocks, and other large masses that occur in the locality, fragments of which become ground off by the surf and incorporated in the sand of the beach. Some of the sand from these clothes is very characteristic and will probably be still more so when I examine it under the microscope.'

'But,' I objected, 'isn't there a fallacy in that line of reasoning? Might not one man have worn the different garments at different times and in different places?'

'That is certainly a possibility that has to be borne in mind,' he replied. 'But here comes my train. We shall have to adjourn this discussion until you come back to the mill.'

As a matter of fact, the discussion was never resumed, for, by the time that I came back to 'the mill', the affair had faded from my mind, and the accumulations of grist monopolized my attention; and it is probable that it would have passed into complete oblivion but for the circumstance of its being revived in a very singular manner, which was as follows.

One afternoon about the middle of October my old friend, Mr Brodribb, a well-known solicitor, called to give me some verbal instructions. When he had finished our business, he said:

'I've got a client waiting outside, whom I am taking up to introduce to Thorndyke. You'd better come along with us.'

'What is the nature of your client's case?' I asked.

'Hanged if I know,' chuckled Brodribb. 'He won't say. That's why I am taking him to our friend. I've never seen Thorndyke stumped yet, but I think this case will put the lid on him. Are you coming?'

'I am, most emphatically,' said I, 'if your client doesn't object.'

'He's not going to be asked,' said Brodribb. 'He'll think you are part of the show. Here he is.'

In my outer office we found a gentlemanly, middle-aged man to whom Brodribb introduced me, and whom he hustled down the stairs and up King's Bench Walk to Thorndyke's chambers. There we found my colleague earnestly studying a will with the aid of a watch-maker's eye-glass, and Brodribb opened the proceedings without ceremony.

'I've brought a client of mine, Mr Capes, to see you, Thorndyke. He has a little problem that he wants you to solve.'

Thorndyke bowed to the client and then asked:

'What is the nature of the problem?'

'Ah!' said Brodribb, with a mischievous twinkle, 'that's what you've got to find out. Mr Capes is a somewhat reticent gentleman.'

Thorndyke cast a quick look at the client and from him to the solicitor. It was not the first time that old Brodribb's high spirits had overflowed in the form of a 'leg-pull', though Thorndyke had no more whole-hearted admirer than the shrewd, facetious old lawyer.

Mr Capes smiled a deprecating smile. 'It isn't quite so bad as that,' he said. 'But I really can't give you much information. It isn't mine to give. I am afraid of telling someone else's secrets, if I say very much.'

'Of course you mustn't do that,' said Thorndyke. 'But, I suppose you can indicate in general terms the nature of your difficulty and the kind of help you want from us.'

'I think I can,' Mr Capes replied. 'At any rate, I will try. My difficulty is that a certain person with whom I wish to communicate has disappeared in what appears to me to be a rather remarkable manner. When I last heard from him, he was staying at a certain seaside resort and he stated in his letter that he was returning on the following day to his rooms in London. A few days later, I called at his rooms and found that he had not yet returned. But his luggage, which he had sent on independently, had arrived on the day which he had mentioned. So it is evident that he must have left his seaside lodgings. But from that day to this I have had no communication from him, and he has never returned to his rooms nor written to his landlady.'

'About how long ago was this?' Thorndyke asked.

'It is just about two months since I heard from him.'

'You don't wish to give the name of the seaside resort where he was staying?'

'I think I had better not,' answered Mr Capes. 'There are circumstances—they don't concern me, but they do concern him very much—which seem to make it necessary for me to say as little as possible.'

'And there is nothing further that you can tell us?'

'I am afraid not, excepting that, if I could get into communication with him, I could tell him of something very much to his advantage and which might prevent him from doing something which it would be much better that he should not do.'

Thorndyke cogitated profoundly while Brodribb watched him with undisguised enjoyment. Presently my colleague looked up and addressed our secretive client.

'Did you ever play the game of "Clumps", Mr Capes? It is a somewhat legal form of game in which one player asks questions of the others, who are required to answer "yes" or "no" in the proper witness-box style.'

'I know the game,' said Capes, looking a little puzzled, 'but——'

'Shall we try a round or two?' asked Thorndyke, with an unmoved countenance. 'You don't wish to make any statements, but if I ask you certain specific questions, will you answer "yes" or "no"?'

Mr Capes reflected awhile. At length he said:

'I am afraid I can't commit myself to a promise. Still, if you like to ask a question or two, I will answer them if I can.'

'Very well,' said Thorndyke, 'then, as a start, supposing I suggest that the date of the letter that you received was the thirteenth of August? What do you say? Yes or no?'

Mr Capes sat bolt upright and stared at Thorndyke open-mouthed.

'How on earth did you guess that?' he exclaimed in an astonished tone. 'It's most extraordinary! But you are right. It was dated the thirteenth.'

'Then,' said Thorndyke, 'as we have fixed the time we will have a try at the place. What do you say if I suggest that the seaside resort was in the neighbourhood of Broadstairs?'

Mr Capes was positively thunderstruck. As he sat gazing at Thorndyke he looked like amazement personified.

'But,' he exclaimed, 'you can't be guessing! You know! You know that he was at Broadstairs. And yet, how could you? I haven't even hinted at who he is.'

'I have a certain man in my mind,' said Thorndyke, 'who may have disappeared from Broadstairs. Shall I suggest a few personal characteristics?'

Mr Capes nodded eagerly and Thorndyke continued:

'If I suggest, for instance, that he was an artist—a painter in oil'—Capes nodded again—'that he was somewhat fastidious as to his pigments?'

'Yes,' said Capes. 'Unnecessarily so in my opinion, and I am an artist myself. What else?'

'That he worked with his palette in his right hand and held his brush with his left?'

'Yes, yes,' exclaimed Capes, half-rising from his chair; 'and what was he like?'

'By gum,' murmured Brodribb, 'we haven't stumped him after all.'

Evidently we had not, for he proceeded:

'As to his physical characteristics, I suggest that he was a shortish man—about five feet seven—rather stout, fair hair, slightly bald and wearing a rather large and ragged moustache.'

Mr Capes was astounded—and so was I, for that matter—and for some moments there was a silence, broken only by old Brodribb, who sat chuckling softly and rubbing his hands. At length Mr Capes said:

'You have described him exactly, but I needn't tell you that. What I do not understand at all is how you knew that I was referring to this particular man, seeing that I mentioned no name. By the way, sir, may I ask when you saw him last?'

'I have no reason to suppose,' replied Thorndyke, 'that I have ever seen him at all'; an answer that reduced Mr Capes to a state of stupefaction and brought our old friend Brodribb to the verge of apoplexy. 'This man,' Thorndyke continued, 'is a purely hypothetical individual whom I have described from certain traces left by him. I have reason to believe that he left Broadstairs on the fourteenth of August and I have certain opinions as to what became of him thereafter. But a few more details would be useful, and I shall continue my interrogation. Now this man sent his luggage on separately. That suggests a possible intention of breaking his journey to London. What do you say?'

'I don't know,' replied Capes, 'but I think it probable.'

'I suggest that he broke his journey for the purpose of holding an interview with some other person.'

'I cannot say,' answered Capes, 'but if he did break his journey it would probably be for that purpose.'

'And supposing that interview to have taken place, would it be likely to be an amicable interview?'

'I am afraid not. I suspect that my—er—acquaintance might have made certain proposals which would have been unacceptable, but which he might have been able to enforce. However, that is only surmise,' Capes added hastily. 'I really know nothing more than I have told you, except the missing man's name, and that I would rather not mention.'

'It is not material,' said Thorndyke, 'at least, not at present. If it should become essential, I will let you know.'

'M—yes,' said Mr Capes. 'But you were saying that you had certain opinions as to what has become of this person.'

'Yes,' Thorndyke replied; 'speculative opinions. But they will have to be verified. If they turn out to be correct—or incorrect either—I will let you know in the course of a few days. Has Mr Brodribb your address?'

'He has; but you had better have it, too.'

He produced his card, and, after an ineffectual effort to extract a statement from Thorndyke, took his departure.

The third act of this singular drama opened in the same setting as the first, for the following Sunday morning found my colleague and me following the path from Sandwich to the sea. But we were not alone this time. At our side marched Major Robertson, the eminent dog trainer, and behind him trotted one of his superlatively educated foxhounds.

We came out on the shore at the same point as on the former occasion, and turning towards Shellness, walked along the smooth sand with a careful eye on the not very distinctive landmarks. At length Thorndyke halted.

'This is the place,' said he. 'I fixed it in my mind by that distant tree, which coincides with the chimney of that cottage on the marshes. The clothes lay in that hollow between the two big sand-hills.'

We advanced to the spot, but, as a hollow is useless as a landmark, Thorndyke ascended the nearest sand-hill and stuck his stick in the summit and tied his handkerchief to the handle.

'That,' he said, 'will serve as a centre which we can keep in sight, and if we describe a series of gradually widening concentric circles round it, we shall cover the whole ground completely.'

'How far do you propose to go?' asked the major.

'We must be guided by the appearance of the ground,' replied Thorndyke. 'But the circumstances suggest that if there is anything buried, it can't be very far from where the clothes were laid. And it is pretty certain to be in a hollow.'

The major nodded; and when he had attached a long leash to the dog's collar, we started, at first skirting the base of the sand-hill, and then, guided by our own footmarks in the loose sand, gradually increasing the distance from the high mound, above which Thorndyke's handkerchief fluttered in the light breeze. Thus we continued, walking slowly, keeping close to the previously made circle of footprints and watching the dog; who certainly did a vast amount of sniffing, but appeared to let his mind run unduly on the subject of rabbits.

In this way half an hour was consumed, and I was beginning to wonder whether we were going after all to draw a blank, when the dog's demeanour underwent a sudden change. At that moment we were crossing a range of high sand-hills, covered with stiff, reedy grass and stunted gorse, and before us lay a deep hollow, naked of vegetation and presenting a bare, smooth surface of the characteristic greyish-yellow sand. On the side of the hill the dog checked, and, with upraised muzzle, began to sniff the air with a curiously suspicious expression, clearly unconnected with the rabbit question. On this, the major unfastened the leash, and the dog, left to his own devices, put his nose to the ground and began rapidly to cast to and fro, zigzagging down the side of the hill and growing every moment more excited. In the same sinuous manner he proceeded across the hollow until he reached a spot near the middle; and here he came to a sudden stop and began to scratch up the sand with furious eagerness.

'It's a find, sure enough!' exclaimed the major, nearly as excited as his pupil; and, as he spoke, he ran down the hillside, followed by me and Thorndyke, who, as he reached the bottom, drew from his 'poacher's pocket' a large fern-trowel in a leather sheath. It was not a very efficient digging implement, but it threw up the loose sand faster than the scratchings of the dog.

It was easy ground to excavate. Working at the spot that the dog had located, Thorndyke had soon hollowed out a small cavity some eighteen inches deep. Into the bottom of this he thrust the pointed blade of the big trowel. Then he paused and looked round at the major and me, who were craning eagerly over the little pit.

'There is something there,' said he. 'Feel the handle of the trowel.'

I grasped the wooden handle, and, working it gently up and down, was aware of a definite but somewhat soft resistance. The major verified my observation, and then Thorndyke resumed his digging, widening the pit and working with increased caution. Ten minutes' more careful excavation brought into view a recognizable shape—a shoulder and upper arm; and following the lines of this, further diggings disclosed the form of a head and shoulders plainly discernible though still shrouded in sand. Finally, with the point of the trowel and a borrowed handkerchief—mine—the adhering sand was cleared away; and then, from the bottom of the deep, funnel-shaped hole, there looked up at us, with a most weird and horrible effect, the discoloured face of a man.

In that face, the passing weeks had wrought inevitable changes, on which I need not dwell. But the features were easily recognizable, and I could see at once that the man corresponded completely with Thorndyke's description. The cheeks were full; the hair on the temples was of a pale, yellowish brown; a straggling, fair moustache covered the mouth; and, when the sand had been sufficiently cleared away, I could see a small, tonsure-like bald patch near the back of the crown. But I could see something more than this. On the left temple, just behind the eyebrow, was a ragged, shapeless wound such as might have been made by a hammer.

'That turns into certainty what we have already surmised,' said Thorndyke, gently pressing the scalp around the wound. 'It must have killed him instantly. The skull is smashed in like an egg-shell. And this is undoubtedly the weapon,' he added, drawing out of the sand beside the body a big, hexagon-headed screwbolt, 'very prudently buried with the body. And that is all that really concerns us. We can leave the police to finish the disinterment; but you notice, Anstey, that the corpse is nude with the exception of the vest and probably the pants. The shirt has disappeared. Which is exactly what we should have expected.'

Slowly, but with the feeling of something accomplished, we took our way back to the town, having collected Thorndyke's stick on the way. Presently, the major left us, to look up a friend at the club house on the links. As soon as we were alone, I put in a demand for an elucidation.

'I see the general trend of your investigations,' said I, 'but I can't imagine how they yielded so much detail; as to the personal appearance of this man, for instance.'

'The evidence in this case,' he replied, 'was analogous to circumstantial evidence. It depended on the cumulative effect of a number of facts, each separately inconclusive, but all pointing to the same conclusion. Shall I run over the data in their order and in accordance with their connections?'

I gave an emphatic affirmative, and he continued:

'We begin, naturally, with the first fact, which is, of course, the most interesting and important; the fact which arrests attention, which shows that something has to be explained and possibly suggests a line of inquiry. You remember that I measured the footprints in the sand for comparison with the other footprints. Then I had the dimensions of the feet of the presumed bather. But as soon as I looked at the shoes which purported to be those of that bather, I felt a conviction that his feet would never go into them.

'Now, that was a very striking fact—if it really was a fact—and it came on top of another fact hardly less striking. The bather had gone into the sea; and at a considerable distance he had unquestionably come out again. There could be no possible doubt. In foot-measurements and length of stride the two sets of tracks were identical; and there were no other tracks. That man had come ashore and he had remained ashore. But yet he had not put on his clothes. He couldn't have gone away naked; but, obviously he was not there. As a criminal lawyer, you must admit that there was prima facie evidence of something very abnormal and probably criminal.

'On our way to the dormy-house, I carried the stick in the same hand as my own and noted that it was very little shorter. Therefore it was a tall man's stick. Apparently, then, the stick did not belong to the shoes, but to the man who had made the footprints. Then, when we came to the dormy-house, another striking fact presented itself. You remember that Hallett commented on the quantity of sand that fell from the clothes on to the table. I am astonished that he did not notice the very peculiar character of that sand. It was perfectly unlike the sand which would fall from his own clothes. The sand on the sand-hills is dune sand—wind-borne sand, or, as the legal term has it, aeolian sand; and it is perfectly characteristic. As it has been carried by the wind, it is necessarily fine. The grains are small; and as the action of the wind sorts them out, they are extremely uniform in size. Moreover, by being continually blown about and rubbed together, they became rounded by mutual attrition. And then dune sand is nearly pure sand, composed of grains of silica unmixed with other substances.

'Beach sand is quite different. Much of it is half-formed, freshly broken down silica and is often very coarse; and, as I pointed out at the time, it is mixed with all sorts of foreign substances derived from masses in the neighbourhood. This particular sand was loaded with black and white particles, of which the white were mostly chalk, and the black particles of coal. Now there is very little chalk in the Shellness sand, as there are no cliffs quite near, and chalk rapidly disappears from sand by reason of its softness; and there is no coal.'

'Where does the coal come from?' I asked.

'Principally from the Goodwins,' he replied. 'It is derived from the cargoes of colliers whose wrecks are embedded in those sands, and from the bunkers of wrecked steamers. This coal sinks down through the seventy odd feet of sand and at last works out at the bottom, where it drifts slowly across the floor of the sea in a north-westerly direction until some easterly gale throws it up on the Thanet shore between Ramsgate and Foreness Point. Most of it comes up at Dumpton and Broadstairs, where you may see the poor people, in the winter, gathering coal pebbles to feed their fires.

'This sand, then, almost certainly came from the Thanet coast; but the missing man, Roscoff, had been staying in Sandwich, playing golf on the sand-hills. This was another striking discrepancy, and it made me decide to examine the clothes exhaustively, garment by garment. I did so; and this is what I found.

'The jacket, trousers, socks and shoes were those of a shortish, rather stout man, as shown by measurements, and the cap was his, since it was made of the same cloth as the jacket and trousers.

'The waistcoat, shirt, underclothes and stick were those of a tall man.

'The garments, socks and shoes of the short man were charged with Thanet beach sand, and contained no dune sand, excepting the cap, which might have fallen off on the sand-hills.

'The waistcoat was saturated with dune sand and contained no beach sand, and a little dune sand was obtained from the shirt and under-garments. That is to say, that the short man's clothes contained beach sand only, while the tall man's clothes contained only dune sand.

'The short man's clothes were all unmarked; the tall man's clothes were either marked or conspicuously recognizable, as the waistcoat and also the stick.

'The garments of the short man which had been left were those that could not have been worn by a tall man without attracting instant attention and the shoes could not have been put on at all; whereas the garments of the short man which had disappeared—the waistcoat, shirt and underclothes—were those that could have been worn by a tall man without attracting attention. The obvious suggestion was that the tall man had gone off in the short man's shirt and waistcoat but otherwise in his own clothes.

'And now as to the personal characteristics of the short man. From the cap I obtained five hairs. They were all blond, and two of them were of the peculiar, atrophic, "point of exclamation" type that grow at the margin of a bald area. Therefore he was a fair man and partially bald. On the inside of the jacket, clinging to the rough tweed, I found a single long, thin, fair moustache hair, which suggested a long, soft moustache. The edge of the left cuff was thickly marked with oil-paint—not a single smear, but an accumulation such as a painter picks up when he reaches with his brush hand across a loaded palette. The suggestion—not very conclusive—was that he was an oil-painter and left-handed. But there was strong confirmation. There was an artist's pencil—3B—and a stump of vine charcoal such as an oil-painter might carry. The silver coins in his pocket were blackened with sulphide as they would be if a piece of artist's soft, vulcanized rubber had been in the pocket with them. And there was the pocket-knife. It contained a sharp steel pencil-blade, a charcoal file and an ivory palette-blade; and that palette-blade had been used by a left-handed man.'

'How did you arrive at that?' I asked.

'By the bevels worn at the edges,' he replied. 'An old palette-knife used by a right-handed man shows a bevel of wear on the under side of the left-hand edge and the upper side of the right-hand edge; in the case of a left-handed man the wear shows on the under side of the right-hand edge and the upper side of the left-hand edge. This being an ivory blade, showed the wear very distinctly and proved conclusively that the user was left-handed; and as an ivory palette-knife is used only by fastidiously careful painters for such pigments as the cadmiums, which might be discoloured by a steel blade, one was justified in assuming that he was somewhat fastidious as to his pigments.'

As I listened to Thorndyke's exposition I was profoundly impressed. His conclusions, which had sounded like mere speculative guesses, were, I now realized, based upon an analysis of the evidence as careful and as impartial as the summing up of a judge. And these conclusions he had drawn instantaneously from the appearances of things that had been before my eyes all the time and from which I had learned nothing.

'What do you suppose is the meaning of the affair?' I asked presently. 'What was the motive of the murder?'

'We can only guess,' he replied. 'But, interpreting Capes' hints, I should suspect that our artist friend was a blackmailer; that he had come over here to squeeze Roscoff—perhaps not for the first time—and that his victim lured him out on the sand-hills for a private talk and then took the only effective means of ridding himself of his persecutor. That is my view of the case; but, of course, it is only surmise.'

Surmise as it was, however, it turned out to be literally correct. At the inquest Capes had to tell all that he knew; which was uncommonly little, though no one was able to add to it. The murdered man, Joseph Bertrand, had fastened on Roscoff and made a regular income by blackmailing him. That much Capes knew; and he knew that the victim had been in prison and that that was the secret. But who Roscoff was and what was his real name—for Roscoff was apparently a *nom de guerre*—he had no idea. So he could not help the police. The murderer had got clear away and there was no hint as to where to look for him; and so far as I know, nothing has ever been heard of him since.

MAURICE LEBLANC (1864–1941)

The Bridge that Broke

1

It was a Tuesday afternoon in midsummer. Paris was deserted—a city of the dead. Jim Barnett sat in his office with his feet on his desk. He was in his shirt-sleeves. A glass of lager beer stood at his elbow. A green blind shut out the blazing sun. To the prejudiced eye, Barnett's appearance would have suggested slumber, and this impression would have been strengthened by his rather loud and rhythmical breathing.

A sharp tap on his door made him bring his feet down with a jerk and sit bolt upright.

'No! It can't be! The heat must be affecting my eyesight.' Barnett affected elaborate astonishment.

Inspector Béchoux, for it was he, closed the door behind him and observed with some distaste his friend's state of deshabille. It was a fad with Béchoux to present at all times a perfectly groomed appearance. On this sweltering day he was cool and immaculate, not a hair out of place.

'How *do* you do it?' Barnett demanded, sinking back wearily into his chair.

'Do what?'

'Look like a fashion-plate off the ice. Damned superior, I call it!'

Béchoux smiled with conscious pride.

'It's quite simple,' he remarked modestly.

'But I take it the case you are working on is *not* quite so simple, or you wouldn't be coming to the enemy camp for assistance, eh, Béchoux?'

Béchoux reddened. It was a very sore point with him that in his difficulties he had several times been forced to accept Jim Barnett's help. For Barnett *was* helpful—almost uncannily so. The trouble was that he always managed to help himself as well as others.

'What is it this time? I've all day to spare—and to-morrow—and the day after. The Barnett Agency doesn't get many clients at this time of year, though it does guarantee "Information Free." I hear that they can't even get any deadheads to go to the theatres—pouf!'

'How would you like a trip into the country?'

'Béchoux, you are a blessing, albeit heavily disguised. What is the case, though?'

Inspector Béchoux grinned involuntarily.

'It's a real mystery—the sudden death of the famous scientist, Professor Saint-Prix.'

'I know the name, but I haven't read about his death in the papers. Has he been murdered?'

Inspector Béchoux's countenance took on a sphinx-like expression.

'That's what I want you to help me to determine. I have my car at a garage near here. Pack a bag and come right along. I'll tell you the facts of the case as we go.'

Reluctantly Barnett got up, drained the last of his beer, and made his simple preparations for the trip.

2

A quarter of an hour later they were spinning out of Paris in Inspector Béchoux's little two-seater.

'I was called in on the case,' said Béchoux, 'by Doctor Desportes of Beauvray—an old friend. He rang up on Monday morning to say there was going to be an inquest at Beauvray—Professor Saint-Prix, the scientist, had been killed by falling into the stream at the bottom of his garden.'

'Nothing very mysterious in that.'

'Ah, but wait. The professor was crossing the stream by a plank bridge, and that bridge gave way under him and precipitated the old man into the water. His head hit a sharp rock and he was killed instantaneously.'

'Was the bridge rotten, then?'

Inspector Béchoux shook his head.

'My doctor friend informed me that though the police had not been called in, they would have to be. The bridge was perfectly sound, but—it had been *sawed through*!'

Barnett whistled.

'And so you went to Beauvray at once?'

'Yes.'

'And what did you find?'

'A queer situation. The professor had a little house where he lived with his daughter, Thérèse Saint-Prix. Joined on to the house was a very fine laboratory. The garden sloped down, first a lawn and then a dense shrubbery, to a stream, sunk deep between rocky banks. A stout plank bridge was the means of crossing from the Saint-Prix garden to the adjoining property of the Villa Eméraude, the home of a married couple, the Lenormands.

'Louis Lenormand is a young stockbroker. His wife, Cécile, is a delicate, beautiful girl. Last Sunday afternoon, Madame Lenormand was going to have tea with Thérèse Saint-Prix. Louis Lenormand was spending the week-end in Paris with his invalid mother, but was expected back that night.

'Madame Lenormand went through the garden of the Villa Eméraude down to the stream. When she got there, she pulled up short and gave a cry of horror! The plank bridge was broken, and in the water lay the body of Professor Saint-Prix. She rushed back to the house for help, and then fainted.'

'Well, where do I come in?'

'Almost as soon as they had got Madame Lenormand to bed, and were breaking the news of her father's death to Thérèse Saint-Prix, Louis Lenormand arrived in his car, driving like a fury. He was pale and trembling. The first words he spoke were: "Am I in time? Tell me—tell me. My God, I've been a fool!" He was like a madman and rushed upstairs to his wife's room without waiting for an answer from the astonished servants. His wife's maid told him what had happened. At first he did not seem to understand. Then he stole to his wife's bedside and kissed her hands passionately, weeping and murmuring, "Cécile, I am a murderer." '

'Still I confess I don't understand. You have your murder—you have your murderer—self-confessed. What more do you want?'

'Well, the thing is this. We checked up on Louis Lenormand's movements while he was away from Beauvray. We know that the bridge was perfectly safe on the Saturday morning, for a gardener crossed by it. Now all Saturday afternoon Lenormand spent at his mother's bedside. He sat with her again after dinner until eleven o'clock, and then turned into bed himself. Old Madame Lenormand's maid and cook heard him kicking off his shoes in the room next to theirs. And the maid swears that in the small hours she heard him switch off his light, so she supposes he must have been lying awake reading. All Sunday morning he did not stir out, so it is out of the question that he could possibly have sawed through the bridge between the gardens at Beauvray.'

'What made you establish such a thorough alibi for your suspect?'

'Madame Lenormand, though still weak from the shock, has recovered consciousness. Her belief in her husband's innocence is absolute. Her one aim is to clear him. She insisted on these investigations being made. He will not say a word in his own defence. It's all very mystifying.'

'You say that Louis Lenormand was not expected back until Sunday evening. Do you know why he left Paris so much earlier?'

'That,' said Béchoux, 'is a curious point. Apparently he was alone in one of the rooms in his mother's flat, reading a book while the old lady had a nap after her lunch. The servants were both in the kitchen, and testify that suddenly, about three o'clock, he rushed in to them and said he was going home at once but would not disturb his mother to say good-bye.'

'And the motive? What reason could Louis Lenormand have to murder his neighbour?'

Inspector Béchoux shrugged his shoulders.

'I have an idea, and Doctor Desportes is making some investigations on my behalf.'

'Is there no one else who comes under suspicion? What about Madame Lenormand?'

3

Inspector Béchoux was silent. The car swung off the main road up a shady avenue. They turned into the drive of the Villa Eméraude. They were met outside the house by Doctor Desportes, who announced:

'The Beauvray police have arrested Monsieur Lenormand, but I have been busy on the telephone to headquarters, and you are now officially in charge of the case.'

'But his alibi—he was in Paris all the time—he could not have sawed through the bridge!'

The doctor looked grave.

'Monsieur Lenormand had a latch-key to his mother's flat. The Paris police have inquired at the garage where he kept his car and they find that he took it out shortly after midnight and told a mechanic that he was unable to sleep because of the heat, and was going to try and get a breath of air in the Bois. He returned after two in the morning.'

'Which,' observed Barnett, 'gave him plenty of time to drive out here, saw through the bridge, and get back to Paris. And what the maid heard was Monsieur Lenormand switching off his light when he really went to bed at last. Both servants must have been asleep when he slipped out of the flat.'

The doctor looked at Barnett in some curiosity, for he spoke in such an assured tone and was so obviously no subordinate of Inspector Béchoux.

Barnett smiled and bowed easily.

'Allow me to remedy my friend Béchoux's deplorable lack of manners. Jim Barnett, at your service, doctor.'

'A friend of mine, who has helped me on more than one occasion,' said Béchoux, not so easily. 'Come, doctor, what news have you for me after your confidential interview with the bank manager at Beauvray?'

'Poor Monsieur Lenormand.' The doctor shook his head sadly. 'I wish it had been a policeman who had found it out. But justice cannot be cheated. I have established that for the past two years Monsieur Lenormand has from time to time paid quite large cheques into the banking account of Professor Saint-Prix.'

'Blackmail?' Barnett and Béchoux came out with the word simultaneously.

'There we have at least the motive!' cried Béchoux, in purely professional triumph. 'Monsieur Lenormand must have had a very good reason for sawing through that bridge——'

'But he did not do it!'

A young woman, deathly pale, wearing a brilliant Chinese wrap, was coming slowly down the stairs into the hall, clutching at the banister for support. A maid followed anxiously behind her.

'I repeat,' she said in a voice trembling with suppressed emotion, 'Louis is innocent!'

'Madame,' said Béchoux, 'allow me to present my friend, Jim Barnett.' Barnett bowed low. 'If any one can achieve the impossible and establish your husband's innocence, it is he! I admit, however, that I originally brought him here because your husband's alibi upset all my deductions. Now that alibi no longer holds, and I have no objection if Barnett transfers his assistance to you. Provided'—he grew thoughtful and did not finish his sentence.

'Oh,' cried Madame Lenormand, taking Barnett's hands impulsively in hers, 'save my husband, and I will give you any reward you care to name.'

Barnett shook his head.

'I ask no reward, madame, beyond the privilege of serving you. Never shall it be said that the Barnett Agency descended to base commercialism in accepting a fee for its labours.'

4

At this point a gendarme came running in from the garden with a pair of rubber boots.

'Where did you find those?' asked Béchoux.

'In a garden shed at the back of the grounds of the villa.'

The boots were covered in fresh mud. In this sweltering weather the only moisture on the ground would be along the channel of the stream. Cécile Lenormand gave a sharp exclamation.

'Your husband's?'

She nodded reluctantly.

'Well,' said Barnett, 'let's go and have a look at the stream—and we ought to take those with us. *A bientôt*, madame.'

Béchoux and Barnett, accompanied by the doctor and the gendarme, walked through the garden and down to the stream. The water was running swiftly over the rocks below.

Béchoux looked unwillingly at the muddy foothold below the broken bridge, and then at his shining new patent leather shoes topped by snowy spats.

'I'll do it!' cried Barnett gallantly, and, seizing a boot from Béchoux, he leapt down, so that he sank ankle-deep in the mud beside the torrent.

'Are there any marks?' asked the doctor eagerly.

'Yes,' said Barnett. 'And they were made by these boots!'

'A clear case!' said Béchoux. 'I need never have brought you along, Barnett, and I'm afraid it's no use your transferring your services to Madame Lenormand. Really, I think you'd better hop back to Paris.'

'My dear Béchoux!' said Barnett, in tones of shocked surprise. 'Go off and leave a client in the lurch? Do you imagine the Barnett Agency shirks what appears to be a losing case?'

'Then you definitely regard Madame Lenormand as your client?'

'Why not?'

He handed up the boot and grovelled a few minutes longer in the mud. Then he clambered up again, somewhat apoplectic of countenance.

'Now,' he said briskly, 'suppose we visit Mademoiselle Saint-Prix and inspect both the properties prior to consuming beef and wine at the village inn.'

'What good can that do? I have my case.'

'And I have my own way of working. If you prefer it, I will pursue my course quite independently on behalf of Madame Lenormand, and you needn't see me again until I, too, have my case.'

But this course Béchoux viewed with some apprehension, so he and Barnett made their way round by the road to the Saint-Prix house.

On the way there Barnett solemnly handed Béchoux a very grubby sealed envelope.

'Will you please keep that carefully for me?' he said, 'and don't let it out of your inner pocket until I ask for it.'

'What is it?'

Barnett smiled mysteriously and laid a finger to his nose.

'A valuable diamond, old horse!'

'Idiot!'

At this point, they had arrived at the late professor's house. Here all the blinds were drawn. Barnett observed that the paint was peeling off the walls, and the matting in the passage was worn and old. A down-at-heel servant girl showed them into a small boudoir where they were received by Thérèse Saint-Prix.

She was quite a young woman—a girl in years, but strikingly poised and mature in bearing and appearance, tall and supple. She wore black, with no ornament of any kind. Her smooth black hair, parted in the middle, was drawn off her ears into a knot low on her neck. Her grave, dark eyes searched the faces of the two men—she had already met Béchoux, and presumed Barnett to be an assistant.

5

She sat, very pale, though calm, in a high-backed chair, carved. Only her strong white hands strained at her handkerchief as if there alone her grief found outlet.

Barnett bowed low.

'Accept my profound sympathy, mademoiselle,' he murmured. 'Your father's death will be felt by all France!'

'Yes,' the girl said, in a low voice. 'Five years ago he discovered the antiseptic which is now used in every hospital. That brought him renown, though it did not mend our fortunes when we lost our money in Russia.' She gave a pathetic little smile.

'How was that?'

'My father was half Russian. He invested everything in his brother's oil-wells near St Petersburg. Revolutionaries burned the factory and murdered my uncle. After that loss, we lived very modestly. But even in poverty my father was generous. And he would take no money for his discovery. He said his reward was to have been able to help in the great war against disease. When my father died, however, he was on the verge of completing another discovery of a different kind—one that would have brought him wealth as well as fame.'

'What was this discovery?'

'A secret process which would have revolutionised the dye industry. But I know scarcely anything about it—my father was secretive in some matters and would not let me help him in his experiments.' Again she smiled sadly. 'I could only be his housekeeper, never his assistant. And my chief occupation was to interest myself in the garden. Cécile and I used to spend hours planning our flower-beds. She was always so kind, helping me with gifts of plants. She was coming to tea on that afternoon, you know, to advise me about some fruit-trees. Poor Cécile! What will she do?'

'You are aware, mademoiselle,' said Béchoux, rather stiffly, as if to recall his presence to her consciousness, 'that Louis Lenormand is under arrest? The case is practically complete against him.'

She nodded.

'What made Louis Lenormand do such a thing? Can you imagine?' Barnett asked abruptly.

'*If* he did it,' said Thérèse gently. 'We must remember that nothing is proved yet.'

'But what reason can he have had? Well off, prosperous, married to a charming wife——'

'Against the wishes of her family,' interposed the girl. 'Louis Lenormand was a penniless clerk, and it was by speculating with his wife's money that he became rich. The family all thought that was why he wanted to marry her, though, of course, it was untrue. And

Cécile was passionately fond of her husband—she grudged every minute he spent elsewhere. Indeed, I used to wonder if she was not a little jealous of the time he spent with my father in the laboratory. I wondered, too, if she minded his helping my father occasionally with loans of money. But I do wrong if I suggest that Cécile is not all that is generous. Only, where her husband is concerned, if you understand, I have often wondered if she can be quite normal.'

Barnett looked distinctly interested, though Béchoux was obviously bored.

'Mademoiselle,' said Barnett, 'I have a favour to ask of you. May I see the laboratory in which your father worked?'

Without another word she led the way down a passage and through a baize door, which opened into the airy, white building.

6

The laboratory was in contrast to the house itself. Here all was new and spotless. Phials were ranged in orderly rows along the shelves; clean vessels sparkled on the benches. In all this dazzling whiteness there was but one dark patch—a muddy coat trailing from a stool.

'What's that?' asked Barnett.

'My poor father's coat,' said Thérèse. 'They carried him in here and removed his coat when they were trying to restore life. But he must have been killed instantaneously.'

'And these are all his chemicals?' Barnett indicated the gleaming phials.

'Yes—to think he will never use them again!' She averted her head slightly. 'Ah, how my father loved this place; and so, I always thought, did Louis Lenormand. Cécile did not, but that was because she did not understand. She loved flowers, everything beautiful; but science she thought ugly and repellant. Why, I have seen her shake her fist at the laboratory windows when my father and her husband were talking there together.'

'Well, mademoiselle, I thank you very much for being so helpful to us in what must be painful and terrible circumstances so far as you are concerned. And I won't hide from you that I have already made one little discovery.'

'What's that?' demanded Béchoux.

'Aha, I thought you would want to know. Well, it is that I am on the track of the motive for the murder. You have the murderer; I shall soon have the motive. And there we are!' Then, hastily dissembling his cheerfulness, he took a dignified farewell of Thérèse Saint-Prix, and departed with Béchoux.

At the garden gate they were met by the doctor and the gendarme.

'We've been waiting for you,' the former observed. 'We have found the instrument of the crime.'

The gendarme held up a medium-sized saw.

'Where did you find it?' asked Béchoux eagerly.

'Among some laurel bushes, near the tool-shed where the boots were discovered.'

'See,' cried Béchoux, turning eagerly to Barnett, 'it is plainly marked "Villa Eméraude." '

'Very interesting,' observed Barnett. 'Béchoux, I feel your case is becoming ever clearer. I almost wish I had never left Paris; it's just as hot here. In fact, I am getting distinctly warm. What about a drink at the local hostelry? I hope you will join us, doctor?' He beamed a comprehensive invitation.

'I shall be delighted to join you and your colleague,' answered the doctor.

At the word 'colleague' Béchoux smiled wryly. He was wishing pretty heartily that he had never brought Barnett into the case.

The sultry, airless evening was followed by a night storm, but Barnett slept through the thunderclaps. The next day dawned clear and much cooler.

Béchoux informed his friend that Louis Lenormand was to be examined by the magistrate up at the Saint-Prix house that afternoon.

'I am going to complete the necessary formalities this morning,' he announced, sipping his coffee. 'Won't you change your mind and pop back to Paris?'

'I'm sorry my society bores you so badly,' said Barnett sorrowfully, and sought solace in a third cup of chocolate.

'Oh, very well!' Béchoux was inclined to be huffy. He left the inn, and Barnett attacked another lightly boiled egg.

When he had finished his breakfast, Jim Barnett spruced himself up and made his way to the Villa Eméraude. Madame Lenormand received him in her sitting-room, and for over an hour he remained talking with her. Towards the end of the interview they moved into Louis Lenormand's study, and Béchoux, coming up the drive, could see through the open window Barnett and Cécile Lenormand bending over an open desk together.

Barnett came out into the hall and greeted his friend as if the Villa Eméraude was his own ancestral hall.

'Welcome, welcome, Béchoux. But I'm afraid you can't see Madame Lenormand. She's feeling over tired already—a little hysterical—and she must rest in view of her ordeal this afternoon. A charming woman; in many ways a delightful woman——' He did not finish, but paused thoughtfully.

Béchoux grunted. 'I came up to find you,' he said, 'to tell you a bit of news.'

'What's that?'

'We searched Louis Lenormand, and found on him a note-book in which he made entries of payments made by him during the past six months or so. One of these, dated three weeks ago, was for five thousand francs, paid to "S," and against it was written "*The last payment*." Investigation has shown that this amount was paid to Professor Saint-Prix. The case is pretty black against Lenormand, Barnett, and I really should advise you to quit now.'

But all Barnett answered was:

'I'm ready for a spot of lunch. Are you?'

The inquiry began at three o'clock. It was held in the narrow dining-room of the Saint-Prix house. Louis Lenormand sat at one end, between two gendarmes, never raising his eyes from the ground. The magistrates and Béchoux conferred together in low tones. Dr Desportes gazed thoughtfully out of the window. Barnett ushered in Madame Lenormand. She was very pale and leaned on his arm for support. She took her seat in a low chair, looking all around her with quick, nervous glances. Her husband seemed not to observe her, so sunken was he in dejection.

Then Thérèse Saint-Prix entered the room. Her presence was like a calming influence. She went over to Cécile Lenormand and laid a compassionate hand on her shoulder, but the other started away violently.

7

Almost immediately the examining magistrate began. He took the medical evidence, which Doctor Desportes gave in even, colourless tones, clearly establishing that the professor had been killed through his fall into the stream.

After this came the questioning of Louis Lenormand.

'Did you take your car out late on Sunday night from the Paris garage?'

'I did.'

'Where did you drive?'

The prisoner was silent.

'Answer me!'

'I really forget.'

Béchoux gave Barnett a significant look.

'Did you pay Professor Saint-Prix large sums of money from time to time?'

'I did.'

'For what reason?'

Louis Lenormand hesitated, and then replied haltingly:

'To assist him in his researches.'

Béchoux's pitying contempt was unmistakable.

A small note-book was produced.

'This is yours?'

The prisoner assented.

'Here you have entered various payments made by you. There is one of five thousand francs dated a month ago which says: "S. *The last payment.*" Was that a cheque paid to Professor Saint-Prix?'

'It was.'

'Won't you tell us why you were being—blackmailed? Perhaps the circumstances——' The magistrate seemed anxious to give Lenormand a chance to defend himself.

'I have nothing to say.'

'Is it a fact that Professor Saint-Prix was in the habit of coming to your house for a game of chess on Sunday afternoons?'

'Yes,' said the young man sullenly.

'Did you saw through the bridge?'

The prisoner was silent.

'You do not deny that these are your boots?' Béchoux produced them. The prisoner looked slightly startled but made no protest.

'I submit,' said Béchoux, 'that the case is clear.'

'Yes, indeed,' said Barnett, 'there never was a clearer. As clear as crystal—as a diamond—Béchoux, won't you produce that little envelope I entrusted to your care?'

With a premonition of disaster, Béchoux extracted the rather grubby envelope from his inner pocket.

'Open it!' commanded Barnett.

He did so, and held up—a diamond earring!

Cécile Lenormand gave a little gasp. Her husband started up and then sank back into his chair.

'Can any one identify this little exhibit of jewellery?' Barnett asked the assembly.

Doctor Desportes looked intensely worried. Poor man, his quiet life was being rudely disturbed!

'Those earrings——' He paused. 'They were given to Madame Lenormand by her husband not very long ago!'

'Is that so?' Béchoux asked of Louis Lenormand.

The latter nodded.

Cécile had bowed her head in her hands. Thérèse reached out a pitying hand to her, but she shook it off wildly.

'You have seen these earrings,' pursued Barnett, 'but you can't guess where I found one of them. Inspector Béchoux will tell you, though. In the mud by the stream, at that point where the body of Professor Saint-Prix was found lying dead!'

'Can you tell us, madame,' inquired the magistrate of Cécile Lenormand, 'whether you were wearing those earrings on Sunday afternoon?'

Looking up, the young woman shook her head.

'I can't—remember—when I last wore them!' she said in a confused manner.

'You must forgive my asking you, madame, but you must tell us now whether you left the villa at any time during Saturday night.'

There was the merest hint of menace in the smooth tones. Louis Lenormand's mouth twitched painfully.

'I—I——' She looked from one face to another of those gathered in the room. 'Why, I believe I did. It was so hot. . . . I went out into the garden for a little. . . .'

'Was this before you retired for the night?'

'Yes—no—not exactly. I had gone to my room, but I had not undressed. I had told my maid to go to bed. Then I felt oppressed by the heat and went out into the garden through the French window of my boudoir.'

'So that no one heard you come or go?'

'No one, monsieur.'

'And, on Sunday afternoon, you were going to tea with Mademoiselle Saint-Prix?'

'Yes.'

'At four o'clock?'

'That's so——'

Thérèse Saint-Prix's voice here interrupted gently, like a low-toned bell.

8

'Don't you remember, Cécile, the arrangement was that you should come over soon after three to me, but that if you did not arrive by four, I was to come up to the villa? Why, I was just getting ready to come when—when *it* happened. You see,' she turned to address the magistrate, 'we were going to make gardening plans together, but just lately Cécile hasn't been feeling too well, and she thought it possible that she might not feel up to walking about the garden in the hot sun. So I was quite prepared for her to stay resting in her boudoir that afternoon, and then we would have had tea together there.'

'Is that true, madame?' asked the magistrate of Cécile Lenormand.

'I—I can't remember. Perhaps that was the arrangement.'

9

'But—but'—Béchoux was stammering under the force of his discovery—'if you, mademoiselle, had been just a few minutes quicker in getting ready to go to the villa, you might yourself have been killed!'

'The question that presents itself,' said Barnett, in a level voice, 'is—for whom was the trap laid? Did Louis Lenormand lay it to kill Professor Saint-Prix? We must remember that the old professor was absent-minded, and was in the custom of going to play chess with his neighbour on Sunday afternoon. Or, was the attack directed by Louis Lenormand against his own wife? Or against Mademoiselle Saint-Prix?'

'Or,' said Béchoux, annoyed to find Barnett calmly taking the floor, 'did Madame Lenormand saw through the bridge because she guessed Professor Saint-Prix would be coming that way? Remember what Mademoiselle Saint-Prix has told us——'

Thérèse Saint-Prix was covered with confusion.

'I never meant you to take it that way,' she cried. 'Why, I only said Cécile sometimes appeared a little jealous of her husband's intimacy with my poor father. But that was nothing! Poor darling, she was always jealous where Louis—Monsieur Lenormand—was concerned. Why, she even at one time——' She broke off and was silent.

'She even what, mademoiselle?' asked the magistrate.

'Oh, it's too silly. But at one time I used to wonder if she were not a little jealous of *me*! I was giving Monsieur Lenormand lessons in Russian—a language he was eager to learn—and so we were naturally together a good deal. I even wondered if Cécile could be—could be spying on us—she seemed so queer. But please don't misunderstand me, I'm not suggesting a thing against her.'

'But mademoiselle is right,' said Barnett gravely. 'Madame Lenormand had the most odd ideas concerning her husband and mademoiselle—almost unbelievable. She imagined—I ask you! that Mademoiselle Saint-Prix had almost forced Monsieur Lenormand into having Russian lessons, in the hope that she might thereby succeed in teaching him something besides Russian! She had the absurd hallucination that she once saw her husband kissing you, mademoiselle, in the little summer-house at the bottom of the garden. And yet, and this is the most unbelievable part of all, she never really doubted her husband—she believed that, like so many men, he was capable of being superficially attracted without being guilty of any serious infidelity. A trusting woman, one would say. But her clemency hardly extended to her supposed rival.

'Now, on Sunday afternoon a woman telephoned from Beauvray to Louis Lenormand at his mother's flat and told him something terrible—so terrible, in fact, as to bring him racing home in his car to try and avert disaster. But he was too late. The tragedy had occurred. Only, it was something quite different from what he had feared! Today you have before you a woman telling a vague, unsubstantiated story of having wandered about on Saturday night in her garden—of having, *perhaps*, asked her friend to come to tea instead of going to tea with her. And, on the other hand, you must picture to yourselves a woman mad with jealousy and fury—a woman telephoning in words of ice-cold rage—"She shall no longer come between us—she and she alone is the obstacle of our love—it is because of her that you have turned a deaf ear to my entreaties, but soon, soon the obstacle will be removed!"

'Gentlemen, which story are you going to believe?'

'There can be but one answer to that,' observed the magistrate, 'if you have proof of what you say. And much is explained if Cécile Lenormand did indeed telephone to her husband in Paris that afternoon!'

'Did I say that Cécile Lenormand telephoned?' asked Barnett, looking most surprised. 'But that would be quite contrary to my own belief—and to the truth!'

'Then what on earth do you mean?'

'Exactly what I say. The telephone call from Beauvray to Paris was made by a woman maddened by jealousy and frustration, by a desire to annihilate her rival in Louis Lenormand's affections———'

'But that woman is Cécile Lenormand.'

'Not a bit of it! I can assure you she had nothing whatever to do with the telephone call.'

'Then whom are you accusing?'

'The other woman!'

'But there were only two—Cécile Lenormand and Thérèse Saint-Prix.'

'Precisely, and since I am *not* accusing Cécile Lenormand, that means that I *do* accuse . . .'

Barnett left the sentence unfinished. There was a horrified silence. Here was a direct and totally unforeseen accusation! Thérèse Saint-Prix, who was at this moment standing near the window, hesitated for a long moment, pale and trembling. Suddenly she sprang over the low balcony and down into the garden.

10

The doctor and a gendarme made to pursue her, but found themselves in collision with Barnett, who was barring the way. The gendarme protested hotly:

'But we shall have her escaping!'

'I think not,' said Barnett.

'You're right,' said the doctor, appalled, 'but I fear something else—something ghastly! . . . Yes, look, look! She's running towards the stream . . . towards the bridge where her father was killed.'

'What next?' came from Barnett with terrible calm.

He stood aside. The doctor and the gendarme were out of the window like lightning, and he closed it behind them. Then, turning to the magistrate, he said:

'Do you understand the whole business now, monsieur? Is it quite clear to you? It was Thérèse Saint-Prix who, after trying vainly to rouse the passion of Louis Lenormand beyond the passing fancy of a flirtation—Thérèse Saint-Prix who, starved for years of all enjoyment and luxury, was suddenly blinded by hatred of Cécile Lenormand.

She was too proud to believe that Louis Lenormand genuinely did not want her love and was devoted to his wife. She thought that if once Cécile Lenormand were out of the way, she would come into her own. So she planned the appalling, cold-blooded murder of her rival, and—compassed the death of her own father! In the night she sawed through the bridge—there was no one to see her. So blinded was she by her passions that next day, just before the tragedy would occur, she telephoned Louis Lenormand to tell him what she had done.

'Confronted by the utterly unexpected result of her strategy, she immediately planned to throw the guilt on to Cécile Lenormand and so at one stroke save herself and get her rival out of the way. It was with this in view that she stole one of Cécile's earrings and dropped it on Sunday night into the ditch, and then told her tale of Cécile having been jealous of the old professor. Then, here in this room, she was struck with a more plausible idea altogether—she tried to get us all to believe that the bridge had been sawed through with the object of killing *her* and not her father at all!'

'How do you account for the boots and the saw?' asked the magistrate.

'The Lenormands and the Saint-Prix shared a tool-shed and their garden implements and so on were used in common.'

'How do you know all about Thérèse Saint-Prix?' asked Lenormand, speaking for the first time.

'I helped him to find out,' said Cécile swiftly. 'My dear, I realised all along how you were placed in the matter, but my pride kept me from speaking to you. I was afraid you would think I was being jealous, and trying to find something to throw in your face because my parents tried to prevent our marriage.'

'Then you forgive me?'

For answer she ran across the room to her husband, and her arms went round his neck.

11

'But,' objected the magistrate, 'that entry in the note-book of "the last payment"—what did that mean?'

'Merely,' said Barnett, 'that Professor Saint-Prix had told Louis Lenormand that this was the last loan he would need, as his discovery was on the verge of completion.'

'And that discovery——?'

'Was something which would have revolutionised the dye industry. Doubtless he was going eagerly up to the Villa Eméraude to show it to his friend, and the stream washed it out of his dying grasp. What a loss!'

'And where *did* Monsieur Lenormand drive that night?'

'He shall tell us himself.'

'I drove,' said the erstwhile prisoner, 'into the country a little way. I honestly could not say exactly where. I did so because it was very hot and I couldn't sleep. But there is no one who could prove the truth of what I say.'

At this point the gendarme came back, rather pale.

Barnett signed to him to speak.

'She is dead!' he faltered. 'She threw herself down—there, where the professor was killed! The doctor sent me to tell you.'

The magistrate looked grave.

'Perhaps, after all, it is for the best,' he said. 'But for you, monsieur,' he turned to Barnett and shook his hand, 'there might have been a grave miscarriage of justice.'

Béchoux stood awkwardly silent.

'Come, Béchoux,' said Barnett, clapping him on the shoulder, 'let's be off and pack our things. I want to be back in the rue Laborde to-night.'

*

'Well,' said Béchoux, when they were alone together again, 'I admit that I do not see how you reconstructed the case so quickly.'

'Quite simple, my dear Béchoux—like all my little *coups*. What faith that woman had in her husband!'

For a moment he was silent in admiration of his client.

'Still,' said Béchoux, 'brilliant as you were, I fail to see where you get anything out of this for yourself!'

Barnett's gaze grew dreamy.

'That was a beautiful laboratory of the professor's,' he said. 'By the way, Béchoux, do you happen to know the address of the biggest dye concern in the country? I may be paying them a call in the near future!'

Béchoux gave a curious gasp, rather like a slowly-expiring balloon.

'Done me again!' he breathed. 'Stolen the paper—the formula of the secret process. . . .'

Jim Barnett was moved to injured protest.

'Dear old chap,' he observed, 'when it's a question of rendering a service to one's fellow-men and to one's country, what *you* designate as theft becomes the sheerest heroism. It is the highest manifestation of duty's sacred fire, blazing within the breast of mere man.' He thumped himself significantly on the chest. 'And personally, when duty calls, you will always find me ready, aye ready. Got that, Béchoux?'

But Béchoux was sunk in gloom.

'I wonder,' Barnett mused, 'what they will call the new process? I think a suitable name might be—but there, I won't bore you with my reflections, Béchoux. Only I can't help feeling it would be rather touching to take out a patent in the name of—Lupin!'*

---

* Jim Barnett is one of the names adopted by Arsène Lupin, Leblanc's central character, and a gentleman-burglar-turned-detective.

PALLE ROSENKRANTZ (1867–1941)

A Sensible Course of Action

Translated from the Danish by MICHAEL MEYER

SHE was very pretty; indeed, she was beautiful. Twenty-six at most, slim, very smart in a foreign style; unpretentious, but the real thing. She turned to Holst as he entered, and her grey dress rustled with the light whisper of silk. It sat as though moulded to her fine body, almost as though cast and not yet set. Her cheeks flushed, a little too redly, and her eyes flickered nervously.

Holst bowed to the Inspector. His eyes rested on her for no more than a second; but he saw much in a glance.

The Inspector asked him to sit. He sounded somewhat embarrassed. He sat at his desk facing the lady, restless as always, toying with a paper-knife, which he put down to scratch his sparse reddish hair.

Holst seated himself and looked at the lady.

'Lieutenant Holst, my assistant,' explained the Inspector in French. Holst bowed slightly.

The Inspector broke into Danish. He was not very fluent in French.

'A ridiculous business, Holst,' he said. 'I'm damned if I know what course of action we should take. This lady says her name is Countess Wolkonski, and that she is from Russia. Her papers are in order.'

He tapped the desk with some documents which had been lying in front of him.

'Countess Wolkonski from Volhynien, to be precise from Shitomir in the district of Kiev. She is a widow. Her husband died in a Russian prison. He was a naval officer who was implicated in the Odessa mutiny—she says. Her only son died too, not long after his father—she says. She is passing through Copenhagen and is staying at the Hotel Phoenix. She arrived the day before yesterday. But, and this is the point, she asserts that her husband's brother, who is also named Count Wolkonski, is trailing her and intends to murder her, because he believes she betrayed her husband to the Russian authorities. She went into a long rigmarole about it, all straight out of a novelette. To cut a long story short, she wants me to protect her. A charming person, as you can see, but I'm damned if I know what to do about her.'

'I am handing this case over to Mr Holst,' he added in French to the lady.

She inclined her head and looked at Holst, as though seeking his help. Her eyes were at the same time searching and pleading. She was very beautiful.

'I have checked,' continued the Inspector, 'that there is a Count Wolkonski staying at the Phoenix. He arrived a few hours ago from Malmö, and asked to see the Countess. When the porter sent up to her she was out, but as soon as she returned and learned that the Count was there she came along here like a scalded cat. I've tried to explain to her that there's really nothing I can do. She practically fell around my neck, which would have been delightful, but how can I possibly help her? We can't arrest the man, for we've nothing against him, we can't take her into custody, and she genuinely seems too terrified to go back to her cab. I've promised her I'll send a man down to the hotel. You must have a word with this Russian fellow and find what it's all about. Of course we could send her papers along to the Embassy, but I can't keep her here. You take her along and do what you can. I know I can rely on you to take a sensible course of action.'

Holst said nothing, but rose and bowed.

'Please go with this gentleman,' explained the Inspector, thinking how much more charming the words sounded in French: 'voulez-vous aller avec ce monsieur?'

The lady protested. She would not go.

'Madame,' said Holst. 'You need have no fear. No harm can befall you if you come with me.' He looked impressively heroic as he said it. He was much better-looking than the Inspector, and spoke much better French. His appearance radiated reliability. He was a handsome man.

She accepted his hand a little timidly and looked at him with two deep black eyes in a way that would have bothered Holst's wife Ulla if she could have seen it. He noticed a small movement at the corners of her mouth, a faint tremor of emotion. She looked very unhappy.

The Inspector seemed impatient.

Eventually the lady agreed to go with Holst; and as they walked through the offices, all the station clerks almost audibly craned their necks.

The Inspector muttered something to himself and, most uncharacteristically, bit one of his nails.

*

Holst drove with the lady towards Vimmelskaftet. As soon as she realized where they were going, she became very nervous.

'Monsieur Olst,' she said. 'You must not take me to the hotel. He will kill me. He has sworn to kill me, and he will do it, at whatever cost. I am innocent, but he is a traitor, a very great traitor. He has killed my little Ivan—do you hear, they murdered my little Ivan!' She was totally distraught, and began a long story which lasted until they reached the corner of Pilestraede. It was a strange story, involving Dimitri Ivanovitch and Nicolai and the police and an Admiral Skrydlov and a Lieutenant Schmidt and others besides.

But she would not return to the Hotel Phoenix, and at the corner of Ny Olstergade she tried to get out of the cab. Is she mad, wondered Holst. But she looked, no, sensible. Hysterical, yes, afraid certainly; this Dimitri Ivanovitch wanted to shoot her, of that she was sure.

Holst did not get many words in. He leaned out of the cab and told the man to drive down St Kongensgade to Marmorpladsen. At least that would provide a temporary respite. Then he explained to her what he had in mind, and that calmed her somewhat. She continued her narrative about Odessa, Lieutenant Schmidt, and several Admirals.

Her voice was deep and rich. When she was calm, her face revealed a certain strength. But she was plainly very frightened, and it seemed unlikely to Holst that these fears could be wholly without foundation. Unless of course, she was mad.

The cab stopped at Holst's house, and he led the lady up the stairs and rang the bell. His wife was at home. It was lunchtime, and he introduced the Russian lady with a brief explanation of her presence. 'Either she is mad,' he said, 'in which case I must get a doctor to her, or she is in genuine trouble, in which case we must try to help her. Talk French to her and see if you can make anything of her. I'll be back in half an hour.'

So Ulla Holst found herself alone with the lady. It was the first time her husband had asked her to do anything like this. However, it seemed to her that if one member of the family had to have a tête-à-tête with so extraordinarily beautiful a woman, it was just as well that it should be she.

The lady accepted a cup of coffee, sat down, and began to talk in a more ordered and logical manner. Gradually but visibly, she regained her self-composure. Ulla Holst sat and listened, blonde and calm, and found the Russian lady's story by no means incredible. As she listened to its ramifications, Holst drove to the Hotel Phoenix and asked to see Count Dimitri Ivanovitch Wolkonski.

He was in his room, and the porter took Holst up.

The Count was a tall man, of military appearance, rather short-sighted, very swarthy, and far from attractive. A real Tartar, thought Holst. But he was courteous, and spoke exquisite French.

'Count Wolkonski?' asked Holst. The man nodded.

'I am from the city police,' continued Holst. 'A lady residing in this hotel has come to us and asked for protection against you, on the grounds that you have designs upon her life.'

Holst smiled politely and shrugged his shoulders. 'The lady was in a very excited frame of mind—'

'Where is she?' interrupted the Russian, looking sharply at Holst.

Holst didn't like his eyes.

'She struck us as mentally confused,' replied Holst. 'So we are keeping her under observation. Her story was so involved and improbable that we felt unable to regard it as anything but a—a hallucination.'

The Russian said nothing.

Holst went on: 'I should appreciate it if you could tell me the truth of the matter. We naturally thought of approaching your Embassy—'

'There is no need for that,' interrupted the Russian quickly. 'No need whatever. My sister-in-law is—not mentally ill—certainly not insane. But my brother's unhappy fate upset her balance. Then her only child died. In my house, unfortunately, and she is convinced that I was to blame. That is the situation—as you have seen. I followed her here. She sold her estates in Russia; she had a fortune—she is very wealthy and spoiled. I traced her in Stockholm. She has made insane dispositions of her property, involving considerable sums that concern me. *Enfin.* I must speak to her, to try to bring her to her senses. Where is she?'

Holst looked closely at the Russian. He thought the fellow was talking jerkily and a little hectically. But he might be telling the truth, and the lady's behaviour had certainly been curious.

'If you could accompany me to the Embassy it is possible that by discussing the matter with His Excellency and the Embassy doctor we might be able to arrange matters to your satisfaction. We cannot possibly take any action in this affair except through the authorities.'

The Russian nibbled his lip.

'You realize, officer, that our position in Russia is not easy. My brother was deeply compromised in a naval mutiny. He died in prison. I myself—God knows, I have been guilty of no crime, but I neither can nor will deal with the representative in your country of a ruler whom I regard as a tyrant. I hope you understand. Yours is a free country. Such political differences of opinion as may exist between the Tsarist régime and myself are no concern of yours, as I think you will agree. But I do not wish to have any intercourse with the Ambassador, or anything whatever to do with our Embassy.'

Holst reflected.

'It is unfortunate,' he said. 'But I appreciate your point of view. I have no official cause to take action against you. We do not perform political errands for foreign governments. I have received no orders in this affair and have no desire to take any step on my own initiative. Your sister-in-law asserts that you have designs on her life, but we cannot act on so vague a charge. But I must warn you that we shall be compelled to contact the Embassy, and it is possible that their reaction may alter the position.'

'Will you arrest me?' asked the Russian sharply.

'Certainly not,' replied Holst. 'I have not the slightest ground or justification for that. But if you feel that any unpleasantness may result for you, my advice is that you should leave immediately. We shall have to speak to the Embassy and—well, I don't know, but it is always possible that—By leaving you will avoid any disagreeable consequences.'

'I shall not leave without my sister-in-law,' replied the Count.

Holst was silent.

'Where is she?'

'At the police station,' said Holst. 'If you care to go there, you can see her there.'

'And meanwhile you will contact the Embassy?'

'My superior has probably already done so,' replied Holst. The Russian's face pleased him less and less.

'Very well. Then I shall come at once with you to the police station. When my sister-in-law has seen me and spoken with me, I hope she may come to her senses, unless—'

He shrugged his shoulders.

Holst felt unhappy. Now the Inspector would have another Russian on his hands. But what could be done? If this sinister character was really at odds with the Tsar, his position was hardly of the kind that could justify any action against him in Denmark. The newspapers had their eyes open, and the government would hardly be anxious to stretch itself to assist the present Russian régime. The main danger was for the Countess, if her brother-in-law really—but that was unthinkable. He scarcely suggested a mad Nihilist with a revolver in his pocket; indeed, she seemed rather the less balanced of the two. Besides, he was under the eye of the police, and if the worst came to the worst Holst could help her to get out of the country while the Count discussed the matter with the Chief of Police, who would have to be brought in where such international issues were involved. Then the two could work out their problems in Malmö or Berlin, which were not in Holst's district.

To gain time, however, he prepared a long report giving the Count's explanation of why he was trailing his sister-in-law. It read very plausibly. She had fled after somewhat precipitately disposing of her estates, to which he apparently had some legal claim; she was in a highly nervous and distraught state. His political opinions made it impossible for him to seek the assistance of the Russian Embassy; he therefore appealed to the police for assistance and, if necessary, medical aid, and undertook to present himself before the Chief of Police that day.

Holst pocketed this paper and returned to his apartment.

*

Ulla Holst had become quite friendly with the Countess. She had a kind heart, and the Countess's story was of the kind to bring two sensitive ladies close together. Countess Helena Wolkonski was the daughter of a Lithuanian landowner; at an early age she had married a naval officer, Count Nicolai Wolkonski, with whom she had spent six happy years. Then her husband, who was attached to the marine depot at Odessa, had become addicted to drink and cards. Marital infidelity had followed, and their home had broken up. The Count had allied himself to the forces of political discontent, thereby threatening the safety of his wife and child. In her despair the young wife had gone to his commanding officer and—she did not deny it—had betrayed him and his brother, who were hostile to the existing régime and were deeply implicated in the revolutionary movement. Count Wolkonski, by now in a state of physical degeneration, had been arrested and shortly afterwards had died in prison. His brother had saved himself by flight, taking with him her son, a boy of seven. Before long he had written to her demanding that she visit him in Vienna, whither he had betaken himself. She had no other relatives to turn to, and had therefore sold her estates. These realized a considerable sum. In Vienna she learned that her son was dead and—she declared—an old woman who had accompanied her brother-in-law on his flight had warned her that he was planning revenge. She said he had sworn to kill her to repay her for her treachery.

Such was her story.

She had fled, and he had followed her. She dared not return to Russia, for fear of the revolutionaries, so had gone to Stockholm, where he had traced her. Now she was fleeing southwards.

Ulla Holst believed her story, and Holst had no evidence to contradict it. He briefly summarized his meeting with the Count and advised the Countess to leave the country with all speed, since she could produce no evidence for her charges against her brother-in-law. Her son's death had been caused by pneumonia, and although it was not impossible that the Count was responsible there could be no means of proving this, or of taking any action against him.

Ulla deplored the masculine indifference of the police, but Holst had to explain that there was nothing they could do in this case.

'And if he murders her?' she asked.

'Well, then we must arrest him,' said Holst. 'But let us hope he won't.'

'And you call that police work?'

Holst shrugged his shoulders. 'We can't put people in custody for things they might do.'

Ulla could not understand that; but women do not understand everything, least of all matters relating to the police. Countess Wolkonski despaired; however, her despair did not express itself in any violent outbursts. Holst explained to her that the police could not take her into custody, since she had not committed any unlawful act, nor could they act against her brother-in-law, for the same reason. But he was willing to help her to leave the country.

'To be hunted to death like a wild beast?' was all she replied.

She calmed down, however. It was almost as though she had conceived some plan. She thanked Ulla warmly for all her kindness, kissed Holst's son, and wept as she patted his curls. Holst got her cab. She refused his offer to accompany her, and drove away.

Ulla was very angry, and Holst not altogether at ease. He hurried back to the police station to keep an eye on the Russian.

*

At three o'clock the police station in Antoniestraede received a report that an elegantly dressed foreign lady had been arrested in a jeweller's shop on Købmagergade while attempting to steal a diamond ring. Holst was in his office: the Russian had not yet arrived. Holst had told him that the Chief of Police was unlikely to be available before three-thirty, since there was a parade at three.

A police van arrived, and Holst stood at the window as it rolled into the gloomy yard. A plain-clothes policeman stepped out, followed by a lady in grey.

It was Countess Wolkonski, arrested for attempted theft. Holst was slowly beginning to believe her story.

When she was brought into the station he went to meet her. She greeted him with a melancholy smile. 'Now you will have to take care of me,' she said.

Holst bowed.

As he did so, he noticed through the window the figure of the Russian standing in the gateway of the yard. At once, with a quick word to the astonished desk sergeant, he ordered the Countess to be taken to the Inspector's office.

A few moments later Count Wolkonski entered and asked in German for the Chief of Police.

He was asked to take a seat.

Holst withdrew into his office to formulate a plan. If Countess Wolkonski had resorted to so desperate a measure as shoplifting to get taken into custody, her fears could not lightly be dismissed. In any case, it would be unpardonable under the circumstances to leave her to her own devices. There was no knowing what she might not do next. Besides, now she was under arrest she could be placed under observation; the magistrate would certainly order this, and in the meantime one might, through official channels, obtain at any rate some information which might throw light on this complicated affair. And the Count was sitting outside. He would certainly demand to be allowed to see her.

A cold shiver ran down Holst's spine. It was a momentary thought, a stupid, crazy, insane notion, but if—if that Russian was a fanatical revolutionary, an avenger—God knows, the whole business might have come out of a Russian novel, but in Russia, as one knew from the newspapers, anything was possible. Certainly a Copenhagen police officer had no right to believe all that is in the newspapers; he has no right to believe that novels can come to life; he must act soberly and professionally. But—Russia is, when all is said and done, Russia, and it cannot all be lies. Suppose that Count Wolkonski before the very eyes of the Chief of Police were to draw a pistol from his pocket and shoot his sister-in-law, or—suppose he took out a bomb, a bomb, that might blow the whole police station with its lord and master into the air?

Of course it was totally impossible, idiotic, crazy, insane. This was Copenhagen, A.D. 1905. But the notion had got inside Holst's head, and was beating away with impish hammers in a way to drive any man from his wits.

He could not possibly say all this to anyone. The Inspector would think he had lost his reason. And so he had; it was an obsession, a foolish obsession from which he could not free himself. In ten minutes the parade would be over, and the case would be on the carpet. The Countess, now a shoplifter caught red-handed, would be confronted with the Count. A flash, an explosion, and the Chief of Police himself might be flying skywards.

Then Lieutenant Eigil Holst, of the Copenhagen police force, on his own responsibility, and at his own risk took a decision which branded him not as a sober, reliable, and trained officer but as a man of dangerous fantasy.

He summoned one of the youngest and most slavishly obedient of the station's constables, went to the window where Count Wolkonski was seated correctly on a bench, formally charged him with being implicated in an attempted robbery committed at a shop in Købmagergade by a woman calling herself his sister-in-law, had the amazed Count marched into an adjacent room, had him, despite some considerable resistance, searched, and found in his right trouser pocket a small American revolver containing six sharp bullets.

Holst drafted a stylish report to his Chief of Police, with the result that the sun set that evening over a cell at Nytorv in which Count Dimitri Ivanovitch Wolkonski sat sadly with sunken head, following a highly suspicious interrogation. And, it must be added, when the sun rose over the same cell, Count Dimitri Ivanovitch Wolkonski was found hanging by his braces dead on a gas bracket.

It is well known that it is easier to enter the clutches of the law than escape from them. Countess Wolkonski had found great difficulty in persuading the police to put her under their protection. She had resorted to a radical method. She had succeeded; but she remained in custody. The Chief of Police dared not set her at liberty. Her theft had been barefaced and her explanation, however truthful it might seem, buttressed by Holst's evidence and a quantity of bonds and jewels in her possession valued at a considerable fortune, at the least required a closer investigation.

She was arrested, to Holst's distress, and Ulla Holst was less than respectful in her comments upon her husband's superior. The Countess spent the night in a cell, not far from the place where her enemy had met his death. The next day she was freed, Count Wolkonski's suicide having weighed powerfully in her favour.

Not everything that was written in the newspapers about this affair was untrue, but the full facts of what happened have not previously been revealed. The Embassy bestirred itself and obtained further details concerning the background of the case. Countess Wolkonski had in fact betrayed her husband. She was not a heroine, and could never be one.

But she was certainly beautiful, and now she had found peace of mind. Count Dimitri Wolkonski was a revolutionary, and as such was entitled to his due share of sympathy from all good and peace-loving Danish citizens who cannot bear to think of a butcher slaughtering a calf but support with all their hearts the bomb-throwing barricade heroes of darkest Russia. In truth, this Dimitri Wolkonski was one of the blackest villains upon whom the sun of Russia has ever shone. His conscience was so heavy with evil deeds that it is a wonder that the gas bracket in the cell at Nytorv did not break beneath his weight.

This must serve as some excuse for the pretty Countess, and may explain why her brother-in-law, once he found himself in the hands of justice, settled his account with his Maker, whether the bill was right or no.

Yet Holst had a lingering suspicion that the Countess's life had never in fact been in danger, nor that of the Chief of Police; and that the Count had been carrying the pistol only in case his own life was threatened by his enemies. And he shared the doubts later drily expressed by the coroner as to whether his arrest and search of the Count had been justified.

Countess Helena stayed for some time in Copenhagen and was a frequent visitor at Ulla Holst's. Ulla enjoyed her company, and refused to believe that she had behaved wrongly in any way regarding those revolutionaries. Ulla was, after all, a policeman's wife, and was therefore opposed to any movement whose activities threatened the lives of policemen anywhere. When the Countess finally left Denmark, accompanied by Ulla's best wishes, the latter expressed her opinion of the affair to her husband. 'It may well be, Eigil,' she said, 'that you had no right to search that Russian, and that as you say it was a stupid idea you got into your head that afternoon in the station. But if you want my opinion, I think you took a very sensible course of action.'

WILLIAM MacHARG (1872–1951)

Murder Makes it Worse

———

'WE got a hot one,' O'Malley said. 'A lawyer knocked off in his office. Krockin, his name was. His secretary and a guy that worked for him was out, and he was alone in the office, and when they come back they found him shot.'

'Have the police any theory about the case?' I asked.

'That's all we got—a theory. They think somebody in some law case pushed him off. This lawyer had a shady reputation. Cops found legal papers there and a lot of telephone numbers. They got the names in the papers and the telephone company give 'em who the phones belong to. Cops are going around to see them people. Identifications cops found a thumbprint on the dead guy's desk.'

'Is it the killer's thumbprint?' I inquired.

'Why, we don't know who.'

He had a small picture of the dead man in a thick envelope. The lawyer had been a little man, shrewd-looking and rather foppish.

'I'm supposed to work on this,' O'Malley remarked, 'but I don't know nothing to do.'

The secretary and the young man who worked for Krockin were at headquarters. They had been brought there for questioning. The man was named Burkil. The girl's name was Miss Melton and she was young and quite pretty.

'What ideas have you got about this murder?' O'Malley asked Miss Melton.

'None at all. I was out of the office. When I came back I found Mr Krockin dead. I screamed and an elevator operator came. Then other people came and the building manager called the police.'

'Who would want to kill the guy?'

'I don't know of anyone.'

'Well, who'd he expect to see this morning?'

'He had no appointments.'

'How about you?' O'Malley inquired of Burkil.

'I don't know anything. Mr Krockin had sent me out to look up some records. When I came back the police were there.'

We went to look at the office. Two rooms, high up in a big building, were luxuriously furnished. A cop was there to take the names of anyone who came to see Krockin.

'Anything happen here?' O'Malley asked him.

'Nobody come here. Some people phoned. I got their names.' He gave us the names. 'One lady wouldn't give her name, so I asked the telephone people could they trace the call, and it turned out they could. It come from a beauty shop, so I told 'em it didn't matter.'

'You won't get no more phone calls. This crime is in the evening papers.'

We inspected the inner office. Its windows looked out onto a courtyard. The police had carried away all the papers and the smaller furnishings. A small safe was still there.

'Could it have been robbery, O'Malley?' I asked.

'Sure, it could be anything. No gun was found here. The safe wasn't locked. Cops found only papers in it and the secretary don't know if there'd been anything else. The building employees didn't see nobody that could be the killer, and so many people get in and out them half dozen elevators there's no chance of getting a description of who got off at this floor. Let's go see that lady that wouldn't give the cop her name.'

'It's a beauty shop,' I objected.

'Sure. We might see some pretty ladies.'

We went to the beauty shop. The lady we saw was very pretty indeed. Her name was Miss Hall and she conducted the shop.

'How come you phoned that lawyer Krockin?' O'Malley asked her.

'I didn't.'

'Yeah, someone phoned from here.'

'Some customer may have done it, but I don't know who.'

'Okay.'

We went back to headquarters.

'Well, there you got the case,' O'Malley remarked to me. 'We got nothing—and we keep on getting it. Let's call it a day.'

I met him next morning.

'So what?' I asked.

'We got a few things. I don't think that secretary is telling everything she knows. That Krockin done a shady business. A lot of his cases never came to court; they got settled privately. Cops that went around and seen the people whose names was in his office report some of 'em claim they didn't even know the guy. We checked up that thumbprint. It wasn't the secretary's or that guy Burkil's, or any employee of the building, or any cop that had went there.'

'Did you get anything more?'

'Sure. Them cops was pretty smart. They had a lot of pictures made of the dead guy, like the one I showed you, and put 'em in envelopes that would protect the surface. When they questioned anyone about Krockin, they give 'em one of the pictures to look at, and they held it in such a way the person had to make a thumbprint on it. You ever hear of a guy named Mr Corvis?'

'I've heard of one,' I told him. 'He's an important man—the head of a big investment company. His son is a well-known polo player and there's been a lot printed about the family lately because his daughter is soon to be married.'

'I'm supposed to see the guy.'

'Was it his thumbprint?'

'That's right,' O'Malley said.

We went and saw Corvis. We found impressive offices. Corvis was a big handsome man. The beautiful young girl whose picture was on his desk I knew must be his daughter.

'A cop seen you yesterday about that dead lawyer, Krockin, Mr Corvis,' O'Malley said.

'Yes.'

'You told him you didn't know the guy.'

'That is correct.'

'How come, then, your thumbprint was on the dead guy's desk?'

'It wasn't.'

O'Malley explained about the thumbprint. Corvis looked straight ahead and didn't say anything. 'Is this a police trick?' he inquired at last.

'No, Mr Corvis.'

'Then it's a police mistake. Some other thumbprint must resemble mine.'

'There ain't no two thumbprints in the world alike.'

'Nevertheless, it's a mistake. I repeat, I didn't know Krockin. To the best of my knowledge I never saw the man, and certainly I never was in his office.'

'This is a miserable affair, O'Malley,' I declared unhappily, when we had left the offices. 'The Corvises are a fine family. Of course, Corvis wasn't telling the truth, and he wouldn't deny being in Krockin's office if he were innocent.'

'Why, innocent guys tell lies like other people.'

Next day I didn't see O'Malley. I bought all the newspapers and I was surprised to find that Corvis' name wasn't even mentioned in them. There had been nothing in any of them about the thumbprint. I found O'Malley at headquarters the following day.

'Well,' I exclaimed, 'I see the Krockin murder never will be solved.'

'Yeah? How come?'

'Corvis has too much influence.'

'Don't kid yourself.'

'Then why hasn't he been arrested?'

'Say, give us time. We're working on it. We been trying to find out what happened in Krockin's office that morning. It shapes up this way: Miss Melton come to work at her usual time of half-past nine. Burkil was in the office and Krockin come in a little later. At ten o'clock Krockin sent Burkil out to look up some records, the same as Burkil told us. At ten thirty he told Miss Melton to go out and stay out an hour.'

'Why was that?'

'She doesn't know why. She says he done that sometimes. She never asked no questions but just figured someone was coming there she wasn't supposed to see.'

'Of course!' I exclaimed. 'Corvis was coming.'

'Well, it might be that way. You'll maybe feel better when I tell you we've pinched Miss Melton.'

'Now I know you're crazy!' I asserted. 'Miss Melton didn't kill Krockin.'

'Have it your own way. I got a place to go to. You might come along.'

We went to a building not far from Krockin's office and went up on the roof, and then across a couple of other roofs, and down a short stairway into a small room where two cops sat wearing headphones.

'You boys getting anything?' O'Malley asked them.

'Not a thing.'

'Let this guy listen in.'

One of the cops gave me his headphone and I listened while O'Malley looked over the notes the cops had taken. I didn't hear anything important. A woman was making an appointment with her hairdresser.

'You ever do much thinking about beauty shops?' O'Malley asked me, after I had given back the headphone.

'What's that got to do with it?' I demanded.

'Why, ladies talk a lot in beauty shops. Some of 'em talk about things to their hairdresser they wouldn't have told to their best friend.'

'You better get this,' one of the cops interrupted.

O'Malley listened, and put down the headphone.

'Come on,' he told me.

We went but we didn't go anywhere. Instead, we stood so long on a street corner that I got thoroughly tired of it. Then I saw Miss Hall, the girl from the beauty shop, approaching. A plain-clothes cop was walking a little behind her, and when the cop saw O'Malley, he wiped his chin with his handkerchief, and O'Malley stopped Miss Hall and showed her his shield, and we all got into a cab. In the cab O'Malley opened Miss Hall's handbag and found $3000 in it.

'Sister,' he said, 'you've got yourself in trouble.'

We took her to headquarters, and we found a woman there whom I hadn't seen before. She was pretty and seemed thirty-some years old, and the two women and a lot of cops went into the Interrogation Room and I was left in the corridor. O'Malley came to the door and spoke to me.

'I'll meet you at dinner.'

I met him at seven o'clock.

'Well,' he said, 'this case come out about like we expected. Burkil killed Krockin.'

'Burkil?' I echoed. 'Why?'

'This was a blackmail ring. Krockin and Burkil and that beauty lady, Miss Hall, was the members of it. When some customer in Miss Hall's shop told something they could make use of, that beauty lady reported it to Krockin. Burkil, who one time had been a private detective, went round and looked the thing up, and if Burkil found enough to make a case out of, Krockin drew up the papers. There wasn't no idea of ever bringing them cases into court, but Burkil seen the guys and made 'em think they meant to prosecute. Then he suggested it could be settled if they saw Krockin.

'When they seen Krockin he told 'em it could be settled secretly for a certain amount of money, and a lot of them people paid rather than take the chance the charges might become public.'

'I see,' I said. 'Then Corvis was one of those blackmailed.'

'You got it. You seen the lady we had there at headquarters? Her name is Miss Darret, and she was one time an actress. Quite a few years ago her and Corvis was friends and they made a trip to Bermuda together. Corvis' daughter's engagement was in the newspapers, and Miss Darret was getting her hair dressed, and she made the remark to the hairdresser that she one time had knew Corvis and they had went on a trip. So Krockin drew up a complaint in Miss Darret's name against Corvis.

'Miss Darret didn't have no idea of making any trouble for Corvis, and she wouldn't have signed the complaint, but when Miss Hall made an appointment with one of her customers she had the customer sign the appointment. So she had all their signatures. Krockin forged Miss Darret's signature on the complaint; then Burkil seen Corvis, and Corvis couldn't afford no scandal when his daughter was being married, and he knew Miss Darret's signature. So he come and seen Krockin and paid him ten thousand to settle the case.'

'I still don't see,' I declared, 'why Burkil killed Krockin.'

'Why, you're kind of simple. Guys like that Krockin are so crooked they can't hardly be square with themselves. When somebody was coming to pay Krockin money, he tried to get Burkil and Miss Melton both out of the office. If he could do that, he took an extra cut out of the money for himself; then he told Burkil and Miss Hall he'd had to settle with the guy for less than they expected. For a long while Burkil suspected Krockin was doing that, and he accused him, but Krockin denied it, and Burkil decided to find out.

'There's a vacant office across the court from Krockin's where you can see into Krockin's windows. Burkil went to the building people and told 'em him and Krockin was thinking of changing their office, and they give him a key so he could look at the office, and he had a duplicate key made. The morning Krockin got killed, Krockin sent Burkil and Miss Melton out, but Burkil didn't never leave the building. He went around and got into that other office. He seen Corvis give Krockin the money, and he seen Krockin put part of the money in his pocket and the rest in the safe. When Corvis had gone, Burkil went and accused Krockin, and they had a big quarrel and Burkil shot Krockin. Then he went back and waited in the vacant office till the police come.'

'What did Miss Melton have to do with it?'

'She didn't have nothing.'

'Then why did you arrest her?'

'Well, that was a piece of police business The case shaped up this way: them legal papers found in Krockin's office hadn't hardly any of 'em ever come into court and they concerned wealthy people. That looked like blackmail. The question was: had somebody that was being blackmailed knocked off the lawyer, or was it something else? Somebody had left a thumbprint on Krockin's desk and it turned out to be Corvis. Still, we didn't never think Corvis had killed Krockin.'

'Why?' I demanded.

'I'll tell you later. We figured Corvis had gone to the office but somebody else had gone there too, and the second guy had killed Krockin. So who? Before it was known Krockin had been knocked off, a beauty shop called up. A beauty shop is all right when it is all right, but it's all wrong if there's a crook in it, and cops know a lot of blackmail originates in crooked ones. The beauty shop give us the idea of a ring.

'So how to find out who was in it? There's an old-time police trick: when several people are mixed up in a crime, you lock up one of 'em and you don't let that one communicate with anybody. You don't let nobody know you suspect 'em, but you keep watch of everybody, and they worry about what you might be getting out of the one you've locked up. When people have worried enough they have to do something. So we locked up Miss Melton.'

'But you said she had nothing to do with it.'

'Why, not with the murder. She knew about the blackmail. She wouldn't tell us nothing because she thought by claiming to know nothing she'd keep out of trouble. Burkil didn't know how much Miss Melton knew. He thought maybe she knew he hadn't went out of the building. He was worried about Miss Hall too, because he had told her he thought Krockin was gyping 'em and he meant to find out. After we pinched Miss Melton, he called Miss Hall up and arranged to meet her, and he told her he hadn't killed Krockin but he had got the money, and he give her three thousand out of what he had got out of Krockin's pocket and out of the safe. Well, you know about that. We'd had her phone tapped. I and you couldn't go to see him and Miss Hall meet because both of 'em knew us, but them cops phoned headquarters, and a couple of plain-clothes guys was there when they met and seen him pass her the money.

'Then we pinched both of 'em. When we got 'em to headquarters we questioned all them people together, and cops brought in seven thousand bucks more that they'd found at Burkil's hotel, and we got how it all was. Now we got a plain murder case.'

'But I still don't see,' I said, 'with so much proof against Corvis why you didn't suspect him.'

'Say, use common sense. He's a smart guy and head of a big company. Guys as smart as him don't do no murder, because they know however much trouble they might be in, murder will make it worse.'

'A nice piece of psychology,' I reflected, 'and Corvis owes you a debt of gratitude.'

'Yeah? Try and collect it. When an innocent guy's in trouble a smart cop looks like an angel to him, but once he's got out of it, the cop only done his duty.'

JACQUES FUTRELLE (1875–1912)

The Stolen Rubens

———

MATTHEW KALE made fifty million dollars out of axle grease, after which he began to patronize the high arts. It was simple enough: he had the money, and Europe had the old masters. His method of buying was simplicity itself. There were five thousand square yards, more or less, in the huge gallery of his marble mansion which were to be covered, so he bought five thousand yards, more or less, of art. Some of it was good, some of it fair, and much of it bad. The chief picture of the collection was a Rubens, which he had picked up in Rome for fifty thousand dollars.

Soon after acquiring his collection, Kale decided to make certain alterations in the vast room where the pictures hung. They were all taken down and stored in the ballroom, equally vast, with their faces toward the wall. Meanwhile Kale and his family took refuge in a nearby hotel.

It was at this hotel that Kale met Jules de Lesseps. De Lesseps was distinctly the sort of Frenchman whose conversation resembles calisthenics. He was nervous, quick, and agile, and he told Kale in confidence that he was not only a painter himself, but a connoisseur in the high arts. Pompous in the pride of possession, Kale went to a good deal of trouble to exhibit his private collection for de Lesseps' delectation. It happened in the ballroom, and the true artist's delight shone in the Frenchman's eyes as he handled the pieces which were good. Some of the others made him smile, but it was an inoffensive sort of smile.

With his own hands Kale lifted the precious Rubens and held it before the Frenchman's eyes. It was a 'Madonna and Child,' one of those wonderful creations which have endured through the years with all the sparkle and color beauty of their pristine days. Kale seemed disappointed because de Lesseps was not particularly enthusiastic about this picture.

'Why, it's a Rubens!' he exclaimed.

'Yes, I see,' replied de Lesseps.

'It cost me fifty thousand dollars.'

'It is perhaps worth more than that,' and the Frenchman shrugged his shoulders as he turned away.

Kale looked at him in chagrin. Could it be that de Lesseps did not understand that it was a Rubens, and that Rubens was a painter? Or was it that he had failed to hear him say that it cost him fifty thousand dollars. Kale was accustomed to seeing people bob their heads and open their eyes when he said fifty thousand dollars; therefore, 'Don't you like it?' he asked.

'Very much indeed,' replied de Lesseps: 'but I have seen it before. I saw it in Rome just a week or so before you purchased it.'

They rummaged on through the pictures, and at last a Whistler was turned up for their inspection. It was one of the famous Thames series, a water color. De Lesseps' face radiated excitement, and several times he glanced from the water color to the Rubens as if mentally comparing the exquisitely penciled and colored newer work with the bold, masterly technic of the older painting.

Kale misunderstood his silence. 'I don't think much of this one myself,' he explained apologetically. 'It's a Whistler, and all that, and it cost me five thousand dollars, and I sort of had to have it, but still it isn't just the kind of thing that I like. What do you think of it?'

'I think it is perfectly wonderful!' replied the Frenchman enthusiastically. 'It is the essence, the superlative, of Whistler's work. I wonder if it would be possible,' and he turned to face Kale, 'for me to make a copy of that? I have some slight skill in painting myself, and dare say I could make a fairly creditable copy of it.'

Kale was flattered. He was more and more impressed each moment with the picture. 'Why certainly,' he replied. 'I will have it sent up to the hotel, and you can—'

'No, no, no!' interrupted de Lesseps quickly. 'I wouldn't care to accept the responsibility of having the picture in my charge. There is always a danger of fire. But if you would give me permission to come here—this room is large and airy and light—and besides it is quite—'

'Just as you like,' said Kale magnanimously. 'I merely thought the other way would be most convenient for you.'

De Lesseps laid one hand on the millionaire's arm. 'My dear friend,' he said earnestly, 'if these pictures were my pictures, I shouldn't try to accommodate anybody where they were concerned. I dare say the collection as it stands cost you—'

'Six hundred and eighty-seven thousand dollars,' volunteered Kale proudly.

'And surely they must be well protected here in your house during your absence.'

'There are about twenty servants in the house, while the workmen are making the alterations,' said Kale, 'and three of them don't do anything but watch this room. No one can go in or out except by the door we entered—the others are locked and barred—and then only with my permission, or a written order from me. No sir, nobody can get away with anything in this room.'

'Excellent—excellent!' said de Lesseps admiringly. He smiled a little. 'I am afraid I did not give you credit for being the far-sighted businessman that you are.' He turned and glanced over the collection of pictures abstractedly. 'A clever thief, though,' he ventured, 'might cut a valuable painting, for instance the Rubens, out of the frame, roll it up, conceal it under his coat, and escape.'

Kale laughed and shook his head.

It was a couple of days later at the hotel that de Lesseps brought up the subject of copying the Whistler. He was profuse in his thanks when Kale volunteered to accompany him into the mansion and witness the preliminary stages of the work. They paused at the ballroom door.

'Jennings,' said Kale to the liveried servant there, 'this is Mr de Lesseps. He is to come and go as he likes. He is going to do some work in the ballroom here. See that he isn't disturbed.'

De Lesseps noticed the Rubens leaning carelessly against some other pictures, with the holy face of the Madonna turned toward them. 'Really, Mr Kale,' he protested, 'that picture is too valuable to be left about like that. If you will let your servants bring me some canvas, I shall wrap it and place it up on this table off the floor. Suppose there were mice here!'

Kale thanked him. The necessary orders were given, and finally the picture was carefully wrapped and placed beyond harm's reach, whereupon de Lesseps adjusted himself, paper, easel, stool, and all, and began his work of copying. There Kale left him.

Three days later Kale found the artist still at his labor.

'I just dropped by,' he explained, 'to see how the work in the gallery was getting along. It will be finished in another week. I hope I am not disturbing you?'

'Not at all,' said de Lesseps; 'I have nearly finished. See how I am getting along?' He turned the easel toward Kale.

The millionaire gazed from that toward the original which stood on a chair near by, and frank admiration for the artist's efforts was in his eyes. 'Why, it's fine!' he exclaimed. 'It's just as good as the other one, and I bet you don't want any five thousand dollars for it—eh?'

That was all that was said about it at the time. Kale wandered about the house for an hour or so, then dropped into the ballroom where de Lesseps was getting his paraphernalia together, and they walked back to the hotel. The artist carried under one arm his copy of the Whistler, loosely rolled up.

Another week passed, and the workmen who had been engaged in refinishing and decorating the gallery had gone. De Lesseps volunteered to assist in the work of rehanging the pictures, and Kale gladly turned the matter over to him. It was in the afternoon of the day this work began that de Lesseps, chatting pleasantly with Kale, ripped loose the canvas which enshrouded the precious Rubens. Then he paused with an exclamation of dismay. The picture was gone; the frame which had held it was empty. A thin strip of canvas around the inside edge showed that a sharp penknife had been used to cut out the painting.

All of these facts came to the attention of Professor Augustus S. F. X. Van Dusen—The Thinking Machine. This was a day or so after Kale had rushed into Detective Mallory's office at police headquarters with the statement that his Rubens had been stolen. He banged his fist down on the detective's desk, and roared at him.

'It cost me fifty thousand dollars! Why don't you do something? What are you sitting there staring at me for?'

'Don't excite yourself, Mr Kale,' the detective advised. 'I will put my men at work right now to recover the—the—What is a Rubens, anyway?'

'It's a picture!' bellowed Kale. 'A piece of canvas with some paint on it, and it cost me fifty thousand dollars—don't you forget that!'

So the police machinery was set in motion to recover the picture. And in time the matter fell under the watchful eye of Hutchinson Hatch, reporter. He learned the facts preceding the disappearance of the picture and then called on de Lesseps. He found the artist in a state of excitement bordering on hysteria; an intimation from the reporter of the object of his visit caused de Lesseps to burst into words.

'*Mon Dieu!* It is outrageous! What can I do? I was the only one in the room for several days. I was the one who took such pains to protect the picture. And now it is gone! The loss is irreparable. What can I do?'

Hatch didn't have any very definite idea as to just what he could do, so he let him go on. 'As I understand it, Mr de Lesseps,' he interrupted at last, 'no one else was in the room, except you and Mr Kale, all the time you were there?'

'No one else.'

'And I think Mr Kale said that you were making a copy of some famous water color; weren't you?'

'Yes, a Thames scene by Whistler,' was the reply. 'That is it, hanging over the fireplace.'

Hatch glanced at the picture admiringly. It was an exquisite copy, and showed the deft touch of a man who was himself an artist of great ability.

De Lesseps read the admiration in his face. 'It is not bad,' he said modestly. 'I studied with Carolus Duran.'

With all else that was known, and this little additional information, which seemed of no particular value to the reporter, the entire matter was laid before The Thinking Machine. That distinguished man listened from beginning to end without comment.

'Who had access to the room?' he asked finally.

'That is what the police are working on now,' said Hutchinson Hatch. 'There are a couple of dozen servants in the house, and I suppose, in spite of Kale's rigid orders, there was a certain laxity in their enforcement.'

'Of course that makes it more difficult,' said The Thinking Machine in the perpetually irritated voice which was so characteristic a part of himself. 'Perhaps it would be best for us to go to Mr Kale's home and personally investigate.'

Kale received them with the reserve which rich men usually show in the presence of representatives of the press. He stared frankly and somewhat curiously at the diminutive figure of the scientist, who explained the object of their visit.

'I guess you fellows can't do anything with this,' the millionaire assured them. 'I've got some regular detectives on it.'

'Is Mr Mallory here now?' asked The Thinking Machine curtly.

'Yes, he is upstairs in the servants' quarters.'

'May we see the room from which the picture was taken?' inquired the scientist, with a suave intonation which Hatch knew well.

Kale granted the permission with a wave of the hand, and ushered them into the ballroom, where the pictures had been stored. From the center of this room The Thinking Machine surveyed it all. The windows were high. Half a dozen doors leading out into the hallways, the conservatory, quiet nooks of the mansion offered innumerable possibilities of access. After this one long comprehensive squint, The Thinking Machine went over and picked up the frame from which the Rubens had been cut. For a long time he examined it. Kale's impatience was evident. Finally the scientist turned to him.

'How well do you know M. de Lesseps?'

'I've known him for only a month or so. Why?'

'Did he bring you letters of introduction, or did you meet him merely casually?'

Kale regarded him with displeasure. 'My own personal affairs have nothing whatever to do with this matter! Mr de Lesseps is a gentleman of integrity, and certainly he is the last whom I would suspect of any connection with the disappearance of the picture.'

'That is usually the case,' remarked The Thinking Machine tartly. He turned to Hatch. 'Just how good a copy was that he made of the Whistler picture?'

'I have never seen the original,' Hatch replied; 'but the workmanship was superb. Perhaps Mr Kale wouldn't object to us seeing—'

'Of, of course not,' said Kale resignedly. 'Come on; it's in the gallery.'

Hatch submitted the picture to a careful scrutiny. 'I should say the copy is well-nigh perfect,' was his verdict. 'Of course, in its absence, I can't say exactly; but it is certainly a superb work.'

The curtains of a wide door almost in front of them were thrown aside suddenly, and Detective Mallory entered. He carried something in his hand, but at sight of them concealed it behind him. Unrepressed triumph was in his face.

'Ah, professor, we meet often; don't we?' he said.

'This reporter here and his friend seem to be trying to drag de Lesseps into this affair somehow,' Kale complained to the detective. 'I don't want anything like that to happen. He is liable to go out and print anything. They always do.'

The Thinking Machine glared at him unwaveringly for an instant, then extended his hand toward Mallory. 'Where did you find it?' he asked.

'Sorry to disappoint you, professor,' said the detective sarcastically, 'but this is the time when you were a little late,' and he produced the object which he held behind him. 'Here is your picture, Mr Kale.'

Kale gasped in relief and astonishment, and held up the canvas with both hands to examine it. 'Fine!' he told the detective. 'I'll see that you don't lose anything by this. Why, that thing cost me fifty thousand dollars!'

The Thinking Machine leaned forward to squint at the upper right-hand corner of the canvas. 'Where did you find it?' he asked again.

'Rolled up tight, and concealed in the bottom of a trunk in the room of one of the servants,' explained Mallory. 'The servant's name is Jennings. He is now under arrest.'

'Jennings!' exclaimed Kale. 'Why, he has been with me for years.'

'Did he confess?' asked the scientist imperturbably.

'Of course not,' said Mallory. 'He says some of the other servants must have hidden it there.'

The Thinking Machine nodded at Hatch. 'I think perhaps that is all,' he remarked. 'I congratulate you, Mr Mallory, upon bringing the matter to such a quick and satisfactory conclusion.'

Ten minutes later they left the house and took a taxi for the scientist's home. Hatch was a little chagrined at the unexpected termination of the affair.

'Mallory does show an occasional gleam of human intelligence, doesn't he?'

'Not that I ever noticed,' remarked The Thinking Machine crustily.

'But he found the picture,' Hatch insisted.

'Of course he found it. It was put there for him to find.'

'Put there for him to find!' repeated the reporter. 'Didn't Jennings steal it?'

'If he did, he's a fool.'

'Well, if he didn't steal it, who put it there?'

'De Lesseps.'

'De Lesseps!' echoed Hatch. 'Why the deuce did he steal a fifty thousand dollar picture and put it in a servant's trunk to be found?'

The Thinking Machine twisted around in his seat and squinted at him coldly for a moment. 'At times, Mr Hatch, I am absolutely amazed at your stupidity. I can understand it in a man like Mallory, but I have always given you credit for being an astute, quick-witted man.'

Hatch smiled at the reproach. It was not the first time he had heard it. But nothing bearing on the problem in hand was said until they reached The Thinking Machine's house.

'The only real question in my mind, Mr Hatch,' said the scientist then, 'is whether or not I should take the trouble to restore Mr Kale's picture at all. He is perfectly satisfied, and will probably never know the difference. So—'

Suddenly Hatch saw something. 'Great Scott!' he exclaimed. 'Do you mean that the picture Mallory found was—'

'A copy of the original,' snapped the scientist. 'Personally I know nothing whatever about art; therefore, I could not say from observation that it is a copy, but I know it from the logic of the thing. When the original was cut from the frame, the knife swerved a little at the upper right-hand corner. The canvas remaining in the frame told me that. The picture that Mr Mallory found did not correspond in this detail with the canvas in the frame. The conclusion is obvious.'

'And de Lesseps has the original?'

'De Lesseps has the original. How did he get it? In any one of a dozen ways. He might have rolled it up and stuck it under his coat. He might have had a confederate. But I don't think that any ordinary method of theft would have appealed to him. I am giving him credit for being clever, as I must when we review the whole case.

'For instance, he asked for permission to copy the Whistler, which you saw was the same size as the Rubens. It was granted. He copied it practically under guard, always with the chance that Mr Kale himself would drop in. It took him three days to copy it, so he says. He was alone in the room all that time. He knew that Mr Kale had not the faintest idea of art. Taking advantage of that, what would have been simpler than to have copied the Rubens in oil? He could have removed it from the frame immediately after he canvased it over, and kept it in a position near him where it could be quickly concealed if he was interrupted. Remember, the picture is worth fifty thousand dollars; therefore, was worth the trouble.

'De Lesseps is an artist—we know that—and dealing with a man who knew nothing whatever of art, he had no fears. We may suppose his idea all along was to use the copy of the Rubens as a sort of decoy after he got away with the original. You saw that Mallory didn't know the difference, and it was safe for him to suppose that Mr Kale wouldn't. His only danger until he could get away gracefully was of some critic or connoisseur, perhaps, seeing the copy. His boldness we see readily in the fact that he permitted himself to discover the theft;

that he discovered it after he had volunteered to assist Mr Kale in the general work of rehanging the pictures in the gallery. Just how he put the picture in Jennings' trunk I don't happen to know. We can imagine many ways.' He lay back in his chair for a minute without speaking, eyes steadily turned upward, fingers placed precisely tip to tip.

'But how did he take the picture from the Kale home?' asked Hatch.

'He took it with him probably under his arm the day he left the house with Mr Kale,' was the astonishing reply.

Hatch was staring at him in amazement. After a moment the scientist rose and passed into the adjoining room, and the telephone bells there jingled. When he joined Hatch again he picked up his hat and they went out together.

De Lesseps was in when their cards were sent up, and received them. They conversed about the case generally for ten minutes, while the scientist's eyes were turned inquiringly here and there about the room. At last there came a knock on the door.

'It is Detective Mallory, Mr Hatch,' remarked The Thinking Machine. 'Open the door for him.'

De Lesseps seemed startled for just one instant, then quickly recovered. Mallory's eyes were full of questions when he entered.

'I should like, Mr Mallory,' began The Thinking Machine quietly, 'to call your attention to this copy of Mr Kale's picture by Whistler— over the mantel here. Isn't it excellent? You have seen the original?'

Mallory grunted. De Lesseps' face, instead of expressing appreciation of the compliment, blanched, and his hands closed tightly. Again he recovered himself and smiled.

'The beauty of this picture lies not only in its faithfulness to the original,' the scientist went on, 'but also in the fact that it was painted under extraordinary circumstances. For instance, I don't know if you know, Mr Mallory, that it is possible so to combine glue and putty and a few other commonplace things into a paste which will effectually blot out an oil painting, and offer at the same time an excellent surface for water color work!'

There was a moment's pause, during which the three men stared at him silently—with conflicting emotions.

'This water color—this copy of Whistler,' continued the scientist evenly—'is painted on such a paste as I have described. That paste in turn covers the original Rubens picture. It can be removed with water without damage to the picture, which is in oil, so that instead of a copy of the Whistler painting, we have an original by Rubens, worth fifty thousand dollars. That is true; isn't it, M. de Lesseps?'

There was no reply to the question—none was needed.

It was an hour later, after de Lesseps was safely in his cell, that Hatch called up The Thinking Machine and asked one question.

'How did you know that the water color was painted over the Rubens?'

'Because it was the only absolutely safe way in which the Rubens could be hopelessly lost to those who were looking for it, and at the same time perfectly preserved,' was the answer. 'I told you de Lesseps was a clever man, and a little logic did the rest. Two and two always make four, Mr Hatch, not sometimes, but all the time.'

The Marshall Murder

―――――

I

'THIS is Mr Duff,' the lawyer introduced them. 'Miss Marshall, Mr Duff.' And Duff shook hands with a very small, a very dark, a very alert and fashionable spinster-lady of middle age, who looked up at him with a sweet and ironical smile.

'Well,' she said softly, 'you're big enough.'

He was huge. He was nearly six feet tall; he weighed some two hundred pounds; and he was solid with muscle.

'It's a disguise,' he assured her. 'I use it to deceive people—the same as you do.' And he met her smile with a shrewd, appraising twinkle.

'The same as I do?'

'Yes,' he said. 'They never suspect me of being a detective, any more than they suspect you of being an autocrat.'

Her smile became sweeter than ever. 'What makes you think I'm an autocrat?'

'The same thing in me that makes me think I'm a detective. Won't you sit down?'

She accepted a chair by the fireplace with a tiny dignity that was not unimpressive. 'I only hope,' she murmured, 'that you're not equally deceived in us both.'

She and Westingate, her lawyer, had come to consult Duff in his rooms, instead of at his office, because they wished to keep their visit to him a careful secret. His rooms were on the second floor of an old brownstone house on Eleventh Street near Sixth Avenue, and the living-room in which they found him, typical of the decayed gentility of the district, had a high ceiling, an old black marble mantelpiece, tall windows, and a hardwood floor. He had furnished it chiefly with a law library, descended from the days when he had been an unsuccessful young attorney. As a living-room, it looked studious and celibate. The chairs were all fat bachelor chairs, upholstered in dark leather, as severe as they were comfortable; and they were so burly that Alicia Marshall, for all her furs, sat in hers like a little fairy godmother in a giant's seat.

The lawyer, Westingate, took a chair on the same side of the fireplace as she, and frowned at the blaze with a forehead that was permanently corrugated. A somber and bilious-looking bald man, he seemed always to be brooding over the obscurities of the law behind a set and worried countenance. 'I suppose you've guessed,' he said, 'that we wanted to see you about this'—he coughed—'murder.'

Duff raised his heavy eyebrows, deprecatingly. 'No,' he admitted. 'I wasn't sure.'

'Well,' Alicia Marshall said, 'we *did*.' She had unbuttoned her sealskin sacque. She threw it open, now, with a gesture of beginning the discussion. Duff sat down. The lawyer cleared his throat.

The murder—the Marshall murder—was one of those picturesque New Jersey murders that happen in the best-regulated families of a state that prides itself on its 'swift Jersey justice'— murders of which no one is ever found guilty, so that they present the fascinating spectacle of an irresistible force meeting an insoluble mystery. The chief victim was a distinguished citizen, Senator Amos K. Marshall, a corporation lawyer and party politician; and his outrageous end may have been more shocking to the popular mind because, after all, the murder of a 'big business' lawyer, who is also a machine senator, contains elements that do not wholly horrify, and it is necessary for many people to be volubly distressed at such a crime in order to overcome a contrary impulse, perhaps. In any case, the public outcry was tremendous, measured either by the amount of newspaper space that was filled with accounts of the Marshall murder, or by the amount of boxwood hedge that was carried away from the Marshall lawn by souvenir hunters.

There was killed with Senator Marshall, a young widow, named Mrs Starrett, who was his housekeeper. When a man and a woman are murdered together, scandal seems inevitable; and in this case, the scandal traveled fast because no evidence was found to support it. It moved as freely as a flying column that lives off the countryside without any need for a base of supplies. And it was followed by the rumor that the man accused of the murder had been in love with the housekeeper, though there was no discoverable basis in fact for that report either.

The man accused was an ex-soldier named Andrew Pittling—a young veteran of the Argonne, suffering from shell-shock—whom Marshall had employed as general utility-man around his suburban home in Cold Brook. Pittling had been voluble in his support of President Wilson's League of Nations, and Marshall had conspicuously helped to defeat Wilson's policies. Hence, many arguments about the murder were warm with the animation of political sympathy.

Hence, also, Alicia Marshall—before her lawyer could get his cleared throat into action—broke out gently to Duff: 'We've decided that there's no use leaving it to the local authorities any longer. They're a lot of Democratic politicians. I believe they're capable of protecting the man who killed Amos, if they knew who he was.'

'You were not in the house, that night?' Duff asked, meaning the night of the murder.

'No, I was not.'

She lived, she explained, in the original Marshall homestead, on Marshall Avenue, in Cold Brook. Her dead brother Amos, when he married, bought an estate in the hills behind the town; he rebuilt magnificently an old Dutch farmhouse on the property and he had lived there ever since. There had been no one in the house on the night of the murder except his daughter, Martha—so ill in bed with influenza that she was too weak to lift her head from the pillow, and a number of servants, all women except this one man, the ex-soldier, Pittling.

'What is the actual evidence against Pittling, do you know?' Duff asked the lawyer.

Well, to tell the truth, there was none. Senator Marshall had been killed, evidently with a hatchet, as he lay asleep in his bed. His housekeeper, Mrs Starrett, had been struck down, apparently with the same hatchet, in the hall outside his door. In the morning, a bloody hatchet was found lying among some rose bushes under an open window that looked out from the dining-room on a side lawn. Either the murderer had dropped his weapon there, as he escaped out the window, or he had tossed it out the window and remained in the house himself. In neither case was there anything to cast suspicion on Pittling except the fact that the hatchet was his. He kept it in the furnace-room of the basement to use when he was building fires; and he had used it earlier in the day to split kindling for a fire in the bedroom of the daughter, Martha. The weather had turned suddenly colder that afternoon, and Martha had complained that her room was chilly even with the furnace on full draught. Pittling and the housemaid built a fire of cannel coal in her bedroom grate, to satisfy her; but neither of them could remember whether Pittling had brought the hatchet up out of the basement then, or whether if he *had* brought it up, he had failed to return it to the cellar. No distinguishable fingerprints were on it when it was found in the morning. There were no footprints outside the window, because the ground was frozen hard and bare of snow. And no one but the dead housekeeper knew whether the window had been left unlocked the night before, or whether it had been opened from the inside after she had locked it. It was her duty to make the rounds at night and see that all the doors and windows were closed and fastened before she went to bed.

'And no one,' Duff asked, 'heard any noise whatever during the night?'

No one. No one could be expected to, except Martha, the sick girl. Her room was next to her father's. The housekeeper was killed in the hall between her father's door and hers. But she had gone through the crisis of her fever that afternoon; she fell asleep, in a weak perspiration, late that evening; and she did not wake till the following dawn. Her door had been closed after she fell asleep, evidently by the housekeeper, to protect her slumber; and she heard nothing. The women servants—that is to say, the cook and the two maids—slept in the kitchen wing, out of hearing of anything that might happen in the main portion of the house. The chauffeur slept over the garage. Pittling, the ex-soldier, had fixed himself a room in the basement, where he lived as if he were in a cement dugout. He was peculiar.

'I see,' Duff said. 'And he heard nothing either?'

'Nothing,' the lawyer replied, 'of any importance.'

'No? What was it?'

Westingate explained impatiently: 'Senator Marshall's home is not supplied with water from the waterworks in Cold Brook. It's too far outside the town. It has its own pumping plant—an air pump, in a driven well, at some distance from the house. Compressed air is stored in a tank in the pumphouse, and the pump is quiet except when any of the faucets in the house are opened; then, as water flows out of the pipe, the mechanism of the pump trips off with an audible stroke. Pittling complains that he was wakened in the night by this sound of the pump working. The main supply pipe to the house runs through the basement just outside his room, and the sound of the pump travels quite loudly along that pipe. It prevented him from sleeping. For half an hour at least, he says, he was kept awake by it. Then it stopped.'

'He doesn't know at what hour this was?'

'No. He thinks he'd been asleep for some time, but of course he can't be sure. It may have happened before all the others had gone to bed.'

'Of course. And he heard nothing else?'

'Nothing until the housemaid screamed when she found Mrs Starrett dead in the hall. Pittling had been up for some time. He'd dressed and tended the furnace—'

'Oh, never mind all that,' Miss Marshall broke in, with a mild impatience. 'You can't possibly suspect poor Pittling. He's the last man in the world to murder anyone. He had enough of that in France.'

Duff had been listening, very much at his ease, his eyes on the fire, asking questions in a voice that was almost absent-minded, his big hands at rest on the massive arms of his comfortable chair. He already knew many of the details of the Marshall murder; he had pieced them together, with a professional interest, from the newspaper accounts. And he had been listening less to what Alicia Marshall and her lawyer said than to the state of mind about the murder which they unconsciously expressed.

Thus far, the most striking fact that he had learned was this: Alicia Marshall was not as deeply concerned about her brother's death as she was about 'poor Pittling.'

'He's been arrested, has he?—Pittling?'

'Yes. He's in the county jail.'

'Has he a lawyer?'

'I'm his lawyer,' Westingate replied.

'I see. I may have to get a talk with him, if you don't mind. And the other servants? Where are they?'

'They're with me,' Miss Marshall said. 'At my house.'

'And the daughter, Martha?'

'She is, too. She's still in bed. We had her moved, the next day. It was impossible for anyone to remain in that house, with the crowds that gathered.'

'Naturally. I suppose you've left some one there to see that they don't carry the house away piecemeal.'

'Yes. The chauffeur has moved in from the garage.'

Duff nodded. 'I'll put in a caretaker and his wife—if you don't object—and relieve the chauffeur.' He turned benignly to Miss Marshall. 'And I'd like to send you a trained nurse, supposedly for your niece, so as to have some one in touch with those servants. They may know something they haven't reported because they don't realize that it's significant. If I tried to cross-examine them myself, I'd only frighten them. I'll not send a detective,' he added, seeing her reluctance in her eyes. 'I have a very nice girl who goes out for me, now and then, on confidential cases—a girl of good family. She's had training as a convalescent nurse. You'll like her.'

'Have you any suspicion,' she asked warily, 'about who did it?'

'No,' he said. 'None. None whatever. If it were a murder of revenge, committed by some enemy from the outside, he'd have brought a weapon with him. He wouldn't've had to use that hatchet—whether he carried it up from the basement or found it somewhere upstairs. On the other hand, if it was a burglar whom Mrs Starrett surprised, he might have killed her, naturally enough, but why should he kill your brother in his bed? And I understand that nothing was stolen?'

'Nothing whatever.'

'If it were Pittling, he'd have taken the hatchet back downstairs and cleaned it off, probably, or concealed it. It's not likely that he'd direct suspicion against himself by leaving his hatchet, covered with blood, lying around where it would be found at once. No. That suggests, perhaps, an attempt to cast suspicion on Pittling.'

'Exactly,' Miss Marshall agreed.

'Or, the whole thing may be just an insane accident. Some madman may have broken in, and found the hatchet, and dropped it again as he ran away.'

'That would be my theory,' the lawyer said.

'I suppose this Mrs Starrett has been looked up?—to see whether *she* had any enemies.'

'Yes, thoroughly. They've found nothing.'

'And Senator Marshall's relations with Mrs Starrett? They've gone into that?'

He asked it casually, reflectively, looking at the fire. The lawyer did not reply. Duff turned to Miss Marshall and found her regarding her shoe tips with a sarcastic smile.

'Well,' she said, 'my brother was no fool. If there was anything going on between him and Mrs Starrett, no one will ever find it out.'

'You think there *was* something, then?'

'It's the last thing I should think. Senator Marshall had about as much private life as the Statue of Liberty.'

'He was a very religious man,' Westingate put in, 'very strict with his family, a leader in the law-and-order movement, and most severe on all this modern—er—laxity.'

'And the daughter? Is *she* religious?'

'Ah, poor Martha,' Miss Marshall sighed. 'She's a saint.'

'I see. Well,' Duff decided, 'I'll start work on it at once. If I send a caretaker and his wife to you, to-morrow morning, you can install them in the house?'

'Certainly,' the lawyer promised.

'And my nurse may come to you, Miss Marshall, to-morrow afternoon?'

'If you wish it.'

'Thanks. I'll arrive in Cold Brook, probably, to-morrow evening, and stop for a few days with the caretaker. That'll make it easier for me to consult with you both the moment I get any sort of clew. If anyone notices me and asks questions, we can explain that Senator Marshall's estate is in the hands of a New York trust company, as his executors, and I'm their agent, appraising the property and making an inventory of the estate. My name is Duffield.'

'Very good.'

They all rose.

'You'll not tell the truth about me, or my operatives, to anyone— the servants, the chauffeur, nor even your niece?'

'Certainly not.'

They shook hands on it.

'I'm beginning to think you really are a detective,' Miss Marshall said.

'Then, at least, I'm not deceived in us *both*,' replied Duff.

II

Cold Brook did not remark the arrival, next day, of a new caretaker at the Marshall home, installed by order of the executors of the estate. The nurse whom Miss Marshall engaged, from New York, to take care of her invalid niece, came unnoticed, in the afternoon, and went silently to work. Duff drove out by automobile, after dark, spent the night in one of Senator Marshall's guest rooms, and appeared next

morning, as the agent of the executors, to look over the other properties which Marshall had owned in Cold Brook, and to consult Alicia
Marshall and her lawyer, Westingate. He ate dinner, that evening, with
Westingate and the County Prosecutor at Westingate's home; and the
following morning a tramp, arrested for drunkenness, was put in the
cell that adjoined Pittling's in the county jail. Duff drove back to New
York in the afternoon, and no one seemed any the wiser. Not even he.

Cold Brook, with its tree-lined residential avenues and its suburban homes, was a commuters' town that had no public opinion of
its own outside of its one business street of shopkeepers, lawyers,
real estate and insurance agents, plumbers, barbers and such. Its
commuters read the New York papers and smiled with the New York
reporters at the provincial animosity of the local authorities to the
metropolitan newspaper men. The business district resented those
smiles. Duff might have walked the streets of Cold Brook openly, for
a week, and none of the reporters would have known that he was a
stranger in the town, because none of the real townsfolk would have
tipped them off. He was not recognized as a detective anywhere,
except in those circles in which he found his clients. He did not, as he
said, 'Hunt criminals with a brass band'—that is to say, he never
advertised. He had served with Military Intelligence during the war—
especially around airplane factories and shipyards—and some of his
war-time friends had urged him to set up a detective agency of his
own when the war ended, and one of those friends was an automobile manufacturer who happened to be a client of Westingate's. The
automobile man advised Westingate to see Duff about the Marshall
murder. That was how he came into the case.

When, after two days of a peculiar dawdling sort of inconspicuous
diligence in Cold Brook, he returned to his office near Union Square,
he telephoned to Westingate: 'I'll have something to report in about a
week, I think. My operatives are busy. I believe we're on the trail of
something.'

'What's your theory?' the lawyer asked.

'Well,' Duff said, 'this murder, you understand, occurred in two
places.'

'In two places?'

'Yes.'

'How so?'

'It occurred in Cold Brook, in the home of ex-Senator Marshall,
but before that, it occurred somewhere else.'

'Somewhere else?'

'Yes. It occurred first in somebody's mind, because it was evidently a premeditated murder.'

'Oh. I get you.'

'And it left a trail in that mind.'

'I suppose it did.'

'And while the County Prosecutor is trying to find its actual trail, I'm going after its mental trail.'

'In whose mind?'

'I'm not sure yet, but I can tell you this much: I don't believe it was Pittling's.'

'I'm glad of that. Then I may expect to hear something definite from you in a week?'

'Or two,' Duff promised.

And it was two.

The tramp who had been shut up with Pittling wormed his way into the ex-soldier's confidence and obtained nothing but indications of innocence. The caretaker and his wife did as much for the chauffeur, with the same result. Mrs Starrett, the murdered housekeeper, had had no enemies, apparently. She had been a respectable young widow who had lived all her life in Cold Brook. Her only surviving relative, an older sister, kept a boarding house; and an operative who went to live there found nothing on which to base a suspicion that there had been anything illicit in Mrs Starrett's relations with her employer, or that there was anyone to resent such relations if they had existed. The nurse, at Miss Marshall's, made friends with the dead man's servants and discovered nothing startling from them. The county authorities were beginning to believe that the crime had been committed by some insane yeggman who had broken into the house to burglarize it and killed two people in a homicidal mania; and they were holding Pittling, merely as a matter of form, until the popular excitement passed.

All these confessions of failure were received cheerfully by Duff in daily conversations over the telephone and in the daily reports which his operatives wrote for his office files. He motored out twice to Cold Brook and consulted with the members of his little field force at night, in Senator Marshall's library, looking blankly meditative and saying nothing. He called on Alicia Marshall to admit that he was making no progress, and he talked with her chiefly about her father, Jeremiah Marshall, with whom she had lived for years in the Marshall homestead. He had died of heart disease, in 1909, at the age of 71, in Senator Marshall's house, where he had gone to live after a quarrel with his spirited daughter. 'My brother always gave way to him,' she said. 'I'm afraid I irritated him. At any rate, the doctor declared his heart was so weak that the excitement of living with me was too much for him. He was too old to live alone. So he went to Amos. And he died there in about a month.' She smiled at Duff placidly. 'You don't think *he* was in any way connected with Amos's death, do you?'

Duff returned her smile. 'Yes,' he said, 'I'm beginning to suspect so.'

She accepted the statement with an air of humorously resigning herself to the fantastic. 'Well,' she sighed, 'I hope you can prove it—he's so safe from the police.'

III

He proved it on the following Sunday night. He proved it to Alicia Marshall and to Westingate, in an after-dinner conversation that took place in the picture gallery which Miss Marshall had added to the old Marshall homestead, in Cold Brook. She had been much abroad after her father's death. She had brought back a collection of Italian primitives and housed them in a gallery that was furnished with medieval chairs, antique carved tables, Oriental rugs, bronzes of the Rodin school and church vestments. In this room that looked like the showroom of a Fifth Avenue picture-dealer, by the light of electric bulbs that had been wired into church candelabra and seven-branched candlesticks, Duff made his report to Miss Marshall and her lawyer, over their after-dinner coffee. And it was a report as grotesque as any utterance of the mind of man that Miss Marshall's curiosities had ever heard in their long association with human life and its dramatic emotions.

He locked the big carved door of the gallery. He looked around to see that there were no windows at which anyone could listen. He warned them: 'I don't want you to worry over anything I tell you. It can't possibly make trouble for anyone, simply because it can't possibly be proved.' He drew from his pocket a modern octavo volume bound in green boards. 'This is my case,' he said, and handed the book to Miss Marshall.

She was sitting, very erect and diminutive, in a pontifical carved chair beside the heavy library table on which their coffee had been served. She was in an evening gown of silver brocade and crimson, and she looked at the volume with the aid of a lorgnette. It was called 'The Roosevelt Myth,' a book published by the author, James Clair Billings, in 1908 and dedicated to 'the enlightenment of all loyal subjects of Theodore, Rex.' On the flyleaf was written, in a girlish hand: 'In memory of my beloved Chester, Dec. 1909.'

Miss Marshall said: 'This is Martha's handwriting.'

Duff replied: 'Yes. It's her book.'

Westingate drew up a Savonarola chair beside her and studied the inscription silently.

'Your father,' Duff said to her, 'your father, Jeremiah Marshall, was a great Roosevelt fan, you remember. This book is an attack on Roosevelt. It's the book that he was reading, the night he died.'

Alicia Marshall turned to him with her sweetest smile. 'Yes? And who was Chester?'

'Chester was a cat.'

'A cat? Well! And that's your case?'

'That's the beginning of it.' He indicated the book with a nod to her to go on. She turned over the pages till she came to a photograph, a snapshot that had been pasted into the book like an extra illustration. It was a faded picture of a young man and a girl in a canoe. 'The girl,' Duff said, 'is your niece, Martha. The man is a young minister, named Keiser, who left Cold Brook some years ago.'

'I'll have to take your word for it,' Miss Marshall replied. 'It's too dim for me to make out.'

'She was in love with him, wasn't she?'

'I believe so.'

'And Senator Marshall interfered.'

'Yes. I'm afraid he did.'

Duff nodded at the book again. She turned the pages to another insertion, a folded letter pasted in like a map—a letter from Senator Marshall to his daughter Martha, telling her that the household expenses were too high and that he intended to employ a house-keeper who was to oversee all expenditures in the future. Miss Marshall read it slowly. 'Yes,' she said, with a sigh, 'it was very foolish. Very foolish.' The letter was dated July of the previous year.

'There's one more exhibit,' Duff said.

She went through the book without finding it. He turned to the inside of the back cover and showed them that something was concealed under the final page of paper that had been pasted down on the cover-lining. He drew out a typewritten note, unsigned, which read, 'I shall arrive, my dear, for our anniversary.' He handed it to Miss Marshall.

'That's my whole case,' he concluded.

She gave the book and its contents to Westingate, with the air of resigning a puzzle to an expert. 'That's your whole case?'

'Yes.'

'But,' she complained, cheerfully, 'I don't at all understand what it means.'

'Well,' he said, 'Let's take the first exhibit, the book itself. Jeremiah Marshall, your father—Martha's grandfather—died of heart disease in your brother's house on the fifteenth of December, 1909. Is that correct?'

'I believe it is.'

'The doctor had warned you all that any excitement would be likely to kill him. That was the reason why he left your house. He was always quarreling with you.'

'Always.'

'When he went to live with your brother, your niece Martha was about seventeen years old. Her mother had been dead about ten years. She was a solitary, eccentric child, with a stern father and an irritable grandfather. The only living thing in the world for which she seemed to have any affection was a pet cat, named Chester. Do you remember that the grandfather had a great aversion to cats?'

'Yes, I do.'

'Did you know that he had Martha's pet cat poisoned?'

'I didn't know. I vaguely remember something of the sort.'

'That's the meaning of the inscription in the front of the book. In order to annoy him, to persecute him for killing her cat, she took into his sickroom and left on his bedside table at night, this attack on his idol, Roosevelt. She may have heard him arguing with Senator Marshall about Roosevelt. Or she may have known that Senator Marshall refused to argue with him about it, for fear of exciting him too much. At any rate, she knew that if he read the book it might irritate him dangerously. And it did. He may have thought that his son had put it there to plague him. He was furious. He jumped out of bed, in a rage, and threw up the window, and flung the book out on the lawn. And the strain of that violent action killed him. They found him dead, next morning, on the floor, with the window open, and his reading lamp still burning at his bedside. One of the servants picked up the book, outside, later in the day, and no one knew where it had come from. When Martha finally got it back, she wrote in it: 'In memory of my beloved Chester, Dec. 1909.'

Alicia Marshall spread her hands in an eloquent gesture which said, 'Well, even so! Supposing it's true. What of it?'

Westingate asked suspiciously: 'Who told you all this?'

'The girl told my nurse.'

'You mean to say that she told the nurse, in so many words, that she had killed her grandfather?'

'No. She described a nightmare that's been persecuting her—a nightmare of a Cheshire cat that showed its teeth in a grin like Theodore Roosevelt's. My nurse asked her if she had ever had a cat, and she recalled a pet cat which her grandfather had poisoned. Subsequently, she asked the nurse to go to her father's house and get this book out of her room. The nurse pretended that she couldn't find it and sent it to me. Later we learned, from Senator Marshall's old cook, about how the grandfather had died in the night beside an open window. She's superstitious about the coincidence, in both cases, of an open window—and in one case a book, and in the other case a hatchet, flung outdoors.'

Miss Marshall drew back in her chair, in an attitude of obstinate defensiveness. 'Well, if Martha really did this to her grandfather,' she said, 'I, for one, can quite understand it. It was time that some one retaliated on him. He'd been making life impossible for everybody, for forty years, to *my* knowledge.'

'Quite so,' Duff agreed. 'And you and I can understand how an angry child could give him that book, with no clear idea of killing him, though with a sort of furious hope that it might pay him back for killing her cat. Quite so. But do we realize what it would mean to her to succeed, and accept her success definitely, and inscribe a book with her triumph, as a Westerner cuts a notch in his gun?'

Alicia Marshall, for the first time, frowned at him. The lawyer rose and put the book on the table and pushed it away from him nervously, as if he were legally refusing any responsibility for its possession.

Duff went on: 'Nothing's as satisfying to one's ego as the death of an enemy. Any soldier can tell you what a godlike feeling of power it gives you. You can't in a moment, and with a wave of the hand, create a human being, but you can destroy one, that way. And the effect on you is almost as great as an act of creation. This girl had already a very sturdy sense of her own importance. She was solitary and eccentric, but she was not timid and depressed. She was an only child. I judge that her mother had been devoted to her and proud of her. I understand that her father thought her spoiled and obstinate. Well, here was this old man, the grandfather, who had been persecuting her with his bad temper. And by a sort of magic act, she had simply wiped him out of the world. That is the sort of youthful experience that makes a unique personality. From this time on, we have to reckon with a human being who has had an experience that may make her superhuman.'

'That,' Miss Marshall said flatly, 'is all nonsense. Martha has never been anything but a devout and simple girl—'

'She became devout,' Duff cut in. 'She became religious, after the death of her grandfather.'

'She became religious, as I did, when she should have been falling in love. If you knew anything about women, you'd know that half of us are like that.'

'Naturally.' Duff leaned forward on the arms of his chair, with a slowly genial smile. 'But—did you ever notice how often religious fanatics are killers? It's my experience that whenever there's a mysterious murder in a decent, respectable family, it's a safe bet that the thing was done by the most religious member of the household. And why? A religious person hates himself. He knows that he's a hateful animal in the sight of heaven, full of low animal impulses that are sinful and nasty. He hates those things in himself, and so he hates himself. An emotion of that sort—an emotion of love or hatred—is almost like a charge of electricity in a person. It either gets drained off naturally in expressions of love or hatred for somebody else, or it stores up as if it were electricity in a storage battery until it's a tremendous charge of suppressed emotion. A religious person can't drain off his hatred freely on people around him because hatred of others is a sin. So he goes on storing up hatred until he's charged full with it. And then—something happens. The hated person blunders into circumstances that make the electric connection, and there's a flash that's murderous, and the thing's done.'

Westingate asked hoarsely: 'Are you trying to prove that this girl killed her father—and the housekeeper—with a hatchet?'

'I'm not trying to prove anything,' Duff smiled. 'I'm trying to tell you privately how this case looks to me.'

'I never heard anything more absurd in my life,' Miss Marshall said.

'Good!' He seemed actually relieved. 'I was afraid I might worry you. I appreciate how absurd it looks, and how safe the girl is from any charge of the kind, but I wasn't sure you'd feel that way about it. Now that you understand how ridiculous the whole thing sounds, I can go ahead with it, more frankly.'

Neither of them replied. The lawyer, having seated himself with the table between them, was staring at Duff with eyes that saw only too clearly the possible implications of his charge. Alicia Marshall, sitting as if her back were against a wall, watched him silently, intent and frowning.

'Let me go ahead,' Duff proposed, 'and tell you the whole story as I see it, without any reservations, or apologies, or anything like that. This girl, Martha, after the grandfather's death was at first defiant, as her inscription in that book shows. Then she began to feel guilty and remorseful, and she fell ill. When she recovered, she became religious, and that annoyed her father. You've spoken of him as a religious man. He wasn't religious. He attended church. And for many years he helped to take up the collection, I know. But that was merely part of his routine of life as a respectable citizen, a leader in the community who had to set a good example to the ungodly and keep himself high in the estimation of his clients and his constituents. He had no patience with his daughter's excess of piety. And when she fell in love with the minister—this young Keiser—he objected to the match. He refused to settle any money on her—so as to keep her from marrying. He used his influence to get Keiser transferred. He told her that Keiser only wanted to marry her for her money. And when Keiser went away, and stopped writing to her, she blamed her father.

'As far as my nurse has been able to find out, this was her only love affair. She was taken ill again after Keiser left, and when she recovered she was more religious than ever, but now her religion began to take a bitter turn. She read mostly the Old Testament, and that's bad reading for anyone who's full of hate; there's too much revenge and murder in it. She became an active worker in all the leagues and associations for the enforcement of Sunday observance laws and prohibition and such—or, at least, she contributed to them every cent she could get from her father or save out of the money he gave her for household expenses. I find that she made herself conspicuous by her opposition to the war and by her refusal to help the Red Cross or the Liberty Loans or anything of the sort. That's significant.'

'Of what?' Westingate asked.

'War,' Duff replied, 'is murder.'

Miss Marshall dropped her eyes, and she did not raise them again. She continued looking at the floor, without a word, her head up obstinately, grasping the arms of her chair.

'Her father quarreled with her about her attitude to the war. He quarreled with her about scrimping on the household expenses so as to give money to the societies in which she was so active. He stopped her allowance, and allowed her to purchase only on charge accounts, paying the monthly bills by check, himself. That was a serious matter for her. She was a proud young woman, silent, repellent in her manner, with none of the magnetism that makes friends. Her ability to contribute money to the causes in which she was interested—that brought people to her, made her important, won her praise. Without that power, she was cut off from everybody. She knew it. She shut herself up in the house. She gave up all her committees, her meetings, her outside work. Then in desperation, she attempted to jockey her accounts, and he found it out. And he wrote her that letter in which he announced that he was putting in a housekeeper who was to have charge of all her expenditures. Did you know that she had to have even her personal accounts—for clothes and books—endorsed by Mrs Starrett?'

Miss Marshall did not answer. She did not look up.

'This long struggle between her and her father was carried on, you understand, in silence. She never spoke to anyone about it. She never remonstrated with him. She set her will against his, obstinately, and never bent to him once. He had deprived her of her lover, of her friends, of her station in life, of everything that a human being— Well, there you are. She began to have these long periods of illness, headaches, attacks of nervous exhaustion. She kept herself shut up in her room, with her thoughts. She expressed them, as far as I've been able to learn, to no one. The servants report of her exactly what you report, Miss Marshall—that she was a saint.'

Miss Marshall raised her hand from the chair arm and dropped it despairingly. 'I had no idea,' she said, 'and my brother could have had no idea. I merely thought her—a peculiar girl. She never told me—'

'Quite so. She never told anyone. And I have no means of knowing what her relations with Mrs Starrett were, or whether she suspected that there was anything going on between Mrs Starrett and her father. I believe she did. I believe that when she got hold of that letter to Mrs Starrett, about their "anniversary," it only confirmed a suspicion that needed no confirmation.'

'You mean,' Westingate asked, 'that this note is from Senator Marshall to Mrs Starrett?'

'Yes. Senator Marshall wrote it on a typewriter himself and left it unsigned, in case it went astray. He addressed the envelope himself on a typewriter, but he made a mistake, absent-mindedly, in the address. He addressed it to "Mrs Agnes Starrett, Brook Farm, New York City." He didn't notice the mistake until he was about to drop the envelope in a mail box, I presume. It was evidently then too late to type another envelope. He struck out the "New York City" with lead pencil and wrote in "Cold Brook, N.J." as you see.' Duff had taken an envelope from his pocket and passed it to Westingate. 'That's Senator Marshall's handwriting. The note was still in its envelope when I found it concealed in the back cover of the book.'

The lawyer offered the envelope to Miss Marshall. She shook her head without looking at it, her eyes averted.

Duff rose from his chair and began to pace slowly up and down the room, as if he were dictating a report. 'The postmark on that envelope shows that it probably arrived at Senator Marshall's home some thirty-six hours before the murder. I judge that the girl intercepted it. She recognized her father's writing in lead pencil and read the note. The fact that it was typewritten and unsigned was sufficient indication that it was a guilty note of assignation. She hid it in the back of the book in which she kept her case against her father, and then she went to bed, ostensibly ill with the grippe, and remained there brooding, in a state of mind that you can imagine. Her father returned on the following forenoon, and found her, as usual, ill in her room. She had been pleading illness, whenever he was in the house, to avoid seeing him. So far, there was nothing unusual.

'But now the circumstance occurred that brought the deadly flash. She complained of being cold. She was probably shaking with a chill of hate and despair. And Pittling was ordered to build a fire in her bedroom fireplace. He brought up a basket of kindling, and in it, I believe, he brought the hatchet that he'd used to split the kindling. It's my theory that he put the hatchet aside as he took the kindling out of the basket and he forgot the hatchet when he returned with the basket to the basement.

'Have you seen that hatchet? It's a real woodsman's broad "razor-blade" of forged steel. I believe that the girl saw it, standing against the fender, after her fire was lit, when she turned in her bed to stare at the blaze. And I believe that when the housemaid came back into her room, she had concealed the hatchet between the mattresses of the bed on which she was pretending to be sleeping in a weak exhaustion.'

Westingate asked, in a shaken whisper, 'Did Pittling tell you—'

'No,' Duff said. 'Pittling won't admit that the hatchet was ever in the girl's room. All he'll admit is the business about the pump. It wakened him, in the middle of the night, and he heard it working slowly, with long intervals between the strokes, as if some one were drawing water in a very small flow. But that flow continued for a long time—for so long that he thought some one must have risen to get a drink and left a faucet running. Then it stopped. The faucet had been turned off. I believe that this water was used by the murderer to wash in. And I'm sure that Pittling suspects it. In the morning when the hatchet was found, outside the open window, he was sure that some one in the house had committed the murder, and this secret suspicion gave him the guilty manner that led the police to arrest him. I don't believe that he suspects the daughter. He doesn't know what to think, so he keeps his mouth shut, and pretends that he doesn't remember whether or not he carried the hatchet upstairs. Or perhaps he doesn't really remember now. He's in a bad state mentally.

'I have no evidence of how the murders actually occurred. I believe that the girl intended to lie in wait for Mrs Starrett and her father and confront them together and threaten them with exposure and disgrace, unless her father gave in to her and discharged Mrs Starrett and ceased to tyrannize over her. She probably seized on the hatchet as a weapon of defense, or perhaps she intended to threaten them with it. While she was waiting to waylay them, she heard Mrs Starrett tiptoeing past her door, and she darted out, under an ungovernable impulse of rage and hatred, and struck the woman from behind. I don't believe she knew the blow was fatal, but her murderous frenzy was now beyond her control. She rushed in to her father—'

Miss Marshall suddenly reached forward to the table and caught up the Roosevelt book. 'It's impossible,' she said, harshly. 'Impossible! I don't believe a word of it. I'll never believe it. Never.'

'Quite so,' Duff said. 'However, you'd better burn that book.'

'Burn it,' she defied him. 'You may be sure I'll burn it.'

He turned to Westingate. 'There's nothing here for the prosecution to base a case on—even if they knew about it. And they'll never find out anything from her. When my nurse first asked her about her cat, she seemed really to have forgotten about it. I believe she'll forget all this in the same way. She'll probably behave about it as if she had a double personality. She'll become, perhaps, even more fanatically religious than she's been in the past. She'll be more proud and inaccessible than ever, with this secret buried in the back of her mind, but she'll bury it, and she'll keep her thoughts away from its grave. She's a very tough-minded young woman, with a Napoleonic ego, and she may break down physically, and become an invalid, but I don't believe she'll ever break down mentally, and though she may be peculiar, I don't believe she'll go insane.'

Westingate asked: 'Do your detectives—? Does your nurse—?'

'No,' Duff assured him. 'The nurse may suspect, but she knows nothing.'

Miss Marshall rose, to end the interview. 'I don't believe a word of it.'

'Good,' Duff congratulated her. 'Then nobody else will. As a matter of fact, so many people kill their parents, in one way or another, that there's a natural resistance to believing a girl like this guilty. If wishes could have killed *your* father, for instance, Miss Marshall—'

'Stop!' She confronted him, in a sort of frightened rage, her head held high but trembling. 'You're a fiend!'

Duff bowed, ponderously. 'I'm a detective.'

She turned and unlocked the door and flung it open. 'You're a monster. I'll not hear another word against my niece.'

'No,' Duff agreed. 'You probably never will.'

And as far as anyone knows she never did. She heard nothing, certainly, from Duff, who closed the case then and there—nor from his nurse who left her charge next morning and never mentioned her again—nor from Pittling who was released from custody a few weeks later and went back to his home in Ohio, discreetly silent. By that time, Miss Marshall had taken her invalid niece to the south of France, and though she herself returned to Cold Brook at various times to attend to selling Senator Marshall's property and storing his goods, her niece has never come back. It is understood that she has joined some sort of lay sisterhood and devoted her fortune to works of piety. And the Marshall murder remains still a mystery.

RAYMOND CHANDLER (1885–1959)

No Crime in the Mountains

THE letter came just before noon, special delivery, a dime-store envelope with the return address F. S. Lacey, Puma Point, California. Inside was a check for a hundred dollars, made out to cash and signed Frederick S. Lacey, and a sheet of plain white bond paper typed with a number of strikeovers. It said:

MR JOHN EVANS,
DEAR SIR:
    I have your name from Len Esterwald. My business is urgent and extremely confidential. I inclose a retainer. Please come to Puma Point Thursday afternoon or evening, if at all possible, register at the Indian Head Hotel, and call me at 2306.

Yours,   FRED LACEY.

There hadn't been any business in a week, but this made it a nice day. The bank on which the check was drawn was about six blocks away. I went over and cashed it, ate lunch, and got the car out and started off.

It was hot in the valley, hotter still in San Bernardino, and it was still hot at five thousand feet, fifteen miles up the high-gear road to Puma Lake. I had done forty of the fifty miles of curving, twisting highway before it started to cool off, but it didn't get really cool until I reached the dam and started along the south shore of the lake past the piled-up granite boulders and the sprawled camps in the flats beyond. It was early evening when I reached Puma Point and I was as empty as a gutted fish.

The Indian Head Hotel was a brown building on a corner, opposite a dance hall. I registered, carried my suitcase upstairs and dropped it in a bleak, hard-looking room with an oval rug on the floor, a double bed in the corner, and nothing on the bare pine wall but a hardware-store calendar all curled up from the dry mountain summer. I washed my face and hands and went downstairs to eat.

The dining-drinking parlor that adjoined the lobby was full to overflowing with males in sport clothes and liquor breaths and females in slacks and shorts with blood-red fingernails and dirty knuckles. A fellow with eyebrows like John L. Lewis was prowling around with a cigar screwed into his face. A lean, pale-eyed cashier in shirt sleeves was fighting to get the race results from Hollywood Park on a small radio that was as full of static as the mashed potato was full of water. In the deep, black corner of the room a hillbilly symphony of five defeatists in white coats and purple shirts was trying to make itself heard above the brawl at the bar.

I gobbled what they called the regular dinner, drank a brandy to sit on it, and went out onto the main stem. It was still broad daylight, but the neon lights were turned on and the evening was full of the noise of auto horns, shrill voices, the rattle of bowls, the snap of .22s at the shooting gallery, juke-box music, and behind all this the hoarse, hard mutter of speedboats on the lake. At a corner opposite the post office a blue-and-white arrow said *telephone*. I went down a dusty side road that suddenly became quiet and cool and piny. A tame doe deer with a leather collar on its neck wandered across the road in front of me. The phone office was a log cabin, and there was a booth in the corner with a coin-in-the-slot telephone. I shut myself inside and dropped my nickel and dialed 2306. A woman's voice answered.

I said: 'Is Mr Fred Lacey there?'

'Who is calling, please?'

'Evans is the name.'

'Mr Lacey is not here right now, Mr Evans. Is he expecting you?'

That gave her two questions to my one. I didn't like it. I said: 'Are you Mrs Lacey?'

'Yes. I am Mrs Lacey.' I thought her voice was taut and over-strung, but some voices are like that all the time.

'It's a business matter,' I said. 'When will he be back?'

'I don't know exactly. Sometime this evening, I suppose. What did you——'

'Where is your cabin, Mrs Lacey?'

'It's . . . it's on Ball Sage Point, about two miles west of the village. Are you calling from the village? Did you——'

'I'll call back in an hour, Mrs Lacey,' I said, and hung up. I stepped out of the booth. In the other corner of the room a dark girl in slacks was writing in some kind of account book at a little desk. She looked up and smiled and said: 'How do you like the mountains?'

I said: 'Fine.'

'It's very quiet up here,' she said. 'Very restful.'

'Yeah. Do you know anybody named Fred Lacey?'

'Lacey? Oh, yes, they just had a phone put in. They bought the Baldwin cabin. It was vacant for two years, and they just bought it. It's out at the end of Ball Sage Point, a big cabin on high ground, looking out over the lake. It has a marvelous view. Do you know Mr Lacey?'

'No,' I said, and went out of there.

The tame doe was in the gap of the fence at the end of the walk. I tried to push her out of the way. She wouldn't move, so I stepped over the fence and walked back to the Indian Head and got into my car.

There was a gas station at the east end of the village. I pulled up for some gas and asked the leathery man who poured it where Ball Sage Point was.

'Well,' he said. 'That's easy. That ain't hard at all. You won't have no trouble finding Ball Sage Point. You go down here about a mile and a half past the Catholic church and Kincaid's Camp, and at the bakery you turn right and then you keep on the road to Willerton Boys' Camp, and it's the first road to the left after you pass on by. It's a dirt road, kind of rough. They don't sweep the snow off in winter, but it ain't winter now. You know somebody out there?'

'No.' I gave him money. He went for the change and came back.

'It's quiet out there,' he said. 'Restful. What was the name?'

'Murphy,' I said.

'Glad to know you, Mr Murphy,' he said, and reached for my hand. 'Drop in any time. Glad to have the pleasure of serving you. Now, for Ball Sage Point you just keep straight on down this road———'

'Yeah,' I said, and left his mouth flapping.

I figured I knew how to find Ball Sage Point now, so I turned around and drove the other way. It was just possible Fred Lacey would not want me to go to his cabin.

Half a block beyond the hotel the paved road turned down toward a boat landing, then east again along the shore of the lake. The water was low. Cattle were grazing in the sour-looking grass that had been under water in the spring. A few patient visitors were fishing for bass or bluegill from boats with outboard motors. About a mile or so beyond the meadows a dirt road wound out toward a long point covered with junipers. Close inshore there was a lighted dance pavilion. The music was going already, although it still looked like late afternoon at that altitude. The band sounded as if it was in my pocket. I could hear a girl with a throaty voice singing 'The Woodpecker's Song.' I drove on past and the music faded and the road got rough and stony. A cabin on the shore slid past me, and there was nothing beyond it but pines and junipers and the shine of the water. I stopped the car out near the tip of the point and walked over to a huge tree fallen with its roots twelve feet in the air. I sat down against it on the bone-dry ground and lit a pipe. It was peaceful and quiet and far from everything. On the far side of the lake a couple of speedboats played tag, but on my side there was nothing but silent water, very slowly getting dark in the mountain dusk. I wondered who the hell Fred Lacey was and what he wanted and why he didn't stay home or leave a message if his business was so urgent. I didn't wonder about it very long. The evening was too peaceful. I smoked and looked at the lake and the sky, and at a robin waiting on the bare spike at the top of a tall pine for it to get dark enough so he could sing his good-night song.

At the end of half an hour I got up and dug a hole in the soft ground with my heel and knocked my pipe out and stamped down the dirt over the ashes. For no reason at all, I walked a few steps toward the lake, and that brought me to the end of the tree. So I saw the foot.

It was in a white duck shoe, about size nine. I walked around the roots of the tree.

There was another foot in another white duck shoe. There were pin-striped white pants with legs in them, and there was a torso in a pale-green sport shirt of the kind that hangs outside and has pockets like a sweater. It had a buttonless V neck and chest hair showed through the V. The man was middle-aged, half bald, had a good coat of tan and a line mustache shaved up from the lip. His lips were thick, and his mouth, a little open as they usually are, showed big strong teeth. He had the kind of face that goes with plenty of food and not too much worry. His eyes were looking at the sky. I couldn't seem to meet them.

The left side of the green sport shirt was sodden with blood in a patch as big as a dinner plate. In the middle of the patch there might have been a scorched hole. I couldn't be sure. The light was getting a little tricky.

I bent down and felt matches and cigarettes in the pockets of the shirt, a couple of rough lumps like keys and silver in his pants pockets at the sides. I rolled him a little to get at his hip. He was still limp and only a little cooled off. A wallet of rough leather made a tight fit in his right hip pocket. I dragged it out, bracing my knee against his back.

There was twelve dollars in the wallet and some cards, but what interested me was the name on his photostat driver's license. I lit a match to make sure I read it right in the fading daylight.

The name on the license was Frederick Shield Lacey.

I put the wallet back and stood up and made a full circle, staring hard. Nobody was in sight, on land or on the water. In that light, nobody could have seen what I was doing unless he was close.

I walked a few steps and looked down to see if I was making tracks. No. The ground was half pine needles of many years past, and the other half pulverized rotten wood.

The gun was about four feet away, almost under the fallen tree. I didn't touch it. I bent down and looked at it. It was a .22 automatic, a Colt with a bone grip. It was half buried in a small pile of the powdery, brown, rotted wood. There were large black ants on the pile, and one of them was crawling along the barrel of the gun.

I straightened up and took another quick look around. A boat idled off shore out of sight around the point. I could hear an uneven stutter from the throttled-down motor, but I couldn't see it. I started back toward the car. I was almost up to it. A small figure rose silently behind a heavy manzanita bush. The light winked on glasses and on something else, lower down in a hand.

A voice said hissingly: 'Placing the hands up, please.'

It was a nice spot for a very fast draw. I didn't think mine would be fast enough. I placed the hands up.

The small figure came around the manzanita bush. The shining thing below the glasses was a gun. The gun was large enough. It came toward me.

A gold tooth winked out of a small mouth below a black mustache.

'Turning around, please,' the nice little voice said soothingly. 'You seeing man lie on ground?'

'Look,' I said, 'I'm a stranger here. I——'

'Turning around very soon,' the man said coldly.

I turned around.

The end of the gun made a nest against my spine. A light, deft hand prodded me here and there, rested on the gun under my arm. The voice cooed. The hand went to my hip. The pressure of my wallet went away. A very neat pickpocket. I could hardly feel him touch me.

'I look at wallet now. You very still,' the voice said. The gun went away.

A good man had a chance now. He would fall quickly to the ground, do a back flip from a kneeling position, and come up with his gun blazing in his hand. It would happen very fast. The good man would take the little man with glasses the way a dowager takes her teeth out, in one smooth motion. I somehow didn't think I was that good.

The wallet went back on my hip, the gun barrel back into my back.

'So,' the voice said softly. 'You coming here you making mistake.'

'Brother, you said it,' I told him.

'Not matter,' the voice said. 'Go away now, go home. Five hundred dollars. Nothing being said five hundred dollars arriving one week from today.'

'Fine,' I said. 'You having my address?'

'Very funny,' the voice cooed. 'Ha, ha.'

Something hit the back of my right knee, and the leg folded suddenly the way it will when hit at that point. My head began to ache from where it was going to get a crack from the gun, but he fooled me. It was the old rabbit punch, and it was a honey of its type. Done with the heel of a very hard little hand. My head came off and went halfway across the lake and did a boomerang turn and came back and slammed on top of my spine with a sickening jar. Somehow on the way it got a mouthful of pine needles.

There was an interval of midnight in a small room with the windows shut and no air. My chest labored against the ground. They put a ton of coal on my back. One of the hard lumps pressed into the middle of my back. I made some noises, but they must have been unimportant. Nobody bothered about them. I heard the sound of a boat motor get louder, and a soft thud of feet walking on the pine needles, making a dry, slithering sound. Then a couple of heavy grunts and steps going away. Then steps coming back and a burry voice, with a sort of accent.

'What did you get there, Charlie?'

'Oh, nothing,' Charlie said cooingly. 'Smoking pipe, not doing anything. Summer visitor, ha, ha.'

'Did he see the stiff?'

'Not seeing,' Charlie said. I wondered why.

'O.K., let's go.'

'Ah, too bad,' Charlie said. 'Too bad.' The weight got off my back and the lumps of hard coal went away from my spine. 'Too bad,' Charlie said again. 'But must do.'

He didn't fool this time. He hit me with the gun. Come around and I'll let you feel the lump under my scalp. I've got several of them.

Time passed and I was up on my knees, whining. I put a foot on the ground and hoisted myself on it and wiped my face off with the back of my hand and put the other foot on the ground and climbed out of the hole it felt like I was in.

The shine of water, dark now from the sun but silvered by the moon, was directly in front of me. To the right was the big fallen tree. That brought it back. I moved cautiously toward it, rubbing my head with careful fingertips. It was swollen and soft, but not bleeding. I stopped and looked back for my hat, and then remembered I had left it in the car.

I went round the tree. The moon was bright as it can only be in the mountains or on the desert. You could almost have read the paper by its light. It was very easy to see that there was no body on the ground now and no gun lying against the tree with ants crawling on it. The ground had a sort of smoothed-out, raked look.

I stood there and listened, and all I heard was the blood pounding in my head, and all I felt was my head aching. Then my hand jumped for the gun and the gun was there. And the hand jumped again for my wallet and the wallet was there. I hauled it out and looked at my money. That seemed to be there, too.

I turned around and plowed back to the car. I wanted to go back to the hotel and get a couple of drinks and lie down. I wanted to meet Charlie after a while, but not right away. First I wanted to lie down for a while. I was a growing boy and I needed rest.

I got into the car and started it and tooled it around on the soft ground and back onto the dirt road and back along that to the highway. I didn't meet any cars. The music was still going well in the dancing pavilion off to the side, and the throaty-voiced singer was giving out 'I'll Never Smile Again.'

When I reached the highway I put the lights on and drove back to the village. The local law hung out in a one-room pine-board shack halfway up the block from the boat landing, across the street from the firehouse. There was a naked light burning inside, behind a glass-paneled door.

I stopped the car on the other side of the street and sat there for a minute looking into the shack. There was a man inside, sitting bare-headed in a swivel chair at an old roll-top desk. I opened the car door and moved to get out, then stopped and shut the door again and started the motor and drove on.

I had a hundred dollars to earn, after all.

I drove two miles past the village and came to the bakery and turned on a newly oiled road toward the lake. I passed a couple of camps and then saw the brownish tents of the boys' camp with lights strung between them and a clatter coming from a big tent where they were washing dishes. A little beyond that the road curved around an inlet and a dirt road branched off. It was deeply rutted and full of stones half embedded in the dirt, and the trees barely gave it room to pass. I went by a couple of lighted cabins, old ones built of pine with the bark left on. Then the road climbed and the place got emptier, and after a while a big cabin hung over the edge of the bluff looking down on the lake at its feet. The cabin had two chimneys and a rustic fence, and a double garage outside the fence. There was a long porch on the lake side, and steps going down to the water. Light came from the windows. My head-lamps tilted up enough to catch the name Baldwin painted on a wooden board nailed to a tree. This was the cabin, all right.

The garage was open and a sedan was parked in it. I stopped a little beyond and went far enough into the garage to feel the exhaust pipe of the car. It was cold. I went through a rustic gate up a path outlined in stones to the porch. The door opened as I got there. A tall woman stood there, framed against the light. A little silky dog rushed out past her, tumbled down the steps and hit me in the stomach with two front paws, then dropped to the ground and ran in circles, making noises of approval.

'Down, Shiny!' the woman called. 'Down! Isn't she a funny little dog? Funny itty doggie. She's half coyote.'

The dog ran back into the house. I said: 'Are you Mrs Lacey? I'm Evans. I called you up about an hour ago.'

'Yes, I'm Mrs Lacey,' she said. 'My husband hasn't come in yet. I—well, come in, won't you?' Her voice had a remote sound, like a voice in the mist.

She closed the door behind me after I went in and stood there looking at me, then shrugged a little and sat down in a wicker chair. I sat down in another just like it. The dog appeared from nowhere, jumped in my lap, swiped a neat tongue across the end of my nose and jumped down again. It was a small grayish dog with a sharp nose and a long, feathery tail.

It was a long room with a lot of windows and not very fresh curtains at them. There was a big fireplace, Indian rugs, two daven-ports with faded cretonne slips over them, more wicker furniture, not too comfortable. There were some antlers on the wall, one pair with six points.

'Fred isn't home yet,' Mrs Lacey said again. 'I don't know what's keeping him.'

I nodded. She had a pale face, rather taut, dark hair that was a little wild. She was wearing a double-breasted scarlet coat with brass buttons, gray flannel slacks, pigskin clog sandals, and no stockings. There was a necklace of cloudy amber around her throat and a bandeau of old-rose material in her hair. She was in her middle thir-ties, so it was too late for her to learn how to dress herself.

'You wanted to see my husband on business?'

'Yes. He wrote me to come up and stay at the Indian Head and phone him.'

'Oh—at the Indian Head,' she said, as if that meant something. She crossed her legs, didn't like them that way, and uncrossed them again. She leaned forward and cupped a long chin in her hand. 'What kind of business are you in, Mr Evans?'

'I'm a private detective.'

'It's . . . it's about the money?' she asked quickly.

I nodded. That seemed safe. It was usually about money. It was about a hundred dollars that I had in my pocket, anyhow.

'Of course,' she said. 'Naturally. Would you care for a drink?'

'Very much.'

She went over to a little wooden bar and came back with two glasses. We drank. We looked at each other over the rims of our glasses.

'The Indian Head,' she said. 'We stayed there two nights when we came up. While the cabin was being cleaned up. It had been empty for two years before we bought it. They get so dirty.'

'I guess so,' I said.

'You say my husband wrote to you?' She was looking down into her glass now. 'I suppose he told you the story.'

I offered her a cigarette. She started to reach, then shook her head and put her hand on her kneecap and twisted it. She gave me the careful up-from-under look.

'He was a little vague,' I said. 'In spots.'

She looked at me steadily and I looked at her steadily. I breathed gently into my glass until it misted.

'Well, I don't think we need be mysterious about it,' she said. 'Although as a matter of fact I know more about it than Fred thinks I do. He doesn't know, for example, that I saw that letter.'

'The letter he sent me?'

'No. The letter he got from Los Angeles with the report on the ten-dollar bill.'

'How did you get to see it?' I asked.

She laughed without much amusement. 'Fred's too secretive. It's a mistake to be too secretive with a woman. I sneaked a look at it while he was in the bathroom. I got it out of his pocket.'

I nodded and drank some more of my drink. I said: 'Uh-huh.' That didn't commit me very far, which was a good idea as long as I didn't know what we were talking about. 'But how did you know it was in his pocket?' I asked.

'He'd just got it at the post office. I was with him.' She laughed, with a little more amusement this time. 'I saw that there was a bill in it and that it came from Los Angeles. I knew he had sent one of the bills to a friend there who is an expert on such things. So of course I knew this letter was a report. It was.'

'Seems like Fred doesn't cover up very well,' I said. 'What did the letter say?'

She flushed slightly. 'I don't know that I should tell you. I don't really know that you are a detective or that your name is Evans.'

'Well, that's something that can be settled without violence,' I said. I got up and showed her enough to prove it. When I sat down again the little dog came over and sniffed at the cuffs on my trousers. I bent down to pat her head and got a handful of spit.

'It said that the bill was beautiful work. The paper, in particular, was just about perfect. But under a comparison microscope there were very small differences of registration. What does that mean?'

'It means that the bill he sent hadn't been made from a government plate. Anything else wrong?'

'Yes. Under black light—whatever that is—there appeared to be slight differences in the composition of the inks. But the letter added that to the naked eye the counterfeit was practically perfect. It would fool any bank teller.'

I nodded. This was something I hadn't expected. 'Who wrote the letter, Mrs Lacey?'

'He signed himself Bill. It was on a plain sheet of paper. I don't know who wrote it. Oh, there was something else. Bill said that Fred ought to turn it in to the Federal people right away, because the money was good enough to make a lot of trouble if much of it got into circulation. But, of course, Fred wouldn't want to do that if he could help it. That would be why he sent for you.'

'Well, no, of course not,' I said. This was a shot in the dark, but it wasn't likely to hit anything. Not with the amount of dark I had to shoot into.

She nodded, as if I had said something.

'What is Fred doing now, mostly?' I asked.

'Bridge and poker, like he's done for years. He plays bridge almost every afternoon at the athletic club and poker at night a good deal. You can see that he couldn't afford to be connected with counterfeit money, even in the most innocent way. There would always be someone who wouldn't believe it *was* innocent. He plays the races, too, but that's just fun. That's how he got the five hundred dollars he put in my shoe for a present for me. At the Indian Head.'

I wanted to go out in the yard and do a little yelling and breast beating, just to let off steam. But all I could do was sit there and look wise and guzzle my drink. I guzzled it empty and made a lonely noise with the ice cubes and she went and got me another one. I took a slug of that and breathed deeply and said:

'If the bill was so good, how did he know it was bad, if you get what I mean?'

Her eyes widened a little. 'Oh—I see. He didn't, of course. Not that one. But there were fifty of them, all ten-dollar bills, all new. And the money hadn't been that way when he put it in the shoe.'

I wondered if tearing my hair would do me any good. I didn't think—my head was too sore. Charlie. Good old Charlie! O.K., Charlie, after a while I'll be around with my gang.

'Look,' I said. 'Look, Mrs Lacey. He didn't tell me about the shoe. Does he always keep his money in a shoe, or was this something special on account of he won it at the races and horses wear shoes?'

'I told you it was a surprise present for me. When I put the shoe on I would find it, of course.'

'Oh.' I gnawed about half an inch off my upper lip. 'But you didn't find it?'

'How could I when I sent the maid to take the shoes to the shoemaker in the village to have lifts put on them? I didn't look inside. I didn't know Fred had put anything in the shoe.'

A little light was coming. It was very far off and coming very slowly. It was a very little light, about half a firefly's worth.

I said: 'And Fred didn't know that. And this maid took the shoes to the shoemaker. What then?'

'Well, Gertrude—that's the maid's name—said she hadn't noticed the money, either. So when Fred found out about it and had asked her, he went over to the shoemaker's place, and he hadn't worked on the shoes and the roll of money was still stuffed down into the toe of the shoe. So Fred laughed and took the money out and put it in his pocket and gave the shoemaker five dollars because he was lucky.'

I finished my second drink and leaned back. 'I get it now. Then Fred took the roll out and looked it over and saw it wasn't the same money. It was all new ten-dollar bills, and before it had probably been various sizes of bills and not new or not all new.'

She looked surprised that I had to reason it out. I wondered how long a letter she thought Fred had written me. I said: 'Then Fred would have to assume that there was some reason for changing the money. He thought of one and sent a bill to a friend of his to be tested. And the report came back that it was very good counterfeit, but still counterfeit. Who did he ask about it at the hotel?'

'Nobody except Gertrude, I guess. He didn't want to start anything. I guess he just sent for you.'

I snubbed my cigarette out and looked out of the open front windows at the moonlit lake. A speedboat with a hard white headlight slid muttering along in the water, far off over the water, and disappeared behind a wooded point.

I looked back at Mrs Lacey. She was still sitting with her chin propped in a thin hand. Her eyes seemed far away.

'I wish Fred would come home,' she said.

'Where is he?'

'I don't know. He went out with a man named Frank Luders, who is staying at the Woodland Club, down at the far end of the lake. Fred said he owned an interest in it. But I called Mr Luders up a while ago and he said Fred had just ridden uptown with him and got off at the post office. I've been expecting Fred to phone and ask me to pick him up somewhere. He left hours ago.'

'They probably have some card games down at the Woodland Club. Maybe he went there.'

She nodded. 'He usually calls me, though.'

I stared at the floor for a while and tried not to feel like a heel. Then I stood up. 'I guess I'll go on back to the hotel. I'll be there if you want to phone me. I think I've met Mr Lacey somewhere. Isn't he a thickset man about forty-five, going a little bald, with a small mustache?'

She went to the door with me. 'Yes,' she said. 'That's Fred, all right.'

She had shut the dog in the house and was standing outside herself as I turned the car and drove away. God, she looked lonely.

I was lying on my back on the bed, wobbling a cigarette around and trying to make up my mind just why I had to play cute with this affair, when the knock came at the door. I called out. A girl in a working uniform came in with some towels. She had dark, reddish hair and a pert, nicely made-up face and long legs. She excused herself and hung some towels on the rack and started back to the door and gave me a sidelong look with a good deal of fluttering eyelash in it.

I said, 'Hello, Gertrude,' just for the hell of it.

She stopped, and the dark-red head came around and the mouth was ready to smile.

'How'd you know my name?'

'I didn't. But one of the maids is Gertrude. I wanted to talk to her.'

She leaned against the door frame, towels over her arm. Her eyes were lazy. 'Yeah?'

'Live up here, or just up here for the summer?' I asked.

Her lip curled. 'I should say I don't live up here. With these mountain screwballs? I should say not.'

'You doing all right?'

She nodded. 'And I don't need any company, mister.' She sounded as if she could be talked out of that.

I looked at her for a minute and said: 'Tell me about that money somebody hid in a shoe.'

'Who are you?' she asked coolly.

'The name is Evans. I'm a Los Angeles detective.' I grinned at her, very wise.

Her face stiffened a little. The hand holding the towels clutched and her nails made a scratching sound on the cloth. She moved back from the door and sat down in a straight chair against the wall. Trouble dwelt in her eyes.

'A dick,' she breathed. 'What goes on?'

'Don't you know?'

'All I heard was Mrs Lacey left some money in a shoe she wanted a lift put on the heel, and I took it over to the shoemaker and he didn't steal the money. And I didn't, either. She got the money back, didn't she?'

'Don't like cops, do you? Seems to me I know your face,' I said.

The face hardened. 'Look, copper, I got a job and I work at it. I don't need any help from any copper. I don't owe anybody a nickel.'

'Sure,' I said. 'When you took those shoes from the room did you go right over to the shoemaker with them?'

She nodded shortly.

'Didn't stop on the way at all?'

'Why would I?'

'I wasn't around then. I wouldn't know.'

'Well, I didn't. Except to tell Weber I was going out for a guest.'

'Who's Mr Weber?'

'He's the assistant manager. He's down in the dining room a lot.'

'Tall, pale guy that writes down all the race results?'

She nodded. 'That would be him.'

'I see,' I said. I struck a match and lit my cigarette. I stared at her through smoke. 'Thanks very much,' I said.

She stood up and opened the door. 'I don't think I remember you,' she said, looking back at me.

'There must be a few of us you didn't meet,' I said.

She flushed and stood there glaring at me.

'They always change the towels this late in your hotel?' I asked her, just to be saying something.

'Smart guy, ain't you?'

'Well, I try to give that impression,' I said with a modest smirk.

'You don't put it over,' she said, with a sudden trace of thick accent.

'Anybody handle those shoes except you—after you took them?'

'No. I told you I just stopped to tell Mr Weber——' She stopped dead and thought a minute. 'I went to get him a cup of coffee,' she said. 'I left them on his desk by the cash register. How the hell would I know if anybody handled them? And what difference does it make if they got their dough back all right?'

'Well, I see you're anxious to make me feel good about it. Tell me about this guy, Weber. He been here long?'

'Too long,' she said nastily. 'A girl don't want to walk too close to him, if you get what I mean. What am I talking about?'

'About Mr Weber.'

'Well, to hell with Mr Weber—if you get what I mean.'

'You been having any trouble getting it across?'

She flushed again. 'And strictly off the record,' she said, 'to hell with you.'

'If I get what you mean,' I said.

She opened the door and gave me a quick, half-angry smile and went out.

Her steps made a tapping sound going along the hall. I didn't hear her stop at any other doors. I looked at my watch. It was after half past nine.

Somebody came along the hall with heavy feet, went into the room next to me and banged the door. The man started hawking and throwing shoes around. A weight flopped on the bed springs and started bounding around. Five minutes of this and he got up again. Two big, unshod feet thudded on the floor, a bottle tinkled against a glass. The man had himself a drink, lay down on the bed again, and began to snore almost at once.

Except for that and the confused racket from downstairs in the dining room and the bar there was the nearest thing you get to silence in a mountain resort. Speedboats stuttered out on the lake, dance music murmured here and there, cars went by blowing horns, the .22s snapped in the shooting gallery, and kids yelled at each other across the main drag.

It was so quiet that I didn't hear my door open. It was half open before I noticed it. A man came in quietly, half closed the door, moved a couple of steps farther into the room and stood looking at me. He was tall, thin, pale, quiet, and his eyes had a flat look of menace.

'O.K., sport,' he said. 'Let's see it.'

I rolled around and sat up. I yawned. 'See what?'

'The buzzer.'

'What buzzer?'

'Shake it up, half-smart. Let's see the buzzer that gives you the right to ask questions of the help.'

'Oh, that,' I said, smiling weakly. 'I don't have any buzzer, Mr Weber.'

'Well, that is very lovely,' Mr Weber said. He came across the room, his long arms swinging. When he was about three feet from me he leaned forward a little and made a very sudden movement. An open palm slapped the side of my face hard. It rocked my head and made the back of it shoot pain in all directions.

'Just for that,' I said, 'you don't go to the movies tonight.'

He twisted his face into a sneer and cocked his right fist. He telegraphed his punch well ahead. I would almost have had time to run out and buy a catcher's mask. I came up under the fist and stuck a gun in his stomach. He grunted unpleasantly. I said:

'Putting the hands up, please.'

He grunted again and his eyes went out of focus, but he didn't move his hands. I went around him and backed toward the far side of the room. He turned slowly, eyeing me. I said:

'Just a moment until I close the door. Then we will go into the case of the money in the shoe, otherwise known as the Clue of the Substituted Lettuce.'

'Go to hell,' he said.

'A right snappy comeback,' I said. 'And full of originality.'

I reached back for the knob of the door, keeping my eyes on him. A board creaked behind me. I swung around, adding a little power to the large, heavy, hard and businesslike hunk of concrete which landed on the side of my jaw. I spun off into the distance, trailing flashes of lightning, and did a nose dive out into space. A couple of thousand years passed. Then I stopped a planet with my back, opened my eyes fuzzily and looked at a pair of feet.

They were sprawled out at a loose angle, and legs came toward me from them. The legs were splayed out on the floor of the room. A hand hung down limp, and a gun lay just out of its reach. I moved one of the feet and was surprised to find it belonged to me. The lax hand twitched and reached automatically for the gun, missed it, reached again and grabbed the smooth grip. I lifted it. Somebody had tied a fifty-pound weight to it, but I lifted it anyway. There was nothing in the room but silence. I looked across and was staring straight at the closed door. I shifted a little and ached all over. My head ached. My jaw ached. I lifted the gun some more and then put it down again. The hell with it. I should be lifting guns around for what. The room was empty. All visitors departed. The droplight from the ceiling burned with an empty glare. I rolled a little and ached some more and got a leg bent and a knee under me. I came up grunting hard, grabbed the gun again and climbed the rest of the way. There was a taste of ashes in my mouth.

'Ah, too bad,' I said out loud. 'Too bad. Must do. O.K., Charlie, I'll be seeing you.'

I swayed a little, still groggy as a three-day drunk, swiveled slowly and prowled the room with my eyes.

A man was kneeling in prayer against the side of the bed. He wore a gray suit and his hair was a dusty blond color. His legs were spread out, and his body was bent forward on the bed and his arms were flung out. His head rested sideways on his left arm.

He looked quite comfortable. The rough deer-horn grip of the hunting knife under his left shoulder blade didn't seem to bother him at all.

I went over to bend down and look at his face. It was the face of Mr Weber. Poor Mr Weber! From under the handle of the hunting knife, down the back of his jacket, a dark streak extended.

It was not mercurochrome.

I found my hat somewhere and put it on carefully, and put the gun under my arm and waded over to the door. I reversed the key, switched the light off, went out and locked the door after me and dropped the key into my pocket.

I went along the silent hallway and down the stairs to the office. An old wasted-looking night clerk was reading the paper behind the desk. He didn't even look at me. I glanced through the archway into the dining room. The same noisy crowd was brawling at the bar. The same hillbilly symphony was fighting for life in the corner. The guy with the cigar and the John L. Lewis eyebrows was minding the cash register. Business seemed good. A couple of summer visitors were dancing in the middle of the floor, holding glasses over each other's shoulders.

I went out of the lobby door and turned left along the street to where my car was parked, but I didn't go very far before I stopped and turned back into the lobby of the hotel. I leaned on the counter and asked the clerk:

'May I speak to the maid called Gertrude?'

He blinked at me thoughtfully over his glasses.

'She's off at nine thirty. She's gone home.'

'Where does she live?'

He stared at me without blinking this time.

'I think maybe you've got the wrong idea,' he said.

'If I have, it's not the idea you have.'

He rubbed the end of his chin and washed my face with his stare. 'Something wrong?'

'I'm a detective from L.A. I work very quietly when people let me work quietly.'

'You'd better see Mr Holmes,' he said. 'The manager.'

'Look, pardner, this is a very small place. I wouldn't have to do more than wander down the row and ask in the bars and eating places for Gertrude. I could think up a reason. I could find out. You would save me a little time and maybe save somebody from getting hurt. Very badly hurt.'

He shrugged. 'Let me see your credentials, Mr——'

'Evans.' I showed him my credentials. He stared at them a long time after he had read them, then handed the wallet back and stared at the ends of his fingers.

'I believe she's stopping at the Whitewater Cabins,' he said.

'What's her last name?'

'Smith,' he said, and smiled a faint, old, and very weary smile, the smile of a man who has seen too much of one world. 'Or possibly Schmidt.'

I thanked him and went back out on the sidewalk. I walked half a block, then turned into a noisy little bar for a drink. A three-piece orchestra was swinging it on a tiny stage at the back. In front of the stage there was a small dance floor, and a few fuzzy-eyed couples were shagging around flat-footed with their mouths open and their faces full of nothing.

I drank a jigger of rye and asked the barman where the Whitewater Cabins were. He said at the east end of the town, half a block back, on a road that started at the gas station.

I went back for my car and drove through the village and found the road. A pale-blue neon sign with an arrow on it pointed the way. The Whitewater Cabins were a cluster of shacks on the side of the hill with an office down front. I stopped in front of the office. People were sitting out on their tiny front porches with portable radios. The night seemed peaceful and homey. There was a bell in the office.

I rang it and a girl in slacks came in and told me Miss Smith and Miss Hoffman had a cabin kind of off by itself because the girls slept late and wanted quiet. Of course, it was always kind of noisy in the season, but the cabin where they were—it was called Tuck-Me-Inn— was quiet and it was at the back, way off to the left, and I wouldn't have any trouble finding it. Was I a friend of theirs?

I said I was Miss Smith's grandfather, thanked her and went out and up the slope between the clustered cabins to the edge of the pines at the back. There was a long woodpile at the back, and at each end of the cleared space there was a small cabin. In front of the one to the left there was a coupé standing with its lights dim. A tall blond girl was putting a suitcase into the boot. Her hair was tied in a blue hand-kerchief, and she wore a blue sweater and blue pants. Or dark enough to be blue, anyhow. The cabin behind her was lighted, and the little sign hanging from the roof said 'Tuck-Me-Inn.'

The blond girl went back into the cabin, leaving the boot of the car open. Dim light oozed out through the open door. I went very softly up on the steps and walked inside.

Gertrude was snapping down the top of a suitcase on a bed. The blond girl was out of sight, but I could hear her out in the kitchen of the little cabin.

I couldn't have made very much noise. Gertrude snapped down the lid of the suitcase, hefted it and started to carry it out. It was only then that she saw me. Her face went very white, and she stopped dead, holding the suitcase at her side. Her mouth opened, and she spoke quickly back over her shoulder: 'Anna-*achtung!*'

The noise stopped in the kitchen. Gertrude and I stared at each other.

'Leaving?' I asked.

She moistened her lips. 'Going to stop me, copper?'

'I don't guess. What you leaving for?'

'I don't like it up here. The altitude is bad for my nerves.'

'Made up your mind rather suddenly, didn't you?'

'Any law against it?'

'I don't guess. You're not afraid of Weber, are you?'

She didn't answer me. She looked past my shoulder. It was an old gag, and I didn't pay any attention to it. Behind me, the cabin door closed. I turned, then. The blond girl was behind me. She had a gun in her hand. She looked at me thoughtfully, without any expression much. She was a big girl, and looked very strong.

'What is it?' she asked, speaking a little heavily, in a voice almost like a man's voice.

'A Los Angeles dick,' replied Gertrude.

'So,' Anna said. 'What does he want?'

'I don't know,' Gertrude said. 'I don't think he's a real dick. He don't seem to throw his weight enough.'

'So,' Anna said. She moved to the side and away from the door. She kept the gun pointed at me. She held it as if guns didn't make her nervous—not the least bit nervous. 'What do you want?' she asked throatily.

'Practically everything,' I said. 'Why are you taking a powder?'

'That has been explained,' the blond girl said calmly. 'It is the altitude. It is making Gertrude sick.'

'You both work at the Indian Head?'

The blond girl said: 'Of no consequence.'

'What the hell,' Gertrude said. 'Yeah, we both worked at the hotel until tonight. Now we're leaving. Any objection?'

'We waste time,' the blond girl said. 'See if he has a gun.'

Gertrude put her suitcase down and felt me over. She found the gun and I let her take it, big-hearted. She stood there looking at it with a pale, worried expression. The blond girl said:

'Put the gun down outside and put the suitcase in the car. Start the engine of the car and wait for me.'

Gertrude picked her suitcase up again and started around me to the door.

'That won't get you anywhere,' I said. 'They'll telephone ahead and block you on the road. There are only two roads out of here, both easy to block.'

The blond girl raised her fine, tawny eyebrows a little. 'Why should anyone wish to stop us?'

'Yeah, why are you holding that gun?'

'I did not know who you were,' the blond girl said. 'I do not know even now. Go on, Gertrude.'

Gertrude opened the door, then looked back at me and moved her lips one over the other. 'Take a tip, shamus, and beat it out of this place while you're able,' she said quietly.

'Which of you saw the hunting knife?'

They glanced at each other quickly, then back at me. Gertrude had a fixed stare, but it didn't look like a guilty kind of stare. 'I pass,' she said. 'You're over my head.'

'O.K.,' I said. 'I know you didn't put it where it was. One more question: How long were you getting that cup of coffee for Mr Weber the morning you took the shoes out?'

'You are wasting time, Gertrude,' the blond girl said impatiently, or as impatiently as she would ever say anything. She didn't seem an impatient type.

Gertrude didn't pay any attention to her. Her eyes held a tight speculation. 'Long enough to get him a cup of coffee.'

'They have that right in the dining room.'

'It was stale in the dining room. I went out to the kitchen for it. I got him some toast, also.'

'Five minutes?'

She nodded. 'About that.'

'Who else was in the dining room besides Weber?'

She stared at me very steadily. 'At that time I don't think anybody. I'm not sure. Maybe someone was having a late breakfast.'

'Thanks very much,' I said. 'Put the gun down carefully on the porch and don't drop it. You can empty it if you like. I don't plan to shoot anyone.'

She smiled a very small smile and opened the door with the hand holding the gun and went out. I heard her go down the steps and then heard the boot of the car slammed shut. I heard the starter, then the motor caught and purred quietly.

The blond girl moved around to the door and took the key from the inside and put it on the outside. 'I would not care to shoot anybody,' she said. 'But I could do it if I had to. Please do not make me.'

She shut the door and the key turned in the lock. Her steps went down off the porch. The car door slammed and the motor took hold. The tires made a soft whisper going down between the cabins. Then the noise of the portable radios swallowed that sound.

I stood there looking around the cabin, then walked through it. There was nothing in it that didn't belong there. There was some garbage in a can, coffee cups not washed, a saucepan full of grounds. There were no papers, and nobody had left the story of his life written on a paper match.

The back door was locked, too. This was on the side away from the camp, against the dark wilderness of the trees. I shook the door and bent down to look at the lock. A straight bolt lock. I opened a window. Screen was nailed over it against the wall outside. I went back to the door and gave it the shoulder. It held without any trouble at all. It also started my head blazing again. I felt in my pockets and was disgusted. I didn't even have a five-cent skeleton key.

I got the can opener out of the kitchen drawer and worked a corner of the screen loose and bent it back. Then I got up on the sink and reached down to the outside knob of the door and groped around. The key was in the lock. I turned it and drew my hand in again and went out of the door. Then I went back and put the lights out. My gun was lying on the front porch behind a post of the little railing. I tucked it under my arm and walked downhill to the place where I had left my car.

There was a wooden counter leading back from beside the door and a potbellied stove in the corner, and a large blueprint map of the district and some curled-up calendars on the wall. On the counter were piles of dusty-looking folders, a rusty pen, a bottle of ink, and somebody's sweat-darkened Stetson.

Behind the counter there was an old golden-oak roll-top desk, and at the desk sat a man, with a tall corroded brass spittoon leaning against his leg. He was a heavy, calm man, and he sat tilted back in his chair with large, hairless hands clasped on his stomach. He wore scuffed brown army shoes, white socks, brown wash pants held up by faded suspenders, a khaki shirt buttoned to the neck. His hair was mousy brown except at the temples, where it was the color of dirty snow. On his left breast there was a star. He sat a little more on his left hip than on his right, because there was a brown leather hip holster inside his right hip pocket, and about a foot of .45 gun in the holster.

He had large ears and friendly eyes, and he looked about as dangerous as a squirrel, but much less nervous. I leaned on the counter and looked at him, and he nodded at me and loosed a half pint of brown juice into the spittoon. I lit a cigarette and looked around for some place to throw the match.

'Try the floor,' he said. 'What can I do for you, son?'

I dropped the match on the floor and pointed with my chin at the map on the wall. 'I was looking for a map of the district. Sometimes chambers of commerce have them to give away. But I guess you wouldn't be the chamber of commerce.'

'We ain't got no maps,' the man said. 'We had a mess of them a couple of years back, but we run out. I was hearing that Sid Young had some down at the camera store by the post office. He's the justice of the peace here, besides running the camera store, and he gives them out to show them whereat they can smoke and where not. We got a bad fire hazard up here. Got a good map of the district up there on the wall. Be glad to direct you any place you'd care to go. We aim to make the summer visitors go home.'

He took a slow breath and dropped another load of juice.

'What was the name?' he asked.

'Evans. Are you the law around here?'

'Yep. I'm Puma Point constable and San Berdoo deppity sheriff. What law we gotta have, me and Sid Young is it. Barron is the name. I come from L.A. Eighteen years in the fire department. I come up here quite a while back. Nice and quiet up here. You up on business?'

I didn't think he could do it again so soon, but he did. That spittoon took an awful beating.

'Business?' I asked.

The big man took one hand off his stomach and hooked a finger inside his collar and tried to loosen it. 'Business,' he said calmly. 'Meaning, you got a permit for that gun, I guess?'

'Hell, does it stick out that much?'

'Depends what a man's lookin' for,' he said, and put his feet on the floor. 'Maybe you 'n' me better get straightened out.'

He got to his feet and came over to the counter and I put my wallet on it, opened out so that he could see the photostat of the license behind the celluloid window. I drew out the L.A. sheriff's gun permit and laid it beside the license.

He looked them over. 'I better kind of check the number,' he said.

I pulled the gun out and laid it on the counter beside his hand. He picked it up and compared the numbers. 'I see you got three of them. Don't wear them all to onst, I hope. Nice gun, son. Can't shoot like mine, though.' He pulled his cannon off his hip and laid it on the counter. A Frontier Colt that would weigh as much as a suitcase. He balanced it, tossed it into the air and caught it spinning, then put it back on his hip. He pushed my .38 back across the counter.

'Up here on business, Mr Evans?'

'I'm not sure. I got a call, but I haven't made a contact yet. A confidential matter.'

He nodded. His eyes were thoughtful. They were deeper, colder, darker than they had been.

'I'm stopping at the Indian Head,' I said.

'I don't aim to pry into your affairs, son,' he said. 'We don't have no crime up here. Onst in a while a fight or drunk driver in summertime. Or maybe a couple hard-boiled kids on a motorcycle will break into a cabin just to sleep and steal food. No real crime, though. Mighty little inducement to crime in the mountains. Mountain folks are mighty peaceable.'

'Yeah,' I said. 'And again, no.'

He leaned forward a little and looked into my eyes.

'Right now,' I said, 'you've got a murder.'

Nothing much changed in his face. He looked me over feature by feature. He reached for his hat and put it on the back of his head.

'What was that, son?' he asked calmly.

'On the point east of the village out past the dancing pavilion.

A man shot, lying behind a big fallen tree. Shot through the heart. I was down there smoking for half an hour before I noticed him.'

'Is that so?' he drawled. 'Out Speaker Point, eh? Past Speaker's Tavern. That the place?'

'That's right,' I said.

'You taken a longish while to get around to telling me, didn't you?' The eyes were not friendly.

'I got a shock,' I said. 'It took me a while to get myself straightened out.'

He nodded. 'You and me will now drive out that way. In your car.'

'That won't do any good,' I said. 'The body has been moved. After I found the body I was going back to my car and a Japanese gunman popped up from behind a bush and knocked me down. A couple of men carried the body away and they went off in a boat. There's no sign of it there at all now.'

The sheriff went over and spit in his gobboon. Then he made a small spit on the stove and waited as if for it to sizzle, but it was summer and the stove was out. He turned around and cleared his throat and said:

'You'd kind of better go on home and lie down a little while, maybe.' He clenched his fist at his side. 'We aim for the summer visitors to enjoy themselves up here.' He clenched both his hands, then pushed them hard down into the shallow pockets in the front of his pants.

'O.K.,' I said.

'We don't have no Japanese gunmen up here,' the sheriff said thickly. 'We are plumb out of Japanese gunmen.'

'I can see you don't like that one,' I said. 'How about this one? A man named Weber was knifed in the back at the Indian Head a while back. In my room. Somebody I didn't see knocked me out with a brick, and while I was out this Weber was knifed. He and I had been talking together. Weber worked at the hotel. As cashier.'

'You said this happened in your room?'

'Yeah.'

'Seems like,' Barron said thoughtfully, 'you could turn out to be a bad influence in this town.'

'You don't like that one, either?'

He shook his head. 'Nope. Don't like this one, neither. Unless, of course, you got a body to go with it.'

'I don't have it with me,' I said, 'but I can run over and get it for you.'

He reached and took hold of my arm with some of the hardest fingers I ever felt. 'I'd hate for you to be in your right mind, son,' he said. 'But I'll kind of go over with you. It's a nice night.'

'Sure,' I said, not moving. 'The man I came up here to work for is called Fred Lacey. He just bought a cabin out on Ball Sage Point. The Baldwin cabin. The man I found dead on Speaker Point was named Frederick Lacey, according to the driver's license in his pocket. There's a lot more to it, but you wouldn't want to be bothered with the details, would you?'

'You and me,' the sheriff said, 'will now run over to the hotel. You got a car?'

I said I had.

'That's fine,' the sheriff said. 'We won't use it, but give me the keys.'

The man with the heavy, furled eyebrows and the screwed-in cigar leaned against the closed door of the room and didn't say anything or look as if he wanted to say anything. Sheriff Barron sat straddling a straight chair and watching the doctor, whose name was Menzies, examine the body. I stood in the corner where I belonged. The doctor was an angular, bug-eyed man with a yellow face relieved by bright-red patches on his cheeks. His fingers were brown with nicotine stains, and he didn't look very clean.

He puffed cigarette smoke into the dead man's hair and rolled him around on the bed and felt him here and there. He looked as if he was trying to act as if he knew what he was doing. The knife had been pulled out of Weber's back. It lay on the bed beside him. It was a short, wide-bladed knife of the kind that is worn in a leather scabbard attached to the belt. It had a heavy guard which would seal the wound as the blow was struck and keep blood from getting back on the handle. There was plenty of blood on the blade.

'Sears Sawbuck Hunter's Special No. 2438,' the sheriff said, looking at it. 'There's a thousand of them around the lake. They ain't bad and they ain't good. What you say, doc?'

The doctor straightened up and took a handkerchief out. He coughed hackingly into the handkerchief, looked at it, shook his head sadly and lit another cigarette.

'About what?' he asked.

'Cause and time of death.'

'Dead very recently,' the doctor said. 'Not more than two hours. There's no beginning of rigor yet.'

'Would you say the knife killed him?'

'Don't be a damn fool, Jim Barron.'

'There's been cases,' the sheriff said, 'where a man would be poisoned or something and they would stick a knife into him to make it look different.'

'That would be very clever,' the doctor said nastily. 'You had many like that up here?'

'Only murder I had up here,' the sheriff said peacefully, 'was old Dad Meacham over to the other side. Had a shack in Sheedy Canyon. Folks didn't see him around for a while, but it was kinda cold weather and they figured he was in there with his oil stove resting up. Then when he didn't show up they knocked and found the cabin was locked up, so they figured he had gone down for the winter. Then come a heavy snow and the roof caved in. We was over there a-trying to prop her up so he wouldn't lose all his stuff, and by gum, there was Dad in bed with a ax in the back of his head. He had a little gold he'd panned in summer—I guess that was what he was killed for. We never did find out who done it.'

'You want to send him down in my ambulance?' the doctor asked, pointing at the bed with his cigarette.

The sheriff shook his head. 'Nope. This is a poor country, doc. I figure he could ride cheaper than that.'

The doctor put his hat on and went to the door. The man with the eyebrows moved out of the way. The doctor opened the door. 'Let me know if you want me to pay for the funeral,' he said, and went out.

'That ain't no way to talk,' the sheriff said.

The man with the eyebrows said: 'Let's get this over with and get him out of here so I can go back to work. I got a movie outfit coming up Monday and I'll be busy. I got to find me a new cashier, too, and that ain't so easy.'

'Where did you find Weber?' the sheriff asked. 'Did he have any enemies?'

'I'd say he had at least one,' the man with the eyebrows said. 'I got him through Frank Luders over at the Woodland Club. All I know about him is he knew his job and he was able to make a ten-thousand-dollar bond without no trouble. That's all I needed to know.'

'Frank Luders,' the sheriff said. 'That would be the man that's bought in over there. I don't think I met him. What does he do?'

'Ha, ha,' the man with the eyebrows said.

The sheriff looked at him peacefully. 'Well, that ain't the only place where they run a nice poker game, Mr Holmes.'

Mr Holmes looked blank. 'Well, I got to go back to work,' he said. 'You need any help to move him?'

'Nope. Ain't going to move him right now. Move him before daylight. But not right now. That will be all for now, Mr Holmes.'

The man with the eyebrows looked at him thoughtfully for a moment, then reached for the doorknob.

I said: 'You have a couple of German girls working here, Mr Holmes. Who hired them?'

The man with the eyebrows dragged his cigar out of his mouth, looked at it, put it back and screwed it firmly in place. He said: 'Would that be your business?'

'Their names are Anna Hoffman and Gertrude Smith, or maybe Schmidt,' I said. 'They had a cabin together over at the Whitewater Cabins. They packed up and went down the hill tonight. Gertrude is the girl that took Mrs Lacey's shoes to the shoemaker.'

The man with the eyebrows looked at me very steadily.

I said: 'When Gertrude was taking the shoes, she left them on Weber's desk for a short time. There was five hundred dollars in one of the shoes. Mr Lacey had put it in there for a joke, so his wife would find it.'

'First I heard of it,' the man with the eyebrows said. The sheriff didn't say anything at all.

'The money wasn't stolen,' I said. 'The Laceys found it still in the shoe over at the shoemaker's place.'

The man with the eyebrows said: 'I'm certainly glad that got straightened out all right.' He pulled the door open and went out and shut it behind him. The sheriff didn't say anything to stop him.

He went over into the corner of the room and spit in the wastebasket. Then he got a large khaki-colored handkerchief out and wrapped the blood-stained knife in it and slipped it down inside his belt, at the side. He went over and stood looking down at the dead man on the bed. He straightened his hat and started toward the door. He opened the door and looked back at me. 'This is a little tricky,' he said. 'But it probably ain't as tricky as you would like for it to be. Let's go over to Lacey's place.'

I went out and he locked the door and put the key in his pocket. We went downstairs and out through the lobby and crossed the street to where a small, dusty, tan-colored sedan was parked against the fireplug. A leathery young man was at the wheel. He looked underfed and a little dirty, like most of the natives. The sheriff and I got in the back of the car. The sheriff said:

'You know the Baldwin place out to the end of Ball Sage, Andy?'

'Yup.'

'We'll go out there,' the sheriff said. 'Stop a little to this side.' He looked up at the sky. 'Full moon all night, tonight,' he said. 'And it's sure a dandy.'

The cabin on the point looked the same as when I had seen it last. The same windows were lighted, the same car stood in the open double garage, and the same wild, screaming bark burst on the night.

'What in heck's that?' the sheriff asked as the car slowed. 'Sounds like a coyote.'

'It's half coyote,' I said.

The leathery lad in front said over his shoulder, 'You want to stop in front, Jim?'

'Drive her down a piece. Under them old pines.'

The car stopped softly in black shadow at the roadside. The sheriff and I got out. 'You stay here, Andy, and don't let nobody see you,' the sheriff said. 'I got my reasons.'

We went back along the road and through the rustic gate. The barking started again. The front door opened. The sheriff went up on the steps and took his hat off.

'Mrs Lacey? I'm Jim Barron, constable at Puma Point. This here is Mr Evans, from Los Angeles. I guess you know him. Could we come in a minute?'

The woman looked at him with a face so completely shadowed that no expression showed on it. She turned her head a little and looked at me. She said, 'Yes, come in,' in a lifeless voice.

We went in. The woman shut the door behind us. A big gray-haired man sitting in an easy-chair let go of the dog he was holding on the floor and straightened up. The dog tore across the room, did a flying tackle on the sheriff's stomach, turned in the air and was already running in circles when she hit the floor.

'Well, that's a right nice little dog,' the sheriff said, tucking his shirt in.

The gray-haired man was smiling pleasantly. He said: 'Good evening.' His white, strong teeth gleamed with friendliness.

Mrs Lacey was still wearing the scarlet double-breasted coat and the gray slacks. Her face looked older and more drawn. She looked at the floor and said: 'This is Mr Frank Luders from the Woodland Club. Mr Bannon and'—she stopped and raised her eyes to look at a point over my left shoulder—'I didn't catch the other gentleman's name,' she said.

'Evans,' the sheriff said, and didn't look at me at all. 'And mine is Barron, not Bannon.' He nodded at Luders. I nodded at Luders. Luders smiled at both of us. He was big, meaty, powerful-looking, well-kept and cheerful. He didn't have a care in the world. Big, breezy Frank Luders, everybody's pal.

He said: 'I've known Fred Lacey for a long time. I just dropped by to say hello. He's not home, so I am waiting a little while until a friend comes by in a car to pick me up.'

'Pleased to know you, Mr Luders,' the sheriff said. 'I heard you had bought in at the club. Didn't have the pleasure of meeting you yet.'

The woman sat down very slowly on the edge of a chair. I sat down. The little dog, Shiny, jumped in my lap, washed my right ear for me, squirmed down again and went under my chair. She lay there breathing out loud and thumping the floor with her feathery tail.

The room was still for a moment. Outside the windows on the lake side there was a very faint throbbing sound. The sheriff heard it. He cocked his head slightly, but nothing changed in his face.

He said: 'Mr Evans here come to me and told me a queer story. I guess it ain't no harm to mention it here, seeing Mr Luders is a friend of the family.'

He looked at Mrs Lacey and waited. She lifted her eyes slowly, but not enough to meet his. She swallowed a couple of times and nodded her head. One of her hands began to slide slowly up and down the arm of her chair, back and forth, back and forth. Luders smiled.

'I'd 'a' liked to have Mr Lacey here,' the sheriff said. 'You think he'll be in pretty soon?'

The woman nodded again. 'I suppose so,' she said in a drained voice. 'He's been gone since mid-afternoon. I don't know where he is. I hardly think he would go down the hill without telling me, but he has had time to do that. Something might have come up.'

'Seems like something did,' the sheriff said. 'Seems like Mr Lacey wrote a letter to Mr Evans, asking him to come up here quickly. Mr Evans is a detective from L.A.'

The woman moved restlessly. 'A detective?' she breathed.

Luders said brightly: 'Now why in the world would Fred do that?'

'On account of some money that was hid in a shoe,' the sheriff said.

Luders raised his eyebrows and looked at Mrs Lacey. Mrs Lacey moved her lips together and then said very softly: 'But we got that back, Mr Bannon. Fred was having a joke. He won a little money at the races and hid it in one of my shoes. He meant it for a surprise. I sent the shoe out to be repaired with the money still in it, but the money was still in it when we went over to the shoemaker's place.'

'Barron is the name, not Bannon,' the sheriff said. 'So you got your money back all intact, Mrs Lacey?'

'Why—of course. Of course, we thought at first, it being a hotel and one of the maids having taken the shoe—well, I don't know just what we thought, but it was a silly place to hide money—but we got it back, every cent of it.'

'And it was the same money?' I said, beginning to get the idea and not liking it.

She didn't quite look at me. 'Why, of course. Why not?'

'That ain't the way I heard it from Mr Evans,' the sheriff said peacefully, and folded his hands across his stomach. 'They was a slight difference, seems like, in the way you told it to Evans.'

Luders leaned forward suddenly in his chair, but his smile stayed put. It didn't even get tight. The woman made a vague gesture and her hand kept moving on the chair arm. 'I . . . told it . . . told what to Mr Evans?'

The sheriff turned his head very slowly and gave me a straight, hard stare. He turned his head back. One hand patted the other on his stomach.

'I understand Mr Evans was over here earlier in the evening and you told him about it, Mrs Lacey. About the money being changed?'

'Changed?' Her voice had a curiously hollow sound. 'Mr Evans told you he was here earlier in the evening? I . . . I never saw Mr Evans before in my life.'

I didn't even bother to look at her. Luders was my man. I looked at Luders. It got me what the nickel gets you from the slot machine. He chuckled and put a fresh match to his cigar.

The sheriff closed his eyes. His face had a sort of sad expression. The dog came out from under my chair and stood in the middle of the room looking at Luders. Then she went over in the corner and slid under the fringe of a daybed cover. A snuffling sound came from her a moment, then silence.

'Hum, hum, dummy,' the sheriff said, talking to himself. 'I ain't really equipped to handle this sort of a deal. I don't have the experience. We don't have no fast work like that up here. No crime at all in the mountains. Hardly.' He made a wry face.

He opened his eyes. 'How much money was that in the shoe, Mrs Lacey?'

'Five hundred dollars.' Her voice was hushed.

'Where at is this money, Mrs Lacey?'

'I suppose Fred has it.'

'I thought he was goin' to give it to you, Mrs Lacey.'

'He was,' she said sharply. 'He is. But I don't need it at the moment. Not up here. He'll probably give me a check later on.'

'Would he have it in his pocket or would it be in the cabin here, Mrs Lacey?'

She shook her head. 'In his pocket, probably. I don't know. Do you want to search the cabin?'

The sheriff shrugged his fat shoulders. 'Why, no, I guess not, Mrs Lacey. It wouldn't do me no good if I found it. Especially if it wasn't changed.'

Luders said: 'Just how do you mean changed, Mr Barron?'

'Changed for counterfeit money,' the sheriff said.

Luders laughed quietly. 'That's really amusing, don't you think? Counterfeit money at Puma Point? There's no opportunity for that sort of thing up here, is there?'

The sheriff nodded at him sadly. 'Don't sound reasonable, does it?'

Luders leaned forward a little more. 'Have you any knowledge of Mr Evans here—who claims to be a detective? A private detective, no doubt?'

'I thought of that,' the sheriff said.

Luders leaned forward a little more. 'Have you any knowledge other than Mr Evans' statement that Fred Lacey sent for him?'

'He'd have to know something to come up here, wouldn't he?' the sheriff said in a worried voice. 'And he knew about that money in Mrs Lacey's slipper.'

'I was just asking a question,' Luders said softly.

The sheriff swung around on me. I was already wearing my frozen smile. Since the incident in the hotel I hadn't looked for Lacey's letter. I knew I wouldn't have to look, now.

'You got a letter from Lacey?' he asked me in a hard voice.

I lifted my hand toward my inside breast pocket. Barron threw his right hand down and up. When it came up it held the Frontier Colt. 'I'll take that gun of yours first,' he said between his teeth. He stood up.

I pulled my coat open and held it open. He leaned down over me and jerked the automatic from the holster. He looked at it sourly a moment and dropped it into his left hip pocket. He sat down again. '*Now* look,' he said easily.

Luders watched me with bland interest. Mrs Lacey put her hands together and squeezed them hard and stared at the floor between her shoes.

I took the stuff out of my breast pocket. A couple of letters, some plain cards for casual notes, a packet of pipe cleaners, a spare hand-kerchief. Neither of the letters was the one. I put the stuff back and got a cigarette out and put it between my lips. I struck the match and held the flame to the tobacco. Nonchalant.

'You win,' I said, smiling. 'Both of you.'

There was a slow flush on Barron's face and his eyes glittered. His lips twitched as he turned away from me.

'Why not,' Luders asked gently, 'see also if he really is a detective?'

Barron barely glanced at him. 'The small things don't bother me,' he said. 'Right now I'm investigatin' a murder.'

He didn't seem to be looking at either Luders or Mrs Lacey. He seemed to be looking at a corner of the ceiling. Mrs Lacey shook, and her hands tightened so that the knuckles gleamed hard and shiny and white in the lamplight. Her mouth opened very slowly, and her eyes turned up in her head. A dry sob half died in her throat.

Luders took the cigar out of his mouth and laid it carefully in the brass dip on the smoking stand beside him. He stopped smiling. His mouth was grim. He said nothing.

It was beautifully timed. Barron gave them all they needed for the reaction and not a second for a comeback. He said, in the same almost indifferent voice:

'A man named Weber, cashier in the Indian Head Hotel. He was knifed in Evans' room. Evans was there, but he was knocked out before it happened, so he is one of them boys we hear so much about and don't often meet—the boys that get there first.'

'Not me,' I said. 'They bring their murders and drop them right at my feet.'

The woman's head jerked. Then she looked up, and for the first time she looked straight at me. There was a queer light in her eyes, shining far back, remote and miserable.

Barron stood up slowly. 'I don't get it,' he said. 'I don't get it at all. But I guess I ain't making any mistake in takin' this feller in.' He turned to me. 'Don't run too fast, not at first, bud. I always give a man forty yards.'

I didn't say anything. Nobody said anything.

Barron said slowly: 'I'll have to ask you to wait here till I come back, Mr Luders. If your friend comes for you, you could let him go on. I'd be glad to drive you back to the club later.'

Luders nodded. Barron looked at a clock on the mantel. It was a quarter to twelve. 'Kinda late for an old fuddy-duddy like me. You think Mr Lacey will be home pretty soon, ma'am?'

'I . . . I hope so,' she said, and made a gesture that meant nothing unless it meant hopelessness.

Barron moved over to open the door. He jerked his chin at me. I went out on the porch. The little dog came halfway out from under the couch and made a whining sound. Barron looked down at her.

'That sure is a nice little dog,' he said. 'I heard she was half coyote. What did you say the other half was?'

'We don't know,' Mrs Lacey murmured.

'Kind of like this case I'm working on,' Barron said, and came out onto the porch after me.

We walked down the road without speaking and came to the car. Andy was leaning back in the corner, a dead half cigarette between his lips.

We got into the car. 'Drive down a piece, about two hundred yards,' Barron said. 'Make plenty of noise.'

Andy started the car, raced the motor, clashed the gears, and the car slid down through the moonlight and around a curve of the road and up a moonlit hill sparred with the shadows of tree trunks.

'Turn her at the top and coast back, but not close,' Barron said. 'Stay out of sight of that cabin. Turn your lights off before you turn.'

'Yup,' Andy said.

He turned the car just short of the top, going around a tree to do it. He cut the lights off and started back down the little hill, then killed the motor. Just beyond the bottom of the slope there was a heavy clump of manzanita, almost as tall as ironwood. The car stopped there. Andy pulled the brake back very slowly to smooth out the noise of the ratchet.

Barron leaned forward over the back seat. 'We're going across the road and get near the water,' he said. 'I don't want no noise and nobody walkin' in no moonlight.'

Andy said: 'Yup.'

We got out. We walked carefully on the dirt of the road, then on the pine needles. We filtered through the trees, behind fallen logs, until the water was down below where we stood. Barron sat down on the ground and then lay down. Andy and I did the same. Barron put his face close to Andy.

'Hear anything?'

Andy said: 'Eight cylinders, kinda rough.'

I listened. I could tell myself I heard it, but I couldn't be sure. Barron nodded in the dark. 'Watch the lights in the cabin,' he whispered.

We watched. Five minutes passed, or enough time to seem like five minutes. The lights in the cabin didn't change. Then there was a remote, half-imagined sound of a door closing. There were shoes on wooden steps.

'Smart. They left the light on,' Barron said in Andy's ear.

We waited another short minute. The idling motor burst into a roar of throbbing sound, a stuttering, confused racket, with a sort of hop, skip and jump in it. The sound sank to a heavy purring roar and then quickly began to fade. A dark shape slid out on the moonlit water, curved with a beautiful line of froth and swept past the point out of sight.

Barron got a plug of tobacco out and bit. He chewed comfortably and spat four feet beyond his feet. Then he got up on his feet and dusted off the pine needles. Andy and I got up.

'Man ain't got good sense chewin' tobacco these days,' he said. 'Things ain't fixed for him. I near went to sleep back there in the cabin.' He lifted the Colt he was still holding in his left hand, changed hands and packed the gun away on his hip.

'Well?' he said, looking at Andy.

'Ted Rooney's boat,' Andy said. 'She's got two sticky valves and a big crack in the muffler. You hear it best when you throttle her up, like they did just before they started.'

It was a lot of words for Andy, but the sheriff liked them.

'Couldn't be wrong, Andy? Lots of boats get sticky valves.'

Andy said: 'What the hell you ask me for?' in a nasty voice.

'O.K., Andy, don't get sore.'

Andy grunted. We crossed the road and got into the car again. Andy started it up, backed and turned and said: 'Lights?'

Barron nodded. Andy put the lights on. 'Where to now?'

'Ted Rooney's place,' Barron said peacefully. 'And make it fast. We got ten miles to there.'

'Can't make it in less'n twenty minutes,' Andy said sourly. 'Got to go through the Point.'

The car hit the paved lake road and started back past the dark boys' camp and the other camps, and turned left on the highway. Barron didn't speak until we were beyond the village and the road out to Speaker Point. The dance band was still going strong in the pavilion.

'I fool you any?' he asked me then.

'Enough.'

'Did I do something wrong?'

'The job was perfect,' I said, 'but I don't suppose you fooled Luders.'

'That lady was mighty uncomfortable,' Barron said. 'That Luders is a good man. Hard, quiet, full of eyesight. But I fooled him some. He made mistakes.'

'I can think of a couple,' I said. 'One was being there at all. Another was telling us a friend was coming to pick him up, to explain why he had no car. It didn't need explaining. There was a car in the garage, but you didn't know whose car it was. Another was keeping that boat idling.'

'That wasn't no mistake,' Andy said from the front seat. 'Not if you ever tried to start her up cold.'

Barron said: 'You don't leave your car in the garage when you come callin' up here. Ain't no moisture to hurt it. The boat could have been anybody's boat. A couple of young folks could have been in it getting acquainted. I ain't got anything on him, anyways, so far as he knows. He just worked too hard tryin' to head me off.'

He spat out of the car. I heard it smack the rear fender like a wet rag. The car swept through the moonlit night, around curves, up and down hills, through fairly thick pines and along open flats where cattle lay.

I said: 'He knew I didn't have the letter Lacey wrote me. Because he took it away from me himself, up in my room at the hotel. It was Luders that knocked me out and knifed Weber. Luders knows that Lacey is dead, even if he didn't kill him. That's what he's got on Mrs Lacey. She thinks her husband is alive and that Luders has him.'

'You make this Luders out a pretty bad guy,' Barron said calmly. 'Why would Luders knife Weber?'

'Because Weber started all the trouble. This is an organization. Its object is to unload some very good counterfeit ten-dollar bills, a great many of them. You don't advance the cause by unloading them in five-hundred dollar lots, all brand-new, in circumstances that would make anybody suspicious, would make a much-less-careful man than Fred Lacey suspicious.'

'You're doing some nice guessin', son,' the sheriff said, grabbing the door handle as we took a fast turn, 'but the neighbors ain't watchin' you. I got to be more careful. I'm in my own back yard. Puma Lake don't strike me as a very good place to go into the counterfeit-money business.'

'O.K.' I said.

'On the other hand, if Luders is the man I want, he might be kind of hard to catch. There's three roads out of the valley, and there's half a dozen planes down to the east end of the Woodland Club golf course. Always is in summer.'

'You don't seem to be doing very much worrying about it,' I said.

'A mountain sheriff don't have to worry a lot,' Barron said calmly. 'Nobody expects him to have any brains. Especially guys like Mr Luders don't.'

The boat lay in the water at the end of a short painter, moving as boats move even in the stillest water. A canvas tarpaulin covered most of it and was tied down here and there, but not everywhere it should have been tied. Behind the short, rickety pier a road twisted back through juniper trees to the highway. There was a camp off to one side, with a miniature white lighthouse for its trade-mark. A sound of dance music came from one of the cabins, but most of the camp had gone to bed.

We came down there walking, leaving the car on the shoulder of the highway. Barron had a big flash in his hand and kept throwing it this way and that, snapping it on and off. When we came to the edge of the water and the end of the road down to the pier, he put his flashlight on the road and studied it carefully. There were fresh-looking tire tracks.

'What do you think?' he asked me.

'Looks like tire tracks,' I said.

'What do you think, Andy?' Barron said. 'This man is cute, but he don't give me no ideas.'

Andy bent over and studied the tracks. 'New tires and big ones,' he said, and walked toward the pier. He stooped down again and pointed. The sheriff threw the light where he pointed. 'Yup, turned around here,' Andy said. 'So what?' The place is full of new cars right now. Come October and they'd mean something. Folks that live up here buy one tire at a time, and cheap ones, at that. These here are heavy-duty all-weather treads.'

'Might see about the boat,' the sheriff said.

'What about it?'

'Might see if it was used recent,' Barron said.

'Hell,' Andy said, 'we know it was used recent, don't we?'

'Always supposin' you guessed right,' Barron said mildly.

Andy looked at him in silence for a moment. Then he spit on the ground and started back to where we had left the car. When he had gone a dozen feet he said over his shoulder:

'I wasn't guessin'.' He turned his head again and went on, plowing through the trees.

'Kind of touchy,' Barron said. 'But a good man.' He went down on the boat landing and bent over it, passing his hand along the forward part of the side, below the tarpaulin. He came back slowly and nodded. 'Andy's right. Always is, durn him. What kind of tires would you say those marks were, Mr Evans? They tell you anything?'

'Cadillac V-12,' I said. 'A club coupé with red leather seats and two suitcases in the back. The clock on the dash is twelve and one half minutes slow.'

He stood there, thinking about it. Then he nodded his big head. He sighed. 'Well, I hope it makes money for you,' he said, and turned away.

We went back to the car. Andy was in the front seat behind the wheel again. He had a cigarette going. He looked straight ahead of him through the dusty windshield.

'Where's Rooney live now?' Barron asked.

'Where he always lived,' Andy said.

'Why, that's just a piece up the Bascomb road.'

'I ain't said different,' Andy growled.

'Let's go there,' the sheriff said, getting in. I got in beside him.

Andy turned the car and went back half a mile and then started to turn. The sheriff snapped to him: 'Hold it a minute.'

He got out and used his flash on the road surface. He got back into the car. 'I think we got something. Them tracks down by the pier don't mean a lot. But the same tracks up here might turn out to mean more. If they go on into Bascomb, they're goin' to mean plenty. Them old gold camps over there is made to order for monkey business.'

The car went into the side road and climbed slowly into a gap. Big boulders crowded the road, and the hillside was studded with them. They glistened pure white in the moonlight. The car growled on for half a mile and then Andy stopped again.

'O.K., Hawkshaw, this is the cabin,' he said. Barron got out again and walked around with his flash. There was no light in the cabin. He came back to the car.

'They come by here,' he said. 'Bringing Ted home. When they left they turned toward Bascomb. You figure Ted Rooney would be mixed up in something crooked, Andy?'

'Not unless they paid him for it,' Andy said.

I got out of the car and Barron and I went up toward the cabin. It was small, rough, covered with native pine. It had a wooden porch, a tin chimney guyed with wires, and a sagging privy behind the cabin at the edge of the trees. It was dark. We walked up on the porch and Barron hammered on the door. Nothing happened. He tried the knob. The door was locked. We went down off the porch and around the back, looking at the windows. They were all shut. Barron tried the back door, which was level with the ground. That was locked, too. He pounded. The echoes of the sound wandered off through the trees and echoed high up on the rise among the boulders.

'He's gone with them,' Barron said. 'I guess they wouldn't dast leave him now. Prob'ly stopped here just to let him get his stuff— some of it. Yep.'

I said: 'I don't think so. All they wanted of Rooney was his boat. That boat picked up Fred Lacey's body out at the end of Speaker Point early this evening. The body was probably weighted and dropped out in the lake. They waited for dark to do that. Rooney was in on it and he got paid. Tonight they wanted the boat again. But they got to thinking they didn't need Rooney along. And if they're over in Bascomb Valley in some quiet little place, making or storing counterfeit money, they wouldn't at all want Rooney to go over there with them.'

'You're guessing again, son,' the sheriff said kindly. 'Anyways, I don't have no search warrant. But I can look over Rooney's dollhouse a minute. Wait for me.'

He walked away toward the privy. I took six feet and hit the door of the cabin. It shivered and split diagonally across the upper panel. Behind me, the sheriff called out, 'Hey,' weakly, as if he didn't mean it.

I took another six feet and hit the door again. I went in with it and landed on my hands and knees on a piece of linoleum that smelled like a fish skillet. I got up to my feet and reached up and turned the key switch of a hanging bulb. Barron was right behind me, making clucking noises of disapproval.

There was a kitchen with a wood stove, some dirty wooden shelves with dishes on them. The stove gave out a faint warmth. Unwashed pots sat on top of it and smelled. I went across the kitchen and into the front room. I turned on another hanging bulb. There was a narrow bed to one side, made up roughly, with a slimy quilt on it. There was a wooden table, some wooden chairs, an old cabinet radio, hooks on the wall, an ashtray with four burned pipes in it, a pile of pulp magazines in the corner on the floor.

The ceiling was low to keep the heat in. In the corner there was a trap to get up to the attic. The trap was open and a stepladder stood under the opening. An old water-stained canvas suitcase lay open on a wooden box, and there were odds and ends of clothing in it.

Barron went over and looked at the suitcase. 'Looks like Rooney was getting ready to move out or go for a trip. Then these boys come along and picked him up. He ain't finished his packing, but he got his suit in. A man like Rooney don't have but one suit and don't wear that 'less he goes down the hill.'

'He's not here,' I said. 'He ate dinner here, though. The stove is still warm.'

The sheriff cast a speculative eye at the stepladder. He went over and climbed up it and pushed the trap with his head. He raised his torch and shone it around overhead. He let the trap close and came down the stepladder again.

'Likely he kept the suitcase up there,' he said. 'I see there's a old steamer trunk up there, too. You ready to leave?'

'I didn't see a car around,' I said. 'He must have had a car.'

'Yep. Had an old Plymouth. Douse the light.'

He walked back into the kitchen and looked around that and then we put both the lights out and went out of the house. I shut what was left of the back door. Barron was examining tire tracks in the soft decomposed granite, trailing them back over to a space under a big oak tree where a couple of large darkened areas showed where a car had stood many times and dripped oil.

He came back swinging his flash, then looked toward the privy and said: 'You could go on back to Andy. I still gotta look over that doll-house.'

I didn't say anything. I watched him go along the path to the privy and unlatch the door, and open it. I saw his flash go inside and the light leaked out of a dozen cracks and from the ramshackle roof. I walked back along the side of the cabin and got into the car. The sheriff was gone a long time. He came back slowly, stopped beside the car and bit off another chew from his plug. He rolled it around in his mouth and then got to work on it.

'Rooney,' he said, 'is in the privy. Shot twice in the head.' He got into the car. 'Shot with a big gun, and shot very dead. Judgin' from the circumstances I would say somebody was in a hell of a hurry.'

The road climbed steeply for a while following the meanderings of a dried mountain stream the bed of which was full of boulders. Then it leveled off about a thousand or fifteen hundred feet above the level of the lake. We crossed a cattle stop of spaced narrow rails that clanked under the car wheels. The road began to go down. A wide undulating flat appeared with a few browsing cattle in it. A lightless farmhouse showed up against the moonlit sky. We reached a wider road that ran at right angles. Andy stopped the car and Barron got out with his big flashlight again and ran the spot slowly over the road surface.

'Turned left,' he said, straightening. 'Thanks be there ain't been another car past since them tracks were made.' He got back into the car.

'Left don't go to no old mines,' Andy said. 'Left goes to Worden's place and then back down to the lake at the dam.'

Barron sat silent a moment and then got out of the car and used his flash again. He made a surprised sound over to the right of the T intersection. He came back again, snapping the light off.

'Goes right, too,' he said. 'But goes left first. They doubled back, but they been somewhere off west of here before they done it. We go like they went.'

Andy said: 'You sure they went left first and not last? Left would be a way out to the highway.'

'Yep. Right marks overlays left marks,' Barron said.

We turned left. The knolls that dotted the valley were covered with ironwood trees, some of them half dead. Ironwood grows to about eighteen or twenty feet high and then dies. When it dies the limbs strip themselves and get a gray-white color and shine in the moonlight.

We went about a mile and then a narrow road shot off toward the north, a mere track. Andy stopped. Barron got out again and used his flash. He jerked his thumb and Andy swung the car. The sheriff got in.

'Them boys ain't too careful,' he said. 'Nope. I'd say they ain't careful at all. But they never figured Andy could tell where that boat came from, just by listenin' to it.'

The road went into a fold of the mountains and the growth got so close to it that the car barely passed without scratching. Then it doubled back at a sharp angle and rose again and went around a spur of hill and a small cabin showed up, pressed back against a slope with trees on all sides of it.

And suddenly, from the house or very close to it, came a long, shrieking yell which ended in a snapping bark. The bark was choked off suddenly.

Barron started to say: 'Kill them———' but Andy had already cut the lights and pulled off the road. 'Too late, I guess,' he said dryly. 'Must've seen us, if anybody's watchin'.'

Barron got out of the car. 'That sounded mighty like a coyote, Andy.'

'Yup.'

'Awful close to the house for a coyote, don't you think, Andy?'

'Nope,' Andy said. 'Lights out, a coyote would come right up to the cabin lookin' for buried garbage.'

'And then again it could be that little dog,' Barron said.

'Or a hen laying a square egg,' I said. 'What are we waiting for? And how about giving me back my gun? And are we trying to catch up with anybody, or do we just like to get things all figured out as we go along?'

The sheriff took my gun off his left hip and handed it to me. 'I ain't in no hurry,' he said. 'Because Luders ain't in no hurry. He coulda been long gone, if he was. They was in a hurry to get Rooney, because Rooney knew something about them. But Rooney don't know nothing about them now because he's dead and his house locked up and his car driven away. If you hadn't bust in his back door, he could be there in his privy a couple of weeks before anybody would get curious. Them tire tracks looks kind of obvious, but that's only because we know where they started. They don't have any reason to think we could find that out. So where would we start? No, I ain't in any hurry.'

Andy stooped over and came up with a deer rifle. He opened the left-hand door and got out of the car.

'The little dog's in there,' Barron said peacefully. 'That means Mrs Lacey is in there, too. And there would be somebody to watch her. Yep, I guess we better go up and look, Andy.'

'I hope you're scared,' Andy said. 'I am.'

We started through the trees. It was about two hundred yards to the cabin. The night was very still. Even at that distance I heard a window open. We walked about fifty feet apart. Andy stayed back long enough to lock the car. Then he started to make a wide circle, far out to the right.

Nothing moved in the cabin as we got close to it, no light showed. The coyote or Shiny, the dog, whichever it was, didn't bark again.

We got very close to the house, not more than twenty yards. Barron and I were about the same distance apart. It was a small rough cabin, built like Rooney's place, but larger. There was an open garage at the back, but it was empty. The cabin had a small porch of field-stone.

Then there was the sound of a short, sharp struggle in the cabin and the beginning of a bark, suddenly choked off. Barron fell down flat on the ground. I did the same. Nothing happened.

Barron stood up slowly and began to move forward a step at a time and a pause between each step. I stayed out. Barron reached the cleared space in front of the house and started to go up the steps to the porch. He stood there, bulky, clearly outlined in the moonlight, the Colt hanging at his side. It looked like a swell way to commit suicide.

Nothing happened. Barron reached the top of the steps, moved over tight against the wall. There was a window to his left, the door to his right. He changed his gun in his hand and reached out to bang on the door with the butt, then swiftly reversed it again, and flattened to the wall.

The dog screamed inside the house. A hand holding a gun came out at the bottom of the opened window and turned.

It was a tough shot at the range. I had to make it. I shot. The bark of the automatic was drowned in the duller boom of a rifle. The hand drooped and the gun dropped to the porch. The hand came out a little farther and the fingers twitched, then began to scratch at the sill. Then they went back in through the window and the dog howled. Barron was at the door, jerking at it. And Andy and I were running hard for the cabin, from different angles.

Barron got the door open and light framed him suddenly as some-one inside lit a lamp and turned it up.

I made the porch as Barron went in, Andy close behind me. We went into the living room of the cabin.

Mrs Fred Lacey stood in the middle of the floor beside a table with a lamp on it, holding the little dog in her arms. A thickset blondish man lay on his side under the window, breathing heavily, his hand groping around aimlessly for the gun that had fallen outside the window.

Mrs Lacey opened her arms and let the dog down. It leaped and hit the sheriff in the stomach with its small, sharp nose and pushed inside his coat at his shirt. Then it dropped to the floor again and ran around in circles, silently, weaving its hind end with delight.

Mrs Lacey stood frozen, her face as empty as death. The man on the floor groaned a little in the middle of his heavy breathing. His eyes opened and shut rapidly. His lips moved and bubbled pink froth.

'That sure is a nice little dog, Mrs Lacey,' Barron said, tucking his shirt in. 'But it don't seem a right handy time to have him around— not for some people.'

He looked at the blond man on the floor. The blond man's eyes opened and became fixed on nothing.

'I lied to you,' Mrs Lacey said quickly. 'I had to. My husband's life depended on it. Luders has him. He has him somewhere over here. I don't know where, but it isn't far off, he said. He went to bring him back to me, but he left this man to guard me. I couldn't do anything about it, sheriff. I'm—I'm sorry.'

'I knew you lied, Mrs Lacey,' Barron said quietly. He looked down at his Colt and put it back on his hip. 'I knew why. But your husband is dead, Mrs Lacey. He was dead long ago. Mr Evans here saw him. It's hard to take, ma'am, but you better know it now.'

She didn't move or seem to breathe. Then she went very slowly to a chair and sat down and leaned her face in her hands. She sat there without motion, without sound. The little dog whined and crept under her chair.

The man on the floor started to raise the upper part of his body. He raised it very slowly, stiffly. His eyes were blank. Barron moved over to him and bent down.

'You hit bad, son?'

The man pressed his left hand against his chest. Blood oozed between his fingers. He lifted his right hand slowly, until the arm was rigid and pointing to the corner of the ceiling. His lips quivered, stiffened, spoke.

'Heil Hitler!' he said thickly.

He fell back and lay motionless. His throat rattled a little and then that, too, was still, and everything in the room was still, even the dog.

'This man must be one of them Nazis,' the sheriff said. 'You hear what he said?'

'Yeah,' I said.

I turned and walked out of the house, down the steps and down through the trees again to the car. I sat on the running board and lit a cigarette, and sat there smoking and thinking hard.

After a little while they all came down through the trees. Barron was carrying the dog. Andy was carrying his rifle in his left hand. His leathery young face looked shocked.

Mrs Lacey got into the car and Barron handed the dog in to her. He looked at me and said: 'It's against the law to smoke out here, son, more than fifty feet from a cabin.'

I dropped the cigarette and ground it hard into the powdery gray soil. I got into the car, in front beside Andy.

The car started again and we went back to what they probably called the main road over there. Nobody said anything for a long time, then Mrs Lacey said in a low voice: 'Luders mentioned a name that sounded like Sloat. He said it to the man you shot. They called him Kurt. They spoke German. I understand a little German, but they talked too fast. Sloat didn't sound like German. Does it mean anything to you?'

'It's the name of an old gold mine not far from here,' Barron said. 'Sloat's Mine. You know where it is, don't you, Andy?'

'Yup. I guess I killed that feller, didn't I?'

'I guess you did, Andy.'

'I never killed nobody before,' Andy said.

'Maybe I got him,' I said. 'I fired at him.'

'Nope,' Andy said. 'You wasn't high enough to get him in the chest. I was.'

Barron said: 'How many brought you to that cabin, Mrs Lacey? I hate to be asking you questions at a time like this, ma'am, but I just got to.'

The dead voice said: 'Two. Luders and the man you killed. He ran the boat.'

'Did they stop anywhere—on this side of the lake, ma'am?'

'Yes. They stopped at a small cabin near the lake. Luders was driving. The other man, Kurt, got out, and we drove on. After a while Luders stopped and Kurt came up with us in an old car. He drove the car into a gully behind some willows and then came on with us.'

'That's all we need,' Barron said. 'If we get Luders, the job's all done. Except I can't figure what it's all about.'

I didn't say anything. We drove on to where the T intersection was and the road went back to the lake. We kept on across this for about four miles.

'Better stop here, Andy. We'll go the rest of the way on foot. You stay here.'

'Nope. I ain't going to,' Andy said.

'You stay here,' Barron said in a voice suddenly harsh. 'You got a lady to look after and you done your killin' for tonight. All I ask is you keep that little dog quiet.'

The car stopped. Barron and I got out. The little dog whined and then was still. We went off the road and started across country through a grove of young pines and manzanita and ironwood. We walked silently, without speaking. The noise our shoes made couldn't have been heard thirty feet away except by an Indian.

We reached the far edge of the thicket in a few minutes. Beyond that the ground was level and open. There was a spidery something against the sky, a few low piles of waste dirt, a set of sluice boxes built one on top of the other like a miniature cooling tower, an endless belt going toward it from a cut. Barron put his mouth against my ear.

'Ain't been worked for a couple of years,' he said. 'Ain't worth it. Day's hard work for two men might get you a pennyweight of gold. This country was worked to death sixty years ago. That low hut over yonder's a old refrigerator car. She's thick and damn near bullet-proof. I don't see no car, but maybe it's behind. Or hidden. Most like hidden. You ready to go?'

I nodded. We started across the open space. The moon was almost as bright as daylight. I felt swell, like a clay pipe in a shooting gallery. Barron seemed quite at ease. He held the big Colt down at his side, with his thumb over the hammer.

Suddenly light showed in the side of the refrigerator car and we went down on the ground. The light came from a partly opened door, a yellow panel and a yellow spearhead on the ground. There was a movement in the moonlight and the noise of water striking the ground. We waited a little, then got up again and went on.

There wasn't much use playing Indian. They would come out of the door or they wouldn't. If they did, they would see us, walking, crawling or lying. The ground was that bare and the moon was that bright. Our shoes scuffed a little, but this was hard dirt, much walked on and tight packed. We reached a pile of sand and stopped beside it. I listened to myself breathing. I wasn't panting, and Barron wasn't panting either. But I took a lot of interest in my breathing. It was something I had taken for granted for a long time, but right now I was interested in it. I hoped it would go on for a long time, but I wasn't sure.

I wasn't scared. I was a full-sized man and I had a gun in my hand. But the blond man back in the other cabin had been a full-sized man with a gun in his hand, too. And he had a wall to hide behind. I wasn't scared though. I was just thoughtful about little things. I thought Barron was breathing too loud, but I thought I would make more noise telling him he was breathing too loud than he was making breathing. That's the way I was, very thoughtful about the little things.

Then the door opened again. This time there was no light behind it. A small man, very small, came out of the doorway carrying what looked like a heavy suitcase. He carried it along the side of the car, grunting hard. Barron held my arm in a vise. His breath hissed faintly.

The small man with the heavy suitcase, or whatever it was, reached the end of the car and went around the corner. Then I thought that although the pile of sand didn't look very high it was probably high enough so that we didn't show above it. And if the small man wasn't expecting visitors, he might not see us. We waited for him to come back. We waited too long.

A clear voice behind us said: 'I am holding a machine gun, Mr Barron. Put your hands up, please. If you move to do anything else, I fire.'

I put my hands up fast. Barron hesitated a little longer. Then he put his hands up. We turned slowly. Frank Luders stood about four feet away from us, with a Tommy-gun held waist high. Its muzzle looked as big as the Second Street tunnel in L.A.

Luders said quietly: 'I prefer that you face the other way. When Charlie comes back from the car, he will light the lamps inside. Then we shall all go in.'

We faced the long, low car again. Luders whistled sharply. The small man came back around the corner of the car, stopped a moment, then went toward the door. Luders called out: 'Light the lamps, Charlie. We have visitors.'

The small man went quietly into the car and a match scratched and there was light inside.

'Now, gentlemen, you may walk,' Luders said. 'Observing, of

course, that death walks close behind you and conducting yourselves accordingly.'

We walked.

'Take their guns and see if they have any more of them, Charlie.'

We stood back against a wall near a long wooden table. There were wooden benches on either side of the table. On it was a tray with a bottle of whiskey and a couple of glasses, a hurricane lamp and an old-fashioned farmhouse oil lamp of thick glass, both lit, a saucer full of matches and another full of ashes and stubs. In the end of the cabin, away from the table, there was a small stove and two cots, one tumbled, one made up as neat as a pin.

The little Japanese came toward us with the light shining on his glasses.

'Oh having guns,' he purred. 'Oh too bad.'

He took the guns and pushed them backward across the table to Luders. His small hands felt us over deftly. Barron winced and his face reddened, but he said nothing. Charlie said:

'No more guns. Pleased to see, gentlemen. Very nice night, I think so. You having picnic in moonlight?'

Barron made an angry sound in his throat. Luders said: 'Sit down, please, gentlemen, and tell me what I can do for you.'

We sat down. Luders sat down opposite. The two guns were on the table in front of him and the Tommy-gun rested on it, his left hand holding it steady, his eyes quiet and hard. His was no longer a pleasant face, but it was still an intelligent face. Intelligent as they ever are.

Barron said: 'Guess I'll chew. I think better that way.' He got his plug out and bit into it and put it away. He chewed silently and then spit on the floor.

'Guess I might mess up your floor some,' he said. 'Hope you don't mind.'

The Jap was sitting on the end of the neat bed, his shoes not touching the floor. 'Not liking much,' he said hissingly, 'very bad smell.'

Barron didn't look at him. He said quietly: 'You aim to shoot us and make your getaway, Mr Luders?'

Luders shrugged and took his hand off the machine gun and leaned back against the wall.

Barron said: 'You left a pretty broad trail here except for one thing. How we would know where to pick it up. You didn't figure that out because you wouldn't have acted the way you did. But you was all staked out for us when we got here. I don't follow that.'

Luders said: 'That is because we Germans are fatalists. When things go very easily, as they did tonight—except for that fool, Weber—we become suspicious. I said to myself, "I have left no trail, no way they could follow me across the lake quickly enough. They had no boat, and no boat followed me. It would be impossible for them to find me. Quite impossible." So I said, "They will find me just because to me it appears impossible. Therefore, I shall be waiting for them." '

'While Charlie toted the suitcases full of money out to the car,' I said.

'What money?' Luders asked, and didn't seem to look at either of us. He seemed to be looking inward, searching.

I said: 'Those very fine new ten-dollar bills you have been bringing in from Mexico by plane.'

Luders looked at me then, but indifferently. 'My dear friend, you could not possibly be serious?' he suggested.

'Phooey. Easiest thing in the world. The border patrol has no planes now. They had a few coast guard planes awhile back, but nothing came over, so they were taken off. A plane flying high over the border from Mexico lands on the field down by the Woodland Club golf course. It's Mr Luders' plane and Mr Luders owns an interest in the club and lives there. Why should anybody get curious about that. But Mr Luders doesn't want half a million dollars' worth of queer money in his cabin at the club, so he finds himself an old mine over here and keeps the money in this refrigerator car. It's almost as strong as a safe and it doesn't look like a safe.'

'You interest me,' Luders said calmly. 'Continue.'

I said: 'The money is very good stuff. We've had a report on it. That means organization—to get the inks and the right paper and the plates. It means an organization much more complete than any gang of crooks could manage. A government organization. The organization of the Nazi government.'

The little Jap jumped up off the bed and hissed, but Luders didn't change expression. 'I'm still interested,' he said laconically.

'I ain't,' Barron said. 'Sounds to me like you're tryin' to talk yourself into a vestful of lead.'

I went on: 'A few years ago the Russians tried the same stunt. Planting a lot of queer money over here to raise funds for espionage work and, incidentally, they hoped, to damage our currency. The Nazis are too smart to gamble on that angle. All they want is good

American dollars to work with in Central and South America. Nice mixed-up money that's been used. You can't go into a bank and deposit a hundred thousand dollars in brand-new ten-dollar bills. What's bothering the sheriff is why you picked this particular place, a mountain resort full of rather poor people.'

'But that does not bother you with your superior brain, does it?' Luders sneered.

'It don't bother me a whole lot either,' Barron said. 'What bothers me is folks getting killed in my territory. I ain't used to it.'

I said: 'You picked the place primarily because it's a swell place to bring the money into. It's probably one of hundreds all over the country, places where there is very little law enforcement to dodge but places where in the summertime a lot of strange people come and go all the time. And places where planes set down and nobody checks them in or out. But that isn't the only reason. It's also a swell place to unload some of the money, quite a lot of it, if you're lucky. But you weren't lucky. Your man Weber pulled a dumb trick and made you unlucky. Should I tell you just why it's a good place to spread queer money, if you have enough people working for you?'

'Please do,' Luders said, and patted the side of the machine gun.

'Because for three months in the year this district has a floating population of anywhere from twenty to fifty thousand people, depending on the holidays and week-ends. That means a lot of money brought in and a lot of business done. And there's no bank here. The result of that is that the hotels and bars and merchants have to cash checks all the time. The result of that is that the deposits they send out during the season are almost all checks and the money stays in circulation. Until the end of the season, of course.'

'I think that is very interesting,' Luders said. 'But if this operation were under my control, I would not think of passing very much money up here. I would pass a little here and there, but not much. I would test the money out, to see how well it was accepted. And for a reason that you have thought of. Because most of it would change hands rapidly and, if it was discovered to be queer money, as you say, it would be very difficult to trace the source of it.'

'Yeah,' I said. 'That would be smarter. You're nice and frank about it.'

'To you,' Luders said, 'it naturally does not matter how frank I am.'

Barron leaned forward suddenly. 'Look here, Luders, killin' us ain't going to help you any. If you come right down to it, we don't have a thing on you. Likely you killed this man Weber, but the way things are up here, it's going to be mighty hard to prove it. If you been spreading bad money, they'll get you for it, sure, but that ain't a hangin' matter. Now I've got a couple pairs of handcuffs in my belt, so happens, and my proposition is you walk out of here with them on, you and your Japanese pal.'

Charlie the Jap said: 'Ha, ha. Very funny man. Some boob I guess yes.'

Luders smiled faintly. 'You put all the stuff in the car, Charlie?'

'One more suitcase coming right up,' Charlie said.

'Better take it on out, and start the engine, Charlie.'

'Listen, it won't work, Luders,' Barron said urgently. 'I got a man back in the woods with a deer rifle. It's bright moonlight. You got a fair weapon there, but you got no more chance against a deer rifle than Evans and me got against you. You'll never get out of here unless we go with you. He seen us come in here and how we come. He'll give us twenty minutes. Then he'll send for some boys to dynamite you out. Them were my orders.'

Luders said quietly: 'This work is very difficult. Even we Germans find it difficult. I am tired. I made a bad mistake. I used a man who was a fool, who did a foolish thing, and then he killed a man because he had done it and the man knew he had done it. But it was my mistake also. I shall not be forgiven. My life is no longer of great importance. Take the suitcase to the car, Charlie.'

Charlie moved swiftly toward him. 'Not liking, no,' he said sharply. 'That damn heavy suitcase. Man with rifle shooting. To hell.'

Luders smiled slowly. 'That's all a lot of nonsense, Charlie. If they had men with them, they would have been here long ago. That is why I let these men talk. To see if they were alone. They are alone. Go, Charlie.'

Charlie said hissingly: 'I going, but I still not liking.'

He went over to the corner and hefted the suitcase that stood there. He could hardly carry it. He moved slowly to the door and put the suitcase down and sighed. He opened the door a crack and looked out. 'Not see anybody,' he said. 'Maybe all lies, too.'

Luders said musingly: 'I should have killed the dog and the woman, too. I was weak. The man Kurt, what of him?'

'Never heard of him,' I said. 'Where was he?'

Luders stared at me. 'Get up on your feet, both of you.'

I got up. An icicle was crawling around on my back. Barron got up.

His face was gray. The whitening hair at the side of his head glistened with sweat. There was sweat all over his face, but his jaws went on chewing.

He said softly: 'How much you get for this job, son?'

I said thickly: 'A hundred bucks, but I spent some of it.'

Barron said in the same soft tone: 'I been married forty years. They pay me eighty dollars a month, house and firewood. It ain't enough. By gum, I ought to get a hundred.' He grinned wryly and spat and looked at Luders. 'To hell with you, you Nazi bastard,' he said.

Luders lifted the machine gun slowly and his lips drew back over his teeth. His breath made a hissing noise. Then very slowly he laid the gun down and reached inside his coat. He took out a Luger and moved the safety with his thumb. He shifted the gun to his left hand and stood looking at us quietly. Very slowly his face drained of all expression and became a dead gray mask. He lifted the gun, and at the same time he lifted his right arm stiffly above shoulder height. The arm was as rigid as a rod.

'Heil Hitler!' he said sharply.

He turned the gun quickly, put the muzzle in his mouth and fired.

The Jap screamed and streaked out of the door. Barron and I lunged hard across the table. We got our guns. Blood fell on the back of my hand and then Luders crumpled slowly against the wall.

Barron was already out of the door. When I got out behind him, I saw that the little Jap was running hard down the hill toward a clump of brush.

Barron steadied himself, brought the Colt up, then lowered it again.

'He ain't far enough,' he said. 'I always give a man forty yards.'

He raised the big Colt again and turned his body a little and, as the gun reached firing position, it moved very slowly and Barron's head went down a little until his arm and shoulder and right eye were all in a line.

He stayed like that, perfectly rigid for a long moment, then the gun roared and jumped back in his hand and a lean thread of smoke showed faint in the moonlight and disappeared.

The Jap kept on running. Barron lowered his Colt and watched him plunge into a clump of brush.

'Hell,' he said. 'I missed him.' He looked at me quickly and looked away again. 'But he won't get nowhere. Ain't got nothing to get with. Them little legs of his ain't hardly long enough to jump him over a pine cone.'

'He had a gun,' I said. 'Under his left arm.'

Barron shook his head. 'Nope. I noticed the holster was empty. I figured Luders got it away from him. I figure Luders meant to shoot him before he left.'

Car lights showed in the distance, coming dustily along the road.

'What made Luders go soft?'

'I figure his pride was hurt,' Barron said thoughtfully. 'A big organizer like him gettin' hisself all balled to hell by a couple of little fellows like us.'

We went around the end of the refrigerator car. A big new coupé was parked there. Barron marched over to it and opened the door. The car on the road was near now. It turned off and its headlights raked the big coupé. Barron stared into the car for a moment, then slammed the door viciously and spat on the ground.

'Caddy V-12,' he said. 'Red leather cushions and suitcases in the back.' He reached in again and snapped on the dashlight. 'What time is it?'

'Twelve minutes to two,' I said.

'This clock ain't no twelve and a half minutes slow,' Barron said angrily. 'You slipped on that.' He turned and faced me, pushing his hat back on his head. 'Hell, you seen it parked in front of the Indian Head,' he said.

'Right.'

'I thought you was just a smart guy.'

'Right,' I said.

'Son, next time I got to get almost shot, could you plan to be around?'

The car that was coming stopped a few yards away and a dog whined. Andy called out: 'Anybody hurt?'

Barron and I walked over to the car. The door opened and the little silky dog jumped out and rushed at Barron. She took off about four feet away and sailed through the air and planted her front paws hard against Barron's stomach, then dropped back to the ground and ran in circles.

Barron said: 'Luders shot hisself inside there. There's a little Jap down in the bushes we got to round up. And there's three, four suitcases full of counterfeit money we got to take care of.'

He looked off into the distance, a solid, heavy man like a rock. 'A night like this,' he said, 'and it's got to be full of death.'

ERLE STANLEY GARDNER (1889–1970)

The Case of the Irate Witness

THE early-morning shadows cast by the mountains still lay heavily on the town's main street as the big siren on the roof of the Jebson Commercial Company began to scream shrilly.

The danger of fire was always present, and at the sound, men at breakfast rose and pushed their chairs back from the table. Men who were shaving barely paused to wipe lather from their faces; men who had been sleeping grabbed the first available garments. All of them ran to places where they could look for the first telltale wisps of smoke.

There was no smoke.

The big siren was still screaming urgently as the men formed into streaming lines, like ants whose hill has been attacked. The lines all moved toward the Jebson Commercial Company.

There the men were told that the doors of the big vault had been found wide open. A jagged hole had been cut into one door with an acetylene torch.

The men looked at one another silently. This was the fifteenth of the month. The big, twice-a-month payroll, which had been brought up from the Ivanhoe National Bank the day before, had been the prize.

Frank Bernal, manager of the company's mine, the man who ruled Jebson City with an iron hand, arrived and took charge. The responsibility was his, and what he found was alarming.

Tom Munson, the night watchman, was lying on the floor in a back room, snoring in drunken slumber. The burglar alarm, which had been installed within the last six months, had been bypassed by means of an electrical device. This device was so ingenious that it was apparent that, if the work were that of a gang, at least one of the burglars was an expert electrician.

Ralph Nesbitt, the company accountant, was significantly silent. When Frank Bernal had been appointed manager a year earlier, Nesbitt had pointed out that the big vault was obsolete.

Bernal, determined to prove himself in his new job, had avoided the expense of tearing out the old vault and installing a new one by investing in an up-to-date burglar alarm and putting a special night watchman on duty.

Now the safe had been looted of $100,000 and Frank Bernal had to make a report to the main office in Chicago, with the disquieting knowledge that Ralph Nesbitt's memo stating that the antiquated vault was a pushover was at this moment reposing in the company files. . . .

Some distance out of Jebson City, Perry Mason, the famous trial lawyer, was driving fast along a mountain road. He had planned a weekend fishing trip for a long time, but a jury which had waited until midnight before reaching its verdict had delayed Mason's departure and it was now 8:30 in the morning.

His fishing clothes, rod, wading boots, and creel were all in the trunk. He was wearing the suit in which he had stepped from the courtroom, and having driven all night he was eager for the cool, piny mountains.

A blazing red light, shining directly at him as he rounded a turn in the canyon road, dazzled his road-weary eyes. A sign, *STOP— POLICE*, had been placed in the middle of the road. Two men, a grim-faced man with a .30–30 rifle in his hands and a silver badge on his shirt and a uniformed motor-cycle officer, stood beside the sign.

Mason stopped his car.

The man with the badge, deputy sheriff, said, 'We'd better take a look at your driving license. There's been a big robbery at Jebson City.'

'That so?' Mason said. 'I went through Jebson City an hour ago and everything seemed quiet.'

'Where you been since then?'

'I stopped at a little service station and restaurant for breakfast.'

'Let's take a look at your driving license.'

Mason handed it to him.

The man started to return it, then looked at it again, 'Say,' he said, 'you're Perry Mason, the big criminal lawyer!'

'Not a criminal lawyer,' Mason said patiently, 'a trial lawyer. I sometimes defend men who are accused of crime.'

'What are you doing up in this country?'

'Going fishing.'

The deputy looked at him suspiciously. 'Why aren't you wearing your fishing clothes?'

'Because,' Mason said, and smiled, 'I'm not fishing.'

'You said you were going fishing.'

'I also intend,' Mason said, 'to go to bed tonight. According to you, I should be wearing my pyjamas.'

The deputy frowned. The traffic officer laughed and waved Mason on.

The deputy nodded at the departing car. 'Looks like a live clue to me,' he said, 'but I can't find it in that conversation.'

'There isn't any,' the traffic officer said.

The deputy remained dubious, and later on, when a news-hungry reporter from the local paper asked the deputy if he knew of anything that would make a good story, the deputy said that he did.

And that was why Della Street, Perry Mason's confidential secretary, was surprised to read stories in the metropolitan papers stating that Perry Mason, the noted trial lawyer, was rumoured to have been retained to represent the person or persons who had looted the vault of the Jebson Commercial Company. All this had been arranged, it would seem, before Mason's 'client' had even been apprehended.

When Perry Mason called his office by long-distance the next afternoon, Della said, 'I thought you were going to the mountains for a vacation.'

'That's right. Why?'

'The papers claim you're representing whoever robbed the Jebson Commercial Company.'

'First I've heard of it,' Mason said. 'I went through Jebson City before they discovered the robbery, stopped for breakfast a little farther on, and then got caught in a road-block. In the eyes of some officious deputy, that seems to have made me an accessory after the fact.'

'Well,' Della Street said, 'they've caught a man by the name of Harvey L. Corbin, and apparently have quite a case against him. They're hinting at mysterious evidence which won't be disclosed until the time of trial.'

'Was he the one who committed the crime?' Mason asked.

'The police think so. He has a criminal record. When his employers at Jebson City found out about it, they told him to leave town. That was the evening before the robbery.'

'Just like that, eh?' Mason asked.

'Well, you see, Jebson City is a one-industry town, and the company owns all the houses. They're leased to the employees. I understand Corbin's wife and daughter were told they could stay on until Corbin got located in a new place, but Corbin was told to leave town at once. You aren't interested, are you?'

'Not in the least,' Mason said, 'except that when I drive back I'll be going through Jebson City, and I'll probably stop to pick up the local gossip.'

'Don't do it,' she warned. 'This man Corbin has all the earmarks of being an underdog, and you know how you feel about underdogs.'

A quality in her voice made Perry suspicious. 'You haven't been approached, have you, Della?'

'Well,' she said, 'in a way. Mrs Corbin read in the papers that you were going to represent her husband, and she was overjoyed. It seems that she thinks her husband's implication in this is a raw deal. She hadn't known anything about his criminal record, but she loves him and is going to stand by him.'

'You've talked with her?' Mason asked.

'Several times. I tried to break it to her gently. I told her it was probably nothing but a newspaper story. You see, Chief, they have Corbin dead to rights. They took some money from his wife as evidence. It was part of the loot.'

'And she has nothing?'

'Nothing. Corbin left her forty dollars, and they took it all as evidence.'

'I'll drive all night,' he said. 'Tell her I'll be back tomorrow.'

'I was afraid of that,' Della Street said. 'Why did you have to call up? Why couldn't you have stayed up there fishing? Why did you have to get your name in the papers?'

Mason laughed and hung up.

Paul Drake, of the Drake Detective Agency, came in and sat in the big chair in Mason's office and said, 'You have a bear by the tail, Perry.'

'What's the matter, Paul? Didn't your detective work in Jebson City pan out?'

'It panned out all right, but the stuff in the pan isn't what you want, Perry,' Drake explained.

'How come?'

'Your client's guilty.'

'Go on,' Mason said.

'The money he gave his wife was some of what was stolen from the vaults.'

'How do they know it was the stolen money?' Mason asked.

Drake pulled a notebook from his pocket. 'Here's the whole picture. The plant manager runs Jebson City. There isn't any private property. The Jebson company controls everything.'

'Not a single small business?'

Drake shook his head. 'Not unless you want to consider garbage collecting as small business. An old coot by the name of George Addey lives five miles down the canyon; he has a hog ranch and collects the garbage. He's supposed to have the first nickel he ever earned. Buries his money in cans. There's no bank nearer than Ivanhoe City.'

'What about the burglary? The men who did it must have moved in acetylene tanks and—'

'They took them right out of the company store,' Drake said. And then he went on: 'Munson, the watchman, likes to take a pull out of a flask of whiskey along about midnight. He says it keeps him awake. Of course, he's not supposed to do it, and no one was supposed to know about the whiskey, but someone did know about it. They doped the whiskey with a barbiturate. The watchman took his usual swig, went to sleep, and stayed asleep.'

'What's the evidence against Corbin?' Mason asked.

'Corbin had a previous burglary record. It's a policy of the company not to hire anyone with a criminal record. Corbin lied about his past and got a job. Frank Bernal, the manager, found out about it, sent for Corbin about 8 o'clock the night the burglary took place, and ordered him out of town. Bernal agreed to let Corbin's wife and child stay on in the house until Corbin could get located in another city. Corbin pulled out in the morning, and gave his wife this money. It was part of the money from the burglary.'

'How do they know?' Mason asked.

'Now there's something I don't know,' Drake said. 'This fellow Bernal is pretty smart, and the story is that he can prove Corbin's money was from the vault.'

Drake paused, then continued: 'The nearest bank is at Ivanhoe City, and the mine pays off in cash twice a month. Ralph Nesbitt, the cashier, wanted to install a new vault. Bernal refused to okay the expense. So the company has ordered both Bernal and Nesbitt back to its main office at Chicago to report. The rumor is that they may fire Bernal as manager and give Nesbitt the job. A couple of the directors don't like Bernal, and this thing has given them their chance. They dug out a report Nesbitt had made showing the vault was a pushover. Bernal didn't act on that report.' He signed and then asked, 'When's the trial, Perry?'

'The preliminary hearing is set for Friday morning. I'll see then what they've got against Corbin.'

'They're laying for you up there,' Paul Drake warned. 'Better watch out, Perry. That district attorney has something up his sleeve, some sort of surprise that's going to knock you for a loop.'

In spite of his long experience as a prosecutor, Vernon Flasher, the district attorney of Ivanhoe County, showed a certain nervousness at being called upon to oppose Perry Mason. There was, however, a secretive assurance underneath that nervousness.

Judge Haswell, realizing that the eyes of the community were upon him, adhered to legal technicalities to the point of being pompous both in rulings and mannerisms.

But what irritated Perry Mason was in the attitude of the spectators. He sensed that they did not regard him as an attorney trying to safeguard the interests of a client, but as a legal magician with a cloven hoof. The looting of the vault had shocked the community, and there was a tight-lipped determination that no legal tricks were going to do Mason any good *this* time.

Vernon Flasher didn't try to save his surprise evidence for a whirlwind finish. He used it right at the start of the case.

Frank Bernal, called as a witness, described the location of the vault, identified photographs, and then leaned back as the district attorney said abruptly, 'You had reason to believe this vault was obsolete?'

'Yes, sir.'

'It had been pointed out to you by one of your fellow employees, Mr Ralph Nesbitt?'

'Yes, sir.'

'And what did you do about it?'

'Are you,' Mason asked in some surprise, 'trying to cross-examine your own witness?'

'Just let him answer the question, and you'll see,' Flasher replied grimly.

'Go right ahead and answer,' Mason said to the witness.

Bernal assumed a more comfortable position. 'I did three things,' he said, 'to safeguard the payrolls and to avoid the expense of tearing out the old vault and installing a new vault in its place.'

'What were those three things?'

'I employed a special night watchman; I installed the best burglar alarm money could buy; and I made arrangements with the Ivanhoe National Bank, where we have our payrolls made up, to list the number of each twenty-dollar bill which was a part of each payroll.'

Mason suddenly sat up straight.

Flasher gave him a glance of gloating triumph. 'Do you wish the court to understand, Mr Bernal,' he said smugly, 'that you have the numbers of the bills in the payroll which was made up for delivery on the fifteenth?'

'Yes, sir. Not *all* the bills, you understand. That would have taken too much time, but I have the numbers of all the twenty-dollar bills.'

'And who recorded those numbers?' the prosecutor asked.

'The bank.'

'And do you have that list of numbers with you?'

'I do. Yes, sir.' Bernal produced a list. 'I felt,' he said, glancing coldly at Nesbitt, 'that these precautions would be cheaper than a new vault.'

'I move the list be introduced in evidence,' Flasher said.

'Just a moment,' Mason objected. 'I have a couple of questions. You say this list is not in your handwriting, Mr Bernal?'

'Yes, sir.'

'Whose handwriting is it, do you know?' Mason asked.

'The assistant cashier of the Ivanhoe National Bank.'

'Oh, all right,' Flasher said. 'We'll do it the hard way, if we have to. Stand down, Mr Bernal, and I'll call the assistant cashier.'

Harry Reedy, assistant cashier of the Ivanhoe Bank, had the mechanical assurance of an adding machine. He identified the list of numbers as being in his handwriting. He stated that he had listed the numbers of the twenty-dollar bills and put that list in an envelope which had been sealed and sent up with the money for the payroll.

'Cross-examine,' Flasher said.

Mason studied the list. 'These numbers are all in your handwriting?' he asked Reedy.

'Yes, sir.'

'Did you yourself compare the numbers you wrote down with the numbers on the twenty-dollar bills?'

'No, sir. I didn't personally do that. Two assistants did that. One checked the numbers as they were read off, one as I wrote them down.'

'The payrolls are for approximately a hundred thousand dollars, twice each month?'

'That's right. And ever since Mr Bernal took charge, we have taken this means to identify payrolls. No attempt is made to list the bills in numerical order. The serial numbers are simply read off and written down. Unless a robbery occurs, there is no need to do anything further. In the event of robbery, we can reclassify the numbers and list the bills in numerical order.'

'These numbers are in your handwriting—every number?'

'Yes, sir. More than that, you will notice that at the bottom of each page I have signed my initials.'

'That's all,' Mason said.

'I now offer once more to introduce this list in evidence,' Flasher said.

'So ordered,' Judge Haswell ruled.

'My next witness is Charles J. Oswald, the sheriff,' the district attorney announced.

The sheriff, a long, lanky man with a quiet manner, took the stand. 'You're acquainted with Harvey L. Corbin, the defendant in this case?' the district attorney asked.

'I am.'

'Are you acquainted with his wife?'

'Yes, sir.'

'Now, on the morning of the fifteenth of this month, the morning of the robbery at the Jebson Commercial Company, did you have any conversation with Mrs Corbin?'

'I did. Yes, sir.'

'Did you ask her about her husband's activities the night before?'

'Just a moment,' Mason said. 'I object to this on the ground that any conversation the sheriff had with Mrs Corbin is not admissible against the defendant, Corbin; furthermore, that in this state a wife cannot testify against her husband. Therefore, any statement she might make would be an indirect violation of that rule. Furthermore, I object on the ground that the question calls for hearsay.'

Judge Haswell looked ponderously thoughtful, then said, 'It seems to me Mr Mason is correct.'

'I'll put it this way, Mr Sheriff,' the district attorney said. 'Did you on the morning of the fifteenth, take any money from Mrs Corbin?'

'Objected to as incompetent, irrelevant, and immaterial,' Mason said.

'Your Honor,' Flasher said irritably, 'that's the very gist of our case. We propose to show that two of the stolen twenty-dollar bills were in the possession of Mrs Corbin.'

Mason said, 'Unless the prosecution can prove the bills were given Mrs Corbin by her husband, the evidence is inadmissible.'

'That's just the point,' Flasher said. 'Those bills *were* given to her by the defendant.'

'How do you know?' Mason asked.

'She told the sheriff so.'

'That's hearsay,' Mason snapped.

Judge Haswell fidgeted on the bench. 'It seems to me we're getting into a peculiar situation here. You can't call the wife as a witness, and I don't think her statement to the sheriff is admissible.'

'Well,' Flasher said desperately, 'in this state, Your Honor, we have a community-property law. Mrs Corbin had this money. Since she is the wife of the defendant, it was community property. Therefore, it's partially his property.'

'Well now, there,' Judge Haswell said, 'I think I can agree with you. You introduce the twenty-dollar bills. I'll overrule the objection made by the defense.'

'Produce the twenty-dollar bills, Sheriff,' Flasher said triumphantly.

The bills were produced and received in evidence.

'Cross-examine,' Flasher said curtly.

'No questions of this witness,' Mason said, 'but I have a few questions to ask Mr Bernal on cross-examination. You took him off the stand to lay the foundation for introducing the bank list, and I didn't have an opportunity to cross-examine him.'

'I beg your pardon,' Flasher said. 'Resume the stand, Mr Bernal.'

His tone, now that he had the twenty-dollar bills safely introduced in evidence, had a gloating note to it.

Mason said, 'This list which has been introduced in evidence is on the stationery of the Ivanhoe National Bank?'

'That's right. Yes, sir.'

'It consists of several pages, and at the end there is the signature of the assistant cashier?'

'Yes, sir.'

'This was the scheme which you thought of in order to safeguard the company against a payroll robbery?'

'Not to safeguard the company against a payroll robbery, Mr Mason, but to assist us in recovering the money in the event there was a hold-up.'

'This was your plan to answer Mr Nesbitt's objections that the vault was an outmoded model?'

'A part of my plan, yes. I may say that Mr Nesbitt's objections had never been voiced until I took office. I felt he was trying to embarrass me by making my administration show less net returns than expected.' Bernal tightened his lips and added, 'Mr Nesbitt had, I believe, been expecting to be appointed manager. He was disappointed. I believe he still expects to be manager.'

In the spectators' section of the courtroom, Ralph Nesbitt glared at Bernal.

'You had a conversation with the defendant on the night of the fourteenth?' Mason asked Bernal.

'I did. Yes, sir.'

'You told him that for reasons which you deemed sufficient you were discharging him immediately and wanted him to leave the premises at once?'

'Yes, sir. I did.'

'And you paid him his wages in cash?'

'Mr Nesbitt paid him in my presence, with money he took from the petty-cash drawer of the vault.'

'Now, as part of the wages due him wasn't Corbin given these two twenty-dollar bills which have been introduced in evidence?'

Bernal shook his head. 'I had thought of that,' he said, 'but it would have been impossible. Those bills weren't available to us at that time. The payroll is received from the bank in a sealed package. Those two twenty-dollar bills were in that package.'

'And the list of the numbers of the twenty-dollar bills?'

'That's in a sealed envelope. The money is placed in the vault. I lock the list of numbers in my desk.'

'Are you prepared to swear that neither you nor Mr Nesbitt had access to these two twenty-dollar bills on the night of the fourteenth?'

'That is correct.'

'That's all,' Mason said. 'No further cross-examination.'

'I now call Ralph Nesbitt to the stand,' District Attorney Flasher said. 'I want to fix the time of these events definitely, Your Honor.'

'Very well,' Judge Haswell said. 'Mr Nesbitt, come forward.'

Ralph Nesbitt, after answering the usual preliminary questions, sat down in the witness chair.

'Were you present at a conversation which took place between the defendant, Harvey L. Corbin, and Frank Bernal on the fourteenth of this month?' the district attorney asked.

'I was. Yes, sir.'

'What time did that conversation take place?'

'About 8 o'clock in the evening.'

'And, without going into the details of that conversation, I will ask you if the general effect of it was that the defendant was discharged and ordered to leave the company's property?'

'Yes, sir.'

'And he was paid the money that was due him?'

'In cash. Yes, sir. I took the cash from the safe myself.'

'Where was the payroll then?'

'In the sealed package in a compartment in the safe. As cashier, I had the only key to that compartment. Earlier in the afternoon I had gone to Ivanhoe City and received the sealed package of money and the envelope containing the list of numbers. I personally locked the package of money in the vault.'

'And the list of numbers?'

'Mr Bernal locked that in his desk.'

'Cross-examine,' Flasher said.

'No questions,' Mason said.

'That's our case, Your Honor,' Flasher observed.

'May we have a few minutes indulgence?' Mason asked Judge Haswell.

'Very well. Make it brief,' the judge agreed.

Mason turned to Paul Drake and Della Street. 'Well, there you are,' Drake said. 'You're confronted with the proof, Perry.'

'Are you going to put the defendant on the stand?' Della Street asked.

Mason shook his head. 'It would be suicidal. He has a record of a prior criminal conviction. Also, it's a rule of law that if one asks about any part of a conversation on direct examination, the other side can bring out all the conversation. That conversation, when Corbin was discharged, was to the effect that he had lied about his past record. And I guess there's no question that he did.'

'And he's lying now,' Drake said. 'This is one case where you're licked. I think you'd better cop a plea, and see what kind of a deal you can make with Flasher.'

'Probably not any,' Mason said. 'Flasher wants to have the reputation of having given me a licking—wait a minute, Paul. I have an idea.'

Mason turned abruptly, walked away to where he could stand by himself, his back to the crowded courtroom.

'Are you ready?' the judge asked.

Mason turned. 'I am quite ready, Your Honor. I have one witness whom I wish to put on the stand. I wish a subpoena *duces tecum* issued for that witness. I want him to bring certain documents which are in his possession.'

'Who is the witness, and what are the documents?' the judge asked.

Mason walked quickly over to Paul Drake. 'What's the name of that character who has the garbage-collecting business,' he said softly, 'the one who has the first nickel he'd ever made?'

'George Addey.'

The lawyer turned to the judge. 'The witness that I want is George Addey, and the documents that I want him to bring to court with him are all the twenty-dollar bills that he has received during the past sixty days.'

'Your Honor,' Flasher protested, 'this is an outrage. This is making a travesty out of justice. It is exposing the court to ridicule.'

Mason said, 'I give Your Honor my assurance that I think this witness is material, and that the documents are material. I will make an affidavit to that effect if necessary. As attorney for the defendant, may I point out that if the court refuses to grant this subpoena, it will be denying the defendant due process of law.'

'I'm going to issue the subpoena,' Judge Haswell said, testily, 'and for your own good, Mr Mason, the testimony had better be relevant.'

George Addey, unshaven and bristling with indignation, held up his right hand to be sworn. He glared at Perry Mason.

'Mr Addey,' Mason said, 'you have the contract to collect garbage from Jebson City?'

'I do.'

'How long have you been collecting garbage there?'

'For over five years, and I want to tell you—'

Judge Haswell banged his gavel. 'The witness will answer questions and not interpolate any comments.'

'I'll interpolate anything I dang please,' Addey said.

'That'll do,' the judge said. 'Do you wish to be jailed for contempt of court, Mr Addey?'

'I don't want to go to jail, but I—'

'Then you'll remember the respect that is due the court,' the judge said. 'Now you sit there and answer questions. This is a court of law. You're in this court as a citizen, and I'm here as a judge, and I propose to see that the respect due to the court is enforced.' There was a moment's silence while the judge glared angrily at the witness. 'All right, go ahead, Mr Mason,' Judge Haswell said.

Mason said, 'During the thirty days prior to the fifteenth of this month, did you deposit any money in any banking institution?'

'I did not.'

'Do you have with you all the twenty-dollar bills that you received during the last sixty days?'

'I have, and I think making me bring them here is just like inviting some crook to come and rob me and—'

Judge Haswell banged with his gavel. 'Any more comments of that sort from the witness and there will be a sentence imposed for contempt of court. Now you get out those twenty-dollar bills, Mr Addey, and put them right up here on the clerk's desk.'

Addey, mumbling under his breath, slammed a roll of twenty-dollar bills down on the desk in front of the clerk.

'Now,' Mason said, 'I'm going to need a little clerical assistance. I would like to have my secretary, Miss Street, and the clerk help me check through the numbers on these bills. I will select a few at random.'

Mason picked up three of the twenty-dollar bills and said, 'I am going to ask my assistants to check the list of numbers introduced in evidence. In my hand is a twenty-dollar bill that has the number L 07083274 A. Is that bill on the list? The next bill that I pick up is number L 07579190 A. Are any of those bills on the list?'

The courtroom was silent. Suddenly Della Street said, 'Yes, here's one that's on the list—bill number L 07579190 A. It's on the list, on page eight.'

'What?' the prosecutor shouted.

'Exactly,' Mason said, smiling. 'So, if a case is to be made against a person merely because he has possession of the money that was stolen on the fifteenth of this month, then your office should prefer charges against this witness, George Addey, Mr District Attorney.'

Addey jumped from the witness stand and shook his fist in Mason's face. 'You're a cockeyed liar!' he screamed. 'There ain't a one of those bills but what I didn't have it before the fifteenth. The company cashier changes my money into twenties, because I like big bills. I bury 'em in cans, and I put the date on the side of the can.'

'Here's the list,' Mason said. 'Check it for yourself.'

A tense silence gripped the courtroom as the judge and the spectators waited.

'I'm afraid I don't understand this, Mr Mason,' Judge Haswell said, after a moment.

'I think it's quite simple,' Mason said. 'And I now suggest the court take a recess for an hour and check these other bills against this list. I think the district attorney may be surprised.'

And Mason sat down and proceeded to put papers in his briefcase.

Della Street, Paul Drake, and Perry Mason were sitting in the lobby of the Ivanhoe Hotel.

'When are you going to tell us?' Della Street asked fiercely. 'Or do we tear you limb from limb? How could the garbage man have?—'

'Wait a minute,' Mason said. 'I think we're about to get results. Here comes the esteemed district attorney, Vernon Flasher, and he's accompanied by Judge Haswell.'

The two strode over to Mason's group and bowed with cold formality.

Mason got up.

Judge Haswell began in his best courtroom voice. 'A most deplorable situation has occurred. It seems that Mr Frank Bernal has—well—'

'Been detained somewhere,' Vernon Flasher said.

'Disappeared,' Judge Haswell said. 'He's gone.'

'I expected as much,' Mason said calmly.

'Now will you kindly tell me just what sort of pressure you brought to bear on Mr Bernal to—?'

'Just a moment, Judge,' Mason said. 'The only pressure I brought to bear on him was to cross-examine him.'

'Did you know that there had been a mistake made in the dates on those lists?'

'There was no mistake. When you find Bernal, I'm sure you will discover there was a deliberate falsification. He was short in his accounts, and he knew he was about to be demoted. He had a desperate need for a hundred thousand dollars in ready cash. He had evidently been planning this burglary, or, rather, this embezzlement, for some time. He learned that Corbin had a criminal record. He arranged to have these lists furnished by the bank. He installed a burglar alarm, and, naturally, knew how to circumvent it. He employed a watchman he knew was addicted to drink. He only needed to stage his coup at the right time. He fired Corbin and paid him off with bills that had been recorded by the bank on page eight of the list of bills *in the payroll on the first of the month.*

'Then he removed page eight from the list of bills contained in the payroll *of the fifteenth*, before he showed it to the police, and substituted page eight of the list for the *first of the month payroll*. It was just that simple.

'Then he drugged the watchman's whiskey, took an acetylene torch, burnt through the vault doors, and took all the money.'

'May I ask how you knew all this?' Judge Haswell demanded.

'Certainly,' Mason said. 'My client told me he received those bills from Nesbitt, who took them from the petty-cash drawer in the safe. He also told the sheriff that. I happened to be the only one who believed him. It sometimes pays, Your Honor, to have faith in a man, even if he has made a previous mistake. Assuming my client was innocent, I knew either Bernal or Nesbitt must be guilty. I then realized that only Bernal had custody of the *previous* lists of numbers.

'As an employee, Bernal had been paid on the first of the month. He looked at the numbers on the twenty-dollar bills in his pay envelope and found that they had been listed on page eight of the payroll for the first.

'Bernal only needed to abstract all twenty-dollar bills from the petty cash drawer, substitute twenty-dollar bills from his own pay envelope, call in Corbin, and fire him.

'His trap was set.

'I let him know I knew what had been done by bringing Addey into court and proving my point. Then I asked for a recess. That was so Bernal would have a chance to skip out. You see, flight may be received as evidence of guilt. It was a professional courtesy to the district attorney. It will help him when Bernal is arrested.'

AGATHA CHRISTIE (1890–1976)

The Adventure of the Egyptian Tomb

———

I HAVE always considered that one of the most thrilling and dramatic of the many adventures I have shared with Poirot was that of our investigation into the strange series of deaths which followed upon the discovery and opening of the Tomb of King Men-her-Ra.

Hard upon the discovery of the Tomb of Tutankh-Amen by Lord Carnarvon, Sir John Willard and Mr Bleibner of New York, pursuing their excavations not far from Cairo, in the vicinity of the Pyramids of Gizeh, came unexpectedly on a series of funeral chambers. The greatest interest was aroused by their discovery. The Tomb appeared to be that of King Men-her-Ra, one of those shadowy kings of the Eighth Dynasty, when the Old Kingdom was falling to decay. Little was known about this period, and the discoveries were fully reported in the newspapers.

An event soon occurred which took a profound hold on the public mind. Sir John Willard died quite suddenly of heart failure.

The more sensational newspapers immediately took the opportunity of reviving all the old superstitious stories connected with the ill-luck of certain Egyptian treasures. The unlucky Mummy at the British Museum, that hoary old chestnut, was dragged out with fresh zest, was quietly denied by the Museum, but nevertheless enjoyed all its usual vogue.

A fortnight later Mr Bleibner died of acute blood poisoning, and a few days afterwards a nephew of his shot himself in New York. The 'Curse of Men-her-Ra' was the talk of the day, and the magic power of dead-and-gone Egypt was exalted to a fetish point.

It was then that Poirot received a brief note from Lady Willard, widow of the dead archaeologist, asking him to go and see her at her house in Kensington Square. I accompanied him.

Lady Willard was a tall, thin woman, dressed in deep mourning. Her haggard face bore eloquent testimony to her recent grief.

'It is kind of you to have come so promptly, Monsieur Poirot.'

'I am at your service, Lady Willard. You wished to consult me?'

'You are, I am aware, a detective, but it is not only as a detective that I wish to consult you. You are a man of original views, I know, you have imagination, experience of the world. Tell me, Monsieur Poirot, what are your views on the supernatural?'

Poirot hesitated for a moment before he replied. He seemed to be considering. Finally he said:

'Let us not misunderstand each other, Lady Willard. It is not a general question that you are asking me there. It has a personal application, has it not? You are referring obliquely to the death of your late husband?'

'That is so,' she admitted.

'You want me to investigate the circumstances of his death?'

'I want you to ascertain for me exactly how much is newspaper chatter, and how much may be said to be founded on fact. Three deaths, Monsieur Poirot—each one explicable taken by itself, but taken together surely an almost unbelievable coincidence, and all within a month of the opening of the tomb! It may be mere superstition, it may be some potent curse from the past that operates in ways undreamed of by modern science. The fact remains—three deaths! And I am afraid, Monsieur Poirot, horribly afraid. It may not yet be the end.'

'For whom do you fear?'

'For my son. When the news of my husband's death came I was ill. My son, who has just come down from Oxford, went out there. He brought the—the body home, but now he has gone out again, in spite of my prayers and entreaties. He is so fascinated by the work that he intends to take his father's place and carry on the system of excavations. You may think me a foolish, credulous woman, but, Monsieur Poirot, I am afraid. Supposing that the spirit of the dead King is not yet appeased? Perhaps to you I seem to be talking nonsense——'

'No, indeed, Lady Willard,' said Poirot quickly. 'I, too, believe in the force of superstition, one of the greatest forces the world has ever known.'

I looked at him in surprise. I should never have credited Poirot with being superstitious. But the little man was obviously in earnest.

'What you really demand is that I shall protect your son? I will do my utmost to keep him from harm.'

'Yes, in the ordinary way, but against an occult influence?'

'In volumes of the Middle Ages, Lady Willard, you will find many ways of counteracting black magic. Perhaps they knew more than we moderns with all our boasted science. Now let us come to facts, that I may have guidance. Your husband had always been a devoted Egyptologist, hadn't he?'

'Yes, from his youth upwards. He was one of the greatest living authorities upon the subject.'

'But Mr Bleibner, I understand, was more or less of an amateur?'

'Oh, quite. He was a very wealthy man who dabbled freely in any subject that happened to take his fancy. My husband managed to interest him in Egyptology, and it was his money that was so useful in financing the expedition.'

'And the nephew? What do you know of his tastes? Was he with the party at all?'

'I do not think so. In fact, I never knew of his existence till I read of his death in the paper. I do not think he and Mr Bleibner can have been at all intimate. He never spoke of having any relations.'

'Who are the other members of the party?'

'Well, there is Dr Tosswill, a minor official connected with the British Museum; Mr Schneider of the Metropolitan Museum in New York; a young American secretary; Dr Ames, who accompanies the expedition in his professional capacity; and Hassan, my husband's devoted native servant.'

'Do you remember the name of the American secretary?'

'Harper, I think, but I cannot be sure. He had not been with Mr Bleibner very long, I know. He was a very pleasant young fellow.'

'Thank you, Lady Willard.'

'If there is anything else——?'

'For the moment, nothing. Leave it now in my hands, and be assured that I will do all that is humanly possible to protect your son.'

They were not exactly reassuring words, and I observed Lady Willard wince as he uttered them. Yet, at the same time, the fact that he had not pooh-poohed her fears seemed in itself to be a relief to her.

For my part I had never before suspected that Poirot had so deep a vein of superstition in his nature. I tackled him on the subject as we went homewards. His manner was grave and earnest.

'But yes, Hastings. I believe in these things. You must not under-rate the force of superstition.'

'What are we going to do about it?'

'*Toujours pratique*, the good Hastings! *Eh bien*, to begin with we are going to cable to New York for fuller details of young Mr Bleibner's death.'

He duly sent off his cable. The reply was full and precise. Young Rupert Bleibner had been in low water for several years. He had been a beach-comber and a remittance man in several South Sea islands, but had returned to New York two years before, where he had rapidly sunk lower and lower. The most significant thing, to my mind, was that he had recently managed to borrow enough money to take him to Egypt. 'I've a good friend there I can borrow from,' he had declared. Here, however, his plans had gone awry. He had returned to New York cursing his skinflint of an uncle who cared more for the bones of dead-and-gone kings than his own flesh and blood. It was during his sojourn in Egypt that the death of Sir John Willard occurred. Rupert had plunged once more into his life of dissipation in New York, and then, without warning, he had committed suicide, leaving behind him a letter which contained some curious phrases. It seemed written in a sudden fit of remorse. He referred to himself as a leper and an outcast, and the letter ended by declaring that such as he were better dead.

A shadowy theory leapt into my brain. I had never really believed in the vengeance of a long-dead Egyptian king. I saw here a more modern crime. Supposing this young man had decided to do away with his uncle—preferably by poison. By mistake, Sir John Willard receives the fatal dose. The young man returns to New York, haunted by his crime. The news of his uncle's death reaches him. He realises how unnecessary his crime has been, and stricken with remorse takes his own life.

I outlined my solution to Poirot. He was interested.

'It is ingenious what you have thought of there—decidedly it is ingenious. It may even be true. But you leave out of count the fatal influence of the Tomb.'

I shrugged my shoulders.

'You still think that has something to do with it?'

'So much so, *mon ami*, that we start for Egypt to-morrow.'

'What?' I cried, astonished.

'I have said it.' An expression of conscious heroism spread over Poirot's face. Then he groaned. 'But, oh,' he lamented, 'the sea! The hateful sea!'

*

It was a week later. Beneath our feet was the golden sand of the desert. The hot sun poured down overhead. Poirot, the picture of misery, wilted by my side. The little man was not a good traveller. Our four days' voyage from Marseilles had been one long agony to him. He had landed at Alexandria the wraith of his former self; even his usual neatness had deserted him. We had arrived in Cairo and had driven out at once to the Mena House Hotel, right in the shadow of the Pyramids.

The charm of Egypt had laid hold of me. Not so Poirot. Dressed precisely the same as in London, he carried a small clothes-brush in his pocket and waged an unceasing war on the dust which accumulated on his dark apparel.

'And my boots,' he wailed. 'Regard them, Hastings. My boots, of the neat patent leather, usually so smart and shining. See, the sand is inside them, which is painful, and outside them, which outrages the eyesight. Also the heat, it causes my moustaches to become limp— but limp!'

'Look at the Sphinx,' I urged. 'Even I can feel the mystery and the charm it exhales.'

Poirot looked at it discontentedly.

'It has not the air happy,' he declared. 'How could it, half-buried in sand in that untidy fashion. Ah, this cursed sand!'

'Come, now, there's a lot of sand in Belgium,' I reminded him, mindful of a holiday spent at Knocke-sur-mer in the midst of '*les dunes impeccables*,' as the guide-book had phrased it.

'Not in Brussels,' declared Poirot. He gazed at the Pyramids thoughtfully. 'It is true that they, at least, are of a shape solid and geometrical, but their surface is of an unevenness most unpleasing. And the palm-trees I like them not. Not even do they plant them in rows!'

I cut short his lamentations, by suggesting that we should start for the camp. We were to ride there on camels, and the beasts were patiently kneeling, waiting for us to mount, in charge of several picturesque boys headed by a voluble dragoman.

I pass over the spectacle of Poirot on a camel. He started by groans and lamentations and ended by shrieks, gesticulations and invocations to the Virgin Mary and every Saint in the calendar. In the end, he descended ignominiously and finished the journey on a diminutive donkey. I must admit that a trotting camel is no joke for the amateur. I was stiff for several days.

At last we neared the scene of the excavations. A sunburnt man with a grey beard, in white clothes and wearing a helmet, came to meet us.

'Monsieur Poirot and Captain Hastings? We received your cable. I'm sorry that there was no one to meet you in Cairo. An unforeseen event occurred which completely disorganised our plans.'

Poirot paled. His hand, which had stolen to his clothes-brush, stayed its course.

'Not another death?' he breathed.

'Yes.'

'Sir Guy Willard?' I cried.

'No, Captain Hastings. My American colleague, Mr Schneider.'

'And the cause?' demanded Poirot.

'Tetanus.'

I blanched. All around me I seemed to feel an atmosphere of evil, subtle and menacing. A horrible thought flashed across me. Supposing I were the next?

'*Mon Dieu,*' said Poirot, in a very low voice, 'I do not understand this. It is horrible. Tell me, monsieur, there is no doubt that it was tetanus?'

'I believe not. But Dr Ames will tell you more than I can do.'

'Ah, of course, you are not the doctor.'

'My name is Tosswill.'

This, then, was the British expert described by Lady Willard as being a minor official at the British Museum. There was something at once grave and steadfast about him that took my fancy.

'If you will come with me,' continued Dr Tosswill, 'I will take you to Sir Guy Willard. He was most anxious to be informed as soon as you should arrive.'

We were taken across the camp to a large tent. Dr Tosswill lifted up the flap and we entered. Three men were sitting inside.

'Monsieur Poirot and Captain Hastings have arrived, Sir Guy,' said Tosswill.

The youngest of the three men jumped up and came forward to greet us. There was a certain impulsiveness in his manner which reminded me of his mother. He was not nearly so sunburnt as the others, and that fact, coupled with a certain haggardness round the eyes, made him look older than his twenty-two years. He was clearly endeavouring to bear up under a severe mental strain.

He introduced his two companions, Dr Ames, a capable-looking man of thirty odd, with a touch of greying hair at the temples, and Mr Harper, the secretary, a pleasant, lean young man wearing the national insignia of horn-rimmed spectacles.

After a few minutes' desultory conversation, the latter went out, and Dr Tosswill followed him. We were left alone with Sir Guy and Dr Ames.

'Please ask any questions you want to ask, Monsieur Poirot,' said Willard. 'We are utterly dumbfounded at this strange series of disasters, but it isn't—it can't be, anything but coincidence.'

There was a nervousness about his manner which rather belied the words. I saw that Poirot was studying him keenly.

'Your heart is really in this work, Sir Guy?'

'Rather. No matter what happens, or what comes of it, the work is going on. Make up your mind to that.'

Poirot wheeled round on the other.

'What have you to say to that, *monsieur le docteur*?'

'Well,' drawled the doctor, 'I'm not for quitting myself.'

Poirot made one of those expressive grimaces of his.

'Then, *évidemment*, we must find out just how we stand. When did Mr Schneider's death take place?'

'Three days ago.'

'You are sure it was tetanus?'

'Dead sure.'

'It couldn't have been a case of strychnine poisoning, for instance?'

'No, Monsieur Poirot. I see what you're getting at. But it was a clear case of tetanus.'

'Did you not inject anti-serum?'

'Certainly we did,' said the doctor dryly. 'Every conceivable thing that could be done was tried.'

'Had you the anti-serum with you?'

'No. We procured it from Cairo.'

'Have there been any other cases of tetanus in the camp?'

'No, not one.'

'Are you certain that the death of Mr Bleibner was not due to tetanus?'

'Absolutely plumb certain. He had a scratch upon his thumb which became poisoned, and septicaemia set in. It sounds pretty much the same to a layman, I dare say, but the two things are entirely different.'

'Then we have four deaths—all totally dissimilar, one heart failure, one blood poisoning, one suicide and one tetanus.'

'Exactly, Monsieur Poirot.'

'Are you certain that there is nothing which might link the four together?'

'I don't quite understand you?'

'I will put it plainly. Was any act committed by those four men which might seem to denote disrespect to the spirit of Men-her-Ra?'

The doctor gazed at Poirot in astonishment.

'You're talking through your hat, Monsieur Poirot. Surely you've not been guyed into believing all that fool talk?'

'Absolute nonsense,' muttered Willard angrily.

Poirot remained placidly immovable, blinking a little out of his green cat's eyes.

'So you do not believe it, *monsieur le docteur*?'

'No, sir, I do not,' declared the doctor emphatically. 'I am a scientific man, and I believe only what science teaches.'

'Was there no science, then, in Ancient Egypt?' asked Poirot softly. He did not wait for a reply, and indeed Dr Ames seemed rather at a loss for the moment. 'No, no, do not answer me, but tell me this. What do the native workmen think?'

'I guess,' said Dr Ames, 'that, where white folk lose their heads, natives aren't going to be far behind. I'll admit that they're getting what you might call scared—but they've no cause to be.'

'I wonder,' said Poirot non-committally.

Sir Guy leant forward.

'Surely,' he cried incredulously, 'you cannot believe in—oh, but the thing's absurd! You can know nothing of Ancient Egypt if you think that.'

For answer Poirot produced a little book from his pocket—an ancient tattered volume. As he held it out I saw its title, *The Magic of the Egyptians and Chaldeans*. Then, wheeling round, he strode out of the tent. The doctor stared at me.

'What is his little idea?'

The phrase, so familiar on Poirot's lips, made me smile as it came from another.

'I don't know exactly,' I confessed. 'He's got some plan of exorcising the evil spirits, I believe.'

I went in search of Poirot, and found him talking to the lean-faced young man who had been the late Mr Bleibner's secretary.

'No,' Mr Harper was saying, 'I've only been six months with the expedition. Yes, I knew Mr Bleibner's affairs pretty well.'

'Can you recount to me anything concerning his nephew?'

'He turned up here one day, not a bad-looking fellow. I'd never met him before, but some of the others had—Ames, I think, and Schneider. The old man wasn't at all pleased to see him. They were at it in no time, hammer and tongs. "Not a cent," the old man shouted. "Not one cent now or when I'm dead. I intend to leave my money to the furtherance of my life's work. I've been talking it over with Mr Schneider to-day." And a bit more of the same. Young Bleibner lit out for Cairo right away.'

'Was he in perfectly good health at the time?'

'The old man?'

'No, the young one.'

'I believe he did mention there was something wrong with him. But it couldn't have been anything serious, or I should have remembered.'

'One thing more, has Mr Bleibner left a will?'

'So far as we know, he has not.'

'Are you remaining with the expedition, Mr Harper?'

'No, sir, I am not. I'm for New York as soon as I can square up things here. You may laugh if you like, but I'm not going to be this blasted old Men-her-Ra's next victim. He'll get me if I stop here.'

The young man wiped the perspiration from his brow.

Poirot turned away. Over his shoulder he said with a peculiar smile:

'Remember, he got one of his victims in New York.'

'Oh, hell!' said Mr Harper forcibly.

'That young man is nervous,' said Poirot thoughtfully. 'He is on the edge, but absolutely on the edge.'

I glanced at Poirot curiously, but his enigmatical smile told me nothing. In company with Sir Guy Willard and Dr Tosswill we were taken round the excavations. The principal finds had been removed to Cairo, but some of the tomb furniture was extremely interesting. The enthusiasm of the young baronet was obvious, but I fancied that I detected a shade of nervousness in his manner as though he could not quite escape from the feeling of menace in the air. As we entered the tent which had been assigned to us, for a wash before joining the evening meal, a tall dark figure in white robes stood aside to let us pass with a graceful gesture and a murmured greeting in Arabic. Poirot stopped.

'You are Hassan, the late Sir John Willard's servant?'

'I served my Lord Sir John, now I serve his son.' He took a step nearer to us and lowered his voice. 'You are a wise one, they say, learned in dealing with evil spirits. Let the young master depart from here. There is evil in the air around us.'

And with an abrupt gesture, not waiting for a reply, he strode away.

'Evil in the air,' muttered Poirot. 'Yes, I feel it.'

Our meal was hardly a cheerful one. The floor was left to Dr Tosswill, who discoursed at length upon Egyptian antiquities. Just as we were preparing to retire to rest, Sir Guy caught Poirot by the arm and pointed. A shadowy figure was moving amidst the tents. It was no human one: I recognised distinctly the dog-headed figure I had seen carved on the walls of the tomb.

My blood literally froze at the sight.

'*Mon Dieu!*' murmured Poirot, crossing himself vigorously. 'Anubis, the jackal-headed, the god of departing souls.'

'Someone is hoaxing us,' cried Dr Tosswill, rising indignantly to his feet.

'It went into your tent, Harper,' muttered Sir Guy, his face dreadfully pale.

'No,' said Poirot, shaking his head, 'into that of the Dr Ames.'

The doctor stared at him incredulously; then, repeating Dr Tosswill's words, he cried:

'Someone is hoaxing us. Come, we'll soon catch the fellow.'

He dashed energetically in pursuit of the shadowy apparition. I followed him, but, search as we would, we could find no trace of any living soul having passed that way. We returned, somewhat disturbed in mind, to find Poirot taking energetic measures, in his own way, to ensure his personal safety. He was busily surrounding our tent with various diagrams and inscriptions which he was drawing in the sand. I recognised the five-pointed star or Pentagon many times repeated. As was his wont, Poirot was at the same time delivering an impromptu lecture on witchcraft and magic in general, White Magic as opposed to Black, with various references to the Ka and the Book of the Dead thrown in.

It appeared to excite the liveliest contempt in Dr Tosswill, who drew me aside, literally snorting with rage.

'Balderdash, sir,' he exclaimed angrily. 'Pure balderdash. The man's an impostor. He doesn't know the difference between the superstitions of the Middle Ages and the beliefs of Ancient Egypt. Never have I heard such a hotch-potch of ignorance and credulity.'

I calmed the excited expert and joined Poirot in the tent. My little friend was beaming cheerfully.

'We can now sleep in peace,' he declared happily. 'And I can do with some sleep. My head, it aches abominably. Ah, for a good *tisane!*'

As though in answer to prayer, the flap of the tent was lifted and Hassan appeared, bearing a steaming cup which he offered to Poirot. It proved to be camomile tea, a beverage of which he is inordinately fond. Having thanked Hassan and refused his offer of another cup for myself, we were left alone once more. I stood at the door of the tent some time after undressing, looking out over the desert.

'A wonderful place,' I said aloud, 'and a wonderful work. I can feel the fascination. This desert life, this probing into the heart of a vanished civilisation. Surely, Poirot, you, too, must feel the charm?'

I got no answer, and I turned, a little annoyed. My annoyance was quickly changed to concern. Poirot was lying back across the rude couch, his face horribly convulsed. Beside him was the empty cup. I rushed to his side, then dashed out and across the camp to Dr Ames's tent.

'Dr Ames!' I cried. 'Come at once.'

'What's the matter?' said the doctor, appearing in pyjamas.

'My friend. He's ill. Dying. The camomile tea. Don't let Hassan leave the camp.'

Like a flash the doctor ran to our tent. Poirot was lying as I left him.

'Extraordinary,' cried Ames. 'Looks like a seizure—or—what did you say about something he drank?' He picked up the empty cup.

'Only I did not drink it!' said a placid voice.

We turned in amazement. Poirot was sitting up on the bed. He was smiling.

'No,' he said gently. 'I did not drink it. While my good friend Hastings was apostrophising the night, I took the opportunity of pouring it, not down my throat, but into a little bottle. That little bottle will go to the analytical chemist. No'—as the doctor made a sudden movement—'as a sensible man, you will understand that violence will be of no avail. During Hastings' brief absence to fetch you, I have had time to put the bottle in safe keeping. Ah, quick, Hastings, hold him!'

I misunderstood Poirot's anxiety. Eager to save my friend, I flung myself in front of him. But the doctor's swift movement had another meaning. His hand went to his mouth, a smell of bitter almonds filled the air, and he swayed forward and fell.

'Another victim,' said Poirot gravely, 'but the last. Perhaps it is the best way. He has three deaths on his head.'

'Dr Ames?' I cried, stupefied. 'But I thought you believed in some occult influence?'

'You misunderstood me, Hastings. What I meant was that I believe in the terrible force of superstition. Once get it firmly established that a series of deaths are supernatural, and you might almost stab a man in broad daylight, and it would still be put down to the curse, so strongly is the instinct of the supernatural implanted in the human race. I suspected from the first that a man was taking advantage of that instinct. The idea came to him, I imagine, with the death of Sir John Willard. A fury of superstition arose at once. As far as I could see, nobody could derive any particular profit from Sir John's death. Mr Bleibner was a different case. He was a man of great wealth. The information I received from New York contained several suggestive points. To begin with, young Bleibner was reported to have said he had a good friend in Egypt from whom he could borrow. It was tacitly understood that he meant his uncle, but it seemed to me that in that case he would have said so outright. The words suggest some boon companion of his own. Another thing, he scraped up enough money to take him to Egypt, his uncle refused outright to advance him a penny, yet he was able to pay the return passage to New York. Someone must have lent him the money.'

'All that was very thin,' I objected.

'But there was more. Hastings, there occur often enough words spoken metaphorically which are taken literally. The opposite can happen too. In this case, words which were meant literally were taken metaphorically. Young Bleibner wrote plainly enough: "I am a leper," but nobody realised that he shot himself because he believed that he had contracted the dread disease of leprosy.'

'What?' I ejaculated.

'It was the clever invention of a diabolical mind. Young Bleibner was suffering from some minor skin trouble, he had lived in the South Sea Islands, where the disease is common enough. Ames was a former friend of his, and a well-known medical man; he would never dream of doubting his word. When I arrived here, my suspicions were divided between Harper and Dr Ames, but I soon realised that only the doctor could have perpetrated and concealed the crimes, and I learnt from Harper that he was previously acquainted with young Bleibner. Doubtless the latter at some time or another had made a will or had insured his life in favour of the doctor. The latter saw his chance of acquiring wealth. It was easy for him to inoculate Mr Bleibner with the deadly germs. Then the nephew, overcome with despair at the dread news his friend had conveyed to him, shot himself. Mr Bleibner, whatever his intentions, had made no will. His fortune would pass to his nephew and from him to the doctor.'

'And Mr Schneider?'

'We cannot be sure. He knew young Bleibner too, remember, and may have suspected something, or, again, the doctor may have thought that a further death motiveless and purposeless would strengthen the coils of superstition. Furthermore, I will tell you an interesting psychological fact, Hastings. A murderer has always a strong desire to repeat his successful crime, the performance of it grows upon him. Hence my fears for young Willard. The figure of Anubis you saw to-night was Hassan, dressed up by my orders. I wanted to see if I could frighten the doctor. But it would take more than the supernatural to frighten him. I could see that he was not entirely taken in by my pretences of belief in the occult. The little comedy I played for him did not deceive him. I suspected that he would endeavour to make me the next victim. Ah, but in spite of *la mer maudite*, the heat abominable, and the annoyances of the sand, the little grey cells still functioned!'

Poirot proved to be perfectly right in his premises. Young Bleibner, some years ago, in a fit of drunken merriment, had made a jocular will, leaving 'my cigarette case you admire so much and everything else of which I die possessed which will be principally debts to my good friend Robert Ames who once saved my life from drowning.'

The case was hushed up as far as possible, and, to this day, people talk of the remarkable series of deaths in connection with the Tomb of Men-her-Ra as a triumphal proof of the vengeance of a bygone king upon the desecrators of his tomb—a belief which, as Poirot pointed out to me, is contrary to all Egyptian belief and thought.

DASHIELL HAMMETT (1894–1961)

Death & Company

———

THE Old Man, meaning the head of the Continental Detective Agency, introduced me to the other man in his office—his name was Chappell—and said, 'Sit down.'

Chappell was forty-five or so, idly built and dark-complexioned but shaky and washed out by worry or grief or fear. I noticed his eyes were red rimmed and their lids sagged, as did his lower lip. His hand, when I shook it, had been flabby and damp.

The Old Man picked up a piece of paper from his desk and held it out to me. I took it. It was a letter crudely printed in ink, all capital letters:

MARTIN CHAPPELL,

DEAR SIR,—If you ever want to see your wife alive again you will do just what you are told and that is to go to the lot at George and Larkin St. at exactly 12 to-night and put $5,000 in $100 bills under the pile of bricks behind the billboard. If you do not do this or if you go to the police or if you try any tricks you will get a letter to-morrow telling you where to find her corpse. We mean business. DEATH & CO.

I put the letter back on the Old Man's desk.

He said, 'Mrs Chappell went to a matinée yesterday afternoon. She never returned home. Mr Chappell received this in the mail this morning.'

'She go alone?' I asked.

'I don't know,' Chappell said. His voice was very tired. 'She told me she was going when I left for the office in the morning, but she didn't say which show she was going to or if she was going with anybody.'

'Who'd she usually go with?'

He shook his head hopelessly. 'I can give you the names and addresses of all her closest friends, but I'm afraid that won't help.

When she hadn't come home late last night, I telephoned everybody I could think of.'

'Any idea who could have done this?' I asked.

Again he shook his head hopelessly.

'I've tried to think of anybody I know or ever knew who might have done it, but I can't.'

'What business are you in?'

He replied, 'I've a manufacturers' agency.'

'How about discharged employees?'

'No, the only one I've ever discharged has a better job now with one of my competitors and we're on perfectly good terms.'

I cleared my throat and said to Chappell, 'Look here, I want to ask some questions that you'll probably think—well—brutal, but they're necessary.'

He winced and took a deep breath.

'I've never had any reason to believe that she went anywhere that she didn't tell me about or had any friends she didn't tell me about. Is that'—his voice was pleading—'what you wanted to know?'

'Yes, thanks.' I turned to the Old Man again. The only way to get anything out of him was to ask for it, so I said, 'Well?'

He smiled courteously like a well-satisfied blank wall, and murmured, 'What do you advise?'

'Pay the money, of course—first,' I replied, and then asked Chappell, 'You can manage the money?'

'Yes.'

I addressed the Old Man. 'Now, about the police?'

Chappell began, 'No, not the police! Won't they——?'

I interrupted him. 'We've got to tell them, in case something goes wrong and to have them all set for action as soon as Mrs Chappell is safely home again. We can persuade them to keep their hands off till then.'

The Old Man nodded and reached for his telephone.

Fielding and an assistant district attorney named McPhee came up. At first they were all for making the George-and-Larkin-Street brick-pile a midnight target for half the police force, but we finally persuaded them to listen to reason. We waved the history of kidnapping from the days of Charlie Ross to the present in their faces and showed them that the statistics were on our side: more success and less grief had come from paying what was asked and going hunting afterward than from trying to nail the kidnappers before the kidnapped were released. At eleven-thirty that night Chappell left his house, alone, with $5,000 wrapped in a sheet of brown paper in his pocket. At twelve-twenty he returned.

His face was yellowish and wet with perspiration and he was trembling.

'I put it there,' he said with difficulty.

I poured out a glass of his whisky and gave it to him.

He walked the floor most of the night. I dozed on a sofa. Half a dozen times at least I heard him go to the street door to open it and look out. Detective-sergeants Muir and Callahan went to bed. They and I had planted ourselves there to get any information Mrs Chappell could give us as soon as possible.

At nine in the morning Callahan was called to the telephone. He came away from it scowling.

'Nobody's come for the dough yet,' he told us.

Chappell's drawn face became wide-eyed and open-mouthed with horror. 'You had the place watched?'

'Sure,' Callahan said, 'but in an all right way. We just had a couple of men stuck up in an apartment down the block with field-glasses. Nobody could tumble to that.'

Chappell turned to me, horror deepening in his face. 'What——?'

The doorbell rang.

Chappell ran to the door and presently came back excitedly tearing a special-delivery-stamped envelope open. Inside was another crudely printed letter:

MARTIN CHAPPELL:

DEAR SIR,—We got the money all right but have got to have more tonight the same amount at the same time and everything else the same. This time we will honestly send your wife home alive if you do as you are told. If you do not or say a word to the police you know what to expect and you bet you will get it. DEATH & Co.

Callahan said, 'What the hell?'

Muir growled, 'Them—at the window must be blind.'

I asked Chappell, 'Well, what are you going to do?'

He swallowed and said, 'I'll give them every cent I've got if it will being Louise home safe.'

At eleven-thirty that night Chappell left his house with $5,000. When he returned the first thing he said was, 'The money I took last night is really gone.'

This night was much like the previous one. Nobody said so, but all of us expected another in the morning asking for still another $5,000.

Another special-delivery letter did come, but it read:

MARTIN CHAPPELL:

DEAR SIR,—We warned you to keep the police out of it and you disobeyed. Take your police to Apt. 313 at 895 Park St. and you will find the corpse we promised you if you disobeyed. DEATH & Co.

Callahan cursed and jumped for the telephone.

I put an arm around Chappell as he swayed, but he shook himself together and turned fiercely on me:

'You've killed her!' he cried.

'Stow that,' Muir barked. 'Let's get going.'

The Park Street address was only a ten-minute ride from Chappell's house the way we did it. It took a couple of minutes more to find the manager of the apartment house and take the keys away from him.

A tall, slender woman with curly red hair lay on the living-room floor in 313. She had been dead long enough for discolouration to have got well under way. She was lying on her back. The tan flannel bathrobe—apparently a man's—she had on had fallen open to show pinkish lingerie. She had on stockings and one slipper. The other slipper lay near her.

Her face and throat and what was visible of her body were covered with bruises. Her eyes were wide open and bulging, her tongue out; she had been beaten and then throttled.

More police detectives joined us and some policemen in uniform. We went into our routine.

The manager of the house told us the apartment had been occupied by a man named Harrison M. Rockfield. He described him: about 35 years old, six feet tall, blond hair, grey or blue eyes, slender, perhaps 160 pounds, very agreeable personality, dressed well. He said Rockfield had been living there alone for three months. He knew nothing about his friends, he said, and had not seen Mrs Chappell before. He had not seen Rockfield for two or three days but had thought nothing of it as he often went a week or so without seeing some tenants.

The police department experts found a lot of masculine fingerprints that we hoped were Rockfield's.

We couldn't find anybody in adjoining apartments who had heard the racket that must have been made by the murderer.

We decided that Mrs Chappell had probably been killed as soon as she was brought to the apartment—no later than the night of her disappearance, anyhow.

A detective came in with the package of hundred-dollar bills Chappell had placed under the brickpile the previous night.

I went down to headquarters with Callahan to question the men stationed at a near-by apartment window to watch the vacant lot. They swore up and down that nobody—'not as much as a rat'—could have approached the brickpile without being seen by them.

I was called to the telephone. Chappell was on the wire. His voice was hoarse.

'The telephone was ringing when I got home,' he said, 'and it was him.'

'Who?'

'Death & Co.,' he said. 'That's what he said, and he told me that it was my turn next. That's all he said. "This is Death & Co., and it's your turn next."'

'I'll be right out,' I said. 'Wait for me.'

Chappell was in a bad way when I arrived at his house. He was shivering as if with a chill and his eyes were almost idiotic in their fright.

'It's, it's not only that—that I'm afraid,' he tried to explain. 'I'm—but it's—I'm not that afraid but—but with Louise—and—it's the shock and all. I——'

'I know,' I soothed him. 'I know. And you haven't slept for a couple of days. Who's your doctor? I'm going to phone him.'

He protested feebly, but finally gave me his doctor's name. The telephone rang as I was going toward it. The call was for me, from Callahan.

'We've pegged the fingerprints,' he said triumphantly. 'They're Dick Moley's. Know him?'

'Sure,' I said, 'as well as you do.'

Moley was a gambler, gunman, and grifter-in-general with a police record as long as his arm.

Callahan was saying cheerfully. 'That's going to be a mean fight when we find him. And he'll laugh while he's being tough.'

'I know,' I said.

I told Chappell what Callahan had told me. Rage came into his face and voice when he heard the name of the man accused of killing his wife.

'Ever heard of him?' I asked.

He shook his head and went on cursing Moley.

I said, 'I know where to find Moley.'

His eyes opened wide. 'Where?' he gasped.

'Want to go with me?'

'Do I?' he shouted. Weariness and sickness had dropped from him.

He asked a lot of questions as we went out and got into his car. I answered most of them with, 'Wait, you'll see.'

'I can't,' he mumbled. 'I've got to—help me into the house—the doctor.'

I spread him on a sofa, brought him water, and called his doctor's number. The doctor was not in.

When I asked if there was any other particular doctor he wanted he said weakly, 'No, I'm all right. Go after that—that man.'

'All right,' I said.

I went outside, got a taxicab, and sat in it.

Twenty minutes later a man went up Chappell's front steps and rang the bell. The man was Dick Moley, alias Harrison M. Rockfield.

He took me by surprise. I had been expecting Chappell to come out, not anyone to go in. He had vanished indoors and the door was shut by the time I got there.

I rang the bell savagely.

A heavy pistol roared inside, twice.

I smashed the glass out of the door with my gun and put my left hand in feeling for the latch.

The heavy pistol roared again and a bullet hurled splinters of glass into my cheek, but I found the latch.

I kicked the door back and fired straight ahead at random. Something moved in the dark hallway then and without waiting to see what it was I fired again, and when something fell I fired at the sound.

A voice said, 'Cut it out. That's enough. I've lost my gun.'

It wasn't Chappell's voice. I was disappointed.

Near the foot of the stairs I found a light switch and turned it on. Dick Moley was sitting on the floor at the other end of the hallway holding one leg.

I picked up his gun. 'Get you anywhere but the leg?' I asked.

'No. I'd've been all right if I hadn't dropped the gun when the leg upset me.'

'You've got a lot of ifs,' I said. 'I'll give you another one. You've got nothing to worry about but that bullet hole if you didn't kill Chappell.'

He laughed. 'If he's not dead he must feel funny with those two .44's in his head.'

'That was dumb of you,' I growled.

He didn't believe me. He said, 'It was the best job I ever pulled.'

'Yeah? Well, suppose I told you that I was only waiting for another move of his to pinch him?'

He opened his eyes at that.

'Yeah,' I said, 'and you have to walk in and mess things up. I hope they hang you for it.' I knelt down and began to slit his pants leg with my pocket-knife.

'What'd you do? Go in hiding after you found her dead in your rooms because you knew a guy with your record would be out of luck, and then lose your head when you saw in the extras what kind of a job he'd put up on you?'

'Yes,' he said slowly, 'though I'm not sure I lost my head. I've got a hunch I came pretty near giving the rat what he deserved.'

'That's a swell hunch,' I told him. 'We were ready to grab him. The whole thing looked phony. Nobody came for the money the first night, but it wasn't there the next day, so he said. Well, we only had his word for it that he had actually put it there and hadn't found it the next night. The next night, after he had been told the place was watched he left the money there, and then he wrote the note saying Death & Company knew he'd gone to the police. That wasn't public news, either. And then her being killed before anybody knew she was kidnapped. And then tying it to you when it was too dizzy—no, you are dizzy, or you wouldn't have pulled this one.' I was twisting my necktie around his leg about the bullet-hole. 'How long you been playing around with her?'

'A couple of months,' he said, 'only I wasn't playing. I meant it.'

'How'd he happen to catch her there alone?'

He shook his head. 'He must've followed her there that afternoon when she was supposed to be going to the theatre. Maybe he waited outside until he saw me go out. I wasn't gone an hour. She was already cold when I came back.'

'Do you think he planned it that way from the beginning?' Moley asked.

I didn't. I thought he killed his wife in a jealous rage and later thought of the Death & Company business.

JAMES THURBER (1894–1961)

The Macbeth Murder Mystery

———

'IT was a stupid mistake to make,' said the American woman I had met at my hotel in the English lake country, 'but it was on the counter with the other Penguin books—the little sixpenny ones, you know, with the paper covers—and I supposed of course it was a detective story. All the others were detective stories. I'd read all the others, so I bought this one without really looking at it carefully. You can imagine how mad I was when I found it was Shakespeare.' I murmured something sympathetically. 'I don't see why the Penguin-books people had to get out Shakespeare's plays in the same size and everything as the detective stories,' went on my companion. 'I think they have different-colored jackets,' I said. 'Well, I didn't notice that,' she said. 'Anyway, I got real comfy in bed that night and all ready to read a good mystery story and here I had "The Tragedy of Macbeth"—a book for high-school students. Like "Ivanhoe."' 'Or "Lorna Doone,"' I said. 'Exactly,' said the American lady. 'And I was just crazy for a good Agatha Christie, or something. Hercule Poirot is my favorite detective.' 'Is he the rabbity one?' I asked. 'Oh, no,' said my crime-fiction expert. 'He's the Belgian one. You're thinking of Mr Pinkerton, the one that helps Inspector Bull. He's good, too.'

Over her second cup of tea my companion began to tell the plot of a detective story that had fooled her completely—it seems it was the old family doctor all the time. But I cut in on her. 'Tell me,' I said. 'Did you read "Macbeth?"' 'I *had* to read it,' she said. 'There wasn't a scrap of anything else to read in the whole room.' 'Did you like it?' I asked. 'No, I did not,' she said, decisively. 'In the first place, I don't think for a moment that Macbeth did it.' I looked at her blankly. 'Did what?' I asked. 'I don't think for a moment that he killed the King,' she said. 'I don't think the Macbeth woman was mixed up in it, either. You suspect them the most, of course, but those are the ones that are

never guilty—or shouldn't be, anyway.' 'I'm afraid,' I began, 'that I—'
'But don't you see?' said the American lady. 'It would spoil everything
if you could figure out right away who did it. Shakespeare was too
smart for that. I've read that people never *have* figured out "Hamlet,"
so it isn't likely Shakespeare would have made "Macbeth" as simple as
it seems.' I thought this over while I filled my pipe. 'Who do you
suspect?' I asked, suddenly. 'Macduff,' she said, promptly. 'Good God!'
I whispered, softly.

'Oh, Macduff did it, all right,' said the murder specialist. 'Hercule
Poirot would have got him easily.' 'How did you figure it out?' I
demanded. 'Well,' she said, 'I didn't right away. At first I suspected
Banquo. And then, of course, he was the second person killed. That
was good right in there, that part. The person you suspect of the first
murder should always be the second victim.' 'Is that so?' I murmured.
'Oh, yes,' said my informant. 'They have to keep surprising you. Well,
after the second murder I didn't know *who* the killer was for a while.'
'How about Malcolm and Donalbain, the King's sons?' I asked. 'As I
remember it, they fled right after the first murder. That looks suspicious.' 'Too suspicious,' said the American lady. 'Much too suspicious.
When they flee, they're never guilty. You can count on that.' 'I believe,'
I said, 'I'll have a brandy,' and I summoned the waiter. My companion leaned toward me, her eyes bright, her teacup quivering. 'Do you
know who discovered Duncan's body?' she demanded. I said I was
sorry, but I had forgotten. 'Macduff discovers it,' she said, slipping
into the historical present. 'Then he comes running downstairs and
shouts, "Confusion has broke open the Lord's anointed temple" and
"Sacrilegious murder has made his masterpiece" and on and on like
that.' The good lady tapped me on the knee. 'All that stuff was
rehearsed,' she said. 'You wouldn't say a lot of stuff like that, offhand,
would you—if you had found a body?' She fixed me with a glittering
eye. 'I—' I began. 'You're right!' she said. 'You wouldn't! Unless you
had practiced it in advance. "My God, there's a body in here!" is what
an innocent man would say.' She sat back with a confident glare.

I thought for a while. 'But what do you make of the Third
Murderer?' I asked. 'You know, the Third Murderer has puzzled
"Macbeth" scholars for three hundred years.' 'That's because they
never thought of Macduff,' said the American lady. 'It was Macduff,
I'm certain. You couldn't have one of the victims murdered by two
ordinary thugs—the murderer always has to be somebody important.' 'But what about the banquet scene?' I asked, after a moment.

'How do you account for Macbeth's guilty actions there, when Banquo's ghost came in and sat in his chair?' The lady leaned forward and tapped me on the knee again. 'There wasn't any ghost,' she said. 'A big, strong man like that doesn't go around seeing ghosts—especially in a brightly lighted banquet hall with dozens of people around. Macbeth was *shielding somebody*!' 'Who was he shielding?' I asked. 'Mrs Macbeth, of course,' she said. 'He thought she did it and he was going to take the rap himself. The husband always does that when the wife is suspected.' 'But what,' I demanded, 'about the sleepwalking scene, then?' 'The same thing, only the other way around,' said my companion. 'That time *she* was shielding *him*. She wasn't asleep at all. Do you remember where it says, "Enter Lady Macbeth with a taper"?' 'Yes,' I said. 'Well, people who walk in their sleep *never carry lights*!' said my fellow-traveler. 'They have a second sight. Did you ever hear of a sleepwalker carrying a light?' 'No,' I said, 'I never did.' 'Well, then, she wasn't asleep. She was acting guilty to shield Macbeth.' 'I think,' I said, 'I'll have another brandy,' and I called the waiter. When he brought it, I drank it rapidly and rose to go. 'I believe,' I said, 'that you have got hold of something. Would you lend me that "Macbeth"? I'd like to look it over tonight. I don't feel, somehow, as if I'd ever really read it.' 'I'll get it for you,' she said. 'But you'll find that I am right.'

I read the play over carefully that night, and the next morning, after breakfast, I sought out the American woman. She was on the putting green, and I came up behind her silently and took her arm. She gave an exclamation. 'Could I see you alone?' I asked, in a low voice. She nodded cautiously and followed me to a secluded spot. 'You've found out something?' she breathed. 'I've found out,' I said, triumphantly, 'the name of the murderer!' 'You mean it wasn't Macduff?' she said. 'Macduff is as innocent of those murders,' I said, 'as Macbeth and the Macbeth woman.' I opened the copy of the play, which I had with me, and turned to Act II, Scene 2. 'Here,' I said, 'you will see where Lady Macbeth says, "I laid their daggers ready. He could not miss 'em. Had he not resembled my father as he slept, I had done it." Do you see?' 'No,' said the American woman, bluntly, 'I don't.' 'But it's simple!' I exclaimed. 'I wonder I didn't see it years ago. The reason Duncan resembled Lady Macbeth's father as he slept is that *it actually was her father*!' 'Good God!' breathed my companion, softly. 'Lady Macbeth's father killed the King,' I said, 'and, hearing someone coming, thrust the body under the bed and crawled into the bed himself.' 'But,' said the lady, 'you can't have a murderer who only appears in the story once. You can't have that.' 'I know that,' I said, and I turned to Act II, Scene 4. 'It says here, "Enter Ross with an old Man." Now, that old man is never identified and it is my contention he was old Mr Macbeth, whose ambition it was to make his daughter Queen. There you have your motive.' 'But even then,' cried the American lady, 'he's still a minor character!' 'Not,' I said, gleefully, 'when you realize that he was also *one of the weird sisters in disguise!*' 'You mean one of the three witches?' 'Precisely,' I said. 'Listen to this speech of the old man's. "On Tuesday last, a falcon towering in her pride of place, was by a mousing owl hawk'd at and kill'd." Who does that sound like?' 'It sounds like the way the three witches talk,' said my companion, reluctantly. 'Precisely!' I said again. 'Well,' said the American woman, 'maybe you're right, but—' 'I'm sure I am,' I said. 'And do you know what I'm going to do now?' 'No,' she said. 'What?' 'Buy a copy of "Hamlet",' I said, 'and solve *that!*' My companion's eyes brightened. 'Then,' she said, 'you don't think Hamlet did it?' 'I am,' I said, 'absolutely positive he didn't.' 'But who,' she demanded, 'do you suspect?' I looked at her cryptically. 'Everybody,' I said, and disappeared into a small grove of trees as silently as I had come.

JORGE LUIS BORGES (1899–1986)

Death and the Compass

Translated from the Spanish by
NORMAN THOMAS DI GIOVANNI

OF the many problems that ever taxed Erik Lönnrot's rash mind, none was so strange—so methodically strange, let us say—as the intermittent series of murders which came to a culmination amid the incessant odor of eucalyptus trees at the villa Triste-le-Roy. It is true that Lönnrot failed to prevent the last of the murders, but it is undeniable that he foresaw it. Neither did he guess the identity of Yarmolinksy's ill-starred killer, but he did guess the secret shape of the evil series of events and the possible role played in those events by Red Scharlach, also nicknamed Scharlach the Dandy. This gangster (like so many others of his ilk) had sworn on his honor to get Erik Lönnrot, but Lönnrot was not intimidated. Lönnrot thought of himself as a pure logician, a kind of Auguste Dupin, but there was also a streak of the adventurer and even of the gambler in him.

The first murder took place in the Hôtel du Nord—that tall prism which overlooks the estuary whose broad waters are the color of sand. To that tower (which, as everyone knows, brings together the hateful blank white walls of a hospital, the numbered chambers of a cell block, and the overall appearance of a brothel) there arrived on the third of December Rabbi Marcel Yarmolinsky, a gray-bearded, gray-eyed man, who was a delegate from Podolsk to the Third Talmudic Congress. We shall never know whether the Hôtel du Nord actually pleased him or not, since he accepted it with the ageless resignation that had made it possible for him to survive three years of war in the Carpathians and three thousand years of oppression and pogroms. He was given a room on floor R, across from the suite occupied—not without splendor—by the Tetrarch of Galilee.

Yarmolinsky had dinner, put off until the next day a tour of the unfamiliar city, arranged in a closet his many books and his few suits of clothes, and before midnight turned off his bed lamp. (So said the

Tetrarch's chauffeur, who slept in the room next door.) On the fourth of December, at three minutes past eleven in the morning, an editor of the *Jüdische Zeitung* called him by telephone. Rabbi Yarmolinsky did not answer; soon after, he was found in his room, his face already discolored, almost naked under a great old-fashioned cape. He lay not far from the hall door. A deep knife wound had opened his chest. A couple of hours later, in the same room, in the throng of reporters, photographers, and policemen, Inspector Treviranus and Lönnrot quietly discussed the case.

'We needn't lose any time here looking for three-legged cats,' Treviranus said, brandishing an imperious cigar. 'Everyone knows the Tetrarch of Galilee owns the world's finest sapphires. Somebody out to steal them probably found his way in here by mistake. Yarmolinsky woke up and the thief was forced to kill him. What do you make of it?'

'Possible, but not very interesting,' Lönnrot answered. 'You'll say reality is under no obligation to be interesting. To which I'd reply that reality may disregard the obligation but that we may not. In your hypothesis, chance plays a large part. Here's a dead rabbi. I'd much prefer a purely rabbinical explanation, not the imagined mistakes of an imagined jewel thief.'

'I'm not interested in rabbinical explanations,' Treviranus replied in bad humor; 'I'm interested in apprehending the man who murdered this unknown party.'

'Not so unknown,' corrected Lönnrot. 'There are his complete works.' He pointed to a row of tall books on a shelf in the closet. There were a *Vindication of the Kabbalah*, a *Study of the Philosophy of Robert Fludd*, a literal translation of the *Sefer Yeçirah*, a *Biography of the Baal Shem*, a *History of the Hasidic Sect*, a treatise (in German) on the Tetragrammaton, and another on the names of God in the Pentateuch. The Inspector stared at them in fear, almost in disgust. Then he burst into laughter.

'I'm only a poor Christian,' he said. 'You may cart off every last tome if you feel like it. I have no time to waste on Jewish superstitions.'

'Maybe this crime belongs to the history of Jewish superstitions,' Lönnrot grumbled.

'Like Christianity,' the editor from the *Jüdische Zeitung* made bold to add. He was nearsighted, an atheist, and very shy.

Nobody took any notice of him. One of the police detectives had found in Yarmolinsky's small typewriter a sheet of paper on which these cryptic words were written:

The first letter of the Name has been uttered

Lönnrot restrained himself from smiling. Suddenly turning bibliophile and Hebraic scholar, he ordered a package made of the dead man's books and he brought them to his apartment. There, with complete disregard for the police investigation, he began studying them. One royal-octavo volume revealed to him the teachings of Israel Baal Shem Tobh, founder of the sect of the Pious; another, the magic and the terror of the Tetragrammaton, which is God's unspeakable name; a third, the doctrine that God has a secret name in which (as in the crystal sphere that the Persians attribute to Alexander of Macedonia) His ninth attribute, Eternity, may be found—that is to say, the immediate knowledge of everything under the sun that will be, that is, and that was. Tradition lists ninety-nine names of God; Hebrew scholars explain that imperfect cipher by a mystic fear of even numbers; the Hasidim argue that the missing term stands for a hundredth name—the Absolute Name.

It was out of this bookworming that Lönnrot was distracted a few days later by the appearance of the editor from the *Jüdische Zeitung*, who wanted to speak about the murder. Lönnrot, however, chose to speak of the many names of the Lord. The following day, in three columns, the journalist stated that Chief Detective Erik Lönnrot had taken up the study of the names of God in order to find out the name of the murderer. Lönnrot, familiar with the simplifications of journalism, was not surprised. It also seemed that one of those tradesmen who have discovered that any man is willing to buy any book was peddling a cheap edition of Yarmolinsky's *History of the Hasidic Sect*.

The second murder took place on the night of January third out in the most forsaken and empty of the city's western reaches. Along about daybreak, one of the police who patrol this lonely area on horseback noticed on the doorstep of a dilapidated paint and hardware store a man in a poncho laid out flat. A deep knife wound had ripped open his chest, and his hard features looked as though they were masked in blood. On the wall, on the shop's conventional red and yellow diamond shapes, were some words scrawled in chalk. The policeman read them letter by letter. That evening, Treviranus and Lönnrot made their way across town to the remote scene of the crime. To the left and right of their car the city fell away in shambles;

the sky grew wider and houses were of much less account than brick kilns or an occasional poplar. They reached their forlorn destination, an unpaved back alley with rose-colored walls that in some way seemed to reflect the garish sunset. The dead man had already been identified. He turned out to be Daniel Simon Azevedo, a man with a fair reputation in the old northern outskirts of town who had risen from teamster to electioneering thug and later degenerated into a thief and an informer. (The unusual manner of his death seemed to them fitting, for Azevedo was the last example of a generation of criminals who knew how to handle a knife but not a revolver.) The words chalked up on the wall were these:

The second letter of the Name has been uttered

The third murder took place on the night of February third. A little before one o'clock, the telephone rang in the office of Inspector Treviranus. With pointed secrecy, a man speaking in a guttural voice said his name was Ginzberg (or Ginsburg) and that he was ready—for a reasonable consideration—to shed light on the facts surrounding the double sacrifice of Azevedo and Yarmolinsky. A racket of whistles and tin horns drowned out the informer's voice. Then the line went dead. Without discounting the possibility of a practical joke (they were, after all, at the height of Carnival), Treviranus checked and found that he had been phoned from a sailor's tavern called Liverpool House on the Rue de Toulon—that arcaded waterfront street in which we find side by side the wax museum and the dairy bar, the brothel and the Bible seller. Treviranus called the owner back. The man (Black Finnegan by name, a reformed Irish criminal concerned about and almost weighed down by respectability) told him that the last person to have used the telephone was one of his roomers, a certain Gryphius, who had only minutes before gone out with some friends. At once Treviranus set out for Liverpool House. There the owner told him the following story:

Eight days earlier, Gryphius had taken a small room above the bar. He was a sharp-featured man with a misty gray beard, shabbily dressed in black. Finnegan (who used that room for a purpose Treviranus immediately guessed) had asked the roomer for a rent that was obviously steep, and Gryphius paid the stipulated sum on the spot. Hardly ever going out, he took lunch and supper in his room; in fact, his face was hardly known in the bar. That night he had come down to use the telephone in Finnegan's office. A coupé had drawn up outside. The coachman had stayed on his seat; some customers recalled that he wore the mask of a bear. Two harlequins got out of the carriage. They were very short men and nobody could help noticing that they were very drunk. Bleating their horns, they burst into Finnegan's office, throwing their arms around Gryphius, who seemed to know them but who did not warm to their company. The three exchanged a few words in Yiddish—he in a low, guttural voice, they in a piping falsetto—and they climbed the stairs up to his room. In a quarter of an hour they came down again, very happy. Gryphius, staggering, seemed as drunk as the others. He walked in the middle, tall and dizzy, between the two masked harlequins. (One of the women in the bar remembered their costumes of red, green, and yellow lozenges.) Twice he stumbled; twice the harlequins held him up. Then the trio climbed into the coupé and, heading for the nearby docks (which enclosed a string of rectangular bodies of water), were soon out of sight. Out front, from the running board, the last harlequin had scrawled an obscene drawing and certain words on one of the market slates hung from a pillar of the arcade.

Treviranus stepped outside for a look. Almost predictably, the phrase read:

The last letter of the Name has been uttered

He next examined Gryphius–Ginzberg's tiny room. On the floor was a star-shaped spatter of blood; in the corners, cigarette butts of a Hungarian brand; in the wardrobe, a book in Latin—a 1739 edition of Leusden's *Philologus Hebraeo-Graecus*—with a number of annotations written in by hand. Treviranus gave it an indignant look and sent for Lönnrot. While the Inspector questioned the contradictory witnesses to the possible kidnapping, Lönnrot, not even bothering to take off his hat, began reading. At four o'clock they left. In the twisted Rue de Toulon, as they were stepping over last night's tangle of streamers and confetti, Treviranus remarked, 'And if tonight's events were a put-up job?'

Erik Lönnrot smiled and read to him with perfect gravity an underlined passage from the thirty-third chapter of the *Philologus*: ' "*Dies Judaeorum incipit a solis occasu usque ad solis occasum diei sequentis.*" Meaning,' he added, ' "the Jewish day begins at sundown and ends the following sundown." '

The other man attempted a bit of irony. 'Is that the most valuable clue you've picked up tonight?' he said.

'No. Far more valuable is one of the words Ginzberg used to you on the phone.'

The evening papers made a great deal of these recurrent disappearances. *La Croix de l'Épée* contrasted the present acts of violence with the admirable discipline and order observed by the last Congress of Hermits. Ernst Palast, in *The Martyr*, condemned 'the unbearable pace of this unauthorized and stinting pogrom, which has required three months for the liquidation of three Jews.' The *Jüdische Zeitung* rejected the ominous suggestion of an anti-Semitic plot, 'despite the fact that many penetrating minds admit of no other solution to the threefold mystery.' The leading gunman of the city's Southside, Dandy Red Scharlach, swore that in his part of town crimes of that sort would never happen, and he accused Inspector Franz Treviranus of criminal negligence.

On the night of March first, Inspector Treviranus received a great sealed envelope. Opening it, he found it contained a letter signed by one 'Baruch Spinoza' and, evidently torn out of a Baedeker, a detailed plan of the city. The letter predicted that on the third of March there would not be a fourth crime because the paint and hardware store on the Westside, the Rue de Toulon tavern, and the Hôtel du Nord formed 'the perfect sides of an equilateral and mystical triangle.' In red ink the map demonstrated that the three sides of the figure were exactly the same length. Treviranus read this Euclidean reasoning with a certain weariness and sent the letter and map to Erik Lönnrot—the man, beyond dispute, most deserving of such cranky notions.

Lönnrot studied them. The three points were, in fact, equidistant. There was symmetry in time (December third, January third, February third); now there was symmetry in space as well. All at once he felt he was on the verge of solving the riddle. A pair of dividers and a compass completed his sudden intuition. He smiled, pronounced the word Tetragrammaton (of recent acquisition) and called the Inspector on the phone.

'Thanks for the equilateral triangle you sent me last night,' he told him. 'It has helped me unravel our mystery. Tomorrow, Friday, the murderers will be safely behind bars; we can rest quite easy.'

'Then they aren't planning a fourth crime?'

'Precisely because they *are* planning a fourth crime we can rest quite easy.'

Lönnrot hung up the receiver. An hour later, he was traveling on a car of the Southern Railways on his way to the deserted villa Triste-le-Roy. To the south of the city of my story flows a dark muddy river, polluted by the waste of tanneries and sewers. On the opposite bank is a factory suburb where, under the patronage of a notorious political boss, many gunmen thrive. Lönnrot smiled to himself, thinking that the best-known of them—Red Scharlach—would have given anything to know about this sudden excursion of his. Azevedo had been a henchman of Scharlach's. Lönnrot considered the remote possibility that the fourth victim might be Scharlach himself. Then he dismissed it. He had practically solved the puzzle; the mere circumstances—reality (names, arrests, faces, legal and criminal proceedings)—barely held his interest now. He wanted to get away, to relax after three months of desk work and of snail-pace investigation. He reflected that the solution of the killings lay in an anonymously sent triangle and in a dusty Greek word. The mystery seemed almost crystal clear. He felt ashamed for having spent close to a hundred days on it.

The train came to a stop at a deserted loading platform. Lönnrot got off. It was one of those forlorn evenings that seem as empty as dawn. The air off the darkening prairies was damp and cold. Lönnrot struck out across the fields. He saw dogs, he saw a flatcar on a siding, he saw the line of the horizon, he saw a pale horse drinking stagnant water out of a ditch. Night was falling when he saw the rectangular mirador of the villa Triste-le-Roy, almost as tall as the surrounding black eucalyptus trees. He thought that only one more dawn and one more dusk (an ancient light in the east and another in the west) were all that separated him from the hour appointed by the seekers of the Name.

A rusted iron fence bounded the villa's irregular perimeter. The main gate was shut. Lönnrot, without much hope of getting in, walked completely around the place. Before the barred gate once again, he stuck a hand through the palings—almost mechanically—and found the bolt. The squeal of rusted iron surprised him. With clumsy obedience, the whole gate swung open.

Lönnrot moved forward among the eucalyptus trees, stepping on the layered generations of fallen leaves. Seen from up close, the house was a clutter of meaningless symmetries and almost insane repetitions: one icy Diana in a gloomy niche matched another Diana in a second niche; one balcony appeared to reflect another; double outer staircases crossed at each landing. A two-faced Hermes cast a monstrous shadow. Lönnrot made his way around the house as he had made his way around the grounds. He went over every detail; below the level of the terrace he noticed a narrow shutter.

He pushed it open. A few marble steps went down into a cellar. Lönnrot, who by now anticipated the architect's whims, guessed that in the opposite wall he would find a similar set of steps. He did. Climbing them, he lifted his hands and raised a trapdoor.

A stain of light led him to a window. He opened it. A round yellow moon outlined two clogged fountains in the unkempt garden. Lönnrot explored the house. Through serving pantries and along corridors he came to identical courtyards and several times to the same courtyard. He climbed dusty stairways to circular anterooms, where he was multiplied to infinity in facing mirrors. He grew weary of opening or of peeping through windows that revealed, outside, the same desolate garden seen from various heights and various angles; and indoors he grew weary of the rooms of furniture, each draped in yellowing slipcovers, and the crystal chandeliers wrapped in tarlatan. A bedroom caught his attention—in it, a single flower in a porcelain vase. At a touch, the ancient petals crumbled to dust. On the third floor, the last floor, the house seemed endless and growing. The house is not so large, he thought. This dim light, the sameness, the mirrors, the many years, my unfamiliarity, the loneliness are what make it large.

By a winding staircase he reached the mirador. That evening's moon streamed in through the diamond-shaped panes; they were red, green, and yellow. He was stopped by an awesome, dizzying recollection.

Two short men, brutal and stocky, threw themselves on him and disarmed him; another, very tall, greeted him solemnly and told him, 'You are very kind. You've saved us a night and a day.'

It was Red Scharlach. The men bound Lönnrot's wrists. After some seconds, Lönnrot at last heard himself saying, 'Scharlach, are you after the Secret Name?'

Scharlach remained standing, aloof. He had taken no part in the brief struggle and had barely held out his hand for Lönnrot's revolver. He spoke. Lönnrot heard in his voice the weariness of final triumph, a hatred the size of the universe, a sadness as great as that hatred.

'No,' said Scharlach. 'I'm after something more ephemeral, more frail. I'm after Erik Lönnrot. Three years ago, in a gambling dive on the Rue de Toulon, you yourself arrested my brother and got him put

away. My men managed to get me into a coupé before the shooting
was over, but I had a cop's bullet in my guts. Nine days and nine
nights I went through hell, here in this deserted villa, racked with
fever. The hateful two-faced Janus that looks on the sunsets and the
dawns filled both my sleep and my wakefulness with its horror.
I came to loathe my body, I came to feel that two eyes, two hands,
two lungs, are as monstrous as two faces. An Irishman, trying to
convert me to the faith of Jesus, kept repeating to me the saying of
the *goyim*—All roads lead to Rome. At night, my fever fed on that
metaphor. I felt the world was a maze from which escape was impossible since all roads, though they seemed to be leading north or south,
were really leading to Rome, which at the same time was the square
cell where my brother lay dying and also this villa, Triste-le-Roy.
During those nights, I swore by the god who looks with two faces and
by all the gods of fever and of mirrors that I would weave a maze
around the man who sent my brother to prison. Well, I have woven it
and it's tight. Its materials are a dead rabbi, a compass, an eighteenth-
century sect, a Greek word, a dagger, and the diamond-shaped
patterns on a paint-store wall.'

Lönnrot was in a chair now, with the two short men at his side.

'The first term of the series came to me by pure chance,' Scharlach
went on. 'With some associates of mine—among them Daniel
Azevedo—I'd planned the theft of the Tetrarch's sapphires. Azevedo
betrayed us. He got drunk on the money we advanced him and tried
to pull the job a day earlier. But there in the hotel he got mixed up
and around two in the morning blundered into Yarmolinsky's room.
The rabbi, unable to sleep, had decided to do some writing. In all likelihood, he was preparing notes or a paper on the Name of God and
had already typed out the words "The first letter of the Name has
been uttered." Azevedo warned him not to move. Yarmolinsky
reached his hand toward the buzzer that would have wakened all the
hotel staff; Azevedo struck him a single blow with his knife. It was
probably a reflex action. Fifty years of violence had taught him that
the easiest and surest way is to kill. Ten days later, I found out through
the *Jüdische Zeitung* that you were looking for the key to
Yarmolinsky's death in his writings. I read his *History of the Hasidic
Sect*. I learned that the holy fear of uttering God's Name had given
rise to the idea that that Name is secret and all-powerful. I learned
that some of the Hasidim, in search of that secret Name, had gone as
far as to commit human sacrifices. The minute I realized you were

guessing that the Hasidim had sacrificed the rabbi, I did my best to justify that guess. Yarmolinsky died the night of December third. For the second "sacrifice" I chose the night of January third. The rabbi had died on the Northside; for the second "sacrifice" we wanted a spot on the Westside. Daniel Azevedo was the victim we needed. He deserved death—he was impulsive, a traitor. If he'd been picked up, it would have wiped out our whole plan. One of my men stabbed him; in order to link his corpse with the previous one, I scrawled on the diamonds of the paint-store wall "The second letter of the Name has been uttered." '

Scharlach looked his victim straight in the face, then continued. 'The third "crime" was staged on the third of February. It was, as Treviranus guessed, only a plant. Gryphius-Ginzberg-Ginsburg was me. I spent an interminable week (rigged up in a false beard) in that flea-ridden cubicle on the Rue de Toulon until my friends came to kidnap me. From the running board of the carriage, one of them wrote on the pillar "The last letter of the Name has been uttered." That message suggested that the series of crimes was *threefold*. That was how the public understood it. I, however, threw in repeated clues so that you, Erik Lönnrot the reasoner, might puzzle out that the crime was *fourfold*. A murder in the north, others in the east and west, demanded a fourth murder in the south. The Tetragrammaton—the Name of God, JHVH—is made up of *four* letters; the harlequins and the symbol on the paint store also suggest *four* terms. I underlined a certain passage in Leusden's handbook. That passage makes it clear that the Jews reckoned the day from sunset to sunset; that passage makes it understood that the deaths occurred on the *fourth* of each month. I was the one who sent the triangle to Treviranus, knowing in advance that you would supply the missing point—the point that determines the perfect rhombus, the point that fixes the spot where death is expecting you. I planned the whole thing, Erik Lönnrot, so as to lure you to the loneliness of Triste-le-Roy.'

Lönnrot avoided Scharlach's eyes. He looked off at the trees and the sky broken into dark diamonds of red, green, and yellow. He felt a chill and an impersonal, almost anonymous sadness. It was night now; from down in the abandoned garden came the unavailing cry of a bird. Lönnrot, for one last time, reflected on the problem of the patterned, intermittent deaths.

'In your maze there are three lines too many,' he said at last. 'I know of a Greek maze that is a single straight line. Along this line so many thinkers have lost their way that a mere detective may very well lose his way. Scharlach, when in another incarnation you hunt me down, stage (or commit) a murder at A, then a second murder at B, eight miles from A, then a third murder at C, four miles from A and B, halfway between the two. Lie in wait for me then at D, two miles from A and C, again halfway between them. Kill me at D, the way you are going to kill me here at Triste-le-Roy.'

'The next time I kill you,' said Scharlach, 'I promise you such a maze, which is made up of a single straight line and which is invisible and unending.'

He moved back a few steps. Then, taking careful aim, he fired.

GEORGES SIMENON (1903–1989)

from *Maigret's Memoirs*

Translated from the French by JEAN STEWART

———

A FEW years ago some of us talked of founding a sort of club, more likely a monthly dinner, which was to be called 'The Hobnailed Socks Club'. We got together for a drink, in any case, at the Brasserie Dauphine. We argued about who should and who shouldn't be admitted. And we wondered quite seriously whether the chaps from the other branch, I mean from the Rue des Saussaies, should be considered eligible.

Then, as was only to be expected, things got no further. At that time there were still at least four of us, among the inspectors in the Detective Force, who were rather proud of the nickname 'hobnailed socks' formerly given us by satirical song-writers, and which certain young detectives fresh from college sometimes used amongst themselves when referring to those of their seniors who had risen from the ranks.

In the old days, indeed, it took a good many years to win one's stripes, and exams were not enough. A sergeant, before hoping for promotion, had to have worn out his shoe-soles in practically every branch of the Force.

It is not easy to convey the meaning of this with any sort of precision to the younger generation.

'Hobnailed shoes' and 'big moustaches' were the terms that sprang naturally to people's lips when they spoke of the police.

And in fact, for years, I wore hobnailed shoes myself. Not from preference. Not, as caricaturists seemed to imply, because we thought such footwear was the height of elegance and comfort, but for more down-to-earth reasons.

Two reasons, to be exact. The first, that our salary barely enabled

us to make ends meet. I often hear people talk of the gay, carefree life
at the beginning of this century. Young people refer enviously to the
prices current at that time, cigars at two sous, dinner with wine and
coffee for twenty sous.

What people forget is that at the outset of his career a public
servant earned somewhat under a hundred francs a month.

When I was serving in the Public Highways Squad I would cover
during my day, which was often a thirteen or fourteen hour day, miles
and miles of pavement in all weathers.

So that one of the first problems of our married life was the problem of getting my shoes soled. At the end of each month, when I
brought back my pay-packet to my wife, she would divide its contents
into a number of small piles.

'For the butcher . . . For rent . . . For gas . . .'

There was hardly anything left to put in the last pile of small silver.

'For your shoes.'

Our dream was always to buy new ones, but for a long time it was
only a dream. Often I went for weeks without confessing to her that
my soles, between the hobnails, absorbed the gutter water greedily.

If I mention this here it is not out of bitterness but, on the
contrary, quite lightheartedly, and I think it is necessary to give an
idea of a police officer's life.

There were no such things as taxis, and even if the streets had been
crowded with them they'd have been beyond our reach, as were the
cabs which we used only in very special circumstances.

In any case, in the Public Highways Squad, our duty was to keep
walking along the pavements, mingling with the crowd from morning till night and from night until morning.

Why, when I think of those days, do I chiefly remember the rain?
As if it had rained unceasingly for years, as if the seasons had been
different then. Of course, it is because the rain added a number of
additional ordeals to one's task. Not only did your socks become
soaked. The shoulders of your coat gradually turned into cold
compresses, your hat became a waterspout, and your hands, thrust
into your coat pockets, grew blue with cold.

The roads were less well lighted than they are today. A certain
number of them in the outskirts were unpaved. At night the windows
showed as yellowish squares against the blackness, for most of the
houses were still lighted with oil lamps or even, more wretchedly still,
with candles.

And then there were the *apaches*.

All round the fortifications, in those days, their knives would come into play, and not always for gain, for the sake of the rich man's wallet or watch.

What they wanted chiefly was to prove to themselves that they were men, tough guys, and to win the admiration of the little tarts in black pleated skirts and huge chignons who paced the pavements under the gas jets.

We were unarmed. Contrary to the general belief, a policeman in plain clothes has not the right to carry a revolver in his pocket and if, in certain cases, a man takes one, it's against the regulations and entirely on his own responsibility.

Junior officers could not consider themselves entitled to do so. There were a certain number of streets, in the neighbourhood of La Villette, Ménilmontant and the Porte d'Italie, where one ventured reluctantly and sometimes trembled at the sound of one's own footsteps.

For a long time the telephone remained a legendary luxury beyond the scope of our budgets. When I was delayed several hours, there was no question of ringing up my wife to warn her, so that she used to spend lonely evenings in our gas-lit dining-room, listening for noises on the stairway and warming up the same dish four or five times over.

As for the moustaches with which we were caricatured, we really wore them. A man without a moustache looked like a flunkey.

Mine was longish, reddish brown, somewhat darker than my father's with pointed ends. Later it dwindled to a toothbrush and then disappeared completely.

It is a fact, moreover, that most police inspectors wore huge jet-black moustaches like those in their caricatures. This is because, for some mysterious reason, for quite a long time, the profession attracted chiefly natives of the Massif Central.

There are few streets in Paris along which I have not trudged, watchful-eyed, and I learned to know all the rank and file of the pavements, from beggars, barrel-organ players and flower-girls to card-sharpers and pickpockets, including prostitutes and the drunken old women who spend most of their nights at the police station.

I 'covered' the Halles at night, the Place Maubert, the quays and the reaches beneath the quays.

I covered crowded gatherings too, the biggest job of all, at the Foire du Trône and the Foire de Neuilly, at Longchamps races and patriotic demonstrations, at military parades, visits from foreign royalties, carriage processions, travelling circuses and second-hand markets.

After a few months, a few years at this job one's head is full of a varied array of figures and faces that remain indelibly engraved on one's memory.

I should like to try—and it's not easy—to give a more or less accurate idea of our relations with these people, including those whom we periodically had to take off to the lock-up.

Needless to say, the picturesque aspect soon ceases to exist for us. Inevitably, we come to scan the streets of Paris with a professional eye, which fastens on certain familiar details or notices some unusual circumstance and draws the necessary conclusion from it.

When I consider this subject, the thing that strikes me most is the bond that is formed between the policeman and the quarry he has to track down. Above all, except in a few exceptional cases, the policeman is entirely devoid of hatred or even of ill-will.

Devoid of pity, too, in the usual sense of the word.

Our relations, so to speak, are strictly professional.

We have seen too much, as you can well imagine, to be shocked any longer by certain forms of wretchedness or depravity. So that the latter does not arouse our indignation, nor does the former cause us that distress felt by the inexperienced spectator.

There is something between us, which Simenon has tried to convey without success, and that is, paradoxical as it may seem, a kind of family feeling.

Don't misunderstand me. We are on different sides of the barricade, of course. But we also, to some extent, share the same hardships.

The prostitute on the Boulevard de Clichy and the policeman who is watching her both have bad shoes and both have aching feet from trudging along miles of asphalt. They have to endure the same rain, the same icy wind. Evening and night wear the same hue for both of them, and they see with almost identical eyes the seamy side of the crowd that streams past them.

The same is true of a fair where a pickpocket is threading his way through a similar crowd. For him a fair, or indeed any gathering of some few hundreds of people, means not fun, roundabouts, Big Tops or gingerbread, but merely a certain number of purses in unwary pockets.

For the policeman too. And each of them can recognise at a glance the self-satisfied country visitor who will be the ideal victim.

How many times have I spent hours following a certain pickpocket of my acquaintance, such as the one we called the Artful Dodger! He knew that I was on his heels, watching his slightest movements. He knew that I knew. While I knew that he knew that I was there.

His job was to get hold of a wallet or a watch in spite of it all, and my job was to stop him or to catch him in the act.

Well, it sometimes happened that the Dodger would turn round and smile at me. I would smile back. He even spoke to me sometimes, with a sigh:

'It's going to be hard!'

I was well aware that he was on his beam-ends and that he wouldn't eat that night unless he was successful.

He was equally well aware that I earned a hundred francs a month, that I had holes in my shoes and that my wife was waiting impatiently for me at home.

Ten times at least I picked him up, quite kindly, telling him:

'You've had it!'

And he was almost as relieved as I was. It meant that he'd get something to eat at the police station and somewhere to sleep. Some of them know the lock-up so well that they ask:

'Who's on duty tonight?'

Because some of us let them smoke and others don't.

Then, for a year and a half, the pavements seemed to me an ideal beat, for my next job was in the big stores.

Instead of rain and cold, sunshine and dust, I spent my days in an overheated atmosphere reeking of tweed and unbleached calico, linoleum and mercerised cotton.

In those days there were radiators at intervals in the gangways between counters, which sent up puffs of dry, scorching air. This was fine when you arrived soaking wet. You took up your position above a radiator, and immediately you gave out a cloud of steam.

After a few hours, you chose rather to hang about near the doors which, each time they opened, let in a little oxygen.

The important thing was to look natural. To look like a customer! Which is so easy, isn't it, when the whole floor is full of nothing but corsets, lingerie or reels of silk?

'May I ask you to come along with me quietly?'

Some women used to understand immediately and followed us without a word to the manager's office. Others got on their high horse, protested shrilly or had hysterics.

And yet here, too, we had to deal with a regular clientèle. Whether at the Bon Marché, the Louvre or the Printemps, certain familiar figures were always to be found, usually middle-aged women, who stowed away incredible quantities of various goods in a pocket concealed between their dress and their petticoat.

A year and a half, in retrospect, seems very little, but at the time each hour was as long drawn out as an hour spent in the dentist's waiting-room.

'Shall you be at the Galeries this afternoon?' my wife would ask me sometimes. 'I've got a few little things to buy there.'

We never spoke to one another. We pretended not to recognise each other. It was delightful. I was happy to watch her moving proudly from one counter to the next, giving me a discreet wink from time to time.

I don't believe that she ever asked herself either whether she might have married anyone other than a police inspector. She knew the names of all my colleagues, spoke familiarly about those whom she had never seen, of their fads, of their successes or their failures.

It took me years to bring myself, one Sunday morning when I was on duty, to take her into the famous house in the Quai des Orfèvres, and she showed no sign of amazement. She walked about as if she were at home, looking for all the details which she knew so well from hearsay.

Her only reaction was:

'It's less dirty than I'd expected.'

'Why should it be dirty?'

'Places where men live by themselves are never quite so clean. And they have a certain smell.'

I did not ask her to the Police Station, where she'd have got her fill of smells.

'Who sits here on the left?'

'Torrence.'

'The big fat one? I might have guessed it. He's like a child. He still plays at carving his initials on his desk.'

'And what about old Lagrume, the man who walks so much?'

Since I've talked about shoes I may as well tell the story that distressed my wife.

Lagrume, Old Lagrume as we called him, was senior to all of us, although he had never risen above the rank of sergeant. He was a tall, melancholy fellow. In summer he suffered from hay-fever and, as soon as the weather turned cold, his chronic bronchitis gave him a hollow cough that sounded from one end of Headquarters to the other.

Fortunately he was not often there. He had been rash enough to say one day, referring to his cough:

'The doctor recommends me to keep in the open-air.'

After that, he got his fill of open-air. He had long legs and huge feet, and he was put in charge of the most unlikely investigations through the length and breadth of Paris, the sort that force you to travel through the town in all directions, day after day, without even the hope of getting any results.

'Just leave it to Lagrume!'

Everybody knew what was involved, except the old fellow himself, who gravely made a few notes on his pad, tucked his rolled umbrella under his arm and went off, with a brief nod to all present.

I wonder now whether he was not perfectly well aware of the part he was playing. He was one of the meek. For years and years he had had a sick wife waiting for him to do the housework in their suburban home. And when his daughter married, I believe it was he who got up at night to look after the baby:

'Lagrume, you still smell of dirty nappies!'

An old woman had been murdered in the Rue Caulain-court. It was a commonplace crime that made no sensation in the Press, for the victim was an unimportant small *rentière* with no connections.

Such cases are always the most difficult. I myself, being confined to the big stores—and particularly busy as Christmas drew near—was not involved in it, but, like everybody else at our place, I knew the details of the investigation.

The crime had been committed with a kitchen knife, which had been left on the spot. This knife provided the only evidence. It was quite an ordinary knife, such as are sold in ironmongers' shops, chain stores or the smallest local shops, and the manufacturer, who had been contacted, claimed to have sold tens of thousands within the area of Paris.

The knife was a new one. It had obviously been bought on purpose. It still bore the price written on the handle in indelible pencil.

This was the detail which offered a vague hope of discovering the tradesman who had sold it.

'Lagrume! You deal with that knife.'

He wrapped it up in a bit of newspaper, put it in his pocket and set off.

He set off for a journey through Paris which was to last for nine weeks.

Every morning he appeared punctually at the office, to which he would return in the evening to shut away the knife in a drawer. Every morning he was to be seen putting the weapon in his pocket, seizing his umbrella and setting out with the same nod to all present.

I learned the number of shops—the story has become a legend— which might possibly have sold a knife of this sort. Without going beyond the fortifications, and confining oneself to the twenty *arrondissements* of Paris, the number makes your head reel.

There was no question of using any means of transport. It meant going from street to street, almost from door to door. Lagrume had in his pocket a map of Paris on which, hour after hour, he crossed out a certain number of streets.

I believe that in the end his chiefs had even forgotten what task he had been set.

'Is Lagrume available?'

Somebody would reply that he was out on a job, and then nobody bothered any more about him. It was shortly before Christmas, as I have said. It was a wet, cold winter, the pavements were slimy, and yet Lagrume went to and fro from morning till night, with his bronchitis and his hollow cough, unwearying, never asking what was the point of it all.

During the ninth week, well into the New Year, when it was freezing hard, he turned up at three o'clock in the afternoon, as calm and mournful as ever, without the slightest gleam of joy or relief in his eyes.

'Is the Chief there?'

'You've found it?'

'I've found it.'

Not in an ironmonger's, nor a cheap store, nor a household goods shop. He had gone through all those unavailingly.

The knife had been sold by a stationer in the Boulevard Rochechouart. The shopkeeper had recognised his handwriting, and remembered a young man in a green scarf buying the weapon from him more than two months previously.

He gave a fairly detailed description of him, and the young man was arrested and executed the following year.

As for Lagrume, he died in the street, not from his bronchitis but from a heart attack.

*

Before discussing stations, and in particular that Gare du Nord with which I always feel I have an old score to settle, I must deal briefly with a subject of which I am not very fond.

I have often been asked, with reference to my early days and my various jobs:

'Have you been in the Vice Squad too?'

It isn't known by that name today. It is modestly called the 'Social Squad.'

Well, I've belonged to that, like most of my colleagues. For a very short period. Barely a few months.

And if I realise now that it was necessary, my recollections of that period are nevertheless confused and somewhat uneasy.

I mentioned the familiarity that grows up naturally between policemen and those on whom it is their job to keep watch.

By force of circumstances, it exists in that branch as much as in the others. Even more so. Indeed, the *clientèle* of each detective, so to speak, consists of a relatively restricted number of women who are almost always found at the same spots, at the door of the same hotel or under the same street lamp, or, for the grade above, at the terrace of the same brasseries.

I was not then as stalwart as I have grown with the passing years, and apparently I looked younger than my age.

Remember the *petits fours* incident at the Boulevard Beaumarchais and you will understand that in certain respects I was somewhat timid.

Most of the officers in the Vice Squad were on familiar terms with the women, whose names or nicknames they knew, and it was a tradition when, during the course of a raid, they packed them into the Black Maria, to vie with one another in coarseness of speech, to fling the filthiest abuse at one another with a laugh.

Another habit these ladies had acquired was to pick up their skirts and show their behinds in a gesture which they considered, no doubt, the last word in insults, and which they accompanied with a torrent of defiance.

I must have blushed to begin with, for I still blushed easily. My embarrassment did not pass unnoticed, for the least one can say of these women is that they have a certain knowledge of men.

I promptly became, not exactly their *bête noire*, but their butt.

At the Quai des Orfèvres nobody ever called me by my first name, and I'm convinced that many of my colleagues did not know it . . . I shouldn't have chosen it if I'd been asked my opinion. I'm not ashamed of it either.

Could it have been some sly revenge on the part of some detective who was in the know?

I was specially in charge of the Sébastopol district which, particularly in the Halles area, was frequented at that time by the lowest class of women, particularly by a number of very old prostitutes who had taken refuge there.

It was here, too, that young servant girls newly arrived from Brittany or elsewhere served their apprenticeship, so that one had the two extremes: kids of sixteen, over whom the pimps quarrelled, and ancient harpies who were very well able to defend themselves.

One day the catchphrase started—for it quickly became a catchphrase. I was walking past one of these old women, stationed at the door of a filthy hotel, when I heard her call out to me, showing all her rotten teeth in a smile:

'Good evening, Jules!'

I thought she'd used the name at random, but a little further on I was greeted by the same words.

'Hullo, Jules!'

After which, when there was a group of them together, they would burst out laughing, with a flood of unrepeatable comments.

I know what some officers would have done in my place. They'd have needed no further inducement to pick up a few of these women and lock them up at Saint-Lazare to think things over.

The example would have served its purpose, and I should probably have been treated with a certain respect.

I didn't do it. Not necessarily from any sense of justice. Nor out of pity.

Probably because this was a game I didn't want to play. I chose rather to pretend I hadn't heard. I hoped they would tire of it. But such women are like children who have never had enough of any joke.

They made up a song about Jules which they began to sing or yell as soon as I appeared. Others would say to me, as I checked their cards:

'Don't be mean, Jules! You're so sweet!'

Poor Louise! Her great dread, during this period, was not that I might yield to some temptation, but that I might bring home an unpleasant disease. Once I caught fleas. When I got home she would make me undress and take a bath, while she went to brush my clothes on the landing or at the open window.

'You must have touched plenty today! Brush your nails well!'

Wasn't there some story that you could catch syphilis merely by drinking out of a glass?

It was not a pleasant experience, but I learned what I had to learn. After all, I had chosen my own career.

For nothing on earth would I have asked to be transferred. My chiefs did what was necessary of their own accord, more for the sake of results, I imagine, than out of consideration for myself.

I was put on stations. More precisely, I was posted to that gloomy, sinister building known as the Gare du Nord.

*

It had the advantage, like the big stores, that one was sheltered from the rain. Not from the cold nor from the wind, for nowhere in the world, probably, are there so many draughts as in the hall of a station, the hall of the Gare du Nord, and for months I had as many colds as old Lagrume.

Please don't imagine that I'm grumbling, or deliberately dwelling on the seamy side so as to get my own back.

I was perfectly happy. I was happy trudging along the streets and I was equally happy keeping an eye on so-called kleptomaniacs in the big stores. I felt that I was getting on a little each time, learning a job whose complexity was more apparent to me every day.

When I see the Gare de l'Est, for instance, I can never help feeling depressed, because it reminds me of mobilization. The Gare de Lyon, on the other hand, like the Gare Montparnasse, suggests holidays.

But the Gare du Nord, the coldest, the busiest of them all, brings to my mind a harsh and bitter struggle for one's daily bread. Is it because it leads towards mining and industrial regions?

In the morning, the first night trains, coming from Belgium and Germany, generally contain a certain number of smugglers, of illicit traders with faces as hard as the daylight seen through the glazed windows of the station.

It's not always a matter of small-scale fraud. There are the professionals in various international rackets, with their agents, their decoys, their right-hand men, people who play for high stakes and are ready to defend themselves by any method.

No sooner has this crowd dispersed than it's the turn of the suburban trains which come not from pleasant villages like those in the West or South, but from black, unhealthy built-up areas.

In the opposite direction, it's towards Belgium, the nearest frontier, that fugitives for the most varied reasons try to escape.

Hundreds of people are waiting there in the grey atmosphere redolent of smoke and sweat, moving restlessly, hurrying from the booking office to the waiting rooms, examining the boards that announce arrivals and departures, eating or drinking, surrounded by children, dogs and suitcases, and almost always they are people who have not slept enough, whose nerves are on edge from their dread of being late, sometimes merely from their dread of the morrow which they are going elsewhere to seek.

I have spent hours, every day, watching them, looking amongst all those faces for some more inscrutable face with a more fixed stare, the face of a man or women staking their last chance.

The train is there, about to leave in a few minutes. He's only got to go another hundred yards and hold out the ticket he's clutching. The minute hands jerk forward on the enormous yellowish face of the clock.

Double or quits! It means freedom or jail. Or worse.

I am there, with a photograph or a description in my wallet, sometimes merely the technical description of an ear.

It may happen that we catch sight of one another simultaneously, that our eyes meet. Almost invariably the man understands at once.

What follows will depend on his character, on the risk he's running, on his nerves, even on some tiny material detail, a door that's open or shut, a trunk that may happen to be lying between us.

Sometimes they try to run away, and then there's a desperate race through groups of people who protest or try to get out of the way, a race among stationary coaches, over railway lines and points.

I have come across two men, one of them quite young, who, at three months' distance, behaved in exactly the same way.

Each of them thrust his hand into his pocket as if to take out a cigarette. And next minute, in the thick of the crowd, with his eyes fixed on me, each of them shot himself through the head.

These men bore me no ill-will, nor did I bear them any.

We were each of us doing his job.

They had lost the game, and there was an end to it, so they were quitting.

I had lost it too, for my duty was to bring them into the courts alive.

I have watched thousands of trains leaving. I have watched thousands arriving too, each time with the same dense crowd, the long string of people hurrying towards something or other.

It's become a habit with me, as with my colleagues. Even if I'm not on duty, if by some miracle I'm going on holiday with my wife, my glance slips from one face to the next, and seldom fails to fall on somebody who's afraid, however he may try to conceal it.

'Aren't you coming? What's the matter?'

Until we're settled in our carriage, or rather until the train has left, my wife is never sure that we're really going to get our holiday.

'What are you bothering about? You're not on duty!'

There have been times when I've followed her with a sigh, turning round for a last look at some mysterious face vanishing in the crowd. Always reluctantly.

And I don't think it's only from professional conscientiousness, nor from love of justice.

I repeat, it's a game that's being played, a game that has no end. Once you've begun it, it's difficult, if not impossible, to give it up.

The proof is that those of us who eventually retire, often against their will, almost always end by setting up a private detective agency.

Moreover that's only a last resort, and I don't know one detective who, after grumbling for thirty years about the miseries of a policeman's life, isn't ready to take up work again, even unpaid.

I have sinister memories of the Gare du Nord. I don't know why, I always picture it full of thick, damp early-morning fog, with its drowsy crowd flocking towards the lines or towards the Rue Maubeuge.

The specimens of humanity I have met there have been some of the most desperate, and certain arrests that I have made there left me with a feeling of remorse rather than of any professional satisfaction.

If I had the choice, none the less, I would rather go on duty again tomorrow at the platform barrier than set off from some more sumptuous station for a sunny corner of the Côte d'Azur.

ELLERY QUEEN (1905–1982)

'My Queer Dean!'

THE queerness of Matthew Arnold Hope, beloved teacher of Ellery's Harvard youth and lately dean of liberal arts in a New York university, is legendary.

The story is told, for instance, of baffled students taking Dr Hope's Shakespeare course for the first time. 'History advises us that Richard II died peacefully at Pontefract, probably of pneumonia,' Dr Hope scolds. 'But what does Shakespeare say, Act V, Scene V? That Exton struck him down,' and here the famous authority on Elizabethan literature will pause for emphasis, 'with a blushing crow!'

Imaginative sophomores have been known to suffer nightmare as a result of this remark. Older heads nod intelligently, of course, knowing that Dr Hope meant merely to say—in fact, thought he was saying—'a crushing blow'.

The good dean's unconscious spoonerisms, like the sayings of Miss Parker and Mr Goldwyn, are reverently preserved by aficionados, among whom Ellery counts himself a charter member. It is Ellery who has saved for posterity that deathless pronouncement of Dr Hope's to a freshman class in English composition: 'All those who persist in befouling their theme papers with cant and other low expressions not in good usage are warned for the last time: Refine your style or be exiled from this course with the rest of the vanished Bulgarians!'

But perhaps Dean Hope's greatest exploit began recently in the faculty lunchroom. Ellery arrived at the dean's invitation to find him waiting impatiently at one of the big round tables with three members of the English Department.

'Dr Agnes Lovell, Professor Oswald Gorman, Mr Morgan Naseby,' the dean said rapidly. 'Sit down, Ellery. Mr Queen will have the cute frocktail and the horned beef cash—only safe edibles on the menu today, my boy—Will, go fetch, young man! Are you dreaming that you're back in class?' The waiter, a harried-looking freshman, fled. Then Dr Hope said solemnly, 'My friends, prepare for a surprise.'

Dr Lovell, a very large woman in a tight suit, said roguishly: 'Wait, Matthew! Let me guess. Romance?'

'And who'd marry—in Macaulay's imperishable phrase—a living concordance?' said Professor Gorman in a voice like an abandoned winch. He was a tall freckled man with strawberry eyebrows and a quarrelsome jaw. 'A real surprise, Dr Hope, would be a departmental salary rise.'

'A consummation devoutly et cetera,' said Mr Naseby, immediately blushing. He was a stout young man with an eager manner, evidently a junior in the department.

'May I have your attention?' Dean Hope looked about cautiously. 'Suppose I tell you,' he said in a trembling voice, 'that by tonight I may have it within my power to deliver the death-blow—I repeat, the death-blow!—to the cocky-pop that Francis Bacon wrote Shakespeare's plays?'

There were two gasps, a snort, and one inquiring hum.

'Matthew!' squealed Dr Lovell. 'You'd be famous!'

'Immortal, Dean Hope,' said Mr Naseby adoringly.

'Deluded,' said Professor Gorman, the snorter. 'The Baconian benightedness, like the Marlowe mania, has no known specific.'

'Ah, but even a fanatic,' cried the dean, 'would have to yield before the nature of this evidence.'

'Sounds exciting, Doc,' murmured Ellery. 'What is it?'

'A man called at my office this morning, Ellery. He produced credentials identifying him as a London rare-book dealer, Alfred Mimms. He has in his possession, he said, a copy of the 1613 edition of *The Essaies of Sir Francis Bacon Knight the kings solliciter generall*, an item ordinarily bringing four or five hundred dollars. He claims that this copy, however, is unique, *being inscribed on the title page in Bacon's own hand to Will Shakespeare*.'

Amid the cries, Ellery asked: 'Inscribed how?'

'In an encomium,' quavered Dean Hope, 'an encomium to Shakespeare expressing Bacon's admiration and praise for—and I quote—"*the most excellent plaies of your sweet wit and hand*"!'

'Take that!' whispered Mr Naseby to an invisible Baconian.

'That does it,' breathed Dr Lovell.

'That would do it,' said Professor Gorman, 'if.'

'Did you actually see the book, Doc?' asked Ellery.

'He showed me a photostat of the title-page. He'll have the original for my inspection tonight, in my office.'

'And Mimm's asking price is——?'

'Ten thousand dollars.'

'Proof positive that it's a forgery,' said Professor Gorman rustily. 'It's far too little.'

'Oswald,' hissed Dr Lovell, 'you creak, do you know that?'

'No, Gorman is right,' said Dr Hope. 'An absurd price if the inscription is genuine, as I pointed out to Mimms. However, he had an explanation. He is acting, he said, at the instructions of the book's owner, a tax-poor British nobleman whose identity he will reveal tonight if I purchase the book. The owner, who has just found it in a castle room boarded up and forgotten for two centuries, prefers an American buyer in a confidential sale—for tax reasons, Mimms hinted. But, as a cultivated man, the owner wishes a scholar to have it rather than some ignorant Croesus. Hence the relatively low price.'

'Lovely,' glowed Mr Naseby. 'And so typically British.'

'Isn't it?' said Professor Gorman. 'Terms cash, no doubt? On the line? Tonight?'

'Well, yes.' The old dean took a bulging envelope from his breast pocket and eyed it ruefully. Then, with a sigh, he tucked it back. 'Very nearly my life's savings. . . . But I'm not altogether senile,' Dr Hope grinned. 'I'm asking you to be present, Ellery—with Inspector Queen. I shall be working at my desk on administrative things into the evening. Mimms is due at eight o'clock.'

'We'll be here at seven-thirty,' promised Ellery. 'By the way, Doc, that's a lot of money to be carrying around in your pocket. Have you confided this business to anyone else?'

'No, no.'

'Don't. And may I suggest that you wait behind a locked door? Don't admit Mimms—or anyone else you don't trust—until we get here. I'm afraid, Doc, I share the professor's scepticism.'

'Oh, so do I,' murmured the dean. 'The odds on this being a swindle are, I should think, several thousand to one. But one can't help saying to oneself . . . suppose it's not?'

It was nearly half-past seven when the Queens entered the Arts Building. Some windows on the upper floors were lit up where a few evening classes were in session, and the dean's office was bright. Otherwise the building was dark.

The first thing Ellery saw as they stepped out of the self-service elevator on to the dark third floor was the door of Dean Hope's ante-room . . . wide open.

They found the old scholar crumpled on the floor just inside the doorway. His white hairs dripped red.

'Crook came early,' howled Inspector Queen. 'Look at the dean's wrist-watch, Ellery—smashed in his fall at 7.15.'

'I warned him not to unlock his door,' wailed Ellery. Then he bellowed. 'He's breathing! Call an ambulance!'

He had carried the dean's frail body to a couch in the inner office and was gently wetting the blue lips from a paper cup when the Inspector turned from the telephone.

The eyes fluttered open. 'Ellery . . .'

'Doc, what happened?'

'Book . . . taken . . .' The voice trailed off in a mutter.

'Book taken?' repeated the Inspector incredulously. 'That means Mimms not only came early, but Dr Hope found the book was genuine! Is the money on him, son?'

Ellery searched the dean's pockets, the office, the ante-room. 'It's gone.'

'Then he did buy it. Then somebody came along, cracked him on the skull, and lifted the book.'

'Doc!' Ellery bent over the old man again. 'Doc, who struck you? Did you see?'

'Yes . . . Gorman . . .' Then the battered head rolled to one side and Dr Hope lost consciousness.

'Gorman? Who's Gorman, Ellery?'

'Professor Oswald Gorman,' Ellery said through his teeth, 'one of the English faculty at the lunch today. *Get him.*'

When Inspector Queen returned to the dean's office guiding the agitated elbow of Professor Gorman, he found Ellery waiting behind the dean's flower-vase as if it were a bough from Birnam Wood.

The couch was empty.

'What did the ambulance doctor say, Ellery?'

'Concussion. How bad they don't know yet.' Ellery rose, fixing Professor Gorman with a Macduffian glance. 'And where did you find this pedagogical louse, Dad?'

'Upstairs on the seventh floor, teaching a Bible class.'

'The title of my course, Inspector Queen,' said the Professor furiously, 'is *The Influence of the Bible on English Literature.*'

'Trying to establish an alibi, eh?'

'Well, son,' said his father in a troubled voice, 'the professor's more than just tried. He's done it.'

'Established an alibi?' Ellery cried.

'It's a two-hour seminar, from six to eight. He's alibied for every second from 6 p.m. on by the dozen people taking the course—including a minister, a priest, and a rabbi. What's more,' mused the Inspector, 'even assuming the 7.15 on the dean's broken watch was a plant, Professor Gorman can account for every minute of his day since your lunch broke up. Ellery, something is rotten in New York County.'

'I beg your pardon,' said a British voice from the ante-room. 'I was to meet Dr Hope here at eight o'clock.'

Ellery whirled. Then he swooped down upon the owner of the voice, a pale skinny man in a bowler hat carrying a package under one arm.

'Don't tell me you're Alfred Mimms and you're just bringing the Bacon!'

'Yes, but I'll—I'll come back,' stammered the visitor, trying to hold on to his package. But it was Ellery who won the tug of war, and as he tore the wrappings away the pale man turned to run.

And there was Inspector Queen in the doorway with his pistol showing. 'Alfred Mimms, is it?' said the Inspector genially. 'Last time, if memory serves, it was Lord Chalmerston. Remember, Dink, when you were sent up for selling a phony First Folio to that Oyster Bay millionaire? Ellery, this is Dink Chalmers of Flatbush, one of the cleverest confidence men in the rare-book game.' Then the Inspector's geniality faded. 'But, son, this leaves us in more of a mess than before.'

'No, dad,' said Ellery. 'This clears the mess up.'

From Inspector Queen's expression, it did nothing of the kind.

'Because what did Doc Hope reply when I asked him what happened?' Ellery said. 'He replied, "Book taken." Well, obviously, the book wasn't taken. The book was never here. Therefore he didn't mean to say "book taken". Professor, you're a communicant of the Matthew Arnold Hope Cult of Spoonerisms: What must the dean have meant to say?'

' "Took . . . Bacon"!' said Professor Gorman.

'Which makes no sense, either, unless we recall, Dad, that his voice trailed off. As if he meant to add a word, but failed. Which word? The word "money"—"took Bacon *money*". Because while the Bacon book wasn't here to be taken, the ten thousand dollars Doc Hope was toting around all day to pay for it was.

'And who took the Bacon money? The one who knocked on the dean's door just after seven o'clock and asked to be let in. The one who, when Dr Hope unlocked the door—indicating the knocker was someone he knew and trusted—promptly clobbered the old man and made off with his life's savings.'

'But when you asked who hit him,' protested the Inspector, 'he answered "Gorman".'

'Which he couldn't have meant, either, since the professor has an alibi of granite. Therefore——'

'Another spoonerism!' exclaimed Professor Gorman.

'I'm afraid so. And since the only spoonerism possible from the name "Gorman" is "Morgan", hunt up Mr Morgan Naseby of the underpaid English department, Dad, and you'll have Doc's assailant and his ten grand back, too.'

Later, at Bellevue Hospital, an indestructible Elizabethan scholar squeezed the younger Queen's hand feebly. Conversation was forbidden, but the good pedagogue and spoonerist extraordinary did manage to whisper, 'My queer Dean . . .'

SEICHO MATSUMOTO (1909–1992)

The Cooperative Defendant

———

1

THE case seemed simple. . . .

On an autumn night, a sixty-two-year-old moneylender was clubbed to death in his own home by a twenty-eight-year-old man. The murderer stole a cashbox from the victim's house and fled. The box contained twenty-two promissory notes. Of these notes, the killer stole five, then threw the cashbox into a nearby irrigation pond. The murdered moneylender's house was located in a western part of Tokyo that was beginning to prosper architecturally, but at the time of the killing, the immediate vicinity was still roughly half agricultural fields.

When the young lawyer, Naomi Harajima, received word from his lawyers' association that he had been designated court-assigned counsel for the case, he did not much like the idea and was on the verge of refusing. He already had three private cases on his hands, and they were keeping him occupied.

The president of Harajima's lawyers' association argued that he would very much like him to take the case. It appeared that one other lawyer had already been appointed but had suddenly taken ill. The trial was scheduled for an early date. The court would obviously be embarrassed if no legal representative for the defendant was found.

The president said, 'Besides, Harajima—this case is nothing much. Come on, now, man—at least give it the once over. All right?'

Section 3 of Article 7 of the Japanese Constitution makes provision for state-assigned legal counsel in cases where the defendant is too poor or for some other reason unable to procure legal advice (Article 36, Criminal Legal Procedural Code).

Since the state pays, the legal fee is extremely low; busy lawyers usually do not want these cases, though sometimes humane reasons for aiding a defendant enter in. The association attempts to divide these duties among its members on a rotational basis, but any attorney is free to refuse. But something must be done. . . .

Accordingly, cases like this usually find their way into the hands of lawyers who are quite young, or who are not too busy.

Because the fee is small, handling of such cases often becomes less careful than it might otherwise be.

Recently the reputation of the system has improved slightly. But actually, these men, often uninterested or very busy, may do no more than give the case a brief run-through before the trial and meet the defendant for the first time in the courtroom. Things will never be completely remedied until fees for court-assigned counsel are raised.

Harajima was urged to defend Torao Ueki in the case of the murder of Jin Yamagishi, because the work was simple. He finally agreed.

In reading the documents pertaining to the indictment, the records of the criminal investigation, Harajima learned the following things.

Originally, the victim, Jin Yamagishi, had owned a rather large amount of agricultural land. But he had sold this to a realtor. With the money accrued, he built a two-storey house and immediately opened a small-scale financing business. This had happened ten years ago. At the time of the murder, Yamagishi lived alone. Childless, his wife had died three years before. Yamagishi rented the second floor of his house to a young primary-school teacher and his wife. The rent was not high, though the old moneylender had a reputation for being greedy. He was impressed because the schoolteacher had a second-dan black belt in judo. In other words, the young man would be a combination tenant and guard.

Any elderly person living alone might want protection. In this case, it was still more important for Yamagishi, since he had made a bad name by charging high interest on the money he lent. Many of his customers were small businessmen trying hard to succeed in a newly developing part of Tokyo. The neighborhood was along one of the private commuter train lines. A good location. But population growth had been slow, and business was not thriving. Some of the people who paid Yamagishi's high rates went bankrupt. There were cases in which older people used their retirement funds to open stores. They put shop and land down as security for loans from

Yamagishi. He took everything when they could no longer keep up their payments.

Customers in other districts along the same train line suffered because of Yamagishi's behavior. It was not alone fear of thieves but also the knowledge of the many people who hated him that encouraged the moneylender to install the young judo expert and his wife in the upstairs apartment.

On October 15, the young teacher received word that his mother was close to death. He and his wife left that day for their hometown. The murder took place on October 18, and Yamagishi's body was discovered by a neighbor on the morning of October 19. This person found the front door open (later it was disclosed that all other windows and doors were firmly secured with rain shutters that were locked from within), entered the hallway, and immediately saw Yamagishi stretched out face down in the adjacent room. Fearful, he called out. There was no answer from the inert form.

He reported the matter to the police.

Autopsy revealed the cause of death to be brain concussion and cerebral hemorrhage, caused by a blow on the head. An area about as large as the palm of an adult hand was caved in and flattened at the back of the skull. The wound had been fatal. Yamagishi had tumbled forward and expired in a crawling position. He had apparently been struck from behind and, after falling, had crawled a short distance on hands and knees.

From the contents of the victim's stomach, it was ascertained that he had died about three hours after his last meal. Yamagishi, who cooked for himself, was in the habit of eating dinner around six. This would mean that the murder took place between nine and ten, an assumption that agreed with the autopsy doctor's estimation of lapse of postmortem time.

Nothing in the room was disturbed. In a smaller bedroom next to the one in which the corpse was discovered, a sliding cupboard door was open. The black-painted steel cashbox in which Yamagishi kept his customers' promissory notes and other documents was missing. Japanese-style bedding was spread out on the floor of this room. The top quilt was pulled partly back. The sheets and pillowcase were wrinkled but not violently disordered. This suggested that Yamagishi must have gotten out of bed and walked into the next room. He habitually retired at nine o'clock (testimony of the young teacher and his wife).

It was apparent that Yamagishi had opened the front door of the house himself, letting the murderer in. Usually the door was locked by means of a stout wooden pole forced against the frame in such a way as to make opening from the outside impossible. When the body was discovered this pole stood in the entranceway beside the door. Only Yamagishi could have removed it and opened up from inside.

Someone Yamagishi knew and who knew his habits well must have come to visit.

Why was the greedy, suspicious old man willing to get out of bed and admit someone at the hour of nine o'clock at night?

There were no reported rumors about Jin Yamagishi's masculinity. He was not prohibitively old. But perhaps because of his curious personality or stinginess, from his youth he hadn't much been interested in women. The person who called at nine that night must have been a man.

Not one of the neighbors had heard anybody knocking on the old moneylender's door or calling out to him on the night of the murder. If he had already gone to sleep, anyone who called loud enough to wake him in the inner sleeping room would have been heard. Possibly the telephone had roused him. The instrument stood on a small table in a corner of the room where he slept. The murderer could have called Yamagishi first to tell him he was coming. Yamagishi then removed the pole from the front door and waited. He must have been quite familiar with the person, if this were true. He did not know he waited for his death.

The stolen cashbox gave some hints about the killer. It contained promissory notes from the people who had borrowed from Yamagishi, plus renewals for payment of interest and other promissory contracts. The murderer obviously knew both the contents and the location of the cashbox. His purpose had been to steal the promissory notes.

Under a Buddhist shrine in the house, the detectives discovered 150,000 yen in cash. But nothing was disturbed; there was no trace of the killer's having tried to find it.

Two days after the crime, the police had arrested Torao Ueki.

One of the investigators learned that a Mr Nakamura, while looking out of his bathroom window, had seen a man hurrying at a run down the street in the direction of Yamagishi's house. This man looked very much like the proprietor of a noodle shop near the train station.

Torao Ueki had opened a noodle shop next to the train station three years earlier. About a year ago, he had purchased some of the neighboring land and expanded and remodeled his shop, not because business was on the upswing, but because he wanted to compete with a new noodle shop in the vicinity. He had hoped that by enlarging and improving his place he would attract more customers. He did not. The number of customers decreased. But to purchase the land and make renovations, he had borrowed money from Yamagishi at a high rate of interest.

With the interest and the drop in business, Ueki was in a tight spot. But he had a hunch that, in a bit, the number of houses in the neighborhood would increase, causing a rise in daily commuters on the trains. His shop was in front of the station, an excellent location. He decided to stick it out. But Yamagishi's exorbitant interest payments were getting the better of him. He couldn't sit back calmly and wait for a brighter tomorrow. From the age of eighteen till twenty-five, he had worked in a second-hand bookshop in the center of town. The restaurant business was completely new to him.

Ueki had suffered deeply because of his connection with Yamagishi. The moneylender was merciless in exacting his due. The note had been renewed a number of times, and the interest came to four times the original loan. When the murder took place, Ueki owed Yamagishi seven and a half million yen. Yamagishi felt that if the debt rose still more, Ueki would never be able to repay, so he would assume ownership of the land and shop, which had been put up as security. This disturbed Ueki terribly and had recently caused trouble. Ueki hated Yamagishi. He told certain persons that he would like to 'kill that old man!'

2

There were many other people who hated Yamagishi enough to kill him. But to be a suspect, there had to be the lack of an alibi for the hour from nine till ten on the night of the crime. The suspect had to be known to the victim and have knowledge that the schoolteacher and his wife were out of town. He had to possess detailed knowledge concerning the layout of Yamagishi's house and the exact location of the cashbox. And, judging from the brutal wound on the back of the victim's head, he had to be quite strong.

No fingerprints belonging to the killer were discovered. There were numerous other fingerprints, but they were smeared, except for some belonging to the couple upstairs. They, though, had the clear alibi of being in Kyushu at the time of the murder. The remaining prints probably were those of people who came to see Yamagishi on financial business. All the prints were old.

The killer left no weapon behind. No suspicious footprints were found, and the entrance hall was floored with concrete, so such prints were unlikely. The pole that latched the front door was considered as a possible murder weapon, yet it seemed too lightweight, slender, to have caused the fatal wound. The only prints on it were Yamagishi's. Yamagishi had been almost completely bald, and had bled little. Neither blood nor hair would be found on the weapon.

Under the eaves at the back of the house was a stack of pine logs, cut for fuel. Town gas had not yet been piped to the area. Most of the residents used bottled propane. Yamagishi, however, in his miserliness and accustomed to farmhouse ways, fired his cooking stove with wood. The pine logs had been carefully split into pieces with roughly triangular cross sections some four centimeters to a side. It seemed that several blows with such a log could cause the kind of wound that killed Yamagishi. Detectives checked the top ten of perhaps thirty bundles of firewood in the stack, but the rough surfaces made it difficult to trace prints. It was, in fact, next to impossible. There were no findings of blood or hair.

With this information on the condition of the body and scene of the crime in his mind, Harajima read the report of the confession made by Ueki:

'Must have been nearly two years ago, I got money from Jin Yamagishi. It was at a damned high rate of interest. Since that time, I suffered because of the debt. Just lately, he made a threat—said he'd auction off my shop and land; they were put up as security for the loan. Everything I had was used to buy the land and open the noodle shop. Later on, I borrowed money from Yamagishi to enlarge and improve my shop. But business didn't go so well. I thought it would be better. That and Yamagishi's crazy demands drove me to despair. Yes. I decided my wife and children, and I, would commit suicide together. But, by God, before I died, I wanted to kill that old man. It would at least be something for the sake of all the other people he brought to grief.

'October 18, I was in the Manpaiso mahjong parlor, maybe two hundred meters from the train station. From maybe seven in the evening, with friends—Nakada, Maeda, and Nishikawa—playing mahjong. Lately, seeing how we don't have many customers, I leave the shop to my wife in the evening, and play mahjong or kill the time one way or the other. We played maybe three games, I think, when Shibata came in and started watching. He comes to the mahjong parlor pretty often. He wanted to join the game. I said, "Look, I've got to run home for something. Why don't you sit in for me?" It made him happy. I left the Manpaiso at maybe nine o'clock.

'But I didn't go home. I went over to the phone booth in front of the station and called Yamagishi. After a time, he answered. I told him I wanted to talk about him taking my property. I told him I'd managed to get together two million yen and I'd bring it with me right now. I said maybe he could postpone his claim on the land and shop, we could talk. At first he was kind of angry, interrupting, saying he'd gone to bed. Then he smoothed out, changed his mind when I mentioned the money. "Okay, c'mon over. I'm waiting." He sounded even impatient.

'It's about a half a mile to Yamagishi's. After a bit there aren't many houses, only fields and two irrigation ponds. I didn't meet anybody. There are twelve or thirteen houses along by Yamagishi's. But Mr Nakamura's house is off the street a ways, some distance. I had no idea he'd be able to see me from his toilet window. He eats at our noodle shop.

'Just like he said he would, Yamagishi had opened the door. I knew the teacher and his woman had gone to Kyushu three or four days ago. The teacher eats at the shop. He told me himself.

'Before I went to the door, I went around behind the house. I hunted around and found a chunk of wood from the pile I knew was there. Nobody was home upstairs, either—I made sure. All the windows were shuttered. No sign of light anywhere through the cracks.

'So I went to the door. I stepped into the hallway and called to Yamagishi. He came to meet me. There was a light in the other room. I held the hunk of wood behind me. It was shadowy.

' "You know, it's late," he said. But he was grinning and didn't seem upset. He was sure as the devil thinking about the two million. "It's okay, though," he said. "C'mon, in."

'I tried to stall, thinking about the piece of wood. I said something about being sorry to disturb him so late, and all. Told him I'd managed to get together two million yen. I didn't want to leave it home for fear of thieves.

' "C'mon, c'mon," he said, moving into the next room. He pulled two seat cushions from a stack in the corner and put them by a table. I kept the wood behind me as I stepped up into the main part of the house from the hall. The second I sat on the cushion, I stuck it underneath, behind me, and said, "I brought the money; how's for writing me a receipt?" I figured the subject of money would keep his attention. I let him see the fake newspaper-wrapped parcel I'd fixed, bulging from my front pocket. He figured it was the money, okay. He jumped up to go into the next room, probably for blank receipts.

'I thought, this is it, and leaped up, too. In one move I smashed him on the back of his bald head with the chunk of wood. I gave it everything. He gave a hell of a yell and fell on his face. I bent down and smashed him three more times on the back of the head. He lay there on his face and didn't move. Then, to make it look like I'd been a thief and not a guest, I put the two cushions back on the pile in the corner.

'Then I went into the next room to look for the cashbox. I found it in the cupboard. I wanted to take it out and tear up the notes like he'd made me suffer, but I didn't know the combination to the lock. I decided to take the box with me. After I left the house, I put the piece of wood on the pile in back. I don't remember exactly where. It was dark. It took maybe thirty minutes, all told.

'The moon was coming up now. I went down the road a little ways, then walked off it into a clump of deep grass. I hunted around, found a large stone, and cracked the lock on the cashbox. I looked quickly through the promissory notes, took the ones with my name on them, along with five or six others. I put these in my pocket. It was hard to see, but I'd been able to make out the names in the pale moonlight. I tossed the box into the irrigation pond on my right. Then I went along to the playground of a life-insurance company, not far away, where I lit a match and burned the notes I'd been carrying in my pocket. I scuffed the ashes into the ground.

'I was plenty surprised when the police told me they had recovered the cashbox from the pond, and that my notes were still there. It turned out that Yamagishi's account book had a customer with a name like mine: Tomio Inoki. The police claimed I must've been mistaken, thinking his notes were mine, in the dark. I'd destroyed the wrong ones. Inoki's notes were missing from the box. I was very excited at the time, so it could have been like that.

'After I'd done all this, I went back to the Manpaiso, where my friends were still playing mahjong. I watched maybe ten minutes, till Nakada won the round. Then I took Shibata's place and played a round myself. None of them knew I'd just murdered a man. If I say so, I was very calm. I guess it was because I had no guilt feelings about having killed Yamagishi.

'I slept well that night. I had burned the notes. Yamagishi had no heirs. The debts would be canceled. I felt happy and relieved.

'The next day, the news of the death caused a big stir in the neighborhood. But there was no one to feel sorry about it. I felt fine when people said it was good he was gone, that he got what was coming to him.

'Two days later, I was watching television in the shop, when two detectives came. They asked me to come to the station. They had a few things to ask me. At the time, I knew it might be the end. Maybe it was wrong to kill him. But he deserved it. I made up my mind to tell the police everything. Of course, if I could, I wanted to make it look like I wasn't guilty.'

Reading all this, Harajima got the impression that the case was indeed simple. It could arouse little interest in any lawyer, private or court-assigned. The best he could do would be to ask for clemency on the basis of extenuating circumstances. But as he went on with the case report, he was surprised. Ueki abruptly changed, and claimed to have nothing to do with the murder. He insisted the confession had been the result of psychological torment and leading questions, plus a promise of leniency on the part of police investigators. Of course, defendants like Ueki made this kind of claim often, especially in cases involving heavy punishment.

Just the same, from the evidence in these documents, Harajima felt reasonably sure Ueki was guilty. The written confession sounded natural and unforced. It agreed with the results of the police investigation on the murder site and environs. It did not appear to have been made under police pressure, as Ueki claimed.

Nonetheless, in front of the public prosecutor, Torao Ueki had issued another deposition containing the following information.

3

'It's true, as stated before, I was playing mahjong with Nakada, Maeda, and Nishikawa in the Manpaiso and that, after two games, Shibata took my place. It's true, I went over to the phone booth in front of the station, called Jin Yamagishi, and told him I had to talk about the securities involved in the loan. It's also true he told me he was up and waiting—and that I went to his house. The rest of the statement I made at the police station, it's untrue.

'I didn't tell Yamagishi on the phone that I'd scraped together two million yen. I could never find that much money. God. But the police kept on insisting Yamagishi wouldn't get out of bed to see me 'less I'd brought money. They claimed, if I'd just told him I wanted to see him, he'd say to wait till the next day. They said I put something in my pocket that looked like a bundle of money, before going to the house. So I thought about what they said. On the basis of Yamagishi's personality, a third person would see eye-to-eye with the police. So I agreed they were right.

'Actually, I simply told Yamagishi I wanted him to wait before taking possession of the securities. If I lost the land and shop, my whole family would have nothing to live on. I said I had an idea for a solution, and I wanted him to listen. He said possession of the securities wasn't really what he wanted—he'd only decided to take such a step because he didn't think there was any hope of my repaying the money. If I had some proposal, he'd consider it. He said I was to come, and that he'd leave the front door open.

'So I walked close to his house, but couldn't go in. I didn't have any damned proposal to make. I was so damned worried about the loss of the land and shop, all I wanted to do was ask him to wait. But I knew this would only make him angrier than ever. I couldn't bring myself to confront him. I felt bad. I just wandered around the neighborhood for maybe thirty minutes, then started back.

'I didn't feel like playing mahjong. I wandered around the playground of the life-insurance company, while thinking over my troubles. It's a country road. I didn't meet anybody. I must've wandered like that for an hour before I went back to the mahjong parlor. The game was nearly over. I took Shibata's place and played for a while. Since I'd done nothing wrong, I was calm. My friends testified to that. My wife says I slept well that night. After all, there was nothing on my conscience. This is really what happened that night. I'll say this about the false confession I gave earlier:

'First off, I told the police I didn't kill Yamagishi. They wouldn't listen. One after the other, detectives came into the room. They said it'd do no good to lie. Said they had all the proof they needed. According to their side, the stolen cashbox had been recovered from one of the two irrigation ponds. The combination lock was smashed. Inside, they found twenty-two water-soaked promissory notes, including mine—for seven and a half million yen. God. They said they compared the contents with Yamagishi's account book. They said promissory notes of a man named Tomio Inoki were missing. They said I'd made a mistake. Intending to steal my own notes, I'd misread the name Tomio Inoki for Torao Ueki. They said it happened because the characters used to write the names are similar. And, also, because there was only a little moonlight that night.

'Then another detective came in. He said did I know Yoshiya Nakamura? I said, sure, because he's a customer at my shop. Then he said Nakamura must know my face pretty well, and I said, sure, that's right. The detective looked real proud of himself then, as if he'd won something, and told me Nakamura had testified to seeing me hurrying in the direction of Yamagishi's house about five minutes after nine, on the night of the murder. Nakamura was looking out his toilet window. The detective was all grins. He said I probably hadn't been aware of Nakamura's watching me, but it was too late to evade. Now they had testimony of a man who'd seen me in the vicinity, the evidence of the cashbox—and my own admission of a motive. They said it was "unshakable evidence." God. Then they said they sympathized with me. If I'd confess, they'd have the public prosecutor release me, arrange to have the case dropped. They were very pleasant to me when they said that I probably wanted to go home to my family and my work as soon as I could.

'I tried to explain why Nakamura had seen me through the window. They wouldn't listen. They kept on promising to have the case dropped if I'd make a false confession. Well, I finally said, all right, I committed the murder. God. They were so happy they let me have cigarettes and ordered in food for me. So then I wrote a confession to their instructions. They wanted something else. A map of the interior of Yamagishi's house. So, I did that.

'Writing, I ran into problems. First, I didn't know what kind of weapon to say I used. One of the detectives said, looking at me like an owl, straight-faced, "How about the stuff used for fuel in a stove?" I said, "Sure, I beat Yamagishi to death with a chip of coal." The detective called me a fool, and said, "Stump-head. The longish stuff they bring from mountain forests. About this long." He gestured. "Oh," I said. "Split logs?" "That's right," he said. "You smacked his shiny old bald pate with a hunk of firewood." Then he said, "C'mon, where's it kept?" I didn't know, you see. So I said, "A corner in the kitchen." Well, he got mad then. He shouted at me, "No! It's a place where rain falls on it. But only drops of rain. Drop, drop, drop!" He was probably trying to be highly descriptive. "Under the eaves?" I said. "Right as rain!" he called out.

'But what is written in the investigation report and that first deposition makes a different impression: "Before I went to the door, I went around behind the house, I hunted around and found a chunk of wood from the pile I knew was there. . . . So I went to the door, I stepped into the hallway and called to Yamagishi." It's true, the general meaning of the two statements is similar. On the end of the confession is the sentence, "I affix my signature to certify that this transcription is identical in content to my oral testimony."

'The detectives took me behind Yamagishi's place and asked me to show them the piece of firewood I used for the murder weapon. But I hadn't murdered anybody! I was at a loss. "How's for this one?" asked a detective, picking a log from about the second row on top. I think he had it in mind from the start. I said, "All right," and it was identified as the murder weapon. Then I said, "But there's no blood or hair on it." They explained that there had been no exterior bleeding and Yamagishi'd been bald. So, obviously there was no blood or hair. Then, like they were making fun of me, one said, "If Yamagishi'd bled, we'd've been forced to paint blood of his type on the log." When I asked about lack of my fingerprints, another said, "Prints can't be detected on a rough surface like that." So he wrapped the log in cloth as a piece of material evidence.

'Then they asked how we'd been sitting when I killed Yamagishi. I said I'd hid the piece of wood in my hand, come in the hallway, and told him I had two million yen with me. He asked me in. I took off my shoes, stepped up into the main part of the house, and abruptly smashed him on the back of the head with the piece of firewood.

'The detectives said it was impossible. So, they had a version. Since I was a guest, Yamagishi must've taken out two cushions, like he would. When I told him I'd come to pay two million, he probably rose to go into the next room for receipt blanks. That was, according to them, when I hit him on the back of the head. They added that I'd put the cushions back in the pile by the wall to suggest the murderer hadn't been a person received as a guest. By this time, I was damned tired of arguing, and just said, "Sure. That's how it was." But they insisted I repeat it all, like they'd said it. So, I did that. Not very well, actually. But I did like I was told.

'Next thing, they asked me how many times I struck him. "Once," I said. They said it wasn't enough to kill. "How many times?" "Six or seven." But that was too many. If I'd hit him that many times he'd have bled more. "Let's see," one said. "You just don't remember, but it's three times, right? Three times." He spoke as if I were a child. Then he muttered, "Three blows with a piece of firewood would make a wound like the one described in the autopsy report."

'Then came the cashbox, breaking it open, taking the notes, mistaking Tomio Inoki's name for mine—all of that was the detectives' suggestion. They asked about the pond where I threw the cashbox. I said, "The one to the left." They told me to think again. "After all, there're only two." So, I said the one on the right. Now, if the real killer's prints could be found on that box, I'd be okay. The investigators said it was impossible to take prints from it, because it got coated with mud from the pond. According to them, I deliberately threw the box in the mud to obscure fingerprints.

'Of course, I didn't know about the ashes they say they found in the weeds in the playground of the life-insurance company. Maybe the police burned some paper like the notes on their own. You can't read printing or writing on ashes.

'I was so eager to go home, I fell into the police trap. They promised to have the public prosecutor release me and have the case dismissed, if I confessed. They said they sympathized with my motive and wanted to help me as much as they could. I believed them.

'They took me right from the jail to the detention house. The detectives said to tell the public prosecutor exactly what I'd said to them. If I said anything different, they threatened to return me to the police and start all over. "This time, we'll really let you have it. You try denying the confession in court, we'll see you get the limit. Play it smart, Ueki."

'They frightened me. So, I told the public prosecutor the things like they're written in the false confession. Then, finally, I found their promises about dropping the case, letting me go home, it was all a lie. I decided to come out with the truth.'

4

After reading this deposition, Harajima couldn't decide whether the claim that the confession had been made under police pressure was exaggerated or true. The first confession sounded unforced, natural. But, in its way, so did the second. There were still some policemen who might resort to tactics of the kind Ueki described. As a lawyer, Harajima was tempted to lean toward the second confession.

The public prosecutor's indictment refused to recognize the second deposition, insisting on considering the confession made before the police as evidence. The constitution (Article 38) states that confessions obtained by means of coercion, torture, or threats, and confessions obtained after unduly long detention are inadmissible as evidence. Confessions given as a result of deceptive interrogation—for instance, claiming that an accomplice has admitted guilt when he has not—or as an outcome of leading questions slanted in favor of the interrogator, are to be regarded as forced. Such evidence is insufficient to establish guilt.

Defendants often plead their confessions were forced in an attempt to prove their innocence. In such cases, corroborating evidence is of the greatest importance in establishing guilt. Such evidence includes material evidence, and testimonies of third parties. It can be divided into direct and indirect, or circumstantial, evidence.

Torao Ueki had borrowed money at high interest from Jin Yamagishi. Unable to pay, he faced the threat of having his securities seized. His desire for murder was circumstantial evidence. He had no alibi for the time of the crime. Testimonies of his friends, Nakada, Maeda, Nishikawa, and Shibata, and the manager and personnel of the Manpaiso mahjong parlor, established the fact that he had left the premises at around nine in the evening and had returned at ten.

Yoshiya Nakamura testified that, shortly after the time Ueki left the Manpaiso, he had been looking out of the window and had seen Ueki. He had not witnessed Ueki's entry into Yamagishi's house, or the murder. Therefore, his evidence was indirect.

Material evidence included the piece of firewood, and the cashbox fished out of the irrigation pond. In searching, the police had dragged the pond and recovered it. Ueki's fingerprints were not on the box. This has been explained. The following police report covers the question of prints on the firewood:

'Question: With what did you strike Jin Yamagishi on the back of the head?

'Answer: A chunk of pine log. Like they use in old-fashioned stoves.

'Question: About how long was the piece of wood?

'Answer: Maybe thirty centimeters.

'Question: Where was it?

'Answer: What?

'Question: Where was the wood kept?

'Answer: Oh. Piled under the eaves behind Yamagishi's place. I'd been thinking of using it ever since I got the idea of killing him.

'Question: You mean you knew there was firewood piled in that place?

'Answer: Yes.

'Question: What did you do with the wood after the crime?

'Answer: I put it back where I got it.

'Question: If we went back to where the wood is stored, could you pick out the piece you used?

'Answer: Sure, if nobody moved it.

'Question: Since the discovery of the body, the house has been in police custody. Everything's just as it was.

'Answer: Sure, then if I went there, I could pick out the piece.'

In this report there are no traces of the association-game hints Ueki claimed were forced on him in the second confession. The defendant was taken back to Yamagishi's house, as the following report reveals.

'The defendant was taken behind Yamagishi's house, where he examined a pile of about thirty-five bundles of wood stacked under the eaves. He promptly picked out a piece from the second row from the top. He said, "This is it. This is the one I used."

'An investigator put on gloves and took the piece indicated. The defendant, too, was given gloves and held the wood in his right hand. Then he swung it two or three times to the right and left and made five or six downstrikes with it. He said, "This is it, all right. I guess once you've used something like this, you know the feel of it, don't you."

'In offering this evidence, the defendant was most cooperative.'

Torao Ueki's efforts to help made it look almost as if he were currying favor with the police.

Harajima had not seen the full initial investigation report. He took time from his busy schedule to visit the police station. From the report, he learned that the police had narrowed their search to Ueki from the moment they received Nakamura's testimony about having seen Ueki from his bathroom window. Ueki confessed immediately after arrest. The police had been comfortably able to send in an early report.

Realizing Harajima was court-appointed counsel, the officer in charge was clearly angry when he said, 'I understand the defendant's now denying his confession. What's he trying to do? It's ridiculous. The police can't be accused of using strong-arm tactics. We'd never promise to set a man free or have the case dropped if he agreed to sign a confession. We don't threaten to fight for the death penalty when a defendant denies his confession in court. When Ueki first came in here, he sat right down—told us everything about the murder, how he went in and talked to Yamagishi, how he killed him. He drew a map of Yamagishi's house, explaining it all on his own. The whole thing about the murder weapon was just as it's written up. He pointed it out to us, made a few swings with it, said he recalled the knot. He even asked us to find out if his fingerprints were on the log. He was friendly. I really don't think he could have described things so well unless he knew what he was talking about.'

This business of Ueki being 'friendly' made Harajima frown. Sometimes defendants cooperate with the police so they can be sent to the detention house quickly. Once there, they change their tune, claiming what they said for the police was made under duress. Maybe this was how Ueki figured things. Still he might pretend friendliness, believing the police would free him and drop the case. He certainly had cooperated.

The trial was drawing near. Stealing time from other cases, Harajima made a trip to the detention house to talk with Ueki.

Ueki was tall, reedy, with a pale, femininely gentle face. Both his shoulders and eyebrows slanted downward, giving him a kind of parallel semblance of dejection. Thin-lipped, he had a tight, narrow forehead, but he was quite polite when he met Harajima, expressing respect and gratitude that the lawyer was representing him. Especially since there was no fee. There was a certain meekness about Ueki, though none of this was in his words.

Harajima was of two minds about the man. Could such a weak-looking fellow commit murder? Still, that girlish face might conceal brutality and cunning. Although he had looked into the eyes of hundreds of defendants, Harajima wasn't always able to tell whether they were sincere.

'Torao, I've taken your case. You want the right kind of defense, you'll have to be completely frank.'

'Sure, yes—understood.'

Harajima hesitated, then said, 'Do you still claim your first confession was a lie?'

Ueki was quick, direct. 'Absolutely. Damn it, I was tricked by the police.'

'Then, it's true, about the leading questions, all that?'

'Yes, yes—'

'They claim you cooperated with them, went so far as to point out the firewood to the investigators.'

Ueki shook his head. 'That's not so. It's like I said in the second deposition. The detectives told me just what to say.'

'You'll testify to that?'

'Certainly.'

'Okay, then. We'll work out a defense on those lines.'

Ueki's tone changed. 'Mr Harajima? I can prove the confession I made was forced from me.'

'Prove?'

'Yes.'

5

A smile touched Ueki's lips. 'I thought of it last night in bed. I'm sure it's because you've been chosen to defend me—God graciously jogged my memory.'

Harajima sighed. 'What d'you mean?'

'Sure. It's about what happened before I'm supposed to have killed the old man. I heard he was on his face, turned in the direction of the next room. Lying there, like that, I mean. When I first talked with the police, I made it up that after Yamagishi'd seen me, he said a couple of words, then invited me in. That he turned to go into the other room. This is when I said I hit him with the log. Well, the police said that story wasn't any good. They kept insisting I must've sat on a cushion Yamagishi pulled out for me. Then I'd put the cushion back after the murder. So it'd look like the crime was by someone who broke in, not by a guest. They kept at it, and finally I went along. But listen—the truth is Jin Yamagishi never offered cushions to people who came to borrow money. I was there a lot and he never gave me one. You'd have to know him. Must've been like that with everybody, I bet. You can ask around.'

'Why'd he have the pile of cushions in the corner?'

'For show, see? None of his customers ever sat on one. If they sat down, they'd stay too long. He liked us to leave right away, after he'd forced his conditions on us. Okay, if the talk lasted a while, then he might maybe show some kind of human feeling. Of course, that's not saying he didn't give a cushion to ordinary visitors. The detectives didn't know this.'

'You have any other proof?'

'The cashbox, Mr Harajima. I didn't know where it had been found. They said something about "water," so I remembered the irrigation ponds. But when I said the one on the left, they called me a fool. So I told them the one to the right. That's in the deposition I made after meeting the prosecutor. Damn it, Mr Harajima, the fact my promissory notes were still there, in the box, should prove I didn't kill him. They said I misread Inoki for Ueki. But, hell—now, would somebody who'd murdered to get those notes back fail to check the names on them? The police said it was dark. But I'm supposed to have burned five notes in the playground a little later. This means I had matches, right? I could've checked the names when I struck a match. Anyway, my prints weren't found on the cashbox.'

'Well. Anything else?'

'Yes. It's important, too. How about this—does the hunk of wood used as the murder weapon match the wound on Yamagishi's head?'

'How d'you mean?'

'Listen, I read the medical report. A copy, that is. There was a flattened spot on the back of Yamagishi's skull, maybe the size of a human palm. The bone was dented in. The log the detectives made me select was triangular, Mr Harajima—in cross-section, I mean—about four centimeters wide on a side.' Ueki shook his head. 'I just don't think three smacks would leave something like that. I mean, the fractures would've been uneven. He must've been hit with something larger, once.' He blinked. 'Naturally, it's only my guess. But, still, you might check it.'

Ueki had been speaking quietly, but with an undercurrent of hope.

Harajima took a taxi home from the detention house. On the way, he thought over what Ueki had said, and could not help becoming excited. Finally, he concluded Ueki's words had considerable significance.

Back at the office, he read the case record over with a different eye. He saw that when the viewpoint alters, so does the impression one gets from the materials. Other possibilities hadn't been investigated. Ueki had confessed, immediately upon arrest. The police had relaxed and consequently were careless about making certain of their evidence. Happy over success, they'd been lax in their very first investigations.

Harajima questioned some ten customers of Yamagishi's about the cushions. He learned that the moneylender never provided them with one when they were at his house. From the young teacher upstairs, however, he found that Yamagishi did, indeed, give courteous hospitality to those who visited on other than business. He seemed to enjoy sitting and chatting. Other associates of Yamagishi attested to this.

The police had considered it only common sense to assume Yamagishi brought out cushions for customers. They required the suspect admit doing this—returning the cushion to the pile after the murder—to suggest the act had been committed by a thief.

Next, Harajima took the coroners' report to a friend who was a doctor of forensic medicine, and asked his opinion.

'It's supposition, remember,' the doctor said. 'But to make a wound of the kind that killed Yamagishi would require a single blow with a weapon more than eight centimeters wide.' Shaking his head, he said, 'It's odd the police don't see this. But, of course, they place more importance on their own intuition and experience than on what we say. They think our reports little more than reference material.' He made a clucking sound with his tongue. 'They actually look down on us, doctors,' he said, smiling quickly.

It would seem that one of the detectives had simply decided the murder weapon should be a split log, lacking anything else suitable. The excitement of conducting an investigation immediately after Ueki confessed probably accounted for much of the laxity. It was different from times when a criminal left so much evidence behind that it confused the police with its very abundance. Nothing was as open to error or powerful prejudice as the educated hunch of an over-confident detective.

Harajima had some notes about this, right on his desk, taken from *Ascertaining the Facts*, by the Judicial Research and Training Institute. It was interesting, and a parallel: 'There have been many cases in which police officers, operating on the basis of a preformed notion, have failed to take into consideration facts that remove suspicions and have used undue methods to force confessions. Almost all judges with long experience have encountered one or two such incidents. Written works on criminal matters often refer to cases of the kind.

For instance, mention is made of police officers who carelessly and hastily overlook facts that prove innocence. In addition, there are remarks to the effect that there is much falsehood in confessions made before police.'

Harajima became enthusiastic. This very case might just be a stroke of good luck. In court, he called the forensic medical expert to give an opinion about the wound. As new witnesses, he summoned several persons who had associations with Jin Yamagishi. He questioned the four police officers who had interrogated Ueki. They all testified that the confession had been given willingly.

— Did you tell the defendant, Mr Ueki, 'We know you killed Yamagishi. You won't get off now. But, if you confess, we'll let you free and get the public prosecutor to drop the case'?

— Witness A: Listen, I never said anything like that.

— In order to prompt a confession, did you allow the defendant to smoke as much as he liked in the interrogation room? And after the confession, did you order food for him on three occasions?

— Witness B: It's customary to allow a defendant two or three cigarettes during questioning. This isn't to 'prompt a confession.' We ordered food once.

— During questioning, did you instruct the defendant with hints about having to put the cushions back in the original place?

— Witness C: No. He told us that, offered it on his own.

— Did you suggest the firewood, exhibit one, as the murder weapon? And, did you lead the defendant to select the log shown here—and to say he struck the victim on the back of the head with it, three times?

— Witness D: Of course not. He confessed all that himself. He chose that piece of wood himself. He said, 'This is it,' or something, and swung it around. Then he said, 'No mistake about it.' He was very cooperative.

Ueki was quite disturbed, indignant, about the testimony of these men during cross-questioning.

'See? They said what I told you. How the devil can they lie like that? Just to make themselves look good. They don't give a damn about who's guilty.'

There was a deadlock. The police officers strongly denied Ueki's accusations.

Three months later, the verdict was handed down. Not guilty, for lack of sufficient evidence.

The verdict was reached for the following reasons:

1. The piece of wood presented to the court as the murder weapon is four centimeters wide at the broadest point. According to testimonies of the autopsy doctor and one other, flattening of the victim's skull would require a weapon at least as wide as an adult palm, eight or nine centimeters. (A report by an expert from a large medical university confirmed this.) Therefore, the pine log offered as evidence cannot have been the murder weapon.

2. Fingerprints of the defendant were not found on the piece of pine log, nor on the cashbox belonging to Jin Yamagishi.

3. According to the confession, the defendant took five of the twenty-two promissory notes from the cashbox. He took these to the playground of a life-insurance company some two hundred meters from the irrigation pond and burned them. Among notes left in the box were those in the name of the defendant, Torao Ueki. It was assumed, after investigation, that the five notes burned had been in the name of Tomio Inoki. The judicial police insist that, in the dark, the defendant must have misread the name Tomio Inoki as his own, Torao Ueki.

This seems likely, but the defense attorney's insistence is also convincing: if the defendant is in fact the murderer, then recovery of the notes would have been his primary concern. He would have made certain he had the right ones.

4. Examination of the written confessions reveals no trace of coercion or undue detention by the judicial police to force the defendant to confess. However, there is an impression that deception and leading questions were employed. The series of depositions submitted by the defendant to this court strongly claim such methods were used. This is not enough to convince the court that the crime was not committed by the defendant. The defendant is unable to account convincingly for his actions and whereabouts for the hour from the time he left the Manpaiso mahjong parlor to the time when he returned. There is doubt because Yoshiya Nakamura testifies to having seen the defendant near the victim's house around that time. This substantiates the first confession.

5. This court has considered the evidence, and come to the following decision. The court concludes that there is insufficient evidence of guilt and, in accordance with Article 336 of the Criminal Actions Law, pronounces a verdict of not guilty.

6

A year passed. Naomi Harajima was in the habit of reading legal volumes during his free time. One night, as he glanced through *Studies of Not-Guilty Verdicts* by the English judge James Hind, his eyes locked on an arresting section. He sat bolt upright in his chair. He read on and experienced an unpleasant thumping in his chest.

In 1923, Peter Cammerton, a worker in a sail factory in Manchester, England, was arrested and charged with murdering a wealthy widow, Mrs Hammersham, and then setting fire to her home. Because he was in need of money, Cammerton planned to kill her and steal whatever he could. Going to her house around seven in the evening, he struck her several times in the face with an iron rod, about fifty centimeters long. He then strangled her with his leather belt, took one hundred and fifty pounds in cash, along with some jewelry from her room, and fled.

To conceal traces of his act, he returned about nine in the evening, intending to burn her house. Lighting a kerosene lamp, he placed it on a book atop the bureau. Half of the lamp-base projected over the edge of the book. The lamp leaned because of unstable support. On the floor, he piled waste paper and clothing, which would ignite when the lamp fell. The fire would spread to the entire house. He knew the lamp would tumble when a freight train passed on tracks behind Mrs Hammersham's house in the next hour. The ground and house foundation trembled whenever a train came along. Three hours later, the house was in flames. Firetrucks raced to the scene. They were unable to extinguish the blaze.

Peter Cammerton was arrested soon after. He confessed, but later denied his confession. He was pronounced not guilty through lack of evidence.

Was Peter Cammerton, in fact, the person who robbed and killed the woman and set fire to the house?

There were no fingerprints or other objective evidence to link him with the crime. More, there was little circumstantial evidence to establish his guilt. Many of his friends testified that he had said and done nothing unusual between the time of the crime and his arrest. On the day of the murder, he had taken a pleasure trip to London. He returned eagerly to Manchester, knowing full well he would undergo a police investigation. This spoke in his favor.

Cammerton confessed to the police, but later denied the confession, claiming he had been coerced into making it. The court uncovered no foundation for coercion and ruled the confession acceptable as evidence.

But close examination of the confession, in comparison with other evidence, revealed serious discrepancies. In the confession, he said Mrs Hammersham first opened the door only a crack. He had waited to strike her with the iron bar when she put her whole face out of the door. Two days after, he claimed she invited him into the house and that they sat opposite each other and talked. He waited for her to be off her guard and then struck her.

When he struck her was a point of major importance. Cammerton would not forget such a major action. Why would he lie? This conflict of statements was difficult to understand.

At first, Cammerton said he struck Mrs Hammersham once in the face with the iron bar. Two days later, he said it had been twice. One week later, he claimed he struck her with all his might once and that, as she lowered her head, he hit her again four or five times. A medical expert said the condition of the bones in the victim's face verified the assumption that the attack really consisted of only one blow.

So, what Cammerton said later also did not agree with his original confession. Lapse of memory was unthinkable. Increasing the number of times he struck the victim could scarcely be to the defendant's advantage. Still, there was little reason to suspect him of deliberately falsifying. All of this cast serious doubt on the veracity of the initial confession.

Immediately upon arrest, the police confronted Cammerton with the steel rod and asked if he'd ever seen it. He said he thought his fingerprints would be on it. He seemed to recall the rod, but there had been several where he picked up the weapon. He could not be certain. Holding the rod, he placed it under his right arm, measured its length, and finally said there could be no mistake—it was the one he had used.

The wound in the victim's face was measured and found to be three times as wide as the rod (2.5 centimeters). This meant that the rod could not be the murder weapon. Why had Cammerton claimed it was? Would the real killer be unable to recognize his weapon? The fact that Cammerton claimed the rod as the weapon and also mentioned fingerprints awakened the possibility that he identified the weapon to please the police, even though he knew it was unrelated to the crime. Why would he do this?

Investigations failed to reveal traces of the kerosene lamp on the floor by the bureau. If it had been there, even though it may not have started the fire, it could scarcely have been overlooked. Had there been no lamp? Many questions remained unanswered. The judge pronounced the defendant not guilty, due to insufficient evidence.

Finished reading this passage, Harajima felt as if the words on the page had leaped out and struck him in the face. The two cases closely resembled each other. Coincidence? It was too close for that. A strong gut feeling told him Torao Ueki had read the same book.

From eighteen to twenty-five, Torao Ueki had worked in a second-hand book store, opening the noodle shop only after getting married.

Harajima checked a copy of the case record, found the name of the book store. He then called a book collector friend, and learned the store specialized in legal volumes. They would certainly have Hind's *Studies of Not-Guilty Verdicts*, which had been translated into Japanese before World War II. As an employee of the shop, Ueki would have had ample time to read it.

It is not easy for a criminal to escape the police. Many criminals have been executed or imprisoned because they have become entangled in their own clever subterfuges. Those who do escape detection often lead lives of anxiety and suffering in some ways worse than a long prison sentence. The ideal thing is to allow the police to make an arrest, then be declared not guilty. When he decided to kill Jin Yamagishi, the moneylender who had caused him much grief, Torao Ueki must have considered this and recalled the volume he once read in a second-hand bookshop.

In the Manchester case, Peter Cammerton claimed that a piece of iron rod the wrong size was the murder weapon. Believing him, the police admitted the wrong item as evidence. Ueki had done the same thing with the firewood. After his arrest, Cammerton identified the iron rod, measured its length under his arm, and suggested his fingerprints would be on it. Ueki had done something very similar with the piece of wood. Learning much from the English murder case, Ueki made self-incriminating statements in his confession, which he later denied. He then created the impression that the confession was made under police pressure.

As the inspector said, Ueki had been cooperative and friendly. The police fell for this and were too pleased with the way things were going to substantiate their evidence. Both Cammerton and Ueki changed the number of times they claimed to have struck their victims. In each case, only one blow had been used. Ueki's knowledge of Yamagishi's habit of never offering cushions to business customers was put to his own advantage when he said he'd been offered such a cushion and had returned it to its corner pile. He had employed the trick of leaving his own promissory notes in the cashbox to convince police he would not have done so if he'd been the murderer. It made no difference that the notes weren't destroyed. Yamagishi had no children, no relatives or heirs. At his death, all debts would be canceled.

What would the police think if they knew Harajima's notions of the truth? In court, when Ueki indignantly accused them of coercing a confession, tricking him with leading questions, bribing him, why had the police allowed it to end in a draw? Had they given up before Ueki's tremendous brass? It was true, when he observed the staunch courage with which Ueki testified, Harajima had become convinced the confession had not been freely given.

Harajima was very nervous. He paced back and forth in his study. At length, trying to calm himself, he removed a slender volume from the bookshelf and thumbed through the pages.

'Never judge the truth or falseness of a defendant's confession on the basis of the excitement he shows in making depositions about the crime, or *by the courage with which he faces police witnesses in court.* Make judgement on the basis of (1) whether the content of the confession agrees with known facts, (2) the personality and nature of the defendant, and (3) the motive that may have induced him to confess. But, after thorough investigation of all evidence, if there is no trace of the defendant's attempting to obscure the uncovering of the truth about his confession, *do not be deceived by distinctive character traits or by the falseness of a servile personality into believing the confession has been forced.* (Special Criminal Report of the Superior Court, March 16, 1944. Kanazawa Branch, Nagoya Superior Court)'

Ueki's whereabouts are unknown. After the trial, he sold his shop and land to a realtor for a good price, and went away. He did not come to thank Harajima. He phoned, instead: 'Can't thank you enough, for getting me out of a tight spot. Mr Harajima, you're tops. The only thing is, I'm embarrassed having to call on your services without paying you.' After a few more inconsequential words he was gone.

If Torao Ueki were killed in a traffic accident, it would be no more than just punishment, or perhaps divine retribution. This, however, is somehow unlikely.

ROBERT VAN GULIK (1910–1967)

The Murder on the Lotus Pond

This case occurred in the year A.D. *667 in Han-yuan, an ancient little town built on the shore of a lake near the capital. There Judge Dee has to solve the murder of an elderly poet, who lived in retirement on his modest property behind the Willow Quarter, the abode of the courtesans and singing-girls. The poet was murdered while peacefully contemplating the moon in his garden pavilion, set in the centre of a lotus pond. There were no witnesses—or so it seemed.*

FROM the small pavilion in the centre of the lotus pond he could survey the entire garden, bathed in moonlight. He listened intently. Everything remained quiet. With a satisfied smile he looked down at the dead man in the bamboo chair, at the hilt of the knife sticking up from his breast. Only a few drops of blood trickled down the grey cloth of his robe. The man took up one of the two porcelain cups that stood by the pewter wine jar on the round table. He emptied it at one draught, then muttered to the corpse, 'Rest in peace! If you had been only a fool, I would probably have spared you. But since you were an interfering fool . . .'

He shrugged his shoulders. All had gone well. It was past midnight; no one would come to this lonely country house on the outskirts of the city. And in the dark house at the other end of the garden nothing stirred. He examined his hands—there was no trace of blood. Then he stooped and scrutinized the floor of the pavilion, and the chair he had been sitting on opposite the dead man. No, he hadn't left any clue. He could leave now, all was safe.

Suddenly, he heard a plopping sound behind him. He swung round, startled. Then he sighed with relief; it was only a large, green frog. It had jumped up out of the pond on to the marble steps of the pavilion. Now it sat there looking up at him solemnly with its blinking, protruding eyes.

'You can't talk, bastard!' the man sneered. 'But I'll make doublesure!' So speaking, he gave the frog a vicious kick that smashed it against the table leg. The animal's long hindlegs twitched, then it lay still. The man picked up the second wine cup, the one his victim had been drinking from. He examined it, then he put it in his wide sleeve. Now he was ready. As he turned to go, his eye fell on the dead frog.

'Join your comrades!' he said with contempt and kicked it into the water. It fell with a splash among the lotus plants. At once the croaking of hundreds of frightened frogs tore the quiet night.

The man cursed violently. He quickly crossed the curved bridge that led over the pond to the garden gate. After he had slipped outside and pulled the gate shut, the frogs grew quiet again.

A few hours later three horsemen were riding along the lake road, back to the city. The red glow of dawn shone on their brown hunting-robes and black caps. A cool morning breeze rippled the surface of the lake, but soon it would grow hot, for it was mid-summer.

The broad-shouldered, bearded man said with a smile to his thin, elderly companion, 'Our duck-hunt suggested a good method for catching wily criminals! You set up a decoy, then stay in hiding with your clap-net ready. When your bird shows up, you net him!'

Four peasants walking in the opposite direction quickly set down the loads of vegetables they were carrying, and knelt down by the roadside. They had recognized the bearded man: it was Judge Dee, the magistrate of the lake-district of Han-yuan.

'We did a powerful lot of clapping among the reeds, sir,' the stalwart man who was riding behind them remarked wryly. 'But all we got was a few waterplants!'

'Anyway it was good exercise, Ma Joong!' Judge Dee said over his shoulder to his lieutenant. Then he went on to the thin man riding by his side: 'If we did this every morning, Mr Yuan, we'd never need your pills and powders!'

The thin man smiled bleakly. His name was Yuan Kai, and he was the wealthy owner of the largest pharmacy in Judge Dee's district. Duck-hunting was his favourite sport.

Judge Dee drove his horse on, and soon they entered the city of Han-yuan, built against the mountain slope. At the market place, in front of the Temple of Confucius, the three men dismounted; then they climbed the stone steps leading up to the street where the tribunal stood, overlooking the city and the lake.

Ma Joong pointed at the squat man standing in front of the monumental gate of the tribunal. 'Heavens!' he growled, 'I have never seen our good headman up so early. I fear he must be gravely ill!'

The headman of the constables came running towards them. He made a bow, then said excitedly to the judge, 'The poet Meng Lan has been murdered, Your Honour! Half an hour ago his servant came rushing here and reported that he had found his master's dead body in the garden pavilion.'

'Meng Lan? A poet?' Judge Dee said with a frown. 'In the year I have been here in Han-yuan I have never even heard the name.'

'He lives in an old country house, near the marsh to the east of the city, sir,' the pharmacist said. 'He is not very well known here; he rarely comes to the city. But I heard that in the capital his poetry is praised highly by connoisseurs.'

'We'd better go there at once,' the judge said. 'Have Sergeant Hoong and my two other lieutenants come back yet, Headman?'

'No sir, they are still in the village near the west boundary of our district. Just after Your Honour left this morning, a man came with a note from Sergeant Hoong. It said that they hadn't yet found a single clue to the men who robbed the treasury messenger.'

Judge Dee tugged at his long beard. 'That robbery is a vexing case!' he said testily. 'The messenger was carrying a dozen gold bars. And now we have a murder on our hands too! Well, we'll manage, Ma Joong. Do you know the way to the dead poet's country place?'

'I know a short-cut through the east quarter, sir,' Yuan Kai said. 'If you'll allow me . . .'

'By all means! You come along too, Headman. You sent a couple of constables back with Meng's servant to see that nothing is disturbed, I trust?'

'I certainly did, sir!' the headman said importantly.

'You are making progress,' Judge Dee observed. Seeing the headman's smug smile, he added dryly, 'A pity that the progress is so slow. Get four horses from the stables!'

The pharmacist rode ahead and led them along several narrow alleys, zigzagging down to the bank of the lake. Soon they were riding through a lane lined with willow trees. These had given their name to the Willow Quarter, the abode of the dancing-girls and courtesans that lay to the east of the city.

'Tell me about Meng Lan,' the judge said to the pharmacist.

'I didn't know him too well, sir. I visited him only three or four times, but he seemed a nice, modest kind of person. He settled down here two years ago, in an old country house behind the Willow Quarter. It has only three rooms or so, but there is a beautiful large garden, with a lotus pond.'

'Has he got a large family?'

'No sir, he was a widower when he came here; his two grown-up sons live in the capital. Last year he met a courtesan from the Willow Quarter. He bought her out, and married her. She didn't have much to commend herself besides her looks—she can't read or write, sing or dance. Meng Lan was able to buy her cheaply, therefore, but it took all his savings. He was living on a small annuity an admirer in the capital was sending him. I am told it was a happy marriage, although Meng was of course much older than she.'

'One would have thought,' Judge Dee remarked, 'that a poet would choose an educated girl who could share his literary interests.'

'She is a quiet, soft-spoken woman, sir,' the pharmacist said with a shrug. 'And she looked after him well.'

'Meng Lan was a smart customer, even though he wrote poetry,' Ma Joong muttered. 'A nice, quiet girl that looks after you well—a man can hardly do better than that!'

The willow lane had narrowed to a pathway. It led through the high oak trees and thick undergrowth that marked the vicinity of the marsh behind the Willow Quarter.

The four men dismounted in front of a rustic bamboo gate. The two constables standing guard there saluted, then pushed the gate open. Before entering, Judge Dee surveyed the large garden. It was not very well kept. The flowering shrubs and bushes round the lotus pond were running wild, but they gave the place a kind of savage beauty. Some butterflies were fluttering lazily over the large lotus leaves that covered the pond's surface.

'Meng Lan was very fond of this garden,' Yuan Kai remarked.

The judge nodded. He looked at the red-lacquered wooden bridge that led over the water to a hexagonal pavilion, open on all sides. Slender pillars supported the pointed roof, decked with green tiles. Beyond the pond, at the back of the garden, he saw a low, rambling wooden building. Its thatched roof was half covered by the low foliage of the tall oak trees that stood behind the house.

It was getting very hot. Judge Dee wiped the perspiration from his brow and crossed the narrow bridge, the three others following behind him. The small pavilion offered hardly enough space for the four men. Judge Dee stood looking for a while at the thin figure, clad in a simple house-robe of grey cloth, lying back in the bamboo armchair. Then he felt the shoulders, and the limp arms. Righting himself, he said, 'The body is just getting stiff. In this hot, humid weather it's hard to fix the time of death. In any case after midnight, I would say.' He carefully pulled the knife out of the dead man's breast. He examined the long, thin blade and the plain ivory hilt. Ma Joong pursed his lips and said, 'Won't help us much, sir. Every iron-monger in town keeps these cheap knives in stock.'

Judge Dee silently handed the knife to him. Ma Joong wrapped it up in a sheet of paper he had taken from his sleeve. The judge studied the thin face of the dead man. It was frozen in an eerie, lopsided grin. The poet had a long, ragged moustache and a wispy grey goatee; the judge put his age at about sixty. He took the large wine jar from the table and shook it. Only a little wine was left. Then he picked up the wine cup standing next to it, and examined it. With a puzzled look he put it in his sleeve. Turning to the headman he said:

'Tell the constables to make a stretcher of some branches, and convey the body to the tribunal, for the autopsy.' And to Yuan Kai: 'You might sit on that stone bench over there near the fence for a while, Mr Yuan. I won't be long.' He motioned Ma Joong to follow him.

They crossed the bridge again. The thin planks creaked under the weight of the two heavy men. They walked round the lotus pond and on to the house. With relief Judge Dee inhaled the cool air in the shadow under the porch. Ma Joong knocked.

A rather handsome but surly-looking youngster opened. Ma Joong told him that the magistrate wanted to see Mrs Meng. As the boy went hurriedly inside, Judge Dee sat down at the rickety bamboo table in the centre of the sparsely furnished room. Ma Joong stood with folded arms behind his chair. The judge took in the old, worn furniture, and the cracked plaster walls. He said, 'Robbery can't have been the motive, evidently.'

'There—the motive is coming, sir!' Ma Joong whispered. 'Old husband, pretty young wife—we know the rest!'

Judge Dee looked round and saw that a slender woman of about twenty-five had appeared in the door opening. Her face was not made up and her cheeks showed the traces of tears. But her large, liquid eyes, gracefully curved eyebrows, full red lips and smooth complexion made her a very attractive woman. The robe she wore was of faded blue cloth, but it did not conceal her splendid figure. After one frightened look at the judge she made an obeisance, then remained standing there with downcast eyes, waiting respectfully till he would address her.

'I am distressed, madam,' Judge Dee said in a gentle voice, 'that I have to bother you so soon after the tragedy. I trust that you'll understand, however, that I must take swift action to bring the vile murderer to justice.' As she nodded he went on: 'When did you see your husband last?'

'We had our evening rice here in this room,' Mrs Meng replied in a soft, melodious voice. 'Thereafter, when I had cleared the table, my husband read here for a few hours, and then said that since there was a beautiful moon he would go to the garden pavilion and have a few cups of wine there.'

'Did he often do that?'

'Oh yes, he would go out there nearly every other night, enjoying the cool evening breeze, and humming songs.'

'Did he often receive visitors there?'

'Never, Your Honour. He liked to be left alone, and did not encourage visitors. The few people who came to see him he always received in the afternoon, and here in the hall, for a cup of tea. I loved this peaceful life, my husband was so considerate, he . . .'

Her eyes became moist and her mouth twitched. But soon she took hold of herself and went on, 'I prepared a large jar of warm wine, and brought it out to the pavilion. My husband said that I need not wait up for him, since he planned to be sitting there till a late hour. Thus I went to bed. Early this morning the servant knocked frantically on the door of our bedroom. I then saw that my husband wasn't there. The boy told me that he had found him in the pavilion. . . .'

'Does this boy live here in the house?' Judge Dee asked.

'No, Your Honour, he stays with his father, the gardener of the largest house in the Willow Quarter. The boy only comes for the day; he leaves after I have prepared the evening rice.'

'Did you hear anything unusual during the night?'

Mrs Meng frowned, then answered, 'I woke up once, it must have been shortly after midnight. The frogs in the pond were making a terrible noise. During the daytime one never hears them, they stay under water. Even when I wade into the pond to gather lotus flowers they remain quiet. But at night they come out, and they are easily startled. Therefore I thought that my husband was coming inside, and had dropped a stone or so into the pond. Then I dozed off again.'

'I see,' Judge Dee said. He thought for a while, caressing his long sidewhiskers. 'Your husband's face didn't show any signs of terror or astonishment; he must have been stabbed quite unexpectedly. He was dead before he knew what was happening. That proves your husband knew his murderer well; they must have been sitting there drinking wine together. The large jar was nearly empty, but there was only one cup. I suppose that it would be difficult to check whether a wine cup is missing?'

'It's not difficult at all,' Mrs Meng replied with a thin smile. 'We have only seven cups, a set of six, of green porcelain, and one larger cup of white porcelain, which my husband always used.'

The judge raised his eyebrows. The cup he had found was of green porcelain. He resumed: 'Did your husband have any enemies?'

'None, Your Honour!' she exclaimed. 'I can't understand who . . .'

'Do *you* have enemies?' Judge Dee interrupted.

She grew red in the face, and bit her lip. Then she said contritely, 'Of course Your Honour knows that until a year ago I worked in the quarter over there. Occasionally I refused a person who sought my favours, but I am certain that none of them would ever . . . And after all that time . . .' Her voice trailed off.

The judge rose. He thanked Mrs Meng, expressed his sympathy, and took his leave.

When the two men were walking down the garden path Ma Joong said, 'You ought to have asked her also about her *friends*, sir!'

'I depend on you for that information, Ma Joong. Have you kept in contact with that girl from the quarter—Apple Blossom is her name, I think.'

'Peach Blossom, sir. Certainly I have!'

'Good. You'll go to the quarter right now, and get her to tell you everything she knows about Mrs Meng at the time she was still working there. Especially about the men she used to associate with.'

'It's very early in the day, sir,' Ma Joong said doubtfully. 'She'll still be asleep.'

'Then you wake her up! Get going!'

Ma Joong looked dejected, but he hurried to the gate. Judge Dee reflected idly that if he sent his amorous lieutenant often enough to interview his lady-friends before breakfast, he might yet cure him of his weakness. As a rule such women don't look their best in the early morning after a late night.

Yuan Kai was standing by the lotus pond talking earnestly with a newcomer, a tall, neatly dressed man with a heavy-jowled, rather solemn face. The pharmacist introduced him as Mr Wen Shou-fang, newly elected master of the tea-merchants' guild. The guildmaster made a low bow, then began an elaborate apology for not having called on the judge yet. Judge Dee cut him short, asking, 'What brings you here so early in the morning, Mr Wen?'

Wen seemed taken aback by this sudden question. He stammered, 'I . . . I wanted to express my sympathy to Mrs Meng, and . . . to ask her whether I could help her in any way. . . .'

'So you knew the Mengs well?' Judge Dee asked.

'I was just talking this matter over with my friend Wen, sir,' Yuan Kai interposed hurriedly. 'We decided to report to Your Honour here and now that both Wen and I myself sought Mrs Meng's favours when she was still a courtesan, and that neither of us was successful. Both of us want to state that we perfectly understood that a courtesan is free to grant or withhold her favours, and that neither of us bore her any malice. Also that we had a high regard for Meng Lan, and were very glad that their marriage proved to turn out so well. Therefore . . .'

'Just to get the record straight,' the judge interrupted, 'I suppose that both of you can prove that you weren't in this vicinity last night?'

The pharmacist gave his friend an embarrassed look. Wen Shou-fang replied diffidently, 'As a matter of fact, Your Honour, both of us took part in a banquet, held in the largest house in the Willow Quarter last night. Later we ah . . . retired upstairs, with ah . . . company. We went home a few hours after midnight.'

'I had a brief nap at home,' Yuan Kai added, 'then changed into hunting-dress and went to the tribunal to fetch Your Honour for our duck-hunt.'

'I see,' Judge Dee said. 'I am glad you told me, it saves me unnecessary work.'

'This lotus pond is really very attractive,' Wen said, looking relieved. While they were conducting the judge to the gate, he added: 'Unfortunately such ponds are usually infested with frogs.'

'They make an infernal noise at times,' Yuan Kai remarked as he opened the gate for Judge Dee.

The judge mounted his horse, and rode back to the tribunal.

The headman came to meet him in the courtyard and reported that in the side hall everything was ready for the autopsy. Judge Dee went first to his private office. While the clerk was pouring him a cup of hot tea the judge wrote a brief note to Ma Joong, instructing him to question the two courtesans Yuan Kai and Wen Shou-fang had slept with the night before. He thought a moment, then added: 'Verify also whether the servant of the Mengs passed last night in his father's house.' He sealed the note and ordered the clerk to have it delivered to Ma Joong immediately. Then Judge Dee quickly munched a few dry cakes, and went to the side hall where the coroner and his two assistants were waiting for him.

The autopsy brought to light nothing new: the poet had been in good health; death had been caused by a dagger thrust that had penetrated the heart. The judge ordered the headman to have the body placed in a temporary coffin, pending final instructions as to the time and place of burial. He returned to his private office and set to work on the official papers that had come in, assisted by the senior clerk of the tribunal.

It was nearly noon when Ma Joong came back. After the judge had sent the clerk away, Ma Joong seated himself opposite Judge Dee's desk, twirled his short moustache and began with a smug smile, 'Peach Blossom was already up and about, sir! She was just making her toilet when I knocked. Last night had been her evening off, so she had gone to bed early. She was looking more charming than ever, I . . .'

'Yes, yes, come to your point!' the judge cut him short peevishly. Part of his stratagem had apparently miscarried. 'She must have told you quite a lot,' he continued, 'since you were gone nearly all morning.'

Ma Joong gave him a reproachful look. He said earnestly, 'One has to handle those girls carefully, sir. We had breakfast together, and I gradually brought her round to the subject of Mrs Meng. Her professional name was Agate, her real name Shih Mei-lan; she's a farmer's daughter from up north. Three years ago, when the big drought had caused famine and the people were dying like rats, her father sold her to a procurer, and he in turn sold her to the house where Peach

Blossom is working. She was a pleasant, cheerful girl. The owner of the house confirmed that Yuan Kai had sought Agate's favours, and that she had refused. He thinks she did so only in order to raise her price, for she seemed rather sorry when the pharmacist didn't insist but found himself another playmate. With Wen Shou-fang it was a little different. Wen is a rather shy fellow; when Agate didn't respond to his first overtures, he didn't try again but confined himself to worshipping her from a distance. Then Meng Lan met her, and bought her then and there. But Peach Blossom thinks that Wen is still very fond of Agate, he often talks about her with the other girls and recently said again that Agate had deserved a better husband than that grumpy old poetaster. I also found out that Agate has a younger brother, called Shih Ming, and that he is a really bad egg. He is a drinker and gambler, who followed his sister out here and used to live off her earnings. He disappeared about a year ago, just before Meng Lan married her. But last week he suddenly turned up in the quarter and asked after his sister. When the owner told him that Meng Lan had bought and married her, Shih Ming went at once to their country house. Later Meng's servant told people that Shih Ming had quarrelled with the poet; he hadn't understood what it was all about, but it had something to do with money. Mrs Meng cried bitterly, and Shih Ming left in a rage. He hasn't been seen since.'

Ma Joong paused, but Judge Dee made no comment. He slowly sipped his tea, his bushy eyebrows knitted in a deep frown. Suddenly he asked: 'Did Meng's servant go out last night?'

'No, sir. I questioned his father, the old gardener and also their neighbours. The youngster came home directly after dinner, fell down on the bed he shares with two brothers, and lay snoring there till daybreak. And that reminds me of your second point, sir. I found that Yuan Kai stayed last night with Peony, a friend of Peach Blossom. They went up to her room at midnight, and Yuan left the house two hours later, on foot—in order to enjoy the moonlight, he said. Wen Shou-fang stayed with a girl called Carnation, a comely wench, though she was in a bit of a sullen mood this morning. It seems that Wen had drunk too much during the banquet, and when he was up in Carnation's room he laid himself down on the bed and passed out. Carnation tried to rouse him in vain, went over to the girls in the next room for a card game and forgot all about him. He came to life three hours later, but to Carnation's disappointment he had such a hangover that he went straight home, also on foot. He preferred walking to sitting in a sedan chair, because he hoped the fresh air would clear his brain—so he said. That's all, sir. I think that Shih Ming is our man. By marrying his sister, Meng Lan took Shih Ming's rice-bowl away from him, so to speak. Shall I tell the headman to institute a search for Shih Ming? I have a good description of him.'

'Do that,' Judge Dee said. 'You can go now and have your noon rice, I won't need you until tonight.'

'Then I'll have a little nap,' Ma Joong said with satisfaction. 'I had quite a strenuous morning. What with the duck-hunt and everything.'

'I don't doubt it!' the judge said dryly.

When Ma Joong had taken his leave Judge Dee went upstairs to the marble terrace that overlooked the lake. He sat down in a large armchair, and had his noon rice served there. He didn't feel like going to his private residence at the back of the tribunal; preoccupied as he was with the murder case, he wouldn't be pleasant company for his family. When he had finished his meal he pulled the armchair into a shadowy corner on the terrace. But just as he was preparing himself for a brief nap, a messenger came up and handed him a long report from Sergeant Hoong. The sergeant wrote that the investigation in the western part of the district revealed that the attack on the treasury messenger had been perpetrated by a band of six ruffians. After they had beaten the man unconscious and taken the package with the gold bars, they coolly proceeded to an inn near the district boundary, and there they had a good meal. Then a stranger arrived; he kept his neck-cloth over his nose and mouth, and the people of the inn had never seen him before. The leader of the robbers handed him a package, and then they all left in the direction of the forests of the neighbouring district. Later the body of the stranger had been found in a ditch, not far from the inn. He was recognized by his dress; his face had been beaten to pulp. The local coroner was an experienced man; he examined the contents of the dead man's stomach, and discovered traces of a strong drug. The package with the gold bars had, of course, disappeared. 'Thus the attack on the treasury messenger was carefully planned,' the sergeant wrote in conclusion, 'and by someone who has remained behind the scenes. He had his accomplice hire the ruffians to do the rough work, then sent that same accomplice to the inn to collect the booty. He himself followed the accomplice, drugged him and beat him to death, either because he wanted to eliminate a possible witness against him, or because he didn't want to pay him his share. In order to trace the criminal behind this affair we'll have to ask for the co-operation of Your Honour's colleague in the neighbouring district. I respectfully request Your Honour to proceed here so as to conduct the investigation personally.'

Judge Dee slowly rolled up the report. The sergeant was right, he ought to go there at once. But the poet's murder needed his attention too. Both Yuan Kai and Wen Shou-fang had had the opportunity, but neither of them seemed to have a motive. Mrs Meng's brother did indeed have a motive, but if he had done the deed he would doubtless have fled to some distant place by now. With a sigh he leaned back in his chair, pensively stroking his beard. Before he knew it he was sound asleep.

When he woke up he noticed to his annoyance that he had slept too long; dusk was already falling. Ma Joong and the headman were standing by the balustrade. The latter reported that the hue and cry was out for Shih Ming, but that as yet no trace of him had been found.

Judge Dee gave Ma Joong the sergeant's report, saying, 'You'd better read this carefully. Then you can make the necessary preparations for travelling to the west boundary of our district, for we shall go there early tomorrow morning. Among the incoming mail was a letter from the Treasury in the capital, ordering me to report without delay on the robbery. A missing string of coppers causes them sleepless nights, let alone a dozen good gold bars!'

The judge went downstairs and drafted in his private office a preliminary report to the Treasury. Then he had his evening meal served on his desk. He hardly tasted what he ate, his thoughts were elsewhere. Laying down his chopsticks, he reflected with a sigh that it was most unfortunate that the two crimes should have occurred at approximately the same time. Suddenly he set down his tea cup. He got up and started to pace the floor. He thought he had found the explanation of the missing wine cup. He would have to verify this at once. He stepped up to the window and looked at the courtyard outside. When he saw that there was no one about, he quickly crossed over to the side gate and left the tribunal unnoticed.

In the street he pulled his neckcloth up over the lower half of his face, and on the corner rented a small sedan chair. He paid the bearers off in front of the largest house in the Willow Quarter. Confused sounds of singing and laughter came from the brilliantly lit windows;

apparently a gay banquet was already in progress there. Judge Dee quickly walked on and started along the path leading to Meng Lan's country house.

When he was approaching the garden gate he noticed that it was very quiet here; the trees cut off the noise from the Willow Quarter. He softly pushed the gate open and studied the garden. The moonlight shone on the lotus pond, the house at the back of the garden was completely dark. Judge Dee walked around the pond, then stooped and picked up a stone. He threw it into the pond. Immediately the frogs started to croak in chorus. With a satisfied smile Judge Dee went on to the door, again pulling his neckcloth up over his mouth and nose. Standing in the shadow of the porch, he knocked.

A light appeared behind the window. Then the door opened and he heard Mrs Meng's voice whispering, 'Come inside, quick!'

She was standing in the doorway, her torso naked. She only wore a thin loin-cloth, and her hair was hanging loose. When the judge let the neckcloth drop from his face she uttered a smothered cry.

'I am not the one you were expecting,' he said coldly, 'but I'll come in anyway.' He stepped inside, shut the door behind him and continued sternly to the cowering woman, 'Who were you waiting for?'

Her lips moved but no sound came forth.

'Speak up!' Judge Dee barked.

Clutching the loin-cloth round her waist she stammered, 'I wasn't waiting for anyone. I was awakened by the noise of the frogs, and feared there was an intruder. So I came to have a look and . . .'

'And asked the intruder to come inside quickly! If you must lie, you'd better be more clever about it! Show me your bedroom where you were waiting for your lover!'

Silently she took the candle from the table, and led the judge to a small side room. It only contained a narrow plank-bed, covered by a thin reed mat. The judge quickly stepped up to the bed and felt the mat. It was still warm from her body. Righting himself, he asked sharply: 'Do you always sleep here?'

'No, Your Honour, this is the servant's room, the boy uses it for his afternoon nap. My bedroom is over on the other side of the hall we passed just now.'

'Take me there!'

When she had crossed the hall and shown the judge into the large bedroom he took the candle from her and quickly looked the room over. There was a dressing-table with a bamboo chair, four clothes-boxes, and a large bedstead. Judge Dee pulled the bed-curtains aside. He saw that the thick bedmat of soft reed had been rolled up, and that the pillows had been stored away in the recess in the back wall. He turned round to her and said angrily, 'I don't care where you were going to sleep with your lover, I only want to know his name. Speak up!'

She didn't answer; she only gave him a sidelong glance. Then her loin-cloth slipped down to the floor and she stood there stark naked. Covering herself with her hands, she looked coyly at him.

Judge Dee turned away. 'Those silly tricks bore me,' he said coldly. 'Get dressed at once, you'll come with me to the tribunal and pass the night in jail. Tomorrow I shall interrogate you in court, if necessary under torture.'

She silently opened a clothes-box and started to dress. The judge went to the hall and sat down there. He reflected that she was prepared to go a long way to shield her lover. Then he shrugged. Since she was a former courtesan, it wasn't really such a very long way. When she came in, fully dressed, he motioned her to follow him.

They met the night watch at the entrance of the Willow Quarter. The judge told their leader to take Mrs Meng in a sedan chair to the tribunal, and hand her to the warden of the jail. He was also to send four of his men to the dead poet's house, they were to hide in the hall and arrest anyone who knocked. Then Judge Dee walked back at a leisurely pace, deep in thought.

Passing the gatehouse of the tribunal, he saw Ma Joong sitting in the guardroom talking with the soldiers. He took his lieutenant to his private office. When he had told him what had happened in the country house, Ma Joong shook his head sadly and said, 'So she had a secret lover, and it was he who killed her husband. Well, that means that the case is practically solved. With some further persuasion, she'll come across with the fellow's name.'

Judge Dee took a sip from his tea, then said slowly, 'There are a few points that worry me, though. There's a definite connection between Meng's murder and the attack on the treasury messenger, but I haven't the faintest idea what it means. However, I want your opinion on two other points. First, how could Mrs Meng conduct a secret love affair? She and her husband practically never went out, and the few guests they received came during the day. Second, I verified that she was sleeping tonight in the servant's room, on a narrow plank-bed.

Why didn't she prepare to receive her lover in the bedroom, where there is a large and comfortable bedstead? Deference to her dead husband couldn't have prevented her from that, if she had been merrily deceiving him behind his back! I know, of course, that lovers don't care much about comfort, but even so, that hard, narrow plank-bed . . .'

'Well,' Ma Joong said with a grin, 'as regards the first point, if a woman is determined on having her little games, you can be dead sure that she'll somehow manage to find ways and means. Perhaps it was that servant of theirs she was playing around with, and then her private pleasures had nothing to do with the murder. As to the second point, I have often enough slept on a plank-bed, but I confess I never thought of sharing it. I'll gladly go to the Willow Quarter, though, and make inquiries about its special advantages, if any.' He looked hopefully at the judge.

Judge Dee was staring at him, but his thoughts seemed to be elsewhere. Slowly tugging at his moustache, he remained silent for some time. Suddenly the judge smiled. 'Yes,' he said, 'we might try that.' Ma Joong looked pleased. But his face fell as Judge Dee continued briskly, 'Go at once to the Inn of the Red Carp, behind the fishmarket. Tell the head of the beggars there to get you half a dozen beggars who frequent the vicinity of the Willow Quarter, and bring those fellows here. Tell the head of the guild that I want to interrogate them about important new facts that have come to light regarding the murder of the poet Meng Lan. Make no secret of it. On the contrary, see to it that everybody knows I am summoning these beggars, and for what purpose. Get going!'

As Ma Joong remained sitting there, looking dumbfounded at the judge, he added, 'If my scheme succeeds, I'll have solved both Meng's murder and the robbery of the gold bars. Do your best!'

Ma Joong got up and hurried outside.

When Ma Joong came back to Judge Dee's private office herding four ragged beggars he saw on the side table large platters with cakes and sweetmeats, and a few jugs of wine.

Judge Dee put the frightened men at their ease with some friendly words of greeting, then told them to taste the food and have a cup of wine. As the astonished beggars shuffled up to the table looking hungrily at the repast, Judge Dee took Ma Joong apart and said in a low voice:

'Go to the guardroom and select three good men from among the constables. You wait with them at the gate. In an hour or so I'll send the four beggars away. Each of them must be secretly followed. Arrest any person who accosts any one of them and bring him here, together with the beggar he addressed!'

Then he turned to the beggars, and encouraged them to partake freely of the food and wine. The perplexed vagabonds hesitated long before they fell to, but then the platters and cups were empty in an amazingly brief time. Their leader, a one-eyed scoundrel, wiped his hands on his greasy beard, then muttered resignedly to his companions, 'Now he'll have our heads chopped off. But I must say that it was a generous last meal.'

To their amazement, however, Judge Dee made them sit down on tabourets in front of his desk. He questioned each of them about the place he came from, his age, his family and many other innocent details. When the beggars found that he didn't touch upon any awkward subjects, they began to talk more freely, and soon an hour had passed.

Judge Dee rose, thanked them for their co-operation and told them they could go. Then he began to pace the floor, his hands clasped behind his back.

Sooner than he had expected there was a knock. Ma Joong came in, dragging the one-eyed beggar along.

'He gave me the silver piece before I knew what was happening, Excellency!' the old man whined. 'I swear I didn't pick his pocket!'

'I know you didn't,' Judge Dee said. 'Don't worry, you can keep that silver piece. Just tell me what he said to you.'

'He comes up to me when I am rounding the street corner, Excellency, and presses that silver piece into my hand. He says: "Come with me, you'll get another one if you tell me what that judge asked you and your friends." I swear that's the truth, Excellency!'

'Good! You can go. Don't spend the money on wine and gambling!' As the beggar scurried away the judge said to Ma Joong: 'Bring the prisoner!'

The pharmacist Yuan Kai started to protest loudly as soon as he was inside. 'A prominent citizen arrested like a common criminal! I demand to know . . .'

'And I demand to know,' Judge Dee interrupted him coldly, 'why you were lying in wait for that beggar, and why you questioned him.'

'Of course I am deeply interested in the progress of the investigation, Your Honour! I was eager to know whether . . .'

'Whether I had found a clue leading to you which you had over-looked,' the judge completed the sentence for him. 'Yuan Kai, you murdered the poet Meng Lan, and also Shih Ming, whom you used to contact the ruffians that robbed the treasury messenger. Confess your crimes!'

Yuan Kai's face had turned pale. But he had his voice well under control when he asked sharply: 'I suppose Your Honour has good grounds for proffering such grave accusations?'

'I have. Mrs Meng stated that they never received visitors at night. She also stated that the frogs in the lotus pond never croak during the day. Yet you remarked on the noise they make—sometimes. That suggested that you had been there at night. Further, Meng had been drinking wine with his murderer, who left his own cup on the table, but took away Meng's special cup. That, together with Meng's calm face, told me that he had been drugged before he was killed, and that the murderer had taken his victim's cup away with him because he feared that it would still smell after the drug, even if he washed it there in the pond. Now the accomplice of the criminal who organized the attack on the treasury messenger was also drugged before he was killed. This suggested that both crimes were committed by one and the same person. It made me suspect you, because as a pharmacist you know all about drugs, and because you had the opportunity to kill Meng Lan after you had left the Willow Quarter. I also remem-bered that we hadn't done too well on our duck-hunt this morning—we caught nothing. Although an expert hunter like you led our party. You were in bad form, because you had quite a strenuous night behind you. But by teaching me the method of duck-hunting with a decoy, you suggested to me a simple means for verifying my suspi-cions. Tonight I used the beggars as a decoy, and I caught you.'

'And my motive?' Yuan Kai asked slowly.

'Some facts that are no concern of yours made me discover that Mrs Meng had been expecting her brother Shih Ming to visit her secretly at night, and that proved that she knew that he had commit-ted some crime. When Shih Ming visited his sister and his brother-in-law last week, and when they refused to give him money, he became angry and boasted that you had enlisted his help in an affair that would bring in a lot of money. Meng and his wife knew that Shih Ming was no good, so when they heard about the attack on the treas-ury messenger, and when Shih Ming didn't show up, they concluded it must be the affair Shih Ming had alluded to. Meng Lan was an honest man, and he taxed you with the robbery—there was your motive. Mrs Meng wanted to shield her brother, but when presently she learns that it was you who murdered her husband, and also her brother, she'll speak, and her testimony will conclude the case against you, Yuan Kai.'

The pharmacist looked down; he was breathing heavily. Judge Dee went on, 'I shall apologize to Mrs Meng. The unfortunate profession she exercised hasn't affected her staunch character. She was genuinely fond of her husband, and although she knew that her brother was a good-for-nothing, she was prepared to be flogged in the tribunal for contempt of court, rather than give him away. Well, she'll soon be a rich woman, for half of your property shall be assigned to her, as blood-money for her husband's murder. And doubtless Wen Shoufang will in due time ask her to marry him, for he is still deeply in love with her. As to you, Yuan Kai, you are a foul murderer, and your head will fall on the execution ground.'

Suddenly Yuan looked up. He said in a toneless voice, 'It was that accursed frog that did for me! I killed the creature, and kicked it into the pond. That set the other frogs going.' Then he added bitterly: 'And, fool that I was, I said frogs can't talk!'

'They can,' Judge Dee said soberly. 'And they did.'

PAOLO LEVI (1919–199?)

The Ravine

Translated from the Italian by DENIS GODLIMAN

───────

WHEN the police commissioner reached the place he found other
policemen already at work, whose shadows moved grotesquely in the
semi-darkness. The scene looked faintly surreal, with the trees and
the manor house silhouetted at the farthest edge of the park.

The lane led to the stream and ended up in a wilderness.

In fact, as the brigadier hastened to explain, the path went another
way. Two large tree trunks were joined by a wooden bridge which
seemed on the verge of collapsing, so rotten was it. So the land-
owners had decided to replace it with a cement structure. The work
had just started.

'A typical accident,' observed the brigadier. 'Should be cleared up
soon.'

'Hmm . . .' said the commissioner. 'No one has thought to put up
a safety railing. And just tonight this chap—the householder, that is,
a certain Mr Rossi—seems to have decided to come out into the park
for a breath of fresh air. And there he is down there.' He pointed
below: the steep slope would have been about ten metres in length,
covered in stones and rough gravel, with nothing to catch hold of.

At the bottom of the slope two crouching shadows were busying
themselves by the side of an immobile figure.

The commissioner looked away and began to grope for a cigarette
in the pocket of his overcoat. Suddenly the darkness intensified as the
moon disappeared behind a cloud.

'Another thing,' murmured the brigadier, striking a match and
proffering it to his companion, 'the fellow was blind.'

The commissioner gazed at him fixedly for a moment in the light
of the tiny flame. 'Blind? Are you sure?'

'Good God, yes! For five years or so, as long as he's been living here. I can't tell you what it was caused by.'

'That's annoying!'

The other man shook the match with a muffled exclamation; he had burnt his fingers. 'But why? On the contrary I should say that it explains the accident.'

'You think so? Have you ever heard tell of a blind man who fell in this way, into a kind of trap like this? The blind are always alert, they can sense obstacles and dangers coming a mile away.'

'That's true,' conceded the other. 'But you must remember that Rossi knew the park like the back of his hand, there was no part of it he wouldn't have hurried through without the smallest hesitation. And there was a bridge on this spot until a couple of days ago.'

'Yes, you're right. Shall we go down and take a look?'

'If you want to,' said the brigadier without enthusiasm. 'This way. Be careful, you don't want to end up like our friend.'

One lens of Rossi's dark glasses had been smashed in the fall and behind it his eye could be seen, half-closed and lifeless. His face was nearly untouched and completely without expression.

'Instantaneous death, I'd say,' remarked one of the shadows standing next to him.

A pocket torch, which, oddly, hadn't shattered, was clutched in Rossi's hand. The commissioner stooped to pick it up and immediately shone a beam of light on to the startled face of the brigadier.

'Well, listen,' said the brigadier in a low voice. 'I assure you that he was blind. Everyone around here was aware of it.'

Righi laughed without merriment. This commonplace accident was beginning to agitate him.

'I don't doubt it,' he said. 'But it remains to be seen what a blind person was doing in the park at night with an electric torch in his hand.'

His colleague didn't reply, but simply shrugged his shoulders, irritated. Righi understood very well what he was getting at; it was nearly midnight. Every small discovery was registered with a bad grace.

Once the two men had reached the top of the ravine, the brigadier noticed that the commissioner was looking around uncertainly, like a pointer that has lost the scent. Then he sat down like a vagrant on a pile of gravel by the side of the pathway, and lit another cigarette.

'Shouldn't you be getting on with interrogating the family?' enquired the brigadier, impatiently.

'Yes. But first . . .' He shook his head and lowered his gaze.

Then suddenly his disgruntled expression gave way to something else, in the shadows; he got to his feet with a jerk and moved towards another pile of gravel a few metres away. He got down on his knees to examine something on the ground which wasn't visible to his companion.

'Have you spotted a clue?'

'Only something as absurd as the torch—more absurd in a way. Someone has moved these piles of gravel. Just a few hours ago. Look here.' He shone the torch on a dark oval stain on the ground. 'This damp stain has been caused by the gravel. Do you see, there was a little heap on this spot a couple of hours ago. The trace will soon dry up.'

The brigadier looked at him wide-eyed. 'Well, then?'

The path was clear; it looked as though the gravel which normally covered it had been swept into piles at the side to allow easier access to the lorries. The imprint of heavy tyres stretched as far as the missing bridge.

'It's clear what has happened,' said the commissioner in a low voice. 'They removed the gravel and heaped it into one . . . two . . . three . . . four piles. Once the work was completed they'd have spread it back over the ground again. Now, why should anyone have tampered with it? I've never heard of gravel that deteriorates and needs to be renewed . . . and in any case, in that event one would not waste time arranging it in heaps.'

'I wasn't thinking that it might have been taken away,' said the brigadier quickly. 'It could have been rearranged in bigger piles, for example. The traces show that there were five to start with, and now there are four; but the quantity could be the same.'

The commissioner looked at him for a moment as if he hadn't quite understood; then he turned round to scrutinize the four heaps and the five dark stains, which were already in the process of evaporating.

'Indeed, you're right, brigadier. But the work has been carried out after dinner—that is, by someone from the house. . . . Who on earth would go to all that trouble, reducing five piles to four, and for what reason? This is a mystery.'

'Do you think,' said the other with a touch of irony, 'that this detail has much bearing on our own enquiry?'

'You think it hasn't?' replied the commissioner, in the same tone of voice. 'A blind man has fallen into a small ravine; in his hand he carried a pocket torch. Then, someone amused himself moving heaps of gravel. Too many incongruities.' He smiled acidly, and then immediately became serious. 'Shall we have a chat with the members of his family? You never know what we might discover.'

He'd hardly had a chance to knock on the front door of the manor house when it opened, as if by magic. An aristocratic, coquettish face appeared. It belonged to a woman of indefinable age—ugly, but with an air of shabby distinction.

'Good evening,' said the commissioner.

'Enough of the chat, young man,' replied the woman. She opened the door a little wider to get a better look at him. 'May I ask who you are?'

'I was about to tell you. I am the commissioner . . .'

'I'm an old madwoman.' She stepped to one side to let him enter. 'My name is Leila Rossi. I'm the sister of poor Arrigo. Arrigo is the dead man. And I know you; I follow your investigations in the newspapers. I'm interested in criminology.'

'Goodness! And what would that be?'

The woman deigned to smile, before ushering him in to a large room literally carpeted with books. The style was heavy and overladen: lots of plush velvet and rugs, and with an immense stereophonic music-centre installed in what looked like an eighteenth-century cupboard.

'This is Arrigo's sanctum,' said the woman. 'He practically lived here. Alone. The rest of the family were courteously requested not to enter. He locked himself in.'

'And the books, who reads them?'

'No one. Who would want to read that stuff? They are classics.'

'Right,' he said, lighting a cigarette and looking around for an ashtray without finding one. 'Now—according to my information, it was you who found the . . . body of your brother.'

'That is so. I always take a short walk in the park before going to bed. I suffer from insomnia.'

'It would have been about eleven o'clock, more or less, would it not?'

'It was twelve minutes past eleven when I found Arrigo.' She stuck out her excessively long neck and added, 'Commissioner, it's possible that this case will strike you as being extremely simple. My brother was blind. He stumbled over the side of a ravine, and so on . . . a commonplace accident.'

'And on the other . . .' said the commissioner with a distracted air, letting the match fall to the floor.

'On the other hand . . . It wasn't an accident. Neither was it suicide.'

'Excuse me,' he interrupted her in a low voice, 'one thing is not quite clear to me. You seem—I don't wish to be impertinent, you understand—but you seem to be more excited than distressed by your brother's death.'

'Ah, well, you're right. Arrigo was anything but lovable. An odious man.'

'I see. There won't be many regrets . . . ?'

'No, none. Before his misfortune he was . . . unpleasant. But after . . . one could only describe him as mad.'

'How long had he been blind?'

'It must be five years. A benign brain tumour. He went to Paris to have it operated on, and came back blind, accompanied by a nurse.'

'No one in the family was aware of his illness?'

'No, not even Maria. Maria is my sister-in-law, Arrigo's wife. Arrigo made out he was going on a business trip.'

'A little strange, wouldn't you say?'

The woman hesitated. She had an aquiline nose and a protruding chin; her once blonde hair, now grey, was dressed like a wig. She looked like a character out of a story by Maupassant.

'Well, you see . . .' She seemed to be hesitating, as if uncertain about how much she should tell him. Then she went on, 'It was at that time that Maria was desperately trying to get him to give her a divorce. She'd fallen in love with somebody else. I didn't learn this from Arrigo, you understand. We never got on. I didn't kill him, however. If I'd been going to do it, I'd never have waited all this time.'

'Let's take things in the proper sequence . . .'

'Aren't you following me? Right, he went to Paris, and came home having lost his sight . . .' She paused, and continued in a different tone: 'After that, there was no more talk about a divorce. Maria gave up the whole idea. She's an old-fashioned girl is Maria.'

'You mean . . .' said the commissioner, 'she stayed with him because she couldn't . . . she found it impossible to walk out on a person afflicted in that way?'

'Yes—but don't get hold of the wrong end of the stick. Maria didn't kill him. I'm a good judge of character; I'm interested in psychology. Two thousand years ago, Maria would have been thrown to the wolves.'

'What do you mean?'

'It's a kind of martyrdom.'

'I understand.' The cigarette butt dropped from his fingers as he went on, 'Besides those you've mentioned, who else lives here?'

'In the house? Giovanni the manservant. But don't imagine he's the guilty party. He went into town and has a strong alibi. I checked it on the phone straight away. Incidentally,' she went on, 'what does the doctor say?'

'Fracture of the cranium . . . not to mention the other injuries.'

'No, no, that's not what I meant,' she interrupted. 'I want to know the time of death.'

The commissioner couldn't help smiling. 'Listen, madame . . . I've often put the question to myself: why did I ever become a policeman? But the thing that puzzles me now is why you didn't become one!'

'I'm only trying to help.'

'Thank you, but look . . .'

'You listen to me, young man. You police are very well equipped to discover common criminals. But what you have here is not a common crime.'

'No? Remember, we haven't ruled out the possibility that it was simply an accident.'

'I knew it! You've already allowed yourself to be influenced. If you're not careful you're going to find yourself making a grave error.'

Righi suddenly rose to his feet and went to the bookshelves. He lifted out a pocket bible bound in red leather. 'When Adam and Eve were chased out of the terrestrial paradise,' he said in a low voice, 'do you know what they were guilty of?'

The question surprised her so much that she lost her composure. 'They had sinned. And so . . .'

'Not sin, madame; an error of judgement. A mistake. We are all condemned to make mistakes.' He hesitated, then went on: 'When this inquiry is completed you will see how many mistakes have been made here. Material and moral.'

'For example,' she said, 'the torch . . .?'

'Well done! The torch. How did you know about the torch?'

'I was staring at Arrigo's body, which had fallen right down to the bottom of the ravine. Then I spotted the torch. Had you noticed it?'

'By chance, yes,' he smiled.

'Well, but have you thought about this detail? Why should a blind man have equipped himself with a torch?'

'Why indeed?'

'There's only one logical explanation.' She paused, well aware of keeping him in suspense. Then she went on: 'He must have been signalling to someone. There are military fortifications near here. I'm almost certain that Arrigo was a secret agent.'

For a brief moment he stood there with his mouth open, then raised his arms in a gesture of disbelief. 'Oh, heavens above! Tell me: how many detective novels have you read?'

'One a night. I suffer from insomnia.' She seemed a bit put out. 'Well, can you come up with a better explanation?'

'You will find that for every occurrence there are at least three explanations. The most likely, the absolutely certain one . . . and the true one. Now I should like to take a look at your brother's room. May I?'

'I'll come with you.'

'Thank you, no. I think I'd rather have Giovanni. Your acumen would disturb me.'

'As you wish,' she said, somewhat offended.

Giovanni was decidedly an unpleasant character, though it was difficult to put one's finger on exactly what it was that produced this impression. If he'd been in an adventure film the audience would have had him down as the villain. He preceded the commissioner up the stairs. The dead man's room was located on the first floor, at the far end of a sombre corridor. The electric light was switched on, the bed undisturbed. On the far side of the room, in front of an alcove, stood a large writing-desk, made of inlaid wood. On it sat a table lamp, switched on, with the light falling on an open novel. A detective story.

'I wonder who would have switched on all these lights,' mused the commissioner.

Giovanni seemed taken aback, as if he had noticed nothing out of the ordinary. 'I've no idea. Perhaps someone was expecting you.'

'I see. And then this book . . . truly a strange thing to find in a blind man's room, wouldn't you say? Who came here with Mr Rossi this evening?'

'No one. He always retired around nine o'clock. Alone. He preferred to go about by himself, indoors and in the park.'

'Strange, then, that he should have taken such a disastrous tumble, is it not?'

Giovanni shook his head sadly; all his gestures seemed false, like the sound of a cracked bell. 'He was too sure of himself.'

'Odd that no one thought to put up a safety railing . . .' the commissioner observed.

'Well, the lady thought that it would have been a good idea, but Mr Rossi himself opposed it. No one could have imagined what would happen. He was always so careful . . .'

'Which makes the accident inexplicable. And no one knows what took him out for a walk in the park after he'd gone to bed. No one saw him leave the house . . . is that so?'

'Well, I certainly didn't. I was in town,' Giovanni said meaningfully.

'And if someone had shouted, down by the river, do you think the sound would have carried as far as the house?'

'Unlikely, with the windows closed.'

'Who does the heavy work here? You?'

'No.' He looked surprised. 'A man comes in from the town. He's also responsible for doing the garden.'

'I'm asking you this because I've noticed your hands are swollen.'

'Are they?' He looked down at them, put them behind his back, then let them drop to his sides. He reddened slightly. 'Well, sometimes I do a bit of sweeping.'

'Strange.'

'What's strange about it?' asked the man with a touch of impatience.

'Strange that your hands should be swollen. You should be used to manual work, yet it seems you're not. As for me, I use my hands very little. If I were to work with any tool, a mattock for example, I'd soon have calloused fingers. But it shouldn't happen to you.'

'I,' Giovanni stated emphatically 'was out of the house when the gentleman died.'

'I know, I know. Don't agitate yourself. It's just that there are too many loose ends in this story. The lights switched on, for example, in a blind person's room?'

'Someone must have gone in after the boss had left.'

'Well. Let's see.' He stroked his chin with three fingers, thinking.

'Mr Rossi comes out, let's say, towards eleven o'clock. The next minute someone enters the room and sits down at the writing-desk. He starts to read a novel which he's brought along . . . Did someone read to your boss every night?'

'No.'

'Strange, then, this evening visitor. He comes in here and sits down calmly to read. Doesn't it occur to him to wonder where Rossi has gone for such a long time? Then he goes, leaving the light on and the book open . . . as if he'd been summoned urgently. I wonder.' He made a grimace and said, to change the subject: 'When I noticed your hands, I wondered if perhaps you'd helped the workers in the park?'

'No.' He shook his head.

'Pity . . . I was hoping you'd be able to explain to me . . . You see, there were five piles of gravel. And now there are four.'

Giovanni didn't answer straight away. He looked at his questioner with open eyes. Then he shrugged. 'What are you getting at?'

'Idiotic, isn't it? Someone has taken the trouble to reduce five piles of gravel to four. This evening.'

'What has that to do with me?' the other shouted.

'Nothing, don't get angry. I was hoping you might be able to explain it. That's all.'

'I don't know anything. I was in town, when . . .'

'I know.' He smiled.

There was a brief pause.

'Listen, commissioner, if you want to interrogate me, then get on with it. But all these pointless things confuse me.'

'I am interrogating you. Hadn't you noticed? You're the only person who could have tampered with the piles.'

'It was me, it was me!' the other shouted. 'Satisfied?'

'Quite. Mr Rossi, was he a decent chap?'

'Oh, yes.'

'Agreeable?'

'As far as I was concerned, yes.'

'However, he seems a bit of an odd bod. Inward-looking, hard, uncommunicative. Would you say he enjoyed being on his own?'

Giovanni shrugged his shoulders. 'Possibly. But he had his good points. He put up with his disability very well.'

'Ah, I can believe it. How long were you in his service?'

'Nearly five years. It was soon after he decided to retire here.' Now Giovanni seemed quite courteous and sure of himself.

'In the circumstances, Giovanni, you must have become something like the confidant of your employer. His eyes, indeed.'

'Well, not that so much. He was very withdrawn, as you said, and he wanted to retain his independence. For this reason he lived shut up in the house. Sometimes he passed whole days in the library, never seeing anyone, and no one dared to disturb him.'

'I understand. He'd created his own domain, small but secure . . .' He broke off. 'Please call the lady of the house.'

'Very well, sir.' He moved away, but turned before reaching the door. 'Don't you want to check my alibi?'

'Oh, no! I accept your alibi absolutely. I wouldn't question an iota of it.'

Giovanni looked relieved, and smiled for the first time. 'Thank you, sir. Excuse me.'

Mrs Rossi was a woman of thirty or thereabouts. It wasn't easy to describe her; she had the kind of face which gave nothing away. She wasn't beautiful, she didn't appear sad or disturbed, her eyes were somewhat blank. She sat in an armchair and waited, her hands in her lap.

'You're the last one I've called,' said the commissioner. 'I wanted to disturb you as little as possible.'

'Thank you.'

'Unfortunately, however, the questions I have to ask you may seem a little . . . intrusive.'

'Ask, by all means.' She arranged her skirt over her knees and then let her fingers fall lifelessly into her lap again.

'I haven't offered my condolences,' the commissioner went on. 'They would sound false on the lips of a neutral official who knew neither you nor your husband. However—you didn't love him.'

'Would that be the first of those questions?' A smile, barely perceptible, appeared on her lips.

'It would.'

'I didn't love him,' she answered calmly.

'You never did love him. That's to say . . . your feelings weren't affected by your husband's illness.'

'Indeed. You could call ours a marriage of convenience.'

The commissioner took a cigarette, went to light it and then changed his mind. Without looking at the woman, he observed: 'I don't think that is altogether true. Your husband loved you. A lot.'

'Is that another question?'

'No, it's an assertion.'

'Then you have been misinformed.'

'I haven't been informed at all. It's a matter of my poor deduction. Well then: perhaps he didn't love you, but he clung to you. Perhaps he was jealous.'

The woman reflected a moment, tranquilly. 'Something like that could be possible. I don't know how you've worked it out.'

'Intuition. It's part of my trade,' said the commissioner. 'And then, one day, it came home to you very forcibly that you had made a mistake in marrying your husband. You'd fallen in love with someone else.'

'Is it really necessary to bring this up?'

'Yes, I'm afraid it is. And then you asked your husband to let you go. What was his response?'

She lowered her head; for a moment her face remained hidden in the shadow. 'He refused to discuss it. He told me that he had to leave for Paris, urgently. It would have to wait until his return.'

'But when he came back, he was blind.'

'Yes.'

'And so you stayed. You felt you couldn't abandon an invalid. There was no more talk about a separation. Because of this, I thought there must have been a strong attachment, at least on your husband's side. Otherwise, you could have gone away without remorse.'

'Indeed.'

'An infernal life,' he said in a low voice. 'I beg you to accept my condolences.'

'It's over now.'

'Yes,' he sighed, finally lighting the cigarette. 'It's finished. Now it's time for a confrontation in the library, with your sister-in-law and Giovanni.'

'Have you reached a conclusion?' She didn't seem very concerned.

'Yes.'

'Was it an accident?'

'No. Neither accident nor suicide.'

'A crime, then.'

'Agreed.'

'But no one could have got into the park. We have electronic alarms, not to mention dogs.'

'No one did get in.'

'But only Leila and myself were in the house. Giovanni was out for the evening.'

'Madame, I would prefer to speak in front of the others.' He smiled. 'I'm something of an actor, I am.'

Ten minutes later, they were all assembled in the library, waiting.

Leila sat on the edge of an armchair, as if preparing to leap to her feet every now and then. 'Now we've really reached the final scene!' she exclaimed. 'I'm so excited.'

'Me too,' said the commissioner, seating himself on a divan in the corner. 'Although we are not dealing here with a materially complicated case. However, from the psychological point of view . . . I must confess, my dear lady, that I also have a weakness for psychology; it fascinates me and at the same time repels me. It's like digging a hole energetically, in search of hidden treasure . . . and bit by bit, as you go on, you start to hesitate for fear of touching the bottom . . .' He paused before continuing in a different tone, 'Miss Leila was very struck by the pocket torch in the hands of the victim. Curious, indeed. However, I was even more struck by the piles of gravel which had been tampered with.'

'The gravel?' asked Leila, craning forward.

'To be precise, in place of the original five piles, we now had four. Why?'

'The boss ordered me to do it,' interrupted Giovanni.

'For what reason?'

'How do I know?'

'Unfortunately, one can't put much faith in your words. You're both untruthful, and a self-deceiver. Your lips work faster than your brain. How much has Mr Rossi left you in his will?'

'I don't know.'

'What do you mean, you don't know?' burst out Leila. 'You know very well. Five million lire.'

'You see? The lips faster than the brain. And with a tendency to lie, because it's easier.'

The man reddened suddenly. 'You can't pin this on me. I have an alibi.'

'It's because of the alibi that you're even suspected. Five million lire! So little, Giovanni. And with devaluation and all . . .'

'I . . .' He bit his lip.

'At the beginning of this century, a famous French physicist, whom undoubtedly you've never heard of, made the following observation:

if an omnipotent demon, at night when everyone is sleeping, took it on himself to increase or diminish in proportion the dimensions of men and everything that surrounds them . . . well, no one would notice a thing.'

'I don't understand what you're getting at,' shouted Giovanni.

'Don't you? But you have carried out something similar yourself. Tell me: how did your employer find his way about? Like all blind people, using points of reference which the senses could recognize. He counted the steps, he felt the wind, he touched the corners of rooms, the trees in the lane . . . the piles of gravel, when they were there. Five. The ravine, with its dangers, followed after the fifth pile. You, Giovanni, had observed Mr Rossi's habits. In the absence of other points of reference, Rossi couldn't possibly have told that the distance between the piles had been slightly increased.'

'I . . .' began Giovanni, and bit his lip again.

'If someone, on some pretext or other, had lured him towards the stream this evening, Rossi would have checked the heaps of gravel with his stick. At the fifth, he'd have stopped.'

'But the fifth wasn't there any more!' exclaimed Leila. She slapped her hand on her knee. 'Isn't it wonderful, Maria!'

'You can't prove any of it,' said Giovanni, who had backed away towards the door.

'Give me another explanation.'

'That's not my business.'

'You're a curious mixture of cunning and stupidity; of ingenuity and evil. I imagine, in order to entice your employer out of the house, you'd come up with some trumped-up charge . . . against signora Maria, I would think. You invented an assignation . . .'

'I've nothing to say.'

'You don't have to say anything. But believe me, Giovanni, five million lire is a small reward for what you've done.'

'The money had nothing to do with it,' said the other in a low voice which became louder, more strident, as if the words were forced out in spite of himself. 'I hated him, that filthy pig . . . that . . .'

'All right, that's enough,' said the commissioner, summoning his men who were stationed outside the door. The two women sat immobilized, Leila agog, Maria with downcast eyes as if she hadn't followed the scene at all.

'I've something to say,' shouted Giovanni, struggling in the clutches of a couple of policemen, 'I want to say it loudly. I'm glad I killed him, do you hear, glad . . . that pig, I hated him . . . I . . .'

The policemen succeeded in hustling him out of the room; the door closed behind them. There was a protracted pause. The commissioner lighted a cigarette.

'Well,' said Leila, finally, 'I'm satisfied that it has ended like this. Although, from a technical point of view, I'm a little disappointed. Merely the manservant . . .'

'Please, Leila', said the other.

'Well, I'm an old half-wit, aren't I? I must be allowed the luxury of speaking my mind.'

'Don't complain too soon, Miss Leila,' said the commissioner; he seemed a little weary. 'Unfortunately it's not yet finished.'

'What are you saying?'

'You've forgotten the pocket torch.'

'Oh my goodness! You're right. How does one explain the torch?'

'Unfortunately the most logical explanation isn't necessarily the true one.'

Maria raised her curious, heavy eyes and looked at him. 'Giovanni has confessed. He's the guilty one.'

'You forgot that Giovanni was far away at the time of death. You believe him to be guilty, because everything fits in as though his plan had worked. But this doesn't mean that it really had worked.'

'I don't understand.'

'You see, the human brain is curious. Miss Leila noticed the torch in the blind man's hand and asked herself what its purpose could be. To make signals: if one assumes he's blind, that is a reasonable explanation. But I, on the other hand, having noted the torch, began to think about the blind man . . . and I said to myself . . .'

'Young man,' declared Leila, 'you're mad!'

'A simple hypothesis, a bit odd, certainly . . . but then, the lights in the room. And the novel open on the writing desk . . .'

'But don't you see that it's absurd? For five years . . . Are you implying that Arrigo faked blindness? I can't believe it.'

'It does seem unlikely, I admit. And yet—is it not even more incredible that a man on the verge of submitting himself to such a serious operation should have left home without saying a word to anyone? Here we have a self-centred, misanthropic fellow, incapable of happiness or of allowing anyone else to be happy. Only one person in the world means anything to him—his wife—and now he learns

he's about to lose her. There is only one way of preventing this catastrophe . . .'

'Good heavens!' exclaimed Leila. 'It can't be true! But for all the . . .
I knew he was vermin, but to go that far . . .'

'Tragic, don't you agree, signorina?' said the commissioner, looking at the widow.

Sitting there in the armchair she hardly raised her eyelids, but he
felt the hostility in her dark eyes.

'You're right. Tragic.'

'Arrigo lived like this for five years. Avoiding everyone's company,
closeted in his library where he knew he was safe from discovery. He
got away with it . . . but he wasn't blind. And so,' he said slowly, 'in
no way would he have fallen into Giovanni's trap.'

'Evidently,' said Leila, 'and now . . .' She stopped short, bringing
her hand up to her lips.

'Well then,' said the commissioner.

'I don't give a damn,' said the wife. 'I don't know why you're hesitating—out of compassion, or cruelty, but . . .'

'Not cruelty, believe me.'

'But in any case, it doesn't matter to me.' Her voice was toneless.
'You think I killed my husband this evening. You're mistaken. I'm the
one who's dead. I understood three hours ago that I was dead. For five
years, I . . .'

'Keep quiet,' interrupted Leila. 'Don't you understand—there's no
proof.'

'Exactly,' said Righi.

'I'm telling you that it doesn't matter! It doesn't matter in the slightest. I was in the garden when I saw him. It was an odd time for him to
leave the house. I watched him hurry towards the river, as if he was late
for an appointment. At the same time, there was something surrepti-
tious in his manner: he kept looking round cautiously, as if to make
sure the coast was clear. I was immediately struck by something not
being right—but I didn't understand what it was, until he took off his
dark glasses . . . and switched on the torch. I understood then what I'd
been tricked out of: happiness, liberty, and life. I gave him a shove. I'd
like to be certain that he recognized me before he went over the edge.'

'Your husband loved you, madame,' said the commissioner in a
low voice.

For the first time she appeared shaken; she stood up suddenly. 'No!
I don't believe it.'

'He loved you, that's the tragedy. Think of the torture he inflicted on himself, just to be near you . . .'

'If he had loved me, he would have let me go.'

'It's hard to judge. If you would follow me.' He stood up in turn.

'Certainly. I don't give a damn. Let's go.'

GWENDOLINE BUTLER (1922–)

Bloody Windsor

IT was the best of times, it was the worst of times.

In Paris the tricolour flew, and the crowds sat watching Madame Guillotine receive her passing guests.

In Windsor all was normal except for a few apprentices and mechanics who held a meeting in Thames Street but were soon dispersed, one or two to the hulks and then on to Australia. The navy was offered as an alternative but few chose it and rightly so, Denny thought . . .

'I can't see that the death of the Queen serves any purpose,' said Major Mearns, over his *Times*, to Sergeant Denny. 'Seeing that she was helpless to hurt anyone and might have served as a hostage with the Emperor of Austria.'

'Ah,' said Denny, drawing on his pipe. 'All quiet here, though.'

'I hear of a bad tumult in Ireland.'

'Ah,' said Denny again. 'There would be. In Ireland.'

The room where the two men were breakfasting, in the deep wards of the great castle of Windsor itself, was warm and comfortable if on the dark side. This did not worry them, they were used to darkness.

The two men were servants of the government rather than the king. They were there to protect the peace, search out criminals and cause them to be arrested. They had served together in India where they had, more by chance than plan, discovered the murderer of a high-ranking officer. Back in London, they had stumbled into a plot against the government. In consequence, they had been sent together to Windsor Castle to keep an eye on the king, the court, and the Prince of Wales.

These were heady times, with revolution afoot in France, and the government trusted no one.

The court, arranged in layers like a very rich cake, had no interest in what lay at the bottom of the cake so that the king, when in his right mind, would bow when he saw the Major but distantly, not knowing that the Major, with Sergeant Denny, was stowed away in his own basement.

When a dead body was found hanging in the wine vaults, it was the Major and Sergeant Denny who sorted the matter out and recognised it for murder and not suicide. When an unknown woman died of a stab wound in the entrance to the silver vaults, it was the same pair who decided it was suicide and got the lady decently buried. It was never discovered who she was.

'Anyone who thinks a royal castle is an orderly place, needs to think again,' declared the Major.

He reported to Lord Charleston in the Government, while knowing that he alone was not the only source of information, his lordship had others. It is the way with governments when there is civil unrest to be feared.

Major Mearns was able to assure his lordship that the king was indeed mad in patches, and then sane again. That the Prince of Wales had married Mrs Fitzherbert but the marriage was a fake, a put-up job, which the poor lady had no idea of. These stories his lordship knew already but the Major knew it was his duty to report them also. Repetition made for truth.

While in Windsor, they had the luck, or bad luck, to trap a murderer of women.

And trap was the word, thought Denny with a shudder, remembering what they had been forced to do.

While never forgetting the difference in rank between them the two men were friends. They had fought together in the American war and then in India. Both had been wounded, both knew themselves to be survivors. They kept details about their lives private, but Sergeant Denny knew that the Major's young wife had died in childbirth, as many did, while he was in Canada and that on the day of her death he wore a white sprig in his lapel. Denny himself had never married but one evening when the wine was red in his veins, he had told the Major that he had left a girl behind him when he went abroad; she had promised to wait, but when he came back, she was gone.

'Into marriage or the streets,' he had said. He was bitter: when a soldier goes to fight, he wants his woman to be there when he comes back. He could write, had written, but got no reply. He had written letters for other men; war was hard on men who could not write. Then he had read the letters as they came back. None for him, though.

'You had plenty of women in India,' the Major had answered. 'Did myself. Splendid creatures.'

'But not to marry.'

'No, not to marry.' Although some men did, but never brought them home to England. 'It doesn't break your heart like the poets make out,' confided the Major, the wine still red in his veins and brain, 'but it cuts it in half. I have but half a heart.'

'A half is better than nothing,' said Sergeant Denny. The big dog stirred by the fire and the cat purred from the windowsill, half a heart was enough for them.

The subject never came up again, although not forgotten. They had but one heart between them, the sergeant thought, and his half was frozen too.

The cat stirred and stretched on the windowsill; Denny rose to join her at the window, running his hand over her plump form. 'What, in kitten, you wretch.'

'I won't drown them,' said the Major from his armchair. 'You must do it.'

Denny could see down the slope to the arched entrance with across the way a view of the houses of the Poor Knights of Windsor. A pretty sight. But not pretty inside, as he knew, for the old soldiers were a drunken, quarrelling lot with no taste for housekeeping.

'There goes old Tossy,' he said, seeing a short, stout, caped figure making an unsteady path up the hill from the gate to where he worked for the Poor Knights.

'Old sot,' complained the major. 'I wonder they employ him.'

'He has his uses.' Sergeant Denny grinned.

'Yes: the best informant in the city, he knows all the dirt and the dirtier it is, the closer it clings to his pockets.'

Denny turned away from the window. 'He is coming over . . .' He held up his right hand, rubbing thumb and forefinger together. 'Money. Spondulick.'

Major Mearns had a rule: never pay him as much as you promise, always keep him short, so that he comes back. A hard man, the Major.

A tap on the door. Tossy was in without waiting for a word. There was a steady grubbiness about Tossy's face, hands and clothes, but hot water and soap did not come his way readily. What money he had, he preferred to use on drink.

The Major stood up, he rattled a few coins in his pocket . . .

'So, what have you got for me?'

Tossy pursed his lips as if debating what to say. The big black dog who unaccountably liked the man, came up to fawn on his boots. 'I 'ave 'eard that a grand lady of the town is about to be taken up . . .'

'Is she a whore?' demanded the Major.

'No, none of that, an important, respectable lady, who is about to be taken up for procuring young girls.'

'Very respectable, indeed,' said Denny. 'So who is this lady?'

At this Tossy had to admit he did not know. 'What I give is worth something.'

When he had gone off, muttering at the smallness of his reward, the two looked at each other.

'He knows more,' said Denny. 'And he is frightened, Tossy is frightened.' And nothing frightened Tossy except death. His own.

'So I suspect, but we shall get at it in the end . . . If it is worth anything. However, it cannot be of importance to us here in the castle.'

In truth, Mearns and Denny took an alert interest in anything that might worry the government. They had honed their skill in America and India and so were a valuable team.

'I don't think we need worry about the poor king . . . he lives in the past.'

'And the Prince of Wales only desires plump middle-aged ladies.'

'Of which there is no shortage willing to oblige . . . however, there is the Duc de Chancey-Melun.'

M. le Duc was a refugee from the French Revolution who had had the good luck to be staying in London, having his London tailor fit his coat, when the Bastille was stormed. Reading the signs accurately, he had decided to stay.

'Could he afford it, they don't come cheap these girls.' M. le Duc had no money but kind friends.

'He might be the procurer himself . . . taking his profit.'

'Both ways?'

The Major laughed. 'He is not a clever man, able to dissemble, and is certainly in debt, but I have never heard of him knowing a notable lady in Windsor, nor of having a liking for young girls . . . his tastes run quite the other way.'

'A pity,' regretted Denny. 'I would like to have got him; I saw him kick a dog the other day.'

'Then we must certainly see he is punished for something,' said the Major, running his hand over the black cat's thick coat. 'I daresay we might manage it between us.'

He got up. 'We must go out into the town and see what we can grub up.'

Major Mearns shrugged himself into a greatcoat while the Sergeant put a muffler round his neck twice, the ends hanging. When they were alone, the rank difference was pretty well ignored, they were working partners, but in the world outside, they marked the social barrier with different clothes.

They passed down the long corridor on whose walls hung some of the less choice pictures of the Royal collection.

One was a female saint with her head in her arms.

'I never fancy that one,' grumbled Sergeant Denny. 'I can't abide a head on the loose. Seen too many in India.'

'They have here the shirt King Charles the First was wearing when his head was cut off. Clean as a whistle, not a bloodstain on it.'

'Washed, I suppose.'

'Or fake,' said the Major sceptically. He believed in very little.

Slowly the two men, well known in the town, walked down the Castle Hill towards the Marlborough Arms, one of the most popular if rowdiest drinking places in Windsor. If you wanted gossip, information, you supped your ale in the Marly . . . for such it was known.

The Major stopped suddenly. 'Denny,' he said. 'Do you know you have blood on your sleeve?'

Denny drew his left sleeve up. 'By God, sir, so I have.' There was a long thin streak of red on the sleeve of his coat. He touched it; his finger came away with blood on it. 'Still wet. I must have rubbed against something.'

'And not long ago,' said the Major. 'I like a bit of blood,' he added thoughtfully. 'You know where you are with blood.'

They looked at each other.

'Was Tossy bleeding?'

'I did not see him bleed.' Denny pursed his lips. 'That's not to say he wasn't. He was worried about something. More than he told us.'

'Not his blood then, I'll have it out of him,' said the Major with decision. He half turned back. 'He will still be with the old soldiers, all as drunk as each other. Where does he drink in the town?' They both knew that Tossy had been drinking.

'Mostly in the Marlborough.'

'They will likely know what he has been up to. Blood, indeed. His own or someone else's?'

The town was busy in its usual quiet way: a donkey pulling a cart with a boy in charge was bearing down on Mr Turvey, owner of the tailor's shop on the corner of Peascod Street, while a smart phaeton was whipped along by a dapper young man, splashing through a puddle and causing the lad with the donkey to shake a fist.

'That's how revolutions start,' said Denny, still cross.

At the bottom of the hill, they could see a slender form leading the procession of twelve young ladies across the road. At their tail came a more imposing form, well bonneted and poking at the pavement with her parasol.

It looked like a poke, the Sergeant decided, as if she was put out, annoyed, even angry.

A stout man was hurrying up the hill as if he had just been speaking to her.

'And there is John Armour coming our way,' said Major Mearns.

Mr Armour was a lawyer who dwelt in the town and managed the affairs of the most prosperous of the citizens from his handsome Queen Anne house where he both lived and kept his office.

A plump, cheerful man with white hair and rumpled clothes, he looked more harmless than he was. Now he came rushing up towards them.

'Major, Major Mearns, sir, I am glad to see you. How do you do, how do you do.' He addressed himself to the Major, ignoring Sergeant Denny but he was one of the few who grasped that Denny was as powerful in the world of keeping the King's Peace as the Major. Possibly more so, since he could go around and gather information in circles closed to the Major. A pot boy or the kitchen cleaning wench would not talk to Major Mearns, a gentleman (which he was not and knew he was not), but they could to Sergeant Denny.

'I was about to call on you, Major.' He did include Sergeant Denny at this point with a swift glance his way, knowing as he did that to consult Mearns was to consult Denny also. 'You are one who knows how to go about finding out where the truth lies, you ask questions and get answers. You investigate, sir.' His eyes did not miss the smear of blood on Denny's jacket sleeve, but he said nothing.

'Yes, sir,' replied Major Mearns in a judicial way. 'I have an investigatory capacity. Learnt in the army, sir.'

'Of course.'

'And honed in civic life.'

—Now what's he up to, Denny thought, he's not usually so pompous.

'We must talk, Major.' He looked around him at the street where a carriage was passing and where a mother with a child spinning his hoop was passing by, and an urchin was kicking something round which might have been a ball or a dead cat or cabbage in the gutter, 'but not here . . .'

'Let's go to the Marly?'

Mr Armour said doubtfully. 'It is not the sort of place that I usually go to.'

The Major ignored this plea. He put his arm firmly round Mr Armour's shoulders. 'Then now is the time to start.'

The Marlborough was crowded as usual.

'My friend and valued client Mrs Breakspere . . . a remote descendant of the famous Archbishop . . .' began the lawyer.

Mearns nodded politely although he had never heard of the said Nicholas Breakspere.

'A lady of dignity . . .'

She must be fat, thought Denny with some cynicism.

'She is the proprietor of the school for young ladies, some six couple follow her to church, St Leonard's in Grancy Road, where I go myself when not at the Chapel Royal in the Castle . . .,' went on Mr Armour.

Wordy as usual, commented Denny silently, and every word on his bill. Mrs Breakspere must pay her bills since he speaks so well of her. Wonder how she pays? He is a bit of an old lecher.

'On this exemplary lady has fallen the most terrible accusation . . .'

Here we go, thought Denny, preparing to look surprised.

'She has been accused of,' the lawyer hesitated, seeking words chaste enough to suit the lady's virtue. 'Of procuring young girls for the stews of London,' he finished with a rush, abandoning all restraint of language.

He had gone quite pink as if even the very words excited him.

'Who accuses her?' asked the Major coolly.

'The father of one of her pupils.'

'Ah.'

'A calumny. A foul calumny.' He leaned forward almost knocking over the glass of gin and water with which the Major had provided him. 'She wishes to engage you in investigating the lie.'

He did not mention the word payment but he knew that the Major would expect to be paid. Never mind how, maybe in information when needed or a patronage when desired but there would be payment.

And I shall expect my whack, decided Denny.

'So we go when it is dark, invisible to the young ladies.' The Major was contemptuous as they marched back to the Castle. Once inside, walking towards the picture of the decapitated saint, the Major said: 'Denny, do you see any blood? Look around for blood.'

No blood.

They had left Mr Armour still in the Marlborough. 'He's a bit of a bum boy, isn't he?' Denny had said idly as they left him behind.

A bleeding saint on the wall, but otherwise no blood.

'Wait.' Denny had caught sight of something on one of the paler of the stone flags which made up the floor. It was the faint shape of a bloody footmark.

'Find and fetch Tossy,' was the Major's order. 'Don't forget the bath house.'

'Tossy does not bath much.'

'Other things go on there, as you know,' said Mearns sharply.

The bath house was a long-established institution in Windsor if not much talked about in polite circles. Some said it went back to Queen Anne. The bath house had baths, hot water and benches for sitting out. It also had more private rooms for those who wished to rest after the hot bath. Those who did so were rarely alone and it was thought that they met by arrangement with the ladies of their choice who made their entrance through a small side door.

The bath house was run at present by a middle-aged couple, Mr and Mrs Jones. He was an old soldier but many thought she was the stouter soldier of the two. Sergeant Denny, not a patron of the baths, approached her with caution.

She emerged from stoking the furnace, red-faced and damp as she always seemed to be from the steam of the baths, to say that she had not seen Tossy, and he should 'ave been here feeding the furnace, a job for which she paid him and if he did show his face she would give him he knew what. One stout red arm suggested she knew what too.

On an impulse, Denny turned back. 'Do you know Mrs Breakspere?'

Sara Jones did not answer, her eyes wary. 'She don't visit here.'

'Never thought she did. But you know her?'

'Know her looks, never had speech, Sergeant.'

'You know who I am?'

'Everyone knows you and knows the Major.'

'Do you find enough young, really young, wimmin to please your customers? Supply running short, is it?'

'Not everyone fancies a slice of chicken.'

'A true word,' and as Denny walked away he thought that word had it that she obliged herself when asked.

The lodgings of the Poor Knights of Windsor did not harbour Tossy, nor did the Marlborough Arms, Ma Bradley's Chop House, and the Watermen's ale house down by the river knew him not. He lodged with many others in a large, run-down house with no drains run by a small dark woman who called herself Mrs Dodge, and was known as the artful dodger.

Nowhere was Tossy to be found, so Denny returned to the castle to report no success.

'I don't care for this disappearing,' said the Major, with a frown. 'He was frightened and he had blood on him.'

Several other matters came up in the day, such as the disappearance of a dozen bottles of the best claret from the royal cellars, and the appearance on the wall of the kitchen of the drawing of a tricolour and the words: Revolution now.

The latter was found to be the work of a drunken scullion who might have been at the claret, although it was suspected he had sold that wine.

He was dismissed the royal service and given the choice between the navy and the army. He chose the navy.

By evening, they were ready to visit Mrs Breakspere. The night was dark and heavy with a small, light rain falling. The Academy for Young Gentlewomen was housed in a sprawling red-brick building hidden behind trees and shrubberies. A heavy iron gate leading to a winding drive protected the young ladies from rude gazes from the road.

The two men pushed through the gate which Sergeant Denny then closed after them. It needed a good shove, and he stepped back a pace to get more force.

His foot hit something which rolled away.

Major Mearns turned back. 'What's that, a ball? Young ladies shouldn't play with balls. It don't do their figger any good . . .'

Denny bent down to look. But he already knew, his feet had told him, they had felt that way before. On the battlefield.

'No, sir. A head.'

There was silence for a moment. 'Are you sure?'

'Yes, sure.'

Another pause.

'Is it Tossy?'

'No, sir, it is not Tossy.'

The bloodied head was that of a younger man, and with a crop of fair hair.

Major Mearns swore under his breath as he made his way to the bushes to look for himself. The head stared up at him, cheeks covered in blood and mud.

'And where is the body?'

There was no body.

The Major did what he would have done in the middle of a battle, he moved the head further into the bushes and nodded towards the house.

'Deal with this later, Sergeant. It'll need the coroner and the town officer and the magistrate. So we will see Mrs Breakspere first.'

'Think she knows anything about it?' asked Denny, stumbling after him. He was out of breath. In spite of the training of war, death for him was still death. He could not accommodate its presence in the garden of an academy for young ladies in the way the Major seemed able to do.

Officers are different, he told himself, although he knew that Major Mearns was an officer like no other.

The door was opened at their approach by an elderly manservant as if they had been watched for. He was wobbly on his feet, frail looking and nearly blind. A poor protector of this household of women. But also too old and weak to do anything to the young ladies, even if he wanted to.

Don't you believe it, Denny told himself, age and weakness are not a bar if you want it enough.

Even if any young lady was likely to fancy Mr Musket . . . that was his name, he was being hailed from the stairs by a tall and handsome young woman and behind her a chain of the young pupils.

They were to get a sight of the inmates and be seen by them after all.

The teacher in charge led her pupils past and round the corner without a glance at the two men, but the young ladies took them in with discreet glances.

Born to it, he thought, the young devils. One especially, with big blue eyes and tiny waist almost gave the sergeant a smile.

Almost but not quite. There was something familiar about her.

He dismissed the thought, there was an air about this place that gave you such ideas.

But the Major's face looked cold and angry, reminding Denny what a strong, hard man he was underneath his cheerful, drinking-companion friendliness.

'The handsome young woman, who is not so young as she looks, is Miss Tong, and she is a wonderful story-teller to the young ladies with a great turn of phrase. She is leaving to live in Chatham with her married sister, a Mrs Dickens.'

'You know her?'

'While you were out looking for Tossy I employed my contacts. I can tell you that Mrs Breakspere is a widow, or calls herself so, who came to Windsor to set up her school with a small inheritance.'

She has done well with it, thought Denny looking around him. The hall and staircase were carpeted with bright Indian rugs, the brass and mahogany on the banisters were well polished. It all said prosperity.

Down the stairs, treading with dignity that became her status, came Mrs Breakspere; there was no mistaking who she was. She was dressed in heavy green silk, well cut and nicely trimmed. Sergeant Denny stared at her as if he could see through the solid flesh and out the other side.

'That's a strong woman,' murmured the Major into the Sergeant's ear. 'Look at the shoulders on her. We could have done with her in the regiment.'

Denny did not answer, but he was thinking that there was a pretty face embedded in all that flesh.

Mrs Breakspere held out her hand, the Major bowed over it. 'Ma'am.' And then as he was rising from the bow: 'A wicked business.'

'You know all?'

Another bow. 'Mr Armour.'

Mrs Breakspere gave a great sigh. 'An adviser and friend. He told me that he would speak to you. I thank you for coming. Of course, you understand that there is no truth in this slander.'

'Never believed it for a minute, ma'am, but we must get to the bottom of it and put an end to it. Who tells this story?'

With another sigh, Mrs Breakspere admitted that it was the father of a pupil. She began to shake a little as she told her story. How the man had come to her, told her that he had learnt what was taking place, he had not shouted at her, no, she could have supported that better, but he had been cold and clear. He would see her school was closed.

'Calm, dear madam. Tell me his name and where he resides. A Windsor man? So, easy to find. And with Sergeant Denny I will talk to him.'

'He lives in Egham, sir, a small town on the river.'

'I know it.'

She added: 'Mr Vavasour.'

'An aristocratic name.' He kept his eyes on her, so Denny noticed.

She hesitated before agreeing that yes, it was indeed an aristocratic name. She had led them into her own room from where she ran the school. There was a large, handsome desk from which she drew a sheet of writing paper on which she wrote an address.

'A good-looking man, is he?' asked Major Mearns, pocketing the sheet. 'Oldish, I suppose.'

'No, young, very pleasant to see, with fair hair and bright blue eyes.'

The major took this in, giving Denny a quick glance. 'I may have seen him, madam. And like his daughter? Eye colour does run in families.'

Mrs Breakspere agreed that the girl was a pretty girl with blue eyes. She seemed to reserve opinion on the family resemblance.

'I must ask if we can move around the school, ma'am.'

Surprised, Mrs Breakspere said she would ring for the butler.

'Better not. Let me make my way alone. Best on my own.'

Outside the door, he paused, then laid his hand on the door knob.

'Back in?' asked Denny, surprised.

'Advice to you: let the ladies think they have got away with something, then go back in and give them a shock.'

Denny, who thought he knew a bit about shocks himself, followed him in.

Mrs Breakspere was sitting at her desk, she jerked her head towards them as they came in.

'Just a question, ma'am. Mr Vavasour . . . he is not the girl's father.' It was not a question, after all, but a statement.

He waited. And waited.

Slowly, Mrs Breakspere rose. 'No,' she said. 'He is . . .' she hesitated. 'He is her guardian, he is educating her to be his wife.'

'And this he told you?'

'I guessed. I have met the arrangement before.' She raised her head high. 'In fact, my own marriage was arranged so.'

Ah, was it, thought Sergeant Denny.

'I so much desired an education. It was a passion with me.'

'And you think this is why he told the story about procuring the girls for the stews of London? A punishment, to keep you quiet?'

She flinched at the words, then nodded, her face white.

Mrs Breakspere seemed about to ask her own questions of the Major but he spoke first. 'Keep your young ladies close in the house, that's my advice. And stay there yourself.'

Before she could speak, he had the two of them out of the door and leading the way down the stairs. 'You think she spoke the truth?'

Denny considered. 'Some of it,' he said with caution.

Major Mearns nodded. 'You are learning, lad.' He was leading the way down the stairs. 'To the servants. Always learn more there.'

In the hall they met Musket who made a feeble attempt to direct them out. 'Stay where you are, Musket,' commanded the Major, although the butler showed no sign of wanting or even thinking of leaving the house. 'Orders.'

A feeble bleat followed them down the winding staircase where carpet gave place to bare stone.

At the bottom of the stair three doors stood wide open. One door led to the kitchen, a second to a pantry and the third to a washhouse. All three were filled with active young women working and shouting. Over all presided a woman of size which dwarfed even Mrs Breakspere. Where she was large, this woman was huge, with muscles standing out on her bare arms. She was beating up a mixture in a large bowl with hard, directed energy. Her complexion was red and sweaty, her eyes cold and blue.

Give her a whip and she would make a fine slave driver. No, thought Denny, observing the kitchen girls at work, she is a slave driver, fully formed and in good working order.

Now how is the guvnor going to introduce himself, Denny

wondered. And the answer was easy: he did not. Just sailed on as if he was an expected visitor.

Perhaps he was.

'Plenty of help, I see.'

'It's my job to train the gals and send them out into the world,' said Mrs Badgett stiffly. 'I am the housekeeper as well as the cook.'

'And do they stay long with you?'

There was a pause. 'Girls always move on, it's their nature.'

'So it is, so it is.' He was most genial. 'Still it's a nuisance for you, always training new girls.'

'I should be obleeged if you would leave my kitchen, sir, we are busy.'

Outside, Mearns turned to Denny. 'You guess where we are? She is the organiser and those poor frightened girls are the ones she transports . . .'

'To where?' But Denny was already guessing. 'But how do you know?'

'Who sent you to the bath house? I always know more about this town than you may guess.'

There was a narrow window high on the wall and rain was beating against it. Denny thought of the bloody head with the curly hair on which the rain was now falling. Was rain merciful and cleansing?

At the door, they found the pretty young girl with big blue eyes, cape drawn down over her head, just opening the door. Musket was nowhere to be seen. No doubt, always bribeable.

Mearns put his hand on her arm. 'Young lady, you must not go out.'

'I am only going to meet my father, sir.'

'Your father? Come, I know better than that.'

She drew in a deep breath.

'What is your name?'

'Nell.'

'And he is not your father, Nell . . .'

There was something in Major Mearns's demeanour that made her hang her head. 'No, sir.'

'And so?'

'John wants me for his wife . . . I was to learn here how to be a lady . . . I am a quick learner, sir. I have performed. On the City Theatre in Bow. That was where Mr Vavasour saw me.' Her voice was proud.

'How old are you, Nell?'

'Thirteen, sir. I think thirteen.'

Mearns looked at her sadly. 'Who is your friend in this place?'

'Alice Ellis, sir. And then Miss Tong.'

'Go to Miss Tong, Nell.' He looked at the Sergeant. 'Denny, set Miss Nell on her way.'

Denny led Nell to the stairs and watched her walk up them, her eyes always looking backward.

Too easy, too malleable, too lost, he thought.

He followed the Major silently down the path.

'I am glad to be out of that house,' said the Major. 'That woman would have killed us if she could.'

'To the bath house, is it?' asked Denny. 'Won't we be in danger there?'

'The two large women are sisters, Badgett and Jones, you saw the likeness?'

Denny nodded. It seemed to him that he had been seeing a likeness of one sort or another ever since they entered the school.

'Yes, we shall be in danger but shall be on our guard,' and the Major drew a pistol from his pocket.

Denny was thinking about the head which must be still lying there, waiting to be rejoined to its body.

He started as a figure crept out of the bushes. 'Tossy! What are you doing here?'

'Followed us, I daresay,' said Mearns.

'I was waiting . . . I knew you would get here, sir.' He was carefully standing well away from where the head of John Vavasour lay.

Mearns dragged him by the shoulder and turned him to see the dead face. 'How did that get here? Tell me all you know or by God you will go to the gallows yourself. There was blood on you, Tossy and you will tell me how you came by it.' He gave Tossy a shake to add force to his words.

Trembling, Tossy admitted that he had been at the bath house when John Vavasour had come there to lay his accusation against the sisters: that girls were brought into Mrs Breakspere's school to work, then sold on to the bath house.

'He shouted out that he had thought Mrs Breakspere guilty, but now he blamed but the sisters. He shouted so loud that Mrs Jones knocked him to the ground with a single blow . . .'

'And who cut his head off?'

'Jones, sir. I was there watching through a crack in the door. He did it with an axe and the blood spurted everywhere, they are washing it still I will say.'

'And the head?'

'Jones carried it up here, meaning to bear witness against Mrs Breakspere. They hate her, sir, say she is a strict, mean mistress.'

'Not strict enough,' said the Major, letting him go. 'Bend over.'

With fear, Tossy did so. Denny waited for the execution. But the Major tore a page from his notebook and wrote on it with a black crayon.

'Here, take this note to the Magistrate, Mr Jennings, and tell him to come down to the bath house with two constables and a cart,' he ordered Tossy. 'And you and I, Denny, will be off to the bath house to start the arrest.'

'What about the head?'

'It will not walk away,' said the Major, beginning to march. 'To the bath house, Denny.'

The bath house was a long, low building with a single flambeau burning over the door. Dim lights could be seen as the two men approached and there was a smell of steam.

'Business as usual,' said the Major.

They looked at each other. The door would have opened at their knock, but the two men were seasoned campaigners and knew you did not approach the enemy at his strongest point.

'Round the back,' murmured Denny.

A cobbled yard lay behind the bath house where the flicker of flames from the furnace which heated the water could be seen from a small window. In one corner of the yard was a wagonette but with no horse, and in the protection of a roofed shed stood a hand cart.

Denny walked over to the hand cart to take a look at the bundle resting within. He raised the sacking and looked, then he shook his head and walked back to Major Mearns.

'The body is there, and an axe . . . it will be buried or else burnt.'

'It would burn,' commented Mearns, 'if jointed, and smell no worse than the Jones's usual supper when cooked.'

The faint hint of cannibalism sickened Denny who turned away. 'God help us,' he thought, 'we must prevent this.' He thought the Joneses, husband and wife, capable of anything. 'Let us break in, and not wait for the constables and the magistrate.'

Mearns nodded and drew out his pistol.

But before they could move, the back door opened and Jones and his wife stood there. She carried a great dish and a jug and he had a cleaver in his hand.

'A fine dish,' said Jones. 'If nicely boiled.'

'It will do for the guests and the gals, jugged with the blood, and an onion or two,' replied his wife. 'But I shan't touch it myself. Get on with it now.'

The Major advanced towards them, his manner easy but his pistol in his hand.

'Well, Jones, so this is what you do with your friends, kill them and cook them for dinner?'

Mrs Jones, brave and huge, raised her great arms and moved towards him.

'Yes, Mrs Jones,' said Mearns, 'and will your sister Mrs Badgett help with the cooking?'

Denny moved up behind the Major in support, but the stamp of the constables' feet announcing the arrival of the magistrate to him, made her draw back, while her husband turned and ran into the house.

'It might have been a near run thing if she had made a fight of it,' said the Major later, 'I swear she is stronger than me.' He turned to Denny. 'You caught the husband, but she's the worst of the two.'

'He's bad enough.' Denny was terse. 'I found him trying to escape from the hatch that lets the coal in, and gave him a blow that made him squeal.'

In a basement of the bath house, next to the coal cellars, was a locked room. Denny dragged Jones to the door, and forced him to open it.

Inside, he saw a huddled group of young girls.

'And who are these?' he demanded of Jones, 'and what do you mean to do with them?'

He gave Jones another blow to help him answer.

Wincing, Jones gasped: 'The plain ones we keep to work Windsor and the pretty ones who will fetch a better price we take to London to be used there.'

'They will hang together, side by side,' said the Major with satisfaction.

As the two men walked back to the castle along the unlit road in the rain, Denny said: 'And what will happen to all the young critters that have been caught up in this, the girls in the kitchen at the school, the ones already down at the bath house, the plain ones and the pretty ones all ready to be sold on?' Tossy too for that matter, but he knew Tossy would survive.

The Major marched on. 'I don't know. We can't know the end of every story.'

Denny was silent. After a minute, he said: 'I know the end of one story now. You remember my girl that I left behind when I went to fight? I saw her again this evening. I believe she recognised me too.'

Major Mearns stopped short. 'Not the lovely Miss Tong?'

'No, the other one. Mrs Breakspere.'

For a moment, all was silence as they walked on, then the Major started to laugh. 'You are a lucky fellow indeed. It is all over.'

Not so. Events seed themselves if they fall on fertile ground and bear fruit. Thus it was with the meeting between Miss Tong, aunt to Charles Dickens, and little Nell.

JOSEF ŠKVORECKÝ (1924–)

The Classic Semerák Case

Translated from the Czech by KÁČA POLÁČKOVÁ

THERE was no talking him out of it. Constable First Class Šinták—the only policeman in all Czechoslovakia who could boast that rank—was firmly convinced that Lieutenant Borůvka wielded powers not entirely in keeping with normal human abilities. But then, Constable Šinták was pushing 60, and had strong religious feelings, though he kept them secret while on duty. In his native village in the Orlice Hills, where he spent his vacations and took part in séances held in the cottage of a former weaver named Potěšil, he felt no such inhibitions, and as far as his superior was concerned, he told all. To Constable First Class Šinták, Lieutenant Borůvka was a wizard.

The Lieutenant proved it, definitely and irrevocably, in the classic Semerák case. That was the investigation to which Borůvka arrived late, having spent the previous evening at his 30-year class reunion at K. After celebrating until the wee hours of the night, he fell prey to depression, and besides, his alarm clock failed to ring.

So early that afternoon, when he arrived at the scene of the crime—a group of bungalows of the sort built before the war by worker-individualists at the cost of their life's savings—Sergeant Málek was just about through with the case, and all he was waiting for were the results of the laboratory tests.

'That,' said the young sergeant to the Lieutenant, 'is the only hitch. From the psychological point of view, you can tell that fellow's a murderer a mile off. But we can't have anybody accusing us of having made an arrest too soon. Psychologically speaking, he's every inch a murderer—just look at him! And then what happens if it turns out we're wrong? The public gets all worked up, and when the Chief gets finished with us we won't even be fit to pound a beat,' declared the sergeant. 'No, sir, a person has to have some insurance, and our insurance is the modern science of criminology.'

While the sergeant was acquainting the Lieutenant with his philosophy of criminal investigation, Borůvka let his mournful baby-blue eyes systematically examine the dismal attic. Hanging by her neck from a rope tied to a beam in the middle of the attic ceiling was an old woman in a dirty plaid dress, her gray hair concealing her face. About the height of the Lieutenant's belt buckle the toes of one foot still balanced a worn bedroom slipper, and the other foot was bare. On the attic floor, under the corpse, lay the other bedroom slipper, like a sad, deserted little animal.

Aside from that, the attic contained only a few musty cupboards, some flowerpots, a few crates, and a stack of yellowed newspapers; the Lieutenant wondered idly if he would find, were he to go through them, reports on the Lindbergh kidnapping, or the Sacco-Vanzetti story. The open skylight let in the cool breeze of Indian summer, and for a moment the breeze blew the hair away from the dead woman's face.

'Suicide?' scoffed the sergeant. 'Pooh. Oh, yes, it all adds up—she had asthma, she had it bad, and she kept threatening that some day she'd hang herself. The neighbors back him up on that. But, Lieutenant, look at the strangulation marks. Wait a minute,' he glanced around, 'we'll get you a chair. Constable, find us a chair, and then you can take a good look at those marks.'

And while Constable First Class Šinták was obeying orders, Málek kept on talking. It was the first case he'd ever had all to himself, and he could thank the Lieutenant's celebration of the previous evening and his unwound alarm clock. He was just quivering to show his superior that he was Johnny-on-the-spot. And so he continued in fine fettle.

'Everything is just too pat. The old lady herself talked about suicide. But what about the strangulation marks? They taught us that strangulation marks from hanging slant from chin to nape. And this one has two sets of marks—at least, I'm willing to bet that's what they are. Just wait till you see for yourself. It's not too clear, and the rope is still in one set of them, but if you look closely, you can see another set just below the rope. Nobody's going to tell me she jerked her head *after* she hanged herself!

'Šinták says there's just one set, or else it's a double set because the old lady tensed her neck muscles, and after they relaxed, she slipped lower in the noose. But I say that's nonsense. And that's why I left her strung up. The doctor wanted to take her down—he said he couldn't be sure of anything until he had her on the autopsy table, but I took it on myself. No, sir, I said, the Lieutenant has to see this just the way it is!'

'Well, thank you for your confidence, Paul,' said the embarrassed Lieutenant Borůvka, and his mournful gaze rested on the eager tanned face of the younger detective. 'Of course—'

'Of course that goes without saying, doesn't it?' interrupted Málek. 'You're in charge here, and you've got to see it. And in the meantime take a look at this,' he added proudly, and unfolded a piece of paper for the Lieutenant to see. 'I made a sketch, a sort of map, you see? I remember in your course on Methods of Scientific Investigation you gave a lecture on that case in Moravia, and you used a map to analyse the crucial times and the topographical situation to put your finger on the murderer.'

'Yes,' said the Lieutenant somberly, 'but—'

'But look,' Málek interrupted again. 'Here you have it black on white, everywhere the murderer—I mean the suspect—claims he went, and all the time and distance factors.'

'Yes, but—'

'But first I've got to report on how we managed the investigation,' and Málek continued with such enthusiasm that he didn't even hear the Lieutenant's resigned sigh. Borůvka capitulated. His smooth round forehead crinkled unhappily, and his sad eyes focused on the sergeant's map, painstakingly executed in colored pencils.

'Old Semerák phoned at 12:45 from the booth down the road,' the sergeant rushed on. 'At 12:57 we were here at the scene of the crime. We found everything just the way you see it—we didn't move a thing. Semerák claims that he left the tavern at 12:00—midnight—found his house empty and his wife hanging from this beam in the attic.

'So he went to phone the police, he says. That in itself is peculiar— home from the tavern at 12:30 and already phoning us at 12:45. And the phone booth a good ten minutes' walk from here. That doesn't sound as if he had to look very hard for his wife. It sounds as if he knew just where to find her and went straight up to the attic.'

'Certainly,' Lieutenant Borůvka made another feeble attempt. 'But—'

'But let's take a closer look at old Semerák's story,' Málek picked up his superior's last word. 'He claims to have left the house at 6:00 p.m. and that's a fact. His neighbor backs him up, a fellow named Pěnkava, a railwayman. He was just arriving home when Semerák was leaving his house. They exchanged a few words, and what do you think they talked about? The weather! And then Semerák remembered he forgot his tobacco pouch. So what do you think he did?'

The Lieutenant shrugged helplessly. 'I don't know. Maybe he—'

'He called his wife!' declared Málek triumphantly. 'Instead of fetching the tobacco pouch himself, he called his wife, and the two of them bickered back and forth over the fence about where she was to look for it. You see? Pěnkava saw her alive! That's perfect, isn't it?'

Lieutenant Borůvka nodded glumly.

'That's what I call an alibi.' The elated Málek rubbed his hands. 'The murderer—I mean the suspect—has a witness to testify when he left the house, who can swear to the exact time, because Pěnkava commutes to work and takes the 5:45 train back every day. And the witness sees the wife too, large as life.

'And that isn't all. There are two other witnesses to back up Semerák's story. One met him at the crucifix by the road, and the other about a quarter of an hour later at the bus stop. He stopped to chat with both of them—can you imagine that, old close-mouthed Semerák *chatting*! And what do you suppose they chatted about? The weather again! A fellow who never says an unnecessary word—and I've got witnesses to back that up—suddenly feels the urge to make small-talk about the weather. With three consecutive passers-by. The very day his wife hangs herself. That's one thing.'

'Yes,' said Lieutenant Borůvka, 'and—'

'And another thing: he makes sure he leaves his house just when he knows Pěnkava always comes home from work, when he knows for certain that he'll meet him. And he needs to meet him, needs Pěnkava to see his wife, alive, and so, on this particular day, the day his wife does herself in, he forgets his tobacco pouch. And he doesn't bother to get it himself—instead he makes his asthmatic old lady do the running around.'

The young sergeant glanced triumphantly at the frail old woman hanging over their heads, and then at the Lieutenant.

'Hm,' the older man cleared his throat, 'your deductions are excellent. Hats off to you there. Nobody puts anything over on you. It's just that—'

'That is not all,' said Málek hurriedly. 'I'll show you a lot of weak spots and tangles and discrepancies in Semerák's story. Like where he claims he went to see a certain Bárta for some beeswax. Bárta is a well-known bee-keeper in these parts, and Semerák keeps bees too. Not very successfully, but he keeps them all the same. You can tell if you look at the hives in the garden back of the bungalow. Honestly, the only bees that could keep alive in those hives are fourth-rate bees. Bum bees,' laughed the sergeant.

'Well, anyway, Bárta and his wife live in a cabin on the edge of the woods about two miles up the road. Semerák arrived there at 6:45, stayed for about three-quarters of an hour, and then took the path through the woods to the tavern. Look at the map I sketched. He arrived at the tavern at about 8:45, and by 9:00 he was sitting at the card table. He played cards till nearly 12:00, then he went home. It's a mile and a half from the tavern to his house and it took him half an hour. That's all right, that's just fine, but—'

'But—' Lieutenant Borůvka looked away from the dead woman, and his gaze rested on the flushed face of Sergeant Málek again.

'But even if a lot of things seem all right in his story,' Málek picked up quickly, 'some of them just don't stand up under examination. Look here—the map of the area he covered.'

'Yes, fine,' said the Lieutenant, 'you did a good job. Still—'

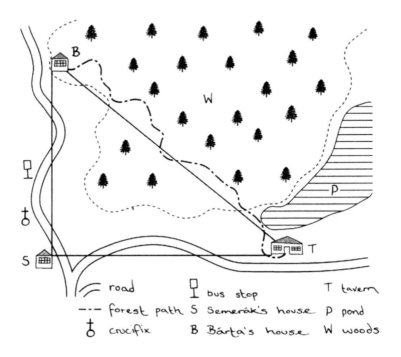

'Still you want to see the time chart, don't you?' He handed the Lieutenant another piece of paper. 'And here, below it, is a chart comparing times and distances.'

Lieutenant Borůvka took a look.

6:00 p.m.—departure from S
6:45 p.m.—arrival at B
7:30 p.m.—departure from B
8:45 p.m.—arrival at T
12:00 p.m.—departure from T
12:30 a.m.—return to S
12:45 a.m.—phoned police
12:57 a.m.—arrival of police on scene of crime

DISTANCES AND CORRESPONDING TIMES

S–B   1.7 miles—45 minutes walk (including two stopovers)
B–T   3 miles—1 hour walk
T–S   1.5 miles—30 minutes walk
B–S–T   3.2 miles—1 hour 4 minutes walk
B–S–B–T 6.4 miles—2 hours 8 minutes walk

'Why did you figure distances B–S–T and B–S–B–T?' asked the Lieutenant in spite of himself after he had studied the charts.

The sergeant grinned. 'I'll tell you. Look, first of all, I'm making the hypothetical assumption that Semerák is a murderer, that the old lady didn't hang herself, that Semerák strangled her and then strung her up on this beam here.'

'But that's—'

'That's jumping to conclusions. I admit I can't prove a thing. Not yet, anyway.'

'I think—'

'I think I have very good reasons to believe that's what happened!'

The older detective relinquished all hope of getting a word in edgewise. He left it to the young sergeant, who took full advantage of this opportunity.

'All right, then, assuming that Semerák murdered her. His alibi is airtight, on first glance. He left his house at 6:00—a witness saw his wife alive at that time. Between 6:00 and 6:45 two other witnesses talked to him, for about ten minutes, at points between S and B. At 6:45 he arrived at B; here the time is right because he claims his watch had stopped and he asked Bárta what the right time was, and wound up his watch and set it. Bárta backs him up there too—6:45. We know just when he left Bárta's because Semerák looked at the wall clock, was surprised that it was already 7:30, and even though Bárta and his wife tried to get him to stay longer, he got up and left.'

The only thing the Lieutenant had the strength to do was to clear his throat, and Málek was off again.

'Let's take another look at beekeeper Bárta and his wife before we follow Semerák to the tavern.' The young sergeant sounded as if he were giving a lecture in a course for beginning criminologists. The Lieutenant let his gaze wander around the attic. 'There's a number of interesting points,' Málek went on. 'First of all, Semerák's continued interest in the exact time. The day his wife hangs herself, his watch stops, and besides, that day of all days, he has to be at the tavern on time, as if he had heaven-knows-what kind of an important date there. And it turns out that all he's going to do there is play cards— and he doesn't even have the reputation of being much of a card player. The tavernkeeper says that Semerák isn't a regular at the card table, and when he does join in, he never stays at it for more than an hour. But yesterday of all days, he stayed at it for three hours.

'But back to the Bártas. Semerák's interest in the time is the first suspicious circumstance—inconspicuously calling the witnesses' attention to the exact time of his arrival and departure. Another interesting thing is the testimony of the beekeeper and his wife. I tried an old trick on them, one I learned from you.' Málek smiled, and the round face of the Lieutenant was momentarily illuminated by an embarrassed smile. 'I remembered,' continued Málek, 'how you told us in a lecture on Interrogation Tactics about the principle of "the confrontation of testimony obtained from separate interrogations of witnesses to the same event"—remember? and so—'

The Lieutenant braced himself for another attempt to halt the flood of words pouring out of the sergeant's mouth. 'Yes, I do recall lecturing on that. But in this case—'

His subordinate's enthusiastic eloquence took over again, and the Lieutenant gave a weary sigh.

'In this case,' the sergeant said impatiently, 'it was all perfectly simple and straightforward. On account of the jacket.'

'Jacket?' breathed the Lieutenant weakly.

'Jacket. And then—listen to this—his bike!'

A significant silence ensued, and Málek gave a sidelong glance at the Lieutenant. The more experienced detective read in his look a craving for recognition. Lieutenant Borůvka grew even sadder. He liked to make people happy. So he asked, with an effort at self-control, 'His bike?'

'His bike.' The sergeant rubbed his hands together. 'That's part of the working hypothesis I finally set up. I mean, my hypothesis uses the bike as the theory's point of departure. And that's the main reason I drew the map.' He tapped the paper the Lieutenant was still holding in his hand. 'First of all, the jacket. I asked the Bártas, each one separately, what Semerák had on when he came to see them last night. And now, listen! Bárta claims Semerák wore a tweed jacket, and his wife insists it was a brown corduroy jacket. When I confronted them, they almost had a fist fight over it. Some couple, those two.' The sergeant laughed. 'Anybody who wants to get married ought to drop in on those two for a chat. Five'll get you ten he'll stay a confirmed bachelor like me, ha ha ha.'

The Lieutenant's smile had a sadness that his subordinate failed to observe.

'They yelled at each other until we just about lost our eardrums, and the two of them were both hoarse, and in the middle of it old lady Bárta said, I mean she screamed, "He had the same brown corduroy jacket on that he wore last week when he rode past here on that bike." So there's another suspicious circumstance for you—a discrepancy between the testimony of two witnesses.

'Of course the discrepancy by itself doesn't mean much—men don't usually notice what a person wears. But all the same, what if the whole thing was planned, you understand? What if it was a fake alibi? What if Semerák didn't go to the Bártas' at all? What if he turned around at the bus stop after he spoke to the witness there, went home, did his old lady in, and then went to the tavern?

'You see, I found something very suspicious when I investigated the tavern—but I'll get to that later. First this: what if they planned this alibi, but got mixed up on the details? You always used to tell us that a false alibi is easy to break down by investigating the details. All I know about all this is thanks to you, Lieutenant.'

Once again the older police officer's countenance assumed a sour smile, and the hand holding the map attempted something that resembled a gesture of rejection. The sergeant responded at once.

'I know it isn't very probable, setting up an alibi for a murder with two people at once, and one of them the biggest gossip for miles around. I don't think too much of that theory myself—I'm just telling you about it so you can follow my thought processes right down the line. What's much more interesting is what the beekeeper's wife said about the bike. There wouldn't be anything odd about that—most of the people around here have bicycles. But the hitch is that Semerák doesn't have a bike! And besides, he denies the encounter with old lady Bárta last week.'

The sergeant's eyes were pleading for praise. Lieutenant Borůvka cleared his throat. 'Yes,' he said somberly, 'that's good work as far as deduction is concerned. In other words, the bike led you to the conclusion that—'

The sergeant, encouraged, launched his explanation with increased verve, 'That the time correlations are false. If Semerák had a bicycle hidden somewhere, then the timetable would be entirely different. Look!' He removed still another piece of paper from his breast pocket, saying, 'I believe in being systematic. Our complete investigative technique is based on system, on strict order, so we criminologists can't allow ourselves to be guided by haphazard ideas the way they do in detective books.'

The timetable was truly systematic:

DISTANCES AND CORRESPONDING TIMES BY BICYCLE

B–S–T	3.2 miles—about 20 minutes
T–S–T	3 miles—about 18 minutes
B–S–B–T	6.4 miles—about 40 minutes

AS ABOVE PLUS 20 MINUTES FOR THE CRIME

B–S–T	about 40 minutes
T–S–T	about 38 minutes
B–S–B–T	about 1 hour

Lieutenant Borůvka took a long time to mull over the information presented in the sergeant's precise handwriting. It looked as if he were undergoing some sort of inner struggle. Then he sighed, cleared his throat again, and asked, 'Why did you figure the times for T–S–T?'

'T–S–T, yes—I was getting to that.' The sergeant took the map from the Lieutenant's hand and indicated point B with his index finger. 'Assuming that Semerák had the bike hidden near the beekeeper's cabin—and that is entirely possible, the cabin is on the edge of the woods, with bushes all around. Well then, there are three possibilities. One: he left Bárta's at 7:30, got on his bike and rode from B to S—back home—committed the crime and then rode the stretch S–T to the tavern. So that B–S–T plus twenty minutes for the murder comes to, say, forty minutes. That means he had plenty of time to get rid of the bike near the tavern and to show up at the tavern at 8:45.'

Lieutenant Borůvka nodded.

'But S–T is a comparatively busy stretch of road that early in the evening. Maybe Semerák didn't dare to risk being seen there, even though it was already dark. He might have taken the road back from S to B, and then the forest path B–T. The stretch B–S–B–T plus twenty minutes for the murder would come to nearly an hour—still giving him plenty of time to reach the tavern by 8:45.'

'Yes,' said Lieutenant Borůvka, but he choked on it, and when he was through coughing, he asked, 'But why figure the stretch T–S–T when you say that he was playing cards from 9:00 till nearly midnight? Besides, I wanted to—'

The Lieutenant didn't get to tell the sergeant what it was he wanted to do. Málek clutched his sleeve, leaned over to him and breathed his cigarette-flavored breath excitedly in the Lieutenant's face.

'That's just it, he wasn't playing cards all that time,' he declared triumphantly. 'He spent more than half an hour in the Men's Room!' The Lieutenant's face quivered as if he were in pain. 'The witnesses don't agree as to just how long it was. We interrogated eight of them, including a couple of kibitzers, the tavernkeeper, and his daughter, who waits on table.

'Semerák claims that it wasn't over a quarter of an hour. One of the cardplayers claims that he was gone for almost an hour. It's all a matter of the relativity of the subjective perception of time,' said Málek slowly, and he blinked his eyes for emphasis. 'If we take an average, it comes to something between forty minutes and three-quarters of an hour. And that's enough for the stretch T–S–T plus time for the murder. Besides, Semerák's long stay in the Men's Room is symptomatic.'

'How?' asked the Lieutenant uncertainly.

'Symp-to-matic,' repeated the sergeant, enunciating every conso-nant. 'It either gives him time to murder his wife, if he uses the route T–S–T, or else it proves that shortly before arriving at the tavern, Semerák experienced something that excited his nervous system considerably. Dr Seifert once told us, in a course on Criminal Psychology, that the human organism frequently reacts to sudden excitement by an uncontrollable urge to move the bowels.'

'Yes, I know.' Lieutenant Borůvka appeared to delve deep into some reminiscence. He had a cool head, and was known to have twisted a loaded pistol out of a murderer's hand, and then when the fellow suddenly pulled a knife on him, to have knocked him down with a single well-aimed blow to the jaw. All the same, though, even Lieutenant Borůvka had occasionally experienced sudden excitement, with the accompanying reaction on the part of the human organism.

'In words of one syllable,' continued Málek, 'after he killed his wife, our friend got the runs. But here is where our criminological laboratory comes on the scene, with chemical and biological analyses.'

The Lieutenant's face twitched. For an instant he was possessed by a fantastic image of some sort of odd laboratory analysis. But the sergeant corrected the error almost at once.

'A careful examination of the scene of the—I mean of the men's toilet at the tavern—proved that somebody had recently climbed in or out of the window, or both. There are a number of items for dactyloscopic examination on the glass of the toilet window,' said Málek importantly, and the older detective blinked. He was used to calling them 'fingerprints,' but then, the sergeant was a member of a younger, more scientific generation.

'And Semerák has some suspicious abrasions on the palm of his right hand. So I ordered a chemical analysis of the paint on the inside wall under the window, and of the suspect's clothes. We ought to have the results of the tests by four this afternoon. Furthermore, I had them fingerprint the suspect and make a comparison with the prints on the window. And finally, I ordered an investigation of the outside wall under the window, in search of human tissue identical with that of the suspect. I also ordered the removal of a sample of skin from Semerák's palm. We had to drive out to the clinic for a dermatome—'

'A which?' breathed the Lieutenant.

'A dermatome. That's a special kind of dermatological instrument—sort of a knife that permits the removal of a thin layer of surface skin as a sample for comparison.'

The Lieutenant said wearily, 'Yes, but still—'

'Still, we ran into more trouble,' said Málek. 'The stucco under the window was badly weathered, and it was doubtful whether it could be removed and transported to the laboratory without destroying it. So we called in a couple of bricklayers and they cut a whole section out of the wall and fixed it into a metal frame, in a cement base. We got the frame at the ČKD plant—they welded it for us in the workshop on the spot—and so we took a whole chunk of wall over to the lab.'

'So the toilet—'

'So the toilet,' laughed the sergeant, 'is temporarily out of order. The tavernkeeper tried to give us a hard time about it, but I convinced him that when we're investigating a capital crime all citizens have an obligation towards society—'

'That's true, but of course—'

'—to contribute to the arrest of the murderer. But I must say that, all told, the citizens of the town were much more helpful. You see, in order to confirm my hypothesis, I had to find Semerák's bicycle.'

The Lieutenant's forehead was moist. 'Did you find it?'

'Not yet,' said the sergeant, but with an undertone of supreme confidence. 'But the entire local Youth Union organization has joined in the search. And the principal of the grammar school was more than understanding. The youngsters in the diving club are searching the pond.' Málek tapped the map. 'There are dense reeds on two sides of the pond, and it's up to twelve feet deep in some places, but there's a fellow in a diving suit hunting down there.'

Lieutenant Borůvka gave something that faintly resembled a groan. 'Listen, Paul, you've got a rare gift for organization, I know that—'

'I know that myself,' grinned the sergeant. 'I did a real job of organizing things here, didn't I? In the meantime the kids from the grammar school, along with the principal and the teachers, are combing the woods. We'll have that bicycle by nightfall or my name isn't Málek.'

'That is, unless—'

'Don't worry,' Málek reassured his superior, who once again was beginning to show signs of extreme nervousness. 'My hypothesis is okay, just wait and see. And I have other evidence. We found soil and bits of moss on Semerák's shoes. At first glance the soil and moss look the same as the stuff under the toilet window. Semerák insists that the same kind of moss grows on the forest path between B and T, where he claims to have walked—from Bárta's to the tavern.

'So we gathered samples of moss from the tavern, and from about fifteen places on the path where he says he walked. We sent it to the Botanical Institute of the Academy of Sciences. They promised to give us a hand—I spoke to Professor Kavina personally by phone this morning.'

There was desperation in Lieutenant Borůvka's glance as it swept the attic again and came to rest on the dead woman's wretched feet. Behind his back, Constable First Class Šinták cleared his throat, and when the two of them turned to face him, they saw that he was now holding a chair in his hand.

'Just a second, Constable. I'll finish giving the Lieutenant the background, and then he'll take a look at the strangulation marks himself,' said Málek, and he turned back to Lieutenant Borůvka. 'Well, while we were collecting the moss, we looked around for tracks. There were a few places along the path where the ground is moist clay, ideal for imprints, and sure enough, there were the tracks of at least five different bicycles. I had plaster casts taken of all of them. When we find Semerák's bike we'll make comparisons, and that'll be first-class proof. All the tracks were made by old bicycles, with characteristic marks on their tires.'

'But—' and that was all the older detective managed to utter when the sergeant took the floor again.

'But, of course, in order to play fair with old Semerák, I had casts made of his shoes as well—I mean, of his footprints—and casts of all the fresh footprints from the forest path. There's an awful lot of them, but since this is a major crime we have to set aside all economic considerations.'

'We wouldn't really have to if—' Lieutenant Borůvka tried to say.

'If that killer hadn't thought things out so cleverly that we're having trouble finding proof conclusive enough to arrest him.' Málek was indignant. 'But there's no such thing as a perfect crime, and we have the latest scientific methods at our beck and call, and that's a mighty weapon. He can't stand up against modern science. I had them bring in the canine squad on the case too,' he added.

'The canine squad,' repeated the Lieutenant.

'Yes, Ajax. You know him, don't you? Magnificent beast. A cross between a dog and a wolf. What a set of teeth! I've never seen a more magnificent set of teeth in all my life.'

'Yes,' replied Lieutenant Borůvka grimly. Ajax's magnificent teeth were not unfamiliar to him. The magnificent beast had attempted to demonstrate his teeth earlier on the Lieutenant's backside when that rotund officer had been rushing from his car to the scene of the crime. It had taken the efforts of two experienced members of the canine squad to calm the beast, who for reasons unknown was excited to a state of ferocity by the Lieutenant's scent.

'We put Ajax on the trail,' continued Málek, 'and the results point to the B–S–B–T alternative, even though there are some confusions. We'll have to wait for the lab tests to clear them up for us. Look,' and

Málek unfolded the map again, 'on the stretch between B and T the dog lost the scent a little way past Bárta's cabin, and couldn't find it anywhere in the woods either. On the stretch B–S he found it, but he had some trouble. But on the stretch between the tavern and Semerák's house, he had no trouble at all. What does that prove?' He turned to the Lieutenant with his rhetorical question, but this time the latter was silent.

'I can see it now, clear as day,' declared Málek with characteristic enthusiasm. 'A little way beyond the beekeeper's cabin old Semerák climbed on the bike, rode home to S along the route B–S, twenty minutes later pedaled back along the same stretch and then took the path B–T to the tavern. That means he walked the stretch S–B once when he went to Bárta's at six o'clock and covered it twice by bicycle. All of—' Málek glanced at his wrist watch—'twenty hours have passed since then, and that's why the dog had trouble finding the trail. Semerák took the stretch B–T only once, and by bike, so it's no wonder that the dog couldn't find the trail there. And he did the stretch T–S on foot, and comparatively recently, less than fifteen hours ago. That trail is still fresh, so a dog can latch onto it and follow it easily.'

'But you mentioned some discrepancies,' ventured Lieutenant Borůvka, and he gave an embarrassed look at Constable Šinták, who was standing almost at attention, with the chair at his feet, and devouring the sergeant's every word. His years of service on the police force had brought the constable a deep respect for superiors.

Lieutenant Borůvka cleared his throat as if to say something more, but Málek started in again.

'It's like this. At the tavern the dog hesitated. He found the trail all right—two trails. One led to the tavern door, and the other under the Men's Room window. Well, that's no contradiction—it just speaks for the T–S–T alternative. The murderer climbed out the window, went for the bike he had left hidden near the road on the stretch T–S, and then at 12:00 he left the tavern by the door and walked home. The only thing that's got me wondering is why the dog couldn't find the scent on the stretch B–T. Unless the murderer hid the bike in the woods near Bárta's cabin, cycled along the stretch B–T, hid it somewhere near the road between S and T so as to have it handy, and waited a while before going into the tavern, so the times would match, and then took the alternative T–S–T.'

'Yes,' said Lieutenant Borůvka groggily, 'all that is possible. Yes,

indeed. You really did a lot of work on this case, there's no denying
that. But of course—'

'But of course,' said Sergeant Málek, pleased, 'now you want to
look at those strangulation marks. Constable!' He didn't have to say
any more. The constable leaped forward with the chair and set it up
at the old lady's feet.

Lieutenant Borůvka looked up. Another breeze wafted in through
the skylight and blew the hair away from the bluish face.

'Go ahead,' urged the sergeant. 'We're going to have to take her
down anyway. She's been up there too long already.'

'I—' began the Lieutenant, when the shaky attic quivered with a
deafening roar. All three looked up. Šinták's face showed an expression of respect, Lieutenant Borůvka looked terrified, and Málek
smiled with satisfaction.

'Helicopter,' he explained, 'The major at the army base gave his
permission. You know,' he turned to the Lieutenant, 'from the air you
can see right down to the bottom of the pond. A lot of time saved for
the divers. Well, any minute now we can expect word that they have
found the bicycle.'

'I—' Lieutenant Borůvka paused, then added determinedly, 'I'm
not going to climb up there!'

'I know you believe me,' said the sergeant, flattered, 'but still—'

'No,' the Lieutenant interposed quickly, 'that's not it. I believe you,
but—I don't have to look. You can go ahead and arrest him,' he said
mournfully, and added, 'for murder.'

'Well,' smiled Málek, 'I'm happy to see that my scientific evidence
has convinced you. But I'd just as soon hold off making the arrest
until we're absolutely certain—until I have the bike, the fingerprint
and lab test results, and the botanical and dermatological reports. You
know how touchy the public is about false arrests. So we'll just wait
until,' and he cleared his throat, 'modern science gives us irrefutable
proof.'

'I don't need proof,' Borůvka said. 'I *know* he murdered her.' He
turned to Constable Šinták. 'Would you please go downstairs and
have them bring Semerák up here?'

That is how it happened that Constable Šinták didn't hear what
Lieutenant Borůvka said to the sergeant. And that is why nobody will
ever convince the constable that Borůvka's certainty as to the
murderer was anything but a product of his strange and supernatural
prowess.

And for that matter, no one ever found out what the Lieutenant told the sergeant that afternoon in the dingy attic under the body of the murdered old woman. Lieutenant Borůvka was a soft-hearted soul, and, whenever possible, he preferred to conceal circumstances that would cast aspersions on the detective abilities of his colleagues.

Two things are certain, however: one is the inexpressible sadness on Lieutenant Borůvka's face when Constable Šinták returned to the attic with Semerák, and the other is that Sergeant Málek was as red as a cooked lobster. Šinták didn't know why. He didn't because he hadn't heard the two questions the Lieutenant had asked the young sergeant during the constable's absence.

The first one was: 'You didn't move a thing—everything is exactly the way you found it?'

And when the sergeant had looked around that bleak attic, in the middle of which, about a yard above the floor and directly over that single sad, deserted slipper, hung the frail old woman, and when he had replied in the affirmative—that everything was exactly the way they found it, that not a thing had been touched—then the older detective asked, 'Then tell me, Paul, how did she get up there all by herself?'

And with a pudgy finger he pointed to the old attic beam over-head, and then, without another word, at the three-foot distance between the old woman's feet and the desolate floor, where the breeze was worrying a few shreds of old newspapers and tiny wisps of dust.

AMANDA CROSS (1926–)

Arrie and Jasper

———

M Y aunt Kate Fansler doesn't care for children. I'm her niece, but I
never really got to know her till we ran into each other when I was a
student at Harvard. It's true my cousin Leo spent a summer with her,
and lived with her a year or so when he was in high school, but he
wasn't really a child in high school, and during that summer she had
a hired companion for him and sent him to day camp besides. Kate
Fansler always refused to become defensive about this. 'I don't much
like children,' she admitted. 'I know it's an eccentric attitude, but not
a dangerous one. The worst fate I've ever inflicted on any child is to
avoid it. As it happens, however,' she added, 'I did once more or less
solve a case for a child. Do you think that will serve to redeem me in
the eyes of those with maternal instincts?'

Kate was in her office at the university, about to conclude that her
office hour was over and the thought of a martini with Reed could be
realistically contemplated, when she heard a timid knock. Kate looked
through the glass in the top half of her door and saw a silhouette
reaching only a few inches above where the glass began. A midget, she
thought. Well, midgets have problems too. But do they have academic
problems, and with me? She opened the door to find herself
confronting a girl child wearing a school uniform, glasses, braces, and
a frown. Kate stared at the child so long, she asked if she might come
in. Kate apologized and ushered her in, closing the door.

'Forgive me,' Kate said. 'I was just a bit startled. You look rather
young for graduate school. Or even for college, if it comes to that. Are
you lost?'

'I've come to hire you as a detective,' the child said. 'I have money.
My father says you probably couldn't find a herd of buffalo in a field
covered with snow, but I figure if he doesn't like you, you must be
good.'

'My dear young woman,' Kate said, dropping back into the chair behind her desk, 'I don't know which misapprehension to confront first. But, in the order in which you offered them: I'm not a detective, either private or police; they work at that job a lot harder than I do; I have detected from time to time, but I never take money, it might cloud the fine, careless rapture of the adventure; I don't know who your father is; and I am somewhat concerned that you hold his opinion in such low regard.'

You might think all this verbiage would have frightened the kid, but she held her ground admirably. 'I hope I didn't offend you about the money,' she said, returning her wallet to her pocket. 'I would be very glad of your help.'

'It doesn't sound to me as though your father would approve of your seeking my help, nor of my offering it. Who is your father? Someone I know?'

'His name is Professor Witherspoon,' the child said, assured that his name was sufficient to establish his identity and credentials in Kate's eyes. She was quite right. Witherspoon was a member of Kate's department, and to say that he and Kate never saw eye to eye on anything was to put their relationship in its least emotional terms. Kate was frank to admit that she could never decide if he was a monster or a lunatic; the best that could be said on her side was that most of the department agreed with her. Kate eyed his progeny with some dismay.

'It sounds to me as though I'm the last person you should come to. Am I to gather that your dislike of your father is sufficient to recommend you to someone he despises?'

The kid had no trouble with this one either, merely nodding. 'I think he's the most awful man I know,' she added. 'I didn't come to you just for that reason, though. My sister took a class with you, and she considered you worthy of recommendation.'

'Well,' Kate said with some relief, 'I'm glad to hear there is one member of your family that you like. But I can't say I ever remember having a Witherspoon in my class. I don't remember all my students' names, but I have a feeling I would have noticed hers.'

'Roxanna has taken our mother's name: Albright. I'm going to do the same as soon as I can. I'll have to wait at least until I leave high school. My sister is a lot older than me; she's very smart and very beautiful, not like me.'

'You look fine to me,' Kate said. She meant it. Kate is the best disregarder of beauty in any conventional sense I've ever met, and if a person is glamorous or studiously well-dressed, they have to go a long way to gain her trust.

'I don't look like my mother,' the child said with evident regret. 'Also, I'm strabismic and have an overbite. Put differently,' she added, 'my eyes have difficulty focusing on the same object, and my upper and lower jaws fail to meet properly. I think it's because I was such a disappointment. I was unexpected, you see, but they hoped—that is, my father hoped—that at least I would be a boy. I wasn't,' she added sadly, in case Kate had any doubt.

Had the kid but known it, she had picked the quickest way to Kate's sympathies. I think Kate asked her what she wanted in order to get her off the topic of her drawbacks.

'I want you to find my dog,' the kid said.

About this time, I'm sure, Kate was beginning to think of that martini with something close to passion. 'I wouldn't know how to begin to look for a lost dog in this city,' she said. 'I'm afraid it may have been snatched by someone, or else wandered off and was hit by a car. Have you tried the ASPCA?'

'He wasn't lost; he was stolen. And not on the streets, out of the apartment. The doorman saw someone leaving with Jasper under his arm. And the apartment wasn't broken into. Which means it was an inside job.'

Kate took the bull by the horns (the same bull Witherspoon no doubt would think her capable of overlooking in a china shop). 'Do you suspect your father?' she asked.

'I don't know who to suspect.' The kid sighed. Kate said later if the kid had said 'whom' she'd have thrown her out. 'But Jasper meant, means, an awful lot to me.' And she began to cry, the tears falling from her eyes as of their own accord. She raised her glasses and wiped her eyes on her other sleeve.

'What kind of dog was he?' Kate asked for something to say. 'I gather not a mastiff if someone could carry him out.'

'He was, is, a Jack Russell terrier. The breed isn't yet accepted by the American Kennel Club, though it is by the English. Jack Russell terriers are small, very low to the ground, white with brown faces and ears, and tough as anything. Don't you see, it had to be someone Jasper knew, someone he thought was taking him out. He loves to go out,' she added, sniffing, 'but he's a fierce watchdog with anyone he doesn't know.'

'You haven't told me *your* name,' Kate said.

'Arabella. It was my father's mother's name. She was a suffragette who chained herself to fences. My father hated her. People like my sister call me Arrie.'

Of course it occurred to Kate that the kid needed a therapist, not a detective, and she also probably needed a new father and a new dog. 'What about your mother?' she asked. 'You haven't mentioned her.'

'She's away trying to stop drinking. She's much younger than my father. She was a graduate student. She's his second wife. Roxanna and I have two much older stepsisters from his first marriage. My father has never been able to produce a son, to his sorrow. I hope my mother gets better. The man where she is says the whole family ought to help, but my father hasn't the time. My sister and I went down there once. . . .' She trailed off.

Poor Kate didn't really know what to do. She wanted to help the kid, but there didn't seem to be any evident practical course of assistance. Arrie seemed to understand her dilemma. 'You could think about it,' she said. 'My sister says you're very good at thinking about things. Only try not to think too long because I'm very worried about poor Jasper. He can be very trying to people who don't understand him.'

'And with that,' Kate said, relating the whole scene to Reed over her second martini, her first having been required simply to calm her down and stop her babbling, 'the kid left with a lot more dignity than I was exhibiting. What the hell am I to do? Could you call some old pal from the DA's office to undertake a dog search on the side?'

Kate's husband answered her real question. 'The doorman saw someone leave with the dog under his arm, as I understand it. The dog wasn't struggling, indicating that it wasn't being nabbed by a stranger, but by someone it knew. You better find out more about the family.'

'It doesn't sound like a family I want to know much more about. Perhaps we should offer to adopt Arrie and get her another Jasper.'

'You have got to begin drinking less,' Reed said with asperity. 'We are a happy, adult couple, let me remind you; you have no trouble remembering it when you're sober. You aren't going to turn maternal on me after all these years?'

'Fear not. Just wait till *you* meet Arrie, not to mention her father, the esteemed Professor Witherspoon.'

'What is he a professor of, exactly?'

'Exactly is the word. He deals in manuscripts, the older the better, and in a foreign tongue. There is nothing about them he doesn't know, to do him justice; the trouble is, he doesn't know anything else. Confront him with an idea, and he turns into a dangerous, oversized porcupine with a very loud voice. He detests every new discipline or theory or concept of teaching, and if he had his way he would never have hired the first woman faculty member. He's done his best to keep our numbers down. Women students, needless to say, are a different matter. He carries on with them in a manner designed to give sexual harassment a bad name. Women students should be grateful to sit at his feet and submit themselves in other suitable poses; he doesn't want them as colleagues. He is also pompous and leering, but we might as well keep this discussion on an impersonal basis, as is my wont.'

'That fills out the picture without getting us anywhere, wouldn't you say?'

'I've *been* saying, ever since I got home. What, dear man, is my next move?'

'Something will occur to you,' Reed said with confidence.

The next day, Arrie's sister Roxanna Albright phoned Kate's office for an appointment. With enormous relief, Kate agreed to see her. Roxanna, being beautiful and older, could be counted on not to get to Kate in the same way Arrie had. No doubt they could arrive at a practical conclusion to the whole problem, insofar as it allowed of one. Perhaps it would be best to begin by advertising for Jasper, hanging plaintive signs on lampposts, that kind of thing.

Roxanna, whom Kate had unsuccessfully attempted to call to mind from some years back, exceeded all expectations. She was gorgeous, there was no other word. She must, Kate thought, have undergone some sort of transformation in the intervening years; not to have noticed her would have been like overlooking Garbo.

'I don't know whether to apologize or implore,' Roxanna said, when they had both sat down. 'Arrie didn't consult me before coming; we'd talked about you once at dinner and I'd expressed my admiration. The fact that you had successfully undertaken some detective commissions was mentioned.'

'As well as the opinion that I couldn't find a herd of buffalo in a white field; I know. But does the fact that your father despises me really qualify me to help Arrie? If so, I hope you'll tell me how.'

'Oh dear. Tact is something Arrie doesn't so much scorn as ignore.'

'I quite agree with her,' Kate said. 'Tact should never interfere with one's getting at the facts. Your father, for example, lacks not tact, but any concept of what the facts are.'

'How well you put it.' Roxanna paused as though considering how to go on. 'I think the world of Arrie,' she said. 'Arrie's convinced she's an ugly duckling; I talk of a swan, which in time she will become. Arrie's going to do just fine. But for me, she doesn't get much undemanding affection, or really, any affection at all. Except from Jasper, of course, which is what made this so awful. Jasper is a very responsive dog; he and Arrie have a relationship I can only call passionate. That's why I wanted to come in person to tell you that he's back, and apparently no worse for his strange adventure. We got a note, printed in capitals on plain paper, saying he could be found at five p.m. tied to the gate of the playground at Seventy-second Street and Fifth Avenue. Of course, Arrie was there on the dot, and so was Jasper. I've really only come to thank you for your kindness, not throwing her out, listening to her. It was a horrible three days; even my father's glad the dog's back, and that's saying a good deal. You've been very kind.'

'There was no ransom asked, no demand at all?'

'None. My father pointed out to Arrie that if she went ahead of time, as she wanted to do, the kidnapper might see her and not return Jasper. It's the only helpful thing he's said in living memory, so I suppose this whole affair is remarkable for that alone.' Roxanna rose. 'I know,' she said, 'that Arrie will write to you and thank you for your sympathy and kindness. I thank you too.'

The next day, however, brought not a letter from Arrie, but Arrie herself. She had waited patiently during Kate's office hour until the last of the students had gone. She had Jasper with her, hidden in a very large sack. She let him out in Kate's office, explaining that she had brought him because she hardly dared leave him alone if she didn't absolutely have to, and because she thought Kate might like to meet him, having been so kind about his disappearance.

Jasper was a bundle of energy, perhaps ten inches high and eighteen inches long; he looked as though he could have taken on with ease anything five times his size. Having dashed about with relief at being out of the sack (necessitated by the university's NO DOGS signs), Jasper sat down at Arrie's feet and looked up at her adoringly. Kate began to feel she was being forced to watch a Disney movie that threatened never to end. Arrie, perhaps sensing this, became very businesslike.

'Jasper and I are not here only to thank you,' she said. 'We wish to engage your services to find out who took him. Unless I know, you see,' she added, 'I'll never be able to feel safe in leaving him again. I'm sure you can understand that.'

Kate was silent—which wasn't, as she was the first to admit, her usual part in a conversation. She had to recognize a clear reluctance to abandon this child to an additional unknown: her father was clearly as reliable as a lottery, her sister affectionate but hardly able, and certainly not obliged, to provide parental attentions. The dog seemed to be the only steady factor, and Kate understood that Arrie's desire for assurance was certainly justified. How, on the other hand, to provide it?

'I have come with a suggestion,' Arrie said, reaching over to stroke Jasper, who sat expectantly—Kate doubted if the dog ever sat any other way—at her side. 'My father is relieved that I have Jasper back; so is my sister. I think they would be willing to agree if I invited you to dinner.'

'To case the joint?' Kate asked. Dinner with Professor Witherspoon, Roxanna, and Arrie, to name only the minimum cast of characters, struck Kate as likely to be bizarre. Apart from everything else, Witherspoon was the sort of man who, alone with three females, becomes either autocratic or flirtatious, neither of them a mode dear to Kate's heart. On the other hand . . .

Arrie had smiled at Kate's question. 'Tomorrow night?' she suggested. 'Seven o'clock? I've written down the address and phone number. Jasper and I will be grateful.'

Kate nodded. What else was there to do? Not for the first time she thanked the gods—Kate, when not agnostic, was firmly polytheistic—that she had very little to do with children in this life.

At least one of Kate's trepidations about the dinner chez Witherspoon was allayed immediately upon her entrance: there were two men in addition to the Professor. At least that cause of Witherspoon's pontification or spriteliness had been removed. Roxanna introduced a young man, almost as gorgeous in his way as she in hers, named Desmond Elliott: an actor. What possibly else? Kate thought, shaking hands; he was good enough to eat. Arrie she greeted with warmth and a wink; Jasper had been, it appeared, exiled for the duration. The other guest was an older man who, it became immediately clear, was allied with Witherspoon and against the others. Why, Kate wondered, was that so clear? Equally clear, somewhat less inexplicably, was the

fact that Mr Johnson was a lawyer who had joined them for dinner
when Arrie's invitation to Kate superseded his planned dinner à deux
with Witherspoon. The Professor had decided upon graciousness. He
was the host, and while in his house Kate would be treated like a
woman guest, neither more nor less. With relief, Kate sank into a
chair, accepted a drink, and embarked upon a sea of meaningless
chitchat. This torture was somewhat ameliorated by Desmond
Elliott's amusing account of the actor's life, made up, it appeared, in
equal parts, of being a waiter and performing in small, unprofitable
companies of great artistic integrity so far 'off' Broadway as to be in
another state.

Roxanna was a pleasant hostess, keeping an eye on everyone's
comfort, but not buzzing about or insisting upon anything. When
they moved in to dinner, she brought things gracefully to the table;
she and Desmond were the mainstays of the conversation, although
Witherspoon made some acidic comments to Kate about their
department which Kate did her best to ignore. It is difficult, while
eating your host's meat, to convey to him that you disagree with
everything he is saying and everything he is likely to say. They finally
reached the blessed subject of the university's administration, in
disdain for which even sworn enemies could agree.

As the company returned to the living room for coffee, Arrie asked
Kate if she would like to say hello to Jasper. Kate eagerly agreed, and
followed Arrie down the hall to a closed door, behind which sharp
barks of anticipation could be heard. 'Quiet, Jasper,' Arrie said, revealing a history of complaints—from whom it was not hard to guess.
'Up.' The dog danced on his short hind legs, and Arrie took from her
pocket a chunk of chicken breast; she tossed it into the air and Jasper
caught and swallowed it in one grateful gulp, then sat, hoping for
more.

'You have a nice room,' Kate said.

'Yes. I used to have a tiny room off the kitchen, but Roxanna took
that since she doesn't really live here most of the time. There's really
just me and my father now.'

'And Jasper,' Kate said, it being the only cheerful fact that occurred
to her. 'Did your father buy him for you?' she added hopefully.

'No. Roxanna did. Dad said I couldn't keep him. But then he
changed his mind. Roxanna made him.'

'Desmond's nice,' Kate observed. It *was* odd how conversation
deserted her in the presence of the very young.

'Very nice. I'm glad he was here. I don't care for Mr Johnson.'

'Does he come often?'

'No, he's never really been here before. I've just talked to him on the phone when he calls my father. Roxanna says he's simultaneously illiterate and imperious.' Kate tried not to grin, and failed. They laughed together, and Jasper rose to his hind legs, joining in.

'I still need to know who took him,' Arrie said before they rejoined the others.

Reed had promised that something would occur to Kate, but all that occurred to her was gossip. And for departmental gossip, the ultimate source was Richard Frankel. Dean Rosovsky, when he became semi-retired from his high post at Harvard, reported in the Harvard magazine that the first duty of a dean was to listen to gossip. Kate, not to be outdone by any dean, took the advice to heart. Richard, reached by telephone, was graciously pleased to make an appointment the following day for lunch.

Kate contemplated his face across the luncheon table with pleasure. Richard combined the best features of an imp and a youthfully aging and gay (in all senses of the word) uncle. He was, in fact, quite heterosexual and a confirmed bachelor, having convinced everyone of this except himself. He still hoped to meet the right woman in the next day or so, and launch himself on a satisfactory career of marriage and fatherhood. Like a number of people Kate had observed over the years, Richard, marvelously suited to his life and vigorously happy, was unaware that his deep satisfaction arose in part from the delusion that he was abjectly in need of passionate love, babies, and a deep and lasting relationship. Kate liked him enormously.

She did not immediately ask about Witherspoon. To have evinced that much interest would have started Richard's investigative motors, and Kate did not wish to reveal her relationship with Arrie. But it was easy to work the conversation around to Witherspoon, whom Richard, together with the greater part of the department, despised with a vigor mitigated only by the pleasure they got in talking about how bloody awful he was. Witherspoon, Kate was forced to realize, had provided a good deal of pleasure in his curmudgeonly life, none of it intended.

Richard knew all about the wife, tucked away in a nearer version of Betty Ford's detoxification facility. 'Before my time of course, but the usual story. He pursued her with tales of his unsympathetic wife; now she's the unsympathetic wife: they never learn, poor dears. One hopes the graduate students these days are too smart to marry him, if not quite smart enough to dodge him entirely. I met the wife once; he had me to dinner in the early days, before I turned out to be too modern altogether. Obviously a lady, and punishing him and herself for her stupid mistake. They have two daughters, an absolutely mouthwatering creature called Roxanna, and an afterthought called Arabella. The names are enough to give you an idea of the marriage. It's widely assumed that Arabella isn't his child.'

Kate stared at him. 'On what grounds?' she finally asked.

'I think it was the poor thing's final attempt to bolt, before she drowned herself in alcohol reinforced by prescription drugs. Considering his record of fornication and adultery, you'd think he'd have turned a blind eye, but not our Witherspoon.'

'Why not?'

'Kate, my sweet, you don't seem your usual quick-witted self, if you'll forgive my observing it. Must you go on grunting monosyllabic questions?'

'I'm sorry, Richard. I'm always astonished at how much life is like prime-time soap operas.'

'Which I'm certain you never watch. They are unreal only in the way outrageous situations follow hard upon each other, if not occurring simultaneously, and in the luxury of the surroundings. Actually, they are, otherwise, just like life, if you're a shit like Witherspoon, which of course most of the characters are. Have you some special interest in him? A renewed fascination with manuscripts?'

Kate laughed. 'If I could take the smallest interest in manuscripts, it wouldn't be renewed. It would be a new and sudden aberration. Actually, I had dinner there the other evening, and was overwhelmed with curiosity. Roxanna used to be a student of mine, and she asked me.' Richard would wonder why she hadn't mentioned this in the first place; the reason was clear to Kate: it had entailed lying.

'Ah. I wondered why your interest was so suddenly awakened. The rumor is that he now wants a divorce and most of what there is of her worldly goods. In exchange, he'll pretend to relinquish with infinite sorrow custody of Arabella.'

'Do you mean he'll get her to pay him alimony?'

'Don't ask me the details, but that's often how it works out these days. The woman gets the children and the man gets the property.'

'Surely the woman gets to keep what she brought into the marriage.'

'No doubt,' Richard dryly said. 'But since all this wife brought in was her misguided affection for Witherspoon, that's unlikely to serve her very well. Of course, she may have some family bonds stashed away, in which case he'll do his best to get them. The men can always afford the better lawyers, alas.'

'No doubt the men look at it differently,' Kate said, her mind elsewhere.

'We certainly can guess how Witherspoon looks at it. And he's got two daughters from the former marriage, both unlikely to have great sympathy with the poor alcoholic. Maybe Roxanna and Arabella will come to her defense. I had the most awful row with him, you know, not too long ago. That's why it's an additional pleasure to contemplate his absolute awfulness. He worked every angle to get tenure for one of his acolytes, a twerp with his nose in manuscripts and his brain in a sling. A born ass-licker and fool. Witherspoon got his way, of course, and I was marked down as an enemy, a mark not of distinction, since there are so many of us, but of honor. The only good part of the story is that the twerp left to devote himself wholly to some manuscript collection. Did Witherspoon behave himself at dinner?'

'Oh yes. The older daughter is very gracious, and I like the younger one. I'm surprised the wife had the gumption to have a love affair.'

'Its end was no doubt the inevitable last straw. Witherspoon made no bones about the fact that if the child had been a boy he would have forgiven everything. He's that kind of monster.'

'Do you think he's really the father?'

'God knows. Roxanna is pretty definitely his, and she's gorgeous, so who has an opinion about genes? Of course, the wife was pretty luscious in those days; he'd never have bothered otherwise, that being all women are good for.'

'Do you know anything about the lover?' He sounds mysterious, like the tutor who might have been Edith Wharton's father.'

'I know the scuttlebutt: he was thin, with glasses and buckteeth, and very sweet. He was an adjunct teacher in art history, which she dabbled in. I don't know what became of him; gossip has it they used to walk around the campus holding hands. I feel sorry for her.'

Kate was amazed, not for the first time, at the extent of her colleagues' interest in one another's lives. Richard was, of course, unofficial keeper of the gossip; since his heart was always in the right place, she was willing to decide that his was a valuable function. What Witherspoon would have thought of it was another question. Did she care what Witherspoon thought about anything, or only what he did? What had he done, apart from being a failure as a human being and a father? Kate decided to walk for a while, after bidding Richard a grateful farewell. She wandered around the city streets, noticing dogs (no Jack Russell terriers) and the general air of menace which by now everyone in New York, and probably elsewhere, took for granted: it seemed the mark of an age. Compared to which, Kate told herself, the momentary absence of a dog was hardly to be counted. And yet, there had been, somewhere along the family chain, a failure of trust, which was how menace began. Was it Kant who had said that trust was the basis of civilization? Letting her attention wander unbidden over the cast of characters at that dinner, and in Richard's account of the Witherspoons, Kate found herself eventually at Central Park at Seventy-second Street; she sat on a bench to observe the spot where Jasper had been tied when Arrie retrieved him. It was a well-chosen location, easily approached and abandoned from four directions, sufficiently crowded with people and dogs entering and leaving the park to make one more man and dog unnoticed. Man? A man had removed Jasper from the building, according to the doorman's report. Dogs were not allowed in the playground, so a number of them were tied to the entrance, waiting, with accustomed patience or anxiety, for their people on the other side of the fence. By the time Kate had to leave to meet her class, she had made up her mind.

'It is, of course, none of my business,' Kate said to Roxanna, as they had a drink before ordering their dinner. 'That phrase is always a sign that someone thinks it is her business, or has determined to make it so. Do you mind?'

'Hardly,' Roxanna said. 'I used to wonder what it would be like to have dinner with Professor Fansler. Thank you for the privilege: my business is your business.'

'Very graciously put. Perhaps you had better order another drink.'

'Oh dear,' Roxanna said.

'I intend nothing more sinister than blackmail,' Kate said reassuringly.

'I know: on behalf of Arrie. Blackmail will not be necessary. From you, that is; I've already employed it on her behalf. Is that what you guessed?'

'It would hardly be fair to get you to tell me what happened, and then claim to have guessed it all.'

'Okay,' Roxanna said. 'You tell me. And I'll take that second drink. May I correct you as you go along?'

'Please do,' Kate said. 'My hope is that you will end up assuring me about poor Jasper's safety.'

Roxanna nodded.

'Your father, the revered Professor Witherspoon, has been after what money he can get out of your mother. Doubtless he has another young lady in tow. I say "lady," because I don't really think a *woman* would have anything to do with him. Did he try to retrieve from your mother something he had given her and now wanted to give to another? A ring, a brooch—it can't have been too big, or Jasper wouldn't have swallowed it, however imbedded in a piece of meat. Although the way he gulps, dancing around on his hind legs, anything is possible.'

'Not a ring,' Roxanna said. 'An emerald. He had had it taken out of the ring. He said he was going to get it reset. It's the most valuable thing my mother had. It was in her family for years; they may have pawned it, but they never sold it.'

'He pretended to her it needed to be reset?'

'Nothing so civilized. She would have been suspicious immediately at any kindly offer, I'm afraid. He talked her out of taking it to the detoxification place, said it might be stolen. She didn't believe him, but when he set his mind on something, she didn't have a chance. I heard them arguing about it one night. So did Desmond, the guy you met; he was there with me. He held me back from interfering; he was right.'

'He's very handsome, even for an actor,' Kate said.

'He's especially handsome for a lawyer, which is what he is,' Roxanna responded. 'We were trying to allay my father's suspicions. He knew we'd overheard him. So when he emerged that evening, we pretended innocence, on Desmond's advice, and I introduced him to Dad as an actor. His looks, as you observed, made that easy.'

'I've lost count,' Kate said, 'but I don't think I'm doing too well. Shall we order dinner?'

'The details need cleaning up, but you certainly seem to be onto the main story line. Go on.'

'There isn't much more. Somehow, later, needing to hide the stolen emerald, the Professor fed it to Jasper. Anyone who observed Jasper's routine with Arrie would have thought of it, whether the motive was greed or detection. Was he going to kill the dog?'

'Of course. Or pay someone else to. Fortunately, I guessed what he was up to. I had caught him examining the stone. I demanded it and he wouldn't give it to me. Sometime later, he came in to promise me he wouldn't take it out of the house. There was something about the exact way he said this that made me suspicious. I pretended to calm down and then went to look for the stone; it wasn't where it was supposed to be. My father went into calm assurances that he didn't have it, and hadn't hid it, urging me to search him. He was so smug about it all; that, and the sight of Jasper dancing around gave me the idea. He had fed it to the dog in a hunk of meat, intending to have the dog "get lost." When I figured this out we really had a knockdown fight. I couldn't believe he'd really do that to Arrie.'

'Where was Arrie?'

'Locked in the bathroom, crying. She hated the fights. She used to stuff her ears with toilet paper. He and I fought about a lot of things, though never as violently as this. In the end, I threatened him. You see, my mother had mentioned her ring when Arrie and I went to see her; she wanted Arrie to have it. Arrie said I should have it because I was beautiful. My mother hugged Arrie and said: "You take care of Roxanna; it's far, far better not to be beautiful, believe me, my darling." '

'And you got Desmond to leave with the dog under his arm. I gather Jasper had got to know him by now.'

'Jasper takes a long time to get to know people well enough to let them pick him up. He may be small, but he's tough. That was me.'

'In drag?'

'Great fun. I got the idea from Sherlock Holmes. "My walking clothes," Irene Adler called them. Desmond borrowed the suit for me from someone my size. I can't remember when I had more fun. The doorman didn't raise an eyebrow.'

'So you took Jasper—where?'

'To Desmond's, where I stay most of the time. I walked him, and never have I used a pooper-scooper more diligently. At first, we thought we'd keep him in, but poor Jasper is well trained. I tell you, retrieving that emerald from Jasper's shit made me feel like someone in a Dickens novel, *Our Mutual Friend* for choice. I well remember your talking about that novel.'

'You said you'd get the emerald back if he behaved?'

'More than behaved. I had Desmond as a witness and advisor. I said Arrie and Jasper were to live with me, that he was to give my mother a divorce under fair terms: he could keep the apartment, he had to continue to support Arrie till she finished her education, my mother was to get half his pension, and if he didn't agree I was going to drag him into court accused of theft and abusive conduct.'

'And he bought it?'

'Not entirely. I had to give him the emerald, and a few other things besides. But I figured I didn't need it, Arrie didn't need it, it hadn't done my mother much good, and it was worth her freedom and ours. I also told him I had a student lined up ready to bring charges of sexual harassment. I scared him. He even cooperated about Arrie's retrieving Jasper. I was going to make him leave the dog at the playground, but I didn't want him to take out his frustrations on the poor beast. So I did that too. Desmond came with me between two closings. Desmond's been great.'

'He sounds rather unusual for a lawyer.'

'He is. He's quitting. He says there's no point spending your life suing about water damage and helping one firm take over another. I don't know what he's going to do.'

'You might suggest acting,' Kate said. 'And being a waiter on the side.'

'He's thinking of becoming a detective,' Roxanna said. 'A private eye. Perhaps he could get in touch with you for pointers.'

Kate decided not to look for irony in this. 'What next?' she asked.

'It's Arrie's vacation next week. We're going down with Desmond to visit my mom. I think with some real encouragement, and the knowledge that the Professor is out of her life, she may actually make it. She never took up drinking, or prescription drugs either, till she met him. But she's going to need a lot of help.'

'Speaking of "none of my business,"' Kate said, 'may I ask an outrageous question? Just tell me to go to hell if you don't want to answer it. Is the Professor Arrie's father, or was there someone else?'

'I'll answer that question on one condition,' Roxanna said. 'That you agree to do me an enormous favor, no questions asked. Is it a bargain?'

'I'll have to think about it,' Kate said. 'I don't believe in blind promises.'

'And I don't believe in gossip, not all of it. My mother did moon around with another guy. His main attraction was that he wasn't lustful. My father is very lustful. He insisted on his rights; that's how he thought of them, as rights. And he still wanted a son.'

'You've been angry at him a long time, haven't you?' Kate said.

'I'm getting over it, with help. I don't want Arrie to go through the same thing. Of course, I couldn't have done it without Desmond, especially since the Professor had that sleazy lawyer on his side. Mr Johnson: you met him too.'

Kate looked into her coffee cup. 'All right,' she said. 'It's a bargain.'

Roxanna looked up questioningly.

'I'll keep Jasper for Arrie while she's gone. Reed will be overjoyed. That is, I'll pretend we have him forever, and when he finds out it's only a week or so, he'll be overjoyed.'

'I think women are reprehensible,' Roxanna said. 'Don't you?' And they laughed together. Kate even found herself wishing Arrie and Jasper had been there.

JANWILLEM VAN DE WETERING (1931–)

The Deadly Egg

THE siren of the tiny dented Volkswagen shrieked forlornly between the naked trees of the Amsterdam Forest, the city's largest park, set on its southern edge: several square miles of willows, poplars, and wild-growing alders, surrounding ponds and lining paths. The paths were restricted to pedestrians and cyclists, but the Volkswagen had ignored the many no-entry signs, quite legally, for the vehicle belonged to the Municipal Police and more especially to its Criminal Investigation Department, or Murder Brigade. Even so, it looked lost and its howl seemed defensive.

It was Easter Sunday and it rained, and the car's two occupants, Detective Adjutant Grijpstra and Detective Sergeant de Gier, sat hunched in their overcoats, watching the squeaky, rusted wipers trying to deal with the steady drizzle. The car should have been junked some years before, but the adjutant had lost the form that would have done away with his aging transport, lost it on purpose and with the sergeant's consent. They had grown fond of the Volkswagen, of its shabbiness and its ability to melt away in traffic.

But they weren't fond of the car now. The heater didn't work, it was cold, and it was early. Not yet nine o'clock on a Sunday is early, especially when the Sunday is Easter. Technically, they were both off duty, but they had been telephoned out of warm beds by Headquarters' radio room. A dead man dangling from a branch in the forest; please, would they care to have a look at the dead man?

Grijpstra's stubby index finger silenced the siren. They had followed several miles of winding paths so far and hadn't come across anything alive except tall blue herons, fishing in the ponds and moats and flapping away slowly when the car came too close for their comfort.

'You know who reported the corpse? I wasn't awake when the radio room talked to me.'

De Gier had been smoking silently. His handsome head with the perfect curls turned obediently to face his superior. 'Yes, a gentleman jogger. He said he jogged right into the body's feet. Gave him a start. He ran all the way to the nearest telephone booth, phoned Headquarters, then Headquarters phoned us, and that's why we are here, I suppose. I am a little asleep myself—we are here, aren't we?'

They could hear another siren, and another. Two limousines came roaring toward the Volkswagen, and Grijpstra cursed and made the little car turn off the path and slide into a soggy lawn; they could feel its wheels sink into the mud.

The limousines stopped and men poured out of them; the men pushed the Volkswagen back on the path.

'Morning, Adjutant; morning, Sergeant. Where is the corpse?'

'Shouldn't you know, too?'

'No, Adjutant,' several men said simultaneously, 'but we thought maybe you knew. All we know is that the corpse is in the Amsterdam Forest and that this is the Amsterdam Forest.'

Grijpstra addressed the sergeant. 'You know?'

De Gier's well-modulated baritone chanted the instructions. 'Turn right after the big pond, right again, then left. Or the other way round. I think I have it right; we should be close.'

The three cars drove about for a few minutes more until they were waved down by a man dressed in what seemed to be long blue underwear. The jogger ran ahead, bouncing energetically, and led them to their destination. The men from the limousines brought out their boxes and suitcases, then cameras clicked and a videorecorder hummed. The corpse hung on and the two detectives watched it hang.

'Neat,' Grijpstra said, 'very neat. Don't you think it is neat?'

The sergeant grunted.

'Here. Brought a folding campstool and some nice new rope, made a perfect noose, slipped it around his neck, kicked the stool. Anything suspicious, gentlemen?'

The men from the limousines said there was not. They had found footprints—the prints of the corpse's boots. There were no other prints, except the jogger's. The jogger's statement was taken; he was thanked and sent on his sporting way. A police ambulance arrived and the corpse was cut loose, examined by doctor and detectives, and carried off. The detectives saluted the corpse quietly by inclining their heads.

'In his sixties,' the sergeant said, 'well dressed in old but expensive clothes. Clean shirt. Tie. Short gray beard, clipped. Man who took care of himself. A faint smell of liquor—he must have had a few to give him courage. Absolutely nothing in his pockets. I looked in the collar of his shirt—no laundry mark. He went to some trouble to be nameless. Maybe something will turn up when they strip him at the mortuary; we should phone in an hour's time.'

Grijpstra looked hopeful. 'Suicide?'

'I would think so. Came here by himself, no traces of anybody else. No signs of a struggle. The man knew what he wanted to do, and did it, all by himself. But he didn't leave a note; that wasn't very thoughtful.'

'Right,' Grijpstra said. 'Time for breakfast, Sergeant! We'll have it at the airport—that's close and convenient. We can show our police cards and get through the customs barrier; the restaurant on the far side is better than the coffee shop on the near side.'

De Gier activated the radio when they got back to the car.

'Male corpse, balding but with short gray beard. Dentures. Blue eyes. Sixty-odd years old. Three-piece blue suit, elegant dark gray overcoat, no hat. No identification.'

'Thank you,' the radio said.

'Looks very much like suicide. Do you have any missing persons of that description in your files?'

'No, not so far.'

'We'll be off for breakfast and will call in again on our way back.'

'*Echrem*,' the radio said sadly, 'there's something else. Sorry.'

De Gier stared at a duck waddling across the path and trailing seven furry ducklings. He began to mumble. Adjutant Grijpstra mumbled with him. The mumbled four-letter words interspersed with mild curses formed a background for the radio's well-articulated message. They were given an address on the other side of the city. 'The lady was poisoned, presumably by a chocolate Easter egg. The ambulance that answered the distress call just radioed in. They are taking her to the hospital. The ambulance driver thought the poison was either parathion, something used in agriculture, or arsenic. His assistant is pumping out the patient's stomach. She is in a bad way but not dead yet.'

Grijpstra grabbed the microphone from de Gier's limp hand. 'So if the lady is on her way to the hospital, who is left in the house you want us to go to?'

'Her husband, man by the name of Moozen—a lawyer, I believe.'

'What hospital is Mrs Moozen being taken to?'

'The Wilhelmina.'

'And you have no one else on call? Sergeant de Gier and I are supposed to be off duty for Easter, you know!'

'No,' the radio's female voice said, 'no, Adjutant. We never have much crime on Easter Day, especially not in the morning. There are only two detectives on duty and they are out on a case, too—some boys have derailed a streetcar with matches.'

'Right,' Grijpstra said coldly, 'we are on our way.'

The old Volkswagen made an effort to jump away, protesting feebly. De Gier was still muttering but had stopped cursing. 'Streetcar? Matches?'

'Yes. They take an empty cartridge, fill it with match heads, then close the open end with a hammer. Very simple. All you have to do is insert the cartridge into the streetcar's rail, and when the old tram comes clanging along, the sudden impact makes the cartridge explode. If you use two or three cartridges, the explosion may be strong enough to lift the wheel out of the rail. Didn't you ever try that? I used to do it as a boy. The only problem was to get the cartridges. We had to sneak around on the rifle range with the chance of getting shot at.'

'No,' de Gier said. 'Pity. Never thought of it, and it sounds like a good game.'

He looked out of the window. The car had left the park and was racing toward the city's center through long empty avenues. There was no life in the huge apartment buildings lining the old city— nobody had bothered to get up yet. Ten o'clock and the citizenry wasn't even considering the possibility of slouching into the kitchen for a first cup of coffee.

But one man had bothered to get up early and had strolled into the park, carrying his folding chair and a piece of rope to break off the painful course of his life, once and for all. An elderly man in good but old clothes. De Gier saw the man's beard again, a nicely cared-for growth. The police doctor had said that he hadn't been dead long. A man alone in the night that would have led him to Easter, a man by himself in a deserted park, testing the strength of his rope, fitting his head into the noose, kicking the campstool.

'Bah!' he said aloud.

Grijpstra had steered the car through a red light and was turning the wheel.

'What's that?'

'Nothing. Just bah.'

'Bah is right,' Grijpstra said.

They found the house, a bungalow, on the luxurious extreme north side of the city. Spring was trying to revive the small lawn and a magnolia tree was in hesitant bloom. Bright yellow crocuses set off the path. Grijpstra looked at the crocuses. He didn't seem pleased.

'Crocuses,' de Gier said, 'very nice. Jolly little flowers.'

'No. Unimaginative plants, manufactured, not grown. Computer plants. They make the bulbs in a machine and program them to look stupid. Go ahead, Sergeant, press the bell.'

'Really?' the sergeant asked.

Grijpstra's jowls sagged. 'Yes. They are like mass-manufactured cheese, tasteless; cheese is probably made with the same machines.'

'Cheese,' de Gier said moistly. 'There's nothing wrong with cheese either, apart from not having any right now. Breakfast has slipped by, you know.' He glanced at his watch.

They read the nameplate while the bell rang: H. F. MOOZEN, ATTORNEY AT LAW. The door opened. A man in a bathrobe made out of brightly striped towel material said good morning. The detectives showed their identifications. The man nodded and stepped back. A pleasant man, still young, thirty years or a bit more. The ideal model for an ad in a ladies' magazine. A background man, showing off a modern house, or a minicar, or expensive furniture. The sort of man ladies would like to have around. Quiet, secure, mildly good-looking. Not a passionate man, but lawyers seldom are. Lawyers practice detachment; they identify with their clients, but only up to a point.

'You won't take long, I hope,' Mr Moozen said. 'I wanted to go with the ambulance, but the driver said you were on the way, and that I wouldn't be of any help if I stayed with my wife.'

'Was your wife conscious when she left here, sir?'

'Barely. She couldn't speak.'

'She ate an egg, a chocolate egg?'

'Yes. I don't care for chocolate myself. It was a gift, we thought, from friends. I had to let the dog out early this morning, an hour ago, and there was an Easter bunny sitting on the path. He held an egg wrapped up in silver paper. I took him in, woke up my wife, and showed the bunny to her, and she took the egg and ate it, then became ill. I telephoned for the ambulance and they came almost immediately. I would like to go to the hospital now.'

'Come in our car, sir. Can I see the bunny?'

Mr Moozen took off the bathrobe and put on a jacket. He opened the door leading to the kitchen, and a small dog jumped around the detectives, yapping greetings. The bunny stood on the kitchen counter; it was almost a foot high. Grijpstra tapped its back with his knuckles; it sounded solid.

'Hey,' de Gier said. He turned the bunny around and showed it to Grijpstra.

'*Brwah!*' Grijpstra said.

The rabbit's toothless mouth gaped. The beast's eyes were close together and deeply sunk into the skull. Its ears stood up aggressively. The bunny leered at them, its torso crouched; the paws that had held the deadly egg seemed ready to punch.

'It's roaring,' de Gier said. 'See? A roaring rabbit. Easter bunnies are supposed to smile.'

'Shall we go?' Mr Moozen asked.

They used the siren, and the trip to the hospital didn't take ten minutes. The city was still quiet. But there proved to be no hurry. An energetic bright young nurse led them to a waiting room. Mrs Moozen was being worked on; her condition was still critical. The nurse would let them know if there was any change.

'Can we smoke?' Grijpstra asked.

'If you must.' The nurse smiled coldly, appraised de Gier's tall, wide-shouldered body with a possessive feminine glance, swung her hips, and turned to the door.

'Any coffee?'

'There's a machine in the hall. Don't smoke in the hall, please.'

There were several posters in the waiting room. A picture of a cigarette pointing to a skull with crossed bones. A picture of a happy child biting into an apple. A picture of a drunken driver (bubbles surrounding his head proved he was drunk) followed by an ambulance. The caption read, 'Not *if* you have an accident, but *when* you have an accident.'

De Gier fetched coffee and Grijpstra offered cigars. Mr Moozen said he didn't smoke.

'Well,' Grijpstra said patiently and puffed out a ragged dark cloud, 'now who would want to poison your wife, sir? Has there been any recent trouble in her life?'

The question hung in the small white room while Moozen thought. The detectives waited. De Gier stared at the floor, Grijpstra observed the ceiling. A full minute passed.

'Yes,' Mr Moozen said, 'some trouble. With me. We contemplated a divorce.'

'I see.'

'But then we decided to stay together. The trouble passed.'

'Any particular reason why you considered a divorce, sir?'

'My wife had a lover.' Mr Moozen's words were clipped and precise.

'*Had*,' de Gier said. 'The affair came to an end?'

'Yes. We had some problems with our central heating, something the mechanics couldn't fix. An engineer came out and my wife fell in love with him. She told me—she doesn't like to be secretive. They met each other in motels for a while.'

'You were upset?'

'Yes. It was a serious affair. The engineer's wife is a mental patient; he divorced her and was awarded custody of his two children. I thought he was looking for a new wife. My wife has no children of her own—we have been married some six years and would like to have children. My wife and the engineer seemed well matched. I waited a month and then told her to make up her mind—either him or me, not both; I couldn't stand it.'

'And she chose you?'

'Yes.'

'Do you know the engineer?'

A vague pained smile floated briefly on Moozen's face. 'Not personally. We did meet once and discussed central heating systems. Any further contact with him was through my wife.'

'And when did all this happen, sir?'

'Recently. She only made her decision a week ago. I don't think she has met him since. She told me it was all over.'

'His name and address, please, sir.'

De Gier closed his notebook and got up. 'Shall we go, Adjutant?'

Grijpstra sighed and got up too. They shook hands with Moozen and wished him luck. Grijpstra stopped at the desk. The nurse wasn't helpful, but Grijpstra insisted and de Gier smiled and eventually they were taken to a doctor who accompanied them to the next floor. Mrs Moozen seemed comfortable. Her arms were stretched out on the blanket. The face was calm. The detectives were led out of the room again.

'Bad,' the doctor said. 'Parathion is a strong poison. Her stomach is ripped to shreds. We'll have to operate and remove part of it, but I think she will live. The silly woman ate the whole egg, a normal-sized egg. Perhaps she was still too sleepy to notice the taste.'

'Her husband is downstairs. Perhaps you should call him up, especially if you think she will live.' Grijpstra sounded concerned. He probably was, de Gier thought. He felt concerned himself. The woman was beautiful, with a finely curved nose, very thin in the bridge, and large eyes and a soft and sensitive mouth. He had noted her long delicate hands.

'Husbands,' the doctor said. 'Prime suspects in my experience. Husbands are supposed to love their wives, but usually they don't. It's the same the other way round. Marriage seems to breed violence—it's one of the impossible situations we humans have to put up with.'

Grijpstra's pale blue eyes twinkled. 'Are you married, Doctor?'

The doctor grinned back. 'Very. Oh, yes.'

'A long time?'

'Long enough.'

Grijpstra's grin faded. 'So am I. Too long. But poison is nasty. Thank you, Doctor.'

There wasn't much conversation in the car when they drove to the engineer's address. The city's streets had filled up. People were stirring about on the sidewalks and cars crowded each other, honking occasionally. The engineer lived in a block of apartments, and Grijpstra switched off the engine and lit another small black cigar.

'A family drama. What do you think, Sergeant?'

'I don't think. But that rabbit was most extraordinary. Not bought in a shop. A specially made rabbit, and well made, not by an amateur.'

'Are we looking for a sculptor? Some arty person? Would Mr Moozen or the engineer be an artist in his spare time? How does one make a chocolate rabbit, anyway?'

De Gier tried to stretch, but didn't succeed in his cramped quarters. He yawned instead. 'You make a mold, I suppose, out of plaster of Paris or something, and then you pour hot chocolate into the mold and wait for it to harden. That rabbit was solid chocolate, several kilos of it. Our artistic friend went to a lot of trouble.'

'A baker? A pastry man?'

'Or an engineer—engineers design forms sometimes, I believe. Let's meet this lover man.'

The engineer was a small nimble man with a shock of black hair and dark lively eyes, a nervous man, nervous in a pleasant, childlike manner. De Gier remembered that Mrs Moozen was a small woman,

386 *Janwillem van de Wetering*

too. They were ushered into a four-room apartment. They had to be careful not to step on a large number of toys, spread about evenly. Two little boys played on the floor; the eldest ran out of the room to fetch his Easter present to show it to the uncles. It was a basketful of eggs, homemade, out of chocolate. The other boy came to show his basket, identical but a size smaller.

'My sister and I made them last night,' the engineer said. 'She came to live here after my wife left, and she looks after the kids, but she is spending the Easter weekend with my parents in the country. We couldn't go because Tom here had measles, hadn't you, Tom?'

'Yes,' Tom said. 'Big measles. Little Klaas here hasn't had them yet.'

Klaas looked sorry. Grijpstra took a plastic truck off a chair and sat down heavily after having looked at the engineer, who waved him on. 'Please, make yourself at home.' De Gier had found himself a chair, too, and was rolling a cigarette. The engineer provided coffee and shooed the children into another room.

'Any trouble?'

'Yes,' Grijpstra said. 'I am afraid we usually bring trouble. A Mrs Moozen has been taken to the hospital. An attempt was made on her life. I believe you are acquainted with Mrs Moozen?'

'Ann,' the engineer said. 'My God! Is she all right?'

De Gier had stopped rolling his cigarette. He was watching the man carefully; his large brown eyes gleamed, but not with pleasure or anticipation. The sergeant felt sorrow, a feeling that often accompanied his intrusions into the private lives of his fellow citizens. He shifted, and the automatic pistol in his shoulder holster nuzzled into his armpit. He impatiently pushed the weapon back. This was no time to be reminded that he carried death with him, legal death.

'What happened?' the engineer was asking. 'Did anybody hurt her?'

'A question,' Grijpstra said gently. 'A question first, sir. You said your sister and you were making chocolate Easter eggs last night. Did you happen to make any bunnies, too?'

The engineer sucked noisily on his cigarette. Grijpstra repeated his question.

'Bunnies? Yes, or no. We tried, but it was too much for us. The eggs were easy—my sister is good at that. We have a pudding form for a bunny, but all we could manage was a pudding. It is still in the kitchen, a surprise for the kids later on today. Chocolate pudding—they like it.'

'Can we see the kitchen, please?'

The engineer didn't get up. 'My God,' he said again, 'so she was poisoned, was she? How horrible! Where is she now?'

'In the hospital, sir.'

'Bad?'

Grijpstra nodded. 'The doctor said she will live. Some sort of pesticide was mixed into chocolate, which she ate.'

The engineer got up; he seemed dazed. They found the kitchen. Leftover chocolate mix was still on the counter. Grijpstra brought out an envelope and scooped some of the hardened chips into it.

'Do you know that Ann and I had an affair?'

'Yes, sir.'

'Were you told that she finished the affair, that she decided to stay with her husband?'

'Yes, sir.'

The engineer was tidying up the counter mechanically. 'I see. So I could be a suspect. Tried to get at her out of spite or something. But I am not a spiteful man. You wouldn't know that. I don't mind being a suspect, but I would like to see Ann. She is in the hospital, you said. What hospital?'

'The Wilhelmina, sir.'

'Can't leave the kids here, can I? Maybe the neighbors will take them for an hour or so . . . yes. I'll go and see Ann. This is terrible.'

Grijpstra marched to the front door with de Gier trailing behind him. 'Don't move from the house today, if you please, sir, not until we telephone or come again. We'll try and be as quick as we can.'

'Nice chap,' de Gier said when the car found its parking place in the vast courtyard of Headquarters. 'That engineer, I mean. I rather liked Mr Moozen, too, and Mrs Moozen is a lovely lady. Now what?'

'Go back to the Moozen house, Sergeant, and get a sample of the roaring bunny. Bring it to the laboratory together with this envelope. If they check, we have a heavy point against the engineer.'

De Gier restarted the engine. 'Maybe he is not so nice, eh? He could have driven his wife crazy and now he tries to murder his girl-friend, his ex-girlfriend. Lovely Ann Moozen, who dared to stand him up. Could be. Do you think so?'

Grijpstra leaned his bulk against the car and addressed his words to the emptiness of the yard. 'No. But that could be the obvious solution. He was distressed, genuinely distressed, I would say. If he hadn't been and if he hadn't had those kids in the house, I might have brought him in for further questioning.'

'And Mr Moozen?'

'Could be. Maybe he didn't find the bunny on the garden path; maybe he put it there, or maybe he had it ready in the cupboard and brought it to his wandering wife. He is a lawyer—lawyers can be devious at times. True?'

De Gier said, 'Yes, yes, yes . . .' and kept on saying so until Grijpstra squeezed the elbow sticking out of the car's window. 'You are saying yes, but you don't sound convinced.'

'I thought Moozen was suffering, too.'

'Murderers usually suffer, don't they?'

De Gier started his 'Yes, yes,' and Grijpstra marched off.

They met an hour later, in the canteen in headquarters. They munched rolls stuffed with sliced liver and roast beef and muttered diligently at each other.

'So it is the same chocolate?'

'Yes, but that doesn't mean much. One of the lab's assistants has a father who owns a pastry shop. He said that there are only three mixes on the market and our stuff is the most popular make. No, not much of a clue there.'

'So?'

'We may have a full case on our hands. We should go back to Mr Moozen, I think, and find out about friends and relatives. Perhaps his wife had other lovers, or jealous lady friends.'

'Why her?'

Grijpstra munched on. 'Hmm?'

'Why *her*?' de Gier repeated. 'Why not him?'

Grijpstra swallowed. 'Him? What about him?'

De Gier reached for the plate, but Grijpstra restrained the sergeant's hand. 'Wait, you are hard to understand when you have your mouth full. What about him?'

De Gier looked at the roll. Grijpstra picked it up and ate it.

'Him,' de Gier said unhappily. 'He found the bunny on the garden path, the ferocious bunny holding the pernicious egg. A gift, how nice. But he doesn't eat chocolate, so he runs inside and shows the gift to his wife, and his wife grabs the egg and eats it. She may have thought *he* was giving it to her; she was still half asleep. Maybe she noticed the taste, but she ate on to please her husband. She became ill at once and he telephoned for an ambulance. Now, if he had wanted to kill her, he might have waited an hour or so, to give the poison a chance to do its job. But he grabbed his phone, fortunately. What I am trying to say is, the egg may have been intended for him, from an enemy who didn't even know Moozen had a wife, who didn't care about killing the wife.'

'Ah,' Grijpstra said, and swallowed the last of the roll. 'Could be. We'll ask Mr Moozen about his enemies. But not just now. There is the dead man we found in the park—a message came in while you were away. A missing person has been reported and the description fits our corpse. According to the radio room, a woman phoned to say that a man who is renting a room in her house has been behaving strangely lately and has now disappeared. She traced him to the corner bar where he spent last evening, until two a.m., when they closed.

'He was a little drunk, according to the barkeeper, but not blind drunk. She always takes him tea in the morning, but this morning he wasn't there and the bed was still made. But she does think he's been home, for she heard the front door at a little after two a.m. opening and closing twice. He probably fetched the rope and his campstool then.'

'And the man was fairly old and had a short gray beard?'

'Right.'

'So we go and see the landlady. I'll get a photograph—they took dozens this morning and they should be developed by now. Was anything found in his clothes?'

'Nothing.' Grijpstra looked guiltily at the empty plate. 'Want another roll?'

'You ate it.'

'That's true, and the canteen is out of rolls; we got the last batch. Never mind, Sergeant. Let's go out and do some work. Work will take your mind off food.'

'That's him,' the landlady with the plastic curlers said. Her glasses had slipped to the tip of her blunt nose while she studied the photograph. 'Oh, how horrible! His tongue is sticking out. Poor Mr Marchant. Is he dead?'

'Yes, ma'am.'

'For shame, and such a nice gentleman. He has been staying here for nearly five years now and he was always so polite.'

Grijpstra tried to look away from the glaring pink curlers, pointing at his forehead from the woman's thinning hair.

'Did he have any troubles, ma'am? Anything that may have led him to take his own life?'

The curlers bobbed frantically. 'Yes. Money troubles. Nothing to pay the tax man with. He always paid the rent, but he hadn't been paying his taxes. And his business wasn't doing well. He has a shop in the next street; he makes things—ornaments, he calls them—out of brass. But there was some trouble with the neighbors. Too much noise, and something about the zoning, too; this is a residential area now, they say. The neighbors wanted him to move, but he had nowhere to move to, and he was getting nasty letters, lawyers' letters. He would have had to close down, and he had to make money to pay the tax man. It was driving him crazy. I could hear him walk around in his room at night, round and round, until I had to switch off my hearing aid.'

'Thank you, ma'am.'

'He was alone,' the woman said, and shuffled with them to the door. 'All alone, like me. And he was always so nice.' She was crying.

'Happy Easter,' de Gier said, and opened the Volkswagen's door for the adjutant.

'The same to you. Back to Mr Moozen again—we *are* driving about this morning. I could use some coffee again. Maybe Mr Moozen will oblige.'

'He won't be so happy either. We aren't making anybody happy today,' the sergeant said, and tried to put the Volkswagen into first gear. The gear slipped and the car took off in second.

They found Mr Moozen in his garden. It had begun to rain again, but the lawyer didn't seem to notice that he was getting wet. He was staring at the bright yellow crocuses, touching them with his foot. He had trampled a few of them into the grass.

'How is your wife, sir?'

'Conscious and in pain. The doctors think they can save her, but she will have to be on a stringent diet for years and she'll be very weak for months. I won't have her back for a while.'

Grijpstra coughed. 'We visited your wife's, ah, previous lover, sir.' The word 'previous' came out awkwardly and he coughed again to take away the bad taste.

'Did you arrest him?'

'No, sir.'

'Any strong reasons to suspect the man?'

'Are you a criminal lawyer, sir?'

Moozen kicked the last surviving crocus, turned on his heels, and led his visitors to the house. 'No, I specialize in civil cases. Sometimes I do divorces, but I don't have enough experience to point a finger in this personal case. Divorce is a messy business, but with a little tact and patience reason usually prevails. To try and poison somebody is unreasonable behavior. I can't visualize Ann provoking that type of action—she is a gentle woman, sensual but gentle. If she did break her relationship with the engineer, she would have done it diplomatically.'

'He seemed upset, sir, genuinely upset.'

'Quite. I had hoped as much. So where are we now?'

'With you, sir. Do *you* have any enemies? Anybody who hated you so badly that he wanted you to die a grotesque death, handed to you by a roaring rabbit? You did find the rabbit on the garden path this morning, didn't you, sir?'

Moozen pointed. 'Yes, out there, sitting in between the crocuses, leering, and as you say, roaring. Giving me the egg.'

'Now, which demented mind might have thought of shaping that apparition, sir? Are you dealing with any particularly unpleasant cases at this moment? Any cases that have a badly twisted undercurrent? Is anyone blaming you for something bad that is happening to them?'

Moozen brushed his hair with both hands. 'No. I am working on a bad case having to do with a truckdriver who got involved in a complicated accident; his truck caught fire and it was loaded with expensive cargo. Both his legs were crushed. His firm is suing the firm that owned the other truck. A lot of money in claims is involved and the parties are becoming impatient, with me mostly. The case is dragging on and on. But if they kill me, the case will become even more complicated, with no hope of settlement in sight.'

'Anything else, sir?'

'The usual. I collect bad debts, so sometimes I have to get nasty. I write threatening letters; sometimes I telephone people or even visit them. I act tough—it's got to be done in my profession. Usually they pay, but they don't like me for bothering them.'

'Any pastry shops?'

'I beg your pardon?'

'Pastry shops,' Grijpstra said. 'People who make and sell confectionery. The rabbit was a work of art in a way, made by a professional. Are you suing anybody who would have the ability to create the roaring rabbit?'

'*Ornaments!*' de Gier shouted. His shout tore at the quiet room. Moozen and Grijpstra looked up, startled.

'Ornaments! Brass ornaments. Ornaments are made from molds. We've got to check his shop.'

'Whose shop?' Grijpstra frowned irritably. 'Keep your voice down, Sergeant. What shop? What ornaments?'

'Marchant!' de Gier shouted. 'Marchant's shop.'

'Marchant?' Moozen was shouting too. 'Where did you get that name? *Emil* Marchant?'

Grijpstra's cigar fell on the carpet. He tried to pick it up and it burned his hand, sparks finding their way into the carpet's strands. He stamped them out roughly.

'You know a Mr Marchant, sir?' de Gier asked quietly.

'No, I haven't met him. But I have written several letters to a man named Emil Marchant. On behalf of clients who are hindered by the noise he makes in his shop. He works with brass, and it isn't only the noise, but there seems to be a stink as well. My clients want him to move out and are prepared to take him to court if necessary. Mr Marchant telephoned me a few times, pleading for mercy. He said he owed money to the tax department and wanted time to make the money, that he would move out later; but my clients have lost patience. I didn't give in to him—in fact, I just pushed harder. He will have to go to court next week and he is sure to lose out.'

'Do you know what line of business he is in, sir?'

'Doorknobs, I believe, and knockers for doors, in the shape of lions' heads—that sort of thing. And weathervanes. He told me on the phone. All handmade. He is a craftsman.'

Grijpstra got up. 'We'll be on our way, sir. We found Mr Marchant this morning, dead, hanging from a tree in the Amsterdam Forest. He probably hanged himself early this morning, and at some time before, he must have delivered the rabbit and its egg. According to his landlady, he has been behaving strangely lately. He must have blamed you for his troubles and tried to take his revenge. He didn't mean to kill your wife; he meant to kill you. He didn't know that you don't eat chocolate, and he probably didn't even know you were married. We'll check further and make a report. The rabbit's mold is probably still in his shop, and if not, we'll find traces of the chocolate. We'll have the rabbit checked for fingerprints. It won't be difficult to come up with irrefutable proof. If we do, we'll let you know, sir, a little later today. I am very sorry all this has happened.'

'Nothing ever happens in Amsterdam,' de Gier said as he yanked the door of the Volkswagen open, 'and when it does, it all fits in immediately.'

But Grijpstra didn't agree.

'We would never have solved the case, or rather *I* wouldn't have, if you hadn't thought of the rabbit as an ornament.'

'No, Grijpstra, we would have found Marchant's name in Moozen's files.'

The adjutant shook his heavy, grizzled head. 'No, we wouldn't have checked the files. If he had kept on saying that he wasn't working on any bad cases, I wouldn't have pursued that line of thought. I'd have reverted to trying to find an enemy of his wife. We might have worked for weeks and called in all sorts of help and wasted everybody's time. You are clever, Sergeant.'

De Gier was studying a redheaded girl waiting for a streetcar.

'Am I?'

'Yes. But not as clever as I am,' Grijpstra said, and grinned. 'You work for me. I personally selected you as my assistant. You are a tool in my expert hands.'

De Gier winked at the redheaded girl and the girl smiled back. The traffic had jammed up ahead and the car was blocked. De Gier opened his door.

'Hey! Where are you going?'

'It's a holiday, Adjutant, and you can drive this wreck for a change. I am going home. That girl is waiting for a streetcar that goes to my side of the city. Maybe she hasn't had lunch yet. I am going to invite her to go to a Chinese restaurant.'

'But we have reports to make, and we've got to check out Marchant's shop. It'll be locked; we have to find the key in his room; and we have to telephone the engineer to let him off the hook.'

'I am taking the streetcar,' de Gier said. 'You do all that. You ate my roll.'

TED WOOD (1931–)

Pit Bull

———

'A BULL TERRIER,' Mr Harris explained again. 'Not a bulldog, that's the kind that looks like Churchill.'

'Churchill?' The policeman narrowed his eyes. He must have been twenty-five, Mr Harris thought, with no knowledge of anything that didn't show up at work or on rock videos.

'Jake is a bull terrier,' he explained again. 'Here, let me get you a photograph.'

The policeman relaxed now the trivia threat had passed. 'Yeah, a photograph would help,' he said and waited, working his chewing gum almost invisibly, while Mr Harris went up the creaking stairs. He looked around the living room with disgust. Christ, the guy only had a black and white TV set. And no stereo at all, just a big old plastic AM radio, tuned to CBC. What did he spend his money on? Not that he made much by the look of him.

Mr Harris came back down the stairs, brown brogues giving way to grey flannel pants, to the Argyll sweater, to the middle-aged face with the pipe. He was holding a photograph in a silver frame, like a wedding photo only this one wasn't, it was the ugliest dog the policeman had ever seen.

'That's a pit bull,' he said excitedly. 'Meanest sonsabitches in the world. How'd anybody steal him? They shoot 'im first?'

Mr Harris shook his head impatiently. 'People always say the same thing. Officer, you have to understand, Jake is not a dangerous dog, he's very sweet natured.'

'Yeah,' the cop said, giving his chewing gum a quick angry bite. 'Yeah. Sure.' Then remembering some distant lecture about public relations he added, 'Sir.'

Mr Harris could see he wasn't going to get much help but he persisted anyway. He reported his bull terrier stolen, gave its value as four hundred dollars, tried to tell the policeman what the dog's full pedigree name was, but gave up finally in the face of the policeman's enormous unconcern.

'You have to realize,' the policeman explained patiently, 'we've got kids missing, we've got homicides, muggers. Dogs don't have very high priority around the station.'

'I see,' Mr Harris said. He was a short, grey-haired man with the hint of an English accent and the kind of face you glimpse in the corner of government offices, out in the areas where the desks don't even have screens around them. 'What would you suggest I do?'

The policeman expanded now. He was the expert, lecturing. 'Well, I'd say the best thing would be to put some signs up around, maybe offer a reward. You've seen what I mean, on light poles an' that. People do it all the time.'

'I suppose so,' Mr Harris said doubtfully. 'But I don't think it will help. He was stolen, you see, let out of the back of my car while I was in the supermarket.'

The policeman nodded. 'Well, if you say. But how come anybody'd steal a pit bull is beyond me.'

'There you go again,' Mr Harris said patiently. 'Pit bull. He isn't a fighting dog. The breed was created for that purpose but dog fights are illegal now. It doesn't happen.'

The policeman did one slow chew on his gum and shook his head seriously. He seemed to have aged ten years as he spoke, giving out information he must have picked up over a beer in the canteen at the police college. 'That's where you're wrong, sir. I heard one time from a guy who grew up in the sticks. They still run dog fights up there all the time. There's nothing else to do half the year, those old farmers love it.' And that was when Mr Harris first realized that Jake was in serious trouble.

The policeman, who had almost failed the California Aptitude test because of his chronic insensibility to other people's problems, was suddenly helpful. 'And you reckon your dog wouldn't fight. I'm telling you. The time they've starved him a while, maybe kept him in a cage, prodding him with sticks, he'd fight anything that moved. And by the look of him I'd say he'd win.'

'Can you imagine?' Harris asked Lucinda at lunch next day. Lucinda was a tall handsome black woman from one of the islands, Harris could never remember which one. She was the only person on staff who was close to his age and they often ate lunch together, sharing his sandwiches and her patty in the corner of the lunch room while the rest of the clerks were over on Yonge Street buying rock records or trying on blue jeans.

'I can,' Lucinda said. 'Back home the men bet on everything, cock-fighting, dogfighting. I didn't think it happened in Canada the same.'

'Well, the officer said it does,' Harris explained. 'He'd heard it from some other policeman from Hornepayne or somewhere. He said there was a traffic in dogs, especially tough dogs, shepherds are favorites, and dobermans of course, even labradors.'

Lucinda divided her orange in two and pushed half over to him. 'And that Jakie of yours, he looks mean.'

'He's not,' Harris protested. 'He looks it but he's a marshmallow inside. Oh, he nipped me once, when he was a puppy, but he was so penitent. You should have seen the look on his face.'

Lucinda laughed. She had a big comfortable laugh that sounded as if it was echoing over a bright beach. 'I've seen the look on his face. You showed me that picture enough times. I'm telling you George, he looks mean.'

It took Harris about a week to realize that she and the young policeman might have been right. Nobody answered his posters or the advertisement he ran. And he called the Humane Society so many times that the receptionist got to recognize his voice and would tell him there was no news of Jake even before he'd asked the question. One night a drunk did call and offer to return his dog for a bottle of rye but the man didn't have the details that would prove he had the dog. He didn't have the inscription that Harris had written on the inside of Jake's collar. He didn't even know that Jake had a black spot under his belly, out of sight so that he still looked like the classic bull terrier, all white. So Harris hung up on him and went back to sleep, dreaming that he was out in the park with Jake, letting him dig his teeth into his leash while Harris swung him around, a foot off the ground, the way he always did.

On the following Saturday he went down to the police station. It was a new building, neat and quiet, totally unlike the bedlam Harris saw on 'Hill Street Blues'. A constable on the desk asked what he wanted and he explained about his missing dog and the constable made all the same comments the first uniformed man had made. And then Harris asked to speak to the sergeant.

He was young, of course. These days, Harris reflected, as he looked into that smooth face with its trim moustache, not just policemen on the beat but even sergeants and inspectors looked young. It was a factor of his age, he supposed.

'Sergeant. I was told by the officer that came to my house that dog fighting still goes on in Ontario. Is that true?'

The sergeant, who was feeling benevolent said, 'Yes sir, I've heard that.'

'In that case,' Harris said, nervously at first, then with growing confidence, 'perhaps somebody's stolen my dog for fighting. And I want to know where it goes on and how I can get close to it.'

The sergeant looked down at him and almost laughed. Where would this little man be, standing in a pack of truckers and farm workers, swearing and drinking rye from mickeys and betting in double sawbucks while dogs like his rolled around killing one another? But he felt kind. So he said, 'Well, it's nothing we hear much about in the city. But maybe if you got in touch with the Provincial Police, the OPP, maybe they have a unit working on things like that, cockfighting too, I'd imagine.'

'Thank you,' Harris said, and straightened up to his full five foot seven. 'Thank you, sergeant. Now I'm getting somewhere.'

It took him three days of phone calls and frustration before he reached the man he wanted, a sergeant with the Parry Sound detachment. The sergeant's name was Malloy and he had the ghost of an Ulster accent. He sounded tough, Harris decided. He liked the sound of Sergeant Malloy.

'Well, sir, we don't have a lot of proof,' Malloy said. 'You can understand these are very cautious people. We know it goes on but we can't find where. If we could, we'd raid them and that would be it.'

'But there have been raids, you must have caught people or had complaints or something,' Harris persisted and he heard Malloy sigh.

'The last time was three years ago, up around Barrie.'

'Oh, but that's hardly any distance at all,' Harris said. 'I could go there myself and look.'

Malloy's sigh was a little gustier this time. 'You sound like an educated man, Mr Harris. You don't sound as if you'd blend in with these people very well at all. They'd never open up to you.'

'Thank you for your concern,' Mr Harris said. 'I don't know how a dogfighter sounds but I can handle myself very well, thank you. I've been in some pretty tough spots in my time.' He didn't add that all his adventures had taken place in the rear turret of a Lancaster bomber forty years earlier. He knew how to look after himself, he was sure of that, even without four Browning machineguns.

He prepared himself very carefully for the part he would play. He went to the Goodwill store and bought some old clothes, the pants from one suit, the jacket from another, a thick woollen shirt with a frayed collar, heavy boots and a cloth cap. Then he gave up his pipe and began rolling cigarettes from makin's. And then the hard part began. He finally got Malloy to give him the name of the convicted dogfighter and his address. It was a rural address and he got up early the following Saturday, dressed in his costume and headed north until he found it.

The farm house was a big old red brick place that looked neglected. The fields were scrappy, filled with brush and a herd of scrawny cattle, and the barn was full of holes where boards had fallen away and not been replaced. Harris didn't stop, instead he went back four miles to the nearest hamlet, a tiny crossroads with a church, a couple of homes and a store with a lunch counter in it. Perfect, he thought. He would start here.

He went in and sat at the lunch counter and rolled one of his homemade cigarettes. He was getting better at it and could carry on with the action as he looked up at the middle-aged waitress who came out of the back, surrounded by a smell of greasy cooking that followed her like a cloud.

He had rehearsed his part and now he played it out carefully. 'G'day,' he said crisply, trying to imitate the accent of Digger Wade, his pilot, who had come from Brisbane. 'You licensed here?'

The woman laughed, a loser's laugh. 'You kidding? You got any idea how much it costs to fix a place up good enough they'll give you a license to sell booze?'

Mr Harris lit his cigarette, trying not to cough. 'Pity,' he said. 'Well, I guess it'll have to be coffee then.'

She poured him a mug and pushed it in front of him. 'Thanks,' he said and beamed at her. 'Tell me, you ever hear of a guy called Dancer. Fred, Ed, Ken, some name like that?'

The waitress had a hard, rural shrewdness. 'Who wants him?' she asked.

'Me,' Harris said and laughed out loud. 'I heard tell that he was interested in some of the same things I'm interested in.'

'Like what?' the waitress asked. She was stubbornly plain, Harris thought, as if she were making a statement to the world, especially the male part of it. She would make a bad enemy, but for someone as unpleasant as this Dancer person, she might make a good hillbilly type friend, loading the shotgun for him while he held off the dogfighting squad of the OPP.

'Like a certain sporting venture I'd like to discuss with him,' he said, speaking around the cigarette.

The waitress flopped a dirty J-cloth around the counter top. 'What makes you think that?' she asked at last.

'Oh, something I heard at work, from one of the truckers,' Harris said. His pulse was racing. He wondered what the little undercover guy in 'Hill Street Blues' would think of his act. Pretty good, probably. But then, he would be carrying a big revolver, he could handle the situation very easily.

The woman tossed the cloth into the sink and sniffed. 'What'd you hear?' she asked innocently enough but with a sudden affected edge to her voice that made Harris realize he was on the right track.

He thought about his answer for a moment, smiling at the woman then said, 'Oh, I hear we're both interested in the same things, I guess you'd say.'

Behind him somebody else came into the store, a farmer with a green co-op store cap and one-piece overalls. The woman went over to the store cash register and Harris drank his coffee while the man bought a tin of Redman snuff, paid and left. When the woman came back he stood up to leave. 'How much is the coffee?'

'Fifty cents,' she said, still studying him, still innocent. Harris put his hand in his pocket and pulled out the roll he had constructed specially for today. It was a wad of bills, folded once and secured with a thick elastic band from the office. On the outside was a fifty, underneath he had some twenties and a couple of tens, then twelve dollars worth of Canadian Tire money. He thumbed at the fifty, then looked up at the woman who was staring at the money. 'Oh, maybe I've got the change,' he said and dropped the roll on the counter casually while he dug out three quarters from his right-hand pocket. He dropped them on the counter and picked up his roll, stuffing it casually into his left pocket. 'If I left you my number, could you mention it to Dancer next time you see him?'

'I suppose so,' she said slowly. 'You from around here?'

'No, Toronto,' Harris said in his nearly perfect Australian accent. He pulled a ball point from his pocket and wrote his phone number on a paper napkin. 'Name's Wade,' he told her. 'Much obliged to you.' He nodded and left, not looking back. When he got into his car he discovered that his legs were still shaking.

He drove home carefully through the golden fall afternoon, not noticing the turning trees or the apple stands on the side of the road. He was going over and over the biggest problem of all. What would he use to intimidate these people? If Dancer phoned and he managed to get himself invited to a dog fight and if he found Jake there and if Jake, whose intelligence was certainly not high, Harris admitted that, would come with him when he called, how could he make sure a circle of big ugly dogfighters wouldn't beat him up?

It wasn't until he saw the liquor store in Richmond Hill, just north of Toronto, that Harris had his idea. He pulled into the parking lot and went in to buy a small bottle of rum. Then he drove home and daringly made himself a large glass of rum and orange juice and thought about his next move while he waited for his phone call.

It came late on Sunday while Harris was shining his shoes for work the next day. A man's voice said, 'You Wade?'

'That's right,' Harris said remembering to do his Australian accent, 'Who's this?'

'I hear you was tryin' a reach me. About a sportin' venture.'

'You the fellah from up Barrie way?' Harris asked.

'S'right. I hear you was askin' around.'

'I was.' Harris let the answer lie there until he realized that Dancer wasn't going to respond. 'Yeah, I heard from a friend of mine, well a guy at work, that you might be interested in a proposition.'

'Depends.'

Good, Harris thought excitedly. He's interested. He kept his voice relaxed. 'Well it happens a mate of mine has a dog, South African ridgeback. Weighs around a hundred pounds, they used to use 'em for hunting lions where he comes from.'

'So?'

'So my mate's away a few months, gone back to the Old Country, he left the thing with me and it's pining here. And I wondered if it was as good as he says.' There, the bait was thrown.

'Makes you think I care?' Harris tried to picture the face that was framing the words. Was it cruel, hawk-nosed, mean, or whisky-smudged and careless? Either way he could sense the excitement over the wire.

'This buddy o' mine says you used to be,' Harris said carefully. 'He was up your place one time for a certain sporting event.'

' 'Big's this thing o' yours you say?' The voice had a sneering quality now. He was hooked, Harris thought triumphantly.

'Big enough. I hear he only ever had a tough time once, in a lot of outings, 'gainst some Limey dog, a pit bull.'

' 'D'e beat him?' The question came so quickly that Harris's heart jumped. This man had Jake, or knew of him, he was positive.

'He did. I figure he'd rip the guts out of anything there is.' The statement sickened Harris slightly. He could remember Jake, jolly and happy, lolling on the chesterfield with him, watching television, barking frantically if he ever heard a dog on the sound track. Maybe Jake was still alive and well, maybe.

'You got any money says he will?' The voice had a snuffling quality and now Harris could picture the caller, smudgy and overweight, probably smoking a cigarette as he spoke, heavy with emphysema.

'A week's pay,' he said, surprised at his own calmness.

'What's that, a hundred bucks?' The voice was sneering openly at him now.

'Try three-fifty,' Harris said. 'Too rich for you?'

The only reply was a laugh.

'Okay then,' Harris said boldly. 'Where and when?'

'I'll see you at the rest'rant, Saturday, 'round noon,' the voice promised. 'Make sure you're not shittin' me.'

'Save up your money,' Harris told him. 'You're in for a surprise.'

'We'll see,' the voice said and the line went dead.

Harris's first impulse was to call Sergeant Malloy and tell him what he had accomplished. He glanced at the clock. It was close to ten. Malloy was probably off duty anyway and if he was working, what would he say? Perhaps he would be able to set up some raid. It wouldn't be possible in a car, not in that country with those wide open fields and the roads so visible from Dancer's farm. No, it would be impossible, unless they planted a bug on him and then followed him with a helicopter, letting down when the dog fighting was at its height. Harris dwelt lovingly on that thought for a while, imagining four or five tough young policemen pouring out of the helicopter behind the barn and storming in with shot-guns. But he soon gave it up. They didn't do things like that for a dog fight. For dope smugglers perhaps, but not for a grungy group of louts doing something that would get them fines of maybe fifty dollars each. No, he was on his own.

*

During the week that followed, he worked out his plan and made all the preparations. It was dangerous, he realized that, but there was a good chance that he would have Jake to help him by the time he had made his move and nobody would interfere with the owner of a pit bull. He repeated the name a couple of times, trying to get the same fear from it that a dogfighter would feel. Perhaps this was the one time that the breed's reputation, wrong though it was, would stand him in good stead. He would win.

Even without the police, he still needed an accomplice. Ideally it would have been a man, somebody tough to come with him and use his fists if it were necessary. But failing that, he needed a woman who would keep her head. So he put the question to Lucinda one lunch hour. She wanted a lot more detail than he would give her but when he insisted it was serious she promised to do what she had to for him. She wished him luck on Friday night when they left work and he was so moved he squeezed her arm and kissed her on the cheek. It was the first time he had ever taken such a liberty and he was surprised when she turned her head at the last moment and kissed him firmly on the lips. It made him a little excited. He hadn't really thought of Lucinda that way, hadn't really thought about any woman that way since his wife died four years earlier.

'Thank you,' he told her. 'Now don't forget, tomorrow, around twelve, one, some time in there.'

'Count on me,' she told him and waved and crossed Wellesley Street and headed for the subway.

He hardly slept all night. Next morning he forced himself to eat a big breakfast, bacon and eggs, a dish his wife had always cooked for him on Saturdays before the day's shopping and chores. In those times the meal had been a treat, the way it once was after his Lancaster landed safely and they had all gone through debriefing and had their tot of rum and laughed too much. But today the food tasted like chaff. When he had finished he was bloated but he allowed himself to smoke one good pipeful of Amphora before finally dressing in his old clothes and going out to his car. He did a last check before leaving. Jake's cage in the rear seat, covered with a blanket, check. Rum bottle, kleenexes, cigarette paper and makin's, lighter, check. Phoney roll of money, check. He sat behind the wheel and took a deep breath, as he had always done before takeoff on an operation, then pulled out of the driveway and headed north, trying not to think about what was going to happen.

He parked outside the store again and went in. The same woman was working there, he guessed she was the owner. He ordered a coffee and she looked at him, as if she expected him to thank her for passing the message along. He carefully said nothing and after a while she went away up the counter and ignored him.

He had been there for a quarter of an hour before he heard a truck pull up outside. He sat with his coffee in front of him, rolling a cigarette, and waited.

The man who came in was short and squat and ugly, in a way that made it seem as if ugliness was his art form. His face was blotched and unshaven and the hair that stuck out under his feedstore cap was greasy grey, stained on the right side with tobacco smoke. He had a short cigarette in the centre of his mouth, between fleshy lips.

Harris looked up then back to his cigarette. 'You Dancer?' he asked.

'Who wants him?' The same boring cunning, Harris thought. How clever did these people really think they were?

'Wade,' he said and licked the paper on his cigarette.

'That your dog in the back of your car?' Dancer asked. The smoke from his cigarette curled up around his face. He gave a final puff on the butt and spat it out, treading on it negligently.

'Well it should've been,' Harris said. He stood up, pleased to find he was no shorter than Dancer, even though the other man outweighed him by forty pounds of bloat.

'Waddya mean?' Dancer stopped in the middle of lighting a fresh cigarette.

'Bastard got hit by a car this mornin',' Harris said angrily. 'Goddamn vet says it'll cost three hundred, maybe four hundred bucks to fix his leg.'

He lit his own handrolled cigarette and waved the match out before dropping it on the floor. This was the tricky part. He had to get over the next couple of minutes.

'You said you hadda dog,' Dancer blustered. Smoke went the wrong way and he coughed convulsively.

'I gotta dog,' Harris said. 'Only he's not here and I gotta find a quick three–four hundred to fix him before my buddy gets back.'

'Bullshit,' Dancer backed off a step. 'You never had no goddamn dog at all, y'ask me.'

'You don't believe me, call the vet yourself,' Harris said. He pulled out his wad of money, unsnapped the elastic band and turned the wad over so he could take a deuce off the inside. He watched the greedy look in Dancer's eyes when he saw the money. 'Here,' he called the waitress. 'Can you gimme some change for the phone?'

The woman came up to the counter to him, looking up and past him at Dancer. She took some signal and picked up the deuce and came back with eight quarters. Harris nodded and went over to the pay phone on the wall. He produced a piece of paper from his pocket and put a quarter in the phone. Dancer came and stood beside him, his eyes squinting at the paper. Harris had written Dr Freemantle and the number of Lucinda's apartment. He asked the operator for the number and then offered the phone to Dancer. 'You don't believe me, you ask yourself. Dog's name's Bruce.'

Dancer looked at the phone for a moment as if it were a loaded gun then snatched it out of Harris's hand. Harris put his hand behind him and crossed the fingers as the phone rang twice. He could hear Lucinda's voice, brisk and confident, through Dancer's hair. 'Doctor Freemantle's office.'

Dancer looked up at Harris who quietly uncrossed his fingers. Then into the phone asked, 'How's Bruce doin', the dog I mean?'

'Let me see, that would be the ridgeback. Well, he's out of the anaesthetic but the doctor says he'll have to stay in the cage for at least three weeks to make sure the cast stays on, he's an exceptionally strong dog, the doctor says.'

Dancer cleared his throat, making his cigarette bob and a quarter inch of ash to fall on the floor. 'What's 'at gonna cost?'

Lucinda was perfect. 'Well, as I told you earlier, sir, our charge is ten dollars a day, plus the operation. Around four hundred dollars.'

Dancer hung up on her without speaking. Then he turned to face Harris squarely. 'So now what?' he growled.

'I'm here,' Harris drawled. 'I figured if you had another event going on, maybe I could make a few bucks, pay the bill. I'm a good judge of dogs.'

'You reckon,' Dancer said contemptuously.

'I know,' Harris said. He dropped his cigarette on the floor and stepped on it. 'So, are you taking me with you or what?'

Dancer thought about it for a long moment, breathing huffily, letting the smoke curl around his head. 'I already got two guys in the truck,' he said. 'You can follow me, I guess.'

He turned and left. Harris took a dollar off his roll and dropped it at the cash register. 'Keep the change,' he said.

He followed Dancer out into the October sunshine and got into his car. Dancer was already pulling out of the lot, doing it fast so Harris had to rush to follow him. He gripped the wheel tightly, trying to ignore the pounding of his heart. The pickup truck turned off on a side road and he followed, then turned again to follow up a rutted road closed almost over with maples. It ran for half a mile, then ended abruptly in front of a farm that looked abandoned. There were a couple of dozen trucks and big old sedans parked around on the grass. Harris parked at the end of the line, making sure he had open space ahead of him as well as behind. If he got blocked in he would be in real trouble.

Dancer got out of his truck and then two other men climbed out, both younger but dressed in the same drab green coveralls. One of them came up to Harris and stopped him, pushing a hard finger into his chest. 'First I make sure you're not a cop,' he said. He had a grinning face that looked friendly except for dead eyes.

'A cop?' Harris blustered. 'What the hell are you smokin', son?'

The kid grinned again and patted him over, stopping when he reached the bottle. 'What's that?'

Harris pulled out the rum bottle, still in its liquor store brown bag. 'That's for later,' he said. 'I get lucky, maybe I'll pass it around.'

The kid laughed. 'Maybe you'll pass it round anyway,' he said. He turned and nodded to Dancer who stood waiting close to the door of the barn. Dancer waved and they went towards him. 'No smokin' inside,' Dancer said. 'I know it's hard but barns is dangerous.'

'I can wait,' Harris said. He was pleased at how calm he sounded. It was no more frightening than sitting in the tail turret while the bomb aimer gave the pilot instructions on that deadly last minute of straight and level flight while all the flak in the sky was aimed right at you. He breathed deeply and went inside.

The noise was surprising. It registered even before he took stock of his surroundings. Dogs were barking and snarling, men were laughing and swearing. Harris looked around quickly. The three who had come in with him ignored him. They went to the side of the ring that had been set up, built out of red snow fence surrounded with bales of straw to a depth of about five feet.

Harris clambered up on the top of the bales and looked down into the ring. Two German shepherds were fighting, one was covered with blood and had an ear torn away, the other was forcing it back, standing half erect, swinging and snarling so fast that Harris could hardly follow it. Then in one almost invisible leap it caught the other dog by the throat and began to shake it. Harris almost vomited but he turned away for a moment until he heard one final yelp of pain and all the snarling stopped. He looked back to see the second dog lying limply, its eyes rolled up in its head, its tongue lying in the dirt.

Beside Harris a man whooped. 'Told ya.' He roared happily. 'Told ya. Pay up.' The man next to him swore and reached into his pocket. Down in the ring a man came in, wearing heavy leather gauntlets and called the winning dog, fussing it and giving it a chunk of meat. Then he snapped a chain on the dog's collar and led him out, stiff-legged and snarling as it passed the corpse of the second dog, then more docile as the handler jerked the chain and pulled it out of the ring.

Harris craned up to see over the bales on the other side to a row of dog cages, set about a yard apart. Each but one held an angry snarling dog. Then another man dragged the dead shepherd out of the ring and tossed it into the empty cage. Harris swept the row of cages with his eyes, hardly daring to breathe. And then he almost wept. A big white bull terrier was standing up in the last cage, its front feet high against the wire as it snarled and plucked at the cage with its fangs. And under its belly he could see the unmistakable black mark. He had found Jake.

Quickly he jumped down and went over to the dogs. Men were all around him, talking at the tops of their voices, swearing, laughing, pointing at the dogs. One of them caught him by the shoulder. 'Hey, Mac. Where you going?'

Harris pulled his shoulder away. 'I wanna see the dogs before I bet,' he said. 'Get your goddamn hands off me.'

The man didn't let go. He was big, six feet tall anyway, and broad and mean looking with an upper incisor missing. 'I never seen you here before.'

'I came with him,' Harris said and pointed at the kid who had frisked him.

The big man let go of his shoulder. 'Okay then,' he said, 'What's your fancy?'

'That mean-looking bastard,' Harris said thickly, pointing at Jake who had stopped snarling and was staring at him out of his tiny, sabre-scar eyes.

'Good choice,' the man laughed. 'He's never been beat yet. I've seen him fight three times. You'll have to give odds on him.'

'I figured,' Harris said. He moved away again, toward the ring. A couple of men came over and took out two more dogs, another shepherd and a big red dog that might have been part Irish setter, part doberman. All the other men were watching, making bets, swearing, ignoring him. Quickly he slipped his rum bottle out of his pocket, unscrewed the top and tossed it aside. Then he lifted it as if to drink, sniffing the rich vapours of the gasoline he had filled it with the day before. He lowered the bottle and pretended to wipe his mouth as he saw Dancer watching him. Then he turned his back quickly and stuffed three folded kleenexes into the neck of the bottle, tipping it up so the paper was dampened with gasoline.

The man who had challenged him had turned away so he crouched beside Jake's cage. 'Good boy. Good Jake,' he whispered and his dog dropped to all fours and wagged his tail. He had scars on his back and a torn ear but he seemed fit. Harris unflipped the catch of the cage, then turned and pulled out his lighter. He saw a man looking at him, framing the words 'No smoking, Mac' as he touched the lighter to the top of the kleenex and hurled the bottle from him into the piled straw bales.

The bottle exploded into a wall of flame. It ran across the floor towards him like a living thing. He ran from cage to cage, unsnapping doors and letting the dogs out to fight and run, then he opened Jake's cage and grabbed his lumpy ugly dog in his arms and ran outside, around the pillar of flame that had been the ring a moment before.

Outside was chaos. Men were jumping into cars and trucks, backing and driving out as fast as they could go. He saw Dancer and the boy coming towards him as he ran, the boy covering the ground faster than he could run. Quickly he unsnapped his belt and strung it through Jake's collar and set the dog down. 'You come closer and he'll kill you,' he shouted and the boy slowed down. Harris hurled himself into his car and drove off. Some other vehicle pulled in behind him, between him and the Dancer truck. Harris pushed his car to the limit, bumping himself and Jake up to the ceiling as he jounced from one rut to another. Behind him he could see the pickup trying to overtake the vehicle between them and he prayed the car wouldn't let him by. As the concession road came up ahead of him he saw the pickup break out, struggling to pass on a road barely wide enough, then to his unutterable relief saw it slip sideways and slam headlong into a maple tree.

The other car kept coming and Harris didn't look back again. He reached out to the other seat and patted his dog. 'Good dog. Good Jake,' he said hoarsely. 'We're OK now, it's all over.' And he stroked the big ugly wounded head and tried to keep himself from weeping with tension and happiness.

He stopped at the first OPP outpost and made a full report, even though the policeman told him it was too late to do anything about it. Everybody would be gone by now. He didn't care. He had his dog back. Dancer didn't know how to reach him, he would never take the time to go all through the phone book looking for the number. Lord there were a million numbers at least in the Toronto book. He had taken them on and he had won, hands down. He drove home down Yonge Street, stopping at a supermarket for a pound of liver which he fed to Jake there and then on the front seat of his car. 'Good dog,' he told him again. 'Clever boy.'

By the time he got home he felt reaction settling about him, clinging like damp clothing. He felt frightened and shaky realizing how close he had come to being caught by the kid who was with Dancer, suddenly afraid that he might meet the kid somewhere again, on the street perhaps. He resolved to go to Church the next day and express his thanks and his concerns properly. The thought made him feel better and less alone. As he walked into the house his phone was already ringing. He looked at it for a long time, wondering if it was Dancer. He would have to change his number, he decided. Finally he picked it up. 'Hello,' he said, stripping his voice of the phoney Australian accent, doing his best to sound like a native Canadian.

'Well hello,' Lucinda said. 'How'd it go? I've been worrying about you.'

'It went well. Thank you. You did marvellously, Lucinda,' he said, and then suddenly he grinned. 'Jake's in no shape to be left tonight. I wondered if you'd like to come around and maybe meet him and watch TV or something. I've got some rum.'

Lucinda laughed. 'Well if that's not the damnedest invitation I ever got,' she said. 'I'll be there in an hour.'

JAMES MELVILLE (1933–)

Santa-San Solves It

'TRY it just once more,' Inspector Kimura said encouragingly. 'Your "Jingle Bells" is fine.'

'Hardly surprising. Everybody knows *Jinguru Beru*; you can't get away from the wretched tune. Television, department stores, coffee shops. They've been playing it twenty-four hours a day since November.'

'True. So you've no worries on that account. All the children will join in at the top of their voices and you'll hardly be heard anyway. No, it's the "Ho! Ho! Ho!" you need to work on.'

Superintendent Tetsuo Otani glowered first at his trusted lieutenant and then at his shoes. 'Ho! Ho! Ho!', he said in an undertone, sounding like an embarrassed Englishman repeating the word 'whore'. 'It's no good, I can't and won't say it. It's not as if it means anything, anyway.'

'Of course you can, Chief, you can't let the Rotarians down. But do try to look a bit more cheerful. It's a Christmas party you're going to, not a funeral. And you'll only be centre stage for twenty minutes or so after all.'

'Half an hour at least, the chairman of the social work sub-committee said. Dressed up like an idiot. All this Santa Claus business is a foreign idea anyway,' Otani complained. 'I don't see why they picked on me. There are two or three foreign Rotarians in other clubs in Kobe who'd probably have been only too glad to volunteer. And lots in Osaka. Ho Ho Ho indeed.'

Kimura sucked in his breath and shook his head. Nothing could be done with the superintendent when he had made up his mind to be mulish. 'Oh, well,' he said, 'I expect it'll be all right if you ring your bell while you say it. And the beard will cover up your expression, I suppose. Now, can I talk for a minute about Mrs Bencivenni?'

Otani sat back in his chair, his black look replaced by one of mild interest. 'I've heard that name somewhere recently,' he said. 'She's . . . yes, of course, isn't she the woman who runs the place?'

'The children's home where your Rotary Club is paying for the Christmas party, yes, but she doesn't exactly run it, she's the president of the committee of management. Fund-raisers, in effect. There are several foreign ladies on it. Goes back to the origins of the place during the occupation, when most of the kids were mixed-blood.'

'Babies bar-girls had by American GI's, you mean. I always felt sorriest for the ones who were half black. Incredible to think some of them must be getting on for forty now. Can't be much of a life for them here, neither the one thing nor the other. We Japanese have a bad record with misfits, Kimura.'

Otani sighed and Kimura nodded briefly, still after years of close association capable of being surprised on occasion by subversive remarks from a man he usually thought of as being a thoroughly old-fashioned Japanese with predictable prejudices. 'Well, it's an odd coincidence that I should be going to this charity place of hers, I suppose, but worrying about foreigners is your job. Why do you want me to hear about this Bencivenni woman of yours?'

'Funny you should mention mixed-blood children, Chief. You must be psychic. Mrs Bencivenni was one of them herself, brought up in that self-same children's home. It was called the Nada Orphanage in those days. Her father couldn't have been black, though, she's fair skinned, looks quite European. Good-looking woman, in fact, speaks perfect Japanese. Middle to late thirties.'

'In that case be specially careful, Kimura. You know how suscep-tible you are. The lady has a husband, I presume?'

'She does indeed. Luciano Bencivenni, an American citizen, aged fifty-six, known as Luke. He's the problem.'

'Ah. Bigger than you, is he? Inclined to be jealous?'

Kimura cast an ostentatious glance heavenwards and pressed on, privately relieved that Otani seemed to be regaining his normal equable humour. 'Mr Bencivenni used to be a bank official, but has been in business on his own account for a number of years as a personal financial consultant. In practice he's a kind of all-round adviser to the western community here in the Kobe-Osaka area. Prepares tax returns for Americans, sells life insurance, arranges long-term investment plans for children's school and college fees and so forth. He's the agent for a number of American and British insurance companies. And Mrs Bencivenni thinks he's planning to kill her.' Kimura paused, wondering whether his chief's renowned poker face would be proof against such an artfully sprung surprise. It was.

'Does she indeed? How do you know?'

'She turned up downstairs here at headquarters yesterday and asked to speak to a senior officer in confidence about a matter involving the foreign community. I interviewed her and she told me herself.'

'Do you believe her?'

'Well, she's certainly not off her head, and she's obviously worried sick. What she told me was disturbing enough for me to organize a certain amount of digging, and I think you ought to know what we've come up with.'

'Stand *still*!' Hanae commanded, and Otani froze. She very seldom used that particular tone of voice, and when she did it was advisable to do her bidding. The Father Christmas outfit had been delivered to the house earlier that day, by Hanae's friend Mrs Hamada, who was also married to a Rotarian and who from time to time spoke vaguely of connections in show business. Hanae took it for granted that it was these which gave her access to such colourful fancy dress.

Over a cup of coffee they had unpacked the exotic garments, shaken out the folds, and agreed that the ensemble must have been made for a giant. They'd both giggled helplessly when Mrs Hamada tied a doubled-up *zabuton* cushion to her tummy and sportingly modelled the voluminous tunic, and after subsiding agreed that it would need a huge tuck in the back. The eighteen inches or so of excess length presented no problem: it could be hitched up as though the garment were a *kimono*.

Three safety-pins later, Hanae rose from her knees, stepped back and surveyed her husband. 'It won't take long to tack up,' she said, obviously having forgiven him for fidgeting.

'Why don't you just leave the safety-pins in? You won't be able to see them under that sash thing.'

Hanae decided to ignore such a heretical suggestion, and eased the ungainly garment off Otani's shoulders. 'Why didn't you tell me that some of the other Rotary wives are going to be helping on the day: I'd have been glad to take some cakes or something along.'

Something remarkably like a blush darkened Otani's naturally swarthy face. 'Because I shall feel quite enough of a fool as it is without you being there to watch,' he mumbled.

'Ah. I thought it might have been that you wanted the glamorous Mrs Bencivenni all to yourself.'

Otani gazed at her in amazement as he slowly lowered himself to the *tatami* matting, reached for the *sake* flask on the low lacquer table and refilled his cup. 'What on earth do *you* know about Mrs Bencivenni?' he enquired as Hanae looked down at him, her arch little smile fading rapidly. 'Have you met her?'

'No. Er, have you?'

'No. So there's no need to look so tragic. But I have been hearing quite a lot about her recently. From Kimura. Presumably you and Mrs Hamada have been discussing her too. What did she say? Sit down and have some *sake.*'

A little over two hours later Otani slid the *shoji* screen in the upstairs room to one side and gazed pensively through the glazed panel behind it at his favourite night view, of the great sweep of Osaka Bay. It was crisp and clear outside, with only a few rags of cloud occasionally obscuring a moon almost at the full. The huddle of tiled roofs with their solar water-heating panels and the forest of television aerials on the houses lower down the foothills of Mount Rokko which offended his eye by day were effectively obliterated, while the navigation lights on ships a mile or so away from where he stood twinkled cheerfully and a distant glow to the left marked the coast of Wakayama Prefecture.

Nothing Hanae had passed on from the gossipy Mrs Hamada contradicted what Kimura had told him about Judy Bencivenni, but his mental picture of the lady was nevertheless now subtly different. Kimura's team had assembled an impressive file of papers about her and her husband. Mrs Bencivenni's real first name as registered by her Japanese mother was Midori, but by the time she won a scholarship to the élite Canadian Academy in Kobe she was Judy, and Judy she remained through its junior and senior high school departments. A Kobe Carnival Queen at eighteen, she had been photographed by the Kobe Shimbun newspaper, whose files yielded a print showing a startlingly pretty girl and a two-paragraph 'interview' in which she spoke touchingly of the loving care she had known at the Kobe Orphanage and her determination to do anything she could to help those less fortunate than herself.

The record showed that she had honoured that pledge. Judy had been a star student both academically and on the sports field, but the orphanage budget could not afford college fees for her and there are no scholarships for higher education in Japan. Her looks and talents stood her in good stead, though, and after graduation from the Canadian Academy she had landed a good job as a bilingual secretary with the American Consulate-General.

She maintained a continuing connection as a volunteer helper with what had by then become known as the International Children's Home. Being technically a stateless alien, at twenty-two she applied for Japanese nationality and was turned down; but strings must have been pulled by her American employers because within six months she had been able to obtain an American passport and move to the United States. During six years there she kept in touch by letter with the children's home, and indeed—according to Mrs Hamada, who was on the committee of management—was reputed to have donated two or three hundred dollars every Christmas to pay for presents for the children. Mrs Hamada thought that she was working at this time as a secretary for Japan Air Lines in Los Angeles, but wasn't sure.

Kimura's file showed that Mr Luke Bencivenni arrived in Japan as a member of the staff of an American bank in 1978, accompanied by his wife Arlene, who drowned while swimming in Lake Chuzenji near Nikko the following summer. After the tragedy Bencivenni returned briefly to America but remained with the bank, being transferred to its Osaka branch. That Christmas he went for a brief holiday to Hawaii, returning with a new bride, the former Judy Nakano.

Kobe Prefectural Police might not have picked up the connection had not the second Mrs Bencivenni almost at once plunged herself into a round of charitable activities which meant that she soon began to figure in the gossip columns of the English-language press (which was routinely scanned by Kimura's staff in the Foreign Residents' Liaison Section). The fact that she was beautiful and had excellent dress sense helped, as did her husband's early retirement from the bank and the rapid expansion of the consultancy business he started immediately afterwards. He did very well, and within a year or two the Bencivennis were leading figures in the western community in Kobe.

Inevitably, such a socially prominent alumna of the children's home as Judy was soon elected to its committee of management, and she had been its president for the past two years; by all accounts an effective manager of committee business and a tireless drummer-up of financial support. Mrs Hamada had told Hanae that it was Mrs Bencivenni's idea to approach the Kobe South Rotary Club to which Otani belonged for a contribution, and Mrs Hamada herself—confound her—who hit upon the idea of a lavish Christmas party financed and organized by the Rotarians.

Otani sighed, turned away from the window, dropped his *yukata* on the *tatami* and slid under the *futon*. Hanae was as usual tranquil and immobile, wearing her own *yukata* which if he knew her would still be mysteriously uncreased when she got up the next morning.

'And I'm stuck with the job of being Santa Claus,' he grumbled. Then he raised himself on one forearm. 'What I don't understand is why he should *want* to kill her. According to both Kimura and your Mrs Hamada they're successful and popular. Luxury apartment, no children—not of their own, anyway. I suppose Bencivenni might have had some by his previous marriage, but there's no note of any and even if he had they'd be adults by now. And he's got this very attractive wife.' A thought struck him. 'Ha-chan, he's a good bit older than her. I wonder, did Mrs Hamada hint that she might be having an affair?'

Hanae had been so still that she might have been asleep, but in the bar of moonlight which lay across their bedding he saw her eyes blink open. 'No. Quite the reverse, if anything. It seems that several of the men in their circle have tried to start something, but she's never given any of them the least encouragement. And of course, a woman in her position, it would be all over town in five minutes if she did. Even Mrs Hamada's obviously a bit jealous of her looks, so I expect the foreign ladies on the committee are too. They're all older, I believe. So they'd pounce on the least suggestion of scandal.'

Otani didn't quite follow, but rolled on to his back and made himself comfortable. 'Sorry to keep you awake. I'm afraid I'm not a bit sleepy. Want a cup of tea or anything?'

'Not really. I don't mind talking anyway, it's interesting. Surely she must have given Mr Kimura some reason for saying such an extraordinary thing about her husband?'

'Oh, she did, but it doesn't impress me. She said she'd discovered that he recently took out a huge insurance policy on her life. A husband can do that, you know. And that he's let slip that he had collected a substantial sum by way of insurance when his former wife drowned. Putting two and two together, Mrs Bencivenni thinks her death might not in fact have been an accident.'

'What an awful thing to suggest! But . . . but why *now*?'

'Well, Bencivenni handles investments for a lot of Americans living here. And you know what happened on the New York stock exchange recently. Here too, of course. She told Kimura she thinks he might have over-committed himself financially and be in urgent need of funds to avoid bankruptcy.'

Hanae reflected in silence for a long time. 'I'm so glad we keep our savings in the bank, dear,' she then said thoughtfully. 'What are you going to do?'

Otani sighed. 'Well, I suppose the least we can do is check the local police report on that drowning in Chuzenji years ago. It might help me sort out my ideas.'

The party at the children's home was a great success. Safely concealed behind an enormous white beard and moustache and with his floppy red hat well down on his forehead, Otani rang his bell with gusto and was delighted to discover what he should have realized from the first, that all the children not only spoke Japanese but that nearly all *were* Japanese.

The extent of the munificence of the Kobe South Rotarians revealed when Otani opened his sack and handed out the presents brought squeals of delight from the children and approving nods from the staff of the home; and afterwards when he had divested himself of his finery Otani was drawn aside by a senior member of his club and gravely thanked for his outstanding contribution to the festivities.

'Such a pity Mrs Bencivenni couldn't be here after all, though. I know she would have wished to thank you personally, but I understand she was unavoidably detained.'

'I can't follow your reasoning, Chief,' Kimura said for the second time. 'All right, so central immigration records indicate that she was in Japan as a tourist at the time the first Mrs Bencivenni was drowned, and the only so-called witness the local police managed to find did have a vague recollection that there had been one other woman swimming in that part of the lake before Arlene Bencivenni went under. But he was a long way away and it proves nothing, even granted that Judy Nakano was an all-round athlete at school. Surely the husband remains the obvious suspect if she really was murdered . . . and that isn't by any means established.'

'I'm not looking forward to it, but I'm going to talk to the poor woman myself,' Otani said. 'I think that with careful handling she'll confess that she accused her husband of planning her murder because she intended to kill him . . . so that when she eventually did so she could claim it was in self-defence. Why otherwise come to the Japanese police with such a tale? What were we supposed to do? Why not simply leave him? She'd proved beyond question that she could earn her own living both in Japan and in America.'

'But there's still no *reason* for it. Remember, he insured her life, not the other way round.'

'Oh, there's a reason. She hates him, you see. With a deep, consistent, murderous hatred that at first sustained her, then fed on itself and brought her to crisis point. When you first described Mrs Bencivenni to me you said she wasn't off her head. Not obviously, perhaps, but in my opinion hopelessly unhinged. More to the point, hopelessly obsessed.'

Otani paused, rubbed his eyes and blinked. 'A victim of circumstance, some would say. I don't know. Anyway, I propose to suggest to her that her years of—not dedicated exactly, calculated perhaps—her years of service to the orphanage where she'd been brought up gave her such a position of trust there that the time came when she could delve into their confidential records more or less at will and turn up a name or names. Have you got a cigarette on you?'

Kimura gave him one and lit it for him. Otani looked tired, but soon began to speak again. 'I'll point out that either when she was working in the Consulate-General here in Kobe or when she went to the United States she was able to check US Army records or hire an enquiry agent to do it for her. I'll suggest that these confirmed—as we can find out for ourselves easily enough—that a certain young GI was serving with the Occupation forces in Japan in 1949 and 1950. And I shall explain that we think her next step was to discover his current whereabouts and circumstances and use her beauty and intelligence to entrap him. Ah, I see it's beginning to dawn on you too, Kimura.'

'I don't believe it, Chief!'

'I don't want to myself, but I do, and I can't help feeling sorry for her. It's a terrible burden she's borne for most of her life, Kimura.

Bottling up all that dark hatred from childhood onwards so success-fully . . . then living with the knowledge that she seduced her own father, murdered his wife and married him with the intention of one day killing him too. A man who still probably has no idea he even has a daughter, much less who she is.'

Find Miriam

_____

'How old would you say I am?'

I looked at the dark handsome man standing next to the railing of his penthouse balcony overlooking Sarasota Bay. He was just a bit bigger than I am, about six feet and somewhere in the range of one hundred and ninety pounds. His open blue shirt, which may have been silk, showed a well-muscled body with a chest of gray-brown hair. The hair on his head was the same color, plentiful, neat. And he was carefully and gently tanned. He had a glass of V-8 in his hand. He had offered me the same. I had settled for water. There was a slight accent, very slight when he spoke and I realized he reminded me of Ricardo Montalban.

I'm forty-four, on the thin side, losing my hair and usually broke or close to it. I'd come to Sarasota two years earlier, just drove till my car gave out and I felt safely in the sunshine after spending my life in the gray of Chicago. I had driven away from a wife who had dumped me and a dead-end investigator's job with the State's Attorney's Office.

Now, I made my living finding people, asking questions, answering to nobody. I had a growing number of Sarasota lawyers using me to deliver a summons or find a local resident who hadn't turned up for a court or divorce hearing. Occasionally, I would turn up some street trade, a referral from a bartender or Dave the owner of the Dairy Queen next door to the run-down two-story office building where I had my office and where I lived. I had a deal with the building manager. The landlord lived in Seattle. By giving the manager a few extra dollars a month beyond the reasonable rent for a seedy two-room suite, he ignored the fact that I was living in the second room of a two-room office. The outer room was designed as a reception room. I had turned it into an office. The room behind it was a small windowed office which I had turned into a living space. I had fixed it up to my satisfaction and the clothes I had brought with me from Chicago would hold out for another year or two. I had a bed, an old dresser, a sink in the corner, a television set and an aging green sofa and matching armchair. The only real inconvenience was that the office, like all the others, opened onto a balcony with a rusting railing facing a parking lot shared with the Dairy Queen and, beyond it, the heavy traffic of Route 301. To get to the bathroom, which had no bath, I had to walk past five offices and take whatever the weather had to offer. I showered every morning after I worked out at the downtown YMCA.

There was nothing but my name printed on the white-on-black plastic plate that slid into the slot on my door. I wasn't a private detective, didn't want to be. I did what I know how to do, ask questions, find people.

'Just a guess,' Raymond Sebastian asked again, looking away from the beautiful sight of the boats bobbing in the bay and the busy bridge going over to Bird Key.

Answering a question like that could lose me a job, but I hadn't come to this town to go back to saying 'yes, boss' to people I liked and didn't like.

'Sixty,' I guessed, standing a few feet away from him and looking him in the eyes.

'Closer to seventy,' he said with some satisfaction. 'I was blessed by the Lord in many ways. My genes are excellent. My mother is ninety-two and still lives in good health. My father died when he was ninety-four. I have uncles, aunts . . . you wouldn't believe.'

'Not without seeing them,' I said.

Sebastian laughed. There wasn't much joy in his laugh. He looked at his now-empty V-8 glass and set it on a glass-top table on the balcony.

'Lawrence told you my problem?' he asked facing me, his gray-blue eyes unblinking, sincere.

'Your wife left. You want to find her. That's all.'

Lawrence Werring was a lawyer, civil cases, injury law suits primarily, an ambulance chaser and proud of it. It had bought him a beautiful wife, a leather-appointed office and a four bedroom house on the water on Longboat Key. If I knew which one it was, I could probably see it from where Sebastian and I were standing.

'My wife's name is Miriam,' Sebastian said handing me a folder that lay next to the now-empty V-8 glass. 'She is considerably younger than I, thirty-six, but I believed she loved me. I was vain enough to think it was true and for some time it seemed true. And then one afternoon . . .'

He looked around as if she might suddenly rematerialize.

'. . . She was gone. I came home and her clothes, jewelry, gone. No note, nothing. That was, let me see, last Thursday. I kept expecting to hear from her or a kidnapper or something, but . . .'

I opened the folder. There were a few neatly typed pages of biography. I skimmed them. Miriam Latham Sebastian was born in Utah, earned an undergraduate degree in social science at the University of Florida and moved with her parents, now both dead, to Sarasota where she worked for a Catholic services agency as a case worker till she married Sebastian four years earlier. There was also a photograph of Miriam Sebastian. She was wearing red shorts, a white blouse and a great smile. Her dark hair was long and blowing in the breeze. She had her arm lovingly around her husband who stood tall, tan and shirtless in a pair of white trunks looking at the camera. They were standing on the wide sands of a Florida Gulf Coast beach, a few apartments or condos behind them.

'Pretty,' I said closing the folder.

'Beautiful,' he corrected. 'Exquisite. Charming.'

'Any guesses?' I said. 'About what happened?'

He shrugged and moved from the balcony back into the penthouse apartment. I followed as he talked. We stopped in front of a painting of his wife on the wall over a big white sofa. The whole room was white, but not a modern white. There was a look of tasteful antique about the place. Not my kind of home, but I could appreciate it.

'Another man perhaps, but I doubt it,' he said. 'We have had no major quarrels. I denied her nothing, nothing. I am far from a poor man, Mr Fonesca and . . .'

He paused and sighed deeply.

'And,' he continued composing himself, 'I have checked our joint checking and savings accounts. Most of the money has been removed. A little is left. I have my corporate attorney checking other holdings which Miriam might have had access to. I find it impossible to believe she would simply take as much money as she could and just walk out on me.'

'You had a little hitch in your voice when you mentioned another man,' I said having decided the chairs in the room were too white for me to sit on.

'She has had a good friend,' he said gently. 'This is very difficult for me. I am a proud man from a proud family.'

'A good friend?' I repeated.

'For about the last year,' he said, 'Miriam has been seeing a psych-iatrist, nothing major, problems to be worked out about her child-hood, her relationship to her parents. The psychiatrist's name is Gerald Bermeister. He's got a practice over one of those antique stores on Palm Avenue. I'm not a young man. I am not immune to jealousy. Gerald Bermeister is both young and good looking. There were times when I could not determine whether my suspicions were simply those of an older man afraid of losing his beautiful young wife or were valid concerns.'

'I'll check it out,' I said.

'Miriam was a bit of a loner,' he went on. 'But because of business connections we belong to a wide variety of organizations, Selby Gardens, Asolo Angels, charity groups, and we're seen at balls and dances. Miriam said that in three years we had been on the *Herald-Tribune*'s society page eleven times. In spite of this, Miriam had no really close friends with one possible exception, Caroline Wilkerson, the widow of my late partner.'

'And what do you want me to do?' I asked.

'Find her, of course,' Sebastian said turning from the painting to look at me.

'Has she committed a crime?' I asked.

'I don't know. I don't think so,' he said.

'So, she's free to go where she wants to go, even to leave her husband, take money out of your joint accounts and wander away. It may be a boyfriend. It may be a lot of things.'

'I just want you to find her,' he said. 'I just want to talk to her. I just want to find out what happened and if there is anything I can do to get her back.'

'She could be half way to Singapore by now,' I said.

'Your expense account is unlimited,' he answered. 'I will want you to keep me informed if you leave town in search of Miriam and I would expect you would, as a professional, keep expenses to a mini-mum and give me a full accounting of all such expenses when you find her.'

'If I find her,' I said. 'I'll do my best to find out why she left. I'll have to ask her if she's willing to talk to you. I'll tell you where she is if she gives me permission to tell you.'

'I understand,' he said.

He moved again. I followed into an office where he moved to a desk and picked something up next to a computer.

'Here's a check in advance,' he said. 'Larry said your fee was nego-tiable. Consider this expenses and, if anything is left, part of your payment. I propose one hundred and twenty dollars a day plus expenses.'

I nodded to show it was fair and took the check. It was made out to me for five hundred dollars. He had been ready and expecting that I'd take the job.

'How long?' I asked.

'How long?'

'Do I keep looking before I give up? I expect to find her, but it may be hard or easy. It may, if she's really smart, be impossible.'

'Let's say we re-evaluate after two weeks if it goes that long,' he said. 'But I want her back if it's at all possible. I'm too old to start again and I love Miriam. Do you understand?'

I nodded, tucked the folder under my arm after dropping the check into it and asked him for the numbers of any credit cards they shared, the tag number and make of her car and various other things that would make my job easier.

While he found what I asked for he admitted, 'I tried going to the police first, but they said they really had no reason to look for Miriam unless I thought she might be dangerous to herself or had been taken against her will. They also said I could file a missing persons report but there was little they could do even if they found her other than inform me that she was alive and well, unless she had committed a crime, which she hadn't. I'm talking too much.'

'It's understandable,' I said as he ushered me to the door and handed me an embossed business card, tasteful, easily readable black script: Raymond Sebastian, Investments, Real Estate. There was an office address and phone number in the lower left-hand corner. He had written his home phone number on the back of the card but I already had that.

'Keep me informed,' he said taking my hand. 'Call any time. As often as you like.'

He waited with me at the elevator. His was the only apartment on the floor, but he was on the twelfth floor and the elevator took a few minutes.

'Anything else I can tell you?' he asked.

'She have any living relatives?'

'No, it's all in the material I've given you,' he said. 'Just me. I don't think she's gone far. We've traveled all around the world, but she considers the Gulf Coast her home. I could be wrong.'

'I'm going to start with her friend Mrs Wilkerson,' I said.

'Good idea though I don't know what Caroline can tell you that I haven't. Yet, maybe there was something said, some . . . I don't know.'

The elevator bell rang and the doors opened. I stepped in and smiled confidently at Raymond Sebastian who now looked a little older than he had on his balcony.

When I'm not working, I bike. Not a motorcycle. A bike. Sarasota isn't that big and it has a good cheap bus system that not enough people use. When I'm on a case, I rent a car and charge it to my client. I had left my bike, an old one-speed, chained to a tree. No one had taken my battered bike pack. It wasn't worth the effort and besides, we were a little off the regular haunts of Sarasota's downtown homeless. I put the folder in the bike pack, took off the chain and dropped it into the second pouch of the pack. I biked. It was summer, the day was hot. I pedaled to my place behind the Dairy Queen on 301. I pedaled slowly. I was wearing my best clothes—sport jacket, pressed pants, white shirt—and I didn't want to get them sweat drenched if I could help it.

When I got back to my office, I made three calls. First, I called the little independent car rental company I used and we agreed on our usual deal. I said I'd be over to pick up a Toyota Tercel within the hour. Then I called Caroline Wilkerson, who was in the phone book, and made an appointment with her that afternoon. She said she was worried about Miriam and Raymond and would be happy to talk to me. I called Dr Gerald Bermeister, got a typical he'll-call-you-back. I told her it was urgent, about Miriam Sebastian. The woman put me on hold for a minute so I could listen to the Beach Boys and then came back on to say Dr Bermeister could see me for fifteen minutes at four-forty-five. I said I'd be there.

I put on my jeans and a black pull-over tee shirt, washed my face and went down to the DQ where I had a burger and a Blizzard and talked to Dave who owned the place. Dave was probably about my age but years of working in the sun on his boat had turned his skin to dark leather. I'm a sucker for junk food and I've got no one to tell me to eat well. Dave doesn't eat his own food, but I knew he kept the place clean. I worked out every day at the YMCA where I biked every day and told myself that covered the burgers, fried chicken, ribs and hot dogs. I could tell myself lies. Who was there to contradict me?

I walked to the car rental office about a mile and a half north on 301, past antique shops, a girlie bar, a pawn shop, some offices and restaurants, a rebuilt and new tire garage and a Popeye's chicken. I had worked up a sweat when I got the car. I turned on the air conditioning and headed for Sebastian's bank where I cashed the check for five hundred. Then I drove back to my office and my room to wash and change into my good clothes.

Caroline Wilkerson met me at the Cafe Kaldi on Main Street. I had no trouble finding her even though the coffee house tables were almost full in spite of the absence of the winter tourists. She sat alone, an open notebook in front of her, reading glasses perched on the end of her nose. She was writing. A cup of coffee rested nearby. I recognized her from the society pages of the *Herald-Tribune*. When I sat across from her, she looked at me over her glasses, took them off, folded her hands on the table and gave me her attention.

The widow Caroline was a beauty, better in person than in the papers. She was probably in her late forties, short, straight silver hair, a seemingly wrinkle-free face with full red lips that reminded me of Joan Fontaine. She wore a pink silky blouse with a pearl necklace and pearl earrings and a light-weight white jacket.

'Would you like to order a coffee?' she asked.

'No thanks,' I said. 'I've had my quota for the day.'

She nodded, understandingly, and took a sip of her coffee.

'Miriam Sebastian,' I said. 'You know she's apparently left her husband?'

'Raymond told me,' she said. 'Called. Frantic. Almost in tears. I couldn't help him. She hasn't contacted me. I would have thought, as Raymond did, that if Miriam did something like this, she'd get in touch with me, but . . .'

Caroline Wilkerson shrugged.

'Did they have a fight?'

A trio of young women suddenly laughed loudly a few tables behind me. When they stopped, Caroline Wilkerson closed her notebook.

'I don't think so,' she said. 'I can't be certain. But Raymond said nothing about a fight and I don't recall ever seeing them fight or hearing from Miriam that they had fought. Frankly, I'm worried about her.'

'Any idea of where she might have gone?' I asked.

The pause was long. She bit her lower lip, made up her mind, sighed. 'Gerry Bermeister,' she said softly meeting my eyes. 'He's her analyst and . . . I think that's all I can say.'

'Mr Sebastian thinks his wife and Dr Bermeister might have had an affair, that she may have left to be with him.'

She shrugged again. I handed her one of my cards, asked her to get in touch with me if she heard from Miriam Sebastian, and said that she should tell her friend that her husband simply wanted to know what happened and if he could talk to her.

She took the card and I stood up.

'I hope you find her,' she said. 'Miriam has had problems recently, depression. One of her relatives, her only close relative, a cousin I think, recently died. That's hardly a reason for what she's done, but . . . I frankly don't know what to make of it.'

At the moment, that made two of us.

'Are you permitted to let me know if you find out anything about where Miriam is and why she's . . .'

I must have been shaking my head 'no' because she stopped.

'I'm sorry,' I said. 'You'll have to get that from her or from Mr Sebastian. Whatever I find is between me and my client.'

'I understand,' she said with a sad smile showing perfect white teeth. 'That's what I would expect if you were working for me.'

When I got to the coffee house door, I looked back at Caroline Wilkerson. Her half glasses were back on and her notebook was open.

One of the criminal attorneys I did some work for had access to computer networks, very sophisticated access. An individual in his office did the computer work and was well paid. Since some of what he did on the network was on the borderline of illegal, the attorney never acknowledged his access to information the police, credit agencies, banks and almost every major corporation had. I had some time before I saw Bermeister so I dropped by the attorney's office. He was with a client but he gave me permission through his secretary to talk to Harvey, the computer whiz. I found Harvey in his small windowless office in front of his computer. Harvey looked more like an ex-movie star than a computer hacker. He was tall, dark, wearing a suit and sporting shot hair of gold. Harvey was MIT. Harvey was also a convicted cocaine user and former alcoholic.

It took Harvey ten minutes to determine that Miriam Sebastian had not used any of her credit cards during the past four days. Nor had she, at least under her own name, rented a car or taken a plane out of Sarasota, Clearwater, St Petersburg, Tampa or Fort Meyers.

'You want me to keep checking every day to see if I can find her?' he said.

'I'll bill my client,' I said.

'Suit yourself,' said Harvey showing capped teeth. 'I like a challenge like this, pay or no pay. Me against her. She hides. I find her.'

'You want her Social Security number?' I asked.

Harvey smiled.

'That I can get and access to bank accounts and credit cards. You want that?'

'Sure. I'll call you later.'

I made it to Dr Bermeister's office with ten minutes to spare. The matronly receptionist took my name and asked me to have a seat. The only other person in the waiting area was a nervous young woman, about twenty, who hadn't done much to look her best. Her hair was short and dark. Her brown skirt didn't really go with her gray blouse. She ruffled through a magazine.

I was reading an article about Clint Eastwood in *People* magazine when Bermeister's door opened. He was in his thirties, dark suit, dark hair and ruggedly good looking.

'I'll be with you in a few minutes, Audrey,' he said to the nervous Audrey who nodded frowning.

'Mr Fonesca?' he said looking at me. 'Please come in.'

I followed him into his office. He opened his drapes and let in the sun and a view of Ringling Boulevard. The office wasn't overly large, room for a desk and chair, a small sofa and two armchairs. The colors were all subdued blues. A painting on the wall showed a woman standing on a hill looking into a valley beyond at the ruins of a castle. Her face wasn't visible.

'Like it?' Bermeister said sitting behind his desk and offering me the couch or one of the chairs. I took a chair so I could face him.

'The painting? Yes,' I said.

'One of my patients did it,' he said. 'An artist. A man. We spent a lot of time talking about that painting.'

'Haunting,' I said.

'Gothic,' he said. 'I'm sorry, Mr Fonesca, but I'm going to have to get right to your questions.'

'I understand. Miriam Latham Sebastian,' I said.

'I can't give you any information about why she was seeing me, what was said.'

'I know,' I said feeling comfortable in the chair. 'Do you know where Mrs Sebastian is?'

'No,' he said.

The answer had come slowly.

'Any ideas?'

'Maybe,' he said.

'Want to share them?' I asked.

He didn't answer.

'This one will probably get me kicked out, but you're in a hurry. Mr Sebastian, and he's not the only one, thinks you and Miriam Sebastian were having an affair.'

Bermeister cocked his head and looked interested.

'And if we were?'

'Or are,' I amended. 'Well, it might suggest that she would come to you. Her husband just wants to talk to her.'

'And you just want to find her for him?' he asked.

'That's it,' I said.

'First,' he said getting up from his desk chair. 'I am not and have not been having an affair with Miriam Sebastian. In fact, Mr Fonesca, I can offer more than ample proof that I am gay. It is a relatively open secret which, in fact, hasn't hurt my practice at all. I get the gay clients, men and women, and I get women who feel more comfortable talking to me. What I don't get are many straight men.'

'Mrs Sebastian,' I said.

'She doesn't want to see her husband,' he said sitting on the sofa and crossing his legs. 'She doesn't want him to know where she is.'

'I told Sebastian that I planned to talk to her if I found her and that I wouldn't tell her husband where she was if she told me she wouldn't talk to him under any circumstances.'

'Which,' said Bermeister, 'is what she would say.'

'I want to hear it from her,' I said. 'Until I do, she can't use a credit card, can't cash a check in her own name, can't use her Social Security number without my finding her. My job is finding people, doctor. I do a good job. If you want references . . .'

His right hand was up indicating that I should stop. He looked up at the painting of the woman looking down at the ruins.

'I made some calls about you after I scheduled this appointment,' he said. 'Actually, Doreen, my secretary, made the calls. You haven't been here long, but your reputation is very good.'

'Small city,' I said.

'Big enough,' he said taking a pad out of his pocket and writing something. He tore the page out and looked at it.

'I have your word,' he said.

'I talk to her. Try to talk her into at least a phone call and then I drop it if she wants to be left alone.'

He handed me the sheet of paper. It had two words on it: Harrington House. I folded the sheet and put it in my jacket pocket.

'I don't want people hounding Miriam,' he said. 'She . . . she can tell you why if she wants to. By the way, I plan to call her the instant you leave. She may choose to pack and leave before you get there.'

'I think it would be a good idea if she just talked to me.'

'I think you may be right,' he said. 'I'll suggest that she do so.'

He ushered me to the door and shook my hand.

'I'm trusting you,' he said.

I nodded and he turned to the nervous young woman.

'I have to make one quick call, Audrey,' he said smiling at her.

She had no response and he disappeared back into his office.

I was parked in front of the hardware store on Main. I stopped at an outdoor phone booth where there was a complete phone book and had no trouble finding Harrington House. It was in Holmes Beach, a Bed and Breakfast. That was on Anna Maria Island. I'd been there to try to find the house where Georges Simenon had lived for a while. The house was gone. I called Harvey the computer whiz.

'Miriam Latham Sebastian has been turning her investments into cash and emptying her joint bank accounts,' he said happily. 'I've got a feeling there's more.'

'Keep at it,' I said.

I hung up and wondered why Dr Gerald Bermeister had been so cooperative. I considered calling Harvey back and asking him to check on the good doctor, but decided that could wait.

I got into my rented car, flipped on the air conditioner and eased back through a break in traffic. I made a left and then another left and then another which brought me right back to Bermeister's office building. I got out fast, ran into the office building, rode the elevator up to Bermeister's floor and then rode back down again and got into my car.

The blue Buick was idling half way down the block near the curb.

He had followed me around the block and was waiting for me now. I hoped I had given the impression of someone who had left something in the doctor's office.

I had noticed the blue Buick when I picked up my rental car, but it hadn't really registered. I hadn't been looking for someone who might be following me. But I had spotted what I thought was the same car when I came out of the Cafe Kaldi. Now I was sure. I eased past the Buick, looking both ways at the intersection and catching a glimpse of the man behind the wheel. This guy was short, wore a blue short-sleeve shirt and looked, from the color of his hair and sag of his tough face, about fifty.

There must have been lots of reasons for someone to follow me, but I couldn't think of any good ones other than that the guy in the Buick was hoping I would lead him to Miriam Sebastian. I could have been dead wrong, but I didn't take chances.

He was a good driver, a very good driver, and he kept up with me as I headed for Tamiami Trail. I pulled into the carry-out lane at the McDonald's across from the airport hoping he would follow me in line. I even timed it so a car would be behind me other than the Buick which was the way the guy who was following me would want it, too. My plan was to order a sandwich and pull away while the Buick was stuck behind the car behind me. If I was lucky, there would also be a car behind him so he couldn't back up.

He was too smart. He simply drove around and parked between a van and a pick-up truck in the parking lot.

Hell. I decided it was all-out now. He had almost certainly figured I had spotted him by now, and I didn't have time to keep playing tag. Miriam Sebastian might be gone by the time I got to Harrington House which was still at least forty minutes from where I took my cheeseburger, put it on the seat next to me and peeled off fast to the right, away from the direction I wanted to go. In the rear-view, I watched the Buick back out as I sailed at sixty down Route 41. He was good, but there's a definite advantage in being the one who is followed. It took me ten minutes to lose him. By then I guessed he knew I wasn't going to lead him to Miriam Sebastian. I ate the burger while I drove.

I took the bridge across to St Armand's, the same bridge you could see from Raymond Sebastian's apartment, and then drove straight up Longboat Key through the canyon of high-rise resorts and past streets that held some of the most expensive houses, mansions and estates in the county.

I went over the short bridge at the end of the Key and drove through the far less up-scale and often ramshackle hotels and rental houses along the water in Bradenton Beach. Ten minutes later, I spotted the sign for Harrington House and pulled into the shaded driveway. I parked on the white crushed shell and white pebble lot which held only two other cars.

Harrington House was a white three-floor 1920s stucco over cement block with green wooden shutters. There were flowers behind a low picket fence and a sign to the right of the house pointing toward the entrance. I walked up the brick path for about a dozen steps and came to a door. I found myself inside a very large lodge-style living room with a carpeted dark wooden stairway leading up to a small landing and, I assumed, rooms. There were book cases whose shelves were filled and a chess table with checkers lined up and ready to go. The big fireplace was probably original and used no more than a few days during the Central Florida winter.

I hit the bell on a desk by the corner next to a basket of wrapped bars of soap with a sketch of the house on the wrapper. I smelled a bar and was doing so when a blonde woman came bouncing in with a smile. She was about fifty and seemed to be full of an energy I didn't feel. I put down the soap.

'Yes sir?' she said. 'You have a reservation?'

'No,' I said. 'I'm looking for Miriam Sebastian, a guest here.'

Some of the bounce left the woman but there was still a smile when she said, 'No guest by that name registered.'

I pulled out the photograph Raymond Sebastian had given me and showed it to her. She took it and looked long and hard.

'Are you a friend of hers?'

'I'm not an enemy.'

She looked hard at the photograph again.

'I suppose you'll hang around even if I tell you I don't know these people.'

'Beach is public,' I said. 'And I like to look at birds and waves.'

'That picture was taken three or four years ago, right out on the beach behind the house,' she said. 'You'll recognize some of the houses in the background if you go out there.'

I went out there. There was a small, clear-blue swimming pool behind the house and a chest-high picket fence just beyond it. The waves were coming in low on the beach about thirty yards away, but still moaned as they hit the white sand and brought in a new crop of broken shells and an occasional fossilized shark's tooth or dead fish.

I went through the gate to the beach and looked around. A toddler was chasing gulls and not even coming close, which was in the kid's best interest. A couple, probably the kid's parents, sat on a brightly painted beach cloth watching the child and talking. Individuals, duos, trios and quartets of all ages walked along the shoreline in bare feet or floppy sandals. Miriam Sebastian was easy to find. There were five aluminium beach loungers covered in strips of white vinyl. Miriam Sebastian sat in the middle lounger. The others were empty.

She wore a wide-brimmed straw hat, dark sunglasses and a two-piece solid white bathing suit. She glistened from the bottle of lotion that sat on the lounger next to her along with a fluffy towel. She was reading a book or acting as if she was knowing I was on the way. I stood in front of her.

'*War and Peace*,' she said holding up the heavy book. 'Always wanted to read it, never did. I plan to read as many of the so-called classics as I can. It's my impression that few people have really read them though they claim to have. Please have a seat, Mr Fonesca.'

I sat on the lounger to her right, the one that didn't have lotion and a towel, and she moved a book mark and laid the book on her lap. She took off her sunglasses. She was definitely the woman in the picture, still beautiful, naturally beautiful though the woman looking at me seemed older than the one in the picture. I showed her the picture.

'Mr Sebastian would like to talk to you,' I said.

She looked at the photograph and shook her head before handing it back.

'We spent two nights here after our honeymoon in Spain,' she said. 'You would think Raymond might remember and at least call on the chance that I might return. But . . .'

'Will you talk to him?' I asked.

She sat for about thirty seconds and simply looked at me. I was decidedly uncomfortable and wished I had sunglasses. I looked at the kid still chasing gulls. He was getting no closer.

'You're not here to kill me,' she said conversationally.

'Kill you?'

'I think Raymond is planning to have me killed,' she said turning slightly toward me. 'But I think you're not the one.'

'Why does your husband want to kill you?' I asked.

'Money,' she said and then she smiled. 'People thought I married Raymond for his money. I didn't, Mr Fonesca. I loved him. I would have gone on loving him. He was worth about one hundred thousand when we married, give or take a percentage or two in either direction. I, however, was worth close to eleven million dollars from an annuity, the sale of my father's business when he died, and a very high yield insurance policy on both my parents.'

'It doesn't make sense, Mrs Sebastian,' I said.

'Miriam,' she said. 'Call me Miriam. Your first name?'

'Lewis,' I said. 'Lew.'

'It makes perfect sense to me,' she said. 'I know that Raymond has been telling people that I am having an affair with Dr Bermeister. Lew, I've been faithful to my husband from the day we met. Unfortunately, I can't say the same about him. I have ample evidence, including almost interrupting a session between Raymond and Caroline Wilkerson in the buff in our bed about five weeks ago. It seems the man almost old enough to be my grandfather married me for my money. After I carefully closed the door without Raymond or Caroline seeing me, I went out, stayed in a hotel and returned the day I was supposed to.'

'Reason for divorce,' I said.

'My word against theirs,' she said. 'He'd drag it on, hold up my assets. I haven't the time, Lew.'

'So . . .?'

'So,' she said, 'I did a little digging and discovered that Caroline was far from the first. I don't know if he is just an old man afraid of accepting his age or if he simply craves the chase and the sex. I know he had no great interest in me in that department for the past year.'

'You waited five weeks after you knew all this and then suddenly walked out?' I asked.

'It took me five weeks to convert all my stocks and my life insurance policy to cash and to withdraw every penny I have in bank accounts. I didn't want a scene and I didn't want Raymond to know what I was doing, but by now he knows.'

'And you think he wants to kill you?'

'Yes. I don't think he knows the extent of what I've done, nor that I've cashed in the insurance policy,' she said. 'Raymond claims to be a real estate dealer. He has averaged a little over twenty thousand dollars on his real estate deals each of the years we've been married. As for his investments, he has consistently lost money. I'd say that at the moment my husband, who is nearing seventy, thinks he'll have millions when, in fact, he has what's left on his credit cards, ten thousand dollars in his own bank account and a 1995 paid-for Lincoln Town Car.'

'And he's trying to kill you before you get rid of your money?'

'Yes. But it's too late. I've put all the money, but the thirty thousand I've kept with me in cash, into boxes and sent the boxes anonymously to various charities including the National Negro College Fund, the Salvation Army and many others.'

'Why don't you just tell him?' I asked. 'Or I can tell him.'

The toddler's mother screamed at the boy who had wandered too far in pursuit of the gulls. The kid's name was Harry.

'Then he wouldn't try to have me killed,' she said.

'That's the picture,' I said. 'You know a short bulldog of a man, drives a blue Buick? He's probably about ten years younger than your husband.'

'Zito,' she said. 'Irving Zito.'

'He was following me today. I lost him.'

She shrugged.

'Irving is Raymond's "personal" assistant,' she said. 'He has a record including a conviction for Murder Two. Don't ask me how he and Raymond came together. The story I was told didn't make much sense. So Irving Zito is the designated killer.'

'If you don't tell your husband your money is gone and you just stay here, he'll find you even if I don't tell him.'

'And you don't plan to tell him?' she asked.

'Not if you say "no." ' I said.

'Good. I say "no," Did he pay you by check?'

'Yes.'

'Cash it fast.'

'I did,' I said, 'I thought it was too easy.'

'Too easy?'

'Finding you. Talk to Caroline Wilkerson at your husband's suggestion. She sends me to Dr Bermeister. He sends me to you and you wait for me. You wanted me to find you.'

'I wanted whoever was going to kill me to find me,' she said. 'I'll just have to wait until Zito and Raymond figure it out. If they don't, Raymond will probably find another private detective with fewer scruples than you who will find me right here. I hope I have time to finish Tolstoy before he does.'

'You want to die?'

'I've left a letter with my lawyer, with documents, proving my husband's infidelity, misuse of my money which I knew about but chose to ignore, and the statement that if I am found dead under suspicious circumstances, a full investigation of the likelihood of my husband's being responsible is almost a certainty. Now that I know Irving Zito is involved, I'll drive into Sarasota with a new letter including Zito's name and add it to the statement I've given my lawyer.'

'You want to die,' I repeated though this time it wasn't a question.

'No,' she said. 'I don't. But I'm going to die within a few months even if Raymond doesn't get the job done. I'm dying, Lew. Dr Bermeister knows it. I started seeing him as a therapist when I first learned about the tumor more than a year ago. I didn't want my husband to know. I arranged for treatment and surgery in New York and told my husband I simply wanted six weeks or so with old school friends, one of whom was getting married. He had no objections. I caught him and Caroline in bed the day I returned. I had hurried home a day early. Obviously, I wasn't expected. Treatment and surgery proved relatively ineffective. The tumor is in a vital part of my brain and getting bigger. Raymond has never even noticed that I was ill. I don't wish to die slowly in the hospital.'

'So you set your husband up,' I said.

Harry the toddler was back with his mother who was standing and brushing sand from the boy who was trying to pull away. There were gulls to chase and water to wade in.

'Yes,' she said. 'You disapprove?'

'I don't know,' I answered. 'It's your life.'

SHIZUKO NATSUKI (1938–)

Divine Punishment

Translated from the Japanese by GAVIN FREW

IT was shortly after six in the morning when Matsuko Torikai rushed into the courtyard of Futami-ga-Ura shrine. It was a cold winter's day and a thick mist sent tendrils swirling through the fields as she covered the hundred yards or so from her house.

'Where is the priest? I've got to see the priest!' she cried to Yamaguchi, a junior priest who was sweeping the garden in front of the shrine. She was wearing slacks, a sweater, and a dirty apron, and from the state of her hair it would appear that she had only just got out of bed.

'What's wrong?'

'Where's the priest? He has to come to my house right away!'

Yamaguchi looked back over his shoulder towards the buildings of the shrine, not sure how to handle the situation. Ignoring him, Matsuko ran to the bottom of the steps leading to the main building and called out in a loud voice, 'Are you there? You've got to help me!'

The priest, Sadamassa Omuro, had just finished the morning devotions and hurried out to see what was the matter. He was a tall, athletic-looking man of about forty-five who had attended graduate school in Tokyo. He was well liked by his parishioners. Ever since Matsuko's husband died, it had become her habit to come and see him nearly every day to talk over her problems.

'Please help me! It's Yuhei! He—he—' She broke into tears and Omuro couldn't make out what she was trying to say. Yuhei was her twenty-two-year-old son.

'What has Yuhei done?' he asked, bending down to look into her face.

'He's been hurt! I found him lying in front of the house, covered with blood. I tried to wake him, but he doesn't move! I don't know what to do!'

'Have you called for an ambulance?'

'Not yet. I thought that if you were to have a look at him—'

Omuro hurried down the steps and, thrusting his feet into a pair of garden clogs lying there, he ran in the direction of Matsuko's house, calling to Yamaguchi to follow.

The shrine was situated on a peninsula on the western side of Fukuoka Prefecture, and as he ran Omuro could see several farm-houses dotted among the brown winter fields. Most of the people in the area made a living from fishing and farming and Matsuko was no exception. She lived in an old single-story house and both it and the small cart parked next to it were covered in white dust from the unpaved road that led to the shrine.

Yuhei was lying face up on the ground next to the verandah, with a straw mat draped over the lower half of his body.

'When did you find him?'

'Just after I woke up. I opened the shutters and—'

'Did he have that mat on him when you found him?'

'Yes. It completely covered him, but I pulled it back, wondering what it could be, and—'

As they moved closer to the body, Omuro and Yamaguchi invol-untarily looked away. Yuhei's face was covered with blood and dirt, the shirt under his leather jacket was soaked in blood, and his legs, visible through gaping tears in his trousers, were a mass of cuts.

Omuro removed the straw mat and called out Yuhei's name in a loud voice. There was no reaction. He put his ear next to Yuhei's mouth for a few moments, then he turned to Yamaguchi.

'He's not breathing and his body is cold. I'd better get in touch with the police straightaway. You stay here.'

Leaving Yamaguchi with Yuhei, he hurried into the house, followed by Matsuko. The living room on the far side of the hall was in a terrible mess, but he spotted a telephone on the floor. He dialed 110 for the emergency service and gave a brief description of the situation. In less than five minutes, two cars arrived from the local police station at Shima.

The man in charge was thirty-six-year-old Assistant Inspector Koizumi and with him were four men, two from the identification section. They established that Yuhei was already dead, and when they told the Inspector it appeared to be murder he called Prefectural Headquarters to notify the homicide division and have them send over a medical examiner.

'At what time did you discover the body?' Koizumi asked Matsuko while his men covered the body with the mat and strung a rope around the scene to prevent unauthorized people from entering.

Matsuko was in her early fifties. Her husband had been a fisherman and since he died she had worked to support Yuhei and herself. The hard work had aged her and her skin was very tanned and wrinkled from her long hours in the sun.

'I got up at six o'clock, as usual, and when I opened the shutters—'

'I see. Where did Yuhei go last night?'

'I don't know. I haven't seen much of him lately. He spends most of his time at his sister's and only drops by here occasionally.'

Matsuko had two children. Her elder, Takako, lived with her husband in a council apartment in Fukuoka City.

'You said that Yuhei was twenty-two and dropped out of high school. What did he do for a living?'

'He worked now and again on construction sites or as a mechanic. You have no idea the amount of trouble he gave Takako and me.' Matsuko spoke quite calmly, but every now and again she covered her face with her hands as a sob wrenched itself from her body.

'So he was basically unemployed, then. If he was going to come back here from his sister's yesterday, how would he have traveled? By bus?'

It was quite a distance to the nearest bus stop, but there was no other way he could have come.

'He used to like bikes,' Matsuko said. 'He went everywhere on his bike until about six months ago.' She went suddenly silent and Koizumi looked over at Omuro questioningly.

'He was involved in an accident and banned from driving,' Omuro said. 'His mother was very worried about it and came to discuss it with me several times.'

'So even though he wanted to drive, he was unable to,' Koizumi said.

'No, that's not true,' Yamaguchi intruded. 'I saw him driving around on someone else's bike occasionally.'

The Chief Investigator and the doctor arrived at almost the same time and the doctor wasted no time in officially pronouncing Yuhei dead. The two then proceeded to examine the corpse and were appalled at what they found.

'Head, shoulder, stomach, knees, legs—he has been stuck seven or eight times with a blunt instrument. The cause of death is probably cerebral concussion received from a blow to the back of the head,' the Chief Investigator explained to the members of the homicide squad when they arrived.

'Can you tell what the weapon was?' one of the homicide squad asked.

'The wounds would indicate he was hit with a bat or club of some kind as well as with a rectangular bar of some kind.'

'You mean that he was hit with more than one weapon?'

'It would appear so.'

'That means that there was more than one of them,' the homicide detective said to Koizumi.

'That's not necessarily true. It would have been possible for the murderer to have struck him on the head first to knock him unconscious, then used another weapon or more to beat him to death,' Koizumi replied.

'True—but he would have to be a big man.'

Yuhei had been five feet ten inches tall and well built, so it followed that whoever had killed him must have been very strong.

'How long since his death?' The man from homicide asked the Chief Investigator.

'Six or seven hours, I think.'

'So that means that at some time between eleven o'clock last night and one o'clock this morning, the victim was murdered and his body carried here to his house.' There was no sign of the murder weapon and no bloodstains in the vicinity of the body. 'The murderer covered the body with the mat and escaped.'

'I think it's also safe to guess that the murderer was known to the victim,' said Koizumi. 'He not only knew where he lived, but whoever it was hated him very much indeed.'

The body was sent for an autopsy.

Although it was a very vicious murder, they had been able to identify the victim from the beginning and so it wasn't necessary for them to set up a separate investigation headquarters and they worked out of the local police station.

Their first task was to try to discover the scene of the actual murder and then search the area for the murder weapons and any other clues. At the same time, they had to check on all the victim's acquaintances, especially those who had reason to hate him enough to kill him. The obvious place to start checking on his friends would be at his home, but it was possible that if he had given someone reason to hate him that much, his family might try to keep it hidden from the police. For this reason, the investigation proceeded along two paths, one group questioning the family, the other the people who lived nearby, a more promising approach in the country, where people tend to know more about their neighbors.

Koizumi started his inquiries at the Futami-ga-Ura shrine. Not only was it very close to the victim's house, but from what he had learned that morning the victim's mother was a regular visitor to the shrine and relied on the chief priest for advice.

Futami-ga-Ura shrine was a medium-sized complex employing twenty priests. In the last ten years, it had seen a huge increase in the number of people who came to worship there. After Omuro took over as chief priest from his father, he had stressed its dedication to the god of traffic safety, and this had led to its sudden rise in popularity. Situated as it was beside the sea, the local fishermen had always come to pray for safety at sea, and Omuro had expanded this to cover all forms of transport. He had even gone so far as to take out commercials on television and radio, and as a result people came all the way from Fukuoka and the surrounding prefectures to pray at the shrine. Owners of transport companies came at the new year to pray for protection over the coming months and people brought their new cars to have them blessed by the priests or simply to buy charms to hang from their dashboards.

'I'm sorry I wasn't able to prevent Yuhei's motorcycle accident,' Omuro said after showing Koizumi through to the shrine's office. He obviously felt some responsibility for the death. 'His mother is a devout believer and came to pray for his safety nearly every day, but unfortunately he never set foot through the gate himself.'

'Can you tell me something about last year's accident?' Of course it would be easy for Koizumi to check the records back at the station, but he thought it could be more enlightening if he were to ask instead.

'It was the end of July last year, I think. Yuhei ran over a twenty-year-old girl in Fukuoka City and killed her. She was crossing the street at a pedestrian crossing, and although Yuhei tried to make an emergency stop his bike skidded and hit her. He had been stopped several times before that for speeding and was worried that he would be sent to prison, but luckily he had not been drinking and wasn't driving very fast. The road had been wet and that was what had caused him to skid, so the judge gave him a one-year sentence suspended for three years. Of course, he was also banned from driving for two years.'

'But as the victim was only twenty years old, he must have had to pay a good deal of compensation.'

'No, he had only the minimum insurance cover. The insurance company paid the maximum twenty-five million yen to the girl's parents, but Yuhei was unemployed and the judge deemed him incapable of paying any more. There was a lot of fuss about it at the time.'

'Didn't he have a house or any land?'

'No, his father was a fisherman, but he died of a stroke about ten years ago and all he left was the house and land. After that, Matsuko worked in a supermarket to earn the money to raise her two children but she didn't have anything extra afterward. The house is standing on only about a hundred and sixty square yards of land, but it is all in Matsuko's name. All the same, the land around here is worth about ten thousand yen per square yard now.'

'Yes, but Yuhei was an adult and she wasn't liable for him under law.'

'That's true. But Matsuko is a very honest woman and she offered to sell the land to pay the girl's parents. They refused, saying they had no desire to impoverish her and even if they took her money it wouldn't bring their daughter back to them.'

'Was she their only child?'

'Yes. She was in her last year at junior college and had already found a job for when she graduated. It was a terrible experience for Matsuko, but even worse for the girl's parents.'

The accident had taken place at approximately five o'clock on the evening of July the twenty-third at the Tajima junction in Fukuoka City. After calling the local police station, Koizumi learned that it had been more or less the way Omuro had described it.

'Normally the parents would have been awarded at least a hundred million in damages, but as the driver was unemployed and there was no way of forcing him to pay the case ended without any clear decision being made,' the chief of the traffic police told him. 'It wasn't just the money the victim's parents found hard to accept, it was the general attitude of the driver. He went to visit them once, but only because his mother forced him to, and he sulked the whole time he was there. Matsuko did everything she could to apologize, and if it wasn't for her efforts the parents would probably have gone to the judge and asked him to remove the suspension from the sentence.'

While Koizumi was questioning the neighbors, the other team was investigating the victim's movements of the previous day and trying to discover where the murder had taken place.

They found a 400cc motorcycle about four hundred yards to the south of Matsuko's house, parked by the side of a narrow lane that branched off the main road. A river ran next to the lane, but the bike was parked in the shadow of the woods on the opposite side. The driver's helmet hanging from one of the mirrors was wet from the rain that had started to fall that afternoon. There were no other houses in the area and the bike looked as if it had been left there for some time, although there didn't appear to be anything wrong with it.

They checked on the number and found it belonged to Sumio Yazawa, 23, of Fukuoka City. They visited his address and found him still at home. He was employed by a bar nearby and didn't start work until four in the afternoon.

'I lent it to Yuhei yesterday afternoon. We were in junior high school together and although I knew he was banned from driving I couldn't refuse when he asked.'

He was a rather weak-looking young man and they guessed that Yuhei had forced him to lend him the bike. At about nine the previous night he had appeared at the bar where Yazawa worked and borrowed the bike, saying he would return it within two or three days.

'His mother lives in the country, but there's nothing there for him to do so he has been staying at his sister's place. She lives in a council apartment in Kashiwabara. That's where he came from yesterday, I think.'

'Why did he want the bike?'

Yazawa shook his head. 'I didn't ask him. I guess he just wanted to go for a drive somewhere.'

At the end of their questioning, the police told him what had happened to Yuhei and asked him if he had any idea who might have wanted to kill him. He turned white and started to tremble, but said he knew of no one.

His statement tied up with the one they had taken from Yuhei's sister, Takako. She had heard about the tragedy from her mother and hurried over to be with her, taking her two young children with her—it was there that she was interviewed.

'Yuhei has been staying at our apartment off and on since last summer. After the accident, he was hounded by the police and by lawyers when he was here at Mother's and, being banned from driving, he couldn't get around, so he stayed with us. Our apartment has only four rooms, and my husband, who works for an electronics manufacturer, comes home early, so it is very cramped. With the two children, there wasn't really room for him, but my husband doesn't like confrontation and Yuhei took advantage of him, acting as if he owned the place. Yesterday he hung around the house all day until about eight o'clock, when he went out, saying something about borrowing Yazawa's bike.'

From this, they had a fair idea of Yuhei's movements the previous night. He had stayed in the apartment until about eight o'clock, then traveled by bus or subway to Yazawa's bar, where he borrowed the motorbike. If he had driven straight to the spot where the bike was found, he could have arrived there in about an hour—but if, as Yazawa suggested, he had wanted to go for a drive there was no telling where he went.

One thing that they did know, however, was that sometime between eleven and one, he had arrived at the spot where the bike was found and parked. It was thought that immediately after he had pulled over to the side of the road and dismounted, he was hit on the back of the head and then beaten to death after losing consciousness.

That afternoon the results of the autopsy came through. The cause of death proved to be a blow on the back of the head with a blunt instrument and the time of death was estimated to be at about eleven o'clock the previous night, backing up the original estimate made at the scene. Yuhei had eaten a meal at his sister's before he went out and more than three hours had passed between then and the time he died.

There were some fields on the other side of the woods next to where the bike was found, and in one corner was a small hut containing farm implements and fertilizer. The door was unlocked, and when they looked inside the detectives saw that this was where Yuhei had been beaten to death.

There were bloodstains on the timber and on the hoes, spades, and other implements in the room, and the ground was spattered with dark stains. The blood was analysed and, predictably, the blood type matched Yuhei's. The only disappointment was that they could find no clear fingerprints on the tools and they guessed that the murderer or murderers must have wiped them clean before leaving the scene.

That night at eight o'clock, a meeting was held to discuss the progress that had been made in the investigation that day.

'We still cannot say for sure whether it was the work of one man or more,' the chief of detectives said. 'However, it does seem very likely that a car was used in the crime. I think it would have taken a car to force the motorcycle to stop. The bike was found about fifty yards from the junction with the main road and at that point it still would not have been traveling very fast. If the killer or killers had parked a car in the middle of the road, the victim would have stopped instinctively. Once he or they had him off the bike, they could chat to him until he took his helmet off, then hit him over the head.'

'But if they were carrying weapons, surely he would have been suspicious and protected himself?'

'Yes, but it was pitch-black.'

'I think there were probably two of them. One could approach him openly while the other came up and hit him from behind.'

Another detective voiced his opinion. 'I don't agree that a car was needed to force him to stop. If a group of people were to stand in the middle of the road, he would have had to stop. Or if one person were to call out in a loud voice—'

'They'd run a certain risk of being run into, but, yes, it is possible.'

It was unlikely that there would be anyone traveling along that road at eleven on a winter's night and there were no dwellings near the spot, so even if Yuhei had called out there would be little likelihood of his being heard. There seemed to be little doubt that for some reason Yuhei was persuaded to get off his bike, then either knocked unconscious and carried or otherwise forced into the hut where he was beaten to death.

'But why did whoever it was bother to carry the body four hundred yards to his house?'

'To show that he was killed for a motive,' one of the senior detectives suggested. 'To show that it wasn't a casual murder, but one that had been planned.'

'I agree it's unlikely that it was the work of a passerby,' Koizumi said. 'They obviously planned to use that hut, and that's why they stopped him where they did. But how did they know he'd be passing that way?'

The room became silent as they all thought about it.

'His mother said he came home every now and again but she never knew when to expect him, and his sister said that it wasn't until eight o'clock that he decided to go out.'

'Maybe somebody telephoned him.'

'No, he didn't receive any calls before he went out,' said the man who had interviewed Takako.

'But it didn't have to be that evening—it could have been during the afternoon, or even the previous day.'

'That's true. If that was the case, there's no way of knowing. Takako went out in the afternoon with the children and he was left in the apartment on his own.'

'Then again, maybe he didn't get a phone call. There's always the possibility that the killer or killers followed him after he left the apartment. They could have been following him for days, waiting for a chance to attack him.'

'Well, whoever it was, they must have had a real grudge against him,' Koizumi said.

'I still half expect her to come through the door and say hello the sweet way she always used to.'

Assistant Inspector Koizumi and one of his sergeants had gone to visit the home of Sumire Tatsumi, the girl Yuhei had killed. They were greeted by the girl's mother, Akie, who still had trouble accepting what had happened to her daughter. There was a picture of the dead girl on the family shrine—she was an attractive, gentle-looking girl.

The detectives were shown into the living room and were told that the father, Hiroaki, was in bed in the next room. The strain of her death had proved too much for him and the previous month he had undergone an operation. It appeared that he was suffering from the beginnings of stomach cancer.

'My husband often said that he would like to kill the man who did that to her,' Akie admitted, 'but he is unable to move from his bed . . .'

During the initial investigation meeting, it had been suggested that the murder might have been committed by a lover of the dead girl, but they had been unable to find any trace of such a person. The girl's parents had also been posed as possible suspects, but neither of them had a driving license or any great physical strength, so it seemed unlikely that they could have done it on their own.

It was at that point that Koizumi came up with an astonishing idea: what if *Yuhei*'s mother had been involved? He suggested that it was unlikely that the murderer or murderers would just happen to come across Yuhei when he was in a place where there was very little likelihood of them being seen and where there was a hut containing the murder weapons so conveniently situated. What if his mother had been so disgusted by his behaviour that she had conspired with Takako or Sumire's parents to lure him there and put him off his guard?

A week passed without any new leads and the police began to grow desperate.

'We have no choice but to bring forward a witness,' Koizumi said. This was on the first Friday in February.

'A witness?' a colleague asked. 'What do you mean? If we had a witness, we wouldn't be having all this trouble.'

'We'll just have to persuade one to come forward.' Koizumi had spent the night working on a plan. 'A cousin of mine lives in an apartment near here. She's twenty-six, single, and works in the restaurant at the golf course. She drives to work every day. I think she's just what we're looking for.'

'But what will she say if we ask her?'

'I *have* asked her—she is very eager to help.'

That night Matsuko stopped off at the shrine on her way back from the supermarket where she worked, and as she was walking to her house from there she noticed two of the detectives walking toward her. One of them spoke.

'Mrs Torikai, I'm sorry it's taken us so long to make any progress, but I think we've got a lead at last.'

Matsuko looked at him expectantly.

'This is still confidential, but we thought you should know. This morning a witness came forward to say that she thinks she saw the murderer. She works in the restaurant at the golf course. On the night of the nineteenth, driving home past the spot where we found the motorcycle, she saw a suspicious figure. Whoever it was, they were so involved in what they were doing they didn't seem to notice her, but she got a good view in the headlights of her car and says she's sure she'd recognize them if she were to see them again.'

'Why did she wait all this time before she came forward to the police?'

'She says she remembered reading about Yuhei's accident and felt so sorry for the victim's parents she decided she wouldn't help. One of her relatives was killed by a bike gang and she's hated all bikers ever since. However, she claims that Yuhei came to her in a dream the other night, covered with terrible wounds, and begged her to help us find the people who killed him.'

A look of horror came over Matsuko's face and she stepped back from the detective.

'She wants to lay his soul at rest as soon as she can,' he continued. 'We've given her photographs of everyone who might have a motive to harm Yuhei, including those who knew Sumire Tatsumi, and she's looking through them, trying to identify the person she saw. If that doesn't work, we'll make a composite sketch based on her description. It's only a question of time before we find the killer now we have a witness.'

'Are you sure you can trust her memory?' Matsuko sounded afraid to hope. 'It has been some time now.'

'Yes,' the detective assured her. 'She's a very bright young woman.'

'You say she works in the restaurant at the golf club?'

'Yes, that's correct. She lives in her own apartment in Imajuku.'

Imajuku was a town situated at the base of the peninsula. The golf club was located in the middle. The detectives answered Matsuko's questions quite openly, telling her the name and address of the witness and the address of the golf club where she worked. What they did not say was whether the person she had seen was male or female or what they had been doing when she saw them.

At the same time they were talking to Matsuko, a different pair of detectives had gone to see the Tatsumi family and told them the same story.

'Although we haven't announced it to the press yet,' one of them said, 'we've found a witness. She is presently going through the photographs of all the likely suspects—we think it's only a matter of time now before the murderer is caught.'

They, too, let slip the girl's name and address but gave no details of the person she was supposed to have seen.

Koizumi's 'witness,' Naomi Kiriyama, carried on her daily routine as before, going to work at the golf club every day. She left her apartment at seven-fifteen in the morning, arriving at the clubhouse on the peninsula at seven-thirty. The restaurant opened at eight in the morning and, during the winter season, closed at six o'clock in the evening. Naomi's working hours varied somewhat, depending on the season and whether she was on the early or late shift.

The road she took to get to the clubhouse led through woods and fields, and the police followed her now at a discreet distance to make sure she wasn't attacked en route. They felt confident that she would be safe while she was in the clubhouse, but at night a watch was kept outside her apartment and a woman constable remained indoors with her.

When nothing happened for the first five days, Matsuko rang the police to find out what progress they had made now that they had a witness.

'We've started by showing her pictures of Sumire Tatsumi's friends, but Ms Kiriyama still hasn't been able to come up with the person she saw,' the chief of detectives told her. 'We're also arranging for her to see the people in person, since it's sometimes difficult to tell from a picture. We're sure we'll have some news for you soon, Mrs Torikai.'

All the while, they kept up their surveillance on Naomi Kiriyama. The apartment block where she lived was open to the elements, which made it easy to watch her door. There was a car park on the opposite side of the road, backed by thick woodland, and they were able to park their cars there without drawing any attention to themselves.

Two days later, things started to happen.

A taxi drove through the woods to the apartment house, where it stopped and a tall thin man in a raincoat got out. The taxi pulled away and the man stood looking up at the building for a moment. He didn't behave as if he were one of the residents, but Koizumi couldn't see his face from where their car was parked.

The man walked in through the entrance, apparently headed for the elevator.

He appeared again on the third floor and walked along the outside corridor until he came to Naomi's door. He paused for a minute as if to get his breath, then reached out to press the buzzer by her door. When he saw that, Koizumi slipped out of the car, leaving the other officer inside. He watched as Naomi came to the door and, after a brief conversation, invited the man in.

Koizumi hurried upstairs and along the corridor until he reached Naomi's door, then took up position outside the half open bathroom window. He couldn't see inside, but there was a woman constable inside, and if Naomi called out he should be able to hear her quite easily.

The man had been in there for a little over a quarter of an hour when Koizumi heard noises on the other side of the door that indicated he was leaving. Koizumi hurried down to the other end of the hall and stepped down into the emergency staircase, leaving the door open a fraction so he could watch what happened. He saw the man come out and turn to say something to Naomi. He only had time to notice that the man had a receding chin before he turned and walked away toward the elevator. After he had disappeared, Koizumi went out to the corridor and signaled for his colleague in the car to follow the man and see where he lived. If need be, he could arrest him en route.

That done, Koizumi went back and entered the unlocked apartment and found Naomi in the living room, talking excitedly with the woman officer. 'Who was he?' Koizumi asked her.

Naomi turned toward him, an excited look on her tanned face. 'Hiroaki Tatsumi, the father of Sumire Tatsumi—the girl Yuhei killed in the accident.'

As soon as she said it, Koizumi realized it was true. When he'd seen Sumire's father at his house, he had been in bed and Koizumi hadn't recognized him standing up.

'What did he want?'

'He brought four pictures of his wife and set them down on the table over there,' Naomi said, nodding toward the table. There was nothing there now. 'He asked if she was the person I'd seen at the scene of the murder and told me that it was his wife. He was worried that she might have killed Yuhei in revenge for their daughter and begged me to keep quiet about it if it was.'

'What?' Koizumi looked at Naomi in amazement.

'He said he'd heard that I also lost a relative to a bike gang, so I must know how he felt. Apparently he's just had an operation for stomach cancer and he said that if his wife is arrested he'll have no choice but to kill himself. He can't bear to think that his whole family could be destroyed because of that man, but he knew that the police would show me a picture of his wife sooner or later and he couldn't just sit back and wait until it happened.'

Koizumi looked over at the woman officer and she nodded in confirmation. She'd been in the next room listening to the conversation, ready to come to Naomi's help if she was needed.

'And what did you reply?'

'I didn't know what to say, I felt so sorry for him. I did say I was pretty sure it wasn't his wife I saw. I stressed that I couldn't be absolutely certain from a photo, but that I was ninety percent sure it wasn't. He looked very relieved and thanked me repeatedly on his way out.'

Koizumi sat down on the sofa dejectedly. 'I never expected this to happen.'

When he had set Naomi up as a fake witness, he'd expected the killer to try to silence her, or at least approach her in some way—as soon as that happened, they could move in. He hadn't allowed for something like this.

'There's nothing for it,' he told her. 'I'm afraid we'll have to stick with it a little longer. I'm sorry to put you to so much trouble.'

'It's okay,' she said.

'Don't let your guard down at the golf club. The killer might approach you there to test you, to see if you recognize him or not.'

'Test me?' Naomi looked at Koizumi questioningly. 'Now that you mention it, one of the guests called me to his table twice last week. No, it couldn't be him—'

'What do you mean?'

'I wear a name badge there. The first time the man called me by name as I was passing. The next time he beckoned me to his table from the other side of the room.'

'What did he want?'

'The first time he simply asked for a glass of water. The second time he wanted some toothpicks—but when I went to his table, he stared at me oddly.'

'Is he a member of the club?'

'Yes. He doesn't come by very often, but last week I saw him twice. I mentioned him to the manager and he told me he was the priest from the Futami-ga-Ura shrine. So no doubt it's meaningless.'

Koizumi didn't give Naomi's comments much thought. There was nothing to connect the priest Omuro with Yuhei's death. It wasn't until after the bank-holiday weekend on February thirteenth that he suddenly realized what the case had been all about.

That morning, one of the other detectives sat at a nearby desk reading the newspaper. 'It says here that last weekend saw the largest number of worshipers since the new year. That's why it seemed so crowded.'

'What are you talking about?'

'The Sugawara shrine. My son will be taking his university entrance exams this year, so my wife and I took him to the shrine to pray for his good luck.'

Sugawara shrine was located to the south of Fukuoka City and was famous nationwide for its dedication to the god of learning. Every year before the exam season it was packed with young people seeking help in their forthcoming tests. It even opened a branch in Tokyo for the season and made a great deal of money selling good-luck charms.

'It must be hell for the children of the priests there. If they fail *their* exams, it doesn't say much for the efficacy of the prayers or the charms they sell.'

'Yes, the priests must take it very seriously, considering the amount of money at stake.'

'It must be the same for the priests at Futami-ga-Ura,' Koizumi said. 'It would ruin the business if any of them were involved in a traffic accident.'

No sooner had he spoken than he felt his pulse quicken.

'That's true. They make a fortune out of their dedication to the god of road safety.'

'Yes. It wouldn't be so bad if it was only a minor accident.' Koizumi sat deep in thought for a while, then telephoned the Chief Investigator at the Prefectural Headquarters.

'If a person was run over by a car, then beaten severely with a blunt instrument, would you be able to tell from the autopsy?'

'It would depend on a number of factors, but to be quite honest I doubt it. When a pedestrian is hit by a car, the bumper hits them at about knee level and they are thrown up into the air. When they come down, they generally hit their head on the road and the most common cause of death is cerebral concussion. However, the wounds are identical to those that would be received if they were hit with a heavy blunt instrument. And if the body was subsequently beaten, it's unlikely we could tell the difference.'

'Could you tell if the subsequent wounds were made after death or not?'

'Not if they were made straightaway. I'm afraid you're going to have a lot of trouble proving this, you know,' the Chief Investigator added as he realized what Koizumi was hinting at.

They made discreet inquiries and managed to discover that on the night of the murder, the priest, Sadamasa Omuro, had attended a party in Fukuoka City and remained there until approximately ten o'clock. He seldom drank much and that night was no exception. He'd had one glass of beer and driven himself home in his BMW.

Further inquiries proved that four days later the same BMW had been put in for repairs at a garage in the center of town, a considerable distance from the shrine. It had a slight dent in the right-hand side of the bumper and the young priest who brought it in told the mechanic that the chief priest had hit the side of the garage as he was parking the previous night.

Once the detectives discovered this, they borrowed the car from Omuro and ran a luminol test on the trunk. Although it looked very clean, the test registered positive—which meant there were invisible traces of blood there.

They asked Omuro to accompany them to the police station.

Soon after they started questioning him, he admitted everything.

'The accident occurred a little after eleven. I turned off the main road toward the shrine and was just accelerating out of the curve when someone ran across in front of me. He must have stopped to relieve himself in the river and was returning to the opposite side of the road and didn't bother to look before he crossed.

'Of course I stopped the car and hurried back to see if he was all right. There was no blood, but he was breathing shallowly. There was no telephone at hand, so I couldn't call an ambulance. I thought it would be best if I took him to the hospital in my car.

'Until I got him to the car, my only thought was to save him. But when I laid him down on the back seat, he'd stopped breathing. I saw then that there was a wound on his head and I realized he must have hit it when I knocked him down.

'I was filled with despair when I thought about what people would say when they heard what I'd done. It would mean the end of the shrine and everything I've worked for all these years.

'That was when I realized that my victim was Yuhei Torikai, who lived near the shrine. He'd had a bad reputation since high school and I knew he had killed a girl in a traffic accident last year. His mother came to discuss her problems with me regularly and so I knew all he had done to hurt her. He'd been banned from driving after the accident, but I knew he still drove around on a bike now and again, and when I looked I saw one parked on the opposite side of the road, a helmet hanging from the handlebars.

'He was hated by the parents of the dead girl and his mother was at her wits' end as to how to deal with him. He was already dead and I thought—'

As soon as he had made his plan, Omuro didn't hesitate to put it into action. He knew there was a shed on the other side of the woods and, carrying the body there, he then proceeded to beat it repeatedly with the tools inside, telling himself that Yuhei was being punished by God. Afterward, he put the bloody body in the trunk of his car and drove it to Matsuko's house, where he laid it out and covered it with a straw mat he'd taken from the shed. He did that to make it look as if Yuhei had been killed in some kind of revenge murder. He also hoped the police would think it was the work of more than one person—which was why he'd used more than one weapon to beat him with.

When he heard that a girl from the golf club claimed to have seen the murderer, he wondered if it could be true. He couldn't bear not knowing if he had been seen or not, and so in the end he had gone to the golf course to check it out. Twice. That had proved his undoing.

He had acted instinctively, without thinking, and realized now what a terrible thing he had done. He wasn't going to hide any longer, he told the police, and was willing to face whatever punishment the law had for him.

'I've heard of people murdering someone and then trying to make it look like a traffic accident, but I've never heard of someone trying to make a traffic accident look like murder.' The chief of detectives shook his head and sipped his sake. 'The god of road safety must have been desperate that night to think up a story like that.'

'Well, at least Yuhei's mother had nothing to do with it, after all,' Koizumi said, his faith in human nature restored.

SARAH CAUDWELL (1939–)

An Acquaintance with Mr Collins

———

THE train has reached Reading, and I still have not decided whether to say anything to Selena concerning the late Mr Collins. It is hardly probable that anything can be proved; it is even possible that there is nothing to prove; and unwarranted investigation might cause undeserved distress. Murder, on the other hand, is a practice not to be encouraged.

I could almost wish that I had not, finding myself with an hour or so to spare before a dinner engagement in central London, chosen to pass it in the Corkscrew. Had I spent it in some other hostelry, I should now be returning to Oxford with a mind untroubled by any more disquieting burden than my responsibilities as Tutor in Legal History at St George's College. It is idle, however, to regret my decision. It was to the Corkscrew that I directed my steps, and indeed in the hope that I might find there one or two of my young friends in Lincoln's Inn.

I am well enough known there, it seems, for the barman to remember who I am and in whose company I am most often to be found.

'If you're looking for some of your friends, Professor Tamar,' he said as he handed me my glass of Nierstein, 'you'll find Miss Jardine right at the back there.' He gestured towards the dimly lit interior.

Selena was sitting alone at one of the little oak tables, in an attitude less carefree than one expects of a young barrister in the middle of the summer vacation: her blonde head was bent over a set of papers, which she was examining with the critical expression of a Persian cat having doubts about the freshness of its fish. Reflecting, however, that in the flickering candlelight she could not in fact be attempting to read them, and that in deliberate search of solitude she would hardly have come to the Corkscrew, I did not hesitate to join her.

Sarah Caudwell

She greeted me with every sign of pleasure, and invited me to tell her the latest news from Oxford; but I soon perceived, having accepted the invitation, that her attention was elsewhere.

'My dear Selena,' I said gently, 'the story I have been telling you about the curious personal habits of our new Dean was told to the Bursar, in the strictest confidence, only this morning, and may well not be common knowledge until the middle of next week. It seems a pity to waste it on an unappreciative audience.'

She looked apologetic.

'I'm sorry, Hilary. I'm afraid I'm still thinking of something I was dealing with this afternoon. I happened to be the only Junior left in Chambers—the others are all on holiday—and the senior partner in Pitkin and Shoon came in in rather a dither, wanting advice in confidence as a matter of urgency. I'm told he's quite a good commercial lawyer, but he candidly admits to being completely at sea over anything with a Chancery flavour. So whenever a trust or a will or anything like that comes his way, he pops into Lincoln's Inn to get the advice of Counsel. And since the sums involved are generally large enough to justify what might otherwise seem an extravagance, one wouldn't like to discourage him.'

I nodded, well understanding that a solicitor such as Mr Pitkin would be cherished by the Chancery Bar like the most golden of geese.

'He's inclined to fuss about things that don't really present any problem, so I thought I'd be able to put his mind at rest quite easily about whatever it was that was worrying him. The trouble is, I wasn't, and I can't help wondering . . . It might help to clear my mind if I could talk it over with someone. If you'd care to hear about it . . .?'

'My dear Selena,' I said, 'I should be honoured. I must remind you, however, that I am an historian rather than a lawyer—on any intricate point of law, I fear that my views will be of but little value.'

'Oh,' said Selena, 'there's nothing difficult about the law. The law's quite clear, I can advise on it in two sentences. But the sequence of events, you see, is rather unusual, and in certain circumstances might be thought slightly . . . sinister.'

The matter on which Mr Pitkin had required advice was the estate, amounting in value to something between three and four million pounds sterling, of his late client Mr Albert Barnsley. Having acted for Mr Barnsley for many years in connection with various commercial enterprises, he was familiar with the details of his background and private life. He had related these to Selena at greater length than she could at first believe necessary for the purpose of her advising on the devolution of the estate.

The late Mr Barnsley (Mr Pitkin had told her) was what is termed a self-made man. Born in Yorkshire, the son of poor but respectable parents, he had left school at the age of sixteen, and after completing his national service had obtained employment in quite a humble capacity with a local manufacturing company. By the age of forty he had risen to the position of managing director—a sign, as I supposed, that he possessed all those qualities of drive, initiative and enterprise which I am told are required for success in the world of commerce and industry.

'Yes,' said Selena, thoughtfully sipping her wine. 'Yes, I suppose he must have had those qualities. And others, perhaps, which moralists don't seem to value so highly—the ability to make himself agreeable, for example, in particular to women. His progress was not impeded, at any rate, by the fact that he had married the chairman's daughter.'

'Perhaps,' I said, 'she was anxious to be married, and he was her only suitor.'

'Far from it, apparently. According to Mr Pitkin, Isabel was a strikingly attractive woman who could have married anyone she wanted, but she set her heart on Albert Barnsley. Her father, as you might expect, was something less than delighted. But Isabel talked him round in the end, and he gave the young couple his blessing and a rather elegant house to live in. Mind you, he didn't take any more chances than he could help—he put the house in trust for Isabel and any children she might have, and when he died he left his estate on the same trusts.'

'So Barnsley did not in fact benefit from his wife's wealth?'

'Not directly, no, apart from living in the house, but that's not quite the point. I don't say that being the chairman's son-in-law would mean he could rise without merit, but it would tend to mean, don't you think, that there was less danger of his merits going unrecognized? And after her father died, of course, Isabel's trust fund included quite a substantial holding in the company, and her husband could always rely on the trustees to support his decisions. Quite apart from that, Isabel was very skilful at dealing with the other major shareholders—after all, she'd known most of them since she was a child. She was a woman of considerable charm and personality, wholeheartedly devoted to her husband's interests, and there doesn't seem to be much doubt that she contributed very significantly to his success.'

'Were there any children?'

'One daughter—Amanda, described by Mr Pitkin as something of a tomboy. The sort of girl, he says, who'd rather have a bicycle for her birthday than a new dress. Actually it sounds as if she'd probably have got both, being an object of total adoration on the part of her parents. Her father in particular was enormously proud of her. People used to ask him sometimes if he wouldn't rather have had a son, and he used to say that Amanda was a son as well as a daughter—she could do anything a boy could do, he said, and do it a damn sight better. But I'm talking of five or six years ago, when Amanda was in her mid-teens. After that things changed.'

Under Mr Barnsley's management the company had flourished, expanded and in due course been taken over by a larger company. The takeover was not one which he had any reason to resist: his personal shareholding was by now substantial, and the price offered—as well as increasing the value of the funds held in trust for his wife and daughter—was sufficient to make him, as Selena put it, seriously rich.

The terms agreed for the takeover included his appointment to a senior position in the company making the acquisition: he was an active and energetic man, still in his forties, and the prospect of retirement held no charms for him. Though his new responsibilities required his presence in London during the working week, he had no wish to sever his connections with his home town or to uproot his family. He accordingly acquired a small bachelor flat in central London and returned at weekends to the house in Yorkshire.

'That is to say,' said Selena, 'he began by doing so. But after a while the weekends in Yorkshire became less frequent, and eventually ceased altogether. You will not find it difficult, I imagine, to guess the reason.'

'I suppose,' I said, 'that he had formed an attachment to some young woman in London—what is termed, I believe, a popsie.'

'I think,' said Selena, 'that the current expression is bimbo. Though in the present case that perhaps gives a slightly misleading impression. Natalie wasn't at all the sort of girl who dresses up in mink and mascara and gets her picture in the Sunday newspapers. There wasn't anything glamorous or sophisticated about her—she was just a typist in Barnsley's office. She was from the same part of the world that he was, and it was her first job in London—I suppose in a way that gave them something in common, and perhaps made him feel protective towards her. She was young, of course—about twenty-two—and reasonably pretty, but nothing remarkable. That's Mr Pitkin's view, at any rate—he found her rather colourless, especially by comparison with Isabel.'

It occurred to me that it might have been the contrast with Isabel that Barnsley had found attractive. It was clear that his wife had given him a great deal; but if it is more blessed to give than receive, then plainly Natalie offered him ampler scope for beatitude.

'No doubt,' said Selena. 'But as you will have gathered, she wasn't the kind of girl who wanted to be given jewellery or dinners at the Savoy or anything like that. It's rather a pity really, because with a little luck and discretion Barnsley could have had that sort of affair without upsetting anyone, and they would all have lived happily ever after. But Natalie was the domesticated sort, and wanted to be married. And he couldn't give her that quite so easily.'

Because Isabel declined to divorce him. Mr Pitkin, having reluctantly and with embarrassment accepted instructions to negotiate with her on Mr Barnsley's behalf, had found her implacable. There was nothing, she said, to negotiate about: she did not want anything from her husband that he was now able to offer her; and she saw no reason to make things easy for him. If she ever found herself in a position, by raising her little finger, to save him from a painful and lingering death, she hoped (she said) that she would still have the common humanity to raise it; but to be candid, she felt some doubt on the matter. Mr Pitkin had perhaps been slightly shocked at the depth of her bitterness.

'Though it seems to me,' said Selena, 'to be quite understandable. It must be peculiarly disconcerting, don't you think, to be left for someone entirely different from oneself? Not just like going into one's bank and being told there's no money in one's account when one thought there was, but like going in and being told one's never had an account there at all. A feeling that all along one must somehow have completely misunderstood the situation.'

I asked what Amanda's attitude had been.

'Extreme hostility towards her father. It was, you may think, very natural and proper that she should take her mother's side, but I gather it went a good deal further than that. She seems to have felt a sense of personal betrayal.'

I thought that too was understandable. When a man forms an attachment to a woman young enough to be his daughter, I suppose that his daughter may feel as deeply injured as his wife; and for Amanda, as for Isabel, it must have been peculiarly wounding that he seemed to love his mistress for qualities precisely opposite to those which he had seemed to value in herself.

'At first,' continued Selena, 'she simply refused to see him or speak to him. But eventually she found that an inadequate way of expressing her feelings, and she wrote him a letter. Mr Pitkin still has a copy of it on his file, but he said rather primly that he couldn't ask a lady like myself to read it. I don't actually suppose that Amanda Barnsley at the age of seventeen knew any expressions which are unfamiliar to me after several years in Lincoln's Inn, but one wouldn't wish to shatter Mr Pitkin's illusions. It was clearly in the crudest and most offensive terms that Amanda could think of, particularly in its references to Natalie, and was evidently designed to enrage her father beyond all endurance.'

'And did it succeed?'

'Oh, admirably. Within an hour of receiving it Mr Barnsley was storming up and down the offices of Pitkin and Shoon demanding a new will, the main purpose of which was to ensure that Amanda could not in any circumstances inherit a penny of his estate. Poor Mr Pitkin tried to calm him down and persuade him not to act with undue haste, but of course it wasn't the least bit of use. So Mr Pitkin, following his usual practice, came along to Lincoln's Inn to have the will drafted by Counsel, and it was executed by Mr Barnsley three days later. The effect of it was that the whole estate would go to Natalie, provided she survived him by a period of twenty-eight days, but if she didn't then to various charities. Not, of course, because he especially wanted to benefit the charities, but to make sure that there couldn't in any circumstances be an intestacy, under which Amanda or her mother might benefit as his next-of-kin.'

'Did Amanda know that she had been disinherited?'

'Oh yes—her father straightaway wrote a letter to Isabel, telling her in detail exactly what he'd done. His letter, I regret to say, was not in conciliatory terms—it made various disagreeable comments on what he called Isabel's vindictiveness in preventing him from marrying the woman he loved and referred to Amanda as "your hell-cat of a daughter". It was written, I need hardly say, without the advice or approval of poor Mr Pitkin. Isabel didn't answer it, and there was no further communication between them for a period of some three years. Perhaps, before I go on with the story, you would care for another glass of wine?'

I wondered, while Selena made her way towards the bar, how she would justify the epithet 'unusual'. The events she had recounted, though no doubt uniquely distressing to the principals, seemed to me thus far to be all too regrettably commonplace. I recalled, however, that she had also used the word 'sinister'; and that Mr Barnsley was dead.

Returning to our table with replenished glasses, Selena resumed her story.

'In the spring of this year Mr Pitkin received a letter from Isabel. She had not written direct to her husband, she said, for fear that he might not open her letter, or if he did that he might have the embarrassment of doing so "in the presence of someone else". But there were matters which she felt they should now discuss, and she did not think that her husband would regret seeing her. She would be most grateful if Mr Pitkin would arrange a meeting.

'I have the impression that poor Mr Pitkin was rather alarmed to hear from her. Though, as I have said, he admired her personality and charm, I think that he was also rather frightened of her, and he was by no means sure that she didn't mean to make trouble of some kind.

'Mr Barnsley himself evidently shared these misgivings, and was more than half-inclined to refuse to see her. But she seemed to be hinting that she might now be prepared to agree to a divorce, and that was enough to persuade him. It would have been another two years before a divorce could take place without her consent, and Natalie was still very unhappy about what she saw as the insecurity of her position.

'He seems to have hoped at first that he would be supported by the presence of his solicitor, but Mr Pitkin very prudently said it was out of the question, since Isabel had asked for a private meeting. Besides, if her husband were accompanied by his legal adviser and she were not, it might look as if they were trying to browbeat her.

'So a week later Mr Barnsley summoned up the fortitude and resolve which had made him a captain of British industry and set forth alone and unprotected to have tea with his wife at the Ritz Hotel. He thought, Mr Pitkin tells me, that the Ritz would be the safest place to meet her—meaning, as I understand it, the least likely place for a woman such as Isabel to make a scene.'

She wanted, it seemed, to talk to him about their daughter. Amanda was now twenty, reading English at a provincial university, and specializing in the nineteenth-century novel—she had formed a great passion for the Brontës. Her academic progress was satisfactory, and she was perfectly well-behaved—almost unnaturally so, perhaps, for someone who had been such a lively and exuberant schoolgirl. Of recent months, however, she had seemed to be out of spirits, and during the Easter vacation had shown such signs of depression as to cause her mother serious concern.

Isabel had questioned her; Amanda had denied that anything was wrong; too anxious to be tactful, Isabel had persisted. Amanda had at last admitted the cause of her dejection: in spite of everything, she still found it unbearable to be estranged from her father. The admission was made with many tears, as evidencing an unforgivable disloyalty to her mother.

Isabel had been dismayed. The bitterness which she had at first felt towards her husband had faded (she said) into an amiable indifference; it had not occurred to her that her daughter's feelings towards him were more intense, and that the girl was still tormented by conflicting loyalties.

It was (said Isabel) a piece of heart-breaking nonsense: when all she minded about was making Amanda happy, she turned out to be making her miserable. If Amanda wanted to be reconciled with her father, then let them be reconciled; if the fact of his still being married to Isabel was in some way an impediment, then let there, by all means, be a divorce.

'Which meant, as I understand it,' said Selena, 'that her consent to a divorce was conditional on Barnsley making friends with Amanda again. This account of Amanda's feelings is all based, of course, on what Isabel told him—you may perhaps choose to take a more cynical view of her motives.'

I remarked that one might expect a study of the Victorian novelists to have reminded her of the practical as well as the spiritual advantages of being on good terms with any relative of substantial fortune.

'Trollope,' said Selena with evident approval, 'is always very sensible about that sort of thing—I'm not quite sure about the Brontës. But be that as it may, Mr Barnsley was quite content to accept Isabel's account of things at its face value. It wasn't only that he was pleased about the divorce—he was really very touched to think that his daughter still cared so much about him. After all, it was a long time since the offensive letter, and until she was seventeen he'd idolized her. He told Mr Pitkin to put in hand the arrangements for the divorce, and wrote in affectionate terms to Amanda to arrange a meeting.'

'Was it,' I asked, 'a successful reunion?'

'Evidently, since shortly afterwards he mentioned to Mr Pitkin that once the business of the divorce was dealt with he would have to do something about changing his will.'

'Did he indicate what he had in mind?'

'He still wanted to leave the bulk of his estate to Natalie, but to give a sufficient share to Amanda to show his affection for her—about a fifth was what he had in mind. Well, with both parties consenting and no arguments about property or children, the divorce went through pretty quickly, and he made arrangements to marry Natalie as soon as the decree was made absolute.

'Mr Pitkin admits to having felt a certain apprehensiveness about the occasion. It was going to be a very quiet wedding in a registry office, with a small reception afterwards, but it was also going to be the first time that Amanda and Natalie had met each other, and he felt Mr Barnsley's view that they would get on like a house on fire might be a little over-optimistic. He remembered Amanda's letter, and he didn't quite trust her not to do something outrageous to show her disapproval. He also had the impression that Natalie was becoming a trifle jealous of Barnsley's renewed affection for his daughter, and might have some difficulty in concealing it.

'But as it turned out his misgivings were quite unfounded. Amanda wore a suitably pretty and feminine dress and was charming to everyone. She and Natalie shook hands, and Natalie said she hoped they would be great friends, and Amanda said she hoped so too, and then they had what Mr Pitkin calls a very nice little conversation about how Amanda was getting on with her studies. So that by the time Mr Barnsley and his bride left to go on their honeymoon, which they planned to spend driving round the Lake District, Mr Pitkin feels able to assure me that everyone was getting on splendidly.

'The only slight embarrassment was the fault of Mr Barnsley himself—he judged it a suitable moment to remind Mr Pitkin, in the hearing of both Natalie and Amanda, that he wanted a new will drawn up. It wasn't, in the circumstances, an entirely tactful remark. But no one else took any particular notice, and Mr Pitkin simply assured him that a draft would be ready for his approval on his return to London.

'As it would have been, no doubt, if Mr Barnsley had ever returned from his honeymoon.'

She fell silent, while at the tables round us there continued the cheerful clinking of glasses and the noise of eager gossip about rumours of scandal in the City. I thought of Mr Barnsley setting forth with his unsophisticated young bride, and reflected that those who lack glamour are not necessarily without avarice.

I asked how it had happened.

'There was an accident with the car. Barnsley and Natalie were both killed instantly.'

'Both?' It was not the contingency that I had envisaged.

'Oh yes,' said Selena, 'both. Something was wrong with the steering, apparently. Well, things sometimes do go wrong with cars, of course. But it was quite a new car, and supposed to have been thoroughly tested, so the local police were just a little puzzled about it. Enough so, at any rate, to ask Mr Pitkin, very discreetly, who would benefit under Mr Barnsley's will. But he gave them a copy of the will made three years before, and when they saw that the beneficiaries, in the events which had occurred, were a dozen highly respectable national charities, they didn't pursue the matter. There are limits to what even the most aggressive fund-raisers will do to secure a charitable bequest.'

She paused and sipped her wine, regarding me over her glass with an expression of pellucid innocence. I have known her too long, however, to be deceived by it, and I had detected in her voice a certain sardonic quality: I concluded that I was overlooking some point of critical importance. After a moment's thought I realized what it was, for the rule in question is one of respectable antiquity.

'Surely,' I said, 'unless there has been any recent legislation on the matter of which I am unaware, the effect of Mr Barnsley's marriage —?'

'Quite so,' said Selena. 'As you very rightly say, Hilary, and as Mr Pitkin discovered for the first time this morning, when he instructed his Probate assistant to deal with the formalities of proving the will, the effect of the marriage was to revoke it. I'm afraid a great many people get married without fully understanding the legal consequences, and in particular without realizing that when they say "I do" they are revoking any will they may previously have made. But there is no doubt, of course, that that is the position under English law. So Mr Barnsley died intestate.'

'I fear,' I said, 'that I have a somewhat hazy recollection of the modern intestacy rules. Does that mean that his estate will pass to Natalie's next-of-kin? There is a presumption, I seem to remember, where two persons die together in an accident, that the younger survived the older?'

'That's the general rule, but actually it doesn't apply on an intestacy if the people concerned are husband and wife. In those circumstances neither estate takes any benefit from the other. But even if Natalie had survived her husband by a short period, her next-of-kin would take relatively little—the widow's statutory legacy, which is a trifling sum by comparison with the value of the estate, and half the income arising from the estate during the period of survival.'

'In that case,' I said, finding myself curiously reluctant to reach this conclusion, 'I suppose that the whole estate goes to his daughter?'

'Who, if her father had died before his marriage, would have taken nothing, and if he had lived to make another will would have taken a comparatively small share of it. Yes. She is, as Mr Pitkin was careful to tell me, entirely ignorant of legal matters and will be even more astonished than he was to learn that that is the case. So naturally he didn't want to give her such momentous news until he'd had it confirmed by Chancery Counsel, and that, he said, was why he'd come to see me. But the question that was really troubling him, you see, was one he couldn't bring himself to ask, and which it would have been outside my competence to answer. That is to say, ought he to mention to the police how very advantageously things have turned out from the point of view of Miss Amanda Barnsley?'

It now for the first time occurred to me that I possessed an item of knowledge of possible relevance to the events she had described. Uncertain whether or not I should mention it, and having had no time to weigh the consequences of doing so, I remained silent.

Selena leant back in her chair and gave a sigh, as if telling the story had eased her mind.

'Well,' she said, 'it's lucky that Amanda's reading a nice harmless subject like English literature. If she'd happened to be reading law it might all look rather sinister. But non-lawyers don't usually know that a will is revoked by marriage, and I wouldn't think, would you, that it's the sort of information she'd be likely to come across by accident?'

The hour of my engagement being at hand, I was able to take my leave of her without making any direct answer. During dinner I put the matter from my mind, thinking that during the journey back to Oxford I would be able to reach a decision. But the train has passed Didcot, and I remain undecided.

It seems extraordinary and slightly absurd that I should find myself in such a quandary on account of an item of knowledge which is not, after all, in any way private or peculiar to myself. Indeed, if the work of the late Mr Wilkie Collins were held in the esteem it deserves, the plot of his admirable novel *No Name*, in which the revocation by marriage of her father's will deprives the heroine of her inheritance, would no doubt be known to everyone having any pretension to being properly educated. As it is, however, I suppose that relatively few people have any acquaintance with it—unless they are studying English literature, and specializing in the nineteenth-century novel.

SUE GRAFTON (1940–)

A Little Missionary Work

———

SOMETIMES you have to take on a job that constitutes pure missionary work. You accept an assignment not for pay, or for any hope of tangible reward, but simply to help another human being in distress. My name is Kinsey Millhone. I'm a licensed private eye—in business for myself—so I can't really afford professional charity, but now and then somebody gets into trouble and I just can't turn my back.

I was standing in line one Friday at the bank, waiting to make a deposit. It was almost lunchtime and there were eleven people in front of me, so I had some time to kill. As usual, in the teller's line, I was thinking about Harry Hovey, my bank robber friend, who'd once been arrested for holding up this very branch. I'd met him when I was investigating a bad cheque case. He was introduced to me by another crook as an unofficial 'expert' and ended up giving me a crash course in the methods and practices of passing bad paper. Poor Harry. I couldn't remember how many times he'd been in the can. He was skilled enough for a life of crime, but given to self-sabotage. Harry was always trying to go straight, always trying to clean up his act, but honest employment never seemed to have much appeal. He'd get out of prison, find a job, and be doing pretty well for himself. Then something would come along and he'd succumb to temptation . . . forge a cheque, rob a bank, God only knows what. Harry was hooked on crime the way some people are addicted to cocaine, alcohol, chocolate and unrequited love. He was currently doing time in the Federal Correctional Institution in Lompoc, California, with all the other racketeers, bank robbers, counterfeiters, and former White House staff bad boys . . .

I had reached the teller's window and was finishing my transaction when Lucy Alisal, the assistant bank manager approached. 'Miss

Millhone? I wonder if you could step this way. Mr Chamberlain would like a word with you.'

'Who?'

'The branch vice-president,' she said. 'It shouldn't take long.'

'Oh. Sure.'

I followed the woman toward Mr Chamberlain's glass-walled enclosure, wondering the whole time what I'd done to deserve this. Well, OK. Let's be honest. I'd been thinking about switching my account to First Interstate for the free chequing privileges, but I didn't see how he could have found out about *that*. As for my balances, I'd only been overdrawn by the teensiest amount and what's a line of credit for?

I was introduced to Jack Chamberlain, who turned out to be someone I recognised from the gym, a tall, lanky fellow in his early forties, whose work-outs overlapped mine three mornings a week. We'd exchange occasional small talk if we happened to be doing reps on adjacent machines. It was odd to see him here in a conservative business suit after months of sweat-darkened shorts and T-shirts. His hair was cropped close, the colour a dirty mixture of copper and silver. He wore steel-rimmed glasses and his teeth were endearingly crooked in front. Somehow, he looked more like a high school basketball coach than a banking exec. A trophy sitting on his desk attested to his athletic achievements, but the engraving was small and I couldn't quite make out the print from where I was. He caught my look and a smile creased his face. 'Varsity basketball. We were state champs,' he said, as he shook my hand formally and invited me to take a seat.

He sat down himself and picked up a fountain pen, which he capped and recapped as he talked. 'I appreciate your time. I know you do your banking on Fridays and I took the liberty,' he said. 'Someone told me at the gym that you're a private investigator.'

'That's right. Are you in the market for one?'

'This is for an old friend of mine. My former high school sweetheart, if you want the truth,' he said. 'I probably could have called you at your office, but the circumstances are unusual and this seemed more discreet. Are you free tonight by any chance?'

'Tonight? That depends,' I said. 'What's going on?'

'I'd rather have her explain it. This is probably going to seem paranoid, but she insists on secrecy, which is why she didn't want to make contact herself. She has reason to believe her phone is tapped. I hope you can bear with us. Believe me, I don't ordinarily do business this way.'

'Glad to hear that,' I said. 'Can you be a bit more specific? So far, I haven't really heard what I'm being asked to do.'

Jack set the pen aside. 'She'll explain the situation as soon as it seems wise. She and her husband are having a big party tonight and she asked me to bring you. They don't want you appearing in any professional capacity. Time is of the essence, or we might go about this some other way. You'll understand when you meet her.'

I studied him briefly, trying to figure out what was going on. If this was a dating ploy, it was the weirdest one I'd ever heard. 'Are you married?'

He smiled slightly. 'Divorced. I understand you are, too. I assure you, this is not a hustle.'

'What kind of party?'

'Oh, yes. Glad you reminded me.' He removed an envelope from his top drawer and pushed it across the desk. 'Cocktails. Five to seven. Black tie, I'm afraid. This cheque should cover your expenses in the way of formal dress. If you try the rental shop around the corner, Roberta Linderman will see that you're outfitted properly. She knows these people well.'

'What people? You haven't even told me their names.'

'Karen Waterston and Kevin McCall. They have a little weekend retreat up here.'

'Ah,' I said, nodding. This was beginning to make more sense. Karen Waterston and Kevin McCall were actors, who'd just experienced a resurgence in their careers, starring in a new television series called '*Shamus, PI*,' an hour-long spoof of every detective series that's ever aired. I don't watch much TV, but I'd heard about the show and after seeing it once, I'd found myself hooked. The stories were fresh, the writing was superb, and the format was perfect for their considerable acting talents. Possibly because they were married in 'real' life, the two brought a wicked chemistry to the screen. As with many new shows, the ratings hadn't yet caught up with the rave reviews, but things looked promising. Whatever their problem, I could understand the desire to keep their difficulties hidden from public scrutiny.

Jack was saying, 'You're in no way obligated, but I hope you'll say yes. She really needs your help.'

'Well. I guess I've had stranger requests in my day. I better give you my address.'

He held up the signature card I'd completed when I opened my account. 'I have that.'

I soon learned what 'cocktails-five-to-seven' means to the very rich. Everybody showed up at seven and stayed until they were dead drunk. Jack Chamberlain, in a tux, picked me up at my apartment at six forty-five. I was decked out in a slinky beaded black dress with long sleeves, a high collar and no back; not my usual apparel of choice. When Jack helped me into the front seat of his Mercedes, I shrieked at the shock of cold leather against my bare skin.

Once at the party, I regained my composure and managed to conduct myself (for the most part) without embarrassment or disgrace. The 'little weekend retreat' turned out to be a sprawling six-bedroomed estate, decorated with a confident blend of the avant-garde and the minimalist: unadorned white walls, wide, bare, gleaming expanses of polished hardwood floor. The few pieces of furniture were draped with white canvas, like those in a palatial summer residence being closed up for the season. Aside from a dazzling crystal chandelier, all the dining-room contained was a plant, a mirror, and a bentwood chair covered with an antique paisley shawl. *Très chic.* They'd probably paid thousands for some interior designer to come in and haul all the knick-knacks away.

As the party picked up momentum, the noise level rose, people spilling out on to all the terraces. Six young men, in black pants and pleated white shirts, circulated with silver platters of tasty hot and cold morsels. The champagne was exquisite, the supply apparently endless so that I was fairly giddy by the time Jack took me by the arm and eased me out of the living-room. 'Karen wants to see you upstairs,' he murmured.

'Great,' I said. I'd hardly laid eyes on her except as a glittering wraith along the party's perimeters. I hadn't seen Kevin at all, but I'd over-heard someone say he was off scouting locations for the show coming up. Jack and I drifted up the spiral stairs together, me hoping that in my half-inebriated state, I wouldn't pitch over the railing and land with a splat. As I reached the landing, I looked down and was startled to see my friend Vera in the foyer below. She caught sight of me and did a double-take, apparently surprised to see me in such elegant surround-ings, especially dressed to the teeth. We exchanged a quick wave.

The nearly darkened master suite was carpeted to a hush, but again, it was nearly empty. The room was probably fifty feet by thirty, furnished dead-centre with a king-sized bed, a wicker hamper, two ficus trees, and a silver lamp with a twenty-five-watt bulb on a long, curving neck.

As Jack ushered me into the master bathroom where the meeting was to take place, he flicked me an apologetic look. 'I hope this doesn't seem too odd.'

'Not at all,' I said, politely . . . like a lot of my business meetings take place in the WC.

Candles flickered from every surface. Sound was dampened by thick white carpeting and a profusion of plants. Karen Waterston sat on the middle riser of three wide, beige, marble steps leading up to the Jacuzzi. Beside her, chocolate-brown bath towels were rolled and stacked like a cord of firewood. She was wearing a halter-style dress of white chiffon, which emphasised the dark, even tan of her slender shoulders and arms. Her hair was silver-blonde, coiled around her head in a twist of satin ropes. She was probably forty-two, but her face had been cosmetically backdated to the age of twenty-five, a process that would require ever more surgical ingenuity was the years went by. Jack introduced us and we shook hands. Hers were ice cold and I could have sworn she wasn't happy to have me there.

Jack pulled out a wicker stool and sat down with his back to Karen's make-up table, his eyes never leaving her face. My guess was that being an ex-high-school sweetheart of hers was as much a part of his identity as being a former basketball champ. I leant a hip against the marble counter. There was a silver-framed photograph of Kevin McCall propped up beside me, the mirror reflecting endless reproductions of his perfect profile. To all appearances, he'd been allowed to retain the face he was born with, but the uniform darkness of his hair, with its picturesque dusting of silver at the temples, suggested that nature was being tampered with, at least superficially. Still, it was hard to imagine that either he or Karen had a problem more pressing than an occasional loose dental cap.

'I appreciate your coming, Miss Millhone. It means a lot to us under the circumstances.' Her voice was throaty and low, with the merest hint of tremolo. Even by candlelight, I could see the tension in her face. 'I wasn't in favour of bringing anyone else into this, but Jack insisted. Has he explained the situation?' She glanced from me to Jack, who said, 'I told her you preferred to do that yourself.'

She seemed to hug herself for warmth and her mouth suddenly looked pinched. Tears welled in her eyes and she placed two fingers on the bridge of her nose as if to quell their flow. 'You'll have to forgive me . . .'

I didn't think she'd be able to continue, but she managed to collect herself.

'Kevin's been kidnapped . . .' Her voice cracked with emotion and she lifted her dark eyes to mine. I'd never seen such a depth of pain and suffering.

At first, I didn't even know what to say to her. 'When was this?'

'Last night. We're very private people. We've never let anyone get remotely close to us . . .' She broke off again.

'Take your time,' I said.

Jack moved over to the stair and sat down beside her, putting an arm protectively around her shoulders. The smile she offered him was wan and she couldn't sustain it.

He handed her his handkerchief and I waited while she blew her nose and dabbed at her eyes. 'Sorry. I'm just so frightened. This is horrible.'

'I hope you've called the police,' I said.

'She doesn't want to take the risk,' Jack said.

Karen shook her head. 'They said they'd kill him if I called in the police.'

'Who said?'

'The bastards who snatched him. I was given this note. Here. You can see for yourself. It's too much like the Bender case to take any chances.' She extracted a piece of paper from the folds of her long dress and held it out to me.

I took the note by one corner so I wouldn't smudge any prints, probably a useless precaution. If this was truly like the Bender case, there wouldn't be any prints to smudge. The paper was plain, the printing in ballpoint pen and done with a ruler.

Five hundred thou in small bills buys your husband back. Go to the cops or the feds and he's dead meat for sure. We'll call soon with instructions. Keep your mouth shut or you'll regret it. That's a promise, baby cakes.

She was right. Both the format and the use of language bore an uncanny similarity to the note delivered to a woman named Corey Bender, whose husband had been kidnapped about a year ago. Dan Bender was the CEO of a local manufacturing company, a man who'd made millions with a line of auto parts called Fender-Benders. In that situation, the kidnappers had asked for $500,000 in tens and twenties. Mrs Bender had contacted both the police and the FBI, who had stage-managed the whole transaction, arranging for a suitcase full of blank paper to be dropped according to the kidnappers' elaborate telephone instructions. The drop site had been staked out, everyone assuring Mrs Bender that nothing could possibly go wrong. The drop went as planned except the suitcase was never picked up and Dan Bender was never seen alive again. His body—or what was left of it— washed up on the Santa Teresa beach two months later.

'Tell me what happened,' I said.

She got up and began to pace, describing in halting detail the circumstances of Kevin McCall's abduction. The couple had been working on a four-day shooting schedule at the studio down in Hollywood. They'd been picked up from the set by limousine at 7 p.m. on Thursday and had been driven straight to Santa Teresa, arriving for the long weekend at nine o'clock that night. The housekeeper usually fixed supper for them and left it in the oven, departing shortly before they were due home. At the end of a week of shooting, the couple preferred all the solitude they could get.

Nothing seemed amiss when they arrived at the house. Both interior and exterior lights were on as usual. Karen emerged from the limo with Kevin right behind her. She chatted briefly with the driver and then waved goodbye while Kevin unlocked the front door and disarmed the alarm system. The limo driver had already turned out of the gate when two men in ski masks stepped from the shadows armed with automatics. Neither Karen nor Kevin had much opportunity to react. A second limousine pulled into the driveway and Kevin was hustled into the back seat at gunpoint. Not a word was said. The note was thrust into Karen's hand as the gunmen left. She raced after the limo as it sped away, but no licence plates were visible. She had no real hope of catching up and no clear idea what she meant to do anyway. In a panic, she returned to the house and locked herself in. Once the shock wore off, she called Jack Chamberlain, their local banker, a former high school classmate— the only person in Santa Teresa she felt she could trust. Her first thought was to cancel tonight's party altogether, but Jack suggested she proceed.

'I thought it would look more natural,' he filled in. 'Especially if she's being watched.'

'They did call with instructions?' I asked.

Again she nodded, her face pale. 'They want the money by midnight tomorrow or that's the last I'll see of him.'

'Can you *raise* 500,000 on such short notice?'

'Not without help,' she said and turned a pleading look to Jack.

He was already shaking his head and I gathered this was a subject they'd already discussed at length. 'The bank doesn't keep large reservoirs of cash on hand,' he said to me. 'There's no way I'd have access to a sum like that, particularly on a weekend. The best I can do is bleed the cash from all the branch ATMs . . .'

'Surely you can do better than that,' she said. 'You're a bank vice-president.'

He turned to her, with a faintly defensive air, trying to persuade her the failing wasn't his. 'I might be able to put together the full amount by Monday, but even then, you'd have to fill out an application and go through the loan committee . . .'

She said, 'Oh for God's sake, Jack. Don't give me that bureaucratic bullshit when Kevin's life is at stake! There has to be a way.'

'Karen, be reasonable . . .'

'Forget it. This is hopeless. I'm sorry I ever brought you into this . . .'

I watched them bicker for a moment and then broke in. 'All right, wait a minute. Hold on. Let's back off the money question, for the time being.'

'Back *off*?' she said.

'Look. Let's assume there's a way to get the ransom money. Now what?'

Her brow was furrowed and she seemed to have trouble concentrating on the question at hand. 'I'm sorry. What?'

'Fill me in on the rest of it. I need to know what happened last night after you got in touch with Jack.'

'Oh. I see, yes. He came over to the house and we sat here for hours, waiting for the phone to ring. The kidnappers . . . one of them . . . finally called at 2 a.m.'

'You didn't recognise the voice?'

'Not at all.'

'Did the guy seem to know Jack was with you?'

'He didn't mention it, but he swore they were watching the house and he said the phone was tapped.'

'I wouldn't bet on it, but it's probably smart to proceed as though it's true. It's possible they didn't have the house staked out last night, but they may have put a man on it since. Hard to know. Did they tell you how to deliver the cash once you got it?'

'That part was simple. I'm to pack the money in a big canvas duffel. At eleven-thirty tomorrow night, they want me to leave the house on my bicycle with the duffel in the basket.'

'On a bike? That's a new one.'

'Kev and I often bike together on weekends, which they seemed aware of. As a matter of fact, they seemed to know quite a lot. It was very creepy.'

Jack spoke up. 'They must have cased the place to begin with. They knew the whole routine, from what she's told me.'

'Stands to reason,' I remarked. And then to her, 'Go on.'

'They told me to wear my yellow jumpsuit—I guess so they can identify me—and that's all there was.'

'They didn't tell you which way to ride?'

'I asked about that and they told me I could head in any direction I wanted. They said they'd follow at a distance and intercept me when it suited them. Obviously, they want to make sure I'm unaccompanied.'

'Then what?'

'When they blink the car lights, I'm to toss the canvas duffel to the side of the road and ride on. They'll release Kevin as soon as the money's been picked up and counted.'

'Shoot. It rules out any fudging if they count the money first. Did they let you talk to Kevin?'

'Briefly. He sounded fine. Worried about me . . .'

'And you're sure it was him?'

'Positive. I'm so scared . . .'

The whole time we'd been talking, my mind was racing ahead. She had to call the cops. There was no doubt in my mind she was a fool to tackle this without the experts, but she was dead set against it. I said, 'Karen, you can't handle something like this without the cops. You'd be crazy to try to manage on your own.'

She was adamant.

Jack and I took turns arguing the point and I could see his frustration surface. 'For God's sake, you've got to listen to us. You're way out of your element. If these guys are the same ones who kidnapped Dan Bender, you're putting Kevin's life at risk. They're absolutely ruthless.'

'Jack, I'm not the one putting Kevin's life at risk. *You* are. That's exactly what you're doing when you propose calling the police.'

'How are you going to get the money?' he said, exasperated.

'Goddamn it, how do I know? You're the banker. You tell me.'

'Karen, I'm telling you. There's no way to do this. You're making a big mistake.'

'Corey Bender was the one who made a mistake,' she snapped.

We were getting nowhere. Time was short and the pressures were mounting every minute. If Jack and I didn't come up with *some* plan, Kevin McCall was going to end up dead. If the cash could be assembled, the obvious move was to have me take Karen's place during the actual delivery, which would at least eliminate the possibility of her being picked up as well. Oddly enough, I thought I had an inkling how to get the bucks, though it might well take me the better part of the next day.

'All right,' I said, breaking in for the umpteenth time. 'We can argue this all night and it's not going to get us any place. Suppose I find a way to get the money, will you at least consent to my taking your place for the drop?'

She studied me for a moment. 'That's awfully risky, isn't it? What if they realise the substitution?'

'How could they? They'll be following in a car. In the dark and at a distance, I can easily pass for you. A wig and a jumpsuit and who'd know the difference?'

She hesitated. 'I do have a wig, but why not just do what they say? I don't like the idea of disobeying their instructions.'

'Because these guys are way too dangerous for you to deal with yourself. Suppose you deliver the money as specified. What's to prevent them picking you up and making Kevin pay additional ransom for *your* return?'

I could see her debate the point. Her uneasiness was obvious, but she finally agreed. 'I don't understand what you intend to do about the ransom. If Jack can't manage to get the money, how can you?'

'I know a guy who has access to a large sum of cash. I can't promise anything, but I can always ask.'

Karen's gaze came to rest on my face with puzzlement.

'Look,' I said in response to her unspoken question. 'I'll explain if I get it. And if not, you have to promise me you'll call the police.'

Jack prodded. 'It's your only chance.'

She was silent for a moment and then spoke slowly. 'All right. Maybe so. We'll do it your way. What other choice do I have?'

Before we left, we made arrangements for her to leave a wig, the yellow jumpsuit and the bicycle on the service porch the next night. I'd return to the house on foot some time after dark, leaving my car parked a few discreet blocks away. At eleven-thirty, as instructed, I'd pedal down the drive with the canvas duffel and ride around until the kidnappers caught up with me. While I was gone, Jack could swing by and pick Karen up in his car. I wanted her off the premises in the event anything went wrong. If I were snatched and the kidnappers realised they had the wrong person, at least they couldn't storm back to the house and get her. We went over the details until we were all in accord. In the end, she seemed satisfied with the plan and so did Jack. I was the only one with any lingering doubts. I thought she was a fool, but I kept that to myself.

I hit the road the next morning early and headed north on 101. Visiting hours at the Federal Correctional Institution at Lompoc run from eight to four on Saturdays. The drive took about an hour with a brief stop at a supermarket in Buellton where I picked up an assortment of picnic supplies. By ten, I was seated at one of the four sheltered picnic tables with my friend, Harry Hovey. If Harry was surprised to see me, he didn't complain. 'It's not like my social calendar's all that full,' he said. 'To what do I owe the pleasure?'

'Let's eat first,' I said. 'Then I got something I need to talk to you about.'

I'd brought cold chicken and potato salad, assorted cheeses, fruit and cookies, anything I could grab that didn't look like institutional fare. Personally, I wasn't hungry, but it was gratifying to watch Harry chow down with such enthusiasm. He was not looking well. He was a man in his fifties, maybe five-foot five, heavy-set, with thinning grey hair and glasses cloudy with fingerprints. He didn't take good care of himself under the best of circumstances, and the stress of prison living had aged him ten years. His colour was bad. He was smoking way too much. He'd lost weight in a manner that looked neither healthful nor flattering.

'How're you doing?' I asked. 'You look tired.'

'I'm OK, I guess. I been better in my day, but what the hell,' he said. He'd paused in the middle of his meal for a cigarette. He seemed distracted, his attention flicking from the other tables to the playground equipment where a noisy batch of kids were twirling round and round on the swings. It was November and the sun was shining, but the air was chilly and the grass was dead.

'How much time you have to serve yet?'

'Sixteen months,' he said. 'You ever been in the can?'

I shook my head.

He pointed at me with his cigarette. 'Word of advice. Never admit nothin'. Always claim you're innocent. I learned that from the politicians. You ever watch those guys? They get caught takin' bribes and they assume this injured air. Like it's all a mistake, but the truth will out. They're confident they'll be vindicated and bullshit like that. They welcome the investigation so their names can be cleared. They always say that, you know? Whole time I'm in prison, I been saying that myself. I was framed. It's all a set-up. I don't know nothing about the money. I was just doing a favour for an old friend, a big wig. A Very Big Wig. Like I'm implying the Governor or the Chief of Police.'

'Has it done you any good?'

'Well, not yet, but who knows? My lawyer's still trying to find a basis for appeal. If I get outta this one, I'm going into therapy, get my head straight, I swear to God. Speaking of which, I may get "born again", you know? It looks good. Lends a little credibility, which is something all the money in the world can't buy . . .'

I took a deep breath. 'Actually, it's the money I need to talk to you about.' I took a few minutes to fill him in on the kidnapping without mentioning any names. Some of Karen Waterston's paranoia had filtered into my psyche and I thought the less I said about the 'victim', the better off he'd be. 'I know you've got a big cache of money somewhere. I'm hoping you'll contribute some of it to pay the ransom demands.'

His look was blank with disbelief. 'Ransom?'

'Harry, don't put me through this. You know what ransom is.'

'Yeah, it's money you give to guys you never see again. Why not throw it out of the window? Why not blow it at the track . . .'

'Are you finished yet?'

He smiled and a dimple formed. 'How much you talking about?'

'Five hundred thousand.'

His eyebrows went up. 'What makes you think I got money like that?'

'Harry,' I said patiently, 'an informant told the cops you had over a million bucks. That's how you got caught.'

Harry slapped the table. 'Bobby Urquhart. That fuck. I should have known it was him. I run into the guy in a bar settin' at this table full of bums. He buys a round of tequila shooters. Next thing I know, everybody else is gone. I'm drunk as a skunk and flappin' my mouth.' He dropped his cigarette butt on the concrete and crushed it underfoot.

'Word of warning. Never confide in a guy wearing Brut. I must have been nuts to give that little faggot the time of day. The money's gone. I blew it. I got nothin' left.'

'I don't believe you. That's bullshit. You didn't have time to blow that much. When you were busted, all you had were a few lousy bucks. Where's the rest of it?'

'Un-uhn. No way.'

'Come on, Harry. It isn't going to do you any good in here. Why not help these people out? They got tons of money. They can pay you back.'

'They got money, how come they don't pay the shit themselves?'

'Because it's Saturday and the banks are closed. The branch VP couldn't even come up with the cash that fast. A man's life is at stake.'

'Hey, so's mine and so what? You ever try life in the pen? I worked hard for that money so why should I do for some guy I never seen before?'

'Once in a while you just gotta help people out.'

'Maybe you do. I don't.'

'Harry, please. Be a prince . . .'

I could see him begin to waver. Who can resist a good deed now and then?

He put his hand on his chest. 'This is giving me angina pains . . .' He wagged his head back and forth. 'Jesus. What if the cops get wind of it? How's it gonna look?'

'The cops are never going to know. Believe me, this woman's never going to breathe a word of it. If she trusted the cops, she'd have called them in the first place.'

'Who are these people? At least tell me that. I'm not giving up half a million bucks without some ID.'

I thought about it swiftly. I was reluctant to trade on their celebrity status. On the other hand, she was desperate and there wasn't time to spare. 'Swear you won't tell.'

'Who'm I gonna tell? I'm a con. Nobody believes me anyway,' he said.

'Kevin McCall and Karen Waterston.'

He seemed startled at first. 'You're kidding me. No shit? You're talking, *Shamus, PI*? Them two?'

'That's right.'

'Whyn't you say so? That's my favourite show. All the guys watch that. What a gas. Karen Waterston is a fox.'

'Then you'll help?'

'For that chick, of course,' he said. He gave me a stern look. 'Get me her autograph or the deal's off.'

'Trust me. You'll have it. You're a doll. I owe you one.'

We took a walk around the yard while he told me where the money was. Harry had nearly two million in cash hidden in a canvas duffel of his own, concealed in the false back of a big upholstered sofa, which was locked up, with a lot of other furniture, in a commercial self-storage facility.

I headed back to Santa Teresa with the key in my hand. Unearthing the money took the balance of the afternoon. The couch was at the bottom of an eight-by-eight foot storage locker crammed with goods. Tables, chairs, cardboard boxes, a desk, a hundred or more items which I removed one by one, stacking them behind me in the narrow aisle between bins. The facility was hot and airless and I could hardly ask for help. By the time I laid my hands on the canvas tote hidden in the couch, there was hardly room in the passageway to turn around. By six o'clock, feeling harried, I had taken all but half a million out of Harry's tote. The rest of the stash I stuffed back into the couch, piling furniture and boxes helter-skelter on top of it. I'd have to return at some point—when the whole ordeal was over—and pack the bin properly . . .

The drop played out according to the numbers, without the slightest hitch. At ten that night, I eased through a gap in the hedge on the north side of the Waterston/McCall property and made my way to the house with Harry's canvas bag in tow. I slipped into the darkened service entry where Karen was waiting. Once the door shut behind me, I shoved Harry's canvas tote into the large duffel she provided. We chatted nervously while I changed into the wig and yellow jump-suit. It was just then ten-thirty and the remaining wait was long and tense. By eleven-thirty, both of us were strung out on pure adrenalin and I was glad to be on the move.

Before I took off on the bicycle, Karen gave me a quick hug. 'You're wonderful. I can't believe you did this.'

'I'm not as wonderful as all that,' I said, uncomfortably. 'We need to talk the minute Kevin's home safe. Be sure to call me.'

'Of course. Absolutely. We'll call you first thing.'

I pedalled down the drive and took a right on West Glen. The cash-heavy duffel threw the bike out of balance, but I corrected and rode on. It was chilly at that hour and traffic was almost non-existent. For two miles, almost randomly, I bicycled through the dark, cursing my own foolishness for thinking I could pull it off. Eventually, I became aware that a sedan had fallen in behind me. In the glare of the headlights, I couldn't tell the make or the model; only that the licence plate was missing. The sedan followed me for what felt like an hour, while I pedalled on, feeling anxious, winded, and frightened beyond belief. Finally, the headlights blinked twice. Front wheel wobbling, I hauled the duffel from the basket and tossed it out on to the shoulder of the road. It landed with a thump near a cluster of bushes and I pedalled away. I glanced back only once as the vehicle behind me slowed to a stop.

I returned to the big house, left the bicycle in the service porch and made my way back across the blackness of the rear lawn to my car. My heart was still thudding as I pulled away. Home again, in my apartment, I changed into a nightie and robe, and huddled on the couch with a cup of brandy-laced hot tea. I knew I should try to sleep, but I was too wired to bother. I glanced at my watch. It was nearly 2 a.m. I figured I probably wouldn't get a word from Karen for another hour at best. It takes time to count half a million dollars in small bills. I flipped on the TV and watched a mind-numbing rerun of an old black-and-white film.

I waited through the night, but the phone didn't ring. Around five, I must have dozed because the next thing I knew, it was eight thirty-five. What was going on? The kidnappers had had ample time to effect Kevin's release. *If* he's getting out alive, I thought. I stared at the phone, afraid to call Karen in case the line was still tapped. I pulled out the phone book, looked up Jack Chamberlain, and tried his home number. The phone rang five times and his machine picked up. I left a cryptic message and then tried Karen at the house. No answer there. I was stumped. Mixed with my uneasiness was a touch of irritation. Even if they'd heard nothing, they could have let me know.

Without much hope of success, I called the bank and asked for Jack. Surprisingly, Lucy Alisal put me through.

'Jack Chamberlain,' he said.

'Jack? This is Kinsey. Have you heard from Karen Waterston?'

'Of course. Haven't you?'

'Not a word,' I said. 'Is Kevin OK?'

'He's fine. Everything's terrific.'

'Would you kindly tell me what's going on?'

'Well, sure. I can tell you as much as I know. I drove her back over
to the house about two this morning and we waited it out. Kevin got
home at six. He's shaken up, as you might imagine, but otherwise he's
in good shape. I talked to both of them again a little while ago. She
said she was going to call you as soon as we hung up. She didn't get
in touch?'

'Jack, that's what I just said. I've been sitting here for hours without a word from anyone. I tried the house and got no answer . . .'

'Hey, relax. Don't worry. I can see where you'd be ticked, but everything's fine. I know they were going back to Los Angeles. She might
just have forgotten.'

I could hear a little warning. Something was off here. 'What about
the kidnappers? Does Kevin have any way to identify them?'

'That's what I asked. He says, not a chance. He was tied up and
blindfolded while they had him in the car. He says they drove into a
garage and kept him there until the ransom money was picked up
and brought back. Next thing he knew, someone got in the car,
backed out of the garage, drove him around for a while, and finally
set him out in his own driveway. He's going to see a doctor once they
get to Los Angeles, but they never really laid a hand on him.'

'I can't believe they didn't call to let me know he was safe. I need
to talk to her.' I knew I was being repetitive, but I was really bugged.
I'd promised Harry her autograph, among other things, and while
he'd pretended to make a joke of it, I knew he was serious.

'Maybe they thought I'd be doing that. I know they were both very
grateful for your help. Maybe she's planning to drop you a note.'

'Well, I guess I'll just wait until I hear from them,' I said and hung up.

I showered and got dressed, sucked down some coffee and drove
over to my office in downtown Santa Teresa. My irritation was beginning to wear off and exhaustion was trickling into my body in its
wake. I went through my mail, paid a bill, tidied up my desk. I found
myself laying my little head down, catching a quick nap while I
drooled on my Month-At-A-Glance. There was a knock on the door
and I woke with a start.

Vera Lipton, the claims manager for the insurance company next
door, was standing on my threshold. 'You must have had a better time
than I did Friday night. You hung-over or still drunk?' she said.

'Neither. I got a lousy night's sleep.'

She lifted her right brow. 'Sounds like fun. You and that guy from
the bank?'

'Not exactly.'

'So what'd you think of the glitzy twosome . . . Karen and Kev.'

'I don't even want to talk about them,' I said. I then proceeded to pour out the whole harrowing tale, including a big dose of outrage at the way I'd been treated.

Vera started smirking about halfway through. By the end of my recital, she was shaking her head.

'What's the matter?' I asked.

'Well, that's the biggest bunch of horsepuckey I ever heard. You've been taken, Kinsey. Most royally had.'

'*I* have?'

'They're flat broke. They don't have a dime . . .'

'They do, too!'

She shook her head emphatically. 'Dead broke. They're busted.'

'They couldn't be,' I said.

'Yes, they are,' she said. 'I bet you dollars to donuts they put the whole scam together to pick up some cash.'

'How could they be broke with a house like that? They have a hot new series on the air!'

'The show was cancelled. It hasn't hit the papers yet, but the network decided to yank 'em after six episodes. They sank everything they had into the house up here when they first heard they'd been picked up . . .'

I squinted at her. 'How do you know all this stuff?'

'Neil and I have been looking for a house for months. Our real estate agent's the one who sold 'em that place.'

'They don't have *any* money?' I asked.

'Not a dime,' she said. 'Why do you think the house is so empty? They had to sell the furniture to make the mortgage payment this month.'

'But what about the party? That must have cost a mint!'

'I'm sure it did. Their attorney advised them to max out their credit cards and then file for bankruptcy.'

'Are you sure?'

'Sure I'm sure.'

I looked at Vera blankly, doing an instant replay of events. I knew she was right because it suddenly made perfect sense. Karen Waterston and Kevin McCall had run a scam, that's all it was. No wonder the drop had gone without a hitch. I wasn't being followed by kidnappers . . . it was him. Those two had just successfully pocketed half a million bucks. And what was I going to do? At this point, even if I called the cops, all they had to do was maintain the kidnapping fiction and swear the bad guys were for real. They'd be very convincing. That's what acting is all about. The 'kidnappers', meanwhile, would have disappeared without a trace and they'd make out like bandits, quite literally.

Vera watched me process the revelation. 'You don't seem all that upset. I thought you'd be apoplectic, jumping up and down. Don't you feel like an ass?'

'I don't know yet. Maybe not.'

She moved towards the door. 'I gotta get back to work. Let me know when it hits. It's always entertaining to watch you blow your stack.'

I sat down at my desk and thought about the situation and then put a call through to Harry Hovey at the prison.

'This is rare,' Harry said when he'd heard me out. 'I think we got a winner with this one. Holy shit.'

'I thought you'd see the possibilities,' I said.

'Holy shit!' he said again.

The rest of what I now refer to as my missionary work I can only guess at until I see Harry again. According to the newspapers, Kevin McCall and Karen Waterston were arrested two days after they returned to Los Angeles. Allegedly (as they say) the two entered a bank and tried to open an account with $9,000 in counterfeit tens and twenties. Amazingly, Harry Hovey saw God and had a crisis of conscience shortly before this in his prison cell up in Lompoc. Recanting his claims of innocence, he felt compelled to confess . . . he'd been working for the two celebrities for years, he said. In return for immunity, he told the feds where to find the counterfeit plates, hidden in the bottom of a canvas tote, which turned up in their possession just as he said it would.

VINCENT BANVILLE (1940–)

Body Count

BLAINE got the call at 2.10. In the a.m. He was in the middle of a dream. Bearing down on the Kilkenny goal with the ball on his hurley stick. Wexford in arrears by two points and the match well into extra time. He side-stepped one last opponent and prepared to strike. The goal would win it for them, and his would be the glory. He gritted his teeth, but by this time the phone was practically jumping off the bedside table.

He gave in, propped himself up, reached across his oblivious wife, Annie, and fumbled the receiver off its moorings.

'Yes?'

'Blaine?'

'Wrong number. No Blaine here.'

'Come on, I know it's you. I need help.'

The voice was familiar, high-pitched and slightly querulous even in its supplicatory tone.

'I'll have you for this, Leo,' Blaine muttered. 'There better be a good reason for waking me at this hour.'

'There is. I need your help in getting rid of a body.'

'A body? A dead body?'

'What other kind is there?'

'Well, at this time of the morning and seeing that it's you . . .'

'It was dumped on me. Now it's just lying there.'

'Couldn't you have it stuffed? Maybe have it exhibited . . .'

'No wisecracks. You owe me.'

Blaine held the phone away from his ear and did some facial kinetic exercises. It was true what Leo had said, he did owe him. Leo was a medical student who had never graduated, but he still carried on a practice and was said to be better than any doctor. On a number of occasions he had ministered to Blaine's many aches and pains, the result of over-zealous poking into other people's affairs in his chosen profession of private investigator. In particular, Leo was a wizard with cuts, and he had restructured Blaine's nose after its encounter with a low-life who had seen 'Chinatown' and imagined himself as Polanski the villain.

Sighing, Blaine put the phone back to his ear and said, 'Okay, I'll be there in twenty minutes. Just give me time to brush my teeth, say goodbye to my wife and daughter, grab a sausage sandwich . . .'

'Ten minutes top. I'm getting the jitters.'

Remembering Leo's penchant for imbibing the rubbing alcohol, Blaine said hurriedly, 'No drinking, Leo. I don't want you in a comatose state. One body at a time is more than enough.'

He replaced the receiver, got out of bed and stood looking down at Annie. She was lying on her back, her mouth open. It amazed him that she could sleep through all that racket. He tip-toed over to the corner of the room and gazed into the cot. His year-old daughter, Emily, was lying as an exact replica of her mother, mouth agape, nostrils fluttering with soft snores. Blaine's input into her conception seemed minimal, to say the least.

He got into some clothes, went downstairs and out the front door. It was May, the sky was clear, and the old Renault, wonder of wonders, started on the first turn of the ignition. He drove out onto the Cabra Road, then down to the North Circular. To his right, the sky over the city was tinged with a red glow. He wondered if, like the song said, he might see a Spanish Lady. In modern-day Dublin? More likely to have a brick thrown through his windscreen.

The streets were deserted and he made good time. In the North Strand the houses wore blind eyes, and were dark and shuttered. Leo owned a three-storey tenement that leaned drunkenly to one side. The upper floors were rented by a Madame named Lil, who sub-let the rooms to working girls who spent most of the time on the flat of their backs. When the forces of law and order called, Leo presented Lil as his secretary and the girls as his patients. Seemingly this dubious arrangement worked, for Blaine had never seen the house shut down.

He parked the car, then went down the stone steps to the basement flat. He was raising his hand to knock when the door was abruptly opened and a beady eye examined him suspiciously.

'Garbage disposal calling for one body . . .' Blaine began, but he was interrupted when a hand reached out, caught him by the front of the jacket and pulled him inside. The door clicked shut behind him.

'Leo . . .'

'In here.'

In here meant Leo's surgery, a surprisingly spick and span room containing an examination table, some glass-fronted cabinets, and a strong smell of antiseptic. The naked body of a fortyish white male lay on the table, his hands discreetly cupping his private parts. His eyes were open, making him look slightly disconcerted, if not to say startled.

'I know him,' Blaine said. 'Isn't he . . .?'

'Yes, Willie "The Kid" Hanton. Fixer for Micky "The Mouse" Lynch. May he rest in peace.'

'He'd better. If he wakes up he'll do us both in.'

They stood looking down at the late fixer. In death, as in life, he was a fine specimen. In contrast, Leo was thin to the point of emaciation, an exclamation mark against the whiteness of the room. His face sagged, his clothes sagged, his whole demeanour cried out for propping up. Blaine took pity on him, opened one of the cabinets, grabbed a glass-stoppered bottle of 100% proof alcohol and handed it to him. The relief on Leo's face was like the late blooming of a winter rose.

He took a deep draught of the contents of the bottle, blanched, staggered, regained his balance, then sucked down another dose of the fiery liquor. A little colour started below his chin, then bled up into the lugubriousness of his features.

'Should we try some of that on Willie?' Blaine suggested. 'If anything'd raise the dead, that should.'

Leo drew in breath like a death rattle, then managed to croak, 'He's been shot.'

'I can see that,' Blaine said, gazing at the blue-black hole in Hanton's chest. 'Heavy calibre.'

'A bank raid,' Leo supplied. 'They went in all tooled up, but the Special Branch were tipped off. Willie came off worst, now I've got to dispose of the remains.'

Blaine gnawed on a fingernail, then he said, 'Was he dead when they left him in?'

'Not quite, but he wasn't telling jokes either.'

'How many were here?'

'Three that I saw. The two dead-beats who carried him in. And Micky Lynch.'

Blaine whistled softly.

'Micky himself was in on it? Must be strapped for cash. He usually plans the job, then sits back and waits for the dividends to flow in. I know a certain police Superintendent who'd like to catch Micky with his hand in the till.'

'Be that as it may,' Leo said, 'the problem still is that I've got to get Willie to a place where he'll look as inconspicuous as a loaf of bread on a shelf.'

'And where might that be, pray?'

'Well,' Leo said, looking devious, 'a loaf of bread would be inconspicuous among other loaves of bread. So . . .'

'The morgue,' Blaine said, tumbling to Leo's stratagem. 'You've made an arrangement with that weirdo friend of yours, the attendant. What's his name . . .?'

'Sugar Ally Hayes. He's making out the papers as we speak. Unknown man 47. Willie'll be in, out and cremated before you can say, "How's your father?"'

'So what d'you need me for?'

'To get him over there, of course. You know I don't drive.'

Blaine sucked in his breath, played with the idea of taking a slug from the medicine bottle, then thought better of it. The sooner they got this over with the better.

'I hope rigor mortis hasn't set in,' he said. 'Otherwise he won't fit in the boot.'

'I thought we'd put him sitting up in the passenger seat,' Leo said drily. 'He'd look more natural that way.'

'Or in the back, your arm draped around him and both of you singing bawdy songs.'

Leo closed Hanton's eyes with a brush of his hand, then he began wrapping him in the white sheet on which he had been lying. Blaine stood and watched, hoping that this was the dream and that the hurling match had been the real thing. The packaging was practically finished when they were both suddenly immobilised into shock by the beep, beep, beeping of a mobile phone. They stared at one another, Leo with his hand on Hanton's naked rump, Blaine like one of Cortez's men staring at the Pacific Ocean.

'The duffel bag,' Leo finally managed. 'Willie's duffel bag. Under the table.'

Blaine bent down, found the bag, unzipped it and took out the mobile phone. It buzzed in his hand like an angry bee. He gazed at Leo, Leo gazed back. Only Hanton remained unperturbed.

They waited, both of them hoping the thing would click off. It didn't. In the end, Blaine pressed the green button and put the phone to his ear.

'Willie had a high-pitched voice,' Leo hissed urgently. He nodded encouragingly. 'Tell them everything's fine.'

Pinching his nostrils between two fingers, Blaine squeaked 'Hello' into the phone.

'Willie?' a voice enquired.

'Yiss.'

'I thought you were done for. How're you managing?'

'How d'you think I'm managing, with a slug up me transom?'

'Will you be able to make the safe house?'

'Huh?'

'The safe house. The heat is on.'

'I'll make it. Where is it?'

'What d'you mean, where is it? Have you lost your marbles?'

'All I know is the Boss said we'd have to go into the wind when this job was over. He never said where.'

'Hold on.'

Blaine stood and listened to his heart beat, while a muttered colloquy beat distantly in his ear. He was depending on the basic stupidity of the common-or-garden low-life to win him some valuable information.

He was about to doze off when a more authoritative voice said, 'What's this about you suffering from amnesia, you dickhead? I told you where the safe house was.'

Taking a chance, Blaine said, 'Is that you, Micky?'

'Who the fuck d'you think it is? The Wicked Witch of the West?'

'Aw, boss, don't be like that. I'm badly injured. Just tell me where you are and I'll be there in a jiffy.'

'In a wha'?'

'I'm feelin' faint. Dark clouds are pressin' in. I might pass out.'

'Someone could be listenin' in. You can't trust these mobile phones.'

'Whisper it, boss. You know you'll feel better if I'm by your side.'

There was a pause, then a reluctant Micky passed on the address of a house in the Liberties. The phone clicked off and Blaine took it away from his ear to an audible plop.

'So?' Leo said.

'He told me to go eat my shorts,' Blaine said. 'No flies on friend Micky.'

Leo finished off his wrapping of Willie, with the result that he looked like Boris Karloff in one of the old Mummy movies.

'D'you think he'd pass for a roll of carpet?'

'Sure he would. Except for the foot sticking out of the end.'

Leo tucked in the offending appendage, then they hoisted up the bundle and made for the door. Blaine opened it cautiously and stuck his head out. The street appeared deserted, the stars low in the sky, and no moon shining. They quickly-marched across to the car and upended their burden into the boot. Willie made no demur, so they presumed all was well with him.

They drove to the morgue in De Valera Terrace in seven minutes flat. It was an imposing cut-stone building, with arched windows and wide double doors.

'Drive around the back,' Leo said in a stage whisper. 'Sugar Ally'll be waiting for us.'

'He'd better be.'

Blaine did as instructed, the car barely making it down the narrow lane. Leo was able to get out, but Blaine's bulk prevented him from squeezing through the narrow opening between the car and the wall of the building. He had to reverse back out into the street.

He sat, drumming his fingers on the steering wheel and wishing, like W. C. Fields on his deathbed, that he was in Philadelphia. After what seemed like an eternity, Leo and his pal Sugar Ally appeared, wheeling a trolley that gave out a distinct squeak. They opened the boot and loaded the well-wrapped Willie onto the mobile stretcher.

'Can I go now?' Blaine asked plaintively. 'Dawn is coming and I've got to be back in my coffin.'

'How am I going to get back?' Leo asked plaintively.

'Sugar Ally'll run you round in the hearse.'

'It's in the garage for a service.'

Resignedly Blaine got out, locked the car and followed the other two as they wheeled their grisly cargo into the building. He had been there before a number of times, but he still found it difficult to prevent a shiver as he went through the main autopsy room. Those steel tables with the channels and sluices, the sinister imagined echoes, the knives and saws laid out so neatly. It was almost a relief to pass on into the storage chamber, with the rows of numbered compartments set into the walls.

'Jesus, it's cold in here,' Blaine complained, wrapping his arms around his body.

'Has to be,' Sugar Ally told him cheerfully. 'Otherwise the lads and lassies'd go off something terrible. Some of 'em stay with me for weeks on end.'

'All right for you, you're well wrapped up.'

Sugar Ally was wearing rubber boots, a rubber apron and a long white coat. On his head was perched a tea cosy hat and over his ears woollen mufflers. His face was long and sallow, and he had an over-bite that made him look as if he had chewed off his chin. An unprepossessing specimen, but one well suited to the job he did and the place he inhabited.

He now made his way over to one of the chambers in the wall and pulled out a long tray. It too gave out an audible squeak. Leo and he slid the wrapped Willie onto this, then Sugar Ally released the same recalcitrant foot that had been sticking out before and tied a label onto the big toe. He then pushed the whole caboodle back into the wall.

'Well, that's that,' Blaine said. He worked his shoulders and flapped his arms. 'Let's get out of here, Leo.'

'Now, now, me dears,' Sugar Ally interjected. 'You can't go without partaking of a little cheer. Something to keep the cold out of your bones.'

Blaine looked at a hopeful Leo and thought that maybe a jolt of firewater might not be a bad idea at that. He was in for a disappointment, however, after following Sugar Ally into his living quarters.

'What's this?' he asked, as he was handed a chipped mug filled to the brim with a liquid that looked distinctly like urine.

'Elderberry wine,' Sugar Ally told him proudly. 'Made by the wife. I drink two quarts of it a day and I'm as healthy as a puma in the jungles of Peru.'

'I didn't know there were jungles in Peru,' Leo said conversationally. He too had been given a mug of the home-made wine, but showed no qualms as he put it to his head and knocked it back.

'Nor pumas, either,' Blaine said.

'No matter,' Sugar Ally assured them. 'Drink up, boys, and have another. I've gallons of the stuff.'

Blaine took a sip, then hurriedly placed the mug back on the chipped formica table. Not alone did the liquid look like urine, it also tasted like it. 'Where's your phone?' he asked Sugar Ally. 'I need to make a call.'

'Who to?' a suspicious Leo asked him.

'The daily papers, of course. To tell them I've just left a shot-to-death man down in the morgue. Don't you think the publicity'd be good for my image?'

'I just wondered.'

'For your information, I'm phoning my wife. She gets up about now to feed the baby and may well wonder about my absence. I merely wish to put her mind at ease by telling her I'm down in the city morgue drinking elderberry wine and swapping morbid tales with you two ghouls.'

'Begod, I could tell you a tale or two, all right,' Sugar Ally agreed. 'There was the time Dr Pat was about to use the circular saw on a cadaver when the bloody man sat up and took notice . . .'

'The phone?'

'Out in the hall.'

Blaine left them, found the phone, put in some change and dialled the private residence of Superintendent George Quinlan of the Dublin Special Branch. After two rings the receiver was picked up and a voice said, 'Yes, what is it?'

'I've always suspected you were a robot, George,' Blaine said. 'That's why you never need sleep.'

'Who is this?'

'A little bird, with some information.'

'I know that voice. It's Blaine, isn't it? Why're you ringing me in the middle of the night?'

'If you shut up and listen, I'll tell you. You'd like to catch Micky "The Mouse" Lynch with his trousers down, wouldn't you? Well, if you hurry around to the address I'm about to give you, you'll find him holed up with the proceeds of the bank he robbed yesterday. Plus his associates, and maybe even the weapons used.'

'How d'you know this?'

'Let's just say the news dropped into my lap like manna from heaven. D'you want the address or not?'

'Of course I do.'

Blaine supplied the relevant information, told George he'd be hearing from him, and rang off. He leaned against the wall and thought about the good deed he had just done. And also about the favour that Quinlan now owed him. Which, of course, he would call in in due course.

Back in the room he had just left, he found Sugar Ally and Leo settling in for the long haul.

'I'm off,' Blaine announced. 'Time and tide wait on no man.'

Leo, already more than halfway into his cups, beamed at him and waved his mug in the air. 'I shall stay here and keep my friend company for a little while longer,' he said grandly. 'In the meantime, I would like to thank you for the aid you rendered me in my hour of need. We must do it again sometime.'

'Will we, fuck,' Blaine said.

He left them, went around the back, down the lane and out into the street. Dawn was just about to break over Dublin town, a rosy sun pushing its way up through the clouds in the eastern sky. Blaine started his car and drove into its brilliance, the satisfaction of a job well done, like its warmth, permeating his bones.

RUTH DUDLEY EDWARDS (1944–)

Father Brown in Muncie, Indiana

———

'CAN it be Father Brown?'

The little black-clad figure sitting in the hotel foyer nodded.

'My God,' said the Magna Cum Murder fan. 'What are you doing here?'

'I don't quite know,' said Father Brown. 'It is a mystery or a miracle. Two very different ideas, but they are of course in their spiritual essence and simplicity essentially the same.'

'I can see you haven't changed,' said the fan. 'I never did understand what you were driving at.'

'That is because the truth so often makes little sense.'

'Yes, yes,' said the fan hastily. 'But metaphysics apart, is there a rational reason for you being in Muncie?'

'Metaphysics and reason are supremely rational.'

The fan was beginning to shift restlessly, when a whirlwind arrived, scooped the little priest into her arms and cried, 'Kathryn Kennison, Father, I just knew you wouldn't let me down.'

The fan nodded. 'Now I understand. I have heard of this from other guests. You find yourself in Muncie without having any real idea why you're here except that Kathryn Kennison seduced you over the phone.'

'Perhaps seduction is a concept which . . .' began Father Brown, as Kathryn Kennison replaced him tenderly in his chair and bounded away to embrace another arrival.

'. . . is inappropriate when applied to a priest,' said the fan.

'Alas, my son, that is not the case. Are priests gods that they cannot be seduced?'

'Yes, but I had thought such talk distasteful to a priest of your generation. You knew nothing of sexual scandals of the kind that grip the ecclesiastical world these days.'

The little head shook. 'You never understood, did you? Spending so much of my life in the confessional box, I knew all the sins of the world. Who better than a priest knows the secrets of human soul?'

'So you're not shockable?'

'No. I am not. That delightful young woman understood that, which is why she asked me to come here to solve the Bobbit case.'

The fan clutched his head. 'The Bobbit case?' he asked wildly. 'The John Wayne Bobbit case? What is there to solve about the Bobbit case?'

'Everything in the world and nothing in the world,' said Father Brown simply, as he picked up his umbrella and glided away towards the lift. 'But the good God may help me to reveal the truth at lunchtime on Saturday.'

'So what happened?' asked the fan's wife when he rang her on Saturday evening to report. 'What did he say?'

'That Lorena didn't do it.'

'Who did?'

'He did.'

'Father Brown did it?'

'No, silly. Bobbit did it.'

The fan's wife's incredulity rendered her momentarily incapable of speech. 'Why would he cut off his own . . .?'

'Because he wanted to be rich and famous.'

'So why didn't he admit he'd done it?'

'Because he would have got a bad press. It isn't something with which one should collude.'

The fan paused to consult his notes. 'Remember Deuteronomy? "He that is wounded in the stones, or hath his privy member cut off, shall not enter into the congregation of the Lord." Even in this secular age, Father Brown points out, men think emasculation renders them outcasts. Therefore they can't admit to outcasting themselves, as it were.'

The fan's wife, who had little patience with her husband's hobby, raised her voice. 'You've bought this crazy idea, you schmuck? Why did Lorena admit to it, then? Not to speak of driving wildly round the country with the missing part.'

'She thought she'd done it, you see. Apparently, she's very very absent-minded, she'd had a few drinks and when Bobbit shouted "Look what you did. Call the hospital," she panicked and made off with the evidence.'

'I cannot believe,' said his wife grimly, 'that even you, whose brains are addled with mystery stories, should have been taken in like this by a man of 140 in a dog-collar.'

'It must be true,' said the fan simply. 'Fictional detectives are always right.'

The fan's wife spoke very slowly and through gritted teeth. 'You mean that because Father Brown doesn't really exist, his explanation is correct?'

'Exactly,' said the fan. 'That's metaphysics.'

SARA PARETSKY (1947–)

Dealer's Choice

―――――

1942

SHE was waiting in the outer office when I came in, sitting with a stillness that made you think she'd been planted there for a decade or two and could make it to the twenty-first century if she had to. She didn't move when I came in except to flick a glance at me under the veil of the little red hat that had built a nest in her shiny black hair. She was all in red; she'd taken the May's company's advertisers to heart and was wearing victory red. But I doubted if she'd ever seen the inside of May's. This was the kind of shantung number that some sales clerk acting like the undertaker for George V pulled from a back room and whispered to madam that it might suit if madam would condescend to try it on. The shoes and gloves and bag were black.

'Mr Marlowe?' Her voice was soft and husky with a hint of a lisp behind it.

I acknowledged the fact.

She got to her feet. Perched on top of her boxy four-inch heels she just about cleared my armpit.

'I've been hoping to see you, Mr Marlowe. Hoping to interest you in taking a case for me. If you have the time, that is.'

She made it sound as though her problem, whatever it was, was just a bit on the dull side, and that if I didn't have time for it the two of us could forget it and move on to something more interesting. I grunted and unlocked the inner door. The muffled tapping on the rug behind me let me know she was following me in.

The April sunshine was picking up the dust motes dancing on the edge of my desk. I dumped the morning paper on to the blotter and reached into my desk drawer for my pipe. My visitor settled herself in the other chair with the same composure she'd shown in the outer office. Whatever little problem she had didn't make her twitch or catch her heels in her rosy silk stockings.

While I was busy with my pipe she leaned forward in her chair, looking at the paper; something on the front page had caught her eye. Maybe the Red Army bashing the Krauts along the Caspian, or the US carving a few inches out of Milne Bay. Or Ichuro Kimura eluding the US Army right here at home, or maybe the lady whose twin daughters were celebrating their first birthday without ever having seen their daddy. He was interned by the Japs in Chungking.

When she caught me watching her she settled back in her chair. 'Do you think the war will end soon, Mr Marlowe?'

'Sure,' I said, tamping the tobacco in. 'Out of the trenches by Christmas.' We'd missed Easter by a day already.

The girl nodded slightly to herself, as if I'd confirmed her opinion of the war. Or maybe me. The bright sunlight let me see her eyes now, despite the little veil. The irises were large and dark, looking black against the clear whites. She was watching me calmly enough but those eyes gave her away—they could light up the whole Trojan backfield if she wanted to use them that way. But something in her manner and that hint of a lisp made me think they didn't play much football where she came from.

'I need some help with a man,' she finally said.

'You look as though you do just fine without help.' I struck a match against the side of the desk.

She ignored me. 'He's holding some of my brother's markers.'

'Your brother lose them in fair play?'

She gave me a shrug that moved like a whisper through the shantung. 'I wouldn't know, Mr Marlowe. All I know is that my brother staked a—an item that didn't belong to him. My brother has gone into hiding, since he knows he can't pay up and he's afraid they'll break his legs, or whatever it is they do when you can't pay your gambling losses.'

'Then I don't see you have a problem. All you have to do is keep supplying your brother with food and water and everyone will be happy. Your gambler will go after easier prey by and by. What's his name?'

I thought I saw a faint blush, but it was such a phantom wave of color I couldn't be sure. It made me think she knew where her brother was all right.

'Dominick Bognavich. And if it were just my brother I wouldn't mind, not so much I mean, since he was gambling and he has to take his chances. But they're threatening my mother. And that's where I need your help. I thought perhaps you could explain to Mr Bognavich—get him to see that—he should leave my brother alone.'

I busied myself with my pipe again. 'Your brother shouldn't bet with Bognavich unless he can stake the San Joaquin Valley. I believe that's all Dominick doesn't own at this point. What did your brother put up?'

She watched me consideringly. I knew that look. It was the kind I used when I wondered if a chinook would accept my bait.

'A ring,' she finally said. 'An old diamond and sapphire ring that had been in Mother's family for a hundred years. My brother knows he'll get it when she's dead, and she could die tomorrow—I don't know—she's very ill and in a nursing home. So he anticipated events.'

Anticipated events. I like that. It showed a certain thoughtfulness with the language and the people. 'And what about your brother? I mean, does he have a name, or do we do this whole thing incognito?'

She studied me again. 'No, I can see you need his name. It's—uh—Richard.'

'Is that his first or his last name? And do you have the same last name or should I call you something else?'

'You can call me Miss Felstein. Naomi Felstein. And that would be Richard's last name, too.'

'And your mother is Mrs Felstein, and your father is Mr Felstein.'

'Was.' She gave a tight little smile, the first I'd seen and not any real sample of what she could do if she were in the mood. 'He's been dead for some years now.'

'And what is it you want me to do for you, Miss Felstein? Shoot Dominick Bognavich? He's got a lot of backups and I might run out of bullets before he ran out of people to send after me.'

One black-gloved finger traced a circle on the arm of the chair. 'Maybe you could see Mr Bognavich and explain to him. About my brother not owning the ring, I mean. Or—or maybe you could talk my brother into coming out of hiding. He won't listen to me.'

Sure I could talk to Bognavich. He and I were good pals, sure we were, and my words carried a lot of weight with him, about as much as maggots listening to protests from a dead body. I didn't like it, any of it. I didn't believe her story and I didn't believe in her brother. I was pretty sure she didn't have a brother, or if she did Bognavich had never heard of him. But it was the day after Easter and I'd been too savvy to let myself get suckered by the Easter bunny, so I owed the rubes one.

I gave her my usual rate, twenty-five dollars a day and expenses, and told her I'd need some up-front money. She opened the little black bag without a word and lifted ten twenties from a stash in the zipper compartment with the ease of a dealer sliding off queens to send you over the top in twenty-one.

She gave another ghostly smile. 'I'll wait for you here. In case you have no success with Mr Bognavich and want me to take you to my brother.'

'I'll call you, Miss Felstein.'

That seemed to confuse her a little. 'I may—I don't—'

'I'd rather you didn't wait in my office. I'll call you.'

Reluctantly she wrote a number on a piece of paper and handed it to me. Her script was bold and dark, the writing of a risk taker. Oh, yeah, her brother lost some big ones to Dominick Bognavich all right.

A guy like Bognavich doesn't start his rounds until the regular working stiffs are heading home for a drink. If I was lucky I'd make it to his place before he went to bed for the day. But when I'd wound my way up Laurel Canyon to Ventura, where Bognavich had a modest mansion on a cul-de-sac, I found he'd become the kind of guy who doesn't make rounds any time of day.

He was slumped against the door leading from the garage to the house. He looked as though he'd felt tired getting out of the car and decided to sit down for a minute to catch his breath but had fallen asleep instead. It was just that he had taken the kind of nap where six small-caliber bullets give you a permanent hangover.

I felt his face and wrists. He'd been dead for a while; if I had a look around without calling the cops it wasn't going to halt the wheels of justice any. The door behind him was unlocked, an invitation for fools to go dancing in and chase the angels out. I listened for a while but didn't hear anything, not even Dominick's blood congealing on the floor.

The kitchen was a white-tiled affair that looked like the morgue after a good scrubdown. I gave it a quick once-over, but Bognavich wasn't the kind of guy who hid his secrets in the granulated sugar. I passed on through to the main part of the house.

The gambler had employed a hell of a housekeeper. She'd left sofa cushions torn apart with their stuffing spread all over the pale gold on the living-room floor. White tufts clung to my trouser legs like cottontails. Marlowe the Easter bunny hunting for eggs the other kids hadn't been able to find.

Bognavich's study was where he'd kept his papers. He'd been a gambler, not a reader, and most of the books dealt with the finer points of cards and horses. They lay every which way, their backs breaking, loose pages lying nearby like pups trying to get close enough to suckle their dam.

I did the best I could with the papers and the ledger. There were IOUs for the asking if I'd been inclined to go hustling for bread, but nothing that looked like a Felstein. I didn't feel like lingering for a detailed search. Whoever had put those six holes into Dominick might be happy for the cops to find an unwelcome peeper fingering the gambler's papers. I gave the rest of the house a quick tour, admired Bognavich's taste in silk pajamas, and slid back through the kitchen.

He was still sitting where I'd left him. He seemed to sigh as I passed. I patted him on the shoulder and went back to the Chrysler. Miss Felstein could have put six rounds into Bognavich without wrinkling her silk dress, let alone her smooth little forehead. It was the kind of shooting a dame might do—six bullets where one or two would do the job. Wasteful, with a war on.

I pulled the pint from the glove compartment and swallowed a mouthful just on principle, a farewell salute to Dominick. He hadn't been a bad guy, he just had a lousy job.

I half expected to find Miss Naomi Felstein, if that was who she was, not just what I could call her, planted in my waiting room like a well-kept jacaranda. I expected her because I wanted her to be there. I wanted to see if I could shake a little fire into those cool dark eyes and get her to tell me why she'd come to me after finding Dominick's dead body lying in front of his kitchen door this morning.

She wasn't there, though. I wondered if she ever had been there, if perhaps she was just an Easter vision, in red the way these visions always appear, leaving the faintest whiff of Chanel behind to undercut the tobacco fumes. I had a drink from the office bottle and the Chanel disappeared.

I didn't have much hope for the number the mirage had left, and my hope began to dwindle after fifteen rings. But I didn't have anything else to do so I sat at my desk with the phone in my ear looking at the front page of the paper, trying again to figure out which of the stories had caught my phantom's attention.

I finished the details of Errol Flynn's cruelty to his wife and why she had to get his entire estate as a settlement and started on why the army thought Ichuro Kimura was an enemy spy. I'd gotten to the part where he'd thrown empty sake bottles at the soldiers who came to arrest him for not reporting for deportation at Union Station last Wednesday when I realized someone was talking to me.

It was a querulous old man who repeated that he was the Boylston Ranch and who was I calling. Without much interest I asked for Miss Felstein.

'No one here by that name. No women here at all.' His tone demanded congratulations for having rid Eden of all temptresses.

'Five feet tall, lots of glossy black hair, dark eyes that could bring a guy back from the grave if she wanted them to.'

He hung up on me. Just like that. I stuck the bottle of rye neatly in the middle of the drawer and stared at nothing for a while. Then I got up and locked the office behind me. Oh, yes, Marlowe's a very methodical guy. Very orderly. He always tidies up his whisky bottle when he's been drinking and locks up behind himself. You can tell he came from a good home.

The army had a roadblock set up just outside Lebec. I guess they were trying to make sure no one was smuggling empty sake bottles in for Ichuro Kimura. They made me get out of my car while they looked under the seats and in the trunk. Then they checked my ID and made me tell them I was looking for a runaway girl and that I had a hot tip she was hiding out on the Boylston place. That made them about as happy as a housewife seeing her cat drag a dead bird into the kitchen. They started putting me through my paces until the sergeant who was running the block came over and told them to let me through. He was bored: he wanted to be killing Japs at Milne Bay instead of looking for old men in Lebec.

The sun had had all it could take of Kern County by the time I got to the turnoff for the Boylston Ranch. It was easing itself down behind the Sierra Madres, striking lightning bolts from the dashboard that made it hard for me to see. I was craning my neck forward, shielding my eyes with my left hand, when I realized I was about to go nose to nose with a pickup.

I pulled over to the side to let the truck go by, but it stopped and a lean, dusty man jumped down. He had on a cowboy hat and leather leggings, in case the gearshift chafed his legs, and his face was young and angry, with a jutting upper lip trying to dominate the uncertain jaw beneath it.

'Private property here, mister. You got any reason to be here?'

'Yup,' I said.

'Then let's have it.'

I got out of the Chrysler to be on eye level with him, just in case being alone with the cows all day made him punch happy.

'You got any special reason for asking, son? Other than just nosiness, I mean?'

His fists clenched reflexively and he took half a step nearer. 'I'm Jay Boylston. That good enough for you?'

'You own this spread?'

'My old man does, but I'm in charge of the range. So spill it, and make it fast. Time is money here and I don't have much to waste of either.'

'An original sentiment. Maybe you could get it engraved on your tombstone. If your old man owns the place I'd better talk to him. It's kind of a delicate matter. Involves a lady's reputation, you might say.'

At that he did try to swing at me. I grabbed his arm. It was a bit tougher than his face but not much.

'What's going on here?'

The newcomer had ridden up behind us on horseback. The horse stopped in its tracks at a short command and the rider jumped down. He was an older, stockier edition of Jay. His face held the kind of arrogance men acquire when they own a big piece of land and think it means they own all the people around them as well.

'Man's trespassing and he's giving kind of smart answers when I ask him to explain himself,' Jay said sullenly.

'Mr Boylston?' I asked. The older man nodded fractionally, too calm to give anything to a stranger, even the movement of his head.

'Philip Marlowe. I'm a private detective from Los Angeles and I'm up here on a case.'

'A case involving my ranch is something I would know about,' Boylston said. His manner was genial but his eyes were cold.

'I didn't say it involved your ranch. Except as a hiding place for a runaway. Big place, lots of places to hide. Am I right?'

'The army's been all through here in the last week looking for a runaway Jap,' Boylston said. 'I don't think there's too much those boys missed. You're a long way from LA if you hope to sleep in your own bed tonight.'

'This is a recent case,' I said doggedly, Marlowe the intrepid, fighting on where others would have turned tail and run. 'This is a woman who only recently disappeared. And she's attractive enough that someone might be persuaded to hide her from the army.'

Boylston had headed back to his horse, but at the end of my speech he turned back to me. He exchanged a glance with his son. When Jay shook his head the father said, 'Who's the girl?'

'I don't have a name. But she's five feet tall, glossy black hair, probably a lot of it but she wears it in kind of a roll or chignon or whatever they're calling them this year. Very well dressed—lots of money in the background someplace.'

'If you don't know her name how do you know she's missing or even what she looks like?'

I smiled a little. 'I can't tell you all my secrets, Mr Boylston. But I will tell you she's wanted for questioning about a murder down in LA.'

Boylston swung himself back onto his horse. 'I haven't seen anyone like that. I can account for all the women around here: my two daughters, and three of the hands are married, and none of 'em has black hair. But if you want to look around, be my guest. There's an abandoned farmhouse on up the road about five miles. We just acquired the land so we only have one hand living out there so far; he can't keep an eye on the house and cover the range, too. That'd be the only place I know of. If you don't see her there you'd best get off my land. Now move your truck, Jay, and let Mr Marlowe get by.'

Jay got into the truck and moved it with an ill will that knocked little pebbles into the side of the Chrysler. I climbed back in and headed on up the track. In the rearview mirror I could see Boylston on his horse watching me, standing so still he might have been a knight on a chessboard.

The road petered out for a while into a couple of tire marks in the grass, but after four miles it turned into a regular road again. Not too long after that I came to the house.

It was a single-story, trim ranch, built like a U with short arms. It was made of wood and painted white, fresh as the snow on the Sierras, with green trim like pine trees. Whoever used to live here had loved the place and kept it up. Or the hand who was watchdogging was a homebody who kept the shrubs trimmed and weeded the begonias.

I rang the bell set into the front door, waited a few minutes, and rang again. It was sunset, not too unreasonable to think the man was done with his chores for the day. But he might be in the shower and not able to hear me ringing. I tried the door and found it unlocked. I pushed it open and went on in with a cloud of virtue wrapped around my shoulders. After all, I wasn't even housebreaking—I had Boylston's permission to search the place.

The hall floor was tiled in brown ceramic with a couple of knotted rugs floating on it. The tiles were covered with a film of dust—the hand who lived there didn't have time for the finer points of house-keeping. Opposite the front door, sliding glass doors led to a garden, a place which the previous owner had tended with care. I stared through the glass at the trim miniature shrubs and flowering bushes. There even seemed to be a pond in the middle.

I turned left and found myself in the kitchen wing. No one was hiding in the stove or under the sink. The other wing held the bedrooms. In one you could see the cowboy's obvious presence, several pairs of jeans, a change of boots, another of regular shoes. The other two bedrooms had been stripped of their furnishings. No one was in the closets or hiding in the two bathtubs.

The only thing that gave me hope was the telephone. It sat next to the kitchen stove, and pasted to it, in neat printing, not my mirage's bold script, was the number I had called. The number where the querulous man had hung up on me after I'd described her.

When I'd finished with the bedrooms I went back to the sliding door leading into the small garden. Sure enough, a pool stood in the middle, bigger than it had appeared from inside the house. I climbed on to a bridge that crossed it and looked down. Immediately a trio of giant goldfish popped to the surface. They practically stood on their tails begging for bread.

'Go work for a living like the regular fish,' I admonished them. 'There's a war on. No one has time to pamper goldfish.'

The fish swam under the bridge. I turned and looked down at them. They'd taken my words to heart—they were hard at work on the face and hands of a man who was staring up at me in the shallow water. In the fading light I couldn't make out his features, but he still had all of them so he couldn't have been in the water long. His dark hair waved like silk seaweed in the little eddies the carp stirred up.

What a detective that Marlowe is. Someone strews bodies all over Southern California and Marlowe finds them with the ease and derring-do of a bloodhound. I wanted a flashlight so I could get a closer look at the face. I wanted a drink and a cigarette, and I was beginning to think I shouldn't stray too far from my gun. All these useful items were in the Chrysler's glove compartment. I headed back through the house, skating on the lily pads on the tile floor, and climbed into the passenger seat. I had just unscrewed the bottle cap when I detected something else—a grand display of pyrotechnics exploding in my retinas. I didn't even feel the blow, just saw the red stabbing lights riding on a wave of nausea before I fell into deep blackness.

My head was a seventy-eight on a turntable that had automatic reset. Every time I thought I'd come to the end of the song and could stop spinning around someone would push the button and start me turning again. Someone had tied a couple of logs behind my back but when I reached around to cut them loose I discovered they were my arms bound behind me. I reeked of gasoline.

The time had come to open my eyes. Come on, Marlowe, you can get your eyelids up, it's only a little less horrible than the old bamboo shoots under the fingernails trick.

I was in the driver's seat of the Chrysler. Someone had moved me over, but otherwise the scene was just the way I'd left it. The glove compartment was open. I could see my gun and the bottle of rye and I wanted both of them in the kind of detached fashion a man lost in the desert wants an oasis, but I couldn't see my way clear to getting them.

Footsteps scrabbled on the gravel behind me. 'You can't set fire to him here,' someone said impatiently. 'You may own the valley, but the US Army is camped on the road and they will certainly investigate a big gasoline fire up here.'

I knew that voice. It was husky, with a hint of lisp behind it. I'd heard it a century or so ago in my office.

'Well, you're such a damned know-it-all, what do you suggest? That we leave him here until morning when the hands will find him?' The sulky tones of the kid, Jay Boylston.

'No,' the woman said coolly, 'I think you should let me drive him into the mountains. He can go over a ravine there and no one will be surprised.'

'Kitty's right,' Boylston senior said authoritatively.

Kitty? She was a kitty all right, the kind that you usually like a good solid set of iron bars around before you toss raw meat to her twice a day. There was a bit more backchat about who would do the driving, but they agreed in the end that the kitten could do it so that no one would wonder where Jay and his daddy were.

'You fired his gun?' Daddy asked.

'Yes,' Jay said sulkily. 'I shot Richard twice with it. When they find him they'll think Marlowe did it.'

'Right. Kitty, just see that his gun falls clear of the car before you set it off. We want to make sure the law doesn't have any loose ends to tie up.'

So she did have a brother named Richard. Or had had. That wavy black hair in the goldfish pond, that was what her dark leopard tresses would look like if she undid that bun.

'Sure, Kurt,' the husky voice drawled.

Kurt and Jay shoved me roughly back into the passenger seat and Miss Kitty took my spot behind the wheel. I tried to sniff the Chanel, but the gasoline fumes were too strong. She drove rapidly up the track, bouncing the Chrysler's tires from rock to rock as though she was driving a mountain goat.

Things looked bad for Marlowe. I wondered if it was worth trying any of my winsome charms, or if I should just roll over on top of her and force both of us flaming into a ditch. It was worth a try. At least it would change the situation—give those cool black eyes something to look surprised about. I was getting ready to roll when she stopped the car.

Her next move took me utterly by surprise: she reached behind me and hacked my arms loose with an efficient woodsman's knife.

'You're kind of pushing your luck, Kitty.' I moved my arms cautiously in front of me. They felt like someone had just forced the Grand Coulee's overflow through them. 'I've been concussed before. I'm not feeling so sorry for myself that I couldn't take that knife from you and get myself out of here. You'd have to explain it to Kurt and Jay as best you can.'

'Yes,' the husky voice agreed coolly. 'I'll tell them something if I have to—if I ever see them again, that is. But I need your help.'

'Right, Miss Kitty. You lure me to Dominick Bognavich's body. You bring me into the mountains and set the sweetest sucker trap I've ever seen, including planting bullets from my gun in what I assume is your brother's body, and now you want my help. You want me to drive my car over a cliff for you so you don't have to chip those bright red nails of yours?'

She drew a sharp breath. 'No. No. I didn't know they were going to knock you out. And I didn't know they had killed Richard until I got here. He—he was the weak link. He always was, but I never thought he would betray me.'

The quiver of emotion in her voice played on my heart like a thousand violin strings. 'The gambler. I know. He gambled away your mother's whoosis and so you had Kurt Boylston drown him in the goldfish pond.'

'It didn't happen quite like that. But I don't blame you for being angry.'

'Gee, sister. That's real swell of you. I'm not angry, though—I love being hit on the head. I came up from LA just to get knocked out. And then have gasoline poured on me so I couldn't miss the cars.'

'That was never supposed to happen,' she said quickly. 'I was trying to get to Grandfather—to the ranch—before Jay did but I couldn't—there were reasons . . .' Her voice trailed away.

'Maybe you could tell me what was supposed to happen. If it wouldn't strain your brain too much to tell the truth. Maybe you could even start with who you really are.'

In the dark I couldn't tell if she was blushing or not. 'My real name is Kathleen Moloney. Kathleen Akiko Moloney. My mother married an Irishman, but her father was Ichuro Kumura. I know I look Jewish to many people and in this climate today it is helpful to let them think so. Dominick—Dominick is the one who suggested it. He suggested the name Felstein. And when I pretended to lose the title to my grandfather's land to him, he kept it under the name of Felstein.' Her voice trailed away. 'I needed help and I was so afraid you wouldn't help me . . .'

'If I knew you were Nisei.' I finished for her. 'And what makes you so sure I will help you now?'

'I don't know.' She leaned close to me and I could smell her perfume again, mixed with the gasoline and a faint tinge of ladylike sweat. 'I saved your life, but that wouldn't count with you, would it, if you thought it was your duty to turn me in and force me to go to Manzanar.'

'You're not in any danger. A girl like you knows how to fight her way out of trouble.'

'Yes. I have to use the gifts I have, just as you do, Mr Marlowe. But we can argue about that later. Let me finish because we must move quickly. If you agree to help me, I mean.'

In the moonlight all I could see was her shape. She'd shed the hat and the suit and was wearing trousers and cowboy boots. I couldn't see her features to tell if she was spinning me another long yarn into which she had somehow appropriated the tale of Ichuro Kimura from the morning paper. I shook a large portion of rye into me to give my brain a fighting edge.

'Don't drink,' she said sharply to me. 'It's the worst thing for a man in your condition.'

'On the contrary,' I said, tilting the bottle a second time. The first swallow had settled the nausea in my stomach and sharpened the pain in my head, but the second one went clear to the base of my spine and worked its way into the brain. 'I think I can stand to hear your tale of woe now. Tell me about Richard, the weakling.'

'Kurt Boylston has wanted to own my grandfather's land for a long time. It's a small ranch, only nine hundred acres, nothing compared to the Boylston spread, but it has the best water. My grandfather worked it as a field hand when he came here from Japan in 1879 and gradually came to own it.

'Boylston has tried everything to get his hands on it. Then, with the internments and the anti-Japanese scare, he saw his chance. He announced that Kimura was a Japanese spy and that his land should be confiscated. Boylston said he would farm it as a service to the government. Of course, in times like these, frightened men will believe anything.'

Her husky voice was shaky with passion. I wanted a cigarette very badly but didn't want to send us up in flames lighting it.

'My grandfather would not go. Why should he? He is no spy. And he knew it was only a ruse, a trick by Kurt Boylston to get his land. I'm sure you saw in the paper how he fought the army and then disappeared. I took the title and gave it to Dominick, but I had to tell Richard. And Richard was weak. Kurt must have bought him. I saw— I saw when I got to Dominick's house this morning, how he had been shot, and knew it was Richard, shooting him six times out of fright, then tearing the house up to find the title. After he turned it over to Kurt, the Boylstons drowned him in my grandfather's goldfish pond. I pretended all along to be in love with Kurt, to be supporting him against my grandfather, but after tonight even he will be able to understand.'

I wondered if even now she was telling the truth. She sure believed in it, but did I? 'Why didn't you tell me this this morning?'

The moonlight caught leopard sparks dancing from her eyes. 'I didn't think you'd believe me. A Japanese spy, written up in all the papers? I thought I would get here ahead of you and explain it all to you, but then I saw Richard's body in the pond and knew that Kurt would figure out my true involvement before long. I had—had to go back to his ranch and—' Her voice broke off as she shuddered. 'I used my special gifts, that's all, and took the title from his pocket while he slept.'

I put one of my gasoline-soaked hands on her soft leopard paw. Why not? She'd told a good tale, she deserved a little applause.

'Bravo. You got your paper back. You don't need me. You want a lift someplace on my way back to LA?'

She sucked her breath in again and pulled her hand back. 'I do need you. To smuggle my grandfather into the city. The army knows my car, and they know my face. They would stop me, but they won't stop you.'

I rubbed the bottle a few times, wondering if her grandfather would pop out of it, a wizened Japanese genie.

'He's been hiding here in an old well, but it's bad for him, bad for his rheumatism, and it's hard for me to sneak him food. And now, he could climb down into the well, but not up, not by himself, but you— you are strong enough for two.'

She was the genie in the bottle, or maybe she just had a little witch blood mixed in with the leopard. I found myself walking across the jagged ground to where a well cover lay hidden beneath the sage. I pried it loose according to the enchantress's whispered instructions. She knelt down on the rim and called softly, 'It's Akiko, Grandfather. Akiko and a friend who will bring you to Los Angeles.'

It wasn't as simple as Miss Moloney thought it would be, driving around to pick up Route Five from the north, but then these things never are. In the first place Kimura wouldn't travel without a little shrine to the Buddha that he'd been keeping in the well with him, and it was a job packing the two of them in the trunk under some old blankets. And in the second place we ran into Kurt and Jay because the only way to Route Five was along the trail that led past the Kimura place. And in the confusion I put a bullet through Kurt Boylston's head—purely by mistake, as I explained to the sheriff, but Miss Moloney had hired me to look for rustlers on her grandfather's old place and when Kurt had started to shoot at us I didn't know what else to do. The sheriff liked it about as well as a three-day hangover, but he bought it in the end.

What with one thing and another the sun was poking red fingers up over the San Gabriels by the time we coasted past Burbank and into the city.

I dropped Miss Moloney and her grandfather at a little place she owned in Beverly Hills, just ten rooms and a pool in the back. I figured Dominick had been a pretty good friend, all right. Or maybe the Irishman who married her mother—I was willing to keep an open mind.

She invited me in for a drink, but I didn't think gasoline and rye went too well with the neighborhood or the decor, so I just left the two of them to the ministrations of a tearful Japanese maid and lowered myself by degrees through the canyons back to the city. The concrete looked good to me. Even the leftover drunks lying on the park benches looked pretty good. I've never been much of an outdoors man.

When I got to my office I tried the air to see if there was any perfume left, but I couldn't detect it. I wondered what kind of detective I was, anyway. There wasn't anything for me in the office. I didn't know why I'd come here instead of finding my shower and bed—that was the kind of thing I could detect all right.

I put the office bottle back in the drawer and locked it. I put yesterday's paper tidily in the trash can and looked around for a minute. There was a scrap of black on the floor underneath the visitor's chair. I bent over to pick it up. It was a little square of lace, the kind of thing a lady with the poise of a dealer would have tucked in her black bag, the kind of thing even the most sophisticated lady might drop when she was peeling off twenties. It smelled faintly of Chanel. I put it in my breast pocket and locked the door.

PENTTI KIRSTILÄ (1948–)

Brown Eyes and Green Hair

Translated from the Finnish by MICHAEL GARNER

———

1

A LOT of people don't know what they want. They may guess, but they usually guess wrong. Such people may have a car or a dog.

What did Timo Karvonen want most in life? He wanted melanin. Melanin was what he wanted, but he didn't even know it. He had never heard the word before an optician enlightened him, telling him that in large doses this very substance turns human eyes brown. When Karvonen had asked where he could get it, the optician had changed the subject.

The most startling revelation in Karvonen's thirty years of life was this: women prefer brown-eyed men to blue-eyed men. But, to his misfortune, he had blue eyes. Another thing he did not know was that the majority of women had to like brown-eyed men, since only a fraction of the world's population has blue eyes. On hearing that there were tinted contact lenses in the shops, Karvonen stepped resolutely into an optician's and announced that he wanted some as brown as possible. The optician enquired about the prescription for the lenses. Karvonen said there was nothing wrong with his eyes, apart from the colour.

The optician was amused. Nevertheless, he recommended a visit to a doctor. When Karvonen simply insisted, the optician thought there must be all sorts of special cases. Actors, for instance. Nor did he want to be an obstacle to people realizing their true selves. His motto was: if someone is prepared to pay 1,500 marks for spectacle frames, why should I sell them for 500 marks? This motto was well applied when Karvonen got his lenses.

So much for Karvonen.

Tiina Salmelainen was seventeen. She was doing very well at school, being a special favourite of her history teacher; the teacher herself said that Tiina had an unusually clear and analytical grasp of the events in history and, what was even more splendid, she also had a capacity for synthesis. There was no other evidence of the reasons for her teacher's partiality.

Tiina was a beautiful, healthy girl, or actually young woman, since she was no longer a virgin. Nor did she lack courage: only a year before, she had once appeared in the schoolyard in a skirt. But not even Tiina was entirely without her problems. She had an unbearable mother. Admittedly, Tiina knew nothing of that. There were other, minor, everyday matters that would not leave her in peace.

One day, Tiina walked into a hairdresser's. Even though people don't generally just walk into hairdressers', she was in luck and the hairdresser had a cancellation. Tiina announced that she wanted a new look: the fair hair flowing over her shoulders was to go, and in its place was to be a short, green cut that stood straight upwards. The hairdresser had not been shocked by anything in years; she had rather been the one who tried to shock others with her new creations. She applied an appropriate mix of scissors, sugar solution, and green hair spray and, a couple of hours later, out of the shop walked a young woman whose history teacher would not have recognized her to say hello to.

So much for Tiina.

Tauno Kurikka lived for the weekends, not with an unnatural fervour, but as though it were the only way to get through life. He was an energetic young man. The acquisition of parents had not gone as well for him as it might have from a material perspective. So, at twenty-four, he worked during the day as a salesman in a watchmaker's shop and in the evenings he went to college. This left only the weekends free and he generally spent them rather wildly in some disco or other.

Everything was actually going fine, he supposed. Except that he hated the name Tauno. He would almost have been ready to kill the priest who christened him, but the priest was already dead. Although, he did actually know it wasn't the priest's fault. And he did actually know whose fault it was. Whenever anyone asked him his name, he introduced himself as Toni. He had to submit to friends calling him

Tauno at odd moments, since constant scuffles would be hard work for anyone.

He got on well with the owner of the watchmaker and goldsmith's shop. He was always on time for work and had a knack for dealing naturally with customers. He occasionally borrowed a 12,000 mark Rolex or some such from the shop's stock to wear over the weekend. He was sure the owner did not know about this, and, if the truth were told, the owner was a bit of a fool. He took advantage of the situation more zealously during the warmer periods of the year, when he paraded out of doors in a short-sleeved shirt. He viewed these borrowings as he would the use of a library card, and saw in it no deeper significance.

So much for Tauno Kurikka.

2

The two young detectives considered it a stroke of luck that the victim's watch had broken as he fell. And when the senior of the two, Sergeant Kankainen, rather enthusiastically reported the matter to the head of the investigation, the time the murder had occurred became the starting point for the investigation. There was nothing else to go on at that stage.

Except, of course, the body.

'Smart watch he had,' said Constable Viiri, as he inspected the body.

'But broken,' Kankainen said. 'And, besides, you can buy those from the market,' he continued, proving that he did not know everything. Kankainen was only a little older than Viiri, but he was stockier and mostly bald, so he gave more the impression of being Viiri's father than an elder brother. Nevertheless, he took a more cheerful attitude to his work, having been in the job that much longer.

'He's a bit broken himself,' Viiri said. 'Blow to the head with a hammer. Fancy using a hammer.'

The detectives inspected the place. It was a very commonplace studio flat, with old furniture, probably built some time in the 1950s and not renovated to speak of since. Nothing smooth and sophisticated, just everyday and ordinary. The body too was ordinary in its way. A lot of people get hit on the head.

The hands of the watch had stopped at ten.

'When did he die?' Kankainen asked.

'If that's anything to go by, he died at ten yesterday evening. At any rate, he didn't die at ten today, or yesterday morning,' the doctor said. He had scrutinized the body like a mechanic would a crankshaft, carefully but without emotion.

Kankainen inspected the sharp corner of the coffee table. The forensics people would have to confirm it, but there might be a mark there, where the falling man's watch had struck it.

'I couldn't have been that exact,' the doctor said. 'God bless the Swiss.'

The doctor rose. Kankainen said to Viiri: 'Right, maybe we should get out the magnifying glass?'

3

'What do we do now?' Karvonen asked.

'You tell me. You're older,' Tiina said.

They were sitting on the sofa in Karvonen's bachelor flat. They had met for the first time a week ago, by chance, so it seemed, and this was more of a surprise to Karvonen than to Tiina.

'What are we actually doing together on this sofa? Just look at us. I'm wearing a shirt with a collar and everything. And you . . .'

'We do have something in common,' Tiina said. 'We're both fakes.'

'Fakes?'

Tiina gave a brief laugh.

'Well? What do you actually mean?' Karvonen insisted.

'You probably think they don't show. Those lenses, I mean. And besides, they don't suit you at all.'

Karvonen was embarrassed, and almost blushed. Computers were familiar to him, but he knew less about people. The optician had claimed that they wouldn't show at all. Karvonen was mortified. He began to dig the lenses out of his eyes.

'Why did you do it, by the way? That Mohican cut.'

'Why did you buy those lenses?'

Karvonen could come up with no answer but the truth, and he didn't have the nerve to tell her that.

'I'm really worried,' he said.

'I can see that,' Tiina agreed.

'And with no good reason?'

'Maybe you have.'

'What do you mean, I have? Both of us have.' Karvonen's hands were trembling.

'Let's say it was an accident. Maybe we shouldn't meet for a little while.' Tiina got up. 'Don't worry, I'm not sure everybody notices. I happen to be more sharp-sighted than most.'

'They don't show!'

'Those lenses, you mean,' Tiina said.

'Jesus Christ!' Karvonen didn't know which way to turn. 'Don't you go anywhere.'

'I don't know anything,' Tiina said. 'I thought you were old acquaintances. I thought you got up to boyish pranks together. He told me to say so. Don't try and get me mixed up in this.'

4

It was the weekend, Saturday, which made things more difficult. It was hard to get hold of people.

They had to find relatives, friends, acquaintances, workmates, teachers (on the table in the bare studio flat was ample evidence that Tauno Kurikka went to evening classes). But first they had to find the men who would do that job.

'Hanhivaara is also off somewhere, fishing,' Kankainen said.

'Is Hanhivaara an angler?' Viiri asked. 'I would never have believed it.'

'It was just a sort of . . .' Kankainen sighed. 'We've found Viktor Onninen, anyway.'

'Who's he?'

'The bloke who owns the flat. Watchmaker, by the way. Let's pay him a visit.'

It was a beautiful, clear day in May. Viiri was peevish, since it was supposed to be his day off.

'Where are we going?' Viiri asked, sitting behind the wheel.

'Go west, young man!' Kankainen said.

'It's all right for you to amuse yourself, when you were on call anyway!' But he nevertheless turned the car to point westwards.

The apple trees were in blossom in the garden of the old ridge-roofed house. The man who opened the door looked to Kankainen just like someone who tinkered about with clocks. Small, round-shouldered, pale, even his reading-glasses hung off his nose.

'Police,' Kankainen said.

'I guessed that,' the man said. 'Onninen.'

The policemen introduced themselves and went in.

'I have a sort of workshop here at home too. Let's go in there,' Onninen said.

The policemen followed Onninen into the workshop, where there must have been as many parts as God used to make the universe. And they were presumably arranged equally precisely.

'Hammers,' Viiri muttered to Kankainen. 'But hellish small ones.'

'What is this about?' Onninen asked. 'I understood you wished to talk about Tauno, Kurikka, that is.'

'Yes. What kind of man was he?' Kankainen asked.

Onninen did not notice the past tense. He said: 'I have been thinking a bit about getting rid of him.'

'Something small disappeared?'

'No. No, it's not that. The boy has simply become a little careless and lazy. Doesn't arrive on time. He's started being overfamiliar with the customers. All sorts of things.'

'He's that bad, is he?' Kankainen thought, taking the plastic bag containing the wristwatch out of his pocket. 'Do you recognize this?'

Onninen took the watch and peered at it. 'Can I take it out of the bag?' Having received tacit assent, he further inspected the watch through an eyeglass and said: 'Yes, it is from the shop. A second, damn it. Where was it found?'

'It was in Kurikka's possession,' Kankainen said.

'Now he'll certainly have to go,' Onninen became so agitated that even his back straightened out.

'Already gone,' Viiri put in.

Onninen again wasn't listening, which was lucky for Viiri, judging by the glare Kankainen gave him. Onninen said: 'So, he's a thief, too. Little rascal, no doubt he thought I wouldn't notice. And to think of all I've done for him. No parents, no trade, every chance of ending up where he will now be going.'

'Where's that?' Kankainen gave Viiri no chance to intervene.

'I'm going to have him put in jail.'

'Not for one watch, surely?'

'You didn't happen to know previously that the watch had disappeared, did you?' Viiri asked.

'How do you mean?'

'You might occasionally visit the shop at the weekend and have happened to notice it.'

'I did actually go back there yesterday after business hours. But I didn't look in all the cupboards and boxes.'

'Would you have been angry if you had noticed?'

'It's a hell of a thing if a person can't get annoyed about his own property being taken like that. I'd have kicked that scoundrel's backside.'

'Like, sort of suddenly from behind?' Viiri said.

Kankainen thought that Viiri might amount to something after all, if a single glare could bring him to heel, and to the point.

'Where were you yesterday evening around ten?' Kankainen asked.

'I must have got home by then. I don't always glance at the clock,' Onninen said.

Kankainen and Viiri looked around, then exchanged looks, but did not laugh.

'What time did Kurikka leave work on Friday?' Viiri asked.

'At five. He'd actually wanted to go earlier.'

'Did you see him after that?'

'No. Where would I have seen him?'

'You didn't happen to visit Kurikka's flat?' Kankainen asked.

'No,' Onninen said sharply.

'Thanks,' Kankainen said. 'Can I have the watch back now?'

'This is my . . .'

'It is evidence in a criminal case,' Kankainen said. 'You will get it back in due course.' Onninen reluctantly surrendered the watch.

Kankainen and Viiri left the building.

5

Saturday was spent trying to establish Kurikka's movements after he left work. He had not had very much time left, just five hours. Kankainen tried the easy way, and phoned the principal of the evening school to question Kurikka's teachers. That was no help, as Fridays had been free since mid-April. It was now May.

A single man with no relatives or workmates is immensely difficult to keep track of. Kankainen called Onninen again and asked about a girlfriend, but that question did not elicit any useful response either.

Kankainen then left with Viiri to ring doorbells. The prognosis was worse than for lung cancer: people who live in blocks of flats don't know each other, don't even say hello, have often never even seen each other, and would very rarely actually want to interfere with each other intentionally. Nevertheless, a law of nature well known to the security police says there is one in every building. It is just rare for the police to be so lucky that this one lives on the same floor as the murder victim, and that this one's door is also opposite the murder victim's door. It is rare for the police to be so unlucky that this one has not seen anyone go into the victim's flat at precisely ten o'clock, has not seen anyone come out of there, and has not even heard anything at precisely that time. Nevertheless, since, in Kankainen's view, the man's level of knowledge merited a pass with distinction, he enquired as to whether Kurikka had a girlfriend.

'He had lots of girlfriends,' came the reply.

'But a more permanent one, one with loose habits, who spent longer periods, months even, in Kurikka's flat,' Kankainen urged.

'Not to my knowledge.'

'To your knowledge?'

'He didn't.'

At that stage, Kankainen, and likewise Viiri, was sure that they would have been in possession of a treasure, if only . . . Kankainen was also tempted to ask whether the man had visited the lavatory around ten.

They did not find a girlfriend. Even though an aggravated college principal provided a list of Kurikka's classmates, and officers were sent out to conduct weekend examinations, nothing came of that either. Night schools were not very close communities.

Saturday was a somewhat unproductive day: a toolkit was found in one of Kurikka's cupboards, but there was no hammer in it. So that was that.

6

It was Monday afternoon. Sergeant Hanhivaara had been through the reports on Kurikka's death. He had seen the photographs of the body. And he had also gone out to buy himself a watch. Kankainen and Viiri came into his room.

'What's the matter with you?' Hanhivaara asked. 'You've been reading too many detective stories and watching too much TV.'

'The minute Hanhivaara arrives on the job, he's better than anyone else,' Viiri said.

'What have you come up with now?' Kankainen asked.

Hanhivaara leaned disgustedly on the edge of the desk. He said: 'Even you should know that the broken wristwatch died the death before Agatha Christie.'

'What do *you* know about watches? Since when did you even have a watch?' Viiri asked.

Hanhivaara took the wristwatch out of his pocket. 'Since today. Solely for the purpose of dramatizing my theoretical exposition, I bought this watch today for 25 marks. Kurikka's watch was more expensive.' He tossed the watch about in his hand. 'Look,' he said. 'It works.' He showed the watch to Kankainen and Viiri. They both stared at him. Viiri was entranced and Kankainen despondent, since, being the smarter of the two, he already guessed what was coming. Hanhivaara flung the watch at the wall, left the desk to stand without support, and plucked the watch from the floor. He inspected it, the expression on his face as blank as only that of someone dramatizing a theory can be. 'It's going,' he said. 'It may no longer be going in a couple of hours. But at least the glass isn't broken. Have you any idea what acceleration they use in the shock tests, how many gs?'

Viiri and Kankainen stared.

Hanhivaara said: 'The world has sunk to the point where only exaggeration and irony work even to some extent. The rest is dross.'

'I've always said Hanhi is a philosopher,' Kankainen declared.

'Here you saw an example of exaggeration. I could have said: "Watches don't break like that nowadays," ' he continued.

Viiri said: 'Do you mean the watch was broken on purpose so we would think . . .?'

'Nail on the head,' Kankainen said, impressed by Viiri's inventiveness. 'That means a new round. Confound it.'

'That must be what Onninen meant when he said the watch is a second. I thought the old fox had fallen into the trap and bought a cleverly made Thai copy,' Viiri said.

Hanhivaara said: 'I don't understand . . .'

'To tell you the truth, neither do I, not now,' Kankainen interrupted him. 'But since it was so easy to start there. Simply to look at the watch for the time of the murder.'

Hanhivaara said: 'There doesn't seem to be anything particularly interesting in this scene-of-crime report. The fact that the body was found as a result of an anonymous phone call does tell us one thing.'

'Such as what?' Viiri asked.

'That the murderer is having conscience problems,' Hanhivaara said.

'That isn't necessarily the case,' Viiri countered. 'Somebody might have a key, but as we know few of them want to get involved.'

'Fingerprints. I'd like to know whose,' Kankainen said. 'The hammer was clean, at any rate.'

'I obviously have to go and look for myself,' Hanhivaara said. 'One generally has to do everything oneself.'

'That's being unfair and you know it,' Viiri said.

'No it's not. I was simply pissing you about.'

Kankainen bit his lip, as he always did when Hanhivaara was in that mood. 'Let's go and see the toad.'

'Who?'

'Hanhivaara doesn't get it,' Kankainen mocked. 'You can't put everything into a report. We have to start making a new timetable. But we still have no way of knowing whether the watch was put forward or back. That depends on when the murderer has the best alibi.'

'I'll go and call,' Viiri said, and left the room.

'But what about the toad?' Hanhivaara demanded.

'There is one person in every block of flats who keeps an eye on all the others. This is, of course, God's gift to the police, if you don't happen to live in the same building. In this case, he happens to look like that. And he croaks, too.'

'Why can't they ever look like just anyone?' Hanhivaara said.

'So it's worth us going and asking him first who he has seen. Last time, we only asked what had happened at ten in the evening. Let's ask something a bit different this time.'

Viiri came back. 'Pure spite. What else do you get here but spite,' he said. 'I asked our esteemed doctor quite innocently what would he think if he hadn't died at ten. And what do I get in reply? Spite. "You're the ones who decided that he died at 10 p.m. You looked at the watch. I didn't say that." That sort of thing. Then he is so gracious as to have the considerable pleasure of giving us at least an hour either way. And he would be prepared to stretch that too, if we like. The man's nothing but chewing-gum.'

7

That's the truth, Hanhivaara thought.

'Ah, you,' said the man whom Kankainen had referred to as the toad. 'Come in. I am retired, you see. Nowhere to go, nothing to do. A week ago, I was abroad, in the Canaries. And I have become attached to my old turnip, to my pocket watch, that is, if you gentlemen are unfamiliar with the expression, and I always take the time from that. That is the source of all the confusion. You gentlemen are three in number. How jolly. Coffee?'

The three gentlemen looked at each other like a trio of punks who had strayed into *The Magic Flute*. Kankainen put the matter into words: 'There may well be a little room for clarification here.'

'No, everything is clear now. Now that I've noticed that my watch needed adjusting to Finnish time. When you last asked, the timetable did not add up. Now things are otherwise.'

'Don't you have a bloody TV?' Viiri thought.

'How is that possible, for an entire week?' Hanhivaara asked. 'That's a lot of television news unwatched.'

'I don't have a television.'

'Then you must have someone in the corner of the room,' Viiri thought. He had a television himself.

'Now that the time is where it should be, for safety's sake the whole story,' the man said. 'So, Friday. That Onninen came a little after seven. Rang the bell and left.'

'Onninen,' Kankainen said. 'How do you know he didn't go inside?'

'Because he didn't. Only rang the bell. Odd that he didn't go in.'

'Why odd?' Hanhivaara asked.

'Since he owns the flat. Went in and out as he pleased, at any time. Strange kettle of fish. He surely had no right to persecute the poor boy, he surely had no right to go in there, whenever he felt like it. Some people make a habit of it. Snooping. And he was an extortionist too.'

'In what way?' Kankainen asked.

'Stopped nearly half the boy's wages in rent. Knew that he wouldn't get a flat anywhere else, anyway. Nasty person.'

The hall was cramped. The three gentlemen shifted their weight to the other leg.

'Will you come in? Coffee?' The man offered.

'No, thank you,' Hanhivaara almost shouted. Then he continued with more control. 'Let's just chat here. What else?'

'Now that I have worked out the times, the girl must have called at nine and then the man at ten.'

The policemen waited. Viiri had been demoted to scribe. The man continued:

'The girl was one of those Red Indians, you see them in the street.

Green hair. While the man was very ordinary. You see them. In the street, too. This one didn't have a briefcase. I don't know about the girl, but the man went in and came out soon afterwards. Or, in fact, immediately.'

'Did you know either of them? Had either of them visited Kurikka before?' Hanhivaara asked.

'I didn't recognize them.'

'Would you know them if you saw them again?' Kankainen asked.

'Yes, for sure. That hair. The man was more ordinary, but I did see his face.'

Hanhivaara failed to comprehend how people could spend their time at the peephole. A television might almost be better . . .

'And the times add up now?' Kankainen continued.

'Yes. Definitely.'

'Why didn't you tell us all this last time?'

'You asked whether anyone visited at ten, and according to my watch nobody had visited at ten. If you had asked . . .'

'Good, good. Thank you,' Kankainen said. 'We may come back, if there is anything.'

'Of course.'

The door banged shut. The men stood in the stairway. Hanhivaara was only there because he wanted to see Kurikka's room. He did not know why, or what he thought he would find there. This was quite a normal situation in police work, but you often found something whose connection to something else became apparent later.

'I think it would be odd if Onninen had killed Kurikka. If things had been the other way round, I could have understood easily,' he said.

'Perhaps they were, but Onninen won this one,' Kankainen said.

'Using what muscles?' Hanhivaara said. 'I think it's strange that just as we decide that Kurikka didn't die at ten, it turns out that someone really did go into his flat around that time. What sense is there in stopping the watch at the right time? Truly a paradoxical way of arranging an alibi for yourself.'

The men stood in the hallway.

Hanhivaara said: 'Give me Kurikka's key. I was thinking of taking a peek at the place.'

'Just by yourself,' Viiri said.

'In the meantime, you go and have another chat with the rest of the occupants,' Hanhivaara said. He didn't particularly care for Viiri's style, yet, on the other hand, he might be partly the cause of it.

8

Timo Karvonen lunged into the phone box and dialled a number. He heard a ringing tone, and gripped the receiver more tightly.

'Hello,' came the reply.

'Can I speak to Jaana?' Karvonen said.

'Who's speaking?'

'Timo Karvonen.'

'There's no Jaana here.'

'Don't mess me about. This is important.'

'Honestly, there is no Jaana here. I just wanted to teach you some manners. You should introduce yourself when you phone a stranger.'

'What number is this?'

The voice at the other end recited the numbers.

'Precisely the number Jaana gave me.'

'Do stop going on about it. Goodbye.'

Karvonen was left staring at the receiver. 'This isn't logical,' he thought.

9

'Do you know what this is?' Hanhivaara asked. The tiny object resting in his palm looked like it had been fished out of the porridge that children eat. Only it was a different colour.

'Looks like a contact lens,' Kankainen said. 'It's tinted. Trendy.'

'What does it tell us?' Hanhivaara continued his grilling.

'What should it tell us?'

'Whose is it?'

'Some woman's, presumably.'

'Who's going to do the opticians?' Hanhivaara asked malignantly.

Viiri looked out of the window. He was thinking that this was an exceptionally beautiful May, spring was early. The winter had been grim.

'Viiri!' Hanhivaara said and threw the lens to the younger man.

Viiri caught it and held the sliver of plastic up against the window. He said: 'Quite a job. I wonder how many opticians there are in this town?'

'Don't let that scare you. Think of the whole country,' Hanhivaara said.

Kankainen consoled him: 'You might strike lucky at the first attempt.'

Viiri left with his hands in his pockets, but in the knowledge that this was only one job among who knows how many.

'You can guess where it came from, Kurikka's flat. I established that it was not Kurikka's. How is it possible that it wasn't found before?' Hanhivaara's voice was without rancour, only genuine amazement.

'Do you know how many jokes there are about lost contact lenses?' Kankainen asked in reply. 'We might be better off asking how you found it?'

'Caught my eye.'

'Well, maybe it wasn't there before. Where did you actually find it?'

'In the hall.'

'Nobody's perfect. Halls get less attention if the murder has occurred in the living-room.'

This was an incontrovertible truth.

'Did you yourself find anything else of interest there?' Kankainen asked.

Hanhivaara said: 'It bothers me that Onninen lied about Friday night. What reason did he have to lie? He could have had any manner of business with Kurikka. Why did he take the risk that he had been seen there, even if he says he hasn't been there?'

'Shall I go and ask?' Kankainen said.

'Not a bad idea at all,' Hanhivaara said.

10

Kankainen entered the watchmaker and goldsmith's shop. A buzzer rang. Onninen appeared from the back room, his shoulders hunched, peering interestedly over his reading glasses at the potential customer.

'And how can I help?' Onninen asked.

'Are you trying to pretend you don't remember me?' Kankainen asked.

Onninen inspected him further and said: 'Indeed. You are the policeman. I was going to telephone you.'

'Why?'

'Since I suddenly remembered that I did go there, to Kurikka's flat, on the Friday evening.' Onninen took off his spectacles and started to clean them.

'Why?' Kankainen asked.

'In the way things just pop into your head. It simply came back to me.' Onninen's movements betrayed the nervousness that the police tend to evoke even in the innocent.

'Why did you go there?'

'I was thinking of asking him to come to work on Saturday. I am generally here myself on Saturdays. But on this occasion I had something to do.'

'But he wasn't in?'

'No. I can't, of course, expect my employees to be at home in their time off.'

'You didn't happen to go in?'

Onninen straightened his back again. 'How could I have gone into another person's flat! That would not be proper.'

'No, it wouldn't. What time did you go there?'

'It would be around seven.'

Kankainen took a watch off the counter and examined it intently. Then he said: 'Now, listen to me. I think it would be sensible for you to tell me everything right away.'

'There is nothing more to tell,' Onninen said.

11

Kankainen was just explaining to Hanhivaara how he had probably drawn a blank, when Viiri bounced into Hanhivaara's room looking highly excited.

'You look highly excited to me,' Hanhivaara said. 'Would to goodness there were a reason for it.'

This cold shower had no effect at all on Viiri. This was his moment.

'Guess what?' Viiri said.

When Hanhivaara did not join in the guessing-game, Viiri continued: 'We were in luck. I found the optician. And, what's more peculiar, this really is definite.' Viiri paused.

Kankainen came in.

'The optician was quite adamant about this lens. With it having nothing but the tint. A sort of stage lens. They don't sell many of them. And it wasn't a woman, it was a man.' Viiri waited for the applause. When none came, he said: 'I've got his name, too.'

12

Timo Karvonen had already been interrogated twice, and Hanhivaara was surprised. At first sight, he had reckoned Karvonen to be a two-hour man. Karvonen was clearly nervous, which was no wonder, and he lacked confidence as a person, which had been Hanhivaara's assessment. Hanhivaara further added a high but narrow-ranging intelligence to this character sketch.

Strangely enough, when Karvonen was led into the interview room for the third time he had not crumbled, but had rather gained in self-confidence. Hanhivaara did not know it, but Karvonen was repeating to himself: this isn't logical. And he drew strength from this irrational banality.

'At least give us one good reason why you did not come to report the body immediately?' Kankainen demanded once again.

'I don't know,' Karvonen said once again. 'It was a sort of blindness that I have never come across before, and I can't explain it, Jaana. . .'

Kankainen lost patience more easily than Hanhivaara, who had been in the business longer and moreover enjoyed interrogations. He said:

'But since we can't find any Jaana.'

'You know she exists. The three of us were in that bar together, Toni, that's Tauno, Jaana, and me. You know that.'

Hanhivaara said: 'We know what the girl at the bar said. She said that you and Kurikka clearly knew each other, but the punk girl may only have been sitting next to you by chance. Didn't seem to fit in with you. And punk circles—believe it or not they do still exist—know of no such Jaana.'

'But seeing as Jaana was with us, go and ask in the other places too. Maybe someone remembers.'

Hanhivaara knew they were on shaky ground here: Jaana existed. He cut in: 'Let's look at what we have, once again. You knew Tauno Kurikka. You say you had met him only once before, and yet you had a key to his flat. Your contact lens is found in Kurikka's flat. You were seen there.'

'But why would I have killed a man I had seen only once?'

Karvonen had by then already perceived a truth, one that would not have occurred to him if it were not for this specific situation: it is a lot easier to prove that you know someone than to prove that you don't know a person in whose company you have been seen. Even the police were unable to point to a single other occasion when their paths had crossed, but Karvonen inevitably knew Kurikka.

'We only have your word for that. Just for the sake of amusement, let's imagine that you are in computers. This or that can happen, which even we don't get to know about, because companies prefer to keep quiet about things like that. Bad publicity, and so on. If you needed an accomplice, for example, a bank account holder, it is better not to be acquainted with that accomplice. Not until you get to the Bahamas.'

Karvonen had walked into a nightmare, one where systems of binary digits did not apply.

'You won't find anything criminal in what I get up to,' Karvonen parried.

Hanhivaara said: 'That may well be the case. But it would have been better if you had chosen your words more carefully, and said: "There is nothing criminal in what I get up to".'

'Just try to find Jaana,' Karvonen muttered. 'She knows I still had the lenses after I had been to Kurikka's flat. She'll tell you how I got the key.'

It troubled Hanhivaara that there was a punk girl somewhere, and he was unable to link her with anything, or even to find her anywhere. Karvonen himself said he had only met the girl twice.

'The man's a born liar,' Viiri said infuriatedly. 'It seems to me that they went around with the girl simply for her appearance. Nobody notices two ordinary-looking blokes when they have someone like that with them. They needed her for something, but then Karvonen here came up with an even better idea. Confound it, the tight-fisted watchmaker must have been right, the watch was a second.'

Karvonen still carried on trying. 'I've admitted that I phoned you about the body. I've told you that I also tried to call Jaana, but that there was no Jaana at that number. You have to understand that someone has played a trick on me that I don't understand at all.'

'Quite a trick,' Viiri said.

Karvonen stood up and said: 'Quite a trick. When I last saw Jaana she said something odd. She said we were both fakes.'

'What does that prove?' Hanhivaara asked.

'It should at least arouse suspicion. I've been set up.'

'Why?'

'That's just what I don't understand,' Karvonen sighed.

Karvonen was taken away.

Hanhivaara said: 'What do you think the prosecutor will say?'

'Almost seems like we have enough evidence,' Kankainen said.

'I would still have liked a clear motive.'

'Maybe they argued over the girl,' Viiri suggested.

Hanhivaara and Kankainen looked at Viiri as though he were a bit of a fool.

13

Tiina Salmelainen had a capacity for analysis and a sense for synthesis. Sometimes history teachers get it just right.

Tiina's mother had wondered why she had got her hair cut. Tiina had said something peculiar: 'My appearance will become mannered too early in life if I am constantly tossing this mop over my shoulder.' Her mother would have fallen dead to the ground if she had just once seen the Mohican cut that had graced her daughter's head for a few days. The ordinary, fair, boy's hairstyle actually suited Tiina quite well. Since Tiina lived in another city, it was highly improbable that any of those involved would bump into her. And only the visually gifted would see the blue eyes under the green hair.

Tiina had met Tauno Kurikka on a weekend trip to a strange town. She had spent the night with him. Getting the key made was no problem: there was a shoe repairer in the department store. On the next day of the same journey, Tiina, who called herself Jaana, had also met Timo Karvonen. The men got on well together. Only Tiina did not fit into the picture, she could see that in the bar girl's eyes.

She had arranged to meet both of them the following weekend. She had met Karvonen at eight on the Friday, and left him for a brief period around nine. Around nine, she had met Kurikka for the last time. The watch, which she had said she liked a great deal, again adorned his wrist. She had broken it to show ten. This proved to be a bigger job than she had expected.

Just before ten, Tiina had given the key to Karvonen and asked him to go to her flat to get a few records. She had only just moved there, and that was why there was a paper nameplate on the door. In the meantime, she herself would go to collect a girlfriend. The girlfriend had not wanted to come out, after all.

Karvonen had gone to the flat, and had found the body. He had been about to go running to the police, but Tiina had got him to see sense. She had admitted that it was not her flat, and said that nobody knew about them. Karvonen had enquired as to whose flat it was, since he had not recognized the man lying face down on the floor. Karvonen had also enquired why Tiina had asked him to get the records from there. Tiina had proposed that they go to Karvonen's place and she would explain everything.

Karvonen had handed Tiina the key, as though it were burning his fingers. But Tiina had left it behind in Karvonen's flat.

After that, there was nothing left for Tiina to do but take one of the contact lenses that an embarrassed Karvonen had taken out and toss it through Kurikka's letter box, make the journey home, wash the spray out of her hair, and devote herself to her studies of history.

Tiina was a touch worried that she had admitted to Karvonen that she was a fake. Otherwise, everything had gone very well. But why did she do it?

Yes, why?

14

It was the slight improbabilities that bothered Hanhivaara most. Slight possibilities, little things, the kind of things that would never resolve the situation in the Middle East.

Too many borrowed things also bothered him: Karvonen had borrowed the colour of his eyes, and Kurikka an expensive watch.

So why couldn't the girl have borrowed her hair colour?

Someone had told him that they do the Mohicans themselves, or for each other. But still.

Hanhivaara looked at Viiri and said: 'Who's going to take the hairdressers?'

GARRY DISHER (1949–)

My Brother Jack

———

IT started at my new place, night-time noises that didn't sound right.

Ironically enough, noise is the reason I had moved there in the first place. Police helicopters, breaking glass, burglar alarms, the bass beat of stereos like repeated explosions underground, car alarms outside my bedroom window—some mornings in Fitzroy I'd wake feeling too wired to write. I was working on *Kickback* then, Jack's first story, and I'd find myself staring out the window, picturing the little place he had near the coast, the clean air, the birds, the silence, the peace of it all before everything went sour on him and he was forced to run. The double irony is, he left the coast, I moved to the coast—not far from where he'd been living, in fact—and before too long things were going bump in the night and robbing me of sleep and composure.

By then I'd written *Paydirt*, his second story, and *Deathdeal*, his third, and there were all those other yarns of his waiting to be shaped into novels, but my concentration was shot. The first wrong note, excuse the pun, was the wind chimes ringing out on a night when there was no wind. It was about 10.30 and I was in bed, reading. There was no wind but those chimes rang out with the kind of abrupt discordancy that made me think *prowler*, someone who didn't know the chimes were hanging there on the verandah. The love/sex interest in this story flung down her Sisters in Crime newsletter, revealing her small but high, low-slung but pointed, melony but round, sloping but curved, tanned but creamy breasts and said, 'What the fuck was that?' I yanked back the curtain and spotlit the verandah with a torch, but all I got was light coming back at me from the glass and by then it was too late. I didn't poke around outside; maybe I should have.

Then there were the other noises. You have to understand that although I grew up on the land I have lived nearly twenty-five years of my life away from it, so I was rediscovering the seasons, the animals, the birds. Especially the birds. They were nesting. I would look up from writing something—some stunt that Jack was pulling; some sentence where I was trying to convey the essence of stillness and dispassion in his face—and see sparrows and wrens angling up into the palm tree, trailing straw four times their length. The willy-wagtails intrigued me the most, their little grey mud egg-cup nests, their devotion to the eggs, the hatchlings, more than anything their fearlessness, the splatter of stuttering, scolding fury that said *back off* if you got too close. So who would they be sounding a warning to at one o'clock in the morning?

Then there were the messages on my answering machine. A couple of times the caller simply clicked off, so it could have been anybody, but twice there was no click, no voice, just a palpable sense of some-one listening to the silence in the house, the silence that said the house was empty and open.

The voiced messages, they were something else. '*You got it wrong, Wyatt.*' Not that *I* had got it wrong, *Wyatt* had got it wrong. If I'd been told that I'd got it wrong, the author had got it wrong, I'd have been able to relate to it, and it wouldn't have been the first time. There had been the gun freak who left a message informing me that revolvers don't have safety catches; the purist who believed Wyatt did things that Richard Stark's Parker would never have done; the safe expert who pointed out that floor safes are bolted down, you don't just wheel them out.

(Where did these people get my number from, that's what I'd like to know.)

I can live with my fuck-ups being pointed out to me. It's my job to get it right (just as it's every crime writer's job, which is why I won't be lifting information about firearms and safes from other crime novels any more), but to say that Jack had got it wrong—Wyatt had got it wrong—is something else entirely. Of course he's fucked up sometimes. He's worked with people he couldn't trust, he's failed to see the wild balls coming in from left field, he's limited himself to old-style bank and payroll heists when he could have made a mint from dealing drugs (if you could call failing to deal drugs a fuck-up). So here was this guy on the machine telling me Wyatt had got it wrong and I didn't know what he meant. Four times he said it, four separate occasions, nothing more, just a low growl, cold and hard: 'You got it wrong, Wyatt.'

There were other things. My cat on a cushion, his ears pricking up, every nerve ending along his spine registering something, someone, outside the house. A garden tap left running. *Two* flat tyres on the elderly Volvo, the twenty-five-year-old car I run because it's built like a tank and show me the writer who can afford a newish car anyway. A gate left open, allowing the old ewe that came with the place to get out, so now I have to plant fruit trees all over again.

I tried to tell myself it was the neighbour's kids, they're a wild bunch, the family has bred horses here for generations whereas I'm new, no better than a Collins Street farmer or a January holidaymaker in their eyes, but you don't see the neighbour's kids with books in their hands, which is why, when I found a page from *Paydirt* knifed to the back door one day, I knew the problem was very real and nasty, the sort of problem that had imagination and flair behind it, which ruled out the neighbour's kids.

The page? It was from Chapter 12, where Wyatt figures out how he's going to ambush and rob a security van on a lonely bush track. It was a good plan, only things went wrong. It's like that for Jack: he's smart but too often he fails to account for the stupidity and duplicity of others. He's preternaturally wary, he keeps his eyes open, his attitude says I'll-believe-it-when-I-see-it, but you can't cover all the bases all the time. Still, things-going-wrong is part of the appeal of his stories.

The knife? It was a kitchen knife. From the knife drawer. You could go into my kitchen and put your hand right on it.

So far I'm talking about gestures here, traces, signs, and all they added up to was a pissed-off character who wanted me to know that he was pissed off. Clearly he was pissed off with Jack, but I was easier to find than Jack and so he was taking it out on me.

Then a month later he stopped making gestures and tried to kill me.

It was a Wednesday evening and I'd driven up to Melbourne to take part in a crime-writing soirée organised by the National Book Council. It was held in Mietta's, a restaurant and bar with the dimpled leather armchair and open fireplace atmosphere of a gentleman's club. Anyway, the place was packed, but they were there to hear Kerry Greenwood, not me, so I got in a couple of gentle digs about the Phryne Fisher type of crime fiction and left to drive home.

I remember that I was somewhere around Abbotsford, stopped at the lights that would take me onto Hoddle Street, wondering how long it takes to establish a series character in the public's eye, when I felt a vehicle bump into the back of the Volvo. Now, the light was red, and this was the gentlest of taps, and my car is old, so I didn't bother to get out. I just waited for the light to change, idly thinking I was in Wyatt territory, things seem to happen to Wyatt in Abbotsford, when I felt another bump, much harder this time. I glanced up at the rear-view mirror and there were two implacable headlights there and an impression of bulk and muscle. It was a four-wheel drive, armoured with a massive bull-bar, and it was backing up, ramming me, backing up, ramming me.

It stopped. There must have been something wrong with the signal box, the traffic lights were still red, so I got out thinking, *Right, I'll have you, mate*. It did me no good. The guy had locked his doors, his windows were tinted, and he'd plastered mud over his plates. He was impregnable. I looked at the damage. There was a pulley on the front of the 4WD, not only a bull bar, and it had scored an expensive-looking dent in the Volvo's boot lid. I got back into the car, determined to U-turn out of there, but the moment I released the handbrake the 4WD rammed me again and this time he just kept going, pushing me metre by metre onto Hoddle Street, into the path of the ceaseless cross-town traffic.

Forget the U-turn. I spotted a gap and planted my foot, merging right, cutting in and out of lanes, heading north away from the freeway. At Langridge Street I turned right. My heart was hammering but by now I was calm enough to think I should do something about this guy. Besides, you're obliged to report accidents. I think. The Collingwood police station is behind the town hall. I pulled in there, went in, stated my case. The scene went something like this:

Cop: Can you describe the vehicle?

Me: It was a four-wheel-drive.

Cop: Toyota? Range Rover? What?

Me: I'm not sure.

Cop: You're not sure. How about the colour?

Me: Dark, possibly blue or black.

Cop: Well, blue or black?

Me: All colours look darker at night under street lights, so I can't be sure.

That earned me a sour look. Then the cop said: What about the driver?

Me: I couldn't see him.

Cop: Registration?

Me: The plates were covered in mud, I think deliberately.

A long look and the cop said: Why deliberately?

This was a tricky area I'd got myself into. I had no proof and there was a risk my explanation would drag Jack's name into it, Jack who has never been finger-printed, photographed or arrested by the cops but who nevertheless is known to them, number one, so I changed my tune quickly: Sorry, I meant to say accidentally.

Cop: Let's take a look at your car.

Outside on the street the Volvo looked every one of its twenty-five years, and when the cop began doing a roadworthy on it, checking tyre tread depth, panel rust, windscreen chips, I began to wish I'd just gone on home with my tail between my legs. Then the cop said: Here's your motive.

He was staring at the back of the car. I joined him. He indicated the *Stop Uranium Mining* sticker in the rear window (that shows you how long I've had the car) and said: There, see?

Me: You think so?

He was a beefy character, puffy and beer-fed, wearing a Merv Hughes moustache. The moustache bristled, that's how I could tell he was grinning, and he said: Just asking for it, weren't you, pal?

Me: It's a free country.

Cop: And the other bloke was expressing his point of view. Look, I'll make out a report if you like, it's what I'm here for, but I'm telling you now, you're wasting your time. We won't be kicking ass on this one.

'Kicking ass.' Kicking *arse* sounds wrong, doesn't it? It sounds weaker than 'kicking ass'. I mean, I have my down-market characters—Sugarfoot, for example—use expressions like 'kicking ass', reality for them being shaped by or filtered through American film and TV, but, really, more and more people are talking like that these days.

Then again, sometimes when I'm writing Wyatt I find myself listening for the beat, the cool flip, wise-ass tone or style or personality that works best and that makes American crime fiction so appealing and distinctive.

Anyway, I drove home then, my tail between my legs. You can understand why I want to give cops a hard time in my crime fiction. I can't see myself writing police procedurals, somehow. Stephen Knight claims there's a national wariness of the police in Australia, so they don't figure very well in crime fiction. Maybe he's right. Maybe this would have been a different story if I'd met a few Morses or

Wexfords along the line or had a few beers with Carella and the guys from the old Eight-Seven.

I pushed through the dark night across the Mornington Peninsula, much as I'd imagined Jack had done in *Kickback*:

The sky was black. When moonlight struggled briefly through the heaped clouds he saw fog wisps like people in the road ahead. Fog hung over dams and creeks. Otherwise he felt that only he was abroad, only he awake. (p.183)

That made me think this was a ghost story, maybe a horror story, I was in. If there was a human agency at work, I hadn't seen the human. All I'd seen was the evidence of evil intent—signs and warnings—and that implacable throbbing 4WD like a living beast. Sure, the windows were tinted, but maybe there was no driver anyway.

It's what you think at night but not in the clear light of day. The next morning I unbolted the house, checked outside—morning sun, the dew like diamonds, a clop of horses along the sunken road—and went back in and phoned Frank Jardine. Frank works with Jack sometimes. He can be trusted. There has to be someone Jack can work with, he can't go a dozen books or even three or four without a reliable sidekick, someone like Grofield in the Parker novels. Jardine lives in Sydney, a hotel on Broadway, and I had to wait till he came on the line.

'Yep.'

I told him who I was.

He sounded pleased. 'Gaz, what can I do for you?'

I couldn't say Jack's name, maybe Jardine's line was tapped, so I said, 'I need to see Wyatt.'

'Trouble?'

'You could say that.'

I knew what Jardine was thinking, he was thinking cop trouble for Jack. Even with the elaborate artifice I've built around Jack—calling him Wyatt; the selection and shaping of the material; the invention; the tightrope walk between a story that is driven by character on the one hand and plot on the other—he still fears the cops might read the books, twig who Wyatt is, and use me to find him. In fact, in the early planning stages that's where I thought this story was headed, it was a cop getting at me, but the evidence didn't really fit that scenario and besides, I needed to bring Jack into it, and it's not likely he'd come in if cops were involved.

'I'll tell Wyatt you called,' Jardine said, and he broke the connection.

A note about the name. Jack wasn't always called Wyatt. He was called Cody at first, as in the story 'Cody's Art'. He was called Cody in the first draft of *Kickback*, the second draft, the third draft, a year's hard slog getting the story and the character to work, and every one of those drafts rejected. But by draft three I thought I'd got it right, so I tried a different publisher, Allen & Unwin, though I was also sufficiently demoralised to submit it under a nom-de-plume: I mean, what if the book *was* bad? I didn't want too many people to know that I'd written a bad book. Fortunately they snapped it up, the book got rave reviews, and the only thing they wanted changed was Jack's name. ' "Cody" is not hard enough,' they said. I thought about it and came up with Wyatt. It sounds right, a whip snap, and a friend told me she's reminded of Wyatt the meticulous architect, and Wyatt the poet: *They flee from me that sometime did me seek / With naked foot stalking in my chamber.* (It can sometimes pay to drop quotes like this. To make it as a writer in Australia you have to become a darling of the English departments.) Jack didn't care either way about the name. 'Mate, you're the writer,' he said.

So I settled down and waited for Jack to contact me. I made notes for the next few Wyatts. It's possible that if Jack didn't exist I'd have been able to invent him, but not his capers. I mean, where can you pick up large amounts of cash these days? I wouldn't have a clue, it's all electronic transfer now. I'd have been able to invent obvious heists for him, banks and payrolls, but that would have been the extent of it. Fortunately Jack has always been able to sniff out other sources: a casino, an ALP frontbencher with $100,000 in his briefcase, a Medicare office in a large regional centre, the grand-final take from the MCG. If Jack can keep pulling these jobs I guess I can keep weaving stories around them. Once he stops, that's it, back to 'literary' fiction, 'blood from a stone' writing as Jean Bedford calls it.

Jack didn't call me, he just showed up the next day. I didn't hear a car, but I saw it later, a Hertz Falcon he probably rented with fake ID, screened from the road and the house by the leaves of the liquidamber. I didn't hear his footsteps on the gravel drive or on the verandah, but then, silence is his element, he would have used the lawn, his shoes are rubber-soled. I didn't hear the back door or any of the inner doors, I didn't hear the boardcreak of his passage through the house, he simply materialised in my study doorway. I looked up and there he was, gazing at me.

'Christ almighty.'

He smiled, a brief twist at the edge of his mouth. 'Not quite.'

'You could've knocked.'

'Jardine said you were in trouble, so I came carefully, looking for the trouble.'

Jack is like that, flat and plain. I nodded. 'Fair enough.'

'You want to tell me about it?'

No small talk, he just gets right down to it. Anyway, he's no good at small talk. He'll engage in it for harmony's sake or to keep someone from losing his nerve, but generally he can't see the point of it.

So I explained what was wrong, all the details, leaving nothing out. Knowing Jack, I kept it clear and economical. 'I want you to find out who's doing it,' I concluded, 'and why.'

He looked at me, thinking it through. My brother is an enigma. I admire him, I always have, but I don't know him at all. No-one does. He left home when he turned sixteen and never came back. I was ten and I felt the absence like an ache. No one knew the life he led, the thoughts he had, what drove him. He was private, like a western loner. Once or twice a year there would be a phone call and something about it, the darkness of the hour, signals from the atmosphere sounding distantly on the line, made me think of my brother in a far off place, the flat planes of his face in the wintry moonlight, the dark and watchful cast of him. I was at school, Joan Baez's *Diamonds and Rust* was getting some airplay, and the line, 'a booth in the mid-west', ran in my head whenever my brother called home.

Years later he started to seek me out. Not often, just once in a while, sometimes hinting obliquely at what he'd been doing before he slipped away again. I know now, but our parents don't, that he spent time in the army. He picked up skills there. He came out knowing how to kill, how to look after himself, but he also came out with a wad of cash—a base payroll, a couple of fleeced poker schools, a few black-market scams involving guns, radios, jeeps. He came out and he went to work. In a good year he'd spend four weeks pulling a couple of big jobs and take it easy for the other forty-eight. That's how he acquired his place on the coast, his home before everything went sour on him. That part of it's in *Kickback*, if you're interested.

He looked at me and I looked back at him. Jack is tallish, six-one, and, like a cowboy archetype, he's as long and hard and supple as a length of rope. He moves well, he thinks well, he perceives well. He doesn't paralyse himself with scruples and inhibitions like the rest of us. People say to me, always with a smartarse look, 'How much of you is in Wyatt?' and I can't tell them about my brother or alter egos or wish fulfilment.

'Find out who and why?' he said. 'So now I'm a private eye, is that it?'

He can make a joke. Hear him talk about yuppies, other crims, contemporary values, and you'll laugh; you'll also go a little cold, recognising an unimpressed and pitiless eye. He can make a joke, but the delivery is flat, the smile if it's there is brief and sharkish, so you have to learn to recognise it.

I smiled back at him. 'You're not so different from a PI,' I said.

'Okay, define the PI.'

I counted on my fingers. 'One, you're a loner, you're not interested in collective solutions. Two, you're sceptical about social redemption. Three, you do have some integrity, even if we can't quite approve of you. Four, you're the seeing eye, looking from below, but you're also a participant, not just an onlooker. Five, you allay middle-class anxieties. There are some nasty people out there and we feel better when you get the better of them.'

Jack cut in. 'Yeah, but I feed other anxieties, like if you happened to have a hundred grand sitting in the safe at home.'

I nodded, grinning. 'True. Six, you're street-wise, all those mental and physical skills we'd like to have.'

'I've learnt them, built on them.'

I knew what he meant. Too often I'm irritated by fictional heroes, all that unexplained know-how, all those abilities. 'Seven,' I said, 'you make sharp observations about contemporary life.'

Jack shook his head. 'That's *you*, Sunshine, intruding into the narrative.' He poked his chest with a strong forefinger. 'Me, I steal, simple as that. I don't give a stuff about values, politics, the way people dress.'

I shrugged. I didn't think he was right, but I said, 'Suit yourself. Eight, the rest of us, we let ourselves get pushed around, we're too polite, but you stand up for yourself. We'd like to be able to do that.'

The look on Jack's face said he couldn't see why that was so hard.

'Nine,' I said, 'our heroes don't let doubts and scruples and uncertainties hold them back.'

Jack's expression said I was generalising. I thought then about V. I. Warshawski, how she carries a bundle of ordinary traits and frailties around with her; how family and friends, affiliation and cooperation, mean a great deal to her. I guess her life is closer to the lives of her readers than is the life of the majority of male heroes, loners, punishing the Scotch, emotionally crippled. Not that you could say Jack's like that. He's not so much socially or sexually blunted or awkward as emotionally unreadable. Not for the first time did I wonder what hurt drove him, if any. Our poor parents, they were convinced it was something they'd done. Anyway, does it have to be explained? Can't he appear on the stage fully formed? This stopped me from listing number ten to him: an element of vulnerability. There's Matt Scudder's drink problem, Fred Carver's gammy leg, Kinsey Millhone's slapdash domestic life. Jack? I don't know. It's the not knowing that makes him appear isolated, unreachable, and I guess that can seem like some kind of ache, deep down inside him.

I don't think of Jack as a reader but he must have read the odd book or two, for he said, 'Private-eye stories are told in the first person. Are you going to have me narrate this story?'

I shook my head. 'I'll use an observer narrator.'

He looked right inside me then, and I blushed. It's as if he knew I'd tried to write about him in the first person but abandoned it: (a) because I didn't know what makes him tick, even though I'd argue that it's my job as a fiction writer to get inside the skin of someone who isn't me, and (b) because a chill comes off the page when Wyatt is around and that chill penetrated like ice when I tried the first person, I felt a bleakness and it scared me. I tried the third-person and that worked, distancing the reader, distancing me.

Even so, people ask me, 'How can a gentle-mannered bloke like you write books like that?' Well, a lot of the material is stuff Jack tells me, but don't these people read the daily papers? Don't they listen to the news? Do they go around with their eyes closed or something? Besides, I'm admitting to private demons. I couldn't write Wyatt if I didn't. I couldn't read Thomas Harris, James Ellroy. Maybe the people who ask me that question haven't got any private demons. Pig's arse they haven't.

Anyway, Jack and I were still there in my study, having this stupid conversation, my years in the classroom showing, and he was getting restless. 'How do you want to go about this?' he said.

I thought about it. Peter Corris says he learned about PI methods from Ross Macdonald and Raymond Chandler. 'Make a few house calls,' I said. 'Ask questions.' Corris also noticed that the trigger in Ross Macdonald is often something way back in the past, now playing out its effects in the present, but I didn't think that was relevant in this case. And Corris claims that 'crime is a sort of backdrop to the real action, which is a resolution of some sort of disorder in the lives of a set of people.' Well, that was true enough here, so I said to Jack: 'Find out who's hassling me, and why, and stop him.'

'Motive, means and opportunity,' Jack said.

'Hell, this isn't a murder story,' I said. 'Not yet, anyway. Just find me a mainspring that I can build plot, structure and storyline around.'

So Jack went to work. When he's working, a film strip runs through my head, black and white, 1950s crime *noir*, something like Kubrick's *The Killing* (1956). One thing was different this time. The question driving Jack—driving Wyatt—was *Who is behind this?* rather than his customary *Can I pull off this robbery without getting caught?*

He returned two days later, mid-evening. There was no hole-and-corner approach this time, he drove openly up the drive to the back of the house, letting his headlights cut across the windows. I went out. The engine was running, the lights still on, and as I approached he opened the passenger door and said, 'Get in.'

'Just a moment,' I said. I went inside, told the love interest I was going out for a while, then returned to the car. 'Where are we going?' I asked, strapping on the seat belt.

'Frankston. His first mistake, lodging in the area he's actually operating in.'

That's one of Jack's cardinal rules: never find a bed near where you're pulling a job. 'Who is he?'

'I'll let him tell you that.'

'How did you find him?'

'I asked around until I came up with a name, someone who'd had his fingers burnt recently.'

I had to be satisfied with that. Jack taps into a network when he wants information or supplies—guns, explosives, getaway vehicles. I don't know who these people are or how it works and he'll never tell me, so I invent it.

Jack drove back across the peninsula to a hotel-motel near the seafront. It was a flash two-storey building with a drive-in bottle shop, restaurants, three bars, rooms. We got out. It was an ugly place, the air smelling of beer and scorched beef. Jack muttered darkly as he led the way across the poorly lit car park.

'See?' I said. 'You *do* comment on people and places and lifestyles.'

'Forget that. We've got work to do.'

I followed him across the foyer. The receptionist smiled automatically but something about Jack, some prohibition, wiped it off her face. We went upstairs. There was a fire alarm at the top. Jack broke the glass, pressed the button, and took me downstairs and out to the car park again. He stood facing the building expectantly.

'Well?' I said.

'You'll see.'

Sure enough, people started yelling *Fire!*, the restaurants, bars and rooms emptied, and everyone came storming out into the car park while sirens started up in the distance. Jack stiffened. 'That's him.'

I saw a guy of about thirty-five, wearing a moustache—not that that is unusual, these guys all watch 'Wide World of Sports'—jeans, Nike runners and one of those vast collarless patterned shirts that look as though they've been inflated with a bike pump. In the darkness Jack pressed his .38 into my hand and said, 'It's up to you, now. You can't be the observer any longer, finally you've got to be the active agent.'

I could see the sense of that, but still, I was shit-scared. I didn't know how I was going to get answers from this guy alone, Jack somewhere around but not about to show his face. I decided to play it as Jack, as Wyatt, would play it. Under the cover of darkness and confusion I became Wyatt, grinding the barrel of the .38 against the hinge of the man's jaw and growling, 'Into the car.'

Fortunately the gun and the sirens subdued the man. He got into the back seat. Wyatt slid behind the wheel. Wyatt didn't do anything, just stared at the man over the seat, the cold mouth of the .38 trained at his gut.

'You know who I am,' Wyatt said, and there was no question mark at the end of it.

The guy nodded.

'You irritated me finally,' Wyatt said, 'so I went looking for you. You're stupid; it wasn't hard.'

'Don't shoot me.'

'That's up to you. What's your name?'

'What?'

Wyatt used psychology in situations like this. When he had the drop on someone it was important to give them back some dignity, some identity, or they'd panic or be otherwise useless to him. 'Your name: what is it?'

The man looked at him suspiciously. 'Steegmuller.'

Well, that was a relief. If it had been Wilson or Collins, for example, the editor would have red-pencilled *Two-syllable Anglo-Saxon names like this are too ordinary, too forgettable, they slide off the page.* 'What do people call you?'

'Steeg.'

'Okay, Steeg, why don't you tell me what's eating you?'

'What are you going to do to me?'

'That depends. You tried to kill me. To stop that happening again I should kill you now.'

'I was just trying to throw a scare into you!'

Wyatt said, flat and cold, 'It doesn't work like that. I have to assume you're serious. That means killing you. So start talking.'

There were red and blue lights in the car park by this stage—two fire trucks and a couple of divisional vans. Those lights were throwing the shapes from bad dreams around the interior of the car. There was enough light for me to see the man's face clearly. If I say his eyes ran over the seats and up the side windows and across the roof of the car the editor will red-pencil *Did they run on their little legs?* so I'll just say he looked around wildly for a way out. There wasn't one. He said:

'Twice you fucked me around. Like giving people valet parking cards outside restaurants so they think you're parking their car for them only you're stealing it. I tried that and the fucking bouncer came and kicked my head in.'

'For Christ's sake,' I said, 'it was only a story.'

He looked at me suspiciously. 'So how did you know how to do it?'

'I didn't. I think I pinched it from an early Elmore Leonard novel.'

'You never tried it?'

'Not me, pal.'

He didn't seem satisfied but went on and said, 'Then when you climbed into the back seat of the car from the boot. I was going to rob this Seven-Eleven night manager on his way to the hole in the wall but I got trapped in the boot, I couldn't fucking get out.'

'I never actually tried it to see if it would work,' I admitted. 'I'd written Wyatt into a corner and I spent hours working out how to get him out of it.'

'You could've written something "With a mighty bound he was free . . ."'

I shook my head. 'Your reader's not going to buy that these days.'

'Or someone turns up in the nick of time.'

Again I shook my head. 'The reader won't buy that, either. The main character has to be the active agent. The answer had to be in Wyatt's hands. So I tried some lateral thinking and had him pushing through the window shelf into the back seat. I mean, I did do a bit of research. I went to car yards and looked in a few boots. It looked feasible. Maybe you chose the wrong sort of car.'

He was gloomy, full of doubt and regret. 'Maybe,' he said. Then some spirit came back into his face. 'So you just like fucking people around?'

'It's not real,' I said. 'I'm not writing about myself, or things that happened to me. I'm making it all up.'

'It seemed real. I went up north, thought I'd try hitting a security van.' He shivered. 'Nothing but saltbush and red dirt.'

Strangely enough the working title had been *Red Dirt Snatch* but the editor pointed out an unfortunate connotation with the word 'snatch', and they wanted uniform titles for the series anyway, so I accepted their suggestion, *Paydirt*. Who was I to quibble? It works for Sue Grafton, it worked for John D. MacDonald. I said to the guy, 'I write entertainments. No message, you're not meant to take it literally. When you put the book down there's the phone bill to pay, it's raining again, you forgot to buy milk.'

Here I was in an ending where the main players are brought together and there's plenty of dialogue and everything's explained and there are no loose ends. Just once in a while you'd like a shoot-out or something downbeat or morally ambiguous. I sighed. I was finished here. 'Stay away from me,' I said, pushing the guy out the door. 'Next time I'll kill first and talk later.' I could have shot him, but the imperative was gone now, it would have been gratuitous. When he was out of sight I wound down the window and called softly, 'Jack?' Nothing, no response, as if my brother wasn't there and had merely been some kind of device all along.

Time to go home. Lawrence Block, bemused by the Best This, That and the Other awards for crime writing every year, said that there were really only two categories, crime stories with cats and crime stories without. I went home to my cat.

And the love interest, of course.

PETER ROBINSON (1950–)

Summer Rain

I

'AND exactly how many times have you died, Mr Singer?'

'Fourteen. That's fourteen I've managed to uncover. They say that each human being has lived about twenty incarnations. But it's the last one I'm telling you about. See, I died by violence. I was murdered.'

Detective Constable Susan Gay made a note on the yellow pad in front of her. When she looked down, she noticed that she had doodled an intricate pattern of curves and loops, a bit like Spaghetti Junction, during the few minutes she had been talking to Jerry Singer.

She tried to keep the scepticism out of her voice. 'Ah-hah. And when was this, sir?'

'Nineteen sixty-six. July. That makes it exactly thirty-two years ago this week.'

'I see.'

Jerry Singer had given his age as thirty-one, which meant that he had been murdered a year before he was born.

'How do you know it was nineteen sixty-six?' Susan asked.

Singer leaned forward. He was a remarkably intense young man, Susan noticed, thin to the point of emaciation, with glittering green eyes behind wire-rimmed glasses. He looked as if the lightest breeze would blow him away. His fine red hair had a gossamer quality that reminded Susan of spiders' webs. He wore jeans, a red T-shirt and a grey anorak, its shoulders darkened by the rain. Though he said he came from San Diego, California, Susan could detect no trace of suntan.

'It's like this,' he began. 'There's no fixed period between incarnations, but my channeler told me—'

'Channeler?' Susan interrupted.

'She's a kind of spokesperson for the spirit world.'

'A medium?'

'Not quite.' Singer managed a brief smile. 'But close enough. More of a mediator, really.'

'Oh, I see,' said Susan, who didn't. 'Go on.'

'Well, she told me there would be a period of about a year between my previous incarnation and my present one.'

'How did she know?'

'She just *knows*. It varies from one soul to another. Some need a lot of time to digest what they've learned and make plans for the next incarnation. Some souls just can't wait to return to another body.' He shrugged. 'After some lifetimes, you might simply just get tired and need a long rest.'

After some mornings, too, Susan thought. 'Okay,' she said, 'let's move on. Is this your first visit to Yorkshire?'

'It's my first trip to England, period. I've just qualified in dentistry, and I thought I'd give myself a treat before I settled down to the daily grind.'

Susan winced. Was that a pun? Singer wasn't smiling. A New Age dentist, now there was an interesting combination, she thought. Can I read your Tarot cards for you while I drill? Perhaps you might like to take a little astral journey to Neptune while I'm doing your root canal? She forced herself to concentrate on what Singer was saying.

'So, you see,' he went on, 'as I've never been here before, it *must* be real, mustn't it?'

Susan realized she had missed something. 'What?"

'Well, it was all so familiar, the landscape, everything. And it's not only the *déjà vu* I had. There was the dream, too. We haven't even approached this in hypnotic regression yet, so—'

Susan held up her hand. 'Hang on a minute. You're losing me. What was so familiar?'

'Oh, I thought I'd made that clear.'

'Not to me.'

'The place. Where I was murdered. It was near here. In Swainsdale.'

II

Banks was sitting in his office with his feet on the desk and a buff folder open on his lap when Susan Gay popped her head around the door. The top button of his white shirt was undone and his tie hung askew.

That morning, he was supposed to be working on the monthly crime figures, but instead, through the half-open window, he listened to the summer rain as it harmonized with Michael Nyman's sound-track from *The Piano*, playing quietly on his portable cassette. His eyes were closed and he was day-dreaming of waves washing in and out on a beach of pure white sand. The ocean and sky were the brightest blue he could imagine, and tall palm trees dotted the land-scape. The pastel village that straddled the steep hillside looked like a cubist collage.

'Sorry to bother you, sir,' Susan said, 'but it looks like we've got a right one here.'

Banks opened his eyes and rubbed them. He felt as if he were coming back from a very long way. 'It's all right,' he said. 'I was getting a bit bored with the crime statistics, anyway.' He tossed the folder onto his desk and linked his hands behind his head. 'Well, what is it?'

Susan entered the office. 'It's sort of hard to explain, sir.'

'Try.'

Susan told him about Jerry Singer. As he listened, Banks's blue eyes sparkled with amusement and interest. When Susan had finished, he thought for a moment, then sat up and turned off the music. 'Why not?' he said. 'It's been a slow week. Let's live dangerously. Bring him in.' He fastened his top button and straightened his tie.

A few moments later, Susan returned with Jerry Singer in tow. Singer looked nervously around the office and took the seat opposite Banks. The two exchanged introductions, then Banks leaned back and lit a cigarette. He loved the mingled smells of smoke and summer rain.

'Perhaps you'd better start at the beginning,' he said.

'Well,' said Singer, turning his nose up at the smoke. 'I've been involved in regressing to past lives for a few years now, partly through hypnosis. It's been a fascinating journey, and I've discovered a great deal about myself.' He sat forward and rested his hands on the desk. His fingers were short and tapered. 'For example, I was a merchant's wife in Venice in the fifteenth century. I had seven children and died giving birth to the eighth. I was only twenty-nine. In my next incar-nation, I was an actor in a troupe of Elizabethan players, the Lord Chamberlain's Men. I remember playing Bardolph in *Henry V* in 1599. After that, I—'

'I get the picture,' said Banks. 'I don't mean to be rude, Mr Singer, but maybe we can skip to the twentieth century?'

Singer paused and frowned at Banks. 'Sorry. Well, as I was telling Detective Constable Gay here, it's the least clear one so far. I was a hippie. At least, I think I was. I had long hair, wore a caftan, bell-bottom jeans. And I had this incredible sense of *déjà vu* when I was driving through Swainsdale yesterday afternoon.'

'Where, exactly?'

'It was just before Fortford. I was coming from Helmthorpe, where I'm staying. There's a small hill by the river with a few trees on it, all bent by the wind. Maybe you know it?'

Banks nodded. He knew the place. The hill was, in fact, a drumlin, a kind of hump-backed mound of detritus left by the retreating ice age. Six trees grew on it, and they had all bent slightly to the south-east after years of strong north-westerly winds. The drumlin was about two miles west of Fortford.

'Is that all?' Banks asked.

'All?'

'Yes.' Banks leaned forward and rested his elbows on the desk. 'You know there are plenty of explanations for *déjà vu*, don't you, Mr Singer? Perhaps you've seen a place very similar before and only remembered it when you passed the drumlin?'

Singer shook his head. 'I understand your doubts,' he said, 'and I can't offer concrete *proof*, but the *feeling* is unmistakable. I have been there before, in a previous life. I'm certain of it. And that's not all. There's the dream.'

'Dream?'

'Yes. I've had it several times. The same one. It's raining, like today, and I'm passing through a landscape very similar to what I've seen in Swainsdale. I arrive at a very old stone house. There are people and their voices are raised, maybe in anger or laughter, I can't tell. But I start to feel tense and claustrophobic. There's a baby crying some-where and it won't stop. I climb up some creaky stairs. When I get to the top, I find a door and open it. Then I feel that panicky sensation of endlessly falling, and I usually wake up frightened.'

Banks thought for a moment. 'That's all very interesting,' he said, 'but have you considered that you might have come to the wrong place? We're not usually in the business of interpreting dreams and visions.'

Singer stood his ground. 'This is real,' he said. 'A crime had been committed. Against me.' He poked himself in the chest with his

thumb. 'The crime of murder. The least you can do is do me the courtesy of checking your records.' His odd blend of naivety and intensity
charged the air.

Banks stared at him, then looked at Susan, whose face showed
sceptical interest. Never having been one to shy away from what killed
the cat, Banks let his curiosity get the better of him yet again. 'All
right,' he said, standing up. 'We'll look into it. Where did you say you
were staying?'

III

Banks turned right by the whitewashed sixteenth-century Rose and
Crown, in Fortford, and stopped just after he had crossed the small
stone bridge over the River Swain.

The rain was still falling, obscuring the higher green dale sides and
their lattice-work of drystone walls. Lyndgarth, a cluster of limestone
cottages and a church huddled around a small village green, looked
like an Impressionist painting. The rain-darkened ruins of Devraulx
Abbey, just up the hill to his left, poked through the trees like a setting
for *Camelot*.

Banks rolled his window down and listened to the rain slapping
against leaves and dancing on the river's surface. To the west, he could
see the drumlin that Jerry Singer had felt so strongly about.

Today, it looked ghostly in the rain, and it was easy to imagine the
place as some ancient barrow where the spirits of Bronze Age men
lingered. But it wasn't a barrow; it was a drumlin created by glacial
deposits. And Jerry Singer hadn't been a Bronze Age man in his previous lifetime; he had been a sixties hippie, or so he believed.

Leaving the window down, Banks drove through Lyndgarth and
parked at the end of Gristhorpe's rutted driveway, in front of the
squat limestone farmhouse. Inside, he found Gristhorpe staring
gloomily out of the back window at a pile of stones and a half-
completed drystone wall. The superintendent, he knew, had taken a
week's holiday and hoped to work on the wall, which went nowhere
and closed in nothing. But he hadn't bargained for the summer rain,
which had been falling nonstop for the past two days.

He poured Banks a cup of tea so strong you could stand a spoon
up in it, offered some scones, and they sat in Gristhorpe's study.
A paperback copy of Trollope's *The Vicar of Bullhampton* lay on a
small table beside a worn and scuffed brown leather armchair.

'Do you believe in reincarnation?' Banks asked.

Gristhorpe considered the question a moment. 'No. Why?'

Banks told him about Jerry Singer, then said, 'I wanted your opinion. Besides, you were here then, weren't you?'

Gristhorpe's bushy eyebrows knit in a frown. 'Nineteen sixty-six?'

'Yes.'

'I was here, but that's over thirty years ago, Alan. My memory's not what it used to be. Besides, what makes you think there's anything in this other than some New Age fantasy?'

'I don't know that there is,' Banks answered, at a loss how to explain his interest, even to the broad-minded Gristhorpe. Boredom, partly, and the oddness of Singer's claim, the certainty the man seemed to feel about it. But how could he tell his superintendent that he had so little to do he was opening investigations into the supernatural? 'There was a sort of innocence about him,' he said. 'And he seemed so sincere about it, so intense.'

' "The best lack all conviction, while the worst / Are full of passionate intensity." W. B. Yeats,' Gristhorpe replied.

'Perhaps. Anyway, I've arranged to talk to Jenny Fuller about it later today.' Jenny was a psychologist who had worked with the Eastvale police before.

'Good idea,' said Gristhorpe. 'All right, then, just for argument's sake, let's examine his claim objectively. He's convinced he was a hippie murdered in Swainsdale in summer, nineteen sixty-six, right?'

Banks nodded.

'And he thinks this because he believes in reincarnation, he had a *déjà vu* and he's had a recurring dream?'

'True.'

'Now,' Gristhorpe went on, 'leaving aside the question of whether you or I believe in reincarnation, or, indeed, whether there is such a thing—a philosophical speculation we could hardly settle over tea and scones, anyway—he doesn't give us a hell of a lot to go on, does he?'

'That's the problem. I thought you might remember something.'

Gristhorpe sighed and shifted in his chair. The scuffed leather creaked. 'In nineteen sixty-six, I was a thirty-year-old detective sergeant in a backwoods division. In fact, we were nothing but a sub-division then, and I was the senior detective. Most of the time I investigated burglaries, the occasional outbreak of sheep stealing, market-stall owners fencing stolen goods.' He sipped some tea. 'We had one or two murders—really interesting ones I'll tell you about someday—but not a lot. What I'm saying, Alan, is that no matter how poor my memory is, I'd remember a murdered hippie.'

'And nothing fits the bill?'

'Nothing. I'm not saying we didn't have a few hippies around, but none of them got murdered. I think your Mr Singer must be mistaken.'

Banks put his mug down on the table and stood up to leave. 'Better get back to the crime statistics, then,' he said.

Gristhorpe smiled. 'So *that's* why you're so interested in this cock and bull story? Can't say I blame you. Sorry I can't help. Wait a minute, though,' he added as they walked to the door. 'There was old Bert Atherton's lad. I suppose that was around the time you're talking about, give or take a year or two.'

Banks paused at the door. 'Atherton?'

'Aye. Owns a farm between Lyndgarth and Helmthorpe. Or did. He's dead now. I only mention it because Atherton's son, Joseph, was something of a hippie.'

'What happened?'

'Fell down the stairs and broke his neck. Family never got over it. As I said, old man Atherton died a couple of years back, but his missis is still around.'

'You'd no reason to suspect anything?'

Gristhorpe shook his head. 'None at all. The Athertons were a decent, hard-working family. Apparently the lad was visiting them on his way to Scotland to join some commune or other. He fell down the stairs. It's a pretty isolated spot, and it was too late when the ambulance arrived, especially as they had to drive a mile down country lanes to the nearest telephone box. They were really devastated. He was their only child.'

'What made him fall?'

'He wasn't pushed, if that's what you're thinking. There was no stair-carpet and the steps were a bit slippery. According to his dad, Joseph was walking around without his slippers on and he slipped in his stockinged-feet.'

'And you've no reason to doubt him?'

'No. I did have one small suspicion at the time, though.'

'What?'

'According to the post mortem, Joseph Atherton was a heroin addict, though he didn't have any traces of the drug in his system at the time of his death. I thought he might have been smoking marijuana or something up in his room. That might have made him a bit unsteady on his feet.'

'Did you search the place?'

Gristhorpe snorted. 'Nay, Alan. There was no sense bringing more grief on his parents. What would we do if we found something, charge *them* with possession?'

'I see your point.' Banks opened the door and put up his collar against the rain. 'I might dig up the file anyway,' he called, running over to the car. 'Enjoy the rest of your week off.'

Gristhorpe's curse was lost in the sound of the engine starting-up and the finale of Mussorgsky's 'Great Gate of Kiev' on Classic FM, blasting out from the radio, which Banks had forgotten to switch off.

IV

In addition to the cells and the charge room, the lower floor of Eastvale Divisional Headquarters housed old files and records. The dank room was lit by a single bare light bulb and packed with dusty files. So far, Banks had checked nineteen sixty-five and sixty-six but found nothing on the Atherton business.

Give or take a couple of years, Gristhorpe had said. Without much hope, Banks reached for nineteen sixty-four. That was a bit too early for hippies, he thought, especially in the far reaches of rural North Yorkshire.

In nineteen sixty-four, he remembered, the Beatles were still recording ballads like 'I'll Follow the Sun' and old rockers like 'Long Tall Sally'. John hadn't met Yoko, and there wasn't a sitar within earshot. The Rolling Stones were doing 'Not Fade Away' and 'It's All Over Now'. The Kinks had a huge hit with 'You Really Got Me', and the charts were full of Dusty Springfield, Peter and Gordon, the Dave Clark Five and Herman's Hermits.

So nineteen sixty-four was a write-off as far as dead hippies were concerned. Banks looked anyway. Maybe Joseph Atherton had been way ahead of his time. Or perhaps Jerry Singer's channeler had been wrong about the time between incarnations. Why was this whole charade taking on such an aura of unreality?

Bank's stomach rumbled. Apart from that scone at Gristhorpe's, he hadn't eaten since breakfast, he realized. He put the file aside. Though there hardly seemed any point looking further ahead than nineteen sixty-six, he did so out of curiosity. Just as he was feeling success slip away, he came across it: Joseph Atherton. Coroner's verdict: accidental death. There was only one problem: it had happened in 1969.

According to the Athertons' statement, their son wrote to say he was coming to see them en route to Scotland. He said he was on his way to join some sort of commune and arrived at Eastvale station on the London train at three-forty five in the afternoon, July 11th, 1969. By ten o'clock that night, he was dead. He didn't have transport of his own, so his father had met him at the station in the Land Rover and driven him back to the farm.

Banks picked up a sheet of lined writing paper, yellowed around the edges. A separate sheet described it as an anonymous note received at the Eastvale police station about a week after the coroner's verdict. All it said, in block capitals, was, 'Ask Atherton about the red Volkswagen.'

Next came a brief interview report, in which a PC Wythers said he had questioned the Athertons about the car and they said they didn't know what he was talking about. That was that.

Banks supposed it was remotely possible that whoever was in the red Volkswagen had killed Joseph Atherton. But why would his parents lie? According to the statement, they spent the evening together at the farm eating dinner, catching up on family news, then Joseph went up to his room to unpack and came down in his stockinged-feet. Maybe he'd been smoking marijuana, as Gristhorpe suggested. Anyway, he slipped at the top of the stairs and broke his neck. It was tragic, but hardly what Banks was looking for.

He heard a sound at the door and looked up to see Susan Gay.

'Found anything, sir?' she asked.

'Maybe,' said Banks. 'One or two loose ends. But I haven't a clue what it all means, if anything. I'm beginning to wish I'd never seen Mr Jerry Singer.'

Susan smiled. 'Do you know, sir,' she said, 'he almost had me believing him.'

Banks put the file aside. 'Did he? I suppose it always pays to keep an open mind,' he said. 'That's why we're going to visit Mrs Atherton.'

v

The Atherton farm was every bit as isolated as Gristhorpe had said, and the relentless rain had muddied the lane. At one point, Banks thought they would have to get out and push, but on the third try, the wheels caught and the car lurched forward.

The farmyard looked neglected: bedraggled weeds poked through the mud; part of the barn roof had collapsed; and the wheels and tines of the old hayrake had rusted.

Mrs Atherton answered their knock almost immediately. Banks had phoned ahead so their arrival wouldn't frighten her. After all, a woman living alone in such a wild place couldn't be too careful.

She led them into the large kitchen and put the kettle on the Aga. The stone-walled room looked clean and tidy enough, but Banks noted an underlying smell, like old greens and meat rotting under the sink.

Mrs Atherton carried the aura of the sick-room about with her. Her complexion was as grey as her sparse hair; her eyes were dull yellow with milky blue irises; and the skin below them looked dark as a bruise. As she made the tea, she moved slowly, as if measuring the energy required for each step. How on earth, Banks wondered, did she manage up here all by herself? Yorkshire grit was legendary, and as often close to foolhardiness as anything else, he thought.

She put the teapot on the table. 'We'll just let it mash a minute,' she said. 'Now, what is it you want to talk to me about?'

Banks didn't know how to begin. He had no intention of telling Mrs Atherton about Jerry Singer's 'previous lifetime,' or of interrogating her about her son's death. Which didn't leave him many options.

'How are you managing?' he asked first.

'Mustn't grumble.'

'It must be hard, taking care of this place all by yourself?'

'Nay, there's not much to do these days. Jack Crocker keeps an eye on the sheep. I've nobbut got a few cows to milk.'

'No poultry?'

'Nay, it's not worth it anymore, not with these battery-farms. Anyway, seeing as you're a copper, I don't suppose you came to talk to me about the farming life, did you? Come on, spit it out, lad.'

Banks noticed Susan look down and smile. 'Well,' he said, 'I hate to bring up a painful subject, but it's your son's death we want to talk to you about.'

Mrs Atherton looked at Susan as if noticing her for the first time. A shadow crossed her face. Then she turned back to Banks. 'Our Joseph?' she said. 'But he's been dead nigh on thirty years.'

"I know that,' said Banks. 'We won't trouble you for long.'

'There's nowt else to add.' She poured the tea, fussed with milk and sugar, and sat down again.

'You said your son wrote and said he was coming?'

'Aye.'

'Did you keep the letter?'

'What?'

'The letter. I've not seen any mention of it anywhere. It's not in the file.'

'Well, it wouldn't be, would it? We don't leave scraps of paper cluttering up the place.'

'So you threw it out?'

'Aye. Bert or me.' She looked at Susan again. 'That was my husband, God rest his soul. Besides,' she said, 'how else would we know he was coming? We couldn't afford a telephone back then.'

'I know,' said Banks. But nobody had asked at the railway station whether Bert Atherton actually *had* met his son there, and now it was too late. He sipped some tea; it tasted as if the teabag had been used before. 'I don't suppose you remember seeing a red Volkswagen in the area around that time, do you?'

'No. They asked us that when it first happened. I didn't know owt about it then, and I don't know owt now.'

'Was there anyone else in the house when the accident occurred?'

'No, of course there weren't. Do you think I wouldn't have said if there were? Look, young man, what are you getting at? Do you have summat to tell me, summat I should know?'

Banks sighed and took another sip of weak tea. It didn't wash away the taste of decay that permeated the kitchen. He signalled to Susan and stood up. 'No,' he said. 'No, I've nothing new to tell you, Mrs Atherton. Just chasing will o' the wisps, that's all.'

'Well, I'm sorry, but you'll have to go chase 'em somewhere else, lad. I've got work to do.'

VI

The Queen's Arms was quiet late that afternoon. Rain had kept the tourists away, and at four o'clock most of the locals were still at work in the offices and shops around the market square. Banks ordered a pork pie, then he and Jenny Fuller took their drinks to an isolated corner table and settled down. The first long draught of Theakston's bitter washed the archive dust and the taste of decay from Banks's throat.

'Well,' said Jenny, raising her glass of lager in a toast. 'To what do I owe the honour?'

She looked radiant, Banks thought: thick red hair tumbling over her shoulders, emerald green eyes full of humour and vitality, a fresh scent that cut through the atmosphere of stale smoke and made him think of childhood apple orchards. Though Banks was married, he and Jenny had once come very close to getting involved, and every now and then he felt a pang of regret for the road not taken.

'Reincarnation,' said Banks, clinking glasses.

Jenny raised her eyebrows. 'You know I'll drink to most things,' she said, 'but really, Alan, isn't this going a bit far?'

Banks explained what had happened so far that day. By the time he had finished, the barman delivered his pork pie, along with a large pickled onion. As Jenny mulled over what he had said, he sliced the pie into quarters and shook a dollop of HP Sauce onto his plate to dip them in.

'Fantasy,' she said finally.

'Would you care to elaborate?'

'If you don't believe in reincarnation, then there are an awful lot of strange phenomena you have to explain in more rational ways. Now, I'm no expert on parapsychology, but most people who claim to have lived past lifetimes generally become convinced through hypnosis, dreams and *déjà vu* experiences, like the ones you mentioned, or by spontaneous recall.'

'What's that?'

'Exactly what it sounds like. Suddenly remembering past lifetimes out of the blue. Children playing the piano without lessons, people suddenly speaking foreign languages, that kind of thing. Or any memory you have but can't explain, something that seems to have come from beyond your experience.'

'You mean if I'm walking down the street and I suddenly think of a Roman soldier and remember some sort of Latin phrase, then I'm recalling a previous lifetime?'

Jenny gave him a withering look. 'Don't be so silly, Alan. Of course *I* don't think that. Some people might, though. People are limitlessly gullible, it seems to me, especially when it comes to life after death. No, what I mean is that this is the kind of thing believers try to put forward as proof of reincarnation.'

'And how would a rational psychologist explain it?'

'She might argue that what a person recalls under hypnosis, in dreams, or wherever, is simply a web of fantasy woven from things that person has already seen or heard and maybe forgotten.'

'But he says he's never been here before.'

'There's television, books, films.'

Banks finished his pork pie, took a swig of Theakston's and lit a Silk Cut. 'So you're saying that maybe our Mr Singer has watched one too many episodes of *All Creatures Great and Small*?'

Jenny tossed back her hair and laughed. 'It wouldn't surprise me.' She looked at her watch, then drained her glass. 'Look, I'm sorry but I must dash.' And with that, she jumped up, pecked him on the cheek and left. Jenny was always dashing, it seemed. Sometimes he wondered where.

Banks thought over what she had said. It made sense. More sense than Singer's reincarnation theory and more sense than suspecting Joseph Atherton's parents of covering up their son's murder.

But there remained the unsubstantiated story of the letter and the anonymous note about the red Volkswagen. If somebody else *had* driven Joseph Atherton to the farm, then his parents had been lying about the letter. Why? And who could it have been?

VII

Two days later, sorting through his post, Banks found a letter addressed to him in longhand. It stood out like a sore thumb among the usual bundle of circulars and official communications. He spread it open on his desk in front of him and read.

Dear Mr Banks,

I'm not much of a one for letter writing so you must forgive me any mistakes. I didn't get much schooling due to me being a sickly child but my father always told us it was important to read and write. Your visit last week upset me by raking up the past I'd rather forget. I don't know what made you come and ask those questions but they made me think it is time to make my peace with God and tell the truth after all these years.

What we told the police was not true. Our Joseph didn't write to say he was coming and Bert didn't pick him up at the station. Joseph just turned up out of the blue one afternoon in that red car. I don't know who told the police about the car but I think it might have been Len Grimond in the farm down the road because he had fallen out with Bert over paying for repairs to a wall.

Anyway, it wasn't our Joseph's car. There was an American lass with him called Annie and she was driving. They had a baby with them that they said was theirs. I suppose that made him our grandson but it was the first time we ever heard about him. Our Joseph hadn't written or visited us for four years and we didn't know if he was alive or dead. He was a bonny little lad about two or three with the most solemn look on his face.

Well it was plain from the start that something was wrong. We tried to behave like good loving parents and welcome them into our home but the girl was moody and she didn't want to stay. The baby cried a lot and I don't think he had been looked after properly, though it's not my place to say. And Joseph was behaving very peculiar. His eyes looked all glassy with tiny pupils. We didn't know what was the matter. I think from what he said that he just wanted money.

They wouldn't eat much though I cooked a good roast for them, and Yorkshire puddings too, but our Joseph just picked at his food and the girl sat there all sulky holding the baby and wanting to go. She said she was a vegetarian. After we'd finished the dinner Joseph got very upset and said he had to go to the toilet. By then Bert was wondering what was going on and also a bit angry at how they treated our hospitality even if Joseph was our son.

Joseph was a long time in the toilet. Bert called up to him but he didn't answer. The girl said something about leaving him alone and laughed, but it wasn't a nice laugh. We thought something might be wrong with him so Bert went up and found Joseph with a piece of string tied around his arm heating something in a spoon with a match. It was one of our silver anniversary spoons he had taken from the kitchen without asking. We were just ignorant farmers and didn't know what was happening in crime and drugs and everything like you do, Mr Banks, but we knew our Joseph was doing something bad.

Bert lost his temper and pulled Joseph out of the toilet. When they were at the top of the stairs, Joseph started swearing at his father, using such words I've never heard before and would blush to repeat. That's when Bert lost his temper and hit him. On God's honour, he didn't mean to hurt him. Joseph was our only son and we loved him even though he was breaking my heart. But when Bert hit him Joseph fell down the stairs and when he got to the bottom his head was at such a funny angle I knew he must have broken his neck.

The girl started screaming then took the baby and ran outside and drove away. We have never seen her again or our grandson and don't know what has become of him. There was such a silence like you have never heard when the sound of the car engine vanished in the distance and Joseph was laying at the bottom of the stairs all twisted and broken. We tried to feel his pulse and Bert even put a mirror to his mouth to see if his breath would mist it but there was nothing.

I know we should have told the truth and we have regretted it for all those years. We were always brought up to be decent honest folk respecting our parents and God and the law. Bert was ashamed that his son was a drug addict and didn't want it in the papers. I didn't want him to go to jail for what he had done because it was really an accident and it wasn't fair. He was suffering more than enough anyway because he had killed his only son.

So I said we must throw away all the drugs and needle and things and take our Joseph's shoes off and say he slipped coming down the stairs. We knew that the police would believe us because we were good people and we had no reason to lie. That was the hardest part. The laces got tied in knots and I broke my fingernails and in the end I was shaking so much I had to use the scissors.

And that is God's honest truth, Mr Banks. I know we did wrong but Bert was never the same after. Not a day went by when he didn't cry about what he'd done and I never saw him smile ever again. To this day we still do not know what has become of our grandson but whatever it is we hope he is healthy and happy and not as foolish as his father.

By the time you read this letter I'll be gone to my resting place too. For two years now I have had cancer and no matter what operations they do it is eating me away. I have saved my tablets. Now that I have taken the weight off my conscience I can only hope that the good Lord sees fit to forgive me my sins and take me unto his bosom.

Yours sincerely,
Betty Atherton

Banks put the letter aside and rubbed his left eye with the back of his hand. Outside, the rain was still falling, providing a gentle background for Finzi's 'Clarinet Concerto' on the portable cassette. Banks stared at the sheets of blue vellum covered in Betty Atherton's crabbed hand, then he cursed, slammed his fist on the desk, went to the door and shouted for Susan Gay.

VIII

'Her name is Catherine Anne Singer,' said Susan the next afternoon. 'And she was relieved to talk to me as soon as I told her we weren't after her for leaving the scene of a crime. She comes from somewhere called Garden Grove, California. Like a lot of young Americans, she came over to "do" Europe in the sixties.'

The three of them—Banks, Susan and Jenny Fuller—sat over drinks at a dimpled, copper-topped table in the Queen's Arms listening to the summer rain tap against the diamonds of coloured glass.

'And she's Jerry Singer's mother?' Banks asked.

Susan nodded. 'Yes. I just asked him for her telephone number. I didn't tell him why I wanted it.'

Banks nodded. 'Good. Go on.'

'Well, she ended up living in London. It was easy enough to get jobs that paid under-the-counter, places where nobody asked too many questions. Eventually, she hooked up with Joseph Atherton and they lived together in a bedsit in Notting Hill. Joseph fancied himself as a musician then—'

'Who didn't?' said Banks. He remembered taking a few abortive guitar lessons himself. 'Sorry. Go on.'

'There's not a lot to add, sir. She got pregnant, wouldn't agree to an abortion, though apparently Joseph tried to persuade her. She named the child Jerry, after some guitarist Joseph liked called Jerry Garcia. Luckily for Jerry, Annie wasn't on heroin. She drew the line at hash and LSD. Anyway, they were off to join some Buddhist commune in the wilds of Scotland when Joseph said they should drop in on his parents on the way and try to get some money. She didn't like the idea, but she went along with it anyway.

'Everything happened exactly as Mrs Atherton described it. Annie got scared and ran away. When she got back to London, she decided it was time to go home. She sold the car and took out all her savings from the bank, then she got the first flight she could and settled back in California. She went to university and ended up working as a marine biologist in San Diego. She never married, and she never mentioned her time in England, or that night at the Atherton farm, to Jerry. She told him his father had left them when Jerry was still a baby. He was only two and a half at the time of Atherton's death, and as far as he was concerned he had spent his entire life in Southern California.'

Banks drained his pint and looked at Jenny.

'Cryptomnesia,' she said.

'Come again?'

'Cryptomnesia. It means memories you're not consciously aware of, a memory of an incident in your own life that you've forgotten. Jerry Singer was present when his grandfather knocked his father down the stairs, but as far as he was concerned *consciously*, he'd never been to Swainsdale before, so how could he remember it? When he got mixed up in the New Age scene, these memories he didn't know he had started to seem like some sort of proof of reincarnation.'

Sometimes, Banks thought to himself, things are better left alone. The thought surprised him because it went against the grain of both his job and his innate curiosity. But what good had come from Jerry Singer's presenting himself at the station three days ago? None at all. Perhaps the only blessing in the whole affair was that Betty Atherton had passed away peacefully, as she had intended, in her pill-induced sleep. Now she wouldn't suffer any more in this world. And if there were a God, Banks thought, he surely couldn't be such a bastard as to let her suffer in the next one, either.

'Sir?'

'Sorry, Susan, I was miles away.'

'I asked who was going to tell him. You or me?'

'I'll do it,' said Banks, with a sigh. 'It's no good trying to sit on it all now. But I need another pint first. My shout.'

As he stood up to go to the bar, the door opened and Jerry Singer walked in. He spotted them at once and walked over. He had that strange naive, intense look in his eyes. Banks instinctively reached for his cigarettes.

'They told me you were here,' Singer said awkwardly, pointing back through the door towards the Tudor-fronted police station across the street. 'I'm leaving for home tomorrow and I was just wondering if you'd found anything out yet?'

IAN RANKIN (1960–)

The Dean Curse

———

THE locals in Barnton knew him either as 'the Brigadier' or as 'that Army type who bought the West Lodge'. West Lodge was a huge but until recently neglected detached house set in a walled acre and a half of grounds and copses. Most locals were relieved that its high walls hid it from general view, the house itself being too angular, too gothic for modern tastes. Certainly, it was very large for the needs of a widower and his unsmiling daughter. Mrs MacLennan, who cleaned for the Brigadier, was pumped for information by curious neighbours, but could say only that Brigadier-General Dean had had some renovations done, that most of the house was habitable, that one room had become a library, another a billiard-room, another a study, another a makeshift gymnasium and so on. The listeners would drink this in deeply, yet it was never enough. What about the daughter? What about the Brigadier's background? What happened to his wife?

Shopkeepers too were asked for their thoughts. The Brigadier drove a sporty open-topped car which would pull in noisily to the side of the road to allow him to pop into this or that shop for a few things, including, each day at the same time, a bottle of something or other from the smarter of the two off-licences.

The grocer, Bob Sladden, reckoned that Brigadier-General Dean had been born nearby, even that he had lived for a few childhood years in West Lodge and so had retired there because of its carefree connections. But Miss Dalrymple, who at ninety-three was as old as anyone in that part of Barnton, could not recall any family named Dean living at West Lodge. Could not, indeed, recall any Deans ever living in this 'neck' of Barnton, with the exception of Sam Dean. But when pressed about Sam Dean, she merely shook her head and said, 'He was no good, that one, and got what he deserved. The Great War saw to him.' Then she would nod slowly, thoughtfully, and nobody would be any further forward.

Speculation grew wilder as no new facts came to light, and in The Claymore public bar one afternoon, a bar never patronised by the Brigadier (and who'd ever heard of an Army man not liking his drink?), a young out-of-work plasterer named Willie Barr came up with a fresh proposition.

'Maybe Dean isn't his real name.'

But everyone around the pool table laughed at that and Willie just shrugged, readying to play his next shot. 'Well,' he said, 'real name or not, I wouldn't climb over that daughter of his to get to any of you lot.'

Then he played a double off the cushion, but missed. Missed not because the shot was difficult or he'd had too many pints of Snakebite, but because his cue arm jerked at the noise of the explosion.

It was a fancy car all right, a Jaguar XJS convertible, its bodywork a startling red. Nobody in Barnton could mistake it for anyone else's car. Besides, everyone was used to it revving to its loud roadside halt, was used to its contented ticking-over while the Brigadier did his shopping. Some complained—though never to his face—about the noise, about the fumes from the exhaust. They couldn't say why he never switched off the ignition. He always seemed to want to be ready for a quick getaway. On this particular afternoon, the getaway was quicker even than usual, a squeal of tyres as the car jerked out into the road and sped past the shops. Its driver seemed ready actually to disregard the red stop light at the busy junction. He never got the chance. There was a ball of flames where the car had been and the heart-stopping sound of the explosion. Twisted metal flew into the air, then down again, wounding passers-by, burning skin. Shop windows blew in, shards of fine glass finding soft targets. The traffic lights turned to green, but nothing moved in the street.

For a moment, there was a silence punctuated only by the arrival on terra firma of bits of speedometer, headlamp, even steering-wheel. Then the screaming started, as people realised they'd been wounded. More curdling still though were the silences, the dumb horrified faces of people who would never forget this moment, whose shock would disturb each wakeful night.

And then there was a man, standing in a doorway, the doorway of what had been the wine merchant's. He carried a bottle with him, carefully wrapped in green paper, and his mouth was open in surprise. He dropped the bottle with a crash when he realised his car was not where he had left it, realising that the roaring he had heard and thought he recognised was that of his own car being driven away. At his feet, he saw one of his driving gloves lying on the pavement in front of him. It was still smouldering. Only five minutes before, it had been lying on the leather of his passenger seat. The wine merchant was standing beside him now, pale and shaking, looking in dire need of a drink. The Brigadier nodded towards the carcass of his sleek red Jaguar.

'That should have been me,' he said. Then: 'Do you mind if I use your telephone?'

John Rebus threw *The Dain Curse* up in the air, sending it spinning towards his living-room ceiling. Gravity caught up with it just short of the ceiling and pulled it down hard, so that it landed open against the uncarpeted floor. It was a cheap copy, bought secondhand and previously much read. But not by Rebus; he'd got as far as the beginning of the third section. 'Quesada', before giving up, before tossing what many regard as Hammett's finest novel into the air. Its pages fell away from the spine as it landed, scattering chapters. Rebus growled. The telephone had, as though prompted by the book's demise, started ringing. Softly, insistently. Rebus picked up the apparatus and studied it. It was six o'clock on the evening of his first rest-day in what seemed like months. Who would be phoning him? Pleasure or business? And which would he prefer it to be? He put the receiver to his ear.

'Yes?' His voice was non-committal.

'DI Rebus?' It was work then. Rebus grunted a response. 'DC Coupar here, sir. The Chief thought you'd be interested.' There was a pause for effect. 'A bomb's just gone off in Barnton.'

Rebus stared at the sheets of print lying all around him. He asked the Detective Constable to repeat the message.

'A bomb, sir. In Barnton.'

'What? A World War Two leftover you mean?'

'No, sir. Nothing like that. Nothing like that at all.'

There was a line of poetry in Rebus's head as he drove out towards one of Edinburgh's many quiet middle-class districts, the sort of place where nothing happened, the sort of place where crime was measured in a yearly attempted break-in or the theft of a bicycle. That was Barnton. The line of poetry hadn't been written about Barnton. It had been written about Slough.

It's my own fault, Rebus was thinking, for being disgusted at how far-fetched that Hammett book was. Entertaining, yes, but you could strain credulity only so far, and Dashiell Hammett had taken that strain like the anchor-man on a tug-o'-war team, pulling with all his might. Coincidence after coincidence, plot after plot, corpse following corpse like something off an assembly line.

Far-fetched, definitely. But then what was Rebus to make of his telephone call? He'd checked: it wasn't 1st April. But then he wouldn't put it past Brian Holmes or one of his other colleagues to pull a stunt on him just because he was having a day off, just because he'd carped on about it for the previous few days. Yes, this had Holmes' fingerprints all over it. Except for one thing.

The radio reports. The police frequency was full of it; and when Rebus switched on his car radio to the local commercial channel, the news was there, too. Reports of an explosion in Barnton, not far from the roundabout. It is thought a car has exploded. No further details, though there are thought to be many casualties. Rebus shook his head and drove, thinking of the poem again, thinking of anything that would stop him focussing on the truth of the news. A car bomb? *A car bomb?* In Belfast, yes, maybe even on occasion in London. But here in Edinburgh? Rebus blamed himself. If only he hadn't cursed Dashiell Hammett, if only he hadn't sneered at his book, at its exaggerations and its melodramas, if only . . . Then none of this would have happened.

But of course it would. It had.

The road had been blocked off. The ambulances had left with their cargo. Onlookers stood four deep behind the orange and white tape of the hastily erected cordon. There was just the one question: how many dead? The answer seemed to be: just the one. The driver of the car. An Army bomb disposal unit had materialised from somewhere and, for want of anything else to do, was checking the shops either side of the street. A line of policemen, aided so far as Rebus could judge by more Army personnel, was moving slowly up the road, mostly on hands and knees, in what an outsider might regard as some bizarre slow-motion race. They carried with them polythene bags, into which they dropped anything they found. The whole scene was one of brilliantly organised confusion and it didn't take Rebus longer than a couple of minutes to detect the mastermind behind it all—Superintendent 'Farmer' Watson. 'Farmer' only behind his back, of course, and a nickname which matched both his north-of-Scotland background and his at times agricultural methods. Rebus decided to skirt around his superior officer and glean what he could from the various less senior officers present.

He had come to Barnton with a set of preconceptions and it took time for these to be corrected. For example, he'd premised that the person in the car, the as-yet-unidentified deceased, would be the car's owner and that this person would have been the target of the bomb attack (the evidence all around most certainly pointed to a bomb, rather than spontaneous combustion, say, or any other more likely explanation). Either that or the car might be stolen or borrowed, and the driver some sort of terrorist, blown apart by his own device before he could leave it at its intended destination. There were certainly Army installations around Edinburgh: barracks, armouries, listening posts. Across the Forth lay what was left of Rosyth naval dockyard, as well as the underground installation at Pitreavie. There were targets. Bomb meant terrorist meant target. That was how it always was.

But not this time. This time there was an important difference. The apparent target escaped, by dint of leaving his car for a couple of minutes to nip into a shop. But while in the shop someone had tried to steal his car, and that person was now drying into the tarmac beneath the knees of the crawling policemen. This much Rebus learned before Superintendent Watson caught sight of him, caught sight of him smiling wryly at the car thief's luck. It wasn't every day you got the chance to steal a Jaguar XJS . . . but what a day to pick.

'Inspector!' Farmer Watson beckoned for Rebus to join him, which Rebus, ironing out his smile, did.

Before Watson could start filling him in on what he already knew, Rebus himself spoke.

'Who was the target, sir?'

'A man called Dean.' Meaningful pause. 'Brigadier-General Dean, retired.'

Rebus nodded. 'I thought there was a lot of Tommies about.'

'We'll be working with the Army on this one, John. That's how it's done, apparently. And then there's Scotland Yard, too. Their anti-terrorist people.'

'Too many cooks if you ask me, sir.'

Watson nodded. 'Still, these buggers are supposed to be specialised.'

'And we're only good for solving the odd drunk driving or domestic, eh, sir?'

The two men shared a smile at this. Rebus nodded towards the wreck of the car. 'Any idea who was behind the wheel?'

Watson shook his head. 'Not yet, and not much to go on either. We may have to wait till a mum or girlfriend reports him missing.'

'Not even a description?'

'None of the passers-by is fit to be questioned. Not yet anyway.'

'So what about Brigadier-General Whassisname?'

'Dean.'

'Yes. Where is he?'

'He's at home. A doctor's been to take a look at him, but he seems all right. A bit shocked.'

'A bit? Someone rips the arse out of his car and he's a *bit* shocked?' Rebus sounded doubtful. Watson's eyes were fixed on the advancing line of debris collectors.

'I get the feeling he's seen worse.' He turned to Rebus. 'Why don't you have a word with him, John? See what you think.'

Rebus nodded slowly. 'Aye, why not,' he said. 'Anything for a laugh, eh, sir?'

Watson seemed stuck for a reply, and by the time he'd formed one Rebus had wandered back through the cordon, hands in trouser pockets, looking for all the world like a man out for a stroll on a balmy summer's evening. Only then did the Superintendent remember that this was Rebus's day off. He wondered if it had been such a bright idea to send him off to talk to Brigadier-General Dean. Then he smiled, recalling that he had brought John Rebus out here precisely because something didn't quite feel right. If he could feel it, Rebus would feel it too, and would burrow deep to find its source— as deep as necessary and, perhaps, deeper than was seemly for a Superintendent to go.

Yes, there were times when even Detective Inspector John Rebus came in useful.

It was a big house. Rebus would go further. It was bigger than the last hotel he'd stayed in, though of a similar style: closer to Hammer Films than *House and Garden*. A hotel in Scarborough it had been;

three days of lust with a divorced school-dinner lady. School-dinner ladies hadn't been like that in Rebus's day . . . or maybe he just hadn't been paying attention.

He paid attention now. Paid attention as an Army uniform opened the door of West Lodge to him. He'd already had to talk his way past a mixed guard on the gate—an apologetic PC and two uncompromising squaddies. That was why he'd started thinking back to Scarborough—to stop himself punching those squaddies in their square-chinned faces. The closer he came to Brigadier-General Dean, the more aggressive and unlovely the soldiers seemed. The two on the gate were like lambs compared to the one on the main door of the house, yet he in his turn was meekness itself compared to the one who led Rebus into a well-appointed living-room and told him to wait.

Rebus hated the Army—with good reason. He had seen the soldier's lot from the inside and it had left him with a resentment so huge that to call it a 'chip on the shoulder' was to do it an injustice. Chip? Right now it felt like a whole transport cafe! There was only one thing for it. Rebus made for the sideboard, sniffed the contents of the decanter sitting there and poured himself an inch of whisky. He was draining the contents of the glass into his mouth when the door opened.

Rebus had brought too many preconceptions with him today. Brigadier-Generals were squat, ruddy-faced men, with stiff moustaches and VSOP noses, a few silvered wisps of Brylcreemed hair and maybe even a walking stick. They retired in their seventies and babbled of campaigns over dinner.

Not so Brigadier-General Dean. He looked to be in his mid- to late-fifties. He stood over six feet tall, had a youthful face and vigorous dark hair. He was slim too, with no sign of a retirement gut or a port drinker's red-veined cheeks. He looked twice as fit as Rebus felt and for a moment the policeman actually caught himself straightening his back and squaring his shoulders.

'Good idea,' said Dean, joining Rebus at the sideboard. 'Mind if I join you?' His voice was soft, blurred at the edges, the voice of an educated man, a civilised man. Rebus tried hard to imagine Dean giving orders to a troop of hairy-fisted Tommies. Tried, but failed.

'Detective Inspector Rebus,' he said by way of introduction. 'Sorry to bother you like this, sir, but there are a few questions—'

Dean nodded, finishing his own drink and offering to replenish Rebus's.

'Why not?' agreed Rebus. Funny thing though: he could swear this whisky wasn't whisky at all but whiskey—Irish whiskey. Softer than the Scottish stuff, lacking an edge.

Rebus sat on the sofa, Dean on a well-used armchair. The Brigadier-General offered a toast of *slainte* before starting on his second drink, then exhaled noisily.

'Had to happen sooner or later, I suppose,' he said.

'Oh?'

Dean nodded slowly. 'I worked in Ulster for a time. Quite a long time. I suppose I was fairly high up in the tree there. I always knew I was a target. The Army knew, too, of course, but what can you do? You can't put bodyguards on every soldier who's been involved in the conflict, can you?'

'I suppose not, sir. But I assume you took precautions?'

Dean shrugged. 'I'm not in *Who's Who* and I've got an unlisted telephone number. I don't even use my rank much, to be honest.'

'But some of your mail might be addressed to Brigadier-General Dean?'

A wry smile. 'Who gave you that impression?'

'What impression, sir?'

'The impression of rank. I'm not a Brigadier-General. I retired with the rank of Major.'

'But the—'

'The what? The locals? Yes, I can see how gossip might lead to exaggeration. You know how it is in a place like this, Inspector. An incomer who keeps himself to himself. A military air. They put two and two together then multiply it by ten.'

Rebus nodded thoughtfully. 'I see.' Trust Watson to be wrong even in the fundamentals. 'But the point I was trying to make about your mail still stands, sir. What I'm wondering, you see, is how they found you.'

Dean smiled quietly. 'The IRA are quite sophisticated these days, Inspector. For all I know, they could have hacked into a computer, bribed someone in the know, or maybe it was just a fluke, sheer chance.' He shrugged. 'I suppose we'll have to think of moving somewhere else now, starting all over again. Poor Jacqueline.'

'Jacqueline being?'

'My daughter. She's upstairs, terribly upset. She's due to start university in October. It's her I feel sorry for.'

Rebus looked sympathetic. He felt sympathetic. One thing about

Army life and police life—both could have a devastating effect on your personal life.

'And your wife, sir?'

'Dead, Inspector. Several years ago.' Dean examined his now empty glass. He looked his years now, looked like someone who needed a rest. But there was something other about him, something cool and hard. Rebus had met all types in the Army—and since. Veneers could no longer fool him, and behind Major Dean's sophisticated veneer he could glimpse something other, something from the man's past. Dean hadn't just been a good soldier. At one time he'd been lethal.

'Do you have any thoughts on how they might have found you, sir?'

'Not really.' Dean closed his eyes for a second. There was resignation in his voice. 'What matters is that they *did* find me.' His eyes met Rebus's. 'And they can find me again.'

Rebus shifted in his seat. Christ, what a thought. What a, well, time-bomb. To always be watching, always expecting, always fearing. And not just for yourself.

'I'd like to talk to Jacqueline, sir. It may be that she'll have some inkling as to how they were able to—'

But Dean was shaking his head. 'Not just now, Inspector. Not yet. I don't want her—well, you understand. Besides, I'd imagine that this will all be out of your hands by tomorrow. I believe some people from the Anti-Terrorist Branch are on their way up here. Between them and the Army . . . well, as I say, it'll be out of your hands.'

Rebus felt himself prickling anew. But Dean was right, wasn't he? Why strain yourself when tomorrow it would be someone else's weight? Rebus pursed his lips, nodded, and stood up.

'I'll see you to the door,' said the Major, taking the empty glass from Rebus's hand.

As they passed into the hallway, Rebus caught a glimpse of a young woman—Jacqueline Dean presumably. She had been hovering by the telephone-table at the foot of the staircase, but was now starting up the stairs themselves, her hand thin and white on the bannister. Dean, too, watched her go. He half-smiled, half-shrugged at Rebus

'She's upset,' he explained unnecessarily. But she hadn't looked upset to Rebus. She had looked like she was moping.

The next morning, Rebus went back to Barnton. Wooden boards had been placed over some of the shop windows, but otherwise there were few signs of yesterday's drama. The guards on the gate to West Lodge had been replaced by beefy plainclothes men with London accents. They carried portable radios, but otherwise might have been bouncers, debt collectors or bailiffs. They radioed the house. Rebus couldn't help thinking that a shout might have done the job for them, but they were in love with technology; you could see that by the way they held their radio-sets. He'd seen soldiers holding a new gun the same way.

'The guvnor's coming down to see you,' one of the men said at last. Rebus kicked his heels for a full minute before the man arrived.

'What do you want?'

'Detective Inspector Rebus, Central CID. I talked with Major Dean yesterday and—'

The man snapped. 'Who told you his rank?'

'Major Dean himself. I just wondered if I might—'

'Yes, well there's no need for that, Inspector. We're in charge now. Of course you'll be kept informed.'

The man turned and walked back through the gates with a steady, determined stride. The guards were smirking as they closed the gates behind their 'guvnor'. Rebus felt like a snubbed schoolboy, left out of the football game. Sides had been chosen and there he stood, unwanted. He could smell London on these men, that cocky superiority of a self-chosen elite. What did they call themselves? C13 or somesuch, the Anti-Terrorist Branch. Closely linked to Special Branch, and everyone knew the trade name for Special Branch— Smug Bastards.

The man had been a little younger than Rebus, well-groomed and accountant-like. More intelligent, for sure, than the gorillas on the gate, but probably well able to handle himself. A neat pistol might well have been hidden under the arm of his close-fitting suit. None of that mattered. What mattered was that the captain was leaving Rebus out of his team. It rankled; and when something rankled, it rankled hard.

Rebus had walked half a dozen paces away from the gates when he half-turned and stuck his tongue out at the guards. Then, satisfied with this conclusion to his morning's labours, he decided to make his own inquiries. It was eleven-thirty. If you want to find out about someone, reasoned a thirsty Rebus, visit his local.

The reasoning, in this case, proved false: Dean had never been near The Claymore.

'The daughter came in though,' commented one young man. There weren't many people in the pub at this early stage of the day, save a few retired gentlemen who were in conversation with three or four reporters. The barman, too, was busy telling his life story to a young female hack, or rather, into her tape recorder. This made getting served difficult, despite the absence of a lunchtime scrum. The young man had solved this problem, however, reaching behind the bar to refill his glass with a mixture of cider and lager, leaving money on the bartop.

'Oh?' Rebus nodded towards the three-quarters full glass. 'Have another?'

'When this one's finished I will.' He drank greedily, by which time the barman had finished with his confessions—much (judging by her face) to the relief of the reporter. 'Pint of Snakebite, Paul,' called the young man. When the drink was before him, he told Rebus that his name was Willie Barr and that he was unemployed.

'You said you saw the daughter in here?' Rebus was anxious to have his questions answered before the alcohol took effect on Barr.

'That's right. She came in pretty regularly.'

'By herself?'

'No, always with some guy.'

'One in particular, you mean?'

But Willie Barr laughed, shaking his head. 'A different one every time. She's getting a bit of a name for herself. And,' he raised his voice for the barman's benefit, 'she's not even eighteen, I'd say.'

'Were they local lads?'

'None I recognised. Never really spoke to them.' Rebus swirled his glass, creating a foamy head out of nothing.

'Any Irish accents among them?'

'In here?' Barr laughed. 'Not in here. Christ, no. Actually, she hasn't been in for a few weeks, now that I think of it. Maybe her father put a stop to it, eh? I mean, how would it look in the Sunday papers? Brigadier's daughter slumming it in Barnton.'

Rebus smiled. 'It's not exactly a slum though, is it?'

'True enough, but her boyfriends . . . I mean, there was more of the car mechanic than the estate agent about them. Know what I mean?' He winked. 'Not that a bit of rough ever hurt *her* kind, eh?' Then he laughed again and suggested a game or two of pool, a pound a game or a fiver if the detective were a betting man.

But Rebus shook his head. He thought he knew now why Willie

Barr was drinking so much: he was flush. And the reason he was flush was that he'd been telling his story to the papers—for a price. *Brigadier's Daughter Slumming It.* Yes, he'd been telling tales all right, but there was little chance of them reaching their intended audience. The Powers That Be would see to that.

Barr was helping himself to another pint as Rebus made to leave the premises.

It was late in the afternoon when Rebus received his visitor, the Anti-Terrorist accountant.

'A Mr Matthews to see you,' the Desk Sergeant had informed Rebus, and 'Matthews' he remained, giving no hint of rank or proof of identity. He had come, he said, to 'have it out' with Rebus.

'What were you doing in The Claymore?'

'Having a drink.'

'You were asking questions. I've already told you, Inspector Rebus, we can't have—'

'I know, I know.' Rebus raised his hands in a show of surrender. 'But the more furtive you lot are, the more interested I become.'

Matthews stared silently at Rebus. Rebus knew that the man was weighing up his options. One, of course, was to go to Farmer Watson and have Rebus warned off. But if Matthews were as canny as he looked, he would know this might have the opposite effect from that intended. Another option was to talk to Rebus, to ask him what he wanted to know.

'What do you want to know?' Matthews said at last.

'I want to know about Dean.'

Matthews sat back in his chair. 'In strictest confidence?'

Rebus nodded. 'I've never been known as a clipe.'

'A clipe?'

'Someone who tells tales,' Rebus explained. Matthews was thoughtful.

'Very well then,' he said. 'For a start, Dean is an alias, a very necessary one. During his time in the Army Major Dean worked in Intelligence, mostly in West Germany but also for a time in Ulster. His work in both spheres was very important, crucially important. I don't need to go into details. His last posting was West Germany. His wife was killed in a terrorist attack, almost certainly IRA. We don't think they had targeted her specifically. She was just in the wrong place with the wrong number plates.'

Ian Rankin

'A car bomb?'

'No, a bullet. Through the windscreen, point-blank. Major Dean asked to be . . . he was invalided out. It seemed best. We provided him with a change of identity, of course.'

'I thought he looked a bit young to be retired. And the daughter, how did she take it?'

'She was never told the full details, not that I'm aware of. She was in boarding school in England.' Matthews paused. 'It was for the best.'

Rebus nodded. 'Of course, nobody'd argue with that. But why did—Dean—choose to live in Barnton?'

Matthews rubbed his left eyebrow, then pushed his spectacles back up his sharply sloping nose. 'Something to do with an aunt of his,' he said. 'He spent holidays there as a boy. His father was Army, too, posted here, there and everywhere. Never the most stable upbringing. I think Dean had happy memories of Barnton.'

Rebus shifted in his seat. He couldn't know how long Matthews would stay, how long he would continue to answer Rebus's questions. And there were so many questions.

'What about the bomb?'

'Looks like the IRA, all right. Standard fare for them, all the hall-marks. It's still being examined, of course, but we're pretty sure.'

'And the deceased?'

'No clues yet. I suppose he'll be reported missing sooner or later. We'll leave that side of things to you.'

'Gosh, thanks.' Rebus waited for his sarcasm to penetrate, then, quickly, 'How does Dean get on with his daughter?'

Matthews was caught off-guard by the question. He blinked twice, three times, then glanced at his wristwatch.

'All right, I suppose,' he said at last, making a show of scratching a mark from his cuff. 'I can't see what . . . Look, Inspector, as I say, we'll keep you fully informed. But meantime—'

'Keep out of your hair?'

'If you want to put it like that.' Matthews stood up. 'Now I really must be getting back—'

'To London?'

Matthews smiled at the eagerness in Rebus's voice. 'To Barnton. Don't worry, Inspector, the more *you* keep out of my *hair*, the quicker I can get out of yours. Fair enough?' He shot a hand out towards Rebus, who returned the almost painful grip.

'Fair enough,' said Rebus. He ushered Matthews from the room and closed the door again, then returned to his seat. He slouched as best he could in the hard, uncomfortable chair and put his feet up on the desk, examining his scuffed shoes. He tried to feel like Sam Spade, but failed. His legs soon began to ache and he slid them from the surface of the desk. The coincidences in Dashiell Hammett had nothing on the coincidence of someone nicking a car seconds before it exploded. Someone must have been watching, ready to detonate the device. But if they were watching, how come they didn't spot that Dean, the intended victim, wasn't the one to drive off?

Either there was more to this than met the eye, or else there was less. Rebus was wary—very wary. He'd already made far too many prejudgments, had already been proved wrong too many times. Keep an open mind, that was the secret. An open mind and an inquiring one. He nodded his head slowly, his eyes on the door.

'Fair enough,' he said quietly. 'I'll keep out of your hair, Mr Matthews, but that doesn't necessarily mean I'm leaving the barber's.'

The Claymore might not have been Barnton's most salubrious establishment, but it was as Princes Street's Caledonian Hotel in comparison with the places Rebus visited that evening. He began with the merely seedy bars, the ones where each quiet voice seemed to contain a lifetime's resentment, and then moved downwards, one rung of the ladder at a time. It was slow work; the bars tended to be in a ring around Edinburgh, sometimes on the outskirts or in the distant housing schemes, sometimes nearer the centre than most of the population would care to think.

Rebus hadn't made many friends in his adult life, but he had his network of contacts and he was as proud of it as any grandparent would be of their extended family. They were like cousins, these contacts; mostly they knew each other, at least by reputation, but Rebus never spoke to one about another, so that the extent of the chain could only be guessed at. There were those of his colleagues who, in Major Dean's words, added two and two, then multiplied by ten. John Rebus, it was reckoned, had as big a net of 'snitches' as any copper on the force bar none.

It took four hours and an outlay of over forty pounds before Rebus started to catch a glimpse of a result. His basic question, though couched in vague and imprecise terms, was simple: have any car thieves vanished off the face of the earth since yesterday?

One name was uttered by three very different people in three distinct parts of the city: Brian Cant. The name meant little to Rebus.

'It wouldn't,' he was told. 'Brian only shifted across here from the west a year or so ago. He's got form from when he was a nipper, but he's grown smart since then. When the Glasgow cops started sniffing, he moved operations.' The detective listened, nodded, drank a watered-down whisky, and said little. Brian Cant grew from a name into a description, from a description into a personality. But there was something more.

'You're not the only one interested in him,' Rebus was told in a bar in Gorgie. 'Somebody else was asking questions a wee while back. Remember Jackie Hanson?'

'He used to be CID, didn't he?'

'That's right, but not any more . . .'

Not just any old banger for Brian Cant: he specialised in 'quality motors'. Rebus eventually got an address: a third-floor tenement flat near Powderhall race-track. A young man answered the door. His name was Jim Cant, Brian's younger brother. Rebus saw that Jim was scared, nervous. He chipped away at the brother quickly, explaining that he was there because he thought Brian might be dead. That he knew all about Cant's business, but that he wasn't interested in pursuing this side of things, except insofar as it might shed light on the death. It took a little more of this, then the brother opened up.

'He said he had a customer interested in a car,' Jim Cant explained. 'An Irishman, he said.'

'How did he know the man was Irish?'

'Must have been the voice. I don't think they met. Maybe they did. The man was interested in a specific car.'

'A red Jaguar?'

'Yeah, convertible. Nice cars. The Irishman even knew where there was one. It seemed a cinch, that's what Brian kept saying. A cinch.'

'He didn't think it would be hard to steal?'

'Five seconds' work, that's what he kept saying. I thought it sounded too easy. I told him so.' He bent over in his chair, grabbing at his knees and sinking his head between them. 'Ach, Brian, what the hell have you done?'

Rebus tried to comfort the young man as best he could with brandy and tea. He drank a mug of tea himself, wandering though the flat, his mind thrumming. Was he blowing things up out of all proportion? Maybe. He'd made mistakes before, not so much errors of judgment as errors of jumping the gun. But there was something about all of this . . . Something.

'Do you have a photo of Brian?' he asked as he was leaving. 'A recent one would be best.' Jim Cant handed him a holiday snap.

'We went to Crete last summer,' he explained. 'It was magic.' Then, holding the door open for Rebus: 'Don't I have to identify him or something?'

Rebus thought of the scrapings which were all that remained of what may or may not have been Brian Cant. He shook his head. 'I'll let you know,' he said. 'If we need you, we'll let you know.'

The next day was Sunday, day of rest. Rebus rested in his car, parked fifty yards or so along the road from the gates to West Lodge. He put his radio on, folded his arms and sank down into the driver's seat. This was more like it. The Hollywood private eye on a stakeout. Only in the movies, a stakeout could be whittled away to a few minutes' footage. Here, it was measured in a slow ticking of seconds . . . minutes . . . quarter hours.

Eventually, the gates opened and a figure hurried out, fairly trotting along the pavement as though released from bondage. Jacqueline Dean was wearing a denim jacket, short black skirt and thick black tights. A beret sat awkwardly on her cropped dark hair and she pressed the palm of her hand to it from time to time to stop it sliding off altogether. Rebus locked his car before following her. He kept to the other side of the road, wary not so much from fear that she might spot him but because C13 might have put a tail on her, too.

She stopped at the local newsagent's first and came out heavy-laden with Sunday papers. Rebus, making to cross the road, a Sunday-morning stroller, studied her face. What was the expression he'd thought of the first time he'd seen her? Yes, *moping*. There was still something of that in her liquid eyes, the dark shadows beneath. She was making for the corner shop now. Doubtless she would appear with rolls or bacon or butter or milk. All the things Rebus seemed to find himself short of on a Sunday, no matter how hard he planned.

He felt in his jacket pockets, but found nothing of comfort there, just the photograph of Brian Cant. The window of the corner shop, untouched by the blast, contained a dozen or so personal ads, felt-tipped onto plain white postcards. He glanced at these, and past them, through the window itself to where Jacqueline was making her purchases. Milk and rolls: elementary, my dear Conan Doyle. Waiting for her change, she half-turned her head towards the window. Rebus concentrated on the postcards. 'Candy, Masseuse' vied for attention with 'Pram and carry-cot for sale', 'Babysitting considered', and 'Lada, seldom used'. Rebus was smiling, almost despite himself, when the door of the shop tinkled open.

'Jacqueline?' he said. She turned towards him. He was holding open his ID. 'Mind if I have a word, Miss Dean?'

Major Dean was pouring himself a glass of Irish whiskey when the drawing-room door opened.

'Mind if I come in?' Rebus's words were directed not at Dean but at Matthews, who was seated in a chair by the window, one leg crossed over the other, hands gripping the arm-rests. He looked like a nervous businessman on an airplane, trying not to let his neighbour see his fear.

'Inspector Rebus,' he said tonelessly. 'I thought I could feel my scalp tingle.'

Rebus was already in the room. He closed the door behind him. Dean gestured with the decanter, but Rebus shook his head.

'How did you get in?' Matthews asked.

'Miss Dean was good enough to escort me through the gate. You've changed the guard detail again. She told them I was a friend of the family.'

Matthews nodded. 'And are you, Inspector? Are you a friend of the family?'

'That depends on what you mean by friendship.'

Dean had seated himself on the edge of his chair, steadying the glass with both hands. He didn't seem quite the figure he had been on the day of the explosion. A reaction, Rebus didn't doubt. There had been a quiet euphoria on the day; now came the aftershock.

'Where's Jacqui?' Dean asked, having paused with the glass to his lips.

'Upstairs,' Rebus explained. 'I thought it would be better if she didn't hear this.'

Matthews fingers plucked at the arm-rests. 'How much does she know?'

'Not much. Not yet. Maybe she'll work it out for herself.'

'So, Inspector, we come to the reason why you're here.'

'I'm here,' Rebus began, 'as part of a murder inquiry. I thought that's why you were here, too, Mr Matthews. Maybe I'm wrong. Maybe you're here to cover up rather than bring to light.'

Matthews' smile was momentary. But he said nothing.

'I didn't go looking for the culprits,' Rebus went on. 'As you said, Mr Matthews, that was *your* department. But I did wonder who the victim was. The accidental victim, as I thought. A young car thief called Brian Cant, that would be my guess. He stole cars to order. A client asked him for a red open-top Jag, even told him where he might find one. The client told him about Major Dean. Very specifically about Major Dean, right down to the fact that every day he'd nip into the wine-shop on the main street.' Rebus turned to Dean. 'A bottle of Irish a day, is it, sir?'

Dean merely shrugged and drained his glass.

'Anyway, that's what your daughter told me. So all Brian Cant had to do was wait near the wine-shop. You'd get out of your car, leave it running, and while you were in the shop he could drive the car away. Only it bothered me that the client—Cant's brother tells me he spoke with an Irish accent—knew so much, making it easy for Cant. What was stopping this person from stealing the car himself?'

'And the answer came to you?' Matthews suggested, his voice thick with irony.

Rebus chose to avoid his tone. He was still watching Dean. 'Not straight away, not even then. But when I came to the house, I couldn't help noticing that Miss Dean seemed a bit strange. Like she was waiting for a phone call from someone and that someone had let her down. It's easy to be specific now, but at the time it just struck me as odd. I asked her about it this morning and she admitted it's because she's been jilted. A man she'd been seeing, and seeing regularly, had suddenly stopped calling. I asked her about him, but she couldn't be very helpful. They never went to his flat, for example. He drove a flashy car and had plenty of money, but she was vague about what he did for a living.'

Rebus took a photograph from his pocket and tossed it into Dean's lap. Dean froze, as though it were some hair-trigger grenade.

'I showed her a photograph of Brian Cant. Yes, that was the name of her boyfriend—Brian Cant. So you see, it was small wonder she hadn't heard from him.'

Matthews rose from the chair and stood before the window itself, but nothing he saw there seemed to please him, so he turned back into the room. Dean had found the courage to lift the photograph from his leg and place it on the floor. He got up too, and made for the decanter.

'For Christ's sake,' Matthews hissed, but Dean poured regardless.

Rebus's voice was level. 'I always thought it was a bit of a coincidence, the car being stolen only seconds before exploding. But then the IRA use remote control devices, don't they? So that someone in the vicinity could have triggered the bomb any time they liked. No need for all these long-term timers and what have you. I was in the SAS once myself.'

Matthews raised an eyebrow. 'Nobody told me that,' he said, sounding impressed for the first time.

'So much for Intelligence, eh?' Rebus answered. 'Speaking of which, you told me that Major Dean here was in Intelligence. I think I'd go further. Covert operations, that sort of thing? Counter-intelligence, subversion?'

'Now you're speculating, Inspector.'

Rebus shrugged. 'It doesn't really matter. What matters is that someone had been spying on Brian Cant, an ex-policeman called Jackie Hanson. He's a private detective these days. He won't say anything about his clients, of course, but I think I can put two and two together without multiplying the result. He was working for you, Major Dean, because you were interested in Brian Cant. Jacqueline was serious about him, wasn't she? So much so that she might have forsaken university. She tells me they were even talking of moving in together. You didn't want her to leave. When you found out what Cant did for a . . . a living, I suppose you'd call it, you came up with a plan.' Rebus was enjoying himself now, but tried to keep the pleasure out of his voice.

'You contacted Cant,' he went on, 'putting on an Irish accent. Your Irish accent is probably pretty good, isn't it, Major? It would need to be, working in counter-intelligence. You told him all about a car—your car. You offered him a lot of money if he'd steal it for you and you told him precisely when and where he might find it. Cant was greedy. He didn't think twice.' Rebus noticed that he was sitting very comfortably in his own chair, whereas Dean looked . . . the word that sprang to mind was 'rogue'. Matthews, too, was sparking internally, though his surface was all metal sheen, cold bodywork.

'You'd know how to make a bomb, that goes without saying. Wouldn't you, Major? Know thine enemy and all that. Like I say, I was in the SAS myself. What's more, you'd know how to make an IRA device, or one that looked like the work of the IRA. The remote was in your pocket. You went into the shop, bought your whiskey, and when you heard the car being driven off, you simply pressed the button.'

'Jacqueline.' Dean's voice was little more than a whisper. 'Jacqueline.' He rose to his feet, walked softly to the door and left the room. He appeared to have heard little or nothing of Rebus's speech. Rebus felt a pang of disappointment and looked towards Matthews, who merely shrugged.

'You cannot, of course, prove any of this, Inspector.'

'If I put my mind to it I can.'

'Oh, I've no doubt, no doubt.' Matthews paused. 'But will you?'

'He's mad, you've got to see that.'

'Mad? Well, he's unstable. Ever since his wife . . .'

'No reason for him to murder Brian Cant.' Rebus helped himself to a whiskey now, his legs curiously shaky. 'How long have you known?'

Matthews shrugged again. 'He tried a similar trick in Germany, apparently. It didn't work that time. So what do we do now? Arrest him? He'd be unfit to plead.'

'However it happens,' Rebus said, 'he's got to be made safe.'

'Absolutely.' Matthews was nodding agreement. He came to the sideboard. 'A hospital, somewhere he can be treated. He was a good soldier in his day. I've read his record. A good soldier. Don't worry, Inspector Rebus, he'll be "made safe" as you put it. He'll be taken care of.' A hand landed on Rebus's forearm. 'Trust me.'

Rebus trusted Matthews—about as far as he could spit into a Lothian Road headwind. He had a word with a reporter friend, but the man wouldn't touch the story. He passed Rebus on to an investigative journalist who did some ferreting, but there was little or nothing to be found. Rebus didn't know Dean's real name. He didn't know Matthews' first name or rank or even, to be honest, that he had been C13 at all. He might have been Army, or have inhabited that indefinite smear of operations somewhere between Army, Secret Service and Special Branch.

By the next day, Dean and his daughter had left West Lodge and a fortnight later it appeared in the window of an estate agent on George Street. The asking price seemed surprisingly low, if your tastes veered towards *The Munsters*. But the house would stay in the window for a long time to come.

Dean haunted Rebus's dreams for a few nights, no more. But how did you make safe a man like that? The Army had designed a weapon and that weapon had become misadjusted, its sights all wrong. You could dismantle a weapon. You could dismantle a man, too, come to that. But each and every piece was still as lethal as the whole. Rebus put aside fiction, put aside Hammett and the rest and of an evening read psychology books instead. But then they too, in their way, were fiction, weren't they? And so, too, in time became the case that was not a case of the man who had never been.

BIOGRAPHICAL NOTES

VINCENT BANVILLE (1940–). Born in Wexford, Ireland. Graduated as a teacher; lived for a time in West Africa. Creator of Dublin private eye and hero of two detective novels, John Blaine; currently crime reviewer for the *Irish Times*. Lives in Dublin.

JORGE LUIS BORGES (1899–1986). Postmodernist Argentinian author; born Buenos Aires. Celebrated for constructing labyrinthine puzzles; his exercises in detective writing push the conventions to an absolute limit, and indeed precipitate them on to a different—metaphysical—plane. Though he greatly admired conventional detective stories, Borges's own concern was more with arcane patterning and cabbalistic enigmas.

GWENDOLINE BUTLER (1922–). Born in South London. Best known for her series of novels featuring Inspector John Coffin, beginning with *Receipt for Murder* in 1956, she also created the first realistic woman police officer, Charmian Daniels (under the name of Jennie Melville). Has also written a few—uncollected—stories. All her detective fiction is full of a kind of picturesque disquiet. Lives in Surrey.

SARAH CAUDWELL (1939–). Born in London, educated in Aberdeen and at St Anne's College, Oxford. Practised for a number of years at the Chancery Bar. Author of three elegantly written novels, beginning in 1981 with *Thus Was Adonis Murdered*, in which the detective figure is Tutor in Legal History at St George's College, Oxford. 'An Acquaintance with Mr Collins' is a rare Caudwell short story.

RAYMOND CHANDLER (1888–1959). Born in Chicago; grew up in London, before returning to the USA. First detective story published in *Black Mask* in 1933. The first Marlowe novel, *The Big Sleep*, followed in 1939 and immediately gained him an avid readership. He is among those authors who are said to have bridged the gap between 'detective' (i.e. genre) fiction, and fiction proper, by turning the 'private-eye' story into an art form.

AGATHA CHRISTIE (1890–1976). Outstanding British author of sixty-six detective novels, starting in 1921 with *The Mysterious Affair at Styles*, and 149 short stories. Unsurpassed as far as technical ingenuity is concerned, and one of the most popular authors of all time.

AMANDA CROSS (1926–). Pseudonym of Carolyn Heilbrun, Professor of English Literature at Columbia University, critic and biographer. A native of New York, she is celebrated as the author of eleven 'Kate Fansler' detective novels, and a handful of stories which come into the 'urbane puzzle' category.

JOHN CHARLES DENT (1841–88). Born in Westmorland; family emigrated to Canada when he was a child. Called to the Bar in 1865; later a journalist in England and then in Boston, Massachusetts, before his return to Ontario. Author of a *History of the Rebellion in Upper Canada*, among other works of history and biography, and a single volume of quasi-detective fiction, *The Gerrard Street Mystery and other Weird Tales* (1888).

GARRY DISHER (1949–). Born in South Australia. Author of more than thirty novels, crime novels, short-story collections, history texts, and children's books.

Writer-in-residence at the University of Northumbria, 1998. Lives near the Victoria Coast, Australia.

ARTHUR CONAN DOYLE (1859–1930). With the first appearance of Sherlock Holmes in *A Study in Scarlet* (1887), the detective genre found both a form and an impetus, and has never looked back. The name of Conan Doyle has remained inextricably linked with the first and most distinctive 'great detective' figure—the daddy of them all.

RUTH DUDLEY EDWARDS (1944–). Born in Dublin. Historian and biographer, and author of a series of wildly entertaining detective novels starring ex-civil servant Robert Amiss and—after the first four—the redoubtable Baroness Troutbeck. Ruth Dudley Edwards lives in London.

R. AUSTIN FREEMAN (1862–1943). Born in London, and—like Conan Doyle—took up the study of medicine. First novel published under his own name was *The Red Thumb Mark* of 1907, which introduced readers to the indefatigably 'scientific' Dr Thorndyke. Many Thorndyke stories followed, and the best of these satisfyingly exploit the 'puzzle' element, and encompass a kind of romantic Edwardian Englishness.

JACQUES FUTRELLE (1875–1912). Born in Pike County, Georgia. On the editorial staff of the Boston *American*, which published many of his early stories. Creator of Professor S. F. X. Van Dusen, known as 'The Thinking Machine', whose cases were collected in two volumes in 1907 and 1908. An urbane and bracing detective writer; critics have often speculated about the effect Futrelle might have had on the genre if he had not gone down with the *Titanic* in 1912.

ÉMILE GABORIAU (1833–73). Born at Saujon, in the Charente-Inferieure, France. A prolific author, whose output included serial fiction for newspapers, novels of the *beau monde*, and the embryo detective novel *L'Affaire Lerouge* (1966). Said to have died from overwork. His story, 'Missing!', has an intricacy and element of surprise that anticipate later exercises in the genre.

ERLE STANLEY GARDNER (1889–1970). Born in Massachusetts; grew up in Oregon and California, before going on to become a Defense Attorney and creating the 'legal detective' Perry Mason who appeared in such adventures as *The Case of the Sulky Girl* (1933). A prolific and successful author, he put his legal knowledge to good use in the Perry Mason stories, which—as Julian Symons put it—'hinge on points of law, forensic medicine or science as clever as a watch mechanism'.

SUE GRAFTON (1940–). *'A' Is For Alibi*, published in 1982, launched Sue Grafton on her investigator's alphabet featuring private eye Kinsey Millhone, the feistiest of them all. Now up to *'O' Is For Outlaw*, 1999), the series has expanded to include the odd short story, written in the same engaging and intriguing manner. Sue Grafton lives in Santa Barbara, California.

DASHIELL HAMMETT (1894–1961). Born in St Mary's County, Maryland. Worked for Pinkerton's Detective Agency and used his experiences there in his detective stories and the series of five novels which began with *The Dain Curse* (1929). Sam Spade and the Continental Op are his series detectives. A formidable creator of atmosphere, widely regarded (along with Chandler) as one of the masters of the 'hard-boiled' genre.

STUART M. KAMINSKY (1934–). Prize-winning detective writer and author of more than forty novels. Professor of Film History and Director of the Florida State University Conservatory of Motion Picture, Television and Recording Arts. Lives in Sarasota, Florida.

PENTTI KIRSTILÄ (1948–). Born Finland. Worked as a journalist before becoming a full-time writer; first novel *Farewell to the Loved One* (the start of his acclaimed 'Farewell' series) published in 1977. Creator of DS Lauri Hanhivaara of Tempere (later Helsinki) CID. His books combine a distinctively deadpan Nordic manner with traditional police investigation. Twice winner of the Finnish Whodunnit Society's prestigious 'Clew of the Year', awarded for the best crime novel published during the previous twelve months. Lives in Helsinki.

MAURICE LEBLANC (1864–1941). Born in Rouen, of Franco-Italian descent. Creator of the Raffles figure, the gentleman-burglar-turned-detective and mastermind, Arsène Lupin, who appears in many novels and stories, often in disguise or going under a different name. The first work to feature this intellectual wizard, *Arsène Lupin: Gentleman-Cambrioleur*, was published in 1907.

PAOLO LEVI (1919–9?). Born Genoa, into a family of Jewish intellectuals. A victim of fascist racial discrimination laws, which obliged him to live for a time in Brazil. In 1946 he returned to Italy, spending the rest of his life in Rome. After a successful career as a playwright, Levi turned to fiction in 1975; his works include detective stories and a family history, *Il filo della memoria* (1984).

WILLIAM MACHARG (1872–1951). A notable contributor to the hard-boiled, laconic American school of crime-writing. Best remembered, perhaps, for *The Achievements of Luther Trant* (1910), written in collaboration with Ewin Balmer—after which he went on to write a succession of 'Officer O'Malley' stories for *Collier's* magazine.

SEICHO MATSUMOTO (1909–92). First Chairman of the Association of Japanese Crime Writers, and an influential and prolific author; produced more than 400 books from the 1950s, including historical fiction, essays on archaeology and other subjects, as well as detective stories. One of the Japanese postwar generation concerned with social realism. Author of the bestselling *Points and Lines* (1970).

JAMES MELVILLE (1933–). For many years a cultural diplomat in Japan, the country in which his detective fiction is set. Creator of Superintendent Otani, the hero of thirteen novels and a couple of short stories, which offer deft plots and striking resolutions.

SHIZUKO NATSUKI (1938–). Graduate of Keio University. Began writing in 1969, and won the 'Mystery Writers of Japan' Award in 1973. Has drawn on her own experiences as a wife and mother—in the 'social realist' mode. Author of *Murder at Mount Fuji* (1984) and *The Third Lady* (1987). Dubbed 'the Agatha Christie of Japan'.

HARVEY J. O'HIGGINS (1876–1929). Born in London, Ontario. Became a reporter on the Toronto *Star*, before moving to New York and the NY city *Globe*. Gave up newspaper work for full-time writing in 1901, becoming a playwright and critic. Died in New Jersey, leaving the posthumously published *Detective Duff Unravels It*, a collection of stories.

SARA PARETSKY (1947–). Born in Iowa. Author of seven 'V. I. Warshawski' novels, beginning in 1982 with *Indemnity Only*, all of them striking contributions to the female private eye genre. There are some Warshawski short stories, but none to match the density and inventiveness of the novels—or the verve of the Chandler pastiche, 'Dealer's Choice'. Sara Paretsky lives in Chicago.

ELLERY QUEEN (1905–82). The original *nom-de-plume* covered the identities of two cousins, Frederic Dannay (1905–82) and Manfred B. Lee (1905–71), both of whom were born in Brooklyn, New York. Their first joint novel was *The Roman*

Hat Mystery of 1929; *Ellery Queen's Mystery Magazine*, which began publication in 1941, provided—and goes on providing—a valuable outlet for all kinds of short detective stories.

IAN RANKIN (1960–). Born in Fife, Scotland. Winner of the Chandler–Fulbright Award, and creator of Inspector Rebus who first appeared in the novel *Knots and Crosses* (1987). Seven Rebus novels and a collection of stories followed, all strongly plotted, with powerful social implications and an energetic approach. Ian Rankin lives in Edinburgh.

PETER ROBINSON (1950–). Born in Yorkshire; lives in Canada. Author of six 'Inspector Banks' novels, set in Yorkshire, and a number of stories. Winner of the Crime Writers of Canada 'Best Short Story' Award.

PALLE ROSENKRANTZ (1867–1941). Born in Copenhagen. Author of many novels, plays, and detective stories, he was called to the Bar in 1909 and began writing to supplement his income—and also to gain an outlet for his views on the Danish legal system, which he considered in need of overhauling. Some of his work was published in English in the early part of the century, but the first translation of a 'Lieutenant Holst' story did not appear until 1971, when Hugh Greene included 'A Sensible Course of Action' in his volume *More Rivals of Sherlock Holmes*.

GEORGES SIMENON (1903–89). Born in Liège, Belgium. Published his first novel at 17, moved to Paris, and subsequently became famous as the creator of Inspector Maigret; his great achievement was to bring a new verisimilitude to the *roman policier*, in contrast to the theatricality displayed by some of his predecessors. Maigret—and by extension, Simenon—is for ever associated with the streets, weather (particularly rainy weather), and *ambience* of mid-century Paris.

JOSEF ŠKVORECKÝ (1924–). Born in Czechoslovakia; emigrated to Canada in 1969 after the Soviet invasion of his country. Lives in Toronto. Creator of the Prague detective Lieutenant Borůvka. 'The Classic Semarák Case' was described by Ellery Queen on its first publication in 1967 as 'a rare detective story—a story from a part of Europe from which you wouldn't expect this kind of story'.

JAMES THURBER (1894–1961). Born in Columbus, Ohio. Associated with the *New Yorker*, Thurber is among the outstanding humorous writers of the twentieth century. Among his best-known collections are *The Beast in Me and other Animals* (1948) and *Thurber's Dogs* (1953). 'The Macbeth Murder Mystery' is a charming spoof.

ROBERT VAN GULIK (1910–67). Dutch diplomat and ambassador to Malaya and Japan. Began by translating a novel from the Chinese, and went on to write a series of novels and stories featuring Judge Dee, who is based on an actual magistrate from the T'ang Dynasty, Ti Jen-Chieh. These add up to a wonderfully imaginative re-creation of Ancient China.

JANWILLEM VAN DE WETERING (1931–). Born in Holland. Served with the Amsterdam police for seven years, before emigrating to Maine, USA. Author of a series of 'Amsterdam Cop' novels, including *Tumbleweed* and *Hard Rain*. A witty and original detective writer.

TED WOOD (1931–). Born in England; educated Worcestershire, but moved to Canada where he served for a time with the Toronto City Police. Has been a freelance writer since 1974. First novel to feature the detective Bennet Reid was *Dead in the Water* (1983). Lives in Toronto.

ACKNOWLEDGEMENTS

The editor and publisher gratefully acknowledge permission to include the following copyright material:

Vincent Banville, 'Body Count'. Copyright © Vincent Banville 2000, first published in this collection by permission of the author.

Jorge Luis Borges, 'Death and the Compass'. Reprinted from *The Aleph and Other Stories*, translated by Norman Thomas di Giovanni (Jonathan Cape, 1971), translation copyright © 1968, 1969, 1970 by Emece Editores, SA and Thomas di Giovanni, by permission of Dutton, a division of Penguin Putnam Inc.

Gwendoline Butler, 'Bloody Windsor'. Copyright © Gwendoline Butler 2000, first published in this collection by permission of the author.

Sara Caudwell, 'An Acquaintance with Mr Collins'. Reprinted from *A Suit of Diamonds* (Crime Club Diamond Jubilee Commemorative Volume, Collins, 1990), by permission of HarperCollins Publishers Ltd.

Raymond Chandler, 'No Crime in the Mountains'. Copyright © Raymond Chandler 1941, first published in *Detective Story Magazine* (US), reprinted by permission of Ed Victor Ltd on behalf of the Estate of Raymond Chandler.

Agatha Christie, 'The Adventure of the Egyptian Tomb'. Reprinted from *Poirot Investigates* (Collins, 1924). Copyright Agatha Christie 1924, by permission of Hughes Massie Ltd.

Amanda Cross, 'Arrie and Jasper'. Reprinted from *Collected Stories* (Ballantine, New York, 1997). Copyright © Amanda Cross (Carolyn G. Heilbrun) 1997, by permission of Ellen Levine Literary Agency, Inc., and Ballantine Books, a division of Random House, Inc.

Garry Disher, 'My Brother Jack'. Reprinted from *Straight, Bent, and Barbara Vine* (Allen & Unwin, Sydney, 1997) by permission of the author and of Allen & Unwin Pty Ltd.

Sir Arthur Conan Doyle, 'The Adventure of the Blue Carbuncle'. Reprinted from *The Adventures of Sherlock Holmes*. Copyright © The Sir Arthur Conan Doyle Copyright Holders 1996, by permission of Jonathan Clowes Ltd, London, on behalf of Andrea Plunket, Administrator of the Sir Arthur Conan Doyle Copyrights.

Ruth Dudley Edwards, 'Father Brown in Muncie, Indiana'. Copyright © Ruth Dudley Edwards 2000, first published in this collection by permission of the author.

R. Austin Freeman, 'A Mystery of the Sandhills'. Reprinted from *The Puzzle Lock* (Hodder & Stoughton, 1925), by permission of A. P. Watt Ltd on behalf of Winifred Lydia Briant.

Erle Stanley Gardner, 'The Case of the Irate Witness'. Copyright © Jean Bethell Gardner 1953, renewed 1981. Reprinted by permission of Thayer Hobson and Company on behalf of the Estate of Erle Stanley Gardner.

Sue Grafton, 'A Little Missionary Work'. Copyright © Sue Grafton 1992, first published in R. Randisi (ed.), *Deadly Allies* (Doubleday, 1992). Reprinted by permission of Abner Stein.

Dashiell Hammett, 'Death & Company'. Reprinted by permission of The Joy Harris Literary Agency, Inc. on behalf of the author.

Stuart Kaminsky, 'Find Miriam'. First published in *New Mystery Magazine* (1997), reprinted by permission of Charles Raisch at *New Mystery Magazine.*

Pentti Kirstilä, 'Brown Eyes and Green Hair'. Translated from the Finnish by Michael Garner, first published in *Suomen Kuvalehti* (1989), English translation first published in this collection, by permission of the author.

Paolo Levi, 'The Ravine'. Translated from the Italian, by Denis Godliman, first published in *Buon Sangue Italiano* (1977), English translation first published in this collection.

James Melville, 'Santa San Solves it'. First published in Jack Adrian (ed.), *Crime at Christmas* (Equation, 1988) reprinted by permission of the author.

Shizuko Natsuki, 'Divine Punishment'. Copyright © Shizuko Natsuki 1991, translation by Gavin H. Frew first published in *Ellery Queen's Mystery Magazine* 1991. Reprinted by permission of WoodBell Co. Ltd, on behalf of the author.

Sarah Paretsky, 'Dealer's Choice'. Reprinted from *Raymond Chandler's Philip Marlowe* (Knopf, 1988) by permission of David Grossman Literary Agency on behalf of the author.

Ellery Queen, 'My Queer Dean'. Reprinted from *Queen's Bureau of Investigation* (Gollancz, 1955), copyright © Ellery Queen, by permission of the author's Estate and its agents, Scott Meredith Literary Agency.

Ian Rankin, 'The Dean Curse'. Reprinted from *A Good Hanging and*

Acknowledgements 587

Other Stories (Century, 1992) by permission of The Orion Publishing Group Ltd.

Palle Rosenkrantz, 'A Sensible Course of Action'. Translated by Michael Meyer and first published in Hugh Greene (ed.), *More Rivals of Sherlock Holmes* (Bodley Head, 1971), reprinted by permission of David Higham Associates.

Peter Robinson, 'Summer Rain'. Copyright © Peter Robinson 1994, first published in *Ellery Queen's Mystery Magazine* (1994). Reprinted by permission of the author.

Georges Simenon, extract reprinted from *Maigret's Memoirs* (*les Mémoires de Maigret*), copyright © 1950 the Estate of Georges Simenon, translation by Jean Stewart (Hamish Hamilton, 1963), copyright © 1963 the Estate of Georges Simenon, by permission of the Administration de l'Oeuvre de Georges Simenon, S. A. on behalf of the Estate. All rights reserved.

Josef Skvorecky, 'The Classic Semerak Case'. Copyright © Josef Skvorecky 1967, translated by Kaca Polackova first published in *Ellery Queen's Mystery Magazine* (1997), reprinted by permission of Westwood Creative Artists on behalf of the author.

James Thurber, 'The Macbeth Murder Mystery'. Reprinted from *My World and Welcome to It* (Hamish Hamilton, 1992), copyright © James Thurber 1942, copyright © renewed 1970 by Helen Thurber and Rosemary A. Thurber, by arrangement with Rosemary A. Thurber and the Barbara Hogenson Agency.

Janwillem Van De Wetering, 'The Deadly Egg' reprinted from *The Sergeant's Cat and Other Stories* (Gollancz, 1988), by permission of Abner Stein and the Smith/Skolnik Literary Agency.

Robert Van Gulik, 'The Murder on the Lotus Pond' reprinted from *Judge Dee at Work* (Heinemann, 1967), copyright © 1967 The Robert van Gulik Estate, by permssion of Prof. Dr. T. M. van Gulik.

Ted Wood, 'Pit Bull'. Copyright © Ted Wood 1987, reprinted from Peter Sellers (ed.), *Cold Blood: Murder in Canada* (Mosaic Press/Calder Publications 1987) by permission of the publishers.

Printed in the United Kingdom by
Lightning Source UK Ltd., Milton Keynes
137966UK00001B/122/P